Hockey coach Scott Christie tells his team, the Waterloo Black Hawks, that they don't play "pansy, wussy-ass 'European style' hockey." Coach wants his men to hit hard enough to kill a whole country. That's the sort of Hockey Grant Tracey plays in this first collection: blue collar tough stories. There's a story about a kid from nowheresville sitting in a Bogey-style fedora watching *The Maltese Falcon*. A story about a Macedonian kid in Canada who desperately wants to be Jewish because Jews have "cultural capital," whereas Macedonians have nothing. A story about a hockey goalkeeper with anxiety attacks. A story about an overweight father trying to connect with his sons in a violent game of touch football in the park. These are stories about people whose lives have gone "a little beyond the grasp." Tracey whacks them at us like perfect slap-shots on goal.

-Brian Daldorph, author of *Outcasts* and
editor of Coal City Review

Given the ego-driven posing and swagger and the self-absorbed stylistics of so many of today's over-schooled faux tales, it's a huge relief to encounter Tracey's clean, honest, unaffected voice and manner. His stories face you square in their natural skins, with no fancy verbal cosmetics or shifty-eyed rhetoric to keep you from seeing them for what they really are. They're not out to impress us with anything but clarity of vision, integrity of voice, and honesty of purpose. As you read, wondering why such straightforwardness so free of pretense should be a rarity rather than the rule, it may occur to you that fabricating a truth is one of the toughest writing jobs around. Lucky for us, Tracey has learned to do it early enough in his career that we can look forward to many more collections from him in future.

-Ben Nyberg, former editor of Kansas Quarterly
and author of *One Great Way to Write Short Stories*

As a story cycle, Grant Tracey's *Parallel Lines and the Hockey Universe* tells it all. Youth, family, country (not just America but Canada and even Macedonia too), sexuality, and the personal identity that's finally formed with adulthood—everything's here, and in a way that makes sense well beyond the limitations of conventional novel form. A love of sports helps hold it together, but Tracey's wonderfully imaginative sense of self is what really does the trick.

-Jerry Klinkowitz, author of *Short Season* and *Owning a Piece of the Minors*

Parallel Lines and the Hockey Universe marks Grant Tracey as natural heir to Sherwood Anderson. But unlike Winesburg, Ohio residents, Tracey's characters, all associates of the Traicheff brothers, are sociable and devoted to pop culture. Likeable without being roguish, these guys live in worlds of asphalt and brick under a low winter sky. They worry over parental divorces, talk with great passion about Iggy Stooge and Lenny Bruce and Humphrey Bogart, play junior league hockey in the upper Midwest, date strippers in small town Ontario, fall innocently in love, and understand that their grandparents' emigration has made the honest, grinding work of the new world. The book is massively complicated without being pretentious or difficult. In fact, *Parallel Lines* is a hoot to read— a hoot and several loud choruses of "All Right Now" after a last second goal slapped in from the blue line. Score!

-G.W. Clift, former editor Literary Magazine Review and author of *Mustaches and Other Stories*

In these linked stories about hockey, family, small-town life, and growing up, Grant Tracey gives us a compelling portrait of a community and a generation. From a Macedonian-Canadian who becomes a teacher, novelist, and sportswriter to the star of a local hockey team and an actress fallen on hard times, all the characters struggle for their moments of grace and transcendence. Hockey, like rock 'n' roll music or the thought of exploding atoms, becomes a metaphor for the elusive and complete joy that the characters are rewarded when they least expect it. Whether we are hockey fans or not, *Parallel Lines and the Hockey Universe,* like all good fiction, gives us the sudden insight into a world full of characters very much like and unlike ourselves.

-Kyoko Mori, author of *Shizuko's Daughter* and *The Dream of Water: A Memoir*

Parallel Lines
and the
Hockey Universe

Grant Tracey

Pocol Press
Clifton, Virginia

POCOL PRESS

Published in the United States of America
by Pocol Press
6023 Pocol Drive
Clifton VA 20124
www.pocolpress.com

Publisher's Cataloguing-in-Publication

Tracey, Grant Annis George, 1960-
    Parallel lines and the hockey universe / Grant
  Tracey.
    p.cm.
    ISBN 1-929763-13-1

    1. Immigrants—Fiction. 2. Waterloo (Iowa)—Fiction.
I. Title

PS3620.R334P37 2003   813'.6
                               QBI133-904

Cover art © 2002 by Gary Kelley.

Acknowledgments

I wish to thank the editors of the following journals in which several of these stories (some in slightly altered form) first appeared: *Aethlon: the Journal of Sport Literature* for "Shot on Goal" and "Truth or Dare"; *AnyKey Review* for "Hat-Trick" (formerly titled "Grey Cup Sunday") and "Mitchell Street Near Midnight"; *Coal City Review* for "Victoria Day" and "Kicks"; *Farmer's Market* for "Public Speaking"; *Kansas Quarterly* for "Hockey Canada"; *Snowbound* for "Ice Skiing" and "Sleigh Ride"; and *Under the Sun* for "Strike."

I'd also like to thank the following people for helping shape these stories. My mother and father provided the voices of the past and had long telephone conversations with me to help nuance "Break and Enter" and "Work in the Garden." Professor Ben Nyberg, who back in 1985 taught me to take myself seriously as a writer, has been a tremendous influence. I often hear his mentoring voice as I strategize story revisions. Ron Sandvik, Managing Editor of the *North American Review*, helped give "King of Noir" its narrative arc. University of Northern Iowa Department Head, Jeffrey S. Copeland provided a supportive work environment in which I could explore the professional directions I wanted to take. Kyoko Mori, Brian Gallagher, and Jerry Klinkowitz read early versions of the manuscript and encouraged me to find a publisher; Colleague and Co-Editor of the *North American Review*, Vince Gotera told me six years ago that I would publish a collection of stories and he's been like a big brother, offering advice and feedback; All of my creative writing students whose own work has helped inform my own; And finally, special thanks to my present family: Caitlin, Elizabeth, Devin and my wife Karen, whose love, enthusiasm and joy fill every page.

For Karen, my Maggie

Table of Contents

Hockey Canada

Matt Traicheff didn't care what Dedo had to say. Canada just had to win.

They were down 1-3-1 to the Soviets in the eight-game Summit Series and had come back to tie it up. A win this afternoon and Canada would be hockey's best, ever, forever.

"*Te tresna penjero,*" Dedo mumbled as he hobbled past, his hands scratches of veins. He tugged at the sweater collar that folded into the furrowed skin at the back of his neck. "Yakushev," he said and then sat somewhat stiffly on the Victorian chesterfield. It was ten years old and still had vacuumed vinyl sealing around the cushions. Zippers were stitched along the edges.

"What did he say?" Matt asked. He never could understand his grandfather, and the radiator next to him was making it even more difficult, rattling as if a bowling ball were loose inside. Anyway, something clanked, and then settled to hum.

"You've got a broken window, a cracked head. You're nuts," Uncle Alec translated. He stood across the room from Matt, hunched over his putter, a collapsed fishing hat pushed against the bald spot on his head. "Why didn't you ever teach this kid Macedonian, Jean?"

Matt's Mom smiled brightly. "I tried, Lac. But at school—"

Uncle Alec shook his head. "It's nothing to be ashamed of."

"He knows that, Lac, he knows."

"He knows but he doesn't know." Al raised the putter on a half-swing. "God damn great putter I got here. Hey, Ma, get me a beer willya? Matt, there's no way that Canada can win three games in Russia. Come on. What are the odds of that?" The putter swung freely above the ball. "Besides, the old man likes Yakushev."

Matt looked out the window. The sun slanted through latticed wood and dried grapevines. Cupped leaves fell to the ground. "No, way. Espo." Matt smiled, his lower lip feeling like an odd squiggle that wouldn't straighten. "He'll do it."

Al lined up the putter and the ball quickly spun across the linoleum, hit the carpet, slowed and stumbled into the Dixie cup. "Damn, I'm good."

"Canada's going to win." Matt's arms tightened across his chest. Everyone at Woodbine Junior High thought so and Phil Esposito was their hero. Espo, a big rangy center with a wide stance and lumbering stride in skates that looked two sizes too small, spoke to the nation after Canada's game four loss in Vancouver. With a thin film of sweat glossing his face and shocks of hair glued over eyes, he said that Team Canada was working real hard, and he was real disappointed that several Canadians booed them—this wasn't about money, this was about country. As Matt watched, a weird feeling spread like a wistful scar—his body stung, his cheeks tingled. Espo connected it all to history and stuff—his words put Matt, hockey and Canada at the center of things. Once Team Canada traveled to Moscow, the mood had shifted. Classes at school were hurried to the gym and library to watch Canada. Matt, who had once dreaded the Led Zep-heads and their black T-shirted friends suddenly found himself welcomed, for a brief time, anyway. Together they yelled at East German officials, stomped their feet at Vladislav Tretiak's saves, and smacked the hard backs of blue chairs when Canada scored. Everyone was pulling for the team, there were no dissenting boos, just feverous adulation. And now with the series tied, his Mom let him skip school for the final game. She said the two of them deserved a break, and besides Babo and Dedo had a color television.

Al picked the ball out of the cup and rolled the gentle nubs against his fingers. "Jimmy Stavro, owns Knob Hill farms, a big shot, I think he's Greek, I don't know, but anyway, a big shot worth millions, Jean, bet against us. A Canadian laid a $100,000 bet in Vegas against Canada."

Mom shook her head, calmly. "That's just a rumor."

Stavro owned acres of real estate in North York. Matt couldn't believe he would lay such a bet, especially after what Espo had said in Vancouver.

"Front page rumor in the *Sun*," Al said.

"Oh, there's a journal with integrity. Doesn't the *Sun* feature the page three girl?" Mom rolled her eyes. "Are we going to trust that rag?"

"I just don't like Canada's chances. It's a bigger surface over there, it's like Lake Erie they're playing on, and they're faster than us and the way they pass—" He snapped his putter on the linoleum and dropped his shoulders with quick jerks. "Zip, zip, whack. Tape to tape and it's in the net."

Shadrin, Kharlamov, Yakushev. They were great, Matt knew that. With their speed, passing, and superb conditioning the Russians challenged the fundamentals of Canadian hockey: dump and chase the puck, forecheck, hit. Steve Johnston and Cameron Wardal, Matt's seventh-grade homeroom pals, weren't as impressed with the Soviets. They never said much about their game, just their looks—Steve said that their bright helmets and square-jawed faces were clearly the sign of a group of unemotional robots, and Cameron called their national anthem a wake-up call for zombies. Hell, Cameron said, the commies' red jerseys with the crooked little CCCP fading across their chests looked like peewee leftovers from the 1950s. But Matt admired the Russians—it was the Canadian team, without helmets and dry discarded hair, who looked like hired hit men, slow-footed wiseguys whacking at Soviet ankles and arms, smearing bodies into the boarded windshields of the rink. Matt disliked his country's chippiness, and how Bobby Clarke with a two-handed slash broke Valeri Kharlamov's ankle 'cause Kharlamov was scoring all these goals, but he didn't say anything about it to his friends. He hated even thinking it.

"*Yahdee*," Babo asked as she held out a plate of *mauslinkee* and *zilnick*. Matt moved out of the sunlight and smiled awkwardly, his hands jammed in his pockets. "No, thanks." The sky and grass were crisp and gold. Stavro was a bum. "I'm okay."

Babo gently grabbed his arm. "You cheer who you like," she said and then handed Al a beer.

Al turned to Matt, his cardigan sweater one long crease. "How smart are ya, kid?" He took a large swig.

"Pretty smart. I do okay on tests and stuff." Al was an engineer at de Havilland aircraft and Matt sensed that another one of his Uncle's logic tests was coming and he wanted to impress him.

"Pretty smart, huh?" Al slyly grinned; his eyes brimmed a darker brown under the hat.

Matt usually failed these tests. The last time the Traicheffs had visited, Al asked Matt a real teaser: if one costs a dollar, twelve, two dollars, and one hundred and twenty four, three dollars, what did I buy? Matt thought and thought and thought and couldn't figure it out. Numbers at a hardware store, address numbers for your house, Al said. Each number—1, 12, 124—costs a dollar per digit.

"Okay, kid. How many people would it take to fill this room before one of them shared the same birthday as you?"

Dedo cupped a hand around his left ear. "Make your par?" he asked as the pins in the radiator crashed over.

"'Make your par,' Jean." Al laughed, his voice colored with respect. "For years Tato said that to the customers who came into his Mom and Pop store and we never could figure out what the hell it meant until cousin Gary set us straight—'beg your pardon. Make your par? Beg your pardon.'" Al pushed back his collapsed hat. "You know, your grandfather brought a lot of people over here from Macedonia. Don't forget that. Helped establish the church."

Matt nodded. "Sure."

"How many people," Uncle Al repeated and Matt wished he had forgotten the question, and he tried real hard to look like he was thinking real hard because he didn't have a clue, really. His eyes were centered on the ceiling. "365?" "Why did you say that, because there's 365 days in the year?" "Yeah." "Now come on. What are the odds of finding 365 people, all with different birthdays?" "Pretty rare." "Pretty rare? *Teekva.* Anyway, twenty-eight. Twenty-eight's the answer. Some guy at work figured it out, using geometric logic, logarithms and a Ouija board. Twenty-eight. And one in twenty-eight are the chances Canada has of beating Russia today."

"Oh, that's lousy logic," Mom said.

Dedo mumbled something in Macedonian. To Matt, his voice was rocks sliding across the bed of a dump truck. Dedo held up two fingers.

"Two goals for Yakushev," Al translated.

"Espo's the best," Matt yelled uncontrollably, leaning toward his grandfather.

"What?" Al's hands were on his hips and suddenly Matt's clothes felt tight. "Are you five years old or something? This is your grandfather."

"So what. This is Canada."

"You're sick." Al's eyebrows arched like the backs of two cats. "Jean, he's sick. Yelling in Dedo's house."

"He roots for his country, that is good," Babo said.

"He learns it in school, Al," Mom said with a shrug.

"The old man loves the Russians because we're their little Slavic brothers. I think you should respect that, Ma."

Matt looked at his shoes. The tips of his Chuck Taylors were covered with splotches of mud and he realized that the chesterfield's vinyl sheen was for little kids like him. He wished he could unzip the vinyl, crawl in, and be left alone. Nobody raised their voice in Dedo's house to Dedo.

"I do, but I also respect the boy," Babo said. Her English wasn't much better than Dedo's, but Matt liked her because he sensed that she thought he'd make good some day. She didn't mind that he still read comic books.

"I respect the boy, too. That's why I feel bad about his father. The boy needs a father."

Matt's Mom looked down at her hands, as dim light glinted off the buttons of her dress. She and Dad had separated in June, but she didn't tell Babo and Dedo until August. Matt knew that there were problems between his parents. He had heard several arguments at night, and once Dad hurled the radio against the wall—chipped plaster and chunky dust sprinkled the floor, and Matt looked at it for a long time the next morning and it made him feel strangely sad because he never wanted to be like his father, but feared that in a lot of ways he already was. They had the same hooded eyes, quick temper, and forceful opinions. Steve and Cameron nicknamed Matt "The Stamp" because he was always stating his opinions like they were the final truth or something.

"Al, I tried to talk to you about this years ago. My husband's a great guy, but he's not great for me. 1964. I called you and you hung up the phone. It was my son's birthday. Do you remember what you said?"

Al sharply exhaled and pressed his lips tight. The putter was slung over his shoulder like a loaded gun. "He was over here, you know. He wants you back."

"You don't know what it was like."

Dedo grumbled. "*Dosta, dosta borvash*," and then he said something about honoring fathers. He tugged at the frayed ends of his sweater and his itchy collar before leaving the room.

Dad was very Macedonian and was well liked. At family get togethers, he became a regular Jackie Gleason, making with the loud jokes and kissing *babushkas* on the cheeks with a "How Sweet it is." Hands full of *zilnick*, he'd add "But, Babo's *zilnick* is not so good. It's no good. Don't eat it. Don't eat the *zilnick*." The ploy never worked because he always had a slice wedged in his mouth, as he repeated his mantra, "Al, don't eat the *zilnick*." Everyone laughed and Aunts Elsie and Frances would brightly say, "Stan sure does love his *zilnick*." Babo charmed by Dad's humor would cut him an even bigger slice. Mom rarely made *zilnick*.

Al stood fixed, seemingly reading the tan underside of his hat's brim. "No, I don't know what it was like. Hey, kid? You wanna try sinking a putt?"

"Yeah, sure," Matt said.

Matt was lined over the ball by Al's thick hands. They gripped his shoulders with a calm trembling. "Esposito, huh?" Al said. "Italian. Well, that's kind of Macedonian."

Matt smiled.

Canada was down 5-3 after two periods.

Matt walked to the radiator to warm his hands. Dedo looked pretty happy, his face a stretched heavy grin. Espo had a goal, but Yakushev netted two. Matt gently rubbed his hands over the heat and imagined his grandfather, forty years ago, standing in the same spot, talking hockey to the group that gathered on Saturday to listen to the game on radio. He wondered what it was like to be that old and to have known "King" Clancy, Charlie Conacher and Harvey "Busher" Jackson.

"Well, it doesn't look good," Al said, slunkered down in the black chair, the putter listlessly leaning against the windowsill.

The heat felt good between Matt's spread fingers and he figured Steve and Cameron were probably pretty bummed and Mr. Halkett had stepped out between periods for a smoke. "I don't know," Matt said. "If we stay out of the box and shoot the puck more, maybe. . ."

Dedo held up two fingers. "Yakushev."

"Forecheck and shoot. That's what we've got to do."

"Harry Sinden beat the Russians before," Mom said about Team Canada's coach. "When he was captain of the Whitby Dunlops."

Matt pressed his hands together and marveled over how Mom knew about the Dunlops and stuff. That was 1958, Mom was only twenty-one, and probably watched the game with Dedo, Al, and the neighborhood regulars on their first television set. Okay, maybe Steve's Mom packed him big lunches with cakes, sparkly things and Sheriff hockey coins, and maybe Cam's Mom gave him lots of extra money to buy *Mad* magazines and hockey cards, but Matt's Mom was really cool because she *knew* hockey.

Matt turned from the radiator, his hands deep in his pockets. Babo brought down drinks and sandwiches on a chunky chrome tray that looked like a bent hubcap. She set them down on the coffee table. Al took off his hat and checked the edges as if he were looking for a fishing hook. "So, Jean. What are your plans?"

"I'm doing some secretarial work and maybe I'll go into real-estate."

Dedo shook his wide head, leaned forward and seemed on the verge of saying something when he stopped, paused and lifted his 7-Up. He flexed the glass until the liquid swirled and lost its bubbles. Babo looked at the stars in boxed buttons on Mom's dress. Al picked at stray thread on his hat. "I think you should give him another chance," he said.

Matt wished the third period would start. He didn't like the way they were pressuring his Mom, but he sure didn't like the idea of his parents getting a divorce. Nobody at school, except maybe some metal-heads, lived with one parent, but Matt couldn't ever remember seeing Mom and Dad kiss. Once when Matt was in the basement looking for Hot Wheels that didn't have bent axles, he found a wet box—corrugated ribs nudging against thinning paper. It was crammed with Mom's books, many of them orange stained and slightly warped. One was kind of different and Mom had written inside it: "If you could only see into the mirrors of my soul, Stan."

"Al, we've been through all this. You don't know what it was like."

"Well, what was it like?"

"That's not your business," Mom said. To Matt, her voice was a skate's edge—sharp, tremulous, strong. Matt wanted to believe that Dad was a swell guy but that just wasn't true. In house league, Dads took their sons to early morning games, talked hockey, told them how to hold their sticks, how to hand-check, how to feather a pass through a defender, but Matt's Dad was never there. It was Mom who used the salt and pepper shakers to explain plays on the breakfast table, it was Mom who taught Matt the value of the wrist shot's control over the slap-shot's randomness.

"Dad and I just think that your place is with, well, you know," Al said.

Matt wondered how much they had talked about his Mom when she wasn't there, and that didn't seem right at all, and then he also wondered if Al would absently flip his hat in the air. He always did that when he got nervous.

Mom shrugged her shoulders and slowly shook her head. "I came to watch hockey."

"Put up your hand," Dedo said, his voice gritted gravel.

Matt was caught off guard and almost flung up his arm to ward off a blow, but Dedo wasn't talking to him. He was leaning forward, his belly against the coffee table, his right elbow resting on glass. He wanted to arm wrestle.

Mom blushed and traced the wet ring left by her drink. "I don't want to wrestle you."

Dedo pumped the fingers of his hand and the scratches of veins filled into red scars. "*Malatah*," he ordered.

Al glanced at Matt and then looked down the shaft of the putter.

"No, Dad. I'm not going to wrestle you."

Dedo threw his hands back in disgust and then pressed them into his thighs. His eyes were hooded with afternoon shadow. Matt wanted to look away, Babo cleared the drinks, Al flipped his fishing hat, and the third period finally started.

Matt watched and watched and then that weird wistful feeling returned, like after the Vancouver game. Matt felt the scar, the sharp spreading tingle, as past voices, all those that said they weren't Canadians because they were immigrants and not English and not Presbyterian, and present voices, those that said he was Canadian because he was Canadian, merged in a strangely wondrous way. The game was his and Canada's, now and then. Matt was Foster Hewitt calling it. Matt was on the ice, taking it to the Russians, checking, hitting, following up shots, pouncing on rebounds. Eyes ablaze, he saw the gangly Peter Mahovlich center the puck to Esposito in the slot. The puck bounced off a skate, Espo knocked it down with a glove, whacked at it with his stick, and then slapped it under Tretiak's pads. Matt threw his arms in the air as if he too carried a stick and Dedo seemed to fade into the couch's plastic. Mom was no longer neutral. "How about that Espo!" she shouted. Al raised an eyebrow.

And the wistfulness didn't let up—Matt felt the scar's mist linger over the ice, over him, and over every slash of skates as Canada applied pressure and doubled the Russian shots on goal. Half-way through the third MattEspo, surround by four surging Russians, lumbered into the slot. He took a snap shot off the wrong foot, and Yvan Cournoyer coralling the loose puck, rolled his wrists, zipping one off of Tretiak's left pad. MattEspo hacked at the rebound as if he were going after a croquet ball, and then Cournoyer, on the back-hand, slid the puck under Tretiak's catch-glove. The game was tied. Cameron and Steve's hands were probably sore from smacking the back of chairs after that one.

"It's a great series, Al," Mom said.

Al nodded, a slight smile on his face. "Yeah. The series should end tied. They're both great teams."

"Yes!" Matt yelled still celebrating the goal. He ran quickly in one spot and then slid across the linoleum on his knees, his hands holding an imaginary hockey stick like a machine gun. "Yes!" He hoped his grandfather was watching. He threw a series of punches. "Yes!"

"You think you're at the rink, or something?" Al asked.

"Yes!" Matt's cheeks felt hot, like before when he had yelled at Dedo, but this time the tingle was in a goofy good kinda way, and several moments later it happened. Everything was red and white, a hard outside cool. With less than a minute to go, Canada pressed the puck in the Russian end. From the blueline, Cournoyer snapped a pass to the streaking Paul Henderson who fanned on the shot, grazing his stick just above the puck, before crashing shoulder first into the boards. Two Russians failed to clear the zone. The puck bounced off an inadvertent skate, and Esposito, once again, croqueted it back to Tretiak who stumbled to make the quick stick save. Henderson, left alone behind the net, was back out front for the rebound and he lifted it over the fallen goalie. Cournoyer hugged Henderson and Matt hugged his mother and they all jumped up and down. "Henderson has scored for Canada," Foster Hewitt, the voice of hockey and a nation, proudly said.

"There's still 26 seconds left," Al warned, leaning at the chair's edge.

"How do you like that Henderson," Mom said. She whacked Al's shoulder. "I wonder if Ballard will give him a raise?" Matt could feel his Mom next to him. It was an incredible stuttering energy that just flowed from her shoulders and hands, and then she kissed his forehead and hugged him so hard that he wished he had on shoulder pads.

Canada won the faceoff and Dedo hobbled off the couch, the vinyl snap-squeaking. He briskly moved across the room, grabbed the putter from Al and whacked the golf ball. It whipped across the floor, flung along the carpet and rattled into the cup, knocking it upright. He slammed the putter on the floor and raised an angry yet seemingly triumphant fist. Then he left the room.

"Boy, was Stavro wrong," Al said.

Victoria Day

Stan Traicheff flipped the football in his hands and watched his son Matt stand awkwardly by the rough uncut grass of Wilket Creek Park. Behind, the car lights on Leslie Street shimmied in circles that looked like the wet undersides of beer mugs. As the evening sun sank, Stan wondered if his son would ever fill out, or if at thirteen he was forever doomed to be a sports outcast, always the last kid picked.

Everything about Matt was awkward. His spindly legs knocked together when he walked. His threadbare cutoffs, the mix of blue stripes and white meteors, looked like a bunch of damp newspapers covering his thighs, and his spit-spikey hair never stayed combed. Matt was Stan twenty-five years before roughing across schoolyards in Cabbagetown, and hanging with the "gang," sharing smokes, the *Hockey News*, and sepia-toned postcards. Of course, like his son, Stan wasn't a tough guy—he had always turtled in a fight, going down, hands over head, after his opponent threw the first punch. Stan hated remembering how he had turtled.

Petey, Stan's younger son, was athletic. He stood by an oak tree, his left eye squinting with twilight, and he caught the ball gracefully—hands to chest. His return pass rotated tightly and had a smooth arc. It hurt Stan's hands.

"Ow. Good job, Petey." Stan smiled and then rolled out of an imaginary pocket. With his left hand waving as if it were trying to shake loose a tight-fitting glove, Stan told Matt to zig-zag and when he broke by a trash can speckled with crumpled fast food wrappers and paper cups, he spiralled the ball. It smashed against Matt's left shoulder, bounded high and then rolled on the ground in that undependable oblong way of a football.

"Sorry, I hit you in the hands, kid." Stan laughed and shook his head good-naturedly. "You're hopeless, Matt. Whatever you do, stay in school. Get an education."

Matt nodded, his shoulders slumped. The tips of his undone shoe laces were dipped in inky, black tar and he looked a little hurt, trudging out there. Petey laughed slightly in his sleeve. Last week, Stan had broken up a fight between them. From what he had later gathered from Petey, they were playing war behind the furniture, lobbing hardened Play-Doh grenades at each other. And when Matt peeked over the edge of the couch to scout the enemy, Petey zapped him in the forehead. Angered and in tears, Matt chased Petey upstairs and pounded on their bedroom door, while Petey leaned against the inside and called him a "Suck." Stan knew that Matt was too upset to talk about it so he let the punishment ride and told them to forget the whole thing.

"Okay, Petey. Your turn. Run a button hook to that trash can and I'll hit you as soon as you turn around."

"Hey, can I join you guys?"

Stan rubbed the beveled ridges of the ball against his palm and glanced over at a short man with big hairy shoulders and a toothbrush-bristled mustache across his upper lip. His striped swim trunks were faded into pastel colors and his muscle shirt and thongs were grimy. He introduced himself as Rick Jason. Stan thought the name was too compact to be real, but it fit his build.

"Sure, pal." Stan flipped Rick the ball. Rick tossed a sharp arcing pass to Petey who handled it deftly and then spiralled one to his brother. Behind Rick, a bunch of twenty somethings celebrated Victoria Day as grills glowed and smoke twisted like bent fingers. Charcoaled hamburger filled the air.

"Are these your kids?" Rick leaned on his left hip to catch a slightly errant pass. His hair was long and his teeth looked too small for his face.

"Yeah, that's Matt."

"He looks like you."

"He better look like me and not the mailman."

Rick laughed and patted the ball's nose.

"Dad, our mailman *is* a woman," Petey said, slightly rolling his eyes.

Stan looked away. "And that's my other son, Petey. He's ten. All boys that age think they're real funny."

"Our mailman *is* a woman, Dad."

"Hi, Pete." Rick smiled and flicked thin strands of hair off his forehead. "You've got good hands. I'll bet you'll play high school ball." Rick's return pass seemed to twist the sky as it momentarily disappeared into the blue night. They had maybe an hour of light left.

After Rick caught another sideways floater from Matt, high, he twisted his neck a little and suggested they play a game—two-hand touch, five-steamboat rush, ten-steamboat dead. He had some buddies, grilling hamburgers and sipping beers, who would love a break.

Stan's knees hurt. He had water on one of them. He was sixty pounds overweight, slow, and his ankles often swelled when he ran, and his two sons were just kids, and maybe they were outmatched but maybe that's why he said sure. "We gonna play so many downs for the field or three to make ten?"

"Three to make ten." Rick looked off through a crook of trees at the picnic tables and a slithering creek. He hollered for his friends and Stan quickly studied them. Chip had shaggy hair, a peace chain around his neck and a tattoo that said "Wheaties" on his left arm. Stan couldn't believe that someone would write a cereal brand on his arm, regardless of how good it tasted, so he figured the guy for one of those fake individualist types who would probably make a play for your wife when a fella wasn't looking. He was also the type that would break from the team once the going got tough. Kirby, who had white-blond hair, was long and lean but only in the upper body. He had real short legs. If the boys played a quick-outs passing game, Kirby couldn't move laterally and would be done. Next to Chip and Kirby floated two girls, pretty in their halter tops and silver glitter around the eyes. Kirby kissed one of them.

After they agreed on ground rules, Rick's team received the opening kickoff. On first down, Kirby sprinted from the huddle, glitter glistening along his left temple, and he smiled at the girls, and then Rick faded back and threw the bomb to Chip, his hair billowing like air foils on a '57 Chevy. The pass caromed ten yards too long.

Stan quickly huddled his kids. His hands were slippery, fat, and his wedding ring felt tight. "Listen. Matt, look at me." Matt was staring at the girls—Stan hoped at their boobs. Maybe he was growing up after all. "Let's play our game. We won't rush the quarterback. We won't even put anyone on the line because he can't run unless he's rushed. These knuckleheads are trying to impress the chicks so we'll play a zone. We'll give 'em the short stuff. You two guys play deep. Pete on the left. Matt on the right. I'll play up."

Two more long passes and the Traicheffs took over.

"Hot dogs," Stan mumbled, grimacing because of his locked-up knee, and glancing at the girls, their nipples showing.

"How come they didn't punt?" Pete asked.

"Not these guys, kid, not these guys. Bunch of hot dogs. Look—" He drew diagrams on his hand, and huffed a little as he talked. He told them to run about five yards, cross like an x, curl back, and he'd hit the open one. His hands had swelled in the heat. His wedding ring dug into the shallow trench in his finger.

They lined up wide and Stan took the snap. Chip jumped up and down, and Stan had a hard time seeing through his weaving arms.

". . . two steamboat. . ." On four, Stan sliced a short pass to Matt who cradled the ball against his shoulder and ran, feet splayed like Charlie Chaplin's tramp, another eight or nine steps to their goal line, a red maple tree. On the next play, Stan spotted Pete on a quick curl by the trash can for a touch.

"Nickel and dime 'em, nickel and dime 'em." Stan spoke loudly, hoping the two girls sitting on faded picnic tables heard. Their knees were solemnly tucked into their chins.

Rick rammed the following kickoff up the middle, deking past Pete, but the ground sloped to the left and he stumbled over rocks and twigs and Matt caught him at midfield. The girls cheered Rick's run and Chip sauntered over for another kiss. Stan was tired of all the kissing, and he yelled as they snapped the ball, and then broke up their first pass with two lunging steps and an angry stab with a stubby hand. The next two passes were bombs that rocketed out of the end zone and knocked into their styrofoam coolers and beers. The girls seemed suddenly bored. One played with her ear, the other said to quit throwing so long. "Yeah, yeah, yeah," Chip said.

Six short passes later the Traicheffs had their second touchdown.

Thirty minutes later the score was 36-6.

Stan hovered over the ball and looked across at Chip who was sipping a beer, his blue eyes flecked with boredom. He wanted to rush Stan and get rid of the five-steamboat rule. "Hey that's what we agreed to," Stan said.

"Shit. It's candy-ass, man." He took another sip. "Let's make it three-steamboat rush."

Rick sighed like air leaking out of a slashed tire. Stan knew that Chip would crumble under the pressure, but now it appeared that Rick would too. He had a hard time keeping Chip reigned in, and Rick's face—jaw slack, lower lip trembling—was surrendering to Chip's wildness. Rick sighed again, a short jabbing puff, and pushed back his long hair and looked at Stan, his eyes tired, yet hopeful.

"Okay," Stan said, "Okay. Three-steamboat rush. Instead of five." Chip was a suck, a real pain in the ass.

Stan took the snap and lobbed a pass to Pete slanting across the open middle. He didn't know what happened after that because Rick shoved Stan sprawling into shards of rock. He felt one of his ankles buckle and he hobbled to his feet.

"Hey, man. I'm sorry," Rick said. "Really. I didn't mean to hit you so hard—"

Stan surveyed the field. Pete stood by a tree stump. "First down," Stan shouted. "First down," he repeated for dramatic emphasis, as he clapped his hands and hop-hobbled across the field and looked at the girls. "Way to go, Pete." He patted his son's head. Rick's anger and violence weren't going to throw Stan-the-Man off his freakin' game. No way.

On the next snap, they rushed two players before the count of three. Stan saw a blur of white cloth and heard the clank of a peace chain. He also smelled beer, but still had enough poise like Johnny Unitas to lace a spiral to a wide open Matt who tucked his head down and kicked up his knobby knees as he busted along the uncut grass for the touch. Stan's chest stung from the slap of Chip's hands just after he had released the ball. When his boys returned to the huddle, Stan saw that they were worried. They didn't want to look anywhere but down, at dull stones, tufts of grass and black ants. Things were careening wildly. Stan's shirt was stained with beer foam. "Hey, don't sweat it, guys. I'm okay."

"I don't know, Dad. I don't know." Matt kicked at wedged stones.

"Yeah," Petey said. "And I'm hungry. Can we stop soon?"

"It's not polite to quit when you've got a big lead, fellas. It's like playing poker and you hold all the chips. You gotta let them decide when to quit."

"Yeah, but—" Matt said.

"I know, kid, I know. They think they're real tough." Stan shrugged and shook his head.

On the following kickoff, Kirby ran low to the ground, his body and shoulders rolling forward like a hurtling bowling ball, as he slugged through Petey's two-handed touch, sending him wobbling like a bunch of pins. Petey got up and wiped blood from his lip. The girls had left. Stan stood and glared at Rick, Chip and Kirby.

Kirby shrugged half-heartedly. "Sorry kid. You're okay, right?" He cracked open another beer.

"Hey, Stan." His wife Jean stood against the darkening trees in her black Capri slacks. Her hair too was black and he loved how it glowed in the dusk and he hoped maybe he'd get lucky tonight. They had spent the past eleven months separated, getting back together, separating, and getting together again, and he wanted everything to run smoothly, this time, this holiday. He didn't want a big scene like two Christmases ago when he bought Jean a $45 banjo instead of the $100 guitar and she got real disappointed because she wanted a guitar and not a banjo, but he couldn't afford a guitar so he broke the damn banjo. And then there were the fat jokes around the table during supper. Right after he'd be needling Matt a little bit and the kid would be crying, Jean would start in about Stan's weight and how he weighed only 138 when they married and look at him now, a "big, fat sweet potato," and how he hated those jokes, but the kids and Jean would laugh, and they were all back together now, and it was Victoria Day, and they'd eat soon and do sparklers and watch the holiday fireworks and everything would be fine. "C'mon, Stan. Everybody else has already eaten. It's late, and the food's finally done, and it's getting cold."

It slightly annoyed him that she was calling him away from the game. "Sure, hon, sure. Twenty more minutes."

"It's ready now."

"Who cares, hon? Do we have to do everything like everyone else?"

"No. But it's getting cold and it's getting dark, and we still have to do sparklers and there's the fireworks. . ."

"Let it wait. We're having fun out here." Stan smiled awkwardly at his sons who were retreating, their eyes looking away, afraid of another fight. Mrs. Traicheff sighed and sat on the edge of a picnic table. "Twenty minutes," she huffed.

"If you quit, you forfeit," Chip said.

"What? C'mon. It's getting dark anyway, and we need to eat."

"Quit you forfeit," Chip repeated.

"Now wait a minute, Chip," Rick interrupted. "That's not right."

"We're not quitting," Matt said, his lower lip determined.

Stan wasn't real sure if after all of his years of quoting Vince Lombardi that the point wasn't lost, somehow misplaced, instilling his sons with false valor and values. So what if they quit. Big deal. The boys knew, deep down, that they were the better team. "Let's play first team to score eleven touches." The score was 42-12.

"Make it a hundred points," Kirby said, bent over, his hands tugging the frayed ends of his shorts.

"Yeah, a hundred," Chip said, a string of sweat running along the chain around his neck.

"Six doesn't divide into a hundred," Matt said.

For the next ten minutes, Stan could tell that Rick's gang was real mad because they played aggressively careless. They were slapping instead of touching, and setting hard picks, and Kirby was tired, the energy sputtering from him like the dying fizz of a fly. He caught a ball on a short route and instead of jerking and spinning from Matt, he hunkered down, and plodded through him, elbows high, as he trotted the field for the touch.

Stan placed his hands on his hips and the tips of his ears shivered with a hot numbness, and suddenly he felt like he was back in grade school readying for a fight and fearing he'd turtle. Mrs. Traicheff stepped away from the picnic table and briskly paced over buzzed tree stumps. Her chin was down, her eyes level. "That's no touchdown," she said. "Matt hit him with two hands." She was shouting. Stan liked the anger and love in her voice. He said something in agreement.

"No way." Kirby wiped sweat from his forehead that left a dirty streak like mud on the side of a car. He rubbed at some of the residue with the end of his "Starvin' Marvin" T-shirt. "He never touched me."

"You ran over him for chissakes," Stan said.

"So? He never touched me. Not with two hands."

Mrs. Traicheff threw up her hands and then walked towards Matt, her shoulders straight, and her breasts and hips in the blueness of night were slight but strong. She told Matt to sit out a couple of downs to catch his wind.

"Hon, Matt's okay. Let him play."

"I'll play," she said, not looking at anyone, her eyes staring off at the cold, dark blue that had filled the sky like a spreading litmus stain.

There was a long pause. Chip crossed his arms, flicked hair from his mouth, and looked over at Rick. "I don't know," Rick said, the spongy tongue to one of his thongs crinkled and frayed. Kirby had his back to everyone.

"Hon, I don't think—"

"No, I want to." She crammed a smile into the left side of her mouth, and Stan knew that she was annoyed because she always smiled like that when she was annoyed.

"Let her play," Rick said.

Jean told Stan to get her the ball and he did. She and Pete ran short curl routes, button hooks and fades. At first the guys gave Jean a lot of room, but when she caught three passes in a row they closed their spacing, and when she caught three more, including a touchdown, they yelled and swore at each other. And the way Jean glided, shoulder and hip-dekeing through the middle of the field, dazzling around their set feet, reminded Stan of when they were teenagers and had first made out in the dank basement of her father's house near the old coal chute. She would run her hands along the sides to the waistband of his shorts, and he'd grace the cups of her bra and she'd move, shift, tuck in her elbows and laugh, and they'd kiss and laugh, and they didn't do much of that anymore.

Moments later, Jean intercepted Rick's pass and ran for another touchdown. She spiked the ball, violently, and it bounded high and haphazardly, and she walked off the field, hands folded across her chest. She kissed Matt's cheek and told him to get back in there.

"Mom's cool," Matt said to his Dad as they lined up for the next kickoff. Stan nodded, but it all felt strange like the time he wrapped her birthday gifts in weird, oblong and short boxes to disguise what was inside, and then dared her to guess and she guessed them all right anyway. He had been so sure of himself and her correct guesses changed all that. And now it was the same. She was mad at him, maybe because she felt that whatever lessons he was teaching the boys had become obscured through the game. And that was definitely true, but she had made it even more difficult to find truth. Midway through the game, Stan had realized that he was wrong for pushing Matt to be tough, insisting that he play to win, but he couldn't quit the game. Yes, the ugliness that winning carries to the losers was obvious by the way Chip and Kirby, and even Rick, carried on, and that's the lesson he wanted the kids to know—that the game should be fun, first, and never ugly, but the Traicheffs also had an obligation to the game, to finish it gracefully, and then Jean got involved, scored 12 points, a regular Victoria Day hero, and the lesson about winning gracefully seemed all messed up, the neat package unraveling, the bright bow knotted, another broken banjo.

Rick carried the following kickoff up the sloped side of the field, near the uncut grass. Matt angled toward him, and when Rick twisted back, spun around, he fell awfully fast, and then he started jumping and screaming.

Rick's left baby toe dropped at an awkward angle, down from the rest. And the tongue of the thong limped forward, bent, the leather ends shattered. He had tripped over a gopher hole and busted his toe. Matt looked away. Stan walked over. Rick grimaced and hobbled on his heel. His whole body bobbed like a broken piston.

"I gotta go, man." He forced a smile.

Stan nodded and tried to keep from laughing. Somehow the whole thing was so damn funny. Kirby and Chip carried Rick from the field like they were in a war movie. Chip shouted something about the game being suspended as they disappeared into blue-black.

"We won, didn't we, Dad?" Matt asked.

Stan shrugged. "You got any homework to do for tomorrow, kid?"

"Yeah, math."

"When we get home, I'll help you with it." He hugged Matt around the shoulders. "Great game, guys."

"I got three touchdowns," Petey said.

Later they sat around the darkness of the picnic table and roasted marshmallows. Jean lit a punk, opened a package of sparklers, and handed them to the boys. Their red tips glowed. Stan asked for one too.

"You should have quit when I told you," she said, passing him a sparkler. "The food got all cold."

"Aw. It's okay honey." He patted her hip. "I thought it tasted great."

"It's not okay. It's not."

She kissed his forehead, and Stan felt the disappointment in her shoulders, as he sat there twirling the sparkler, absently writing the names of his sons.

Public Speaking

When I was fourteen my classmates wanted to be accountants, lawyers, hockey players. Me, I wanted to be Jewish.

I didn't know much about Chanukah or Yom Kippur, but I did know some really cool words—*shiksa, goy, schmuck*—and the *Mad* magazine iconoclasm of Lenny Bruce. Bruce's comedy was all Jewish, an irreverent send up of popular forms that affirmed and denied the world we lived in. When Bruce suggested that the Lone Ranger was on the take he showed a love for the western genre while also questioning our icons of justice. His humor captured the outsider's identity: our desire to be a part of and apart from the mainstream.

And that's the way I was. Hopelessly nerdy and not-yet-proud to be ethnic, I didn't fit into WASP valley; I couldn't skate or fire a slapshot, I dreaded shop class, fearing I'd lose an arm in a lathe, and I knew that one day the Led Zep heads would take me out because I insisted on carrying a thermos lunch instead of the standard paper bag. My only chance was to be funny, so I read *The Essential Lenny Bruce* during homeroom, recess, lunch, and dreamed of being liked. Anyway, the standup comedy part wasn't working out either, as on a lazy Thursday afternoon I had to tell Mom about the "*schmuck*" thing.

She was standing against the kitchen table, flour dotting the outside of her arms like dried mud, as she rolled out pizza crust. Tomato sauce sputtered on the range and dishes clung over a wet towel on the counter. Dad, who was usually still delivering milk to the east-end suburbs, was home early that day and was crashed on the couch, looking at vague patterns on the ceiling. In front of him was a jar packed with celery and water and a loaf of bread, the bag folded underneath because he had lost the twist tie.

"Whattya mean, Matt?" Mom asked, anger in her voice, her forehead wrinkling. She rolled the crust too thinly, stopped, scratched a large lump off the table, smacked it together like an icy snowball, and rolled it out again.

"I can't perform tomorrow." I had made it to the finals for Woodbine Junior High's public speaking contest, but Mrs. Thatcher, our coach and coordinator, whose hair looked like a scoop and a half of ice cream and voice traced with *Leave it to Beaver* kindness, thought my send up of Superman was in poor taste. "Whenever I broke into my Broom-Hilda shtick, Mrs. T. turned away and looked out the exit door. All week she did that."

"She didn't like the bit where Superschmuck goes into the closet to change and Broom-Hilda attacks him?"

"No, she didn't."

Dad stretched and struggled to his feet. His hair was spiked like a defensive puffer fish. I hoped he hadn't been drinking.

"She also didn't like my joke about Bentover Kent wearing high-heeled shoes."

"Oh, that's a funny joke," Mom said, and then shook her head. "Cross-dressing is hip. Very hip." Actually, Mom gave me that joke. She ran a boutique and listened to glam rock: the New York Dolls, David Bowie, Queen, so she was into that whole gender-bending thing that was so big in the early-to-mid seventies. Dad thought she was nuts when she said that it wouldn't bother her any if he wanted to wear lipstick. Not that he did want to wear any, not my Dad, but she was open to the possibility.

"But mainly she didn't like the word, '*schmuck*,'" I said. After our final practice, Mrs. Thatcher kneeled next to me on the stage, a hand clasped around a bracelet on her wrist. Pipes ran along the wall, hard klieg lights dipped above, and a blue curtain slashed behind. "The '*schmuck*' reference might offend our Jewish friends," she had said.

"This is fucking ridiculous," Dad blurted, the words sleep graveled. He shook his head and swept back black hair, as his forehead beaded up with rectangular sweat. "They censoring my kid?"

Suddenly we didn't say nothing, because he was doing all the yelling. He spoke in broken Macedonian, calling Thatcher a *drislo*—that means she shits her pants, and a *gusz*—that means an ass. He also said that she had a *te tresna penjero*—a broken window, or in plainer terms, a cracked head. The outburst surprised us. I'd practiced all week and Dad, looking at the ceiling, had never bothered to really hear the routine. Mom coached me on the punchlines, but when I told Dad that I'd made it to the finals, he smiled and suggested that I put some Clearasil on my face.

"What was it she said, 'our Jewish friends'?"

"Yeah, Dad. She said it would offend them."

"That's bull." He hitched up his work pants. His T-shirt had sand-colored stains under the arms. "Bullshit. That's what it is. Bullshit."

"How do you know? You haven't heard my speech," I said with the cockiness of adolescence trying to find its voice in the world. "Maybe it is offensive."

"No. Your Mom's told me all about it. Sounds funny. Although I don't know about that high-heeled shoes bit."

"Oh, come on, Stan. That's a riot. The kids go for that."

"Okay, okay. But where I work, they beat you up for that."

Mom shook her head and rolled her eyes. She now had flour dust in her hair and along the left side of her face. "Matt, you've performed the speech for a lot of people and no one, except this Mrs. Thatcher, has ever been offended."

"But I haven't performed it for Jews."

"Yes, you have. Moe and his daughter Miriam."

"They're Jewish?"

"Yes." Mom smiled brightly.

"Oh."

"Well there you go," Dad said. "I told you it was funny."

We waited outside Principal Allan's office. This was Dad's idea. He even put on a plaid sportcoat to look respectable. We were going to argue my case, and get me reinstated to speak at the assembly tomorrow. Mom agreed. She said than in last year's yearbook message Allan emphasized tolerance for all of the new immigrants to Canada. Allan hoped that Toronto was cosmopolitan not only in look but also in attitude. Mom felt that Allan was a hip guy and all we had to do was appeal to his hipness. Dad wasn't sure about the hip part of the plan. "We're second generation Slavs. What does he care about us?"

"Shh—he might hear you," Mom said.

"I don't care if he hears me. He ain't shutting up my son. That ain't right, it ain't right."

Mr. Allan had heard the speech earlier in the week and when Mrs. Thatcher removed me from the program, he kept rubbing his upper lip with a pensive finger as he walked me to homeroom. His hair, a flat red, looked like a dab of fresh paint. "I thought parts of the speech were very funny, very creative," he said. So maybe, I figured, if Dad just calmed down, things could work out. And then Dad said that *teekva* word again as Mr. Allan opened the door. "Mr. and Mrs. Traicheff? Matt. Come in."

We entered. His office was crammed with boxes and boxes of books that had yet to be shelved. Fanned across his desk were file folders, memos, unopened mail, stacks of recent literary magazines and a World War One aviator's hat, the goggles resting back on the leather. I had heard that he wore that hat whenever he rode his red bicycle, which was also in the room, propped along a wall, the handlebars and front wheel twisting outward. Behind hung civic pictures of Mr. Allan shaking hands with various educators and members of parliament. Cornering us were empty metal bookshelves. He leaned in a cozy chair. The arms were padded. "I'm glad you came."

Our chairs weren't as comfortable. They were cobalt blue, and the backs looked like thick glass lenses. But Dad didn't mind. He hunched forward and spoke with an eloquence I had never heard before. He told a story about being an immigrant, the 1950s, and church-going. Back then the church elders frequently argued about their roots, what part of the old country they hailed from. Laszlo and Spiro had lived in the same village, tilled the same field, but when Laszlo called it Zehlevoh, and Spiro, who recognized the Greek occupation, called it Antartikon, my father interrupted their reminiscences and said, "Antartikon, Zehlevoh. You're still standing on the same spot of ground, only now it's Canada." Canada was our country, and we should be proud of it, and think like Canadians, not Bulgarians, or Macedonians, or Albanians, or heaven help us, Greeks. So his son used a Jewish word? So what? Aren't Jews Canadians? Can't one Macedonian-Canadian borrow a word from another Jewish-Canadian?

"I understand," Mr. Allan said, his eyes steady and gentle. He paused and raised his chin. "But we're not a melting pot, like the U.S. Canada is a cultural mosaic. We are pieces of a quilt, a fabric joined— many people, many quilts, separate, distinct, together." He rolled up his sleeves. "If one person complains about the word '*schmuck*,' Mrs. Thatcher, myself, we could damage that fabric."

I wasn't following where he was going with that mosaic stuff, and neither was Dad, for we were both looking at Dad's left foot, turned awkwardly—stiff, sharp—I was damn sure that it was suddenly going to snap.

"But the *schmuck* reference has nothing to do with Jews. Kent is a gentile," Mom said, her voice tentative, distant. "It's not like Matt's making fun of Jews."

"No, he isn't, and I don't have a problem with the speech because I know how to interpret it." He leaned over and tied the laces to his ankle-top sneakers. "Your son's very funny, but Mrs. Thatcher and I are concerned about the students. Do *they* know how to interpret it? That's the question." He stood and walked to the window, his back strong and broad. "Look, everyday I deal with intolerance. The intercom rings and there's blacks and whites fighting in the gym, 'Paki' jokes in the halls. Some, the school superintendent for example, might see '*schmuck*' as furthering those divisions."

"I didn't, I mean, I meant to use the word like he's a dufus. You know, a *schmuck*?" My cheeks were hot.

Mr. Allan moved from the window, smiled, and picked up his aviator's hat. "I know." He touched the goggles, sat down, and I wondered as he pedaled the city's blue streets, if he too had wanted to be a flyer, a knight of the air, dipping over no-man's land in Billy Bishop or Raymond Collishaw's squadron.

There was another awkward pause. Mom didn't know what to say. Dad spoke. "How? How can '*schmuck*' offend anyone? It's just a word that means a dork."

"There's two problems with Matt's use of the word." He pushed aside the hat. "The first concerns sending a message of intolerance. The second concerns cultural appropriation. *Schmuck* is a Jewish word, and your son isn't Jewish."

Yes, I wasn't Jewish, but I couldn't believe I was actually in trouble for wanting to be. Lenny Bruce once said that everyone in New York was Jewish, and everyone outside of New York was not, and since I was a Yankees fan that made me an honorary Jew. Anyway, what was I supposed to do? Come up with a Macedonian word—Super*teekva*, Super*gusz*, Super*tetresnapenjero*? Nobody would get it. To be Jewish was hard and wild, to be Macedonian was lost and invisible. Jews existed. They had cultural capital: Stan Lee and Jack Kirby created an entire Marvel Universe and they were Jews; William M. Gaines of *Mad* and nearly all of the Hollywood producers were Jews. The dominant popular narratives of our time were Jewish. And I wanted to borrow those voices and engage in their dialogue because as a Macedonian I had nothing, not even a flag—my grandfather's country was annexed by the Yugoslavians and Greeks. We had no Lenny Bruces.

"Jewish word? My kid can't use a Jewish word because he's not Jewish?"

"Yes. It's theirs, not his." Mr. Allan shrugged. "I'm sorry, but I'm trying to be sensitive."

"Sensitive? You're talking segregation."

"No. I'm not."

Back then I didn't know what Dad's point was, and maybe I don't agree with it now, but one thing's for sure: I admired him, sitting upright in that damn sportcoat that he hated to wear, rapidly talking way cool, his voice a chattering tommygun. Dad and Mom believed in assimilation, in leaving the past behind, putting Canada first. Dad saw no problem in using a Jewish word because we were all part of the same country, and we were immigrant brothers, the 1890-1915 wave, who came over at the same time. But fitting in wasn't so hot. In my mid-twenties, I learned how much Dad resented his Macedonian roots, telling me that he still felt that his Slavic speech rhythms had denied him promotions and a house in the suburbs. He never liked who he was and that's why he drank.

"Besides," Dad said, standing, looking at the loop of his belt, the leather slightly frayed, as he tried to harness one last phrase of eloquence. "I don't think it's right to stop him from speaking the day before he goes on. It isn't right."

"It's unfortunate."

"'Unfortunate?' How many kids speaking tomorrow aren't English-white?"

Mr. Allan slid out his top desk drawer and looked at a list of speakers. "Well, there's a Chinese girl."

"Debbie Chao?" I said. "Yeah. Debbie loved my speech." And she did, but I'm embarrassed to admit now that there was an Asian joke in the piece. Debbie never said anything about that there, but the joke had something to do with Bentover buying his Lee jeans in Chinatown and getting four eggrolls and a Bruce Lee poster free. Something like that. Lee was big back then—*Fists of Fury, Chinese Connection, Enter the Dragon*. I dug the guy, but anyway, we were so focused on the "Jewish friends" thing that some of the more questionable gags—including several homophobic ones—got overlooked.

"You have one Oriental kid," Dad said, looking at Allan's list. "But the rest are Scotch and English. I don't see no Italians, Macedonians or Jews."

"Well, I see your point. Perhaps the selection committee—"

Dad sighed heavily. He wanted to say something else, but he had too much pride. He sat, his face like chunked-up asphalt, exposed.

"I want to do the right thing." Mr. Allan couldn't look at Dad. He smiled at Mom. "Let me tell an anecdote as a way to explain my position."

I don't remember the story very well. Maybe I wasn't listening carefully. Dad's pain had thrown me back into myself, my family and who I am. Mr. Allan's story had something to do with a Board of Education meeting and some old guy who didn't like foreigners very much. The old guy supposedly said "fuck them" about immigrants. Mr. Allan paused after saying the "f" word. My parents said nothing. They didn't even flinch. They used the world all the time at home so it was no big deal.

"I'm a principal. I just used that word in this office. Now some people might be alarmed at that."

Dad shrugged, his eyes ceiling glazed.

"You see my point?"

"No," Dad said. "No, I don't see it."

Mr. Allan rubbed the back of an ear. "Fuck. I just said that word in this office."

"Yeah. Okay, so?"

"In this context it's not appropriate. In front of parents, students. No. At home, if you choose, at the pub, it's okay to use that word. 'Schmuck' is the same way. It's a word that means penis, after all."

"It does?" I said.

"Well, yes. 'Penis' or in the street vernacular, 'prick.' Anyway, within the context of this school and our educational goals and the problems we have, I can't allow such a word."

There was a long silence and we sat like that there for awhile. I read and reread the spine of the *Evergreen Review* and wondered when Mr. Allan's bicycle would fall over. I knew that Super*teekva* wouldn't work, but maybe something else would. "What if I changed the character from Superschmuck to Super Sap? Instead of getting power from bagels and matzo crackers he gets them from pancakes and maple syrup."

"That might work," Mr. Allan said. "That might work." He suggested that I revise the routine and run it by Mrs. Thatcher tomorrow. Maybe I could still be part of the show.

Years later, Mom says that Mr. Allan, an individualist—a man who wore black Chuck Taylors, wrote poetry and rode a red bicycle— smiled when we got to the door, admiring our individualism, our desire to stand and question the system. Maybe that's true, but what I remember is not Mr. Allan but Dad, squeezing my hand as we left the office and then saying nothing more about it.

The next day Mrs. Thatcher and Mr. Allan okayed the revised presentation and I spoke at the assembly. Super Sap, wearing high heels and gaining power from pancakes, took on the evil forces of Captain Commode and his lackey Toilet Paper Roll, flushing them down the john and saving the world. Only once, I think, I slipped and called Sap, *Schmuck.*

I was glad to perform.

I finished third.

Davey Walker, who talked about his stuttering problem, took second, and Sheila Carter, who discussed life in a family of twelve, took first. My parents were there (two years later they were divorced) and Dad gave me a standing ovation when I finished. My eyes burned when I saw that and I wanted him to sit down, but I wanted him to keep standing, too, to stand even after it was done.

Later, we were all in the main hallway, planning to go to the Peanut Plaza, a small mall, to celebrate. "That was great, fucking great," Dad said. "And funny. I told you it was funny. Did you hear those people laughing, didja kid?"

"Yeah."

"I mean, that's something. It means something, you know?"

I nodded and Mom said I could get a record and Dad said, "Let's get some ice cream, too."

At the mall we had Neapolitan ice cream. Mom bought a new Eric Clapton record. I couldn't find anything by Lenny Bruce. At least nothing I didn't already own.

"Hawks Hopes High Heading into New Season"

General Manager Scott Christie is smiling.

At least for now.

The preseason has just ended, and the USHL's Waterloo Black Hawks swing into action next Saturday here at Young Arena against the Des Moines Buccaneers. Junior A hockey is back!

Christie thinks that this might be the best bunch he's ever put on the ice. "We got a gritty team. A good mix of veteran grinders and young kids with speed, and we're going to challenge this year and offer Waterloo some great hockey," the thirty-five year old Christie, a former USHL official said.

Let's hope so. The past three years haven't been kind to the locals. They failed to make the playoffs and they haven't had a winning season in ten years.

Christie thinks that's about to change. "This is the fifth year out of our five-year plan, and everything's in place to make a serious run for the Clark Cup," the championship of the USHL.

Head Coach Scott Michaels agrees. "Last year we had some guys, frankly, who just didn't want to play. And weren't dedicated. This year's bunch is focused. These guys really busted their butts in summer tryouts and the preseason."

The Hawks were 6 and 3 in preseason games.

Owner and President Raymond Southworth, who had threatened to move the team last year if a new arena wasn't built, expects big things. "I think we'll finish in the top three. We had a strong draft and got a good mix of kids."

So who are the stars to watch?

Goalie Francis Koslov, Massapequa, Long Island, returns in the pipes and Coach expects he'll see a lot of offers during the early signing period in November. "Francis is a strong angle goaltender, stand-up style, quick with the glove," Michaels praised. "He's kept us in a lot of games, and I expect he'll be an All-Star."

Seventeen year-old Kevin Ogilvie, an import from Canada (the USHL allows each team to carry two import players), has the front office buzzing. "He's probably the fastest skater in the league, and has nice, soft hands. He'll be our second-line center and help put the puck in the net," Coach Michaels said.

Christie, too, sees potential in the Canadian youngster, but feels the kid needs "just a little more grit."

Joining Ogilvie on left wing is another newcomer, Austin, Minnesota's Isaiah Sullivan, who's all grit. "He's a banger," Christie grins. "The kind of guy that fights in the corners, runs goalies, and makes space for our players."

In other words, Sully's the feisty, instigator type that Christie admires and stockpiles his teams with. Let's just hope this team isn't as slow and plodding as last season's.

And back on the blueline, for his fourth season, is veteran rearguard Ryan Chatham, the team captain. "Ryan's the team's heart and soul," Coach Michaels says. "He logs twenty-eight minutes a game—plays the power play, the penalty kill, and often double shifts."

Christie agrees. "The kid's all Black Hawk. A Hall-of-Famer. We'll probably retire his number four when he moves on to the next level."

So will the team finish over .500? Will they make the playoffs? "Hockey's a game of emotion," Christie says. "And this team's got it. If you want to watch pretty skating and dancing, then go to Europe. The Black Hawks play a bruising style, and we're going to do that skillfully."

The Hawks will be at Younkers, Wednesday at 6 p.m., to sign autographs. Smiling Scott Christie will also be there, handing out schedules, signing team posters, and no doubt demonstrating the art of the body check.

--Matt Traicheff
Waterloo Courier, September 6, 1995

Ice Skiing

Ryan Chatham hates being labeled a goon.

But he hears it on the road. One lady in Sioux City wobbles a hooked rubber chicken across the ice every time Chats is in the box. The chicken dangles and squats like a runny poached egg, and when she reels it up and down, the crowd spazzes like Iggy Pop on "Raw Power," but how can Chats be a chicken when he leads the league in penalty minutes every season? Hell, Ryan's a hard-nosed defenseman. He carries the puck up the middle of the ice so that he can't be trapped along the boards. He also throws crisp hip checks at center. But he's no chicken. And, despite the rantings of Sioux City's fans, he's certainly no "Hey, Mr.ElbowsKingoftheGoon Squad. Asshole."

Ryan shrugs, his shoulder pads tight and heavy like manhole covers, and he and his teammates circle in the neutral zone, listening to Coach Michaels' long and short whistles, shifting the skating from mid-tempo to fast flow. As he crosses over, arcing left to right, Ryan watches his teammate Isaiah Sullivan. Sully's crossovers are white cap choppy, arms dragging him down. Last night, the team lost again, 7-1 to Sioux City's Musketeers. The Waterloo Black Hawks are now 2 and 7, last in the USHL's North Division. And Coach Michaels has had them skating side to side for over an hour.

"You guys looked terrible last night," he yells after calling them to center. "Just terrible. A bunch of candy asses." Coach has a square jaw and his chin, the chunky clunk of a kindergarten eraser, now rests on the wedged knob of his stick. He wears a baseball cap and white lining streams through his threadbare sweats.

Yesterday, Ryan heard that if coach isn't at .500 by the all-star break, owner Raymond Southworth will have Coach fired. Several of the guys are homesick enough and they're not real comfortable with rumors and instability. Ryan looks down at Coach's inky thick diagrams of a pinch forecheck with the forwards digging low. Hell, most of these Black Hawk kids are only 17 and 18. Chats is a little more laid back about change and all that. When he was a kid, his Dad, a truck driver, slept and drank and slept a lot, and often Mom drove Ryan to early morning hockey practices. Mom also took him to father and son Boy Scouts banquets because Dad was too road- or booze-wobbly. So, Ryan figures he can handle all this damn instability, but as captain, he knows that a lot of his teammates can't. Junior A Hockey isn't supposed to be that damn complicated.

Coach Michaels tells the defense to not let the forwards get the puck back to the point. Ride them hard into the boards, if you have to. They nod, and for Ryan, it seems odd, that in a few weeks they might be listening to someone else, someone who draws different smudges, maybe thick ice-picked blocks or scratchy pubic wisps on a white board. Fuck. Coach gets his kids into good colleges and knows the game, but when Ryan had barged into GM Scott Christie's office and asked if the rumors were true, Scott said, yes winning is important, and yes there's pressure from upstairs. "But do we have to get to .500 by January 17th?" Ryan demanded. Scottie, his thick hair matted like wet paint on his forehead, leaned back in his padded chair, and glanced at pictures of Gordie Howe taken in the 1940s. He stared at the crisscrossed hairlines on the ice and only said something or other about old-time hockey, desire and emotion.

Coach goes over the details again, and Ryan's group of yellow-for-D-and-red-for-O- jerseyed players glide to the South End of Young Arena. Ryan waits his turn, gently rocking on the back of his blades. In front of him slants Sullivan, tipping left, waving up toward Section P and Annie Riordan. Her red hair sticks out from her black beret like thin pipe cleaners. Eight-year old Annie's cute, with her freckled face and eyes that always seemed freckled too. And she sure has a crush on Sullivan. Chats knows it, everyone knows it. And they tease Sully relentlessly about it: "When are you going to take her out," "Boy she's hot." "Don't forget to have her home by ten."

Sullivan seems to love the attention. He talks a lot to Annie about the game, and her parents are big fans too. Two months ago, they complained to Coach about Sullivan's playing time. Early in the preseason, Michaels sat Sully against the faster, more Euro-style teams. But after the left winger worked on the bike and weights, Michaels put him on the second line, as an enforcer protecting the Canadian Kevin Ogilvie from taking cheap hits. Anyway, Sully's real close with the Riordans, and one time Ryan and K. O. visited and they all played Parcheesi in a basement out of a 60s time capsule—lava lamps, formica tables, and psychedelic-looking LOVE posters. Ryan dug the posters, and imagined getting it on with a groupie under a drooping mushroom, and then he set up a blockade against Annie. He raced his pawns around the board and won. Shit, he hates to lose at anything.

Annie smiles back at Isaiah, but she wasn't smiling that day. Man, she was pissed. And so was Sully and K. O. And now her beret hangs over her eyes like the edge of a billowed parachute. She and Scott Christie are the only fans there. At least Scottie's always watching; it's kinda cool to know that they've always got the GM there. The guys have never even seen Southworth. He also owns a team in the ECHL, the Tennessee Titans, or Titties, or something or other, and that's where he spends all his time, threatening from Knoxville.

Ryan and Sully line up along the edge of the near circle, and Coach yells, "Go!" They slash around the net, a ridge of snow dust spraying, and a quick snick-snick as Sullivan pulls ahead and backhands the puck to Michaels at the point. Coach snaps a wrister that goalie Fran Koslov kicks free with his skate and paddle of his stick.

"Hey, Chatham. Take a little sharper angle and once he's beat you to the corner, finish your check." Coach's eyes are a pair of flat lines.

Ryan nods, his helmet tightening around his ears and the top of his head. Several forwards rib him about not even getting a glove on Sullivan. "Yeah, yeah, yeah," Ryan says, spitting all over his yellow practice jersey. Up in the reds, Annie jump-slides across her seat. Sullivan waves and points again.

Next, Ogilvie glides around the net, his skates kicking up small puffs of white. The defender has the angle, lunging slightly, slighting leaning, but K. O. dekes with the shoulder, spins left, puck cradled on his backhand, forehand, and then a bank pass off the boards to Michaels, who snaps a wrister that Kos gloves nonchalantly. Ryan is impressed by Ogs' moves. If only he had that talent.

Coach praises Ogs on the pass and the young seventeen-year-old glances at the ice, adjusts the straps to his helmet and skates by Sullivan, tapping the winger's shin pads with his stick. "How's our number one fan?" The cold air has quilted Kevin's face into red splotches.

Isaiah talks about Paul Kariya, Mike Modano, and Joe Sakic and how Annie thinks that he's as good as them, maybe even Gretzky. She's writing a report on Sully for class called "Isaiah Sullivan: My Best Friend," and he's going to go to Kingsley School in a few days to talk hockey.

"That's pretty cool," Ogs says.

Ryan listens and says nothing. Annie writes with broad strokes. Ryan likes visiting the Riordans because they let the guys hang out and listen to the Doors and watch *Slap Shot*. But, one thing's for sure, he never wants to be mistaken for a Hanson brother.

Several other players finish the drill and it's Ryan's turn again, this time from the far circle. Before Michaels yells "Go," Ryan has powered into his skate, digging the front tips of his blades into the ice to accelerate. Sully curves around the net, a step ahead of Chats and the far post. Ryan raises his stick and crosschecks him into the boards.

The plexiglass shudders and Sullivan braces back with his stick, but Ryan lowers his head, drives with his legs, and rubs the wet underside of his glove into Sully's face. Sullivan curses. Their arms tangle, push and shove. And then Ryan throws a punch, nicking Sully's left ear. Sullivan drops his gloves and punches Ryan in the neck. Koslov props his mask on the upper meshing of the net and tries to stop the fight by holding his blocker between their punches. Coach's whistle sounds like a truck with bad brakes.

"That's enough." Michaels separates them. "What the hell's with you, Chatham?" His eyebrows snake together into one bushy zipper. "Go sit and cool off."

"Huh?" There's more fights in practice than in a real game. What's the big deal?

"Sit down."

Christie, bending forward from a seated position, stands up in the end reds. He presses his hands into his thighs and slightly smiles, his eyes crescent moons. "Hell, Ryan. You didn't even drop your gloves."

Ryan wipes his lips and glides sulkily toward the bench. He slams the door and sits. Sweat from his hair drips onto his hands and he looks at his skates. Maybe not dropping the gloves when Sullivan dropped his was sucky, but at least he didn't whack him over the head with his stick. Shit, everybody protects Sullivan and likes him. Probably because he's black and they're all afraid of looking like a bunch of racists. Ryan can't look up at Annie.

Michaels starts another drill, a series of two-on-ones from just outside the blueline. Ogilvie, smoothly skating, freezes the defenseman into a twist of licorice by faking the pass with a dip, and then fires a wrister over Koslov's glove. Moments later, Bobby Torrio, the team's first-line center, squat and strangely lithe, floats over the blueline. He saucers a pass to Sullivan who snaps it under Koslov's right pad. Koslov shakes his head.

"Don't back up so far into the net," Coach says. "You're giving the shooter too much to shoot at. Come out a little bit, challenge."

Koslov nods, tugs off his helmet, tightens some straps, readjusts them, pokes hair behind the plate in back of the mask, and takes it off again to wipe sweat from his eyes. The joints of his fingers are wrapped in gritted white tape that looks like wet streaks of ocean sand.

Ryan sneaks a glimpse at Annie. She's not glowering or looking down his way. Her eyes are at the blueline. Shit, he shouldn't have punched Sullivan with his gloves on. That wasn't right. The gloves. Damn. That's worse than a Parcheesi blockade. Maybe Ryan Chatham is a goon.

But Annie doesn't seem to mind, she's just concentrating, her knees nudging her chin. Ryan wishes he had some fans. Most of the guys have girlfriends. Jeff Paplowsky, the left winger on Torrio's line, has folks who attend every home game. Annie writes more broad strokes. That's going to be some report. Southworth's a dick.

Coach follows up the two-on-ones with three-on-twos. Shit, it wasn't even that big of a fight, for chrissakes. Maybe that's the problem with this year's Black Hawks—too few genuine tough guys. Helmets say a lot about personalities and most players are wusses, wimps or waldos. Wusses wear the wire-caged mask and helmet trying to hide from the world. Seventeen year-old kids and flashy centers with no guts wear that baby. And boy do they like to get their sticks high, because they think they're invincible. No payback. You can punch them in the face all you want, and all you'll do is hurt your fingers. Wimps wear the full-faced shield. They look good but take no risks. Waldos, well, they wear the half-shields. Wingers, glamour boys, Paplowsky. The few, the really cool players, are Marlboro Men, usually defensemen who have to get down and block shots. They wear helmets without visors, and they'd wear no helmet if the league rules would allow it.

The PA system breaks into "Bad to the Bone," the cue for the players to leave the ice, and Ryan dreams of looping in some Black Sabbath "Supernaut." Tony Iommi's rubbery bass lines would smack opponents into a series of post-concussion syndromes. Coach hurriedly writes on a clipboard. "Chatham, my office. Twenty minutes."

Ryan sees Sully at the exit door and quickly glances away. Ryan sits down on the bench and hears voices along the runway. Sully's pretty tough. He wears a defenseman's helmet. And he may take choppy crossovers, but he's a defensive-minded winger, always forechecking and clogging up the opponent's breakout.

Annie, too, sits, watching from section P, as the end boards open and the bright blue gleam of the Zamboni shimmies. Two rookies lift the west net off its posts and slide it along the boards. Then they lumber across ice; green buckets in hand, picking up loose pucks before removing the other net. For chrissakes, Scottie is driving the Zamboni! The GM doing double duty—another one of Southworth's cost cutting measures, no doubt. Christ. "Let's go surfin' now / everybody's learning how / C'mon safari with me" segues through the fading Thorogood.

Just then, Ryan figures he'll ice ski.

He hops the boards and skates to the opening. For Ryan, the Beach Boys have as much punch as James Taylor at a grunge festival. Oldies music lacks guitar crunch—forget this singer-songwriter shit, rock 'n' roll is two guitars, battering bass, drums and Iggy Pop on vox. He walks along wet concrete to a large wooden box, and imagines overlaying Beach Boy harmonies with a Stooges' riff, a psych-garage surge of "Search and Destroy" that would push Brian Wilson, his homeys, and their damn 409 into the ocean. As he rummages through the hockey accessories, he chuckles at the notion of a bloated Wilson tendrilled under Mag wheels and napalm. In the storage bin, Ryan finds tires, ropes and the Tommy Hawk mask.

Tommy or T-Hawk, the team mascot, entertains fans during intermissions. He's a muppet on skates. Ryan puts the mask on. It feels loose, but so does he, and he returns to the ice. "We're loading our Zambonies for the Alamo this year / so come on let's hurry along," Wilson croons, or something or other. Ryan can't quite make out the words with that mask on.

He glides behind the Zamboni, shouts to Scottie, and tosses him the water ski tow lines. Scottie grins and hitches the rope to a blue post. Ryan skis on one skate and then the other. With a free hand, he waves at Annie. She smiles.

As the Zamboni makes a second turn, the line slackens, and Ryan, the T-Hawk mask bobbing, spins a slow eight. When the Zamboni stretches in the straightaway, the line tightens. Ryan, now ten yards aside, pretends to lose control, spinning skates, flapping arms. He releases the rope and thuds against the boards. He gets up, holds both hands to his head and gets another laugh. He shakes his head, places a hand on his hip and taps a skate as if thinking, and then chases the Zamboni at top speed. He tries to pick up the rope, but as he bends, he kick-skitters it away.

Ryan stands back, does a large dramatic shrug, and then dives for the rope, letting it drag him across the dashed centerline. He rolls and grapples with the rope, but it shakes past, a twisting lariat. Again he stands, shrugs his head, power dives, and gets dragged like a Western outlaw hitched to a wild horse.

Everything looks distorted through the mask. The T-Hawk nose bobs like a bent windshield wiper, and Annie laughs. Ryan thinks it's a kind of laugh that says he's weird and silly, a laugh that worries maybe the weirdness is in the silliness.

Ryan rights himself for his exit, knees bent and shoulders hunched. The orange nose flaps. He waves to Annie one last time before being towed from the rink.

Shot On Goal

So much in this game depends upon the referee.

That's what Fran Koslov thinks as he smacks both posts with the broad side of his stick and readies for a face-off. This ref, a rookie, has called a tight game to get respect. In the opening ten minutes he had called three-ten minute misconducts—two against the Waterloo Black Hawks, and just moments ago when Rochester's league-leading scorer Jimmy Damon pulled a Greg Louganis, Wes Johnson got a two minute tripping call. In a 2-1 game, late, you can't call phantom trips. Waterloo is a hard-checking team, lunch-bucket grit, and they can't afford an official who's too particular. And following Friday's 5-1 loss in Omaha, the team needs a boost to even begin to think about playoffs.

Kos shrugs his shoulders and crouches. He hasn't played that well, really. Pucks hit his body, but he's not seeing them and Rochester's best scoring chances have rocketed wide.

"You set?" Kevin Ogilvie, the Canadian guy, asks. He leans, sweat dripping from his chin liked discarded coins.

"Yeah, sure." Kos wonders if Kevin knows. He's pretty perceptive, always reading—hockey books of the '60s, working-class novels of the '30s—and talking about how there's a fundamental contradiction at the heart of the American ethos: we believe in a classless society and the success myth. But if you're successful then society can no longer be classless.

"Your mask all right?" Ogilvie smiles.

Kos adjusts the straps. "Yeah. You bet." That's the first thing Kos picked up when he arrived from Massapequa, Long Island to Iowa to play tier-two Junior A. People in the Midwest throw "you bet" at the end of everything. At restaurants: "Is everything all right over here, sir?" "You bet." At the bank after taking out $20.00: "you have a good weekend, Fran." "You bet." And when you make a great save off an opponent who shouts and swears he'll score next time. "Yeah, you bet."

Ogs smacks Kos's pads with his stick. "Let's get this one."

"Sure." Kos notices that Ogilvie uses a pretty flat stick. It may take away from his shot—a wrister elevates more quickly off a curved stick, but Kos likes Ogilvie's choice—it gives him an edge in face-offs and a greater control in stick handling. Besides, Ogs is a set-up guy. He fed Ryan Chatham on a nifty behind the legs drop for the go-ahead goal.

Kos isn't outgoing. Unlike a lot of his teammates—Torrio, Sully, Paplowsky—he's an observer. From the crease he loves to watch the game, especially when it's down in the other end. Just before the penalty, Coach had been working a two-man forecheck. Two forwards picked low, holding the puck in and the third was high, covering board to board. If he couldn't hold the puck, he left the zone, conceding, and the Hawks had three men at center—a good defensive situation. But now, killing a powerplay, the Hawks play the box and stand up the Mustang forwards before they cross the blueline. Several goalies tell reporters they need shots on goal to stay sharp. Not Kos. If the action's in the other team's zone, cool. When the puck's in his zone, Kos flops and makes butterfly saves and then the leg pads bloat like heavy sponges, the mask itches across his face, and the chest protector constricts and he can hardly breathe.

Kos shoves his pads together, protecting the five-hole, as the linesman stands over the left circle and then drops the puck. Ogilvie wins it cleanly and Kirby Davis banks it off the boards to the winger, beating Rochester's two-man forecheck.

Kos exhales sharply and watches Isaiah Sullivan stand up Damon at center, knocking the puck back in. Waterloo's two forwards continue to press, breaking up passes, and Ogilvie steals the puck from the right winger and lobs it deep and Coach Michaels hollers for a line change. Rochester's goalie glides out of his net to play Ogs's lob and quickly rattles it up left wing, which the Mustangs have flooded with three players. They bust over the blueline and fly up the strong side. Chatham skates backwards, readying, and Chris Stanzack, twelve goals in last year's playoffs, fakes a pass to Damon, who Chats has tangled with gloves and stick away from the flow, and snaps a quick wrister. Koslov catches it high with the blocker and redirects it into the meshing above the plexiglass. Whistle.

Kos shakes his head and undoes his mask, re-tightens the straps.

"Way to go man," Chatham says. "Way to go." He then slaps his pads. Chats always slaps Kos's pads.

Kos looks up at the clock. 2:21. Ten seconds left in Johnson's penalty. "Yeah." He reaches for the water bottle and backs into his net, crouching under the top meshing and wondering when he first discovered his peculiar affliction. He had no problems last year, nor the first few games of this season, but lately he feels trapped, short of breath. Ogilvie once said that Jacques Plante was asthmatic, Glen Hall threw up before every game, and Mr. 100 shut-outs, Terry Sawchuck, was an emotional recluse—simultaneously needing to be loved and left alone. So, maybe it's just a goalie thing. It's not like Kos is scared of the puck or anything like that—he's a good goalie, third best goals against average in the USHL, even with last night's disaster in Omaha, and he's going to play for Northern Michigan University next year. And it can't be that he's claustrophobic—Kos has no problems riding elevators and he even locked himself in a bedroom closet, just to check it out, and he did fine. But his equipment never feels right. Sometimes he wonders if it's the foods he eats, haunting him with a big processed food payback. Kos doesn't like much— Campbell's Tomato Soup with water, not milk; Kraft macaroni and cheese, no off-brands; Franco-American spaghetti, not Chef Boyardee, or God forbid, Shur-fine; grilled cheese sandwiches with Kraft American slices, white Wonder Bread and three or four sweet pickles; Oscar Mayer bologna sandwiches and hot-dogs. To drink, Pepsi, not Coke, never RC. Yup, it must be a processed food thing, nitrite-MSG revenge warping his reflexes, driving him back, back, back into the net to confront that which confines him. One game, maybe real soon, he's going to strip right in the middle of a play and dance naked around the rink.

Ogilvie hops back on the ice, and Coach shouts, "Kevin, if you lose the draw, push Stanzack out of the slot. The rest of you play the box and give Fran a clear sight. Got it?"

The players nod, and Kos readies.

Ogs wins the draw, and Chats slaps it around the boards to Ronnie Stevenson who lifts it down the ice. The crowd, standing, cheers tight and hard, and Johnson's back on and Waterloo is full strength. Michaels makes a series of quick line changes and the Black Hawks return to the two man forecheck, keeping the Mustangs from advancing the puck and now Kos looks quickly at the clock, twenty-seconds to go. Sullivan slaps at a guy's skates and stick and kicks the puck free but the shaft of his stick has broken. He hangs onto the Rochester player's jersey and then throws away the stick. Ogilvie picks up the loose puck, weaves and lobs it back in. A Mustang defenseman slaps the puck the length of the ice and the horn sounds as the puck hits Kos's pads and then several teammates rush and tackle him. Coach Michaels, too, is on the ice and the crowd, a jet trapped in a hub-cap.

"Great game," Sullivan says, hugging Kos, who's finding it a little hard to breathe. He's not sure if it's the claustrophobia-type thing or if Sullivan is just holding him that tight.

The Mustangs, dejected, chin straps loose, heads down, skate toward the exit but are stopped by a linesman. The referee skates to the scorer's table and motions toward the Black Hawks bench. Then he stands in front of the penalty box his arms folded. Suddenly Young Arena's rattling roar, becomes less assured, breathy, full of hesitant pauses, like Koslov at confession. "Hey, it's over," fans shout. Kos wonders if Sullivan got called for playing with a broken stick.

The referee skates to both benches. He's called a penalty shot. Waterloo left too early to celebrate. Coach Michaels, hands on hips, argues that the Mustangs had no chance to score, but the referee says, if in the last two minutes a player leaves the bench early a penalty shot can be awarded. He even cites the page and rule number. Michaels calls him a "fucking rookie."

The fans, feeling oil-slicked, are anxious, angry. They throw popcorn boxes. Two others unfurl a twenty-foot banner featuring a cartoon sketch of a ref with a head up his ass. The first time Kos saw it he laughed, but now he finds it just bizarre Comedy Central stuff. Another fan in Section R waves a white flag. The announcer explains that the Rochester Mustangs have been awarded a penalty shot. From the fourth row Vice President and General Manager Scott Christie lobs a soda drink. The drink explodes into a tongue of caramel. Several other drinks are lobbed like grenades and stretches of scorched soda-beer flames fill the ice. There's even a bra and some panties at the blueline. Kos doesn't quite get that one.

"Francis William," Coach motions Kos to the bench. He always calls him by his full Catholic names whenever it's serious. "Francis William." Coach smiles, a hand on Kos's shoulder. "Go make the save," and then he winks.

Kos chuckles, looks down at slits of foam bleeding from his pads, and heads to the net.

"Oh, Francis." Coach calls him back. "Nothing too technical now. Let's just make sure you get out of the net a little bit. Don't get caught back in too deep right away. Come out and then come back with the shooter."

Kos nods and looks at Jimmy Damon, number 15, arcing behind his end of center. Kos hopes that maybe Damon's hands will tense, that he'll be a little nervous. After all, his team needs the goal to tie. The worse Kos can do is send it to overtime.

The crowd chants "bullshit, bullshit," and the announcer asks them to cheer on Koslov. "Kos, Kos," "Bull-Kos, Kos-shit" chugs around the glass like an air carrier, and the ice gleams brightly.

Kos shrugs and thinks about his game, and how he doesn't want to give Damon a chance to make a good move. With Damon's hands tensing, chances are the puck might just roll off his stick. All right, that's pretty doubtful, but he's not going to let Damon make a killer deke, that's for sure.

Kos has been susceptible to the short side lately. Usually he just knows where the net is, but over the past two, three games, he has had to look over both shoulders to make sure there are no large openings. The game's finer nuances haven't felt right, and now his mask itches like a new wool sweater, and his chest protector feels like a tightly wound Ace bandage.

Damon touches the puck at center, and Kos lets go a wild scream, a repressed rage, as he races out of his net, twelve, thirteen feet in front of the crease. He doesn't look back, but feels instead a sense of joyful abandon. Damon, a left-handed shot, crosses the blueline, dips his right shoulder, but Kos, backing slowly, doesn't buy the deke, and when Damon moves to his forehand, Kos moves with him, falling, stacking the pads and stopping the puck.

The crowd shakes the glass, and the ref and his crew stand at the scorer's table as the Mustangs leave the ice.

Coach Michaels is at center, waving his jacket over his head like a checkered propeller, and GM Christie, held back by Chats and Sully, shouts 'Rookie,' and several players maul Kos, who has collapsed in the crease, his mask, gloves, jersey and chest protector discarded remnants.

"Great save," somebody says.

Kos works on loosening his pads. "You bet."

Hat-Trick

Kevin Ogilvie sits in the lobby of Thunder Bay's Empress Hotel and worries that he looks too much like his mother and younger sister. All three Ogilvies have Scottish eyes, freckled faces and short chins. None have Dad's fiery black eyes—at least they look fiery in the old photographs Kevin's seen. Maybe they're not even black.

Dad disappeared when Kevin was four, sister Shawna two, and Kevin has always feared that because he was brought up in a house full of women he has an overly romantic sensibility, one that idealizes, sentimentalizes the world, rather than seeing it as hard and wild, but Mom was emotionally tough and did all she could to fulfill a boy's needs. Every Saturday, Mrs. Ogilvie, Kevin and Shawna watched the Toronto Maple Leafs on *Hockey Night in Canada*. As they ate popcorn and apples, Mom talked hockey, lecturing Kevin on how to shield the puck with his body from his opponents. Together they argued over who would be the three game stars. Shawna always picked one of the goalies.

"You're not getting in anybody's face," Mrs. Ogilvie says. She looks older, the lines around her eyes looser, since the last time he saw her in July before he left Cobourg, Ontario for summer tryouts in Waterloo, Iowa. "You need to be gritty in the corners and get inside the slot." She wears a red sweater and black slacks and Kevin watches her watch him. Her forehead is smooth, her face resonates relaxed seriousness.

Mom and Sis have made the fourteen-hour trip from Cobourg and it hasn't gone well. Two Junior A games at the Thunder Bay Tournament Centre, two losses, 8-4 and 4-3. Kevin had a goal and an assist earlier in the afternoon, but he missed Isaiah Sullivan on two odd-man rushes and never could zip the puck to his new winger Johnny Gilmour, frequently open in the Flyers zone.

Across the room, high on the bulky television over the reception desk, CBC announcer Scott Oake in brittle gloves stutters during pre-game analysis at Winnipeg Stadium. "You couldn't ask for a better host city. The volunteers all week have given us a warm Winnipeg welcome and hospitality. Unfortunately the weather didn't cooperate." Oake contends that -18 degrees Celsius is just too cold for football.

Kevin smiles and thinks it's odd that the snowstorm delayed his departure long enough for him to watch part of the Grey Cup, the championship of Canadian football. Outside, transparent stripes crystallize cars, and a dry November snow covers the gloss as people at red lights stamp their feet and flex fingers to keep from freezing. Once the sanders clear the streets the Black Hawks will bus back to Waterloo, Iowa. In Winnipeg, play-by-play anchor Don Witman says that the Calgary Stampeders will try to beat the Toronto Argonauts with the six-pack, an offensive combination of four wide receivers and two slot-backs.

"I think Sullivan plays with a lot of heart, but everybody else seems to be just standing around, waiting for the puck to come to them," Shawna says, her face dimpled, her hair high and puffed up like curled ocean waves.

Kevin doesn't look at Shawna. "Huh? I do dig in the corners, Mom, what are you talking about? I have guys on me all the time. It's hard to make plays."

"That's just it, you're thinking too much about making plays instead of just doing it."

Kevin shrugs and it bothers him how he never really gets to see the cities he visits. From Highway 61, Thunder Bay looked like an exciting resort town, full of fir and birch trees and ski slopes that shrouded the sky with a resilient majesty. He had wanted to walk in Ouinet Canyon and along Lake Superior, but he didn't get beyond the bus window, hotel ice buckets, carpeting and vending machines.

"How did Sullivan feel about the game?" Shawna says, and Mom asks how he likes living in the U. S. and Kevin says fine, and he hopes to sign with a U. S. college after next year, but there's weird stuff to get used to, like when the checker at Quik-Trip asks if he wants a sack instead of a bag. And Shawna's fifteen, the sharp awkward angles have curved, and Kevin hopes she isn't dating any hockey players. To hear the fellas on the bus talk they're getting action, or at least always looking for action, and looking at women as if it's a male right to look. No matter what a woman wears—five layers of sweaters or even a parka over another parka—a guy can undress and know her. Last night, GM Christie caught two groupies in Ryan Chatham's bedroom.

Shawna points at Kevin's black fedora, baggy green pants and blue Adidas sneakers, "Your clothing style ain't doing nothing for me, babe. Salvation Army Grunge is like, over." She chuckles while stirring her coke, ripples in the glass.

To Kevin it's all weird. He and Shawna used to talk hockey. He'd go into her room late at night and sit next to orange bear and tell her about his dreams of being an NHLer and how he loved the nubby, scratchy feeling of tape against his fingers and the smells of the wet leather undersides of his gloves and the rink, a frozen chlorinated pool. He'd also discuss how the puck snapped around the boards, thudding with its own authority, separate from the sudden slash of stopping skates or the dented twine of a wrister, top shelf. She'd listen and boost his confidence and relive all his goals and assists with vivid descriptions. About today's game Shawna would have said something like, "I thought you looked pretty cool on your goal. Nice rush from center and then the give-and-go to Sullivan, and then, zip, high over the stick side. Awesome," but now instead, she's older, needling him about his working-class clothes, and then Burton Cummings saunters out on the Winnipeg stage and sings the national anthem, and Kevin hopes she isn't dating any hockey players.

"Sullivan's a hard worker and he's cute."

Kevin has told Shawna all about Sully in his letters. At first they were four to five pages, but when she seemed to write less about hockey and more about school dances, math, and how men victimize women, he didn't know what to say. He hadn't written in two weeks.

"So, you seeing anybody?" Kevin doesn't ask, he sort of interrogates and feels a little bit embarrassed.

"You mean like a friend?" She sits back brightly. "Dates, that sort of thing? What do you want, a list of names?"

"No, I—" Kevin plays with his hat. It's so hard to talk about stuff like that. "Anybody, I know, that's all."

"Pass the puck more, Kevin," Mom says.

"I do pass the puck. Coach tells me to shoot more."

"Well, you do have only four goals in 13 games."

"Yeah, but I've got seven assists."

"Eight," his sister says, firmly.

Kevin smiles and then in the "God Keep our Land / Glorious and Free" stretch to "O Canada" Cummings extemporizes, holding "Stand on guard for thee" through more bars than he should and dropping several words for a funky "Canada" that carries over half a verse.

"What the hell's he doing?" Kevin feels his lower lip quaking with anger.

"What?" Shawna asks.

"Cummings. He never could rock and now he's messing with the national anthem."

"Kevin, please," Mom says. "I heard what he did. And the Guess Who *does* rock!"

"He changed the words." Kevin tells her what they should have been.

"Yes, I know the anthem, Kevin. Maybe he's singing it the old way, the way he learned it in school. They changed the anthem a few years ago, you know."

"Or maybe he's an atheist, and has trouble saying 'God,'" Shawna says.

"Who cares, Ma? If he can't sing it right, then don't sing it." Kevin smacks his hat against the edge of the table as the song fades and CBC cuts to ten fighter jets crossing the stadium like a shrouded cloak.

"That doesn't sound very tolerant."

Kevin makes a face. "It ain't right."

"Hey, Kev," Isaiah Sullivan rushes into the room and stands between two mahogany desk lamps. He wears torn gray sweats and an Icehouse beer T-shirt. Half his hair is matted with awkward sleep. "I need your help. Oh, I . . . Hi, Mrs. Ogilvie, Shawna."

"What's up?"

There's a bat flapping in their hotel room, Isaiah says. Front desk told him to keep the door closed. They'd call Animal control or the Royal Canadian Mounted Police, or maybe even Michael J. Fox. Shawna laughs at Sully's jokes. "Coach says we're leaving in twenty minutes, and I still need to pack."

"A bat?" Kevin says.

"Yeah. Flap, flap. A bat. I don't like them. Rats with wings, you know?"

"So, what do you want me to do?"

"Help me get it out of the fucking room. Oh, excuse me Mrs. Ogilvie, Shawna."

"That's okay," Shawna says. "I don't like them much, either."

"I knew your sister was cool." He taps her shoulder. "I've already broken a lamp trying to shoo it out the door."

"All right." Kevin hitches his pants. "Mom—"

"I ain't going to catch that bat, Kevin."

"I will," Shawna says.

"I'm not asking you to catch the bat, Mom. Whattya mean, you will?"

Shawna shrugs. "No big deal." She tells how they had one in gym during volleyball practice and she and three other girls gathered towels and coweled the bat against hardwood, easing it outside.

"I thought bats were nocturnal. What are they doing in daylight?"

"It's dark out, the snow and shit. The sun went down a half hour ago," Isaiah says.

"I meant in the gym, at volleyball practice." Kevin turns to Shawna.

"I don't know, but are we gonna stand here or get that bat out of the room?"

Kevin shrugs, nods, and thinks he shrugs too damn much. He's got to be more assertive, and then, Shawna leading, they run red stairs to the third floor. When they get to room 309, Shawna leans against the door. She looks like a cop on a drug bust.

"Shawna, this ain't *NYPD Blue*," Kevin says.

"Funny." She listens intently. "I'll go in."

"Nothing doing. We'll all help."

She nudges the door and a bat stutters across the carpet, its wings folded Vs. It crawls, hovers briefly, and crawls again. Kevin nimbles back, and Isaiah curses as the bat flutter flaps between the wall and a twin bed.

Isaiah was sure right about the lamps. Two are knocked over, and a black hole burns through one of the shades. Kevin places it on the desk next to the television. The Argos lead 15-0. Long pass and an interception return for touchdowns.

"The towels are all wet," Shawna says, returning from the bathroom, her hands on hips.

"Is that a problem?" Kevin asks.

"I don't know. Last time I did it the towels were dry. I don't know what a bat might do with a wet towel."

"Oh, come on, admit it, you never touched that bat in the gym. You and the girls maybe tossed some towels back and forth but you didn't, not really, somebody else, a janitor maybe, did."

Shawna scrunches her face and gives Kevin a lean look. "Oh, I didn't did I?"

"No you didn't." Kevin thinks she's just showing off, trying to be cool for Isaiah, and then she seizes his black hat, and in two steps smacks it over the bat. The bat dully bumps against the hat's lining.

"My hat." Kevin can't believe it.

"Get me a pillow case to slip under this," she says.

"That's way cool," Isaiah says. "She's trapped it."

"Good job, Hon," Mrs. Ogilvie says.

"My hat."

Isaiah hands Shawna a pillow case and she lifts the front brim carefully and then scrapes the slip through to the far end and Kevin looks, marveling at Shawna's subtle grace and wonders why he's never noticed it before.

Swiftly, she carries the hat across the room, the pillow case shuttled along the underside. Outside, dry snow swirls against the fire ladder and gray-stained sky. Kevin opens the window and Shawna unsheathes the slip and the bat, funnel whipped wind, flies above the Empress.

Truth or Dare

Geoff Kelly hunched over his hockey stick and huffed out curves of air that seemingly darted around his eyes and nose like snakes. He didn't feel the cold tightness in his lips. He couldn't. He was Rocket Richard ready to blaze down the ice and blast a shot in the right-hand corner of the net.

"Geoff, you gonna shoot, or what?" Cindy asked, her wrist bent over the black knob of her goalie stick. Foam dripped out of the thick pads she wore. Cross-patched electrical tape covered up smaller slits.

Geoff wondered how a girl like her who liked hockey, slugged a tether ball around with the guys, and sat in back of the school with a smoke, had a soft name like Cindy. She wasn't like the other girls in junior high who giggled when they snapped at the backs of those who wore training bras and snickered when they passed around happy-face notes during history class. She was different. For one thing, she didn't look funny in baggy hockey pants.

"Yeah, yeah." He breathed deep, imagining his eyes intense, ablaze like the Rocket's. He had never seen Richard play and he suspected his father hadn't either, but to hear Dad talk—the Rocket was the deal. "Greatest player in the clutch I ever saw," his Dad said, pausing to adjust the TV's rabbit ears and to sip from his Molson Golden. "The best. Back when hockey was tough—3-1 games, not like these blowouts today—Rocket scored 4 goals against the Leafs and was chosen not one, not two, but all three game stars." Geoff felt awed by the power of this feat. Not even the pride of Parry Sound, Bobby Orr, had been so honored.

"Geoff!" She pounded the ice with her stick.

He pushed back his wool cap and tugged on the edges of his CCM hockey gloves. He and Cindy had been playing showdown on the school's outdoor rink all that Saturday afternoon, and it was now dark. He had scored 50 goals. She had made 50 saves.

"You can't get it by Tony Espo this time." She slapped her stick against the posts and backed up into the net, leaning forward in a crouch, her catch glove poised. "No way. You're not going to get it by the Big O, Espo. No goal Espo, here."

Geoff wanted to say "uh-huh," or something equally cool sounding, but he was afraid he'd mess up and look like a dufus. So instead, he curled his tongue, jammed it out of the left side of his mouth, and sped down the ice. He knew he wasn't really speeding, he knew that the edges of his ankles nicked the ice's rough kinks, but he visualized himself as the great Rocket, hair billowing, skate blades slashing up puffs of white.

She slapped the stick again and glided out of the crease, cutting down the angle. He hitched his shoulders and concentrated on not seeing her. All he wanted to see was the net. He deked to the left, brought the puck flat upright on his backhand and saw a large opening above the catch glove. He leaned on the bottom half of his stick and suddenly felt a whap at his ankles. His arms jerked and his body sprawled forward as the puck fluttered over the endboards.

"Shit!" Geoff mumbled, flakes of snow caught inside his gloves and slivered his cheeks.

"What a blast," Cindy said, holding her arms high and rigid, the stick raised in triumph. Air blew out of her lips, as she mimicked the hair-dryer drone of a cheering crowd. "Yes . . . haaaah. Esposito has . . . haaah . . . done it! What a save sports fans, what a save!" She pounded her gloves together and skittered on the tips of her blades. "Haaahhhh!"

Geoff shook his head.

She punched his shoulder, laughed, and discarded the wire-caged mask. Her freckled face had reddened from the brisk air and her eyes seem strangely freckled too. Her blond grainy hair, tied back in a pony tail, looked to Geoff like a long hunk of rope. "Sorry about the stick, but I had to stop you." She wiped mucus from the tip of her nose into the upper arm of her Chicago Black Hawk sweater.

"Tony Esposito, my butt. More like Lizzie Borden, with that stick."

She laughed and covered her mouth.

Geoff figured she was embarrassed because of the front tooth that stuck out. He pulled himself up. "Damn it. The puck went over the boards, again." It happened a lot and it would take at least five minutes to find.

Cindy skated backwards into the net, undid her pads, tied their leather straps together and dropped them in the crease. She plopped down in a small puddle of water and undid her skates. "Your wrist shot has some zip."

"Thanks," Geoff said, really wanting more praise but deciding on aloofness. They had played showdown for months—out on the roads in the summer and on the rinks in winter. Since moving from Toronto to podunk Norwood six months ago, Geoff had made no real friends besides Cindy. He wasn't cool enough in jeans and sweatshirts for the partying football crowd, and he was too bright for the shop crowd, but not bright enough for the chess-playing browners. Dad had said that all these set backs stemmed from Mom's refusal to join the Ladies Auxiliary Curling Team. Geoff doubted that but he wished he was more like Cindy, who didn't seem to care about belonging to any crowd.

She kicked aside her helmet, packed her mouth with three chunks of Dubble Bubble and chomped them in half. "Truth."

Geoff looked for a break in the drifting snow. His feet were cold. "Truth."

"Huh?"

"You heard me, dummy. Truth. I'm challenging you."

"Okay, what?"

"Who you have a crush on?"

"Crush? Whattya mean?" Geoff blushed slightly. "I don't know. No one." How ridiculous. Crush. In the middle of the hockey season.

He trudged through knee-high drifts cursing himself for not taking his skates off first. She had been acting strange lately, different, talking about crushes and stuff. "Why? Do you have a crush on someone? Randy?" He had heard rumors that Cindy had kissed Randy at the Public School monkey bars, and that they had done maybe a little more than that.

"No way." She pulled down the sleeves of her sweater and looked indignant. "That guy's a toad." She blew a pink transparent bubble and it popped against her face. "I thought I saw you making eyes at Sarah Reynolds."

"Me? I was just borrowing some pencil crayons to label my geog maps with." Sarah was nice. She liked watching old war movies and Bugs Bunny cartoons. She also laughed at his jokes. But that didn't feel like a crush, whatever they felt like. Geoff was sure that he didn't have one. He trudged on.

"I thought you were awful polite."

He shrugged. Yep, she was acting different. "Hey, stupe. Did you see where the puck went?"

"No." She lifted her left shoulder and reached between her Black Hawks sweater and red sweat top to loosen the chest protector's buckle and clips. She tugged at the jagged edge in back, huffed, and grimaced, squinching her nose until it crinkled her forehead. She undid the buckle, let the corrugated protector fall to the ice and pulled the hockey sweater up to her neck where it tangled up in her hair. By now Geoff had looked away, embarrassed at having glimpsed patches of sweat draped around the small lumpy outlines of her chest.

"Geoff, my arms are stuck."

"I'm looking for the puck," he said.

She wriggled and tugged, yanking the short strands of hair caught inside the sweater's collar. She pulled it back down over her sweats and hitched her shoulders until the fabric was smooth and comfortable.

"Guess what? I found the puck," he said with a shrug.

"Te-riff."

"You got another hunk of gum?"

She spat over her blocker and threw him a pack.

He sat on an end of the boards, unpeeled the bow tie of wax, and plopped a chunk in his mouth. "Gum's the greatest after playing hockey."

She nodded. "It's okay."

"I like Dubble Bubble best."

"Yeah. I'd rather have a smoke."

Geoff knew she smoked but still he was surprised to hear her talk so openly about it because he had never actually seen her light up. "Smoking gives you cancer."

Cindy smiled, her front tooth sticking out. She flipped the bulky pads over her left shoulder. Geoff grabbed the chest protector, the blocker, and her goalie stick, wondering what else about her he didn't know. "You wanna come to my place and watch *Hockey Night in Canada*?" One thing was certain about Cindy, she didn't have a color television.

She flicked back her hair with a soft roll of her neck. "Yeah, sure."

"Let me take those pads."

"I can handle them."

Geoff shrugged and they headed out across the field to his home on Cedar Street. Cindy lagged behind because of those damn pads—he heard their bulky bumping against her chest—while he cut a swathe through the snowdrifts with his goalie stick, splaying powder which sprinkled his ear.

Suddenly, his back hurt. He turned around. "Cindy."

She packed another snowball. Her eyes freckled behind her wire-caged goalie mask.

"That mask is unfair." Geoff laughed.

She giggled and lobbed two more salvos. One missed Geoff's shoulder, the other stung his leg. He got down in a battle crouch and ran towards her like Lloyd Nolan, machine gun tucked against his hip, storming the beach in *Guadalcanal Diary*. A final snowball whizzed by his head.

"Geoff, no!" She turned to run, but her laughter slowed her down.

Geoff caught her shaking shoulders and pushed her into the snow, where he fell on top of her, pinning back her arms, and removing her helmet.

"Geoff . . . no." She giggled and flailed with her feet.

He rubbed a mound of snow in her grainy hair. She blinked her eyes and blew steam through her lips, and he dumped another mound down her sweater. Her back felt warm. "I gotcha, now."

"Oww . . . that's cold. Let me up."

"You promise no more snowballs?"

"Yes, yes," she giggled.

"Promise?"

"My back's cold," she yelled. "Yes."

He let her up and she arched and shivered. He rubbed her back.

"Easy. God. It's like sharp glass." She rolled her shoulders. "That's good."

They said nothing for awhile as they walked under the streetlights. Her back was warm, Geoff thought.

Cindy wiped her forehead and her eyes flickered as that mischievous look that Geoff knew all too well took over. She rubbed her lower lip. "Dare."

"What, now?" Last week she dared him to climb the school roof to gather tennis balls, and the week before that she dared him to wrap himself up in a tire and roll himself down Main Street.

"A twosy."

"Teamwork. Great. No more throwing snowballs at Mr. Smith." Smith had caught Geoff nailing his bulldog with 20-foot bombs and Geoff mysteriously flunked his History test.

"That was funny," she said.

"It wasn't funny. Flunking History of Confederation was not funny."

"No," she suppressed a giggle. "It wasn't."

"How did we get started on this game, anyway?"

"Last summer you dared me to walk along the railroad tracks across the CN bridge."

"Oh, yeah."

"And the week before that you gave me a Death, daring me to streak across Mr. Smith's backyard. Geez, that was base."

"Well, you didn't do it."

"Of course not."

Geoff smiled. He was glad she hadn't. After that challenge there were no more "deaths," just "truths" and "dares." "Okay, what's the plan, maestro?"

She told him. Behind the public school parking lot ran a dried-out gully surrounded by trees. From there they could play "I Spy" and watch the high school students make out by the monkey bars.

"What? . . . I mean, why there, it's cold out."

"They can't do it at home, dummy."

"Okay, expert. How do you know so much about this place?"

She frowned. "I walk Burger at night and I seen them," she said.

Geoff nodded. "Yeah, sure." Burger. What a name for a dog.

"You don't believe that I?"—she huffed and crossed her arms— "You've been listening too long to that retard Randy. Shit, he still thinks the Leafs have a shot at winning the Cup."

Geoff laughed. "Okay. So we go there. What are we going to do?"

She bit her lower lip and shoved her hands insider her hockey sweater. "We throw a snowball or two."

"That's a blast," he said, half-heartedly.

"Let's drop my equipment off at your garage."

"No, no." The streetlights were on and Geoff's parents would make him stay home. And Cindy's place was out because Mrs. Jablonski had company for the evening and had told her daughter not to be back before nine. "Adults need adult time," Cindy told Geoff her mother had said. He wondered where her father was. She said that he had died in the great Canada-China war, but Geoff knew there was no such thing. If they were going to play "I Spy," they would just have to avoid their parents and take the damn pads with them. "Make a great fortress, sitting on end, against a counter attack, wouldn't they?"

She laughed.

They'd sat behind the car curbs for twenty-five minutes and the insides of his hockey gloves were damp and cold. The laces dangling the skates around his chest and back irritated him. He could be at home watching the Leafs get blown out by the Blues instead of freezing his tail off. "This is stupid," he said.

"Sh—I think I hear something."

"You've been saying that for the last twenty minutes."

"I mean it this time."

He rolled his eyes and glanced at the outlines of trees behind him and the goalie pads and gloves, sticks and helmet, and chest protector, sitting under gnarled branches. He spat and thought about being grounded for staying out late. He could leave now, but that would be un-cool. "First intermission."

"Will you relax about the game, we'll watch it."

He sighed.

"Duck!" Cindy's voice was excited and strangely high-pitched. She grabbed him by the back of the neck and pushed his face into the snow.

"You're breaking my nose."

"Sh—there's two of them."

He dug himself down behind the curb. "Let go, willya?"

Cindy told him she saw two people standing in front of the concrete window ledge by the outer gymnasium wall. She loosened her grip and Geoff took a peek.

The girl wore a suede jacket and blue jeans. Her hair was curled at the ends. The guy wore a down-filled vest and jean jacket. He had a stud in his left ear. "Sh—" Geoff said, watching the girl's shoulders slide up as the guy kissed her. It was like a Black Velvet ad or something.

Geoff noticed that she seemed to like the kiss, as she swayed her head and flipped her hair back with a lazy wave. The guy kissed her neck and his hands slipped down, hooking on the backs of her jean pockets.

"That's why she has a short jacket on, I guess," Cindy said, to say something.

Geoff smothered a nervous laugh on his sleeve. He didn't want to giggle, not out loud; he didn't want to say anything. Suddenly, he knew a girl was next to him and he felt like he shouldn't be doing this.

She kissed the guy hard on the lips and he pulled her towards him clutching his hands into her back. They stumbled onto the window ledge.

Geoff stared into the ground and his fingers tensed inside the hockey gloves. He wondered what it would be like to kiss Cindy and then his cheeks flushed and he thought better of the idea.

Cindy's face, too, looked a little red in the splash of streetlights, flooding in from behind the school. Maybe it was just the cold air. Well, maybe it wasn't just that. He tugged on her sweater. "Let's go."

Cindy nodded, her jaw slack.

They kissed again and the guy had a hand inside the girl's jacket. Geoff saw the coat flap and flatten, and he wasn't about to ask Cindy if that was what "felt-up" was all about.

The coat bulged again and he hoped that Cindy wasn't watching. He especially hoped that Cindy wasn't watching him watching. He looked away.

"Do that again . . . she likes it," Cindy shouted, her voice cracking with nervous excitement.

"Cindy!"

The guy in the down-filled vest jumped while the girl did up her suede jacket and tucked her legs into her chest. "Huh?" He stepped forward and loomed tall and large. His voice was terse. His eyes looked mean. "Why, you little pricks." He packed a snowball.

"C'mon," Geoff screamed, pulling Cindy backward. They tumbled down the incline, crashing into broken chunks of cattails and chips of rock at the bottom of the gully.

"Shit," Cindy said as a snowball whizzed by Geoff's ear. Another one smacked the side of her head. "Oww—"

"Maybe you should put on your helmet."

"Funny. Grab the pads," she ordered as she picked up the sticks and chest protector.

He dropped the pads, picked them up again, and two snowballs crashed at his feet. "What did you have to say something for?"

"I don't know."

He tucked the bulky pads under his arms and they took off through the field. The white plastic skateguards pounded against his chest as they ran. He didn't look behind.

They stumbled out by Old Miller's tobacco field, climbed the barb-wired fence with its ten inch rusted nails that Geoff was sure would give him gangrene one day, and made it to the street. Geoff lapsed against a stop sign and dropped the pads. He fell on top of them, laughing.

Cindy exhaled sharply, laughed, and sat next to him.

"Man," he shook his head. "Man . . . that was a blast."

"Yeah."

He folded his hands under his armpits and shook his head. It was silly to ever think of kissing Cindy. Getting all that guck and junk on your teeth and lips wasn't for him.

She looked at the brick-covered street. "I better get home. It's past nine."

He wiped the corners of his lips. The second period would be halfway over by now. "Doncha wanna watch the game?"

She made large half circles on the street with her goalie stick.

"Mom's gonna give me shit for being late," he said. "Probably take away my allowance. But if you're there. . ."

Afraid to show the front tooth that stuck out, she pulled her lips tight and smiled. "Okay." She shoved the helmet under her arm and picked up one of the pads.

Geoff smiled. The street light dappled across her hair and the curve of her neck and she seemed—kinda cute. He felt a strange tingle that he tried to suppress. He picked up the other pad and chest protector. "Truth."

"Huh?"

"Truth."

She looked through his shoulders and he thought better of asking her what she'd felt when she'd seen what she'd seen. "Uh, do girls . . . really? Well, do they . . . like that?"

She bit her lower lip and drew half-circles again. She shrugged. "I don't know. She did, I guess."

They walked silently along the sides of the shoulder. Cindy hurled some odd pieces of limestone and chunks of glass she had found.

"Do you think she did?"

"Geoff, I don't know. I guess so."

"Yeah . . . weird." He sighed and the tingle spread.

Cindy nodded and they walked silently, the breeze numbing their cheeks.

"You really have a good wrist shot," she said.

"Yeah?"

"It's improving."

"Seriously?"

"Yeah." She grinned.

He nodded. "I'm gonna score sixty goals tomorrow," he said.

Get a Move On

"So, Matt, whatcha doing? Writing Shira's name? Again?" asked Steve Johnston. He spoke in a loud, loping voice that demanded that everybody else slumped in early morning homeroom take note, like what he was saying was something real funny. Matt Traicheff shyly covered up the blue margins of his math book. Her name was like a flower puffed aloft by the wind.

"Why don't you just ask her out? Or better yet, get Marina Hays to tell her that you like her, and then find out if she likes you." Steve glanced down at a problem he was puzzling over, the smudged rubber tip of his pencil crammed in the left corner of his mouth.

"No, thanks Steve, that's cool, but—" Marina wasn't silly or nothing. And she had long black hair that kind of glowed like underwater moonlight. But Matt didn't want to talk to Marina because then it would be out there and there would be no going back. Besides, if Shira said, "No," would he ever be able to talk to her again in English class? They sat next to each other in Mr. Fitzpatrick's class, and he often feigned Bruce Lee's moves in *Chinese Connection* while she sang the *Mary Tyler Moore* theme song. She also read *Seventeen* regularly during class and she laughed when Matt joked about David Cassidy's all-too-cool-nipple look.

"Hey, I'll ask her, for ya," Cameron Wardal said. He was a real big kid with soft edges, a freckly face, and a trace of moustache across his upper lip. He was definitely not a nerd like Matt and Steve, but he was real into Professional Wrestling, and strangely, hydrogen bombs, always reading up on megaton this and megaton that. When he grew up, he wanted to be either a nuclear physicist or a gym teacher. That was if the science thing didn't work out.

"No, I—"

Cameron shrugged. His "Keep on Truckin" T-Shirt was hunched around his shoulders like the folds in a walrus' face, and looked mighty uncomfortable. "Shit, you don't have a date for the big dance yet."

"Hey, guys," Steve interrupted. "I still can't figure out this math problem, guys. 3X=17. But then X isn't an even number but a fraction." Steve's red hair was tangled over his eyes, and his face, when he removed his glasses, looked like a peering turtle. Often the fellas, namely Cam, asked Steve to do a turtle, and he never liked to, but at the threat of being beaten up, he did. Math was a tough subject for Steve, and in English class he was always on the wrong page.

"Look. I'm taking Marina. You know, you gotta ask her," Cameron said. "Steve, it's not 3X=17, it's 3X=18, you subtracted wrong." Cameron snatched the pencil out of Steve's mouth and started writing over his problem, scratching penciled dirt out, carving a slight tear in the center of the page. "There. Like that."

"Oh, yeah, sure, Cam, sure. So X=6. Right. Cool. I wonder if we'll feel any tit. I mean, at the dance, you know? Get a feel, you know?"

"Sure, Steve." Cameron shook his head.

Steve was always looking at *Playboy* magazines at the mall, or grabbing hall health pamphlets and studying how to insert diaphragms and things, and telling Matt to get hip, quit reading the *Hockey News*, check out the tits. Grow up Traicheff kid.

"So you want me to ask her?" Cameron said.

"No. I'll do it."

"When?"

"After Music class. Before English."

Shira entered the room. She was laughing with Marina and her shoulder blades dipped like sharp-angled oil derricks.

"You gotta."

"Yeah."

"She's got a great ass, that Shira," Steve said, leering in her direction.

"Steve. You can't see nothing. She's sitting down."

"I know, Cam, I know. But I'm just saying, in the abstract sense. Wow."

Cameron leaned forward across his desk. "Do a turtle."

"No, Cam, no."

"C'mon, Steve, or else I'm going to give you the killer headlock and then the mega-airplane spin."

"No, Cam, please."

"Steve."

Steve sighed, tipped down his head and took off the glasses. He stuck out his neck and awkwardly grinned. The pads from his glasses had indented the sides of his nose with small Frankenstein looking feet. "Look out for the turtle!" he said.

Near the end of library hour Matt found out that Shira already had a date.

He never could get up the nerve to directly ask her out. Instead, he had hung back by the Perry Mason book rack and watched her at the far table, talking to Marina, and heard them say something about Dave Hornsby, a short, tough, halfback on the school football team. Dave was real wiry, and strong—he did a killer flex arm hang in Phys. Ed. class, his body shaking, eyes above the bar for over two minutes, cheeks puffed like oblong balloons. By contrast, Matt lasted only as long as it took Mr. Darcy to say, "Okay gentleman, ready, go." Matt hated the Canadian Fitness Test. Dave got the certificate of excellence signed by the Governor General and the Prime Minister. Matt and Steve were always handed participatory pins.

And besides, Dave fancied himself as a real sexy guy. His hair was always combed and he smelled good, and some time last winter, Matt had seen him kissing Pam Waters, a tall angly blonde, by the side of the school. It was a dark, gray day, and Dave's woolen hat clung high along the bricks of the school wall, and they were necking, and she had a hand inside his pants, and he had this real goofy look on his face like a cartoon character who had just circled out from under a falling safe.

"Hey, Traicheff kid," Steve shouted, jumping on Matt's back. He knocked a Perry Mason book from his hand, and sent him crashing into a hard metal edge of the book rack. Steve had Matt in a headlock. "You can't get out of this one, loser!" Steve always had a way of putting Matt down, and pulling macho stuff that Matt hated.

"C'mon, let go, Steve. Let go. You're pulling my hair."

Steve tightened his grip. "No way, Traicheff kid, no way. Say Uncle, say it." Matt shrugged and then swung both arms high, knocking Steve at the elbows, and spinning himself free. He was surprised at how mad he felt. He was ready to pop Steve in the freakin' glasses.

"Did you ask her?"

"No."

"Hey, Shira!" Steve yelled. "You going to go out with this guy?"

Shira looked over at Matt, her face puzzled like someone lost at a hockey game trying to find her seat.

"She's going out with Dave, you dumbass," Matt mumbled, embarrassedly.

"You're the dumbass, Traicheff kid." Steve pushed Matt hard in the chest. "You never got around to asking her out. Loser."

"I don't see you going out with anybody."

"Fuck you, Traicheff." Steve pushed Matt again and then announced that he was leaving to look at the *National Geographics*. Steve had probably already torn out most of the good pictures.

Shira and Marina smiled and nodded at Matt, and then continued talking. Matt heard Shira laughing, her voice like change jangling in a subway turnstile, and he suddenly remembered Dave at the side of the wall with the woolen hat and Pam, and what he might do to Shira. Dave always jived with the faster kids—girls like Pam, who brought a lipstick tube to biology class—it was her Mom's or something—and when Miss Fogels left the room, Pam rolled the tube out and it had a fake penis in it. Anyway, lots of kids touched it, and Matt wondered if maybe his parents had stuff like that because one time, real recently, in the middle of the night he woke up and heard them actually doing it, and his Mom it seemed didn't want to do it, maybe, but his Dad kept doing it, and Matt tried not to hear by imagining himself playing hockey—that was a real joke, he couldn't skate worth a damn— anyway, he was playing hockey and the crowd was really loud and he was scoring a lot of goals.

Sometime during the second set, Matt and Cameron were leaning against the radiator and talking in the bathroom about atomic weaponry and the futility of the 1950s duck and cover drill. Shira and Dave had left the dance floor awhile ago. Matt didn't know where they went.

"Geez," he interrupted Cameron, "I keep rubbing my hands, but they don't seem to be getting dry." The automatic dryer thunk-thudded like a roll of pool balls falling in pockets.

"Technology. What can I say?" Cameron laughed. "We can make a megaton bomb, kill millions of people, but we can't make a machine to dry our hands."

Steve was banging around inside a bathroom stall—he couldn't get the door open, and then there was a clatter of glass, and Matt smelled beer.

"Shit, Steve, did you bring one of those here? From Mrs. Hornsby's?"

"Sure."

"We could get suspended, you asshole."

"We only got two days left, Traicheff. Relax, willya? Shit, you're so squeaky clean, like Greg Fuckin' Brady."

"Matt's right," Cameron insisted, his hands on his hips. "It was really dumb to bring a soldier here. Marina could get in trouble. And if she gets in trouble, you're in trouble."

"Oh yeah. Sorry Cam." Matt heard Steve kick and scrape glass into a pile. It sounded like grits of sandpaper rubbing together, and he figured that Cam was kind of mad at Steve because Marina, his date, hadn't shown up. She had gotten sick at Mrs. Hornsby's. Before the party, Dave's mother had invited everyone over, and she had left beers across the kitchen table for the ninth graders to enjoy. Cameron and Matt didn't drink, but Shira had one, Marina three or four. "Damn," Steve said. "There's no toilet paper in here to wipe this up. Ouch!" He was picking up chunks with his hand.

Suddenly, the outside door stuttered open. Matt was at first relieved to see that it wasn't Mr. Halkett, one of the chaperons, but then his stomach flipped into his chest and stayed there as Dave strolled into the room. His feet were splayed out, his hands in his pockets. He was wearing a blue and gold football jacket. Next to him were a defensive end and a linebacker. All three had their hair parted down the middle in two even waves, and their faces looked real relaxed, as if they were gangsters in a movie in which the world were theirs. "How you guys doing?" Dave nodded at Matt, and then Cameron.

"Fine," Cameron said, leaning against a mirror, the glass of which had dulled, as spidery silver tendrils shone from behind. "Fine."

"You getting laid in there, Johnston?"

The guys on the football team laughed.

"No, no." Steve stumbled out of the stall, his shirt half in and half out, his glasses crooked across his face. "I mean, I wish."

"Hey, Cam, I'm sorry about the Marina thing." Dave shrugged sheepishly. "But Geez, her friend Shira's pretty hot." He smiled knowingly, and then turned away from Matt and leaned into one of the urinals. "She can really put out." His voice sounded strange, like an apologetic politician who had been caught in a scandal but still hoped to win an election, and Matt felt like he was being challenged with all this sexy stuff, that he was supposed to stand up for Shira and say something, tell Dave to quit bragging, that it wasn't right, that she was nice, and that, whatever happened is private, and then he really wanted to slug him across the jaw, like James Cagney throwing a right cross at some sorry-assed gangster in one of those old movies that Mom always watches on CBC, but life's never like the movies, and there's always going to be guys like Dave, macho jerks, always suggesting more than they really know.

"Geez." Steve stumbled toward the sink, a large trough in the center of the room with black rubber rimming along the base. The ends of his hair were wet with beer sweat and the tip of one of his fingers was spackled red. He threw a mound of glass into the trash bin, and then stepped on the ribbing, a jet of water slicing his hands. "Did you get some, Dave?"

Matt gave Steve a lean look: apparently his friend was even less sensitive than Dave. Steve sort of looked away with his left eye, while his right eye was looking through Matt's shoulder.

Dave stepped away from the urinal, zipped, glanced at Steve, and then his teammates, and said something about how wet she got down there, and how she liked to be touched there, and she touched him too, there.

The football players hollered and high-fived, and Steve, his hands dripping, laughed too, like he was wanting to be a part of the football group instead of the nerds, but his laughter was hard and high, too wild to ever fit with their laconic cool.

"That's pretty funny, ain't it, Johnston?" Dave said.

"Yeah, yeah it is." Steve said, trying to swagger off Dave's mood.

"Come on, Steve." Cameron pushed him gently to the door, and looked at Matt. "Let's get out of here. Matt—"

"You're pretty funny, yourself, Johnston. That's what I hear, anyway."

Steve said nothing, and Matt could tell that he was pretty embarrassed for deserting his friends, but also embarrassed because he could never be one of the cool kids, ever, and the tips of his shoulders were shaking and his hands were in his pockets.

"Hey, Johnston," one of the football players shouted as they reached the door. "Give us a turtle."

Steve, shook his head, the lower half of his jaw trembling and colorless. "No," he said. "No."

"He doesn't want to," Cameron said. "See you around."

The next day, Matt rode his bicycle by Shira's split-level home on Houston Crescent, near the corner of Van Horne. He had ridden by it many times before, hoping to catch a glimpse of her, running after a Frisbee, glints of star-points in the sun, or sitting on a lawn chair, her braided yellow hair glimmering as she read a paperback.

He hadn't seen her in class after lunch that day, and sure hoped she wasn't too sick. He also wanted to apologize for not asking her to dance, but after Dave said what he did, Matt got real mad and huffed out of the gym, through the dark parking lot, running and running and running, the lights dipping behind him like bent Q-tips. It was all so melodramatic. He knew that at the time, but that couldn't stop him from running and looking up at dark, hazy skies, the stars hushed in the city's lights.

Dave probably told a bunch of lies anyway, but yesterday they really hurt. And Matt was hurting even more for not trying to punch Dave's lights right there in the bathroom. Anyway, he didn't want to feel small all the time and feel like he shouldn't feel nothing, because he can't succeed at nothing anyway, so why feel at all, but that was too easy, and Matt wasn't going to do that no more, nothing easy for him, not after last night. Anyway, maybe he wasn't cool and a jock, but he was going to start saying how he felt, tell Shira how he felt, how he liked her and all that kind of stuff, but when he saw Shira out front, leaning slightly to the left, her yellow hair flowing with the driveway's blacktop, he slowed his bike, and then slid off his banana seat. The setting just wasn't right. The sky was kind of weird for that time of day, sort of a pink lavender like the inside of a sea shell.

And everything else was weird, too. A police car was parked out front, up on the curb, flashing red, its right rear tire a little low, and the Friedman's refrigerator was sitting on the front lawn, the doors open. All around the threadbare grass were frozen cartons of vegetables and butcher-wrapped packages of meat. Matt, straddling his bicycle, walked toward Shira. "Hey— "

She nodded and put up a hand to shield the sun. Her lower lip was a funny squiggle, like maybe she'd been crying.

"W-what happened?" He reached down and snapped a hockey card from his rear spokes and stuffed it in his pocket.

Shira glinted in the sun, her eyes bright, her nose slightly pinched. Dad had dragged the refrigerator outside, she said, and plopped it there. The guys from Sears weren't going to take it back, weren't going to fix it for free. Mr. Friedman said he had a warranty, but they weren't going to do it for nothing because it was his fault in the first place that the condenser or the freon gas was all busted. "He was defrosting it and stabbed it with a knife," she said. She was wearing shorts and a black cowgirl shirt with red trim.

"Stabbed what?"

"The inside or something. Where the freon is."

"Oh."

"He was trying to defrost it and the ice wasn't melting. It smelled really bad after he punctured it. And then Mom started trying to cook all the veggies and meat. Make a big stew, I guess, but Dad said the hell with that. They could pay for it and all the groceries when they got him a new fridge. He was really mad." She shook her head.

Next door, eight or nine neighbors, in front of a crooked sprinkler, were watching. They wore faded shirts and jeans. One little kid bounced a rubber ball on a wooden paddle. "But it's his fault," Matt said.

"That's what they and the police said, but Dad says if it defrosted like it should have he wouldn't have gone and got a knife and got all impatient. The defrost thing wasn't working. So they can pay for the fridge and the groceries."

"Hey, Matt," Mr. Friedman shouted at him. His hair was dark red, his forehead freckled. "Grab yourself a popsicle, kid. Enjoy."

Matt waved, let his bike fall to the ground, and he and Shira walked to a caved-in carton. One of the corners was damp and sticky. Matt opened a bomb pop and red gummy stains ran along the inside curve of his wrist. "Why weren't you back at school after lunch? You don't look sick—"

"Dad was worried about the gas, that maybe I had got sick and didn't know it or something, so he wanted to keep an eye on me, I guess. Anyway, Mom got a really bad headache. Actually she's had several headaches the last couple of weeks."

Matt ate the popsicle, it dripped at the corners of his mouth, and a few spots splashed his shirt. All around him, food looked to be sweating in the hot sun. Bubbles of water dotted everything. "Geez," he said. The inside of his left wrist was sticky and icky and he rubbed it on his pants and now they were sticky and icky too.

"'Hey, Matt.'" Again Mr. Friedman, strands of hair like broom bristles over his forehead, peered through the cop. "Help yourself. Have another." Mr. Friedman waved once more and then turned to the cop. Matt heard the cop say something about getting the fridge back inside, or if he was going to keep it on the front lawn he had to take off the doors so that no kids could get inside it and suffocate.

Mr. Friedman nodded and slumped to the house, probably to get his toolbox.

Matt couldn't understand why Shira's Dad didn't just leave the fridge inside. The fridge part still worked and they could at least save that food, but it was all melting in the heat, and the air was starting to smell like puked-up milk. "I don't get it." He rubbed the itchy part of his hand on his pants again. "There's good food there."

"You wanna go inside and wash your hands?" Shira smiled, but her thoughts seemed to be elsewhere. She had a friendship bracelet around her neck.

"No, I'm fine."

"My Dad lost his job."

"When?"

"Two weeks ago."

The cop, his back stiff, jaunted back to his car, his black heels bending barely. He spoke into a radio, and wrote something down. Mr. Friedman, shoulders slumped, limped back with his toolbox. "Goddamn fridge. Have another popsicle, Matt, please."

"He's gotta wash his hands, Dad." She pulled Matt toward the front door, with a desperate urgency—it was as if she didn't want him to leave. Inside, there wasn't much food anywhere, just a crowd of pop bottles on the counter. Matt washed his hands at the sink. The bar of grimy soap by the window ledge looked like it had chunks of leeches in it. Mrs. Friedman, the lines around her eyes loose, was lying on the couch. "Oh, Shira." She smiled somewhat brightly. "Why don't you guys have a pop?"

"You want one?" Shira asked, her face a bemused smirk. "It's pretty warm, Matt."

"Sure. That's fine."

She poured them each a drink, and then he followed her to her bedroom. On the walls were pictures of rock stars, TV actors, and an autographed picture of Paul Henderson, the Leafs' left winger and star of the '72 Summit Series. On her bed was a pink diary and a hockey stick and gloves. The pop *was* warm.

"I didn't know you liked hockey," Matt said.

"Yeah. You want to play showdown sometime?"

"Sure. I've got a net and goalie stuff at home, but we can ride by my place."

She sat on the bed, and moved the stick and gloves aside. The tips of her Keds were touching each other. "I was wanting to ask you to dance last night, but Dave was a real possessive jerk and when I finally got free of him, you were gone."

"Really?"

"Yeah."

Matt sat down next to her, but not too close. He didn't want to be presumptuous. "I wanted to ask you too. I don't know."

Outside in the hallway, Matt heard Mr. Friedman pacing. "Shira, you forgot to put the pop away," he shouted.

"Oh, sorry." They left the room, and Matt slightly bumped a bookshelf in the hallway.

"And don't run. Your mother's got a headache." A cigarette dangled from Mr. Friedman's lower lip. Grease stains were on his forehead, his left cheek, and along his arms. His voice was tired and flat, not at all bright like it was outside.

Matt leaned against the wall, waiting for Shira to finish wiping pop stains off the counter. "You wanna go outside and play some road hockey? We'll go to my place and get my stick."

Mr. Friedman stacked towels in the closet at the end of the hall. "Hey, don't lean against that wall," he said in a stern, angry voice.

It seemed to come from nowhere. Matt stiffened.

Mr. Friedman sighed as if he were trying to blow up a tight balloon. "You know how long it'll take me to scrub this?" He raised his hands, cursed, and frowned at Matt.

Matt stepped away and looked for Shira, who had just tightened a dented metal cap onto a glass pop bottle.

Mr. Friedman's back shook as he rubbed the wall with a J-cloth. He was careful not to remove the paint. "Goddamn fridge and the next thing you'll know, I'll need to repaint these walls. All the time it's something."

"Harold, leave them alone," Mrs. Friedman said feebly, from the couch.

Mr. Friedman turned to Shira. "You done in the kitchen? Get going." He tossed the J-cloth in the sink and exhaled sharply off his cigarette. "Go outside and play. Get a move on."

Matt swallowed hard and Shira grabbed his hand, clamping her fingers around his, and hurrying him out the door. They forgot about his bicycle, and her stick, and ran and ran down the street to the city park.

A little later, she blew hair back from her forehead. "Man," she said. The sun was a low, red disk in the sky.

"Geez." Matt thought about her hand and how hard and tight it felt in his and the way her fingers trembled.

They walked along the gravel path to the playground and stopped at the swings.

She leaned against a swing post and then sat on the swing and he sat next to her. They didn't say anything for a long time. Matt looked at the kids playing on the red, metal rocketship. He wished it would blast off.

"Thanks for the coke and everything," he said.

"Sure." Shira looked at her shoes. "It was pretty warm."

"Yeah." Matt smiled. He rubbed the tips of his shoes into the ground, nubbing their ends with dirt.

She smiled. "I had a terrible time last night, how 'bout you?"

They both laughed, and as the sun dipped they started swinging, soft and gentle at first, and then with a more rhythmic strum, and Matt looked at the red twisting sky, his feet bobbing below, slicing the ground, and she looked, and he looked at her looking at him, blurring black, cowgirl red, Shira sky, and then they let go.

King of Noir

"You got any wrapping papers?"

She stood against the door frame, her left hand flecked over her head.

Matt Traicheff backed into his dorm room and stumbled. He hadn't done any Christmas shopping yet, but he may have a roll or two in back from having wrapped his brother's b-day gift in mid-October. "Yeah. Uh, I'm not sure. Hang on."

She nodded, smiled, and briefly leaned into the room. Matt figured that she was probably peering at the 1940s floor lamp slanting against the window, or the heavy embroidered chair with scooped curves, spindly legs and gold trim that he had picked up last week at St. Vincent De Paul's Thrift Shop.

He took a philosophy class with her last year, and he knew that she lived on the floor above him, but what was her name? Karen? Kirsten? He liked her faded bell-bottom jeans and the casual ease of her flannel shirt, a low-key mix of patchy blue lines and black plaids.

But there were no wrapping papers in his closet, or below the set of cubbyhole drawers he kept dirty laundry in. He pushed back black winter boots, and an-oil stained box of crackers, potato chips, and peanut butter. Eventually, he found a purple roll, the foil scratched, the upper end slightly elbowed. "Yeah. I got some." *Ciara O'Brien*. A Heidegger, Sartre, and Existentialism class. One time during a break in Boundas' lecture, she told him that she wanted to be a secondary school teacher. Matt was terrible with names, and he was pleased that he had remembered hers. "Here it is, Ciara."

She smiled when he recognized her, reached for the roll, dropped her hand, and smothered a laugh in her soft fold-over flannel sleeve. "No, I didn't mean gift wrap." She gently tapped her foot on the floor, keeping time in eighth notes to the music snaking down the hallway. It was XTC's song about Nigel. "I meant like papers to roll a joint. You know?"

"Oh, shit." Matt looked down at the tips of his Chuck Taylors, the purple roll dotted with spider webbing and pieces of cardboard lint, and then the split ends of her bell bottoms. "Oh, no. I'm sorry."

"Oh, that's okay." She smiled again. "Me and a bunch of the gang are going to go to the pub and dance, I guess. You wanna join us?"

The pubs were held every third Saturday in the eating halls of Ottonabee College. Matt had often wanted to go but never made it. He bit his lower lip and nodded his head up and down. "No. Uh, thanks, but I've got a lot of work to do. *Moby-Dick* to read for Stollicker. Man, that's a killer."

Ciara agreed (she had Professor D. S. Stollicker last year), and she said that she liked him in spite of his having left his wife and two kids in search for some kind of Transcendentalism. "He really believes in that Thoreau, Emerson stuff. And I could tell you some stories. I baby sit his kids."

"Cool."

She nodded and stood awkwardly, her left foot arced over her right. "Well, I better get going. I guess, if I have any gifts to wrap, I'll come knocking, eh?"

"Yeah." He smiled sheepishly, and she turned back up the stairs, her hips twisting peppy and neat.

Matt closed the door. He sort of liked being alone. This was now his second year at Trent University, and all throughout his first year he skipped the parties and worked on his essays, and readings, and his grades, a B+ average, A- in American History up to the Crash of '29. He had been an A student in high school and was thus able to get a single dorm room and avoid having a roommate, but he felt lost in the wider dimensions of university life. He thought Trent's size, 2400 students, and small tutorials would encourage his participation, but he often left class frustrated by discussions absorbed with circular tangents and detours. It was almost as if loneliness for Matt were a choice, something he couldn't fully articulate or understand, but something that he vaguely believed in, as if before a man could begin to talk in and out of class and say sensible and intelligent things, he had to spend a period of time in isolation, reading, listening, observing the ideas of others, and saving his words, his thoughts, until he felt ready to speak, to explore the world.

Besides he couldn't dance tonight. He was going to see *The Maltese Falcon* playing at Trent's Wenjak Theatre. He loved Bogey's laconic stoicism and how cool he looked in those stylish, 1940s fedoras.

The next Monday, Matt walked along the crowded aisles of St. Vincent De Paul's looking for something, he wasn't sure what, but something that would help further convert his dorm room into a replica of Sam Spade's hard-boiled office. Outside snow fell like pebbles of crushed Styrofoam, and the sky was a hazy gray. At the back entrance of the store, by the thin-curtained dressing rooms, an elderly black man turned an old waffle iron over as if it were a tennis racket. He was humming to a tune about a girl on a beach that lilted over the radio. "Tall, tan, warm and lovely, the girl from Ipanema. . ."

Matt glanced at the LP's discarded atop one another, and shuffled several from the mid 60s, their dull, gray surfaces covered with cross-sliced scratches. It was as if dust were trapped in the grooves like cat hairs on a pair of black slacks. Maybe one day he'd find a collection of torch songs by a sultry saloon singer like Julie London or Sarah Vaughan, but today, as was the case yesterday, the best of the batch were the Carpenters, Nancy Sinatra, and Herb Albert and the Tijuana Brass. Across from the LP's and .45s, in a wire rack, were a smattering of stuffed animals, orange bears and lopsided looking raccoons and even some snakes. Matt picked up one of the bears, it had poached-egg eyes, and he wondered what had happened, why a child had given up on this one.

High above the stuffed animals was a jittery looking collection of puzzles and board games—Life, Masterpiece, Ker-Plunk. The edges on the boxes were creased, broken, and the once-bright colors faded. And the Masterpiece set was missing all but three of its art cards! He chuckled and enjoyed the smells of St. Vincent, a kind of wet wool comfort like his mother's porridge. She often served it Saturday mornings before Matt spent the day dekeing on the streets of North York, playing hockey with a group of neighbor kids. He missed his Mom's porridge, and the conversations about movies. She always said that she liked Henry Fonda, because he was one of the good ones, a brave man who stayed liberal even when it wasn't so cool to do so during the socially repressive 1950s. Anyway, Mom used to say that Matt's lean frame and angly walk looked a bit like Fonda, and he'd just shake his head. "Bogart, Mom. Bogart."

Now, Matt ambled behind another counter, the loose tie to his hood flapping against one of the shelves' metal supports, and among the $10 pink Barbie vans and chunky plastic corvettes—the seat belts slightly frayed or missing—he spotted a red, Hungry-Hippos game tray. He snapped down on the black handles. They clacked in place. None of the parts were broken, and although all of the marbles were gone, Matt decided to buy it for $1.00.

Two days later, after a grueling discussion of Joseph Conrad's narrative structure to *Heart of Darkness* and a generally pervasive feeling of his own strange Kurtz-like aloofness, Matt was back at St. Vincent's. He wished he had more to say in class, because he loved Conrad's novella, but as usual, he never could find the graceful turn in the discussion, or the on ramp to the existing traffic of language. Actually that wasn't quite true. At one point, Matt said that the story's ending, Marlow's visit with Kurtz's wife, read like a scene from a Film Noir. Matt felt that if he filmed the book, he'd have Neolithic shadows on the walls, potted palm trees in her apartment, Lucky Strike cigarette smoke filtering the room, and a series of eerily focused off-centered and canted compositions. The professor arched an eyebrow, nodded his head briefly, cordially intoned, "How interesting," and then turned his attention to another student. Although a standout in high school (and a standup comic and a writer for his school paper), Matt felt he was real nowheresville in college.

Maybe he never would find his schwerve, Matt feared, as he passed a series of old Zenith and Admiral televisions, all stamped with orange-dated stickers that claimed they worked. A tall, jaunty man with a gray toque and a fringe beard was stirring through a bucket of mixing beaters, looking for something more precise than what he held in his hand. All of the mixing beaters looked the same to Matt, but to this man his idea of what a beater should be wasn't to be found.

Matt smiled, rummaged through a tray full of extension cords, largely brown, thought about the waffle irons, and was struck by how much the Thrift Shop smelled like his grandparents' basement: a mix of damp mold, coffee, and fresh laundry soap. Matt loved his grandparents, but their old world ways (neither of them spoke much English) embarrassed him a little. Matt was fluent in Macedonian up until he was four, but when kids at nursery school laughed at his accent (a competing combination of Slavic and Scottish rhythms), he insisted that his parents only speak English at home. And slowly, he passively lost touch with a part of his past. Whenever someone at school asked him where he came from, he always said Canada, as if he were taking pride in being Canadian, but secretly he knew that he was running from being Macedonian. And although he respected his Babo and Dedo—they had founded a church, brought other immi-grants to Canada, and ran a Mom and Pop Variety Store along Old Weston Road—Matt still felt a backward ripple in the tips of his ears and a slight flood of tension in the upper part of his back, as he thought about them, then and now.

The following week, Matt bought a floor ashtray. It had a ridged column, heavy iron grating, and looked like it belonged in a 1940s hotel frequented by Brigid O'Shaunessy. He just had to have it.

That Saturday, Matt watched *The Big Sleep* at the Wenjak, and he wanted a Bogart hat for sure, a brown felt fedora with a crisp brim that would shade his face and make him look like he were a step ahead of everyone else's moves. And he loved Bacall in that film, too—the sleek dresses, the bedroom eyes, the hair angled with jaunty cool. She was so much Bogey's equal, trading barbs with him, acting insolent, and telling him in a sexy, sultry way that he was like a race horse and she wanted to see how well he ran before she committed to him. After Monday's Intro to Brit Lit class—a discussion of Irish/Anglo relations and Yeats' "Easter 1916" —Matt was back at St. Vincent's.

A family of five—their father wearing a creased vinyl jacket with a fur collar, their mother huddling in a green chair in a skimpy down vest—were drinking black coffee and saying little. Matt had overhead something about the heat in their mobile home trailer not working, and they were looking for a space heater, a cup of coffee, and just some conversation as they tried to keep warm. The older woman who supervised the store gave the kids coloring books and a plastic cup full of crayons. They scribbled, using the top of an old television set as a table.

Matt walked head down, practicing Bogart's sneer, the facial twitch, his upper lip tight against the teeth. In the front window was a yellow Gibson guitar like Chuck Berry played on for his Chess recordings. $75. It had only three strings. Behind it were racks of clothes hung in a circle, like a limped lariat. Suits, blue jeans, khaki slacks, dangled on bent hangers. Below, slammed in A&P boxes, were a haphazard volcano of dress shoes. A pair of black Oxfords were worn bare on the sides from a set of wide feet. Matt couldn't find any hats.

"Hey, Matt. What's happening?"

He looked up from the shoes. It was Ciara. She was shoving the stiff hangers on the rack, probably searching for bell bottoms. "I didn't know you shopped here," she said, looking at the seams, checking for any signs of fraying. "This is where I get a lot of my clothes."

Matt nodded. "Cool." He pushed his hands in his pockets and tried to overcome a feeling of awkwardness. He was so damn skinny and tall, and his arms were often full of awkward gestures, his face wrinkled with embarrassment. And his angly slimness was unfortunately further highlighted by a heavy-set man, who nudged Matt's shoulder while looking at crinkled pinstripe pants. He pressed them against his waist, hoping the legs were long enough. Matt glanced back at Ciara and then over at a series of souvenir glasses crowded on a nearby table. Some said Niagara Falls, and one Smuckers jar had figure skater Toller Cranston shaving the ice, sending up a wave of shuddering snow. For Matt, in the presence of Ciara, it was as if the snow were falling on him, and he tensed, his hands cold at the ridges of his pockets like ice trapped inside the lining of a pair of mittens, and he found himself worrying about the pimples daubing his chin, the blackheads caught in the large crease of his neck, and the red honker of a zit curled in the curve between the outside of his nose and upper lip. "Yeah. I like this place. I don't know."

Ciara smiled. Her teeth were small and very straight. "So? How was *Moby-Dick*?"

"Oh, okay, I guess. I wish Queequeg didn't die."

"Yeah. I thought the whole novel was kind of a big bore." She shrugged her shoulders, apologizing for her lack of interest in it. "Anyway." She paused. "What are you looking for?" She held her hands on her hips, her arms two sideways V's.

"A hat. You know a felt hat, like Bogart would wear in those old movies of the 1940s?"

Ciara said that she had seen some in back, under the sporting goods section, mixed in with some fishing tackle, poles, and baseball and feed caps. As they walked along Matt briefly stared at the roundness of her small breasts, and wondered if anybody saw them walking together, and it felt good to be walking with her. Ciara kneeled down on the floor, her flannel shirt flaring out around her hips. She tugged a box from under a display of footballs and bruised-looking golf clubs. Lefties. Of course. "Right here," she said.

"Cool." Matt felt like an idiot. Was this all he could say, *cool, yeah,* and *you know*?

"Here try this one." She extended the hat as if it were a church offering plate.

Matt let it fall in his hand, feeling the weight, and the plush and sharp contours. The hat was light beige with brown trim. He skid it on, letting it rest high and on the back of his head. That placement felt less aggressively suggestive, a more friendly and open posture. "I like it," he said, "but it feels loose." He nudged it off and glanced inside at the silk-weaved lining: Blue Palace Clothiers. The size was a 7 ½ . "Is there a 7 and 3/8's in there?"

"There is," Ciara said, spinning the hat from the soft inside along her index finger, as if the fedora were a basketball. The twirling hat was dark brown with black trim, and she said, "Let me," and then fixed it on his head, and if felt right, too. "That's pretty hip," she said. "When you go dancing, you don't have to put on a fez, or a lampshade, just that hat. It's fucking cool."

Matt wasn't sure if she was needling him a little or just being real sincere. "You think so?" He readjusted it slightly and felt his eyes squinching with doubt. "I don't want to look like a loser, or have people think I'm lame or something."

"No. It's not lame. It's retro. Totally. And you love old movies. It's you."

He smiled, and self-consciously looked at his shoes, and the large grayish white tiles on the floor that needed to be waxed. "So, you getting jeans? I should've known you got your bell bottoms from here, They're so seventies."

"Actually, those pants you saw me in the other night are the ones, believe it or not, my Mom wore in the 60s."

"No."

"Yeah. Fifteen years old those pants. Shit. Mom was a real flower child. Into incense, psychedelia, Bob Dylan—electric not acoustic—and lava lamps."

"Your Mom sounds cool. My Mom was into Englebert Humberdinck, I think. My Dad, Johnny Cash." That wasn't really quite true. His Mom was also pretty hip, but Matt wanted to say something funny to keep the mood light.

She shoved her right hand in her pocket, and bent it at the wrist. "Cash is cool," she said, and then she rolled up the left sleeve of her brown and tan flannel shirt. "So you gonna go to the dance this Saturday?"

"I don't know."

"I'll look for you."
"Sure."

On Saturday, Matt bought a set of Stanford luggage, brown leather suitcases from the 1950s. The lock on the right side of one didn't quite snap firmly, but the suitcases had a square-edged look that Matt preferred over the smoother, vinyl finish and space age curves of most present-day Samsonite sets. And they definitely could carry a Maltese falcon. Later in the evening, after reading a large portion of James Joyce's *Stephen Hero*, Matt walked to the Wenjak. The final Bogart film in the festival series, 1948's *Key Largo*, a classic Film Noir with a hardened war veteran who redeems himself, was playing. It costarred Bacall and Edward G. Robinson. The film was also directed by the legendary John Huston.

Matt slunk down in his seat. Sometimes he wished he were born in the 1940s. But chances are if he was he wouldn't be going to school. Instead, he'd be working in a Macedonian Bakery in Cabbagetown, or driving a small route sales truck, delivering bread or milk, like his Dad did for years, to Mom and Pop stores all along Queen Street. He often felt responsible, that he needed to get good grades in order to honor all the hard work his father and immigrant grandfather did so that he could have the opportunity to attend school. And as he dangled a pencil on the bottom of his lower lip, Matt remembered Dad softly thunking around at four am, shaking Mom awake, drinking a cup of coffee, and leaving, the screen door snapping, the whisk of his Old Spice after shave filling the house with a brisk kind of love, and he figured some day soon he'll find a way to talk more in class. Maybe in a few weeks he'd even go to the dance in his felt hat.

Why was the theater so damn empty? There were maybe fifty people there. The whole place felt cavernous, and the two overhead projectors, on carts situated at opposite sides of the stage, filled the space around the screen with an open emptiness. Matt was surprised. Bogart was a wonderful performer, an embodiment of 1940s self reliance, the man alone, a professed cynic who was really a sentimentalist. Unfortunately, most people liked the newer, Me Generation 70s types like Alan Alda, Jon Voigt, and Robert Redford.

He sat forward, re-crossed his feet, tipped down his hat, and chewed on the end of a pencil as if it were a cigarette. A tinny rubbery taste spackled his tongue, and he decided to put out the pencil. A few more people trekked in slowly, and then the screen was lowered with a metallic yawn.

Five more minutes passed, and a girl, in a blue sweatshirt with a white turtleneck, sat behind Matt. He quickly and awkwardly glanced over his shoulder at her, and then back at the blank screen. She had wide-set eyes, and her date, a large guy in a Montreal Canadiens sweater, kept ragging Bogart, saying he was just a skinny-ass nothing in a toupee who wasn't nearly as cool as John Wayne. John Wayne's a racist she said, and he didn't really want to argue—must have been a first date—so they agreed that James Dean was cooler than both Bogey and Wayne, and he asked her if she wanted to grab a Pepsi, a pizza, or something when the show was over. They could even watch the third period of the Habs versus North Stars' game in his dorm room. She suggested instead that they go to Tim Horton's for donuts and coffee. And then they talked some more about how they both hated the sociology lectures that took place in this lecture hall, and the guy in the Canadiens' sweater confessed that he only attended the first and last fifteen minutes. "That's all you need," he said. "Sure, it is," she said. "I'm telling you, it works," he said, and then she tapped Matt on the shoulder.

"Excuse me. Could you remove your hat?"

Matt couldn't believe it. There were hundreds of empty seats in the theater, and she had to sit right behind him, and then she had to wreck his party by asking him to take off his hat. Was this some kind of etiquette thing, a regular Emily Post deal, or did she not like the hat, or not like Matt's individuality for wearing it, or was she just into power games and petty displays of false forthrightness?

"The hat. I can't see the screen."

Matt's cheeks tightened and he felt pressed in his seat like hardened dough caught in the patterns of a cookie cutter. He struggled to find words, but all he kept thinking about was a damn, empty pail of melted ice. He didn't want to remove the hat, but the words weren't there, and he sure wasn't going to move—he was sitting there first—and he sure didn't want to pick a fight, especially with the guy in the Canadiens' sweater who could probably crosscheck Matt clear into Ottawa. But then, just as suddenly, there was a strange feeling of calm, like wading at the edge of a glimmering lake, and his tense shoulders rolled and angled up and his lower back arched and straightened, and he regally turned towards them. "*Yus se tsaro ot*

Makedonia," he said, his tongue comfortably Slavic. "*Yus ne govorum po Angleetsee.*"

"He said something about kings," the girl said, her face flecked with confusion.

"He doesn't speak English," the guy said. "Shit, must be right off the boat or something."

"*Yus ne govorum po Angleetsee,*" Matt repeated, gently smiling, and nodding his head.

The couple said nothing else about lecture halls or John Wayne, or hats for that matter, and in a few seconds they awkwardly bumped and banged into the backs of seats on their way to the far end of the row.

Matt crossed his arms and grinned. Suddenly the room darkened, a wedge of light split the theater, and the embossed Warner Bros. shield jutted the screen. Matt tugged the curved edge of his hat to the left and fell into a dark lit kingdom of Noir.

Two Artists

She was slumped across the front seat of his hack, the red tip of her cigarette burning a hole.

Peter Traicheff didn't know how to wake her up. He nudged her heavy shoulder, shouted, and even shook her a little bit, but she didn't move.

Frustrated, he grabbed the radio speaker snaked around the cab's rear view mirror and told Robbie, the dispatcher, that his fare wouldn't wake, couldn't, and he had no idea where she lived.

"Look, cowboy, just drop her on the corner. I'm backed up seven, nine calls."

"Robbie, it's freezing out there." Peter's hands had numbed along the nubs of the steering wheel, and the sky looked like streaks of gray piping. Cold shadows danced above Lake Kawartha. It must have been -20 or something.

Robbie conceded with a low sigh and grunt.

Peter had picked up his ride outside of the Trent Inn just before the beer store closed at 8 p.m. From there, they sliced down Stewart Street—it had no lights and but one stop sign—bought a two-four, and cruised for hours. She spent her Thursday's money, sharing egg rolls and KFC and spilling beer on her coat. But she never told him her name, or where she lived. "Just drive," she repeated, and they curved down by the ball diamonds, the Quaker Oats plant, and the water locks. She said that her husband had left and that she had some kids. It was now 10:30. Peter gently shoved her, as beer drool dotted the edge of her lips. He removed the cigarette from her fingers, and Norm's voice, snick-snicking like ice skates, scratched over the intercom. "What does she look like, car five?"

Peter gave a quick description as he idled at the side of Charlotte Street. Frost clung along the facade of the University bookstore like silver satin. She was oldish, forty-something, bleached hair, a little heavy.

"Does she have a red hat," Norm asked.

"Yeah. A big floppy hat." The front of it was crushed against the seat. Peter had failed to notice it before, but it was childlike, almost soft with round curves and a few wedged edges.

"I know who it is. That's Sadie. I'll be right over."

Moments later Stormin' Norman arrived. His silver Diplomat had rusty pock-marks along the doors' edges. Norm, an independent hacker, worked for Bruce's City Cab, but he made 80% off the meter, as opposed to Peter's 40% company rate. Norm loped from his car, his beer gut seemingly balancing him like a ship's ballast. He leaned in the window. "Oh, she's had a bender, eh? Yup, that's old Sadie." Norm laughed. He seemed to know everyone.

"Where does she live?" Peter's breath danced in the air like curved snakes.

"427 Water Street. I'll come over with ya, help get her inside."

Four-twenty seven was a strip of Ontario Housing along the river. Welfare District.

"Hey, Normie," said a woman with a low-pitched voice. She stepped out of the Diplomat. She had long legs, red hair, and a mole on her right cheek. She wore a fur-fringed jacket with puffed sleeves and designer jeans. "Can I see the drunk?" she asked.

Norman shrugged and raised an eyebrow at Peter. "Stripper" he mouthed so that she couldn't hear. "This is Inge." He told Peter that he had wanted to take her home first, but she insisted on going on the call. He also said, as way of introduction, that Inge worked at B. J's, the club out on Highway Seven, and that she was brought to the club by Ned, the owner, who had seen her act in Kingston. Ned said that Inge was the most beautiful woman he had ever seen, and Norman was inclined to think Ned was right.

"Don't you just hate drunks?" she said, smiling at Peter, looking for confirmation.

Peter looked at the front end of his cab. The swirling snow had layered on his front bumper in a series of small upright megaphones.

"I get a lot of drunks in my profession," she said. "Let me tell you. Always wanting to touch the merchandise."

Peter nodded to do something. He was never real good at flirting with strippers. And because of that they never tipped him real well. He wasn't sure if Inge was flirting with him or not.

"Actually, my name's not Inge. It's Cindy. Cindy Jablonski. Inge's my stage name." She held out her hand.

Her fingers were elegant and surprisingly long. Peter figured she could easily play two or three notes over an octave on the piano. "Hi," he said.

"Hi."

"Well, let's get Sadie home," Norm said, walking toward his cab.

Inge followed, her shoulders down, her steps brisk. "Hey!" She spun on her black stilettos and flung open her jacket. "Whattya think?"

Underneath, she wore a silver-sequined bikini with spaghetti straps. Her breasts were rounder than Peter thought breasts could possibly be. Not that he had seen a lot of breasts, a few, back in high school when he played football and later at college during post-pot parties, but none since he graduated last spring with a B. A. in Ojibway Studies. One professor was so sure that Pete was Native Canadian. He kept tugging at the cuffs of his tweed jacket and leaning forward in a friendly and spirited way. "So, Pete where are your people from?" "Uh, originally Toronto. My brother now lives in the States." "Yes, but where are you *from*? Your people?" Pete just couldn't bring himself to tell the prof that he was just a Macey with a strong forehead. As a matter of fact, it was kind of cool to be thought of as being authentically Indian. Peter Traicheff of the First Nation's Peoples.

"They're, uh, great," he said about the breasts, slightly abashed. He didn't know why he was thinking about that professor right about now.

"I won a contest tonight. At B. J's. 'Best dancer.'"

"Yeah," Norman said. "She does a Billy the Kid number with water pistols that gets me all wet." Norman laughed uproariously and she playfully smacked his shoulder.

Ten minutes later they arrived at Sadie's on Water Street. The steps to her front porch caved to the left, and a big wheel with a split plastic tire was turned over on its side. Next to the big wheel was a hula-hoop, snow tipped along the inside arc.

Norm cradled Sadie off of the front seat and carried her up the broken steps. Peter was amazed at Norm's strength and grace. He moved quick and nimbly for a big guy.

"Do you have exciting stuff like this happen every night?" Cindy asked, leaning against Peter's shoulder. "Christ, it's cold. I guess I should have dressed more appropriately, huh?" She smelled of green apples and strawberries.

Peter said that yesterday he drove a guy who had turned the bluest he'd ever seen to the hospital. Asthma attack.

They didn't say much more once they followed Norman into the row house. Two kids, between seven and ten, huddled around the door. They wore adult T-shirts for pajamas and one might have been a girl. Their eyes looked like they were crying on the inside. They had probably often seen Mom like this. Norm placed Sadie in an orange-flowered recliner. A folded diaper was next to a steam heater. Wood blocks were flecked along the throw rug, and an empty two-liter bottle was propped on its side by her feet.

"I'll pick up your money for you tomorrow, Pete," Norm said.

"Sure." Peter told Norm that she owed him $21.30. He felt bad about asking for the money because he had often seen kids like that. Early in the mornings, as his graveyard shift wound down, gangly kids walked to Mac's Milk, pop bottles in their hands, looking for breakfast money.

Back outside Cindy let go of Peter's arm. "Geez," she mumbled.

"See you tomorrow, Cowboy," Norm said with an apologetic shrug.

Peter watched them drive off.

"Hurry up," she said.

"What the hell are you doing?" Peter said, trying to keep up, his left knee stiffening in the cold. She walked with quick strides. In her left hand dangled a mud flap, black, with a silver-silhouetted woman with one long leg and a huge set of tits. In Cindy's other hand was a pair of shears.

The blue-gray 18-wheeler idling next to them, chugged out diesel vapor. The driver must have been taking a shower or something, but Peter kept looking back over his shoulder, wondering when the truckie would emerge from the Truck Stop, a red glare that glowed like a chunk of hard candy.

"Help me with this one," Cindy said. She was bent over a rear flap, her back stretched tarpaulin.

Peter hesitated, and bit the back of his right hand. He had picked Cindy up outside of B. J's about twenty five minutes ago, and she was pissed. She kept swearing, and said that Ned was a real fucking jerk, and how there were these two truckers who gave the girls a hard time. They danced on the stage during their numbers, squeezed asses, grabbed tits, and Ned just laughed along with them. "No," Peter said.

"Hurry." She glanced at the mud flap. "Women just don't look like this. Shit." She stamped her foot.

Peter couldn't believe that a stripper cared how a woman's body was perceived or presented, but Cindy was serious. Her upper lip curled under her teeth as she squeezed the sheers and the blades shuddered. A slight split outline appeared but the flap wouldn't snap.

"Don't be such a candy-ass. These fuckers think they can get away with anything. Touching me. Shit." She let out a short sharp sigh. "My hands are freezing."

Peter didn't know why, but he grabbed the shears. Maybe it was the sexy sincerity behind her pleas, maybe it was just a general sense of having to do something, but he quickly severed the mud flap. It plunked on the snow like a plastic straw slipping into a tall drink.

"Oh, fuck," Cindy said.

Behind them, their half-adjusted jackets flapping like stretched flags, ran two truckies. Cindy grabbed Peter's hand and they crunched over grainy snow. She spoke in hushed hues, and Peter started the taxi before he even sat down. Cindy tossed the shears in the back seat. The engine slurred, spit, and rattled like wet heavy clothes in a dryer.

Peter pulled out of the truck stop, chunks of ice smacking and sliding up the rear windshield.

Cindy howled and squeezed Peter's shoulder. "That was a blast!" She kissed him on the cheek, and then tucked her knees up against her chin. She drummed a quick series of quads on the dashboard.

Peter nodded, worried that the truckers got his license number and might radio the police. He tried not to think of the kiss.

Moments later they were sitting in the diner of the Chateau Hotel. Cindy leaned against a Formica table, stirring her rum and coke with a red swizzle stick. Peter looked at the ice cubes thinning in his Pepsi.

"So what do you do? I mean, a cabbie's really not your future, right?" The lines around her eyes looked a little heavier in the yellow track lighting of the Chats.

Peter smiled. He said he wasn't sure what he wanted to do. He didn't want to work in business that was for sure. Maybe get another degree? He had played football in high school, was a pretty good defensive end, loved spinning off the outside of the tackle's shoulder and rushing the quarterback and thudding into him with a gasping jolt. There was an artistry to it all, but he hated all the shit that went with football—the coach smacking you on the helmet with his clipboard if you made the wrong play; the offensive players who felt up any girl in the halls because they could get away with it and figured they could fuck any girl, too, because they played varsity; and all the fucking trophies in the glass case by the Principal's office, and the ring of honor, yellowing photographs of past superstar jocks, hanging around the assembly hall, just because they could tackle or run fast, shit, that just seemed wrong. And after he hurt his knee in his junior year, Peter really didn't try to get back into playing shape. "I used to bench 375. Now I do 300." He shrugged. "Who cares, right?"

She nodded, saying "No, no. People care. I care, I guess," and then she looked through his left shoulder, and then up at the deep lines around his mouth.

"My final year at Trent I started writing some poetry. Nothing much." Actually, Peter was being too modest. He had a couple of poems published in big-time literary magazines. One, in *Canadian Poetry Review*, was about date night at the Shoppers Drug Mart, and was printed next to an Earle Birney. That was pretty cool. But he spent most of his spare time writing and watching reruns of *Kojak* on television. "The latter's a joke," he said. "I don't watch *Kojak*. Much."

She laughed. "I thought you seemed, well, innocent, I guess." She sipped her drink. "I hear *Kojak*'s real big in Hong Kong. Or maybe it's India. They make fun of it or something. View it as a joke. Parody. I don't know. Got a girlfriend?"

"No. I just drive people around." He laughed self-consciously and glanced over at the jukebox which was playing a Thin Lizzy song.

"Boy, Ned's an asshole. I can't believe he let those guys do that. Fuck."

"Do you like doing what you do? I don't mean to be judgmental or nothing, I just, I mean—"

She shrugged and flicked hair in front and back of her shoulders. Dancing was a form of control and she made good money at it, but she really wanted to be an actress she said. She had a one-line speaking part in a recent episode of the *Amazing Stories*, and she was in an anti-smoking ad, playing the sexy vamp smoking in a black corvette. But at twenty-five she worried that her moment was passing. "I'm certainly not going to be doing this shit when I'm thirty-five or forty." She stirred her drink, and small ripples arced in the glass. She looked at the back of her hands. "I might be on *Toronto Tonight*," she said. Cindy had an audition next week for the quirky variety show. She had a shot at a Slobber Boy sketch. Slobber was a weird guy who had a ten-foot pole jabbed in his head and the pole acted like an antenna tapping Slobber into Wall Street data bases and Prime Minister Trudeau's private phone calls with ex-wife Margaret. His speech—a mix of borrowed ideas and non-sequiturs—made for great comedy.

"*Toronto Tonight* rocks," Peter said. His brother Matt, two years ago, had been called back for several auditions and re-auditions, or

whatever the fuck they call them, a short list or something, but he
didn't quite make the final lineup.

"Yeah." She touched his hand. "I had a lot of fun tonight. You
wanna do it?"

"Huh?"

"I won't say anything to Ned." She shrugged and looked back at the
jukebox. "I won't."

Peter wondered if this was another control thing, a fantasy or
something, as his chest burned with a pleasantly painful tingle. He
shook his head gently. "No. I don't think so."

"Come on."

The next week Peter was in a terrible mood. Bruce added four new
cars to the graveyard shift, and Peter had to work fourteen-hour
nights just to make what he had earned hacking 12 hours. And now he
didn't even kibbutz with the fellas. He even told Norm to mind his
own biz when the veteran tried to help him find a call on a separated
stretch of Charlotte Street. But the worst of it was how dirty he felt. It
was as if all of his body, his joints, his eyelids were brushed with dirt.
His knees, his swollen fingers, his sore wrists cracked with mud, and
the smell of her apple-strawberry hair lingered along his upper lip. He
couldn't believe that he had gone to her room, that they fooled around
to some Stevie Wonder songs, and she had jerked him off with KY
jelly. He didn't want to have sex, not that soon, and she knew that,
and she eased him into a compromise.

Days later, whenever Cindy requested Petey to pick her up at B. J's,
he drove her back to the Chateau not saying much, ashamed. She
tried to talk about it, but he'd only say "whatever," and she said,
"Come on. You enjoyed it. What's the big frikkin' deal?" When he
didn't answer she changed the subject by asking about his poetry, but
he said he wasn't writing much lately.

Now, Peter was parked out front of a huge two-story home on
Parkhill Drive. The house had long angular windows and three Dorian
columns. Bright floodlights glanced across the driveway, and long
elbow shaped bricks were dug into the patio. Ned had requested
Peter, and told him to keep the meter running. Peter had never met
Ned before so the whole request-call thing made him a little nervous.

He looked down at the ticking shakes of the meter. The red flag
vibrated. $3.50. $3.55. $3.60. To shake off the hollow thud in his
stomach, Peter started to write a poem on the back of his clipboard. It

had something to do with the talons and beaks of blackbirds burrowing into his chest.

Suddenly in the window's sheathe curtains, Peter saw a curved hip, an arched back, and a man, Ned probably, sweaty and naked, hunched over a woman with long red hair. It may have been Cindy. Ned nuzzled his chin between her breasts and then the floodlights blackened.

Peter returned to his poem about hecatombs and the dead. The meter vibrated. $5.40. Again the floodlights burst brightly, and Peter saw naked bodies. The sheer white curtain was being held back by Ned's hand, and Peter tried to look away from Cindy's belly, breasts, chin, kisses. The lights flashed off $6.10. $6.15.

He couldn't return to his poem.

Ten more minutes past by, and then Ned, his hair slicked back, strolled outside. He shoved the wrinkled cuffs of his Ralph Lauren shirt into his silk pants. His shoes were crisp and black. He hopped in the cab. "Take me to the club, kid."

Peter nodded and eased away from the C-shaped, evergreen-lined drive. Why would Cindy be doing that shit? Was this some kind of game?

Ned leaned back in his seat, rubbed after-shave on his chin, and adjusted his tie. "So how did you like the show?"

Peter glanced in the rear view, not quite getting what the point was. Maybe Ned knew about Peter's misadventure with Cindy the other night and this was his way of saying the stripper was his girl and get lost.

"I never see you at the club, kid. Norm's there all the time. Knows all the girls first hand. He's quite a card. But Inge's the best, eh?"

"Yeah. Norm's a good guy."

They curved down a steep road, and emerged on Lansdowne Drive, the Memorial Center where the Peterborough Petes played, and then a stump of Motor Inns.

"Did you hear what happened the other night? Shit." Ned leaned forward, his heavy hands resting on the back of Peter's bench seat. He rolled his right shoulder and spoke about a bunch of truckers who got a little rowdy the other night. They juked to the stage, and danced with the girls, and Inge liked it and encouraged it, and they were all having a party. The truckers were even twirling their tire irons around like batons. Sure there was a little groping, some butt pinching. But what the fuck, you know? Yes, the truckers got a little too fresh, but when they told Inge that her tits sagged and so did her ass and she should do something about it she got mad. Quit right in the middle of her Billy the Kid bit. Later that night she was cutting mud flaps off of a parked rig. "Does that make any sense, kid? One moment like that?"

"No." Peter looked at the perpendicular flag of the meter vibrating. "No. It all doesn't make much sense, I guess." His face felt raw and his eyes itched.

"It's a business, right?"

"Sure."

They pulled up in front of B. J's, a long ranch style club with wood planks splayed along the front. Icicles dipped from the edges of the corrugated roofing. A couple of strippers in light wind breakers were smoking.

Ned moved into the light. "Cost me a couple of hundred." His jaw was strong, his lower chin tight. "But I squared it with the truckers. Never did find out who the cabbie was. Bet it wasn't a City Cab guy, eh?"

"No. Probably not."

Ned tapped Peter on the shoulder and tossed him a McKenzie King, $50. "Keep the change, kid. Hope to see you around some day. Inge's worth it." He left the cab quickly. His aftershave felt cold and wild, like a hard slap to the side of a football helmet.

Two nights later, Peter was at the bus station watching Cindy board for Toronto. He hadn't seen her since the night with Ned, and he was still confused about everything, especially about how he still really cared about her and all. His stomach felt like a block of ice had melted inside. Cindy had won the *Toronto Tonight* audition and had a speaking part. The sketch had something to do with *Leave it to Beaver*.

"Gee, Wally," Peter kidded her and she smiled back as the line crunched closer to the bus door. The sky was expectant with snow, the wind bitter. Cindy had her chin tucked in.

"*Leave it to Beaver*." She shook her head and laughed at herself, wrinkles at the corners of her eyes. "I'm certainly not a Cleaver."

"Hey." Peter looked down at the edges of his wrists that he couldn't jam in his pockets. They felt numb. "I'm sorry about the other night, how I acted—"

"Don't worry about it. It didn't mean anything."

"Why do you say that?"

"Pete, I like you and everything. You're a nice guy. I knew that that night with Sadie, how you looked at those kids. But what happened was just a moment. Fuck, let's not argue about it, okay?"

He couldn't look at her. "Okay."

They stood for awhile not saying anything, her red beret curling like a flat muffin in the wind. "Maybe, you'll write a poem about me."

"Yeah. Maybe."

She kissed him on the cheek. "Well, wish me luck." She buttoned the top of her wool jacket and glanced over at the angular bus driver collecting tickets. "You know, my name sucks."

Peter nodded. "Yeah. I don't like Inge. Too exotic."

"No, no. I meant Cindy. Girls with that kind of name never wind up lawyers, doctors or leaders. They raise kids, or work at A&P, or do shit like I do." She shrugged "Shit, it's cold out here."

Peter smiled at her, and wasn't sure if she would ever make it.

Peter numbed with No-Doz and having finished a twenty-four hour shift, collapsed against the vinyl chair in his apartment and ate dry Cheerios out of a plastic stadium cup. The newspapers across his windows were yellowing and ripped.

He rewound the video, and then sped through the Leafs' game and several sketches for *Toronto Tonight*. And then there was Cindy in "Leave it to Cleavage." She was a checker in a tight red blouse that squished her chest, and Slobber Boy was the Beaver and Keith Macdonald played a Dean Martin type of Wally. Slobber Boy kept saying he wanted cans, cans, cans, and Gee Wally what's happening? I don't want soup anymore. Remember when you were in fifth grade and you didn't dig Geometry, kiddo, Dean-Wally said. Now you do dig it? Well, now, it's the same with chicks. Oh, I like that, slobbered Slobber, the pole in his head banging into magazine racks as Cindy bent forward, her breasts in the camera, the UPC light flashing over Campbell's' Soup cans, and Slobber shouting, cans, cans, cans.

Suddenly Dino tossed aside his fedora and sang, "Like the fella once said, ain't love a nine-foot pole in the head? My life is spinning." And then Cindy slammed the cash drawer, and jumped over the conveyer belt. She grabbed Dino's hand and they twirled with symmetry and sang, "Bea-u-ti-ful." And it was. Peter wasn't totally sure because he was starting too drift off, but Cindy's voice was a smooth haunting alto, sung from the shallow part of her chest instead of down deep, but echoing with elegance. Her harmonizing transcended the sketch's lewdness into an air of dignity.

And then stock boys in smocks and clutching spaghetti-stringed mops sang too, and Slobber boy couldn't get out of the checkout aisle, the fence post in his head clashing into the cash register, shopping carts, and a ream of *National Enquirer*s.

Strike

If I didn't care so much about winning I might have made a great baseball manager—no, no, check that—I might have made a good intramural softball manager.

It was 1985, I was a Master's student, and I was coaching the English Department's Co-Rec intramural team, and when our third baseman Donna Tyler, couldn't complete the throw from third to first, I moved her to the outfield.

Two days later, Donna and our catcher went on strike.

That afternoon, the remaining nine of us were huddled in the cold green of the Davis seminar room talking about it. Well, actually, four or five of us were doing most of the talking. I think everyone else was stunned.

"Matt, you hurt Donna's feelings," Linda said, her left hand poised like a sharp scythe. She was the ringleader, I figured, because she always spoke with such eloquence against workshop stories that had cardboard women. I, too, sometimes, fell under her shrapnel because my women were either too naive or castrating. The "her legs moved like scissors" reference in my last story—something I stole from Nathanael West—just had to go, according to Linda. And she was right.

"Her feelings? She's hurting the team. The ball bounces, rolls, and never gets to first," Mike said, his glasses pushed back tight on the bridge of his nose. His red hair, combed sideways on his forehead, looked like a huge snowdrift and suggested an intense distrust of social graces. "We can't give up that many infield hits." Mike was probably our best player, and he was the one who gave me advice on how to run the team, where to position everybody: weakest players in right field, second base, first base, catcher, and pitcher. And that's where I put a lot of them. A lot of women.

I ran my finger along the gritted edge of the table. The sun, through the blinds, cut bars that looked like wedges of chocolate across hard tile. "I thought we played to win," I said, and as soon as the words slid out of my mouth like Jell-O through fingers, I knew that I sounded like an idiot, but I said it—win. And I meant it. I guess we all denied that part of the gig when we signed up, we pretended like it was all about having fun—playing hard and partying in Aggieville afterwards—but for many of us, myself and Craig, we were never Little League stars and playing intramural softball was our chance to redeem ourselves, to feel what we had missed out on as kids. And for others, like Jane, playing hard held greater significance. I remember, early in the season, how she jumped up and down on home plate after I drove her in from third to win a game. "I'm an epic hero, I'm an epic hero," she shouted with joyous irony, but for a woman who had missed out on Title IX, the benefits of gender equity, and playing Little League, such victory dances were earned.

"I thought we played to have fun," Linda corrected. Her hair was black and cropped. The tips of her angular shoulders were unyielding and thrown forward.

"Well, you can't have fun, if you're not winning," Craig said. His eyes behind thick glasses were usually luminescent dots, his face forever brimming with jokes to tell, but right now he wasn't joking, his voice edgy, maybe because he was the new third baseman.

"Yes, I agree with Craig and Matt," Jane said, a stack of Blake books held against her chest. Her face was blush-freckled with impatience. She must have thought that this whole meeting was crazy. Shit, she had a paper to write, and if we weren't going to play for real, then she'd not waste her time dallying and busy herself instead with writing her MA thesis. "If we're going to play, I do want to play with the best intentions and that being to win," she said, absently flicking her ponytail over her left shoulder.

I smiled at her, recalling the darkened musky glove in her lower desk drawer, and how on many a cold March morning Jane coaxed Mike and me to leave our student papers and play catch on the quadrangle, limestone walls and tall trees, silences in early dawn. We enjoyed the leathery slip of the dewy ball in our hands, and the loud, wet smack it made hitting our gloves. Further and further apart we stood, throwing, trying to see how far we could arc the sky with contrails, and when it ended we looked into our gloves and the names written there: Cesar Cedeno, Brooks Robinson, George Brett. It was during such moments that we felt connected, writing ourselves into the game.

"I still don't think it's right," Linda said. "Matt promised that she could play there."

"She can't make the throw," I said.

"That doesn't matter." She shrugged, and then said we were sexist, that we weren't being sensitive to women's concerns. I didn't know what to say, because I thought I was pretty sensitive. I'd done a whole unit on images of women in advertising for my comp class, and I had real problems with Maidenform's "You Never Know Where She'll Show Up" campaign in which a woman doctor poses around an operating table in a frilly magenta bra and panties. Anyway, I don't ever remember seeing the Maidenform woman in cleats.

"Donna's feeling hurt, and Stacy's sitting out as a sign of protest and support. Changes need to be made, or else we've got problems, Saturday."

Linda was referring to the threat of forfeit and a subsequent one-year suspension from league play. I was bummed. I probably should have just sat down with Donna and told her how I felt, the team, well most of the team, felt, but instead, I didn't. Managers are supposed to have interpersonal skills. I just made the change during the game and said nothing.

Mike scraped his chair against the tile floor and slid away from the table. He grabbed some chalk and wrote in big block letters, "I WANT TO BE TRADED." And then he left the room.

"I guess his feelings are hurt, too," Craig said.

The next day, I sat down in a hard chair, and wondered what the hell I was doing in Linda's office. Frankly, her mixing of gender politics with my desire to field a strong softball team left me feeling somewhat disrespected and embarrassed. I wanted to set up a meeting, with Donna, maybe Stacy, and Linda, to talk about it some more, and as I waited, I thought about all these contradictions. I started getting real mad, like if we throw the ball soft to a woman cutoff man, some of them complain that we're being patronizing and sexist, but if we throw it hard, then they complain that their hands hurt. What are we guys supposed to do?

When Linda finished with a student, I thought better about complaining about cutoff throws, so we yakked about music—The Blasters, Los Lobos, Elvis the C, and then I talked about the workshop, and figured I'd work our way back to softball. "I don't think your last story got treated fairly," I said. "The Visionary" was about a man, a New Age guy, trying to possess a woman and make her think just like him. Actually, the point of view was the woman's perspective, and it was her story, her battle for independence and autonomy. Strange that I inverted Linda's story, then and now.

She grinned, eyebrows arching. "It wasn't very good. All interior, like you guys said. Characters' thoughts. No physical description.

That's what I like about your stories—very visual and plot oriented. But, when I critique your characters' sensibilities, I hope you don't think I'm picking on you."

"No. No." But I did take her critiques personally. One time she said that my prose style was "prosaic." I didn't know what that meant, but I knew it was bad by her tone, and after the workshop I looked it up, and felt even worse. And right then I figured for sure that Linda saw this whole strike thing as an extension of my fictional sensibilities: Matt Traicheff just doesn't respect women.

And we sat there and talked some more about fiction and music and fiction and music.

It was a cold Saturday, and the ground was sharp stones wedged in bald grass. The sky looked like faded blue jeans.

Maggie was standing by a sycamore tree, a Franklin batting glove on her left hand. I, under Jane's suggestion, had called her the night before, and asked, as a favor, if she would play for us. I knew we were going to be short and I didn't want to forfeit. I told her everything, but she already knew the story. I guess it had been talked up somewhat among the secretaries in our English department. Anyway, Maggie didn't like the idea of being a scab, but she showed up, because she was Jane's best friend, and as I later found out, she liked me quite a bit so that was way cool.

"Boy, you look swell," Craig said. "The batting glove is a nice touch."

Maggie flecked hair behind her left ear. "I play to win."

"Okay, okay, maybe I'm a bit overly competitive," I said.

"Overly? Does Hemingway leave a cat out in the rain?" She smiled. All of us—Maggie, Linda, Craig, Mike, and me—were in Professor Johnston's Ernest Hemingway seminar that semester. Jane had more sense—she was studying William Blake.

"Can't winning be fun? It is to me."

"Where do you want me to play, Matt?"

"Second. Okay?"

"Sure." She pushed her Kansas City Monarchs hat back, licked a finger, and stabbed the air. "Wind's blowing north. I'll shade it closer to first."

She winked, and then headed to the diamond to field grounders. Mike made some joke about Maggie being a ringer, and told me not to put her too deep in the lineup, and I nodded, and then it got real quiet, as Linda, thick bricks of charcoal smeared under eyes, stepped from her Camaro. Donna and Stacy were no-shows.

Once the game got started I wasn't thinking about the strike anymore. The issue just sort of vanished like ice cubes thinning in a glass. I wanted to win. I wish I could say that that wasn't the case, but I was focused on the game.

For four innings Linda's high arcing change-up had the opponents baffled and we were up 4-3. We threatened to pull away in the fifth when Jane hit a ball that sliced and twisted the sky. But she was called out, upon appeal, for missing first base. I couldn't fucking believe it. Appeal? In this game—slow pitch for chrissakes?

Jane was mad, red, I mean, she had more freckles than usual, even her eyes were freckled over. I thought she was going to empty our bench of all three bats. "I did *so* touch the base. I did!"

I walked to the umpire and told him to get his head in the game, and he threatened to toss me if I didn't cool it. I kicked at wedged stones and envisioned throwing first base at his head, but the rubber square was more suited for a bath mat than a dramatically torquing weapon.

Linda stepped forward, sunlight filling the curve of her shades. "It was a homer. She stumbled over the bag, but she touched it."

"You're warned, too." The umpire said. He wore a "Party Naked T-shirt" and pushed two stubby fingers in Linda's face. "Anymore and you'll be tossed. The both of you."

We returned to the backstop. "Bullshit call," Linda mumbled as we bent over to pick up our gloves. "Jane's homer was a beaut."

"Yeah," I said, and then we momentarily looked at each other, like maybe we understood something about this game, and this moment, and ourselves, and then we walked into the sun.

If only I had my mind off the game. If only I had been thinking about interpersonal relationships, instead of losing myself in the feeling of competition, but that's where I was, stuck with adrenaline's needle, a sort of twisted fist of excitement in the gut, and when the Vet students tied the game in the bottom of the sixth, I felt a sense of urgency.

But we had something going in the seventh. Maggie lead off with an infield single and then sprinted to third on Craig's two-out slash to right. And when Maggie slid, I knew then that I was going to marry her some day: it was like one of those intense moments of clarity where you get a glimpse of the future and the past and everything. Her right arm flexed above her head echoed Joe DiMaggio's dust-filled slides in Yankee stadium, her legs sprawled fluently looked like Paris water colors, and her body, a sepia-toned Conlon snapshot, circa 1929, glinted brown and orange under the sky's brim.

"Great slide," Linda said, spitting into her hands, breaking my epic reverie. "Fucking great." She walked to the plate, hunched the sleeves of her T-shirt around her shoulders and let her sunglasses slide down her nose. She took the first pitch and then winked at the pitcher. I couldn't believe it. The gesture was so elfin-like and yet cocksure, sort of a blend between Audrey Hepburn and Jimmy Cagney, and the pitcher got really pissed and threw a flat, fast one that Linda tomahawked up the middle, scoring Maggie. Way cool. I leaped in the air and so did Jane and our caps were twisting propellers.

But in the bottom of the seventh, after striking out the first batter, Linda gave up back-to-back singles and was now behind 2-1 on the Vets' weakest hitter, their catcher. Mike in left, glove tucked under arm, kicked at wedged stones. "You gotta do something. She's losing control."

"Give her a chance."

Linda's next pitch missed by a foot; the other one after that bounced three feet short of the plate, and Mike raised an eyebrow and I called time. I slowly ambled in, crossed the mound, and didn't look at her. "Craig, pitch."

I wish I didn't have to tell you that part. I wish I handled it all differently, but I didn't. Two years later, in early 1987, Donna Tyler visited Maggie and me and our daughter Caitlin in our basement apartment. She brought gifts for the baby—a spinning top, an outfit, and a blanket—and we talked, not baseball, but about her love for North Carolina basketball and how she used to drive a school bus there before coming to Kansas State, and how when she finished her Master's she wanted to do social work for her church. And then we talked about Linda. Donna said that Linda had a copywriting job lined up in Kansas City. It was with a nonprofit organization.

"Craig, pitch."

When I pulled Linda, I was real scared that there'd be a scene or something, so I became trembling cool, all Jake Barnes restraint and no apparent feeling. For years, I have thought about that moment, and the lack of closure surrounding my mediocre managing stint. I admit that maybe there was a sick thrill, a wobbly strength in forcing my will on that pitching mound, but I believed that I had acted justly, morally, for the team. A few years ago, I felt my morals were all wrong, that I had put an empty concept such as winning before a woman's dignity, that I had hurt Linda by pulling her, that I should have just quietly stood in left center and let her pitch—win or lose—pitch, let her maintain her independence. Today, I believe that such a non-move would have been the cruelest move. Linda had nothing left to give, her concentration had wandered, and because of our team's gender differences, she could never remove herself. The only way to preserve her dignity was for me to intervene. Perhaps that's the truth. Perhaps it's all false testifying on my part. I really don't know. But I would know, if I had looked at her when I crossed the mound, if I had asked her how she felt, if I had acknowledged her.

Craig shaded closer to the bag and frantically shook his head, the blips of his eyes a bright blue.

For the third time, I told him to pitch, and he moved to the mound, his shoulders down, his hands limp at their sides. Linda adjusted the black band on her shades and went to third.

"C'mon, buddy. You can do it." I handed him the ball, and then remembered something Earl Weaver once said about managing: always remind the reliever of the situation. "Fresh count. Bases loaded. One out." Oh, I was some manager, all right.

Craig nodded and the infielders were quiet, until Jane, crouched at first base, pounded a fist into her glove. "C'mon, Craig. Let's do it. Shut 'em down. Throw heat, pal. Throw heat."

"This is slow pitch. What heat?"

Several infielders laughed and I ran back to my spot in left center, where the ground sloped to the right.

Craig strangely struck out one of the Vets' power hitters—he couldn't throw an arc and the guy, waiting on one, swung through three illegal pitches. And I'm not sure, but I think Craig forced the next batter, on an inside pitch, to pop to third. Linda caught it.

We stamped our feet, slapped backs, and Mike and I, gloves against our chests, ran in from the outfield. I looked for Linda, but she was gone.

"Great game, huh, Matt?" Maggie wiped sweat from her forehead.

"Yeah, your slide was great."

"You liked it?"

"Too bad about Jane's homer." I said, to say something, while looking for Linda's Camaro.

Jane shrugged and smiled. "Yeah, that sucked. But you guys know that it was one."

"Sure it was," Craig said. "Lousy fucking ump. I certainly don't want to see him naked at any party, any time soon."

"Yeah." I nodded. "Where's Linda?"

"She left," Maggie said. "I think she has an exam to write up for Monday."

"Oh." I rubbed at the dust and grass stains on the tips of my Chuck Taylors, and my stomach still felt like a twisted fist, but in a different way. "You did all right."

"Thanks. You want to go get a beer," she said.

"Yeah. Let's go get a beer," I said.

A Crack in the Universe

I didn't know what to say. Seventy-seven CDs were missing.

Frank didn't know what to say either. His duplex had been broken into. Beer foam had dry-bubbled across the shag carpeting, and old albums were splayed along kitchen cabinets like flung guitar picks. Pushed against the coffee table was a green screen door, with white concrete and wood shavings still grooved in the hinge screws. As Frank glanced absently at the robbery fallout, he spoke in a clipped, deliberate way. "I can't believe this shit. All the M's are gone." He stamped his feet and then kicked over a trash can. Cigar ash puffed like dandelion seed.

I shrugged apologetically. Frank housed a lot of music—over 12,000 records, 900 CDs, a regular Smithsonian of rock 'n' roll. The LPs crammed his bedroom in musty wood crates with bottoms bowed. A box fan blew air to stop the warping.

"Somebody must have known I wasn't here," he said. "Doesn't it seem weird that they took only the M's? Marble Orchard. Mudhoney. The Mortals. My last name starts with M."

"Maybe," I said. We had just done our show, "Let it Bleed," on Community Radio, WEFT Champaign, 90.1 FM, like we did every Tuesday from ten to midnight, spinning garage rock and psychedelia. Our show was popular with the college crowd. Frank had developed a fan base working at the local Mom and Pop record store, and I taught four sections of freshman composition at the University. On air, we talked in a 'zine sort of way, offering insights on how various bands achieved their sounds, and we were committed to the music, knew a lot about band histories, and the students dug that. Anyway, we, too, were in a band once—Frank played guitar and I shout-sang like a low-rent Iggy Pop.

Maybe a listener did the Break and Enter. We answered phones but rarely played requests outside our canon. One high school Chemistry teacher, Mr. Delgarno who had a South-Side Chicago voice, loved Jerry Lee Lewis. We figured he was joking the first time he made a Killer request, but he had called every Tuesday night for three years.

Frank grabbed two Pepsis out of the fridge, popped their caps on a counter edge, and handed me one. He took a large gulp and collapsed into the couch covered with a fading green throw. "I thought our Stones set was pretty good," he said.

I nodded. Keith's work on "Stray Cat Blues" was incredible. All fills, no leads until the end. "You think maybe a fan did this?"

Frank pressed the cold soda bottle against his forehead and cocked his head to the left. "I don't know. The M's are missing. My last name starts with an M. Maybe we should have played that one guy's request for Ministry." He smiled. My first name, Matt, also started with an M.

"Shit, Frank. Did I tell you that I got another article rejected today?"

"Really?"

"Yeah."

"Damn."

"Mono Men," Frank said, his face covered with mustard sauce and penciled shavings of Hardee's biscuits.

"Huh?" We were parked out front of Paulie's pawnshop in downtown Rantoul. The store's plate glass window was smeared with insects. Three iron balls hung from the front awning. It was early morning—the streets were blue.

Frank took off his Sub-Pop hat, the bill of which looked beer stained. "*Wrecker*," he said, another one of the missing CDs. "'Took that Thing.' What a blasting song."

"Yeah." I had made the comment before on our show.

Frank glazed out the window. He was a heavy-set guy, sort of a bigger Michael Douglas with grungy black and silver hair. He had called just as I'd fallen asleep. Maggie, my wife and a great drummer, wasn't too pleased, but she knew how worked up Frank got about things, especially seventy-seven missing CDs. "Go ahead. You're friends and you hung out a lot together your first four years," she said. I headed to his place across from the high school on Race, watched him call every record owner in town, waking them at home too in order to give out a wanted list of the missing seventy-seven in case the jokers tried to unload them. With Champaign-Urbana covered, we drove, the cool September breeze numbing my left elbow as it propped outside the car window.

Anyway, here I was looking at Frank and I wondered how lonely his life must be, listening to music, writing record reviews for the *CU Optimist*, a granola press that couldn't tell the difference between James Taylor and James Brown, and never finishing his dissertation on Charles Brockden Brown, the male domestic story, and proto-revivialism. There are a lot of people like Frank in the academe, talented people who can develop their thesis forever without finding the finish and fit for all the parts. Detoured, they return to more passionate interests like rock 'n' roll. Hell, I'm one to talk. I had finished my dissertation on Screwball Comedies of the 1930s and couldn't get a real job. I couldn't even get an interview, and I still hadn't published a damn thing. Adjunct work. That's all I was doing.

Frank finished his biscuit. "How are things with Maggie and Caitie?"

"Fine." Maggie was finishing up her dissertation on 19th Century American Women writers and she was also a copy-editor at N.C.T.E. Her money kept me afloat in the adjuncts-who-wannabe-assistant-professors game. Caitlin was my little daughter, who loved the MC5 because the number in the band's name equaled her age. Often, with a bowl of cereal in her left hand, and her right arm swinging like a shaking crash symbol, Caitie hollered out the lyrics to "American Ruse" while watching NFL football with me. "They're great. Cait would like you to come over some time and play action figures with her."

Frank smiled. He did such wonderfully elaborate games with Caitie, involving Spidey, Doctor Octopus, Cap, the Joker, and a bunch of stuffed animals converted into earth-destroying aliens who projected sub-atomic death rays.

"She's a great kid." He nodded, and then looked at Paulie's and the 1960s paean to modernity, the Urban Shade, dulling next door. It had orange and blue panels and perforated metal along the trim, and we had always wanted to play in a bar like that. Man, could Frank groove. He'd hunch over his guitar like a dipping dolphin and play licks that made you want to jump and bleed, but he never stayed in bands. I ought to know, because me, him, Maggie, and two other cats formed the Jodie Foster Four, and rocked for fourteen weeks, storming through covers and originals. We were pretty good. Even did some swing and punked-up Sinatra. We had a gig all set, but Frank, who Maggie says is terminally shy, thought we didn't sound right or something so he canceled and we just faded along like bright colors dulling in sunlight. John, the bass player, real rubbery funky groove-meister, still practices with Frank, but they haven't formed a band. One day Maggie and I dropped in on a session and we did a reggae, for lack of a better word, version of "Fortunate Son." And as the analog hum cleared, I knew, and so did they, that we would never do anything that cool again.

"Hey— " Frank pointed a stubby finger. Across the street stood a blonde in blue jeans with a wide black belt. A large box was pressed to her chest, and her shoulders exuded a kind of stubborn resiliency. "My CDs," he said.

"Huh? How can you tell? From here it looks like a box piled with books, maybe."

The car door metronomed on its hinge and then jostled shut as Frank ran across the blue street, engulfing the woman like a spreading stain. I couldn't tell what he said, but his hands were on the box and she pulled it and then he yelled and she yelled and I got out of the car.

"They don't have your name on them, do they?" she said, her eyes kelly green. She was probably nineteen.

"Hell no," Frank said with pride. He hated messing up anything. Damn, one name on one CD, a Mychek somewhere on the label, and he could prove ownership. He seized three off the top of the box. "Mono Men, Mortals, Marble Orchard. Where did you get these?"

"The mall." Her jaw was severe.

"You stole them from my apartment."

Paulie kicked open the pawnshop door and held a shotgun that glinted an arc of orange light. "You stop that, fella," he said to Frank. Paulie was a small angular man, with sticky black and white stubble along his upper lip that looked like the insides of jellybeans. His eyes were kind of glassy suggesting that he didn't see too well.

"What's going on here?" asked a man who carried a briefcase. He had bushy eyebrows. His left eye was higher than his right.

"I want my CDs."

"They're mine," the woman said, the box against her stomach.

"Maybe we ought to get some law," said the sensible guy with the briefcase.

"I love the Mortals." She started singing the lyrics to "I Want More," and she had them right. "Steve 'the Tongue' Gash sounds like Iggy Pop. And Bill Grapes' guitar licks have a 60s sound," she said.

Frank looked perplexed.

"See, Mr., they're hers," Paulie said.

"Marble Orchard. What can you tell me about them?"

"Psychedelic. Big fat guitar sound," she said. "They groove. 'Sickness' kicks."

Frank's jaw slackened like chicken innards sliding across a plate. "Sickness" was his favorite song and she seemed to know what we knew—damn, she talked just like us—and then Paulie and the guy with the briefcase and three others gave Frank a collective why-are-you-bothering-this-woman-with-*her*-box-of-CDs look.

He screamed and lunged for the box. The five of them tackled Frank and Paulie raised the butt-end of the shotgun but I stumbled between them. The woman walked down the street into a gray car. And then I didn't see her.

On Thursday night we were called over to the high school across from Frank's. Seems Johnny Rocket, an English professor at the University of Illinois, had a new lead on the robbery. Rocket, when not writing scholarship, scribbled pithy anecdotes for the *Chronicle* on the job crisis in higher education, and also penned postmodern poetry for the little magazines. Anyway, the Rocket wasn't his real name, just a character he played on Cable Access who interviewed people from a drum kit, told jokes, and thud-thunked away on the skins and tins whenever things got slow. He also said that the reason I didn't get a job was because my dissertation wasn't any good. What does he know? He couldn't even keep time.

"Rocket seems to know of some woman or something," Mr. Delgarno said as we strolled sullenly through the corridor. The school was getting ready for the big dance tomorrow night and Delgarno, as faculty advisor to the Student Council, was making last-second arrangements. Rocket was going to interview some faculty members about rock 'n' roll, Fenders versus Gibsons, and preferred chip dips for his access show. At the end of hard tile glowed a sharp, steel door with a big wheel that could ballast a ship. "Forget Presley. Jerry Lee's the real King."

"Forget 'em both," Frank said. "The girl's probably in Kankakee by now."

We entered a gymnasium. "High School Confidential" was blasting. The bleachers were locked flat against cinder block, but the parquet floor was filled with Urbana West teachers: women in baby grand dresses, art-deco black and white with piano key patterns everywhere. Men wore "Killer" T-shirts and blue jeans. Bamboo curtain hung along most of the walls and around the wet bar were exotic plants: one had crescent-shaped leaves with holes that looked like sad faces, and another had long, narrow stalks with fat-folded-elephant ears. Leaning against the bar was Johnny Rocket, a Presley fan. He wore gold lamé, a thin tie, and Italian disco shoes that signified a practitioner of Straight-Queer Theory. Maggie and a police officer were next to him.

"Hey," I said in Lou Reed cool, "What goes on?" A deejay who looked like Alan Freed spun 45s from a built up sound stage. Basketball twine limped from a hoop over his head.

Rocket snapped his fingers to the Lewis boogie. "I'm surprised to see you in town. What are you doing now?"

"I'm an adjunct in the department."

"Oh."

Maggie kissed my cheek. Her hair smelled of strawberries and she looked swell in her long art-deco dress, piano keys running along the sides. I hadn't told Frank yet that Maggie was ten weeks pregnant. It hardly showed.

"Any luck?" she asked.

I shook my head and told her what had happened. Officer O'Rourke, a skinny guy, seemed to be talking into a small headset that curved around his left ear.

"Kim from my 'Keats and Colonialism' class thinks she knows somebody who might have done this," Rocket said, his hair two identical waves.

"Huh?" Frank seemed transfixed by the large cardboard cutout of the Killer dangling from the ceiling. It was Lewis from 1958, eyes ablaze like the devil, hair wild, dangerous, foot up on the keys.

Kim, her skin glistening like wet lip gloss, leaned forward on her stool. She wore a long red and white hat. It looked like it belonged on a Dr. Seuss character. "There's some chick who charts all your shows, writes down all the songs you spin."

"Redhead with green eyes?" Frank said.

"She was blonde," I said.

"Redhead."

"No, brunette with blue eyes. The fan, I mean," Kim said. "She said you played ten songs by bands whose names started with M."

Rocket shrugged. "I thought it might be important."

O'Rourke asked Kim some more questions, spoke into his headset and left. Frank wandered from the bar and stood directly under the life-size Lewis. He leaned right and stared, and I wasn't sure what he was thinking.

"Matt, Frank's pretty shook up," Maggie said.

"Yeah, I know."

"Hey," Mr. Delgarno squeezed between us, elbows up. He wore flared pants with checkered patterns, a wide-open shirt, and thin chains. "Like the music?"

"Great," I said.

"Fund-raiser. You know, for Frank."

"Oh."

"We've raised $400. The money goes to get back those CDs. Tomorrow this place will be crowded with students. Frank used to work for us, you know?"

"No, I didn't."

"Yeah, back in the 80s, won a teaching award. Anyway, we had to do something, and, well, I couldn't resist a little delicious irony. Killer style. Oh, listen." He held up a hand. "The Lewis pause. 'Breathless!' Brilliant! That pause and then that emotion. Wow."

"Do you think the woman who took them is a fan?" Maggie said.

"The *Live at the Star Club, Hamburg* may be one of Lewis' best, perhaps the definitive album," Mr. Delgarno said.

"We don't know for sure if it was a woman," I said. "I mean, his screen door was torn in half—"

"But the footprint the cops found. Woman's size. What if she had a crush on Frank and this is her way of getting to meet him? You know Frank's not a very approachable guy. We were in the band. He quit because he couldn't play out. Maybe she figures this is the only way to reach him," Maggie suggested.

"That's too fucking weird," I said.

"No weirder than what happened in Rantoul." Dimples formed at the sides of Maggie's face.

"One other thing about Lewis," Mr. Delgarno said. "He kept rocking and still rocks. Presley was finished after the *G.I. Blues* thing, but nothing can kill the 'Killer,' the death of his son, nothing. Hey, 'Great Balls of Fire.' My song."

"Every song's your song," Maggie said.

"You gotta dance with me." He grabbed her wrist. "Please?"

Maggie sighed with low-key surrender and she was off twirling. Frank walked away from Jerry Lee, shoulders slumped, as if he were afraid to upset whatever it was the partygoers waited for. Maggie, well, she waited for the song to end, her face angling for a tow-line, and I wondered how did I ever get to know Frank and what was it that connected us beyond our anger about no futures, no jobs. Music was something, a way to understand, feel good about ourselves, I don't know, but together we listened to Radio Birdman's use of the wah-wah and rediscovered the Chocolate Watch Band. But I really didn't know Frank. When was his birthday? He never did tell me.

"Yeah, that's pretty awesome," some guy said to Frank. The stranger sipped Evian water by the punch bowl, and I tried not to stare, and then suddenly I knew. It was Wayne Kramer of the MC5, now rocking on Epitaph with *The Hard Stuff*. His face was slightly fuller with age, a federal stretch for drug possession adding wrinkles around the eyes, but he remained brimmed and bemused, and I envisioned a younger dirt-sweated twenty-something raging across Detroit gym floors, hammering activist slogans with his guitar. He and the Five were all about "kicking out the jams," freeing yourself of repression and doing what felt right.

"Wayne Kramer?" I said.

"Yeah. You teachers sure know how to party." He made a face and then laughed before sipping more Evian. Back in 1968, the MC5 had swagger and energy as they poised to take over the rock 'n' roll establishment. It didn't work out, but the jazzy buzz was still there, although now obscured with Blue Note cool.

"I was telling Frank, I play at the high school tomorrow." Wayne said.

"I haven't seen any advertising," I said.

He smiled, said something I didn't catch, and then said he'd be at the Cabaret Metro, Chicago, Saturday. I wondered what it was like to have played with Fred "Sonic" Smith, to have two great guitar players in the same band and how it felt to later lose "Sonic" and "Rocking" Rob Tyner. I figured if 1971's *High Time* were released today it would be a big hit, *Billboard* easily, but back then it was too early—music hadn't caught up with them.

"You know on *Kick Out the Jams*, the fold-out sleeve, did you guys really pin those buttons to your chests?"

Frank shook his head, and Wayne arched his eyebrows and grinned. "Sure." He winked. "We're the original punks."

I shouldn't have asked the question. That picture with the bare-chested Five staring into the camera, arms defiantly folded, evoked adolescent angst and power: the demand for recognition, respect and radical commitment. And now it was all reduced to a joke. "But in Australia, your impact. Radio Birdman—"

"Hey," Wayne smiled. "It's only rock 'n' roll." He shrugged, his face again bemused. "Besides Radio Birdman got their name from a Stooges' song. It's the Stooges the Aussies really dig."

"Yeah, but— "

He then said that he loved our radio show, someone had sent him tapes, and he'd like to get us backstage passes and do an interview some time.

"Cool."

"But right now I gotta head upstairs, make some calls, see if I can find a place to crash." He left apologetically.

The "Killer" music stopped and Maggie reappeared. She hugged my waist and gave it two gentle pats, telling me we've got to leave soon, because it was getting late for the sitter. "Wayne Kramer," I said. "That was Wayne Kramer."

"He always was the best player in that band," Frank said.

"Oh, c'mon. 'Sonic' Smith did some great work."

"Kramer had the best solos. Anybody who knows anything about rock 'n' roll knows Kramer was the best."

I smiled. Maybe I'd revise the article on Barbara Stanwyck, temptation, and *The Lady Eve* and send it to *Journal of Film and Video*.

"Eat donuts, die fat," I said into a microphone. "It can work for you."

"Funny," Maggie said, and Caitlin, who was curved into the edge of the couch, grinned at me with her "Dad-you're-being-too goofy" face.

We were all crowded in the heat of Frank's duplex. Wayne hadn't found a place so Frank told him to come on over, and then he invited me and Maggie and we all watched Thursday Night Football, studied old records, and copied a bunch of riffs.

"Hey, Reservoir Dog, move over a little," Frank told Wayne. "I'm picking up a lot of hum from your amp."

"Sure." Wayne wore dark shades and pushed the Peavey amp across the room, leveled it on a chair, and then tuned his Fender, while I checked the connections to the eight-channel mixer. I tweaked knobs and Maggie pounded the drum's kick. To give the music less bottom I brought up the kick's treble and adjusted the snare's snap into a whapping stutter.

"Nothing flat or hollow now," I said.

Wayne pushed back his glasses with a forearm and played some low chords, and my body lurched to the rhythm. Frank filled Wayne's sound and suddenly Maggie was pounding the drums, and we were hurtling into "Crack in the Universe."

The music was loud and feedback filled. Frank hunched over his guitar, fingers pressing chords as he whipped black hair. I slid between his and Wayne's amps, just to singe my ears, and shouted about a girl in Queens tight in "designer jeans."

Wayne took the first break, coolly pressing the guitar against his gray T-shirt, his face calm trembling, and I no longer cared about English departments, neighbors, or CDs. This was loud, and I jumped up and down, Maggie smiled from the kit, and Caitie, wearing yellow welder's ear plugs, was waving her hands like a pair of crashes, and I recalled something that Iggy once said about the buoyancy and power that happened when guitars were hitting the same sound at the same time—a joyful and dangerous abandonment.

Frank, who had filled every momentary space with barbed licks, took the second break. He let loose a string of notes that burned hotter than a urinary tract infection and Wayne nodded with approval, the shades sliding.

"A crack— " Loud guitars flailed through my body like sunlight on sand. "A crack—" We ended together.

"That fucking rocked," Maggie said. "Sorry, Caitie."

Frank shrugged and then slightly smiled before rubbing away sweat. "What's next?" he said. "'Sister Anne?'"

"Wow." I sipped cold beer. "That would be cool."

Caitie asked if we could rock out to "American Ruse."

"Yeah," Wayne nodded, wiping steamed shades against thighs. "That would be cool, Cait the Skate. Goddamn." He walked toward the front door. "How do you do it Frank, without any AC?"

"Well, Wayne, we all can't be rich like you."

Wayne laughed, and then opened the door, and we saw them. They stood at sidewalk's edge, blurred by the green banner of high school grass, hands in pockets, staring, wondering, waiting. Through streetlights shimmering with humidity I watched as they watched, a series of faint spots. Mr. Delgarno, with an orange beagle on a leash, blinked tired eyes. Ten down was O'Rourke, his headset now twisted around the right ear. Next to him was Johnny Rocket, doodling notes on a Big Chief tablet. I couldn't see the girl with green eyes, but I was sure we'd hear from her soon, or maybe I already heard her in the music and she was sitting at the roadside, the lip of her wide belt hanging violently from her jeans. I wasn't quite sure because of the lights, but she may have been there, turning and slipping through the crowd, but the rest had come and Frank had played. And if the cops decided to shut us down 'cause of the noise, well, it was worth the wait.

"Any requests?" I said.

Sleigh Ride

"I'm religious and three's the Trinity," Deaner says, and General Manager Scott Christie hopes they don't hit their third deer.

Deaner, Ted Dean, formerly of John Deere, retired 1977, and part-time bus-driver, defends his choice in music, his beloved Holiday Tape which blasts over the sound system. The guys had already heard the Frank Sinatra and Bing Crosby versions of "Hark the Herald Angels Sing," and now it's Perry Como's turn. Each song on "Deaner's Rockin' Christmas" comes in rushes of three. "The Trinity you know, and I just feel lucky with it, that's all, and odds are nothing bad will happen, but if it does, I think having the music helps square me with God." Christie can tell the guys hate the damn thing, especially Chatham who points his hockey stick like an M-16 at the back of Deaner's hunched head, but even if they all think the music is sentimental hooey, Deaner doesn't, and he's had a ten-year run of good luck driving Black Hawk coaches. Sinatra and Crosby make him feel better, drive better, so what the hell. Chats, who has his own weird rituals like listening to punk rock, slapping Kos on the pads before every faceoff, and carrying his hockey stick aboard the bus just to have a damn air-guitar, should, well, understand Deaner's point.

Christie shrugs and wonders when someone will emerge as the leader of this team. Every summer it's the same. He brings together eighty guys, trims to twenty-four by August and hopes that two, three players will create the team's personality. Chatham, the team captain, *is* a leader—digs in corners, shoves forwards out of the crease, and falls to the ice, blocking shots. He also gets along with the black guy, Isaiah Sullivan, and is great to rookies off ice. But Christie's favorite player can't make the big offensive play under pressure and carry the team when it's in trouble. Kevin Ogilvie, who three months ago played Ontario Junior C in some lake town called Cobourg, is the guy to do that. He has the speed, the quickness and peripheral vision, but, well, he's always reading—not the usual things, either—*Swank* and *Penthouse Letters*—but old-time hockey books, and some Irish guy Studs Lonigan or something or other. Studs. A good hockey name.

Deaner suddenly curses, speeds up, and crushes his third deer full on, sending a shower of blood, guts and bone all over the windshield that sparkles like entering warp-speed on *Star Wars*.

"What the hell you doing, Deaner?"

He shrugs, an unlit cigar chomped between his lips. "Hell, I didn't want to maim the thing."

The players howl, applaud Deaner, the collision, and some call play-by-play.

"That bus hits like Chatham," Sullivan says.

Chats laughs and Christie looks down the aisle. "Joyful all ye Nations Rise." Lots of the guys are in their underwear, readying to sleep during the long ten-hour ride home to Waterloo. Several are finishing dinners—spaghetti, with salad, rolls, and milk. Koslov, who sits next to Ogilvie, has hardly touched his.

"Hey, Kos, I can't order Franco-American. You gotta eat."

"I will." He sips milk. "I will."

Jeff Paplowsky and Billy Nelson are playing poker. Looks like Paplowsky's got more chips. Ogilvie is reading some damn book on Roosevelt and the New Deal. "Hey, Ogilvie, what the hell's that? I mean there's no tits or ass or anything cool like that here. You're wasting your time."

Ogilvie shrugs.

"Hey," Christie leans against the fake wood-grain finish on back of a seat. "I'm just teasing you a little bit. I'm sorry we didn't play any better when your Mom and sister visited."

Ogilvie grins and tells how his Mom said he needed more grit in the corners and how she might come visit him in Waterloo next spring. Wes Johnson and Kirby Davis, eight rows down, are reading Marvel Comics and arguing over who's tougher, the Hulk or Thor.

"She knows her hockey."

"We all need to dig more and get inside the box," Coach says. "We're great on the outside but we're not getting high or low in the slot." He stands in the aisle, his hands resting inside the waistband of his sweats. Rectangular-shaped sweat dots his forehead. "C'mon guys, don't just leave that shit here for everyone to kick all over."

Michaels has sworn more in the past two days than all season. The four-game losing streak is really getting to him. And the whole team is down. It always takes a team a while to gel, and the recent trades— Gilmour for Harris—and owner Raymond Southworth's get-to-.500-by-Christmas-or-else-I-fire-the-coach ultimatum hasn't helped. Playing Junior A, Christie figures, ought to be the culmination of a dream, but instead it leads to shattered dreams. When the young guys come from Midgets they're the best players on their teams. And within weeks of joining the Waterloo Black Hawks most of these players know that they're just one player amongst many great players and that they can't make money at this game and this is it. At least half of them will play only one season. Nine or ten will play Division One. Perhaps three out of the twenty-four, Chatham, Torrio and Sullivan maybe, will earn cash playing in the Colonial or Eastern League. Perhaps two or three, Paplowsky, if he grows up a little and converts more scoring chances, Ogilvie if he really wants it, and Fran Koslov if he can bring up his level of concentration, can play in the NHL. When players realize these odds, it's hard to stay focused, to do what's necessary to bond.

"Hey, it wasn't me, homey," Chats says about the mess, as snow swirls across windows like white tracer fire.

"Captains, pick three rookies to clean up the aisle and collect the garbage." Michaels speaks with precision, and then he reads off scores from other USHL games. The Hawks are in last place in the South Division.

"Hey, uh, Scott, we got a problem." Deaner's red Black Hawk vest has bunched up his back.

Christie lumbers to the front of the bus. The tips of his shoes are wet and salt-stained. "Yeah, what's up?" He looks through the windshield. Chalky snow twists above the highway like floating silverfish.

"The brake light's on."

Christie looks down at the dash and sees a faint red glare. "Yeah, so we take it a little easy, don't make any sudden stops."

"No, you don't understand, the light's *on*. We have no brakes."

"We have no brakes?"

"No. None. I can't stop this thing."

The bus is somewhere south of the Canadian border and North of Duluth. That stretch of Highway is a twisting two-lane, hilly, with narrow shoulders, and run-offs—one slip, like a skate edge on the heel of a hockey stick, and everybody's down. He wants to scream at the sky, but instead, pulls Michaels to the front of the bus.

"I can't believe this shit, I mean I can't believe it." Coach, head down, straddles the cooler in the aisle. "Pull over."

"I can't. I can downshift, but I can't pull over."

The roads look black under white-outs, slick like a goalie's crease, and Christie says it's important to stay cool, they've got twenty-four players on the bus to protect, kids.

"What's up, Chief," Sullivan calls out.

Christie spins around. His shoulders ache with tension. "Look fellas, we need everybody to sit down and balance this bus. We've got no brakes. I need everyone to sit down so that we can equally distribute, I said sit down, damn it!"

All of the players look sharply ahead. Deaner turns down the deck. Sinatra: "I'll be Home for Christmas / You can Count on Me."

"We must have busted the brake line after we hit that deer," he says, his hands steady, the wipers swishing.

Suddenly the bus slides side-to-side on hardened slicks of ridged slush and they slam down a steep hill at 55 m.p.h., and Christie envisions himself, alone, late at night, dimly skating on the ice at Young Arena, backwards, turning, shooting the slapper from inside the blueline. Fortunately the hill has an equally steep incline and Deaner levels the speed at 40 m.p.h. and they cruise fifteen miles, downshifting, into Grand Marais, Minnesota, a casino town, before stopping at a Holiday gas station. Deaner says he's going to work on the bus, see if he can heat up the brake sack or some damn thing. He grabs a tool box and a blow torch. "You better get the fellas gear from down below, 'cause I'm gonna have to shut the engine off." Christie shakes his head. Everyone's half-naked, but the temperature will drop real fast with the engine off. Michaels nods and assigns six rookies, including Ogilvie, Sullivan and Gilmour, to brave the cold and bring gear back on the bus. "I'm Dreaming of a White—"

Christie, hands in pockets, walks to the gas station. It's blue and white with a big neon sign that seems to turn in the wind. He calls three hotels. No luck. Next to the bus Christie sees Ogilvie, Davis, Paplowsky and Sullivan hustling, grabbing gear, tossing it aboard, and then one motel clerk tells him to drive down the road, a few miles or so, and there should be a spot available in Two Harbors. Christie buys a Twix bar.

Outside, the wind whips his face, and traces of snow trap in the back collar of his jacket. Deaner lies under the bus, and there's red-green fluid everywhere, spilling toward the diesel pumps. "Uh, Deaner." Christie's hands are in his pockets.

"I think I've almost got it."

"How long will it take?"

"Oh, about half an hour."

"Is all that fluid—"

"Brake stuff—"

"I mean, is it, flammable? I mean are we all going to blow up like

Cagney in *White Heat*? There's pumps behind us."

Deaner adjusts the blow torch's nozzle, narrowing the flame. "Damn, that's a good film, but I wish the O'Brien character would have got taken out in the end, the rat. He should have got shot in a crossfire or something."

Christie nods and re-boards the bus. The guys are leaning together. The windows have frosted over and Christie's toes hurt. "Shit, it's cold."

"Goddam right, Chief," Sullivan says.

"You guys bundled?"

They all nod, saying nothing, their lips cold slivers. He walks down the aisle and makes sure everyone's zipped. "C'mon Ogilvie," Christie taps his left shoulder twice. "Do that zipper all the way to your chin, and button it. It's too fuckin' cold."

"Sure, Scott."

Christie rubs his hands between his legs, stamps his feet, and tells Michaels that he had no luck getting a hotel. Seems there's a high school reunion or something, but that sounded like bullshit, it's Sunday night for crying out loud—probably just afraid to house a bunch of rowdy hockey players. Michaels suggests that they all go inside the gas station to keep warm.

Christie isn't sure there's enough space in the small store, but what the hell. "Sure." He reaches into his pocket and pulls out $85. "Here, let the fellas get a couple of things, up to $3.00 each. And guys, you're hockey players, you represent Waterloo. I want you to behave in there. Be polite and no looking at the skin mags."

The guys quietly trudge into the store. Christie returns to Deaner who still lies under the bus. "What's the coolest scene in *White Heat*?"

Forty minutes later they're back on the road, the bus feels more like an outdoor sleigh ride with Mom, Dad, and Perry Como. And that Winter Wonderland thing is really starting to happen as Christie senses the heater ain't putting out much heat.

Deaner says nothing.

The players seem contemplative, some talk about how wild it all is, others reflect, realizing just how dangerous things might have got. Ogilvie's intensity suggests that he's looking for more deer.

"See anything, K. O.?"

"Hell, no."

Deaner curses and slams his hands along the outer edge of the steering wheel.

"Don't say it," Michaels says.

Christie walks to the front of the bus. "Damn, the light's on again."

"Look, we gotta get off this bus." Michaels is insistent and several players sit up in their seats.

"Deaner, we're ten miles from Two Harbors. When we get there stop along the route and we'll find a hotel."

"Sure, Chief."

Christie shrugs and within minutes the wipers stiffen, the front window frosts over and the heater blows cold air.

Deaner says something or other about having shut off the engine and now being unable to regain pressure. Sinatra slurs through "Silent Night." Two miles later they're pulled over on the side of the road, five miles from town. Michaels bumps his briefcase off the seat and it explodes on the floor. Christie tells the fellas to conserve their candy bars, keep bundled, huddle next to each other, rub shoulders, "Don't worry I won't think you're queers" and stamp your feet and rub your hands. "Keep your feet moving. Stamp them." Christie saw a war film when he was a kid where the guys where holed up in a cave in Korea and they stamped their feet to keep from getting frost bit, and it's at least minus 20 on the bus, and the guys are now stamping and the bus rocking like a tank riding over a half-track or some damn thing. On the cellular phone he calls the USHL offices, the highway patrol, the transit commission and the public works people to let them know that a hockey team, the Waterloo Black Hawks, are stranded five miles from town and how they might just become the first franchise in USHL and all hockey history to freeze to goddamn death.

Ten minutes later they arrive. Two Harbors' winter road crew: large sanders, plows and pick-ups. Their lights gleam curves like wet slices of oranges against the glass of the bus. Several workers, dressed in padded vests, hop aboard and run up the aisle, quickly checking for frostbite or any emergencies. "We got a place for you in town, a resort. You can sleep on the convention room floor," a guy with a beard says.

"Swell," Christie says, "That's swell."

They exit slowly. The colder players, those with possible frostbite on their ears and feet, ride up front in the rigs of the road crew. The rest climb in back of one of five black pick-ups.

Ogilvie rolls over the gate and rests against the back of the bed. "Scott, this is something else. I never—"

"Yeah," Christie rubs Ogilvie's shoulders, "Yeah."

As snow swirls like lint shook loose from a dryer, they pull away, and Chatham clutches his stick, Paplowsky and Koslov stamp their feet, and Sullivan hums a few bars to "Dueling Banjos." "I think these road crew guys are okay and everything, but do we really know them? They might not be okay, they might be getting ready to carve us up, or feed us to the gimp under the stairs," Kos says.

Christie shrugs his shoulders, raises an abrasive fist into pencil streaks of snow, and Chatham shout-sings like a demented punk rocker, "Hark the Herald Angels Sing." Christie and then several Black Hawk voices follow, hard and spit-spikey cool.

Dragonflies

Late last night Annie's father left home.

He and his wife Mrs. Riordan had argued from the bedroom in gasps of contoured violence: sideways words, electric anger, and the shy, awkward aftermath of suitcases shut with cramped clothes. Isaiah Sullivan heard it all from the living room couch, where he and Annie were watching *Get Smart*.

Now, Isaiah and Annie sat behind a round, block table at the Waterloo Public Library. Outside, rain fell in lanky lines the size of gray pencil streaks, and the seventeen-year old felt unsure of how to help Annie with her third-grade project on dragonflies. Every Saturday morning he drove her to the library to hang and read, and in the early afternoons they played Parcheesi and Easy Money in Annie's basement, and then invited over a bunch of Waterloo Black Hawks to eat pizza rolls and watch *Slap Shot*. But this Saturday was different. Isaiah didn't want to hear his teammates howling at the Hanson brothers. Instead, he just wanted to watch Annie scratch heavy lines into loose yellow paper.

"Did you know that a dragonfly can zoom along at thirty-five miles per hour?" Annie looked up from her red angular book, the metal end of her pencil nudging sideways at the left corner crease in her lips. The pencil's rubber end was worn down. "And its two ginormous eyes can see as far as 42 feet."

"'Ginormous,' huh?" Isaiah smiled. "Not bad. That's about as third as fast as a slap shot." Isaiah, who played left wing on the Hawks's second line, was always searching for connections between life and hockey. The Riordans were his house parents, and Annie had become a kind of linemate, a new kid sister. She often slumped into his room late at night, the white picot trim of her pink pajamas stretched and twisted into loose lariats around her wrists, as she pleaded with him to read another chapter from Beverly Cleary's *Ramona and Her Father*. Annie also talked hockey, and wondered why on the penalty kill the Black Hawks played a kind of "laid-back square" instead of skating out toward the offensive players who held the puck on the edges. "So why did you pick the dragonfly for your project?"

"I don't know." Annie shrugged, her right shoulder rising higher than her left, her lips squiggling together. Her face was freckled, and her right eyebrow was dotted with a small hammer-shaped scar. "Dad used to take me to Hartman Reserve and we'd see them dancing, skating like helicopters over the pond. They were cool."

"They're way cool." Annie's imagery was impressive and accurate. Dragonflies *did* kind of dance, or hover like helicopters. Isaiah was from Austin, Minnesota, and when he was a kid his parents took him camping along lakes and ponds and they caught dragonflies in filmy Mason jars. "If you stand right behind them, they can't see you, because their eyes are on the sides of their heads. And then snap. I've got 'em."

"No way."

"Way, dude. I'll show you some time. This spring."

Annie's father never really said much to Annie or anybody when he was home. He talked about hockey, complaining about coach's tough style of play, and huffed that the Hawks needed more finesse up front and less brawling grit. When he wasn't talking hockey, Mr. Riordan hesitantly scowled behind a newspaper or fell asleep on the couch, the television clicker clutched in his left hand. Isaiah figured that there were problems between the Riordans but he wasn't prepared for last night's kind of sudden death overtime.

A bunch of nine- and ten-year old boys were playfully shoving by a water fountain and bumping up next to a dull-colored poster featuring Michael Jordan in a Chicago Bulls uniform. Jordan had a foot balanced on a bench, an accordion of books next to him, and he was telling everyone to read. It was old—Jordan had hair.

A librarian, in a dark dress and low-heel shoes, saw the commotion, directed the children to three shelves of collected Christmas stories, and then told them that they could each check out two. The kids laughed at some of the illustrations. "Finding anything else about dragonflies, kiddo?"

"Yeah, they zigzag when they fly." Annie held her left hand out like a flat stone and it skipped up and down in her efforts to capture the darting dance of a dragonfly. "And," she read from the book, "'their spiny legs form a basket' and that's how they catch mosquitoes."

"So, a dragonfly is one of the good guys? They're like spiders taking care of the nasty bugs?"

"Yeah. I guess so."

"That's ginormously cool," he said. "I'm a dragonfly."

"Huh?"

"No really. That's how I play, that's my role on the team." Isaiah explained to Annie how he wasn't a great goal scorer, but he was strong on his skates, flung himself into corners with elbows high, and made sure, like those dragonflies taking care of us humans by eating mosquitoes, that no one messed with center Kevin Ogilvie, the team's playmaker.

"Dragonflies," she said, her voice thinning.

Isaiah smiled. He had often heard road fans shouting in voices dipped with battery acid, "Hey, Sullivan, go back to Harlem, you can't dribble a puck," but the words only made the hard-checking winger hit harder and crash the net more forcibly. His aggressive play opened up spaces for Kevin, allowing him to skate more freely, and to pass and to score. Last night, before Mr. Riordan left with his blue suitcases, Ogs scored two goals in a 5-2 win over Sioux City at Young Arena.

Annie bit her upper lip and gritted out words with the metal end of her pencil. A faint scratchy hole appeared inside the yellow-gray smudges, and then she was crying. She didn't want her Mom and Dad to divorce. Her father hadn't said much to Annie as he left, except that he would see her every other weekend.

"Look," Isaiah took the book from her fingers. "It's a trial separation. Sometimes parents get back together after a trial separation, after they've thought it over."

Annie's upper lip curled back like a stretched rubber band. "No. They've already thought it over. It's over."

"Well maybe he'll stick around. Maybe he'll say, no."

"No. Mom . . . she said, no."

"Oh." Isaiah was struck by the book's images, the dragonflies' wings, the porous membrane looking like the insides of human lungs. "You wanna go get a Pepsi or something?"

"My tummy's sore."

"Yeah." He flipped pages, searching, and they sat still for awhile, and the rain had stopped. The sky was the green of wet grass cuttings.

Annie then said something about splinters and how Dad was always gentler at removing them than Mom.

"Hey— " Isaiah looked through Annie's shoulder. "Did you know Japanese farmers believed that the dragonfly represented the spirit of the rice plant and that if you saw them they were a welcome sign of a good rice harvest? It says that right here. Pretty cool, huh?"

Annie nodded, and Isaiah hoped that maybe on their way to the car they'd see them, thousands, hovering soundlessly.

Mitchell Street Near Midnight

Francis Koslov can't remember ever seeing his parents kiss.

So it feels kind of good right now, Mrs. Maroucheff kissing his cheek in that Eastern European way and everything, pinching his chin and smiling. "*Guolomo*."

"That means big." Wanda smiles as she leans against a rusty sink. Her hair is black, long and sleekly shines.

"Me?" Kos is six-four, one-hundred and sixty-five pounds, long and lithe maybe, but never *guolomo*, well, pretty *guolomo*, maybe, when he's in the nets with his hockey pads and chest protector on.

Wanda buttons her jacket and tightens a bootstrap that looks like a bungee chord. "We'll be back soon, Ma."

Mr. and Mrs. Maroucheff say *guolomo* a few more times, pinch Kos's cheeks, and direct the young couple to the door. Boy, Wanda wasn't kidding when she wrote that her Mom could sure fix him a great meal. She had written Kos several fan letters care of the Waterloo Black Hawks, commenting on his style of play—perceptively she noted how he was an angles goalie who liked to flop to the ice to protect the bottom half of the net. She also suggested that he looked like he needed a square meal, so why not meet her, her family and have some real ethnic Macedonian food—stuffed peppers, *zilnick*, and tomato salad, heavy with olive oil. After the Thunder Bay trip, Kos called her on the phone, and then she met him at the rink, watched practice, and they went for Pepsis afterwards.

Outside on Mitchell Street the snow crunches under their boots. It's a cold sky, and all of the stars look like the bruise on the inside of Kos's left arm—courtesy of a rising slap shot that he mishandled. But he feels real funny, weirdly happy. It's something new to him.

"Let's go down to 'Adams,' I want to get something." Wanda's lips glisten in the arc of streetlights.

She reaches for his hand, and he holds it awkwardly. They haven't kissed or anything. Kos has sort of wanted to, but he's afraid of spoiling everything, of not doing it right or something, and then embarrassing her and himself. He hasn't had many dates and once in ninth grade a girl kissed him, wishing him "Merry Christmas" but she was Jewish so he figured it was all a joke.

They cross 9th Street and enter Adams', a big Mom and Pop independent grocery store that's shaped like a barn.

"Hey, Wanda," says one of the checkers, wearing a finger-splotched smock. "You gonna work tomorrow?"

"Can't—there's a game on." She looks up at Kos. Wanda's a year older, nineteen. She graduated from West High last year and takes part-time classes at Hawkeye Community College. Several nights a week she works as a checker at Adams'. Kos thinks that after practice yesterday she had really wanted to kiss him, because she was doing the leaning-toward-him thing outside the dressing room as they talked. It wasn't a listen-more-intently lean, but the come-on-get-close-put-your-arms-around-me-stupe type of lean.

"Wanda, how are ya?" Gary, the manager, grins. He's wearing a dress shirt, with the sleeves rolled up. Around his wrist are several rubber bands. "Can I get you to baby-sit on Thursday? The wife and I want to go to a movie."

"Sure." Wanda picks up a Hershey bar and some Tic-Tacs.

"How's the folks?" He jams carts together and stacks cardboard boxes.

"Fine, fine."

Kos enjoys watching Wanda talk to Gary and others, and then they walk down an aisle. The whole supermarket seems to glow like wet lip gloss under track lighting and everyone likes Wanda and he likes being with her, and in turn, being liked.

Back outside, down Mitchell to 8th, they cross snow-covered sidewalks, faintly layered with ice. Despite the slick spots, Wanda walks quickly, her shoulders huddled, chin down. "I thought you played great last night."

Kos nods. Forty stops, 1-0 win. "Yeah, I saw the puck real well."

"Tic-Tac?" She shakes the container. It rattles like a can of spray paint.

"Uh, no." They walk down the hill to Liberty Park and along wet, dark trees. All around them are small, squat homes built during World War Two. The people who live in the homes have been there for generations, giving the area a sense of stability, security. Kos's home wasn't like that. Dad was always asleep on the couch after a hard, dusty day working construction. Mom was usually at Doris' house, eating day-old donuts and watching reruns of old sitcoms. He likes walking by these homes.

"So, when, you're seeing the puck real well, do you always know where you are in relation to the net? Is it easy to see the angles?"

They stand next to a slide streaked with hardened mud. Glasses of grass stretch through cracks in the cement. Kos wipes his lips with the back of a gloved hand. "It's easier at home. At home you have advertisements on the dashers and you have columns, staircases, around the rink that I use as sights—you have twenty, twenty-five sights around the rink so when you're concentrating on the puck your peripheral vision will see these markers, and you'll know you're lined up, or whether you're off six inches, one way or another."

"Cool."

"Angles become second nature, but it's difficult on the road. A place like Sioux City where the rink is real tiny—that's very difficult to adjust to."

Wanda nods, and far behind the playground, along the fence and wood-chipped path, and wet almost cellophane-streaked trees, Kos sees an old man picking at garbage with a harpoon-like cane that clicks and stabs. The man carries a white bucket and around his left shoulder hangs an orange bag that glows like a radiated leech. The old man pushes back his cap, pauses, and then stabs at a wrapper with the stick. He bends slowly, inspects the wrapper, and places it in the bucket. Kos thinks it's weird that he's working past ten o'clock. Nobody at the Park District works after nightfall, not even when they built the new baseball diamonds last summer.

"I wonder what he's up to?" Wanda suggests they move farther away, down the hill, toward the bridge.

They climb over rocks, sharded-slabs of concrete, and cross the thin slick of the creek to stand under the bridge. Overhead is the steady slapped slush of cars and all around them graffiti in big block letters. Across the wall "Marianne loves Derek" jags in angular lines, and Kos stands against a column and feels a little tense. The bridge thuds with knocking tires.

"You don't say much on the ice." She leans forward.

Kos looks away. "I'm supposed to, but I'm not very good at it."

She places a hand on his chest and starts drawing small circular patterns. "What sorts of things do you want to say?"

"Well, uh—" Wanda's hair smells great. "Uh, when the defense comes back to pick up the puck you're supposed to tell them how much time they've got, if there's a guy on them. On rushes, let them know where our backcheckers are—"

More thudding overhead and Kos gets that tight Ace bandage feeling around his chest. He feels like he wants to take off his goalie mask, but he doesn't have it on.

Wanda throws her arm around his shoulder and kisses him. Kos staggers slightly and wonders if it was something he said, and then puts a hand around her back and another on her waist. As he kisses her he thinks her lips are soft, and as she leans back, it all seems like a perfume ad or something and he wonders if she's bending her left leg at the knee like one of those super-models and he keeps kissing.

Wanda catches her breath. "Now, do you want a mint?" She laughs.

Over by the play structures, Kos sees a blue jacket with two white stripes draped across a silver duck. A ball cap limply rests under a swing. Parachute-shaped monkey bars swirl with snow, and the old man leans, catches his breath and then clicks the cane at shadows under a red horse. "That's why you got the mints."

"Duh. A girl can't be subtle with you. I've got to practically throw myself at you. The girl is not the one who's supposed to do all the leaning."

"You mean you want me to lean?"

They kiss again, and then, across the park they watch the quiet man. His stick clicks and slowly drags from under the red horse. As he lifts the stick, they see that it is heavy. He bends and removes a small animal. He looks at it, opens the orange bag and drops it in. He reaches into his white bucket and pulls out shucked corn. He looks them over, too, and then tosses them like grenades under the swings and slide. Tired, he sits on a bench and lights a cigarette. The orange bag on his shoulder is heavy.

"Shit," Wanda says. "I wonder how many animals he's found?"

"Yeah. I don't know."

"We should get back. My parents are expecting us."

They walk out from under the bridge toward the wet trees and back across the play structures.

"Who goes there?" The old man leans forward, both hands creased at the knuckles like V-shaped wedges. One holds the cane poised, like a switchblade. "You trying to sneak up on my blind side?" The cigarette bobs like a lake buoy on his lower lip. The bucket in his right hand has 'HELP' written across in red letters.

Wanda seems startled. She and Kos stand motionless. "No, I—" she says.

"You shouldn't be out this late. Where's your parents?"

"I'm eighteen, she's nineteen," Kos says.

"Oh." He looks away and pushes back his cap. He takes a long drag off his cigarette, and walks slowly over to the swings and picks up a soda bottle. He sits on a swing, absently running a finger around the bottle's opening. "I know what that's like." He nods. "I thought you were trying to sneak up on me. I can't see out of this eye." Years ago a man who was high on drugs or something, came out of the evergreens and surprised him on his blind side. "Even then, I was old, but this cane, here— " He jumps ahead, both feet balanced. "This cane, this cane is a weapon." He clicks it twice, steps up, and jabs it forcefully toward Kos's ribs.

Kos throws up his right arm as if defending a wicked wrist shot.

"That's what I did. Called the cops. They took him away in an ambulance." He turns his back and walks by the posts of the swings looking for more wrappers.

"There's a coat over there," Wanda points, "by the duck."

"Yeah, I know. Blue coat. Green lining. Two white stripes on the left sleeve. There's also a cap under the swings. I found them last night with a bunch of half-torn deposit envelopes. I wonder if Adams across the street got robbed. I keep listening to the news, but—" He tosses the cigarette and wipes the corners of his mouth. He moves quickly, more quickly than Kos had noticed from a distance. He picks up a brown bag and two beer bottles.

"Why are you working so late?" Kos asks. Adams couldn't have got robbed. They were just there. Gary would have said something.

The old man smiles and shrugs. "I'm retired."

Kos wants to get going, but Wanda pauses, absently studying salt gritted on her boots. "Do you find a lot of animals, dead, I mean?"

"Uh-huh. Just found a squirrel."

"They always crawl away to die?"

"I find a lot of them." He starts to say something, hesitates, and points across the park, to the fence and the wood-framed homes. "I've been there, too," he announces, "have you?"

"I live there." He squints in the moon. "Do you see it, the lights—"

Most of the lights along Mitchell have shut off, except for two or three around Seventh Street. "Yeah—"

"Squirrels get into attics, chew wires. The lights, take a look at the lights."

Kos wonders what the man is talking about. Wanda seems to wonder the same thing. "Do they kill the squirrels," she asks.

He shakes his head as if in disbelief. "I've gotta be going. Perhaps, I'll see you again tomorrow." He picks up his cane and wipes his thinning hair.

"I want to hear more about the lights."

"My wife died yesterday."

Kos and Wanda say nothing as he turns and walks off, well coordinated, bending slightly but moving briskly toward the evergreens. They watch him, without speaking until he is only a speck in the distance. He stops, maybe to pick up another animal—they aren't sure.

They walk back up the hill, snow crunching under their feet. Kos shoves his hands in his pockets and doesn't know what to say. Wanda kicks at snowball stones at the side of the street.

"Man," Kos says. "Wow."

"Yeah." The arc of light from Adams' cuts a swath in the snow. "Yeah."

"Hey, you got another mint?"

"Sure." Wanda reaches in one pocket, then the other, and they stroll briskly toward her house. She takes off a glove and looks again. "Shit, I can't find them. I must have left them there."

"WWF on Skates"

Coach Scott Christie is no Scotty Bowman.

He's Hulk Hogan and, as an interim coach, he's made the USHL a ringside circus.

Two ejections in three games.

$1000 in fines.

"Hockey's an emotional game and I'm an emotional guy," he says.

But under his interim guidance (absentee owner Raymond Southworth fired Coach Michaels last month), the Hawks continue to spiral out of control. The team record has dipped three games below .500 (21-24-3), and with four games to go they'll miss the playoffs unless they win 2 and get some help from other teams.

What went wrong? Is it having a president who lives in Tennessee making key decisions? Is Christie's brand of grinding hockey as outmoded as the "Broadstreet Bullies," 1974's Philadelphia Flyers who featured such distinguished gents as Dave "the Hammer" Shultz and Andre "Moose" Dupont?

Frankly, Christie's team looks slow, lethargic, and confused. And a season that started with such promise appears destined to be shutout from the second season.

Christie's a fine motivator, the players like him, but he's not a coach.

The past three games have been a debacle with Christie shouting at officials and getting tossed from two games for giving rival coaches, fans, and refs the one-fingered salute. Just last week, against Rochester, Christie threw a bucket of pucks onto the ice. It makes for great showmanship, WWF fireworks on skates, but this town is hungry for a winner. . .

--Matt Traicheff
excerpt from *Waterloo Courier*, March 16, 1996

Four Minutes for Crosschecking

Coach Scott Christie.
What a weird sound.
Coach.
The Black Hawks huddle, readying themselves for the final one minute and fourteen seconds of the third period. Coach Christie, his shirt collar itching the sides of his neck, plunks a leg up on the boards and leans over the ice, as the rowdy crowd of 2600 at Sioux City Auditorium cheer the Musketeers. It's "Boom Box Night" and the fans turn up KWSL, the Fox 91, whenever their team scores or the Black Hawks try to regroup like during this "You-Shook-Me-All-Night-Long" timeout. The Fox deejays all sound like Midwestern Fabios, milkshake smooth with a touch of sun-block. And they stood at all the entryways prior to the game, handing out boom boxes, toothbrushes, and bikinis. All three periods Christie has had to hear sweaty-testosterone-fuck 'n' run rock—AC/DC, Led Zeppelin, Steppenwolf, the Stones. How the league office ever let Musketeer coach and GM Hugh "Two-Fisted" Farrell get away with the boom-box gimmick is beyond Christie. In an indoor arena for chrissakes. And to think, just months ago the league office fined Christie $500 for putting the names of fathers and daughters, family values, on his home jerseys.

"Okay, fellas, we're down 3-2," Christie shouts above the din of Slade's "Gudbuy T' Jane." I want to go to the pinch forecheck with Chats and Ogs, for some offensive punch, on D. Let's force a faceoff in their zone, and then Sully you're going to come off the bench as our extra attacker. Okay, Kos? You be looking to come half way. Pinch forecheck with Chats and Ogs. Got it?" The crisp leather of Christie's new shoes digs into his insteps.

Matt Murphy, who has a short abrupt face, no chin, nods as do his linemates. Stanzack, another new guy, has an almost shark-like stare, dim blank and yet vaguely intense.

"I'll set up in the slot," Stanzie says.

"Great. Murphy, Nelson double down low and rotate to the point."

The players nod, squirt water over their faces, and GM Christie feels that Stanzie—nine goals in eight games—was perhaps one of his best acquisitions since nabbing Chats three years ago in a draft day deal. Now, if Coach Christie can only win some hockey games and find scholarships and jobs for his soon-to-be-overage players. He's yet to find a spot for Chats. Alaska-Anchorage has expressed some interest, but have yet to sign the Coach's fave.

Referee McMahon holds the puck in the neutral zone and the players line up for the faceoff.

Coach. Shit. Southworth fired Michaels two weeks ago.

Scottie preferred just being a GM and doing radio broadcasts with the Shado, Jack Shadoin, and shining forth with his own local color persona—the *bon vivant*, let's-all-have-a-cold-Mountain-Dew guy. He loved being the Midwest promo man, and his chuck-a-puck-for-a-buck contest was a big hit with the Young Arena faithful, as two hundred fans would crowd the ice between periods and take their chances, throwing a puck toward the center circle. The closest puck in the circle's center would win a Waterloo Black Hawks team cap and dress shirt. That was cool, and then there was the time he camped out on a billboard for three weeks, urging each passerby to go to the home games, sellout the arena so that he can come down and sleep in a warm bed. That campaign got a lot of air time on KQMG and the Hawks did sell out against Dubuque.

But he sure hopes he doesn't have to do this coaching gig much longer. He has one candidate that the team is actively pursuing, Morris "The Titanic" Lysevich, a bruising big winger formerly of the Winnipeg Jets, who in the early 1980s scored 29 goals in six years. Scott had wanted to hire one of Mick's assistants, but Southworth said no. The president wanted "new blood, new energies." Truth is Southworth never liked Michaels much and therefore doesn't care for people associated with the Mick.

The puck drops, Murphy kicks at it with his skates, and then shuttles it back to Chatham who fires it to Ogilvie who lugs the puck across center and dumps it in. A minute to go, and Christie awkwardly paces behind the bench, the program rolled in his hand. It just feels too weird, as if everything he is doing is mannered. He shouldn't be thinking about how he looks, or about hiring Lysevich or plotting his next promo campaign: "Night of the Pogs, coming March 19th." He should be thinking about winning this hockey game, but his mind channel surfs to images from his past. He's not a real coach; he's more like Pat O'Brien playing the role of Knute Rockne, sounding tough. The rolled-up program doesn't illustrate his coaching skill but his attempts to look the part. "Hey guys, stand up. Let's not sit. I don't see any of the Sioux City guys sitting. Look at them. Stand up. Let's get some fire, let's play with some intensity. Hockey's a game of emotion."

The guys stand, leaning over the bench as Nelson pinches low and the cross-crease pass hops over Stanzack's stick.

Scottie likes aggressive, hard-hitting hockey. He calls the passing, free-wheeling game, "European style," which is his code phrase for pansy, wussy-ass hockey. There's no greater insult that he can hurl at a player than saying, "he plays a good European game." "North American," that's the style Christie loves. He wants his team to dump and chase the puck, play defensively, two men always on their one, and to hit so hard as to kill a whole country. He hasn't changed Michaels' schemes, relying a lot on intimidation and a two-man forecheck, but sometimes Scottie feels that the players don't really listen. As GM, he was the affable avuncular figure, offering advice about girls, homework and haircuts, giving the players jackets sponsored by the U.A.W. and meals, securing them jobs, lending insights to their problems, but teaching X's and O's and inspiring victory has not gone well. The Hawks during his tenure are 1-4. They picked up a bonus point for losing another shoot-out, but they have lost three close games at home for zero points, and the media, especially *Courier* reporter Matt Traicheff, have accused Scottie of WWF intimidation tactics. The criticism surprises Scottie a little bit because Traicheff is writing a novel, *Young Ice* or something or other, on the team, a sort of arty documentary in which the sports writer fictionalizes some games and tells stories from a variety of points of view. It's not bad—it's pretty good actually, and Scottie's flattered by his own likeness in the novel for the most part, but the WWF references? In two of the last home games, Scottie, who Traicheff views as the USHL equivalent to Hulk Hogan, was tossed for arguing with officials. His dramatic exits—yelling, shouting, broad gestures, the occasional finger when the referee wasn't looking, fired up the crowd, and in Traicheff's reading, no doubt boosted ticket sales. Scottie disagrees. "I'm just an emotional guy," he had said. "And sometimes I get emotional."

Suddenly behind the play, low in the Musketeer end, Andrew Walters whacks Chatham in the back of the head with a vicious two-handed crosscheck. Chats slips to the ice like a drifting parachute, his gloves propping him up and then he rolls over on his side. Ogilvie touches the puck up at the blueline and the whistle sounds.

Murphy, behind the Musketeer net, frantically waves for the trainer as he looks at Chatham, and a linesman seems to be telling him not to touch his neck. Scott jumps over the boards and hurries across ice. Trainer Bob Davidson, black shoes sliding, is at his side.

The crowd cheers like a rising slap-shot and then turn up the boom boxes, rocketing Scottie's skull with Led's "Rock 'N' Roll." Scott feels his forehead collapsing like wet cement into his eyes, as bells and horns blast, and John Bonham's drumming has just given him his nineteenth nervous headache. A crazy woman, who sits next to the scorer's table, now tosses a wobbling rubber chicken onto the ice. It's attached to a fishing pole and it squats and twists. Man, these people are sick. Ten years ago, when Scottie was a USHL official, he took a slap shot in the heart, in this very arena. All he saw was himself skating on an outdoor rink, spinning, turning in blue light, arcing— which means, of course, he thought he was going to die. As they wheeled him off on a stretcher and the crowd laughed and gave a standing O.

Scottie shrugs his head and kneels down beside Chats who's curved like a fingernail clipping. The horns and bells have ebbed, but not the Zeppelin boxes and that damn chicken on a string that drags its sorry ass across the ice. Scott wishes he had a .357 Magnum.

"Chats—"

"Cheevers, Johnston, the Cat, Low and who are the other guys?" Chatham murmurs.

"Huh?"

"The goalies who became NHL Head Coaches. Gerry Cheevers—"

"There's six of them," Kevin says, leaning in, his face puzzled. He shrugs at Christie. "Emile 'the Cat' Francis—"

"Yeah. Eddie Johnston and Ronnie Low, and who are the other guys?"

"Uh, Vachon. Rogie Vachon," Sully says. "And uh—"

"I don't know—" Ogs says.

Scottie shakes his head. Chats hates stats and shit. He's always giving Ogs a hard time for being into old-time hockey, and now he's asking about old-time goalies! Shit, he must be badly hurt. "Are you okay, Ryan? Ryan where are you?"

"There's one more. Damn, I can't think. Cheevers, Johnston, Francis, Low, Vachon, and—"

"Did McMahon call a penalty?" Ogs asks.

"No." Scott looks over at McMahon who's doing small arcs, high in the slot. No indication. Nothing.

"Damn." Ryan winces. "Cool music, huh?"

"Chats, how many fingers have I got up?"

"Two, Chief."

"I'm not holding up my hand, Chats."

McMahon, skating a larger arc, glides to Scottie and through his shoulder studies Chatham. "Is he okay?"

"Ask Walters. The guy just whacked him. A vicious crosscheck. Head-hunting for chrissakes." Christie tries to catch his breath. "Is there no fucking penalty?"

Christie and McMahon had a run-in earlier in the season during the famed "beer party" game, the one where Kos made the big save off a penalty shot, and Christie called McMahon a "Fucking Rookie." Both were reprimanded by the league. Christie was fined $1,000 and McMahon suspended four games for "failure of judgment." "Hell, I'll gladly pay the fine just to see him sit," Christie told the reporters. Matt Traicheff raised an eyebrow at that comment, but printed it.

Davidson, a towel around his neck, asks Chats if he has feelings in his legs and Chats rolls left, right, back to the left.

"I didn't say to do that," Davidson snaps.

"It happened away from the play. I didn't see it," McMahon confesses. "I'm sorry."

The apology shocks Scottie. Usually referees avoid admitting they missed anything, let alone something this big. "Walters gave him a vicious two-handed whack. Crosschecking, intent to injure, five minutes. Shit. At least he should get a double minor." He turns to Walters who hovers along the near boards. "You're an asshole." Walters says nothing and looks at the lettering on his stick. "And you, too, Farrell," Scott screams at the Musketeer bench. Head Coach "Two Fisted" Farrell, former IHL goon, throws up both hands and shouts, "It was a clean hit."

"Yeah, right, Farrell." Scottie cups his right hand and makes a rapid jerking-off gesture. "'Two-fisted.' More like one-fisted."

McMahon shrugs and skates toward the linesmen.

"Can't *they* call a penalty, McMahon?"

He turns around, his red eyebrows looking like two fat caterpillars. "There's no blood, Coach."

"I'm fine." Chatham strains forward and props on his elbows.

"What's my name, Ryan?" Scott asks.

"Chief."

"That's my nickname. Who am I?"

"Scott Christie, the Kansas City Chief. I know who you are. I know who I am. Ryan Chatham. This is the third period in a 3-2 hockey game and I've got to get my ass off the ice and we've got to score a goal to send it to overtime. But who was the sixth goalie?"

Scott smiles. "I think he's okay, Bob."

"My head sure hurts."

"I think he should have a stretcher," Davidson says.

"Hey—" Ryan smiles. "Listen." His face contorts into a zigzag grin, as Scottie cringes from the heavy bass lines that seem to envelop him like a pair of blue jeans that are three sizes too small. "I want to reach out and touch the sky. Toni Iommi. Black Sabbath."

Coach shrugs and looks at Davidson who also shrugs. Ryan sits up without the help of his elbows and says some more words about "Supernaut," *Black Sabbath Vol. IV*, and then raises a thumb at the fans. Maybe the boom boxes weren't such a bad idea.

"Ogs, Sullivan, lug this guy off the ice, okay?" They skate-push Chats to the boards.

"He's pretty wobbly," Davidson says, following with a series of short slip-hops. "We'll take him to the hospital and check it out."

"I'm going with you."

"No, you've gotta coach."

"Look, Bob. Just between the two of us, I'm not much of a coach."

"Bring the team over as soon as this thing ends." Bob taps Scottie's shoulder. "He'll be okay."

Scottie nods.

"And find out who that sixth guy was."

Scottie laughs. Coach Christie. Weird.

He slides toward McMahon. "He's hurt bad, man. Geez. Wouldn't it be nice to see the end of goon hockey, Jayme?"

"Yeah, I suppose you'd like a purer, 'European' game."

"I ain't into European hockey, that's for wusses, but my kid got hurt."

"Yeah, it's just awful."

Scottie says nothing and as he walks back to the bench, he's tempted to kick that damn rubber chicken across the rink, kick it into goddamn Nebraska, but he keeps calm and calls for the Sullivan, Ogs, Paplowsky line with Murphy and Stevenson at the points. Stanzie will be the extra skater. Thirty-eight seconds. "Let's tie this thing up. Let's do it for Chats."

The classic rock channel fades, and Ogs wins the draw and slithers the puck back to Murphy who fakes the slapper, cruises into the slot and zips the puck to Stanzie at the left side of the net. Stanzie tries to jam the puck between the post and pad, but the goalie slides across quickly, covering the area, and a Musketeer defender picks up the loose puck and lobs it over the blueline. Stevenson circles back and gets stood up in the neutral zone. Murphy corrals the end-over-end puck and Sullivan hooks Walters and gives him an elbow to the face and Walters falls against the boards and McMahon shoots up an arm.

Twenty-four seconds and now two minutes for elbowing. Shit. Scott yells Ogs over to the bench. "Kevin, take the face-off with the butt end of your stick."

"Huh?"

"I want to protest the call. Take the face-off with the butt end."

Kevin nods, as Sully throws his gloves in the penalty box and spits. McMahon flips the puck at a linesman.

Kevin leans in at the face-off circle, the black knob of his stick touching the ice.

"That's it, Christie," McMahon shouts, his hands on his hips, as he skates toward the Black Hawk bench. His face is all stretched out, the left eye higher than the right.

"What? What's a matter?"

"Two minutes. Bench minor, unsportsmanlike conduct."

"What did I do?"

"Don't give me that, that stick thing, that's your idea."

"I didn't do nothing."

"Bullshit, Christie. You're out of here."

"Don't swear at me. Have some respect."

"Get going."

"Don't swear at me!"

"Don't fuck with me, Christie. You're out of here!"

"Don't you fucking talk that way to me, McMahon. Don't you fucking talk that way." Christie grabs a stack of sticks and heaves them on the ice. They fan out like the steel fingers on Freddy Krueger's right hand.

"Get going, before I get you suspended."

"Oh, you'd like that, wouldn't you?" He grabs a water bottle and tosses it. Then a bucket of pucks. "You're the one who is suspended, in suspended animation, like Buck 'Fuckin' Rogers and Captain 'Fuckin' America. Gone. Gone in the fucking head. What are you smoking, anyway? Colombian pot? Our guy gets hurt and you don't call nothing. What do you expect? It's payback, you sonuvabitch."

McMahon stands sternly at the Hawk bench, arms folded across his chest.

The Sioux City crowd bunches around the Black Hawks, their boom boxes blasting bass lines. Hendrix and "Purple Haze": "Acting funny and I don't know why / 'scuse me while I kiss the sky." The fans also shout obscenities, ring bells and shove signs in players' faces. One, in faded black marker on corrugated cardboard, reads "The Black Hawk formula: Scott Christie = Shit Christie." Another: "Waterloo is Wussyloo." And Scott knows what signs Matt Traicheff will post in the *Courier* tomorrow: "Christie takes his WWF show on the road. Tag Team or Bad Team?" He only hopes the WWF show doesn't make tonight's ten o'clock news.

Well, maybe that would be cool.

Busload of Faith

Scott Christie worries that he might never win another game. A loss in Fargo-Morehead, Minnesota and the Black Hawks are out of the playoffs, and Christie just might be out of a job. There have been hints about it anyway.

"Hockey has always been a game of emotion. You've heard me say that before," he tells the *Courier*'s Matt Traicheff as the bus drifts into an arcing turn along Highway 218. The bright lines of the road are a hunch-backed spine, sort of like Deaner, the bus driver, who appears to have no neckline because his shoulders are a berm pushing into his ears. Deaner's tapping a left hand on the ridges of the steering wheel, keeping time to his "rocking faves," Frank Sinatra and Perry Como. "Controlled emotion. Grace under pressure is what our new Coach Hebenton preaches to the guys and with a win today, we're in." Scott's voice sounds upbeat, but he feels that his dark, faraway eyes belie the truth.

Traicheff nods, standing in the center aisle. He has a round face, high cheekbones, and slightly hooded eyes. "How has all the turmoil on this club affected everyone? I mean, you lose your coach, you coach for awhile—a debacle—the owner's absent all year, but is back in town for the past three games—"

Scott bites at the inside of his lower lip. He dislikes Traicheff's use of the word "debacle." That feels like purple prose, and he had to read that very word in the paper a few days ago in a feature about Christie, the WWF, and "Tag team or Bad team." "Yeah, yeah. It's been tough. But we're professionals. Michaels wasn't' getting it done. Hebenton's won two of the three games, and he's always leaving Hemingway quotes in the locker room to inspire the guys. It's amazing." Christie glances through the murky film of the window behind Traicheff to catch traces of sky. It looks like a storm is twisting in from the west.

In back, the fellas are making ruffles of noise, playing poker or downloading pix of internet babes on Paplowksy's laptop. Coach Hebenton told them to have fun, kick up a ruckus until they reach Mason City. Once on I-35, they're to quiet down and visualize themselves succeeding: hitting opponents, clearing the slot of any opponents in front of Kos, and scoring goals at the other end. "Visualize and believe," Coach had said. "I want all of you to picture yourselves being successful. Belief, hockey, faith, will get us into the playoffs."

"We got a busload of faith to get by," Chatham shouted in a New York inflected voice, and the fellas laughed. Christie had heard him playing that damn Lou Reed CD over and over the past few weeks. His getting-in-the-zone music.

"Fargo-Morehead's in second place. Can you beat them, at their rink?" Traicheff sits down. His hands are very small. "It's tough to win in this league, on the road."

"Yes." The question seems a little cheeky, and Scott wonders why he's feeling so defensive. After all, he invited Traicheff along for the road trip, to be a part of history, but he didn't invite Southworth, the southern owner who's sitting in back, reading *Forbes* and not saying nothing, but expecting a win nonetheless, and if they don't win Scott will be out of the league. Hell, Southworth aside, this team's too good to miss the playoffs. Many reporters, including Traicheff, had the Black Hawks tagged for third or fourth in the preseason, and now they're struggling to make the eighth and final spot. "Yes, I think so. With all the adversity, we've had, we're struggling and we'll be close to .500. Coach Hebenton? What can I say? He came here and said, 'Get me three wins in four games and we'll make the playoffs,' and he was right. His style, what with the quotes about bullfighting and those goofy plaid jackets he wears, is a little unorthodox, but—you heard about the Hemingway reports each player had to write?"

Traicheff nods. "Thank god he didn't ask them to read Henry James."

"Yeah." Scott's not sure he knows who this James guy is. Did he write about erotica, and tits and ass in Paris? "Anyway, he's got real communication—well, at times he's kind of wordy—but he reaches the players, and they've learned to respect each other and the game more. And the fans love Heb. All of the players had to do two reports: one on Hemingway and another on our hockey fans, interviewing them, finding out what they liked about the Black Hawks and this great game. Anyway, those reports brought people together, as the players learned the respect a lot of the fans had for the game. It's just amazing! We've got a bus load of boosters, a hundred fans going to this game!"

Scott sits back in his seat, his right foot resting atop of his left knee. It feels like the old days, the 1960s, before Christie's era when the Black Hawks were a semi-pro team, winning three consecutive championships, packing old McElroy Arena every night, chartering flights for their away games, and having a boisterous club, the "Gay Blades," following them everywhere. "Wanda Maroucheff has done a wonderful job with the boosters arranging this trip. That's Maroucheff, M-A-R-O-U-C-H-E-F-F. And people in Waterloo are excited again. The last two home games were sellouts. Hell, Minnesota is supposed to be a great hockey state, but the Rochester Mustangs, The Twin City Vulcans, and the Fargo Morehead Bears all struggle to make payroll and get a thousand fans a game. We're averaging over 2500."

"Hey, Scott," Deaner shouts through his right shoulder, his voice heavy. "Scott." The tone is reminiscent of the night he hit three deers and then lost his brakes.

"So, you have a quote on Minnesota for me?"

"Whiners. They want an NHL team but they can't support three USHL franchises. Iowa is a great hockey state—Dubuque, Sioux City, and us. We all pack them in. Nebraska's good too, with Lincoln and Omaha, but I don't know what's up with Minnesota. Maybe too much *Lake Wobegone* in their diet. Hockey's a blue collar game—tough river towns like we got in Iowa. It's not for Garrison Keillor types—wimps with wit. It comes back to emotion. We've got it in Iowa. They don't."

"That's quotable."

"Scott! We got a problem."

"Not the damn brakes again." Scott struggles out of his seat. He knows that he has to lose weight but he can't let go the Moutain Dew and Twinkies. He turns to Traicheff. "Stick around. I've got a story to tell you about our Thunder Bay trip last November. The story from hell, but it has a happy ending." He approaches the front of the bus. The red dashboard glows like spinning bike spokes and he finds his breath trapped in his upper chest. "What's up?"

"Nothing wrong with the bus, Chief. But look in my side mirror."

A police cruiser, red lights flashing arcs that look like glass stains left on a coffee table, appears alongside the bus. "And you're not even speeding."

Christie wonders if maybe he needs to get the speedometer calibrated or if the tires are overinflated, or if he failed to renew the charter's license. "I don't know." Shit, surely it has to be something that he forgot to do. As a GM, there are so many responsibilities and not enough time to get to everything. Christie can't remember the last time that he had a day off, when he wasn't thinking hockey, when he wasn't scouting some new young talent, contacting college coaches, or managing the business of running the arena and paying the bills. "Pull over."

"Well, I'm not going to race a cruiser, Chief."

They slow down along the highway's edge as gravel klinks and spits underneath the bus. Moments later a cop talks to Christie outside. He has light blond hair and a face that looks like construction paper that sat out in the rain—all of the dull colors run together. "There's no game tonight, Scottie." A large tree hooks like an "F" in the distance and the clouds in the darkening sky don't seem to be moving

"What?" Christie leans against the closed bus door. He's impressed that the cop knows who he is.

"Fargo-Morehead had to forfeit. They couldn't pay their operating expenses." He goes on to explain how they hadn't paid on the lease for the arena the past two months, and the city closed down their operations.

Christie heard rumors of under funding, but he can't believe that this is happening to the Bears. "They're in second place! What about those kids and how hard they worked all season?"

"I'm sorry, Scottie. I'm just reporting what I know. We tried to reach you on the cell phone, but you must have left it in the office."

"Damn, damn, damn." Twenty-four players with no second season. One, an ex-Black Hawk. "I can't believe this. Can't the league do anything?"

"That's all I know, Scottie. There's a fax at the office for you from the league. I guess, it came just a few minutes too late."

Scottie glances at the gravel dusting the tips of his shoes. The sky is a cold, frozen bruise. "We've got another bus full of boosters. Probably ten, twenty minutes ahead of us, up the road. Could you flag them down, too?"

"Sure." He mumbles into a speaker curled around his mouth. "No problem. Good luck." He shakes Scott's hand. The GM wishes he hadn't heard what he did, wishes he got pulled over for a fucking speeding ticket instead.

As the cruiser fades off into the cold sky, Christie reboards the bus and tells the players the news. Fargo's out of the playoffs. At first there's a raucous cheer as the Black Hawks realize that they're in— Southworth is even pumping Hebenton's hand—and then everything gets real reverent. Ogilvie, Kos, Chatham, and Sully quit their card game, Paplowsky's laptop snaps down, and even Deaner, shaking his head, his red Black Hawk sweater bunching at the nape of his neck, silences his song tape. The quietude is a mood of awe and disappointment, sort of like what kids feel when they discover for the first time that Santa Claus is all imaginary and adults have been lying to them. It's as if the entire city of Waterloo had been lied to. Southworth stumbles back to his seat and gnaws at the bristled edging of his peppered mustache. He glances out the window, his eyes dim and vague.

The bus sits at the side of the road for a good fifteen minutes, and then Coach Hebenton stands up, his plaid jacket flared open from the stress on the bottom button. He pushes back his felt hat. "Fellas. I know you're disappointed right now. But nobody can tell me that we backed into the playoffs. You deserve to be there. You put yourself in this position to allow this to happen. If we didn't win last week, if Kos didn't get that shutout, if we didn't win eight days ago, two months ago, we wouldn't be here. I'm proud of you. I believe Hemingway said it best, "It takes a man to walk up the mountain. But the mountain isn't going to come to the man.' We walked that mountain, fellas."

The players nod and fill the bus with low-wattage cheers that give it a momentary glow. Christie's not sure if Hemingway really wrote that bit about the mountain and stuff but it seems appropriate that he should have.

"Now let's keep our noise level down, and pay our respects to the fans of Fargo-Morehead," Coach says, the hat twirling in his hands. "They deserved better."

Traicheff skiffs some notes and smiles sheepishly at Christie. "*Lake Wobegone* is too funny for this situation. 'Wimps with wit.'" He laughs nervously. "Shit." He scratches out what he had written, crumples up the page and starts writing anew.

Christie is surprised at how the reporter feels. He figures the guy was just a suit, working at copy, coming up with stories, such as the WWF angles to make Scottie and the Black Hawks look entertaining, but he too cares about these kids, Fargo-Morehead's kids, and the integrity of the game.

"Home, Scottie?" Deaner asks.

"Yeah, home."

Forty-five minutes later, the two busses are parked outside the Country Kitchen on Highway 63. The sky's a cracked umbrella, and several boosters have joined the players on the players' bus and players have joined the boosters on the boosters' bus. Wanda and Kos slow dance in the aisle, his hands hooked on the back of her jean pockets, her head resting on his chest. Their movements look odd, off kilter with the fast song that's playing, something about wanting to be sedated. Chatham had talked Deaner into letting him play his punky tape of "New York songs," and he's happily slapping the back of a seat to the beat of the music. Annie Riordan sits next to him, hopping up and down, not wanting to go home. Mrs. Riordan, her hair pulled back from her forehead and done up in a tight bun, gives Scottie a congratulatory hug and tells him it's not too bad to win this way, and he should be proud of his team. Scottie nods, saying something about having to turn up the intensity level for the second season, as Sully and Ogs lean forward, sporting pretend microphones, belting out the lyrics to the song about sedation.

The players and the boosters on this bus seem happy, sort of, a little bit, anyway, and Christie wishes he, too, felt happy.

And then he sees Southworth, wading through empty styrofoam boxes—leftovers from dinner—that crowd the aisle. The owner, gray hair askew, face a contorted wrinkle, topples a little, as he tries to make sense of it all.

Kicks

The coach in a yellow fishing hat held up an open fist, and Matt Traicheff feared that his daughter wasn't doing well.

Elizabeth had kicked three balls into the far corner of the net, between the orange neon cone and the inside of the post, and they could have earned nine points for the drill, but, because she used the side of her foot instead of the laces knitted along the top, none of the goals counted.

"Is that your daughter?" asked a curvy woman who smelled of cocoa butter and polar-fresh chewing gum. She had white-blond hair, slight wrinkles at the corners of her eyes, and her face was shrouded under the nylon hood of her jacket that creased at the top of her forehead like a tent. Matt nodded and they commented on how cold it was for May. It didn't seem possible, but the wind draped around them like frozen curtains.

Matt shoved his hands deep in his pockets and tried to smile, as she discussed how she wished they had soccer when she was a kid, but the edges of his chin were numb, and the ends of the last two fingers on his left hand stung as if coated with quick-drying plaster. "Yeah. I'm from Canada. I played a lot of soccer as a kid. Must be the English influence, I don't know." He shrugged. "My daughter's the one out there who keeps getting an open fist. I don't think that's good." The sky was full of bleeding purple swirls.

"Oh, she's doing fine," the woman said, but her well-meaning tone wasn't completely convincing.

The coach rolled Elizabeth another ball. She trapped the ball high against her ankle, her right foot flailing up and outward, tapped it with her left foot, and then kicked it hard with her right. The back of the net billowed, but because she had used the tips of her toes, the coach held up another empty fist, and a lean man in an Amoco hat, standing to the side, scribbled something on a clipboard. Matt had never learned that style of power kicking. The kick relied on a quick snap motion, as the shooter snubbed the ball with a piercing thrust. He would work on it with Elizabeth tomorrow.

"You look familiar," the woman said.

"I'm a sports reporter for the *Courier*. I write on hockey, mainly," Matt explained, figuring she'd probably seen his picture next to the byline. Matt hated posing for pictures. Before a camera, he often felt a kind of Junior-High gawkiness, and his general modesty mixed with gently askew glasses stamped him as a nebbish. Matt's soulful nerdiness made it hard for him to be taken seriously by some of the more cocky Junior-A hockey players and most of the USHL coaches.

"No. No. Didn't you used to live at the townhouses on Briarwood?"

"Yeah. When we first moved here."

"I thought I recognized you." The woman smiled while grabbing her jacket between neckline and front zipper as if to let the air out of a tupperware container. She introduced herself as Betty Bronson and once again self-consciously commented on the cold. Seems as a kid, Betty was always goose-bumped and blue at swimming lessons. She laughed at herself and said that the ten-year old girl with the red pony tails, freckles, and two-tone socks was her daughter Lindsey. "Doesn't she look like Pippi Longstocking?"

Matt nodded. He was impressed with Lindsey's touch. On several of the dribbling drills Lindsey had cut the cones sharply, keeping the ball tight in front of her.

"Your wife works at the university?"

Matt looked over at the stretched corner flags and the tall grass rippling backward. "Yeah. She's a professor of English."

"You were a kind of Mr. Mom back then?"

"I was under employed, yeah." Matt, like his wife, also had a Ph.D. When they first moved to Cedar Falls from the graduate program at Champaign, Illinois, Matt did a lot of writing and childcare, seeing Caitlin off to the bus in the mornings, and taking Elizabeth to the parks in the afternoons to play. At first, he did some adjunct work for the English department, teaching Personal Essay and College Reading and Writing, but in his spare time he wrote a hockey novel, *Young Ice*, and started submitting hockey stories to literary journals and feature articles on the Waterloo Black Hawks to *Courier* Editor Sal Yanosky. Yanosky liked Matt's visual storytelling style and eventually offered the freelancer a full-time slot on the paper.

Betty recalled watching Matt walk Elizabeth to preschool and playing with her in the backyard of the townhouses, by the swings. "I wish I had had more time to spend with Lindsey, when she was little."

"I hope they don't only do drills," Matt said. "My daughter's really a great game player. She knows how to get to the open spaces, how to get back on D. Matt smiled awkwardly over his words, and felt like he was saying too much, making an apology or something, but he was a

Rec. team co-coach, with Chris Kanger who had played some soccer in Europe, and he knew what Elizabeth could do.

"Lindsey always said that your daughter had a great imagination. The games she played in the backyard. With her dinosaurs and action figures."

The comment surprised Matt. He couldn't remember Betty or Lindsey at all, but the feelings behind her words suggested an intimacy between daughters that he was unaware of. "Yeah. She likes to write." The coach lobbed a ball at Elizabeth and she gingerly leaned and headed it. The ball bounced four times before trickling into the net. "She's written a lot of stories. Surprise, huh?"

An hour later, Elizabeth and her father were walking to their minivan. Matt enjoyed the in-step sounds of gravel under their shoes—a short, sharp crunch followed by a longer slide. "How do you think you did?"

"Oh, I don't know." Elizabeth pushed blond-dark hair away from her eyes. She used to have bangs, but in the past year she had decided to grow them out. "He was annoying."

"The coach?"

"Yeah. Chris says any goal's a good goal, but he kept saying mine weren't because I wasn't kicking them with my laces."

"We can work on that." Matt had always kicked with the left inside of his foot, never the very top, but he could see how it gave a shooter a lot more power. "Tomorrow after work, okay? We'll get it right for the next practice." There was one more competitive-team tryout on Wednesday.

She nodded and Matt looked at their shadows stretching together in the bald grass. Elizabeth's eyes behind her blue-framed glasses seemed disappointed.

"Kicking's never been your strength, hon. But I thought you dribbled real well. And you had speed going around the cones. No jumbo jet turns. Real sharp. And on those one-on-ones, you rocked. Taking the ball off those other girls' feet. That was awesome." Like himself, Elizabeth had a lot of passion for the sports she played, and she flung herself into the game with an utterly joyful abandon. Matt's oldest daughter Caitlin had tried softball and didn't care much for competitive sports, and Devin, his youngest, was still too little for organized play.

"There's only 21 girls trying out. He told us that eighteen make the team. If I don't make it, then that means I'm terrible."

"No. I wouldn't say that. I only saw five or six girls that were better than the rest. All of the other girls are going to be hard to choose from. There's about fifteen girls who are all pretty comparable." And Elizabeth was one of them.

"Still."

"You want to come to the second practice on Wednesday?"

"Yeah, I guess."

"Whattya mean, 'I guess'? If you don't want to, you don't have to."

"It's just, I don't know any of the girls." Elizabeth pulled on the edges of her windbreaker that clung like shrink wrap around her elbows and arms. Because the soccer complex was built in a lowland region between a highway and scattered wet lands, it felt as if you were caught in an airport runway. Wind briskly twisted and swirled.

"That kind of sucks," Matt said. There were no other Cedar Heights kids at the tryout, and he suspected that there were little pockets of three-to-four girls from various teams, pockets that Elizabeth was not a part of. "But don't worry about it. Work hard."

"So what do you want for your birthday?"

They reached their red minivan. Matt rolled Elizabeth's ball in the hatch. It knocked against the back, and she sprawled her knee on the top of the bench seat, and quasi-hurdled to her place in the second row. Liz's legs were angly, lean, like a poised cricket. "I was proud of how you played today," Matt said.

"I'm working on a new story for your birthday," she said.

That night Matt couldn't sleep. The bathroom light—that Elizabeth and her younger sister Devin liked to have on—burned a sharp arc around the edges of his bed. He rolled over and folded a pillow in half around his head and tried not to think about soccer.

"Honey, go to sleep," Maggie said.

"I can't." He sighed, flipped on his back, and looked at a faded yellow curve spreading across the ceiling. "I keep thinking about that damn practice."

"Well, maybe she shouldn't play competitive at all. You're taking it too seriously, and that's going to rub off on her."

"Well, yeah. But she can play at that level. I just don't think that they saw what she can do." And then Matt told Maggie how there were all these clicks and how Elizabeth wasn't in any of them. It reminded him of high school and how all the popular kids always got the best parts in plays and positions on the football team, and always won unknown Kiwanis Club awards for essays their mothers helped them write on Civics and Canadian History. It was like a secret society and the same people held all the mega-membership cards.

Maggie sat up, her blue teddy scooping a little in front of her neck. "Matt, this isn't about you. It's about Elizabeth."

"I know. But I feel like I didn't do a good job as a coach. I didn't even teach her that damn kick all year."

"Has she not improved as a player?"

"Yes. A lot, I think."

"Yes, you and Chris are doing a great job. You've taught the girls to have fun. More importantly, you guys aren't serious about winning but you take the girls seriously. You listen to what they have to say, you and Chris respect them, and that's the main thing for girls at this age, to know that men—and yes it has to be men—respect them for who they are. Not for how they look or how they kick."

Matt nodded and glanced at the dim light glinting off his index fingers, and noted how his fingers weren't straight, but curved out to the left, and then he glanced toward his wife, her hair scraggled and slightly bumped up like a cone because of a cowlick. "Yeah, I guess we do do that, don't we?" He kissed her forehead. "But what if she doesn't make the team?"

"Who cares? Is this such a great thing to be a part of? It's too damn intense. I won't have it. I don't want you getting intense, or her."

"Okay, okay."

"Rating the kids with stopwatches and point systems? These aren't Olympic tryouts."

Matt agreed, but there was a part of him that wanted Elizabeth to make the team to right his own failings as a player. He had been cut from several grade school teams—softball, basketball (he had one long jumper that rimmed and rattled out, and he still believes that if he had made that shot he'd have earned a spot on the fourth-grade team). And even though Matt was born in Canada and played a lot of exuberant street hockey in sneakers, he couldn't skate worth a damn, and thus ice hockey, the national pastime, was never a real part of his childhood experiences. Maybe that's why he wrote so much about the game. In his junior year, he played midget baseball, but sat on the bench. In his limited plate appearances, Matt went 5 for 10 (all singles), but his role was that of insurance marker. If anyone got thrown out of a game or broke an ankle or something, Traichefff was there, assuring that his team would never forfeit. As a senior, he played football for Cobourg West, but the school was so small that almost everyone who tried out made it. His kid brother Pete was the real star, a wicked defensive end who led the Kawartha League in sacks. "You're right, Maggie. I guess I am thinking about me. I never made any teams. I played Rec. league. I was a pretty good soccer goalie, but I never made a school or traveling team. I just wasn't *that* good."

"Well, I know something that you're good at." She kissed his cheek, and then pulled him down toward her.

"You want to fool around?"

"Matt, is there no subtlety with you?" She ran her fingers down his back, and pushed her knees gently against his legs. "Let's just snuggle and we'll see."

Three days later Matt was at the *Waterloo Courier* tapping out the final paragraph to a hockey story, when the partition around his desk shook slightly from having been nudged. Maggie stood behind him, her hair curled around her ears, the lines in her forearms noticeably raised. "Hey, what are you doing here," he asked, revising his next-to-last sentence. The Waterloo Black Hawks forthcoming tryouts were just weeks away, and once again the summer looked promising. The Hawks, who had only one winning season in their nearly twenty in the USHL, had a promising head coach—Andy Hebenton—and two star players out of Minnesota high schools.

"You want to go for a walk or something? Get a Pepsi?" she asked.

He shoved aside his USHL media guide and held up a diet pop. "Just had one." Then he tossed some phone books on the floor and slid his wife a wooden chair that swiveled and clanked when she sat in it. Her cheeks were slightly splotched, like she had been exercising or angry.

"Elizabeth didn't make the team." Maggie snapped a letter on Matt's keyboard. It was plain looking with a tulip-stamp in the corner. "Today, all these other girls in town are getting big packages, 'welcome to the team,' and all that, and Liz gets this."

"What? I thought Coach Rider said the decision would take several weeks. At least until after the Cedar Valley Cup."

"Well. Apparently not for Elizabeth." Maggie crossed her arms and huffed.

"Has she seen it, yet?" Matt bit the inside of his lower lip. He felt his daughter did real well at the second practice, and they even approached Coach Rider and his staff afterward and asked if Elizabeth could re-do the kicking drill and they said yes. With the laces of her left and right foot, she tightly kicked several balls between cone and post.

"No. She's going to feel terrible when she reads those scores—"

Scores? Matt opened the envelope, absently paused, and glanced up at the series of 8 by 10 photographs that seemingly danced along the makeshift partition behind Maggie. The photographs were taken during the Christmas skating party the *Courier* threw at Young Arena months ago. Matt was captured in several photographs skating awkwardly, his left ankle buckled, his right straight, his daughters— Cailtin, Elizabeth and Devin—close by lunging, laughing as Dad clunked and clattered on the ice. Matt loved skating, even though he was hopeless at it. There was something about gliding along open space that placed Matt wonderfully at the center of things, instead of on the fringes, or in the doldrums thinking about the next day and all the work that he still had to do.

Matt returned to the letter and in a spat of self-defensiveness quickly spotted two typos and some formatting problems:

Elizabeth Traicheff
1616 Hawthorne Dr
Cedar Falls, IA 50613
Dear Elizabeth,

I want to thank you for taking time to come to the tryouts for the U11 CVYSA girl's team. I hope you found the two days well spent. There were 21 girls that tried out for 18 positions on the team and as a coach it was very difficult to make a decision on whom to invite and who would better benefit by playing an additional season in the recreational league.

At the conclusion of the tryouts, Coaches Kevin, Jim and I reviewed the scores for everyone who came. Scores were based on running with the ball, turning the ball, speed, speed dribbling the ball, heading, shooting, 1 verses 1 ability, working with a group 4 verses 4, and full team skills. There were a possible 100 points, 50 for skill and 50 for field play. The average score for skill was 35 and your score was 25. The average score for field play was 37 and your score was 17.

At this time in your soccer career. . .

"Seventeen! Seventeen out of Fifty! That's ridiculous," Matt's mouth suddenly had gone dry.

"I rather they had just said that she didn't make the team," Maggie said.

"This is so typically American." Matt often felt a thin-anti-American streak prick his skin whenever an injustice struck him personally. "You try to make a decision appear fair by throwing in some arbitrary numbers. Just like there's too many X's and O's in American coaching and American hockey, now we have to have numbers and percentages placed on ten-year old girls. How can they gauge her a 17? On what scale? For what reason? They only had one damn scrimmage, and Elizabeth was overshadowed on defense by a much more aggressive defense partner. But she got to the ball, kept it outside the triangle—" He shook his head. "She is a *good* player."

"A part of me didn't want her to make that team, Matt. It was just too competitive. But that letter. I don't know."

"It sucks. And this part gets me." He pointed at Coach Rider's prose. "'Touch can be improved by spend'—not spending— 'spend 10 minutes juggling the ball, 10 minutes dribbling and turning the ball and 10 minutes kicking the ball. If you will follow this routine 5 of 7 days a week you will build into a good player.' Five to seven days? This isn't the Olympics. Like the girls don't have other things going on in their lives?"

Maggie shrugged. "You want to go get a Pepsi?"

"No, I'm fine. Thanks."

"Well, Scoop Traicheff, do you want to go get a Pepsi, with me? I'm not fine. That's such a Hemingway word. 'Fine.' And we're all so 'terribly fine.'"

"This is another one of those subtlety things that I'm missing, right? The Pepsi question?" He laughed. "Okay. Let's go get some Pepsis."

Later at home, Elizabeth was writing in front of the television and snatching sideways glances of *Dexter's Laboratory* on the Cartoon Network. Five year-old Devin was coloring by the recliner, and Caitlin was off doing her newspaper route. Maggie looked at Matt over her shoulder and asked him "to tell her," and then she retreated into the kitchen, where she opened the fridge and shuffled leftovers. Matt stood against the kitchen door with his hands on his hips, and he watched Elizabeth watching the television. "Dad don't look, I'm writing your story," she said, covering the pages with crocheted fingers and hands. He half smiled and walked into the kitchen and poured a glass of water.

Maggie sighed. "We've got to quit shoving things into the back of this fridge. Here's some more leftovers gone bad. Ka-ching, ka-ching. That's the sound of our money. Ka-ching." She backed out of the refrigerator, turned toward him, and pressed two fingers to the inside of left forearm. "We've got to stop the bleeding."

Matt laughed. "I get it honey. Ka-ching, We're throwing money away. I'll work on it." Matt gasped on the water. It was too cold.

"Slimy chicken and rice anyone?" Maggie dramatically held out the small Revere pot as if it were an exotic French cuisine. The top of the lid was splattered with the upper shelf's runoff of Juicy-juice and chocolate syrup.

"Sorry about that," Matt said.

"Put leftovers in containers, they're easier to find."

"I know. Next time." Matt wiped his lips. "Hey, Liz, hon. You didn't make the team. The letter came today."

"Good," Elizabeth said.

Maggie flashed a surprised grin, and muffled a chuckle into the back of her wrist. Matt entered the living room. He too was laughing. "'Good'?"

"Yeah. It was annoying." Elizabeth tucked her knees up into her chin and smiled as Dee-Dee pirouetted in Mandark's lab. Computers were blowing up, and then there was a double mushroom cloud as Dexter sighed with glee. "I didn't like the other girls much. They weren't interested in getting to know me. And I just don't want to watch games all year. I want to play. I don't think I would have played much if I had made the team."

"Yeah, that's probably true, hon. And I don't think the coaches knew you either. They gave you some scores, and they're just ridiculous. Seventeen out of 50 for field play. Please."

"Seventeen?" Her voice dipped with sudden hurt.

Why did Matt have to tell her that score? His face felt numbed by his own words, and the lower left side of his lip quivered slightly with rising anger and disappointment. "Yeah, that's bullshit. Seventeen. You always get to the open spaces. Cut the angles on defense. Ride forwards outside and out of bounds. These coaches are out of it." He didn't want his daughter to see him blaming the coaches for her not making the team, but he couldn't help himself. "I don't know how many times I saw you girls standing around doing nothing. Kids need to move on the field, not watch. And on the drills they always had you backing up instead of moving forward. On defense you should play outside the box, keeping the offense out. Not sagging in, like they taught."

"Yeah. Those coaches were out of it," Elizabeth said.

"You don't have to try out next year if you don't want to."

"I don't know. Unless someone I know tries out with me, I probably won't."

"Problem is that jerk Les Rider is always going to be your coach. He has a daughter the same age. So you'll always be trying out for his team."

"Really?"

"Yeah. I'm going to call that coach."

"No, Dad. Don't."

"He doesn't know who you are."

"Don't call," Elizabeth pleaded, and Maggie rushed into the living room, her hands wet with soap bubbles. "What good would calling do? It will only make you and Elizabeth look bad," she said, drying her hands on a nearby checkered towel.

"Well. I want him to know that I don't think he was fair."

"Matt—" She paused so that the full effect of her position would register.

"Okay, okay."

"Why don't you call Chris? Find out what he thinks."

Two days later near the end of practice the girls gathered round in a circle for their head-it/catch-it drill (an exercise in which the players do the opposite of what the coach directs as he tosses a ball at an appointed individual). Matt stood on the circle's outside edge, hands behind his back. Dust carved off an adjacent baseball diamond, and the transformers in the distance looked like pencil tips. Chris shouted "catch it" to Tori, and the spunky third-grader, smiled, leaned forward with the edges of her shoulders and headed the ball hard back to the circle. "Great, Tori, great." Next, he quickly spun to Elizabeth, "Catch it!"

Elizabeth paused. Matt saw the slight hesitancy in her upper back, and she shouted "I rebel," as she deliberately caught the ball. The other girls laughed and yelled "You're out," and "Down," and

Elizabeth said that that's what she wanted, and she sat with her legs crossed under her. The sky was a dark curtain, and the lighter green undersides of the tree leaves curled in the strong wind.

Chris glanced over at Matt with a "what's wrong with Elizabeth" expression etched across his wavering upper lip. He had talked to Liz before practice started, asked her what she learned at the competitive tryouts, and when she shrugged saying, "Nothing," he corrected her gently, reminding her that she probably learned "some new skills." "Sure," Elizabeth agreed, "but it was annoying. I didn't kick right. I didn't dribble right. What's the point?" "I bet you're a better playing for having gone," Chris had said, nudging the worn bill of his ball cap. But now he wasn't saying anything, his eyes filled with shades of bemused annoyance. Matt glanced away, over at the utility company, the transformers, and the backside of a satellite dish that looked like the inside of an open umbrella.

In a few minutes Matt sat next to his daughter. "Liz, what are you doing?"

She rolled a golf ball around in her left hand. It was muddy, scarred, and had a red stripe. She was always finding them on the practice field—a golf course was on the east side of the river. She shrugged. "I didn't want to head it. My head hurts."

"You have to try. Everyone else does it."

"I didn't want to," she said, with a pouty edge, the golf ball wedged back between her index and middle fingers as if she were about to hurl a Roger Clemens forkball.

"Liz, you're my daughter. I'm a coach. You have to set a good example."

She nervously laughed into the sleeve of her blue jersey.

As they drove out of the parking lot and thudded across the train tracks, Matt turned to his daughter and fought back his anger. "Liz, why didn't you head the ball?"

"I didn't want to."

"What do you mean, you didn't want to?"

"My head hurt. I told you about it."

"What?"

"At school. We played softball and Mr. Daoust over threw first base and it bounced and hit me in the head. So I didn't want to head it."

"Oh, yeah. Sorry. That's right you did tell me." He drove with the inside of his right wrist and glanced at the Cedar Falls Utilities smoke stack staining the sky and the black mounds of coal covered in what looked like giant Glad bags. "Still, I don't think you're being totally honest with yourself."

"What do you mean?"

"You tell Chris you learned 'nothing.' You shrugged like you didn't care, like it was all a waste of time. 'Nothing.' I don't think you're being honest with how you really feel about not making that team." He drove under an overpass and stopped at a set of lights.

"Why do you keep bringing it up? I don't care about the competitive team. I didn't think about it all day today. But you keep bringing it up and it makes me feel bad."

"I don't want you to feel bad, I just don't want you to be in denial."

The light changed, and Elizabeth was crying, her glasses were in her left hand, the golf ball in her right. "I don't care about it."

"Liz. I'm sorry. I—"

The next day it was Matt's birthday, and although Elizabeth hadn't said much to him the evening after practice, that morning she cracked open her parents' bedroom door and whispered, "Happy, birthday, Dad," beating her sisters and Maggie to the punch.

Matt rubbed his gritted eyes, and nudged his wife who was sleeping with an arm twisted over her head. "Did you hear that?"

"Yes, birthday boy."

"She was the first one to say it."

Maggie smiled. "You have to read her story. It's on the table. It's marvelous."

Matt stuttered out of bed and within minutes picked up Elizabeth's story "Alina" that was covering his latest issue of the *Hockey News*. Maggie was right—it was a marvelous tale about a lonely girl, different from the rest, who wanted her imaginary friend Packy, a stuff toy, to come to life. She wishes and wishes for a miracle, and suddenly Packy emerges from a basket in the bedroom closet. But Packy has a strong will and brings darkness to the world, covering the sun, and making the planet cold and the earth's colors change. Matt smiled with pride over Elizabeth's sentence structure. He couldn't believe that a ten-year old wrote this.

"It's amazing isn't it," Maggie asked, patting the side of his waist and drinking a strong cup of chocolate-flavored coffee.

"It's really good," Matt said. "Liz, I love this," he shouted.

"You do?" She ran into the kitchen, her hair partially over her glasses, and looked at where he was in his read. "Wait until you get to Chapter 7," she said, and then ran back to the living room to play with her sisters.

Maggie kissed Matt on the neck. "Hmm. Your shaving cream smells nice."

"Oh, please."

"Happy birthday."

He hurried ahead to the last two chapters and read how Packy made elephants shrink, the sun hide behind clouds, and tornadoes show up on television. Even the springs in the couch broke. Alina wished that Packy had never come alive, and then it happened: the sun returned in front of clouds, elephants were bigger than rats, Alina and her father were playing checkers on a raised up couch—even the springs were back to normal! Matt smiled at the final sentence: "Alina became closer to her dad and never glanced at the closet."

Later that afternoon Matt was coaching Elizabeth out at field eight of the soccer complex. The sun was bright, and the sky a cloudless light, blue like faded denim. Elizabeth was on defense, standing on top of the box, challenging one of the gray team's forwards. She kicked the ball between the forward's legs, and then dribbled outside the triangle, her knees kicking high as she rushed up the side of the field. Along the wing, Elizabeth loped gracefully, her legs tap-tapping the ball, her arms flowing with fun, and her ponytail dipping. Coach Kanger grinned over at Matt, shouted, "look at that Elizabeth go," and then Liz cross-passed perfectly to Keely who drove the net and kicked one hard into the goalkeeper's hands. As his daughter rotated back on defense, Matt smiled, for Elizabeth's long, leggy glide up the wing had looked, ever so briefly, as if she were skating.

Parallel Lines

Peter Traicheff wasn't so sure that attending his high school's centennial was such a good idea.

He stood in the middle of Cobourg arena, crammed with doubts, the back of his neck cramped with tension. His belly dipped over his jean belt, and blue and gold streamers dripped around him. The ice had been removed from the Junior C hockey rink, and the floor, crowded with high-school graduates dating as far back as 1951, was a dull gray and water stained. Black scuffs of pucks and body checks darkened the boards, and the glass above the dashers was splotched with hand prints. Several of Peter's '83 class were at the party, including Gary Hlapchek, a second-string halfback on the Cobourg West Vikings' football team. "Disco" Happy now worked as an industrial engineer at Cobourg Plastics, but the past clung to him in the stretched fabric of his tense, white leisure suit.

"Peter. Hey, what's up, my man?" Several wisps of black-gray hair, chipped links of Brillo pads, curled around Gary's exposed chest.

"Not much." The nine-piece band, off in a far corner of the rink, spritzed through a Chicago tune. One of the trumpeters was singing, but when he hit the high-end notes his voice quavered off key. The band's rhythm section, however, sounded like boisterous bubbles skipping in a champagne glass.

"So whatcha doing now?"

"I'm still working at the post office in Toronto."

"Mailman, eh? How about your brother? God he was funny." Gary's face was heavier when he smiled, and then he swished about the last chug of beer in his plastic cup before drinking.

"He's fine. A sports writer. Married an American."

"Man, remember that play your brother wrote? *Rocky and Jules*? I was the Friar. 'Hey, baby. What's happening, cats?' My character was into herbs and stoned all the time. Not much of a stretch for me to play, I tell ya."

Peter smiled. *Rocky and Jules* had won some local awards and went on to the Southern provincial finals.

"And doing that part helped me get laid. Girls go for actors."

"You would've got laid, no matter what, Disco."

"True, true. Actually a lot of the chicks I rendezvoused I've seen here tonight. Cynthia Stuckenberg. Remember her? Short. Nice tits? Looks exactly the same. Married now, two kids."

"You ever gonna get married, Gar?"

"No. How about you?"

"I don't know. I'd like to, I guess."

"Well anyway, I gotta get another cold one. Too bad your brother wasn't here."

"Yeah." Peter shrugged. He really didn't have much to celebrate. Some of his former classmates, like Gary, had high-profile jobs or were now district managers, foremen, executives, but he was just a hard-working postie. But Cobourg West had a lot to celebrate. In the early 70s it was almost closed down because of declining enrollment, but here it was, one-hundred years young and ushering back alums, teachers, and hosting a series of "Vikings Forever" events—soccer games, reunion dances, and "blue and gold flashbacks" on campus. Peter visited the school earlier that afternoon to honor the past and down in the old typing rooms that still smelled of coffee, thick ink and spilled correcting fluid, he passed poster-board displays of former classes. The 1975-79 display highlighted his older brother Matt in a series of photographs: playing Mercutio in *Rocky and Jules*, performing stand up comedy in the assembly hall, and leaning by his locker, talking to Karim, the only black kid in the school. By contrast, in the 1980-84 set of pictures Peter was only glimpsed in a reprint of his senior photograph. Peter felt like he just hadn't made much of an impact, and while lost in the typing rooms, he felt a sharp urge to grab a slag of chalk and scrawl on the board, "Peter Traicheff did exist." But hell, the past's the past. You can't go back. No point living with regrets. Yes, as students Matt was an idealist and a wheel, whereas Peter was moody, somewhat of a dark iconoclast, and not particularly motivated. He was a solid defensive end, but besides excelling at football Peter was a drifting rebel. Angry over his parents' divorce and his father's alcoholism, Peter rarely did his homework, smoked a lot of pot, wore crisp black T-shirts with "Still a Virgin—this is a very, very old T-shirt" written on them, and was often sent home by Principal Williams for "inappropriate attire." Once, Peter even got the heave from a Halloween dance for dressing like a Baseball Bopper, a gang character in the *Warriors* who sported Kiss makeup and toted a baseball bat. Another time he was suspended three days for telling Mr. Taylor to go fuck himself, after Mr. T. held Peter's 12-out-of −50-

geometry test up for the whole class to gawk at. But those were his angry young man days. Now he was working steady, hoping to buy a house outside of T.O., and enjoying the duh-da-duh-duh, duh-da-duh-duh drum thump as the band thudded into "Zoot Suit Riot."

Peter faded back along the hazy glass of the rink, conscious of his own clumsy gait, the extra pounds around the midsection, and how he slid side-to-side as he walked. The glassed hand prints along the upper edges looked like puffs of cold winter breaths. He eventually stopped by the penalty box and stared up at the high school pennants, Kiwanis club banners, and radio ads. Across the back of the press box, hung an uneven banner, scooped in the middle with "Vikings Forever" sloppily scrawled like an afterthought. As he looked, the top of his stomach tightened like a cramped fist, and he wondered why had he come. He was also a little miffed at his brother for not being there. Matt, school president of 1979, member of the drama club, and humor writer for the school paper, could have smoothed over introductions for him. Oh, well. From a distance Peter watched Dieter, his old chem-lab partner, talking over old times with a Dan Dagg, a weight lifter. At another table, her face resting in her right hand, sat Cynthia Stuckenberg, her blond hair green in the lights. She was a popular girl that Gary had once dated, and she still looked young but her breasts were much more fulsome with middle age. Peter had danced with Cindy once in ninth grade, and he fantasized a lot about her during sleepless tenth-grade nights, her yearbook picture tucked under the ridge of dim light blipping from his clock radio as he masturbated.

The memories of those nights burned bright guilt in the edges of Peter's ears, and his eyes quickly darted from Cynthia back to the loping Viking banner, and then to the score clock. 9:30. The Prestige Picture Company was snapping photographs of each Vikings decade, starting at 9:30, and the 1980s were planned for 11:00. Peter decided to see if the pictures, in the accompanying arena for house league hockey, were on schedule. Outside, between arenas, the July wind had picked up and the air was no longer humid but a lanky kind of cool like strips of wet cloth draped around his neck. The sky was plum black, and the gravel smelled as if it had been hosed down with industrial oil. Peter leaned against an old 1950s cola machine, and heard people saying that the damn photographers were still unfolding front-row metal chairs and were a good 45 minutes behind. He talked to some more old classmates whose names he couldn't remember, and then he drifted away, back along the corrugated outside ridge of the house-league arena, and down toward the low-level lights that cast conical shadows.

A woman was crying.

It was soft, almost like a wounded animal hiding in forest underbrush. He wasn't sure what to do at first, but he moved in the direction of the sound, the hurt filling him with a chivalric tenderness. And in a dark recess, along corrugated rims, he saw her angular shoulder blades and the small cherry point of a cigarette curved up in her right hand. "Miss, are you all right?"

"Peter?" She turned and sobbed against his shoulder. He felt her chest heaving against him, and he glanced down at the fine outline of her jaw, her black hair, smoothly graying, and the wet sweaty spots behind an ear. It was Brenda Coull, the 1983 newspaper editor for the *Westerly* and his dissection partner in biology. Five or six years ago she had married a veterinarian who ran a small practice on Division Street.

"Brenda? What's up?"

She was wearing a modest white blouse and black slacks. "I'm sorry, Peter. I'm—I didn't want to come here. But I didn't want people to think that something was wrong, but if everything's not white picket fences, then something is wrong. If we don't fit, you know, then everyone knows."

"Slow down, it's okay."

She stepped away from his chest and took a quick drag from her cigarette. The veins in her arms were raised. "I know I'm not making any sense. That happens to me when I'm upset. I talk too fast and then everything runs together." She paced and ran a hand through her hair. "Damn parallel lines."

"No need to rush." He placed a hand on her shoulder, and it trembled under his palm. "C'mon, let's move away from here. We can sit over by that exit door. That's where they keep the Zamboni. No one's over there."

They walked quickly, in and out of the light, their steps in time to a Kenny Aronoff-inflected "Hurts So Good," drum beat.

"I suppose our pictures aren't going to be for another hour or so. I can pull myself together by then," she said, her wide-set eyes briefly squinting. "Got to be in the picture for history's sake. Shit." She inhaled quickly off her cigarette, and puffed out with a quick spasm that she had intended to control but couldn't.

"Who cares about the pictures?" Peter had liked Brenda a lot in high school, but hell, back then everybody's hormones were working at cross-purposes. Jocks dated only jocks, nerds wanted to date populars instead of the more compatible nerdish girls, and the populars wanted the jocks or the college-bound business kids. Peter had wanted to date Brenda, a nerd, but although he was a really good football player, he wasn't really a jock (he didn't feel up girls in the halls like several of the other football players did). Peter was a nerd who didn't know he was a nerd, and she was dating John Langway, one of the populars, a student council treasurer and an MBA-bound guy.

"Is it okay if I smoke?"

"I don't care. Sure." He pressed his hands against the tops of his thighs. "Go ahead."

She butted the cigarette against the concrete wall. And then sat up on the edge, by the docking doors. He joined her. "You were always a nice guy. You don't want me to smoke, but you want me to be comfortable, so you're not saying what you really want, which is for me to put out the cigarette, which I don't mind doing if that's what you want."

"Bren, I don't care. It's okay." He brushed hair lightly away from her eyes and the bridge of her nose. His hand now smelled like Sea Breeze, a brisk smelling astringent that his last girlfriend had used. Brenda probably had tried to compose herself in the bathroom just before he had found her crying.

"Why'd you do that?"

"I don't know. I wanted to." He shrugged. "I guess I wanted to say I care about you, that I'm sorry that you were crying and that I want to help. I guess that sounds corny."

"No." She glanced down at gravel glinting in hexagonal splotches of light. "That's okay. That was nice."

"I look around and I see a lot of people, like Gary, hanging onto the past, and they aren't happy, and I guess, I'm not too far from them, either. I'm 38. I work at a post office." He looked at a trace of dirt trapped under his left index finger like an eyelash. "Almost every day I'm delivering something good, you know, but I'm not doing so good."

"You're doing all right, now." She held his hand, he smiled, and the exit light arced around them like a hula-hoop. Brenda swung her legs freely, and then confessed to Peter how in a desperate fear of growing old and dying alone and without children, she had married six years ago, a man in his forties, and now he had left her. "You knew I had kids?"

"Yeah. A boy and a girl, I believe. Five and four years old?"

She nodded. "Vic's been gone for five months. 'Trial separation.' Yeah, right. He doesn't want me back. He just wants to humiliate me." Brenda's husband had insisted that she quit her job at the bank and stay at home with the kids, but Brenda's doctor even said that she needed work for her own identity and contentment. And when she did return to work, Vic belittled her in front of the children, calling her "Mrs. Selfish," and "Bad Mama." Brenda huffed and twisted the leather watchband on her left wrist. "At my wedding, I took a vow to submit to my husband. Submit. Shit, I never believed in it. I never should have done it."

"Do you want Vic back?"

"I used to. I'm not so sure anymore." She relit the crumpled cigarette. "I don't think so. Maybe, he's right. I *do* have too much pride. I haven't been able to tell anyone that I'm separated. No one knows. They all think I'm happy. And so, I came to this party and I just couldn't keep up the pretenses anymore. Everyone's lives here have such neat, parallel lines, no gaps—the kids, the car, the mortgage. Everything running on a smooth, even track." She shook hair off of her forehead. The lids to her eyes were rigid.

"Kiwanis Club. Church."

"Yeah."

"But you know something? They don't have it so great. Look at me. I got gaps. I haven't been on a date for five years. At work, I get disrespected by some of my more well-heeled points of call in Rosedale. If I don't put the mail through the door slot neatly and exactly the way they want (whatever way that might be, I have no frikkin' idea), they run me down in the street and holler. I'm allowed a 1% error per week. One percent. That means out of 650 to 900 homes, 8,000 pieces of mail a day, I can screw up on 80 addresses, but when I get one or two wrong, and a Well Heel calls, my supervisor's on my back. Parallel lines? I wish the lines in my life were so neat."

"I'm sorry." She took a quick drag from her cigarette and flicked it away into the wet, bald grass that glazed behind them. Bits of candy wrappers, styrofoam boxes, and paper cups were wedged up against a fence that shimmered in the dull light like spider webbing. "I didn't know."

"It's okay." He gently squeezed her hand. "I'm just going postal. It comes with the job."

She laughed. In the recesses between arenas her eyes looked blue, slightly gray.

And they talked some more about her married life, and how there were early warnings of Victor's troubles—headaches, mood swings, dark interiors—but she denied the dangers, figuring she could heal him. "God, what an Ego trip that was. Florence Nightingale."

Peter slowly nodded, and found himself looking for the cigarette that was no longer burning between her fingers. He could no longer look at her eyes, so he glanced at her slender hands, and said that he didn't have any warning signs in his relationship with Julie. She was his next-to-last girlfriend, the one he had while he was a cab driver, and everybody liked her, she was "so nice." But after she had moved into his apartment, she was sullen, often sleepy, avoiding his kisses, and saying that his lack of ambition had made their relationship stale. She was on the pill, but never wanted to have sex. To save the relationship, Peter thought he should go into business for himself, buy his own cab, but driving hack wasn't what he wanted, long term. So he decided to become a postie, started out as a non-union employee doing the overrun drops, was eventually invited to join the union, and bought Julie flowers, wrote her poetry, and tried impromptu surprises such as candlelit dinners to prove that he was earnest and intense. "I think after my thing with Julie, I lost some of my romantic shwerve. I was never a very romantic guy to begin with, but I'm afraid to try that stuff, you know? I'll never again sing to a girl outside her window."

"You did that for Julie?"

"Yeah. Ladder, flowers, champagne. The whole bit."

"Wow. That's very romantic."

Peter shrugged. "I guess." He quickly peered into Brenda's blue eyes, and saw her own frequent rejections from Victor and her need for romantic nuances, and then he looked at her shoulder. "Oh, hell, we don't want to stick around for pictures, do we? Who cares about history? Let's get something to eat."

Together they walked a short distance to Sheldon's Pizzeria. There, Peter and Brenda sat in a back booth, talking, and eating an olive-oil-slick cheese-combination of mozzarella, provolone, cheddar and brick. She talked some more about her husband, how he often got headaches, was depressed, and always seemed to want sex when he was in a terribly frightening mood. When she refused him, he'd berate himself for being over sexed, and thrashed about on the couch, rubber bands wrapped around his testicles as he demanded to be castrated. On those rare occasions when he was in a stable mood and they did have sex, it was quick and he rarely kissed her. Brenda apologized for being "too revealing," but Peter said it was okay and that he was really sorry, and that when Julie used to take the pill, she'd never swallow it. Instead she'd lie in bed, crunch on it, and then go to sleep. "That's weird," Brenda said. "I thought so," Peter quipped. "The crunching part. That was it? It wasn't a prelude to anything?" "No."

After pizza, they walked toward Brenda's house on Princess Street, a few blocks between the pizzeria and the arena. Brenda was angled up on the curb, her shoulders leaning to the right, and Peter walked along the street at the curb's outside edge. She said that he had a big heart and that he was one of the kindest people she knew. He was sensitive and sincere. He smiled dimly, his hands sticky from the grease at Sheldon's, and he looked down, glancing at the lake-sized oil stains around the buttons of his shirt. He felt a little clumsy, having made such a mess, but he also felt a kinetic connection with Brenda, like atoms swirling, colliding, a fuzz guitar kind of prolonged buzz, that made his self-consciousness seem unimportant. "I feel like I'm back in high school, at one of those parties, you know? Where the loser guys hang out by a car listening to a tape of the latest Clash or Elvis Costello albums, and a really cool, nonjudgmental chick abandons the party, joins the guys, and rocks out to "Mystery Dance" or "Death or Glory," or something equally kick ass. That's what it's like right now, walking, talking with you."

Brenda laughed, her arms anchored behind he back, as she leaned forward. "I wasn't a cool chick. I was a nerd. You were cool." The lines around her eyes were slightly wrinkled as she looked at him with kind abandon.

"I was not. My brother was cool. Everyone still talks about *Rocky and Jules*. You know? That play *was* funny. Me, I was always in trouble with some teacher or something. Man, I was mad at my Dad."

"How come?"

"He just. I don't know. I didn't like the way he treated my Mom, I guess."

The street lights cast short diffused shadows around them, stunting their figures, and the moon, shrouded by clouds, looked like the bottom of a drinking glass.

"You know Peter, there were just one or two times that I remember you being in real trouble. That time in Taylor's class, but he deserved it." She smiled. "Rhombuses and Trapezoids. Who cares? They're just lines."

"Yeah," he chuckled into his wrist. "I didn't know how to diagram a rhombus. And he went atomic."

"But I don't think you should think of your brother as being the only cool one. You *were* cool. You started up the whole football program. The School Board had banned it, and for four years we didn't have a team, until you and Karim had gone around getting signatures from possible players and teacher coaches, and the Board let us restart the program."

"Oh, yeah."

"I remember you with that petition. I was the first one to sign it, in Man and Society with Paul Forhan." Her eyes glinted as she recalled the afternoon.

"That's right. You sat next to me it that class. Shit, I forgot that you signed it first."

They walked along in the mist. The grass smelled liked dogs that had been rolling in the rain. "And remember the time you and Gary went down to East High in the middle of the night and painted their goal posts blue and gold and sprayed 'Go Vikings' on their field?"

"Yeah. They kicked our ass that game, 41-16, but at least we got a minor victory from playing on their field under our colors."

They laughed and recalled football rallies in the gym and post-game parties along King Street and beers on the beaches, and bonfires burning at the edges of the lake. Eventually they reached her small house. It was a gray and green wartime home with a slightly sagging front porch. The porch light glinted wanly and moths fluttered in the glow. Brenda asked him in.

Once inside, she introduced Peter to Sally the baby sitter, who sat on the couch, her thin white legs curled under, as she ate microwave popcorn and watched Much Music. She was a little over fourteen and Peter waved at her.

"Oh, hi, Mrs. Haley."

"How were the kids?"

"Fine. Real good," she said, her eyes on the television.

"This is my friend, Peter. Peter, Sally."

"Hi. How ya doing? I work at the post office," he said somewhat sheepishly. *Mrs. Haley*? He knew Brenda had a married name, but it felt cryptically weird coming from Sally just then.

Sally lightly smiled at Peter in that friendly but spiritedly aloof and disinterested teenage way. Brenda reached into her hip wallet for money, and realizing that she was a little short, said that she'd have to go to the back room to get more. She invited Peter to join her, and they walked across fresh-stained hardwood floors, past a small shelf of Disney videos and a series of black-framed photographs on the wall. In one, Vic, in white vet scrubs and hair askew with controlled eccentricity, hugged both children in his La-Z-Boy. His tight face and jaw looked stern, proud, and strangely defiant.

Brenda recovered some money from under a set of pale pink socks in a top dresser drawer, and then opened the door to the next room. "I wanted to show you the kids," she whispered to Peter.

Over Brenda's shoulder he could see them sleeping in a bunk bed. Courtney, hands tucked under her chin, had brown hair that spread across her pillow like disjointed pieces of spun cotton candy. Michael, his back to the door, was bent like an elbow joint under a bulky down-filled comforter. Peter couldn't see much of him but together the children radiated a kind of calm lake effect that he wished he could sit and relax by for hours.

"It's only a two-room house," Brenda explained.

"Hey, that's okay. It's nice. The kids are nice."

"When Michael gets older, we'll have to set something up in the living room. Our basement is unfinished." She closed the bedroom door. "Well, as a matter of fact, it's dirt."

"A lot of these old houses are like that."

Brenda kissed Peter on the cheek, and returned to Sally, who collected her money, said thanks, and waited for the Fuel video to end before leaving. "Sally's a pretty popular girl, I think," Brenda said.

The living room had a couple of other chairs besides the La-Z-Boy, a red and green throw rug, and a 1960s low-riding coffee table. "She's definitely got that teenage ennui thing down," Peter said. "I was just like that when I was fourteen. Interested in the adult world because I knew that they were having sex and I wasn't, but I always acted vague and aloof to maintain my own sense of cool."

Brenda laughed. "I wonder if she thinks we're having sex?"

"I don't know."

"I think she figures something's up with Vic, anyway. I'm always telling her that he's out on a call. But he runs a small animal practice, not large. Small animals have office appointments." She shook her head, and with a hand on her hip, opened the refrigerator. The door was covered with a lot of her children's drawings, bright circular lines, snow-flaked asterisks, sideways V's, and the odd recognizable dog or cat with a big head and feet. "She probably thinks we're going to have sex."

"Yeah. Maybe so. That's all I thought about at that age."

"You want something to drink? I have Pepsi. A beer? Labatt's Blue?"

"I'll have a Pepsi, thanks." Peter sat on the red and green couch that was covered with Aztec designs and shapes, glanced at the TV listings, and asked if he could change the channel. He clicked to TSN. CFL highlights were coming up soon, Toronto Argonauts versus the Montreal Allouettes. Brenda brought him a plastic stadium cup, capped with volcanic ice, and she sat next to him, and they talked some more about high-school football, and the post-game cruising up and down King Street.

"Cars full of girls," she said. "I occasionally was in one of those cars with the football players." She smiled. "Just occasionally. Are you going to go back to Toronto, tonight?"

"Probably." It was a 90-minute drive to his apartment. "I have to work the day after tomorrow."

She sipped her Pepsi, put it down on the coffee table, and leaned forward, hands on her knees. "You can stay here. On the couch, if you want. It's late."

"No. I probably should go." A dull spot, on the baseboard, running behind the television and the cable wires, hadn't been coated with wood stain. Peter wanted to stay, but he wasn't sure on what terms. Was she interested in a relationship, or a confidante-type of friendship, or was she just fearful of being lonely and was attracted to him for just this brief moment of time? He looked at the dull spot.

He definitely wanted her more than Julie or the other two women that he had slept with, but Victor's hovering presence made everything vaguely unsure and incomplete. The lines of their lives weren't parallel but unstable, closed at one end and gaping, perhaps, at the other. And as Peter pondered this open-ended problem, Brenda leaned forward and kissed him quickly. Her lips were soft, and then he leaned into her, pushing her gently into the arm rest of the couch, kissing her nose, her heavy eyebrows, the mole on her left cheek, her lips, and she kissed back, whispering, "Oh, Peter," as his fingers slid down along her sides, and hers along his, feeling the urgency of each other's breathing, before resting on the pockets of each other's hips. She hugged him hard, and then Peter broke the grasp by torquing his neck, gasping, and sitting up. "I can't, Brenda. This isn't right. You're not sure of what you really want, yet."

"I just wanted to kiss. That's all. What did you think I wanted? My kids are down the hall."

"I'm sorry. I mean with Victor and you, and, everything's happening too fast." Peter hadn't wanted to ruin the moment, he didn't want her to go too far, and have her full of regrets in the morning, but now he felt embarrassed for having been presumptuous and for underestimating her. "I'm really sorry."

"I just wanted a kiss."

Peter turned toward the blue glow of the television. He really cared about Brenda and he wanted to see her again, but he didn't want to get hurt like he did with Julie. He felt a need to hold back. "Can I call you, tomorrow? You and the kids? We can go to a park or something?" He stood up.

"Yes. I'd like that."

He moved to the door.

"Peter?"

"Yeah?"

"You can stay. I want you to."

"My car's back at the arena, I should go, I," He paused, looking for clarity between the lines. "I guess, I can get the car tomorrow." He returned to the couch and sat next to her, the thought of her Sea-Breeze skin and the smell of her body fresh on his mind. "You got wool blankets? I'm always cold when I sleep. It doesn't matter how hot it is, I get cold."

"I'll bring some blankets for you." She laughed. "The couch pulls out."

"Those springs tend to hurt my back. I'll sleep on it, as is."

"All right, Peter." She looked gently at his eyes. "And I wasn't being honest. I did want more than a kiss. How much more, I don't know," she said.

"I want you to know, Brenda, I'll be thinking about you as I sleep tonight. And I'll think about you tomorrow, and when we're ready, we'll know, I guess."

"I guess." She curled into his shoulder, and together they held hands, drank Pepsi, and watched an Argonaut wide receiver desperately running under an arcing football that seemed just a little beyond his grasp.

Break and Enter

Babo Sophie didn't know what to do with her daughter.

At least that's what Mom tells me and my wife Maggie years later during one of our late night summer reminiscences when we and our three daughters are up visiting from the States. The time was 1944, Canada was at war retaking Antwerp from the Axis, the Maple Leafs had a decent hockey team with slick-skating Syl Apps and hard-nosed Babe Pratt, and my seven-year old Mom, Jeannie, and her nine-year old brother Alec were visiting Uncle Risto Mitanis. Risto was also a newcomer from the old country, and since he was christened after Jesus, every Christmas Eve dinner was celebrated at his modest home on Adelaide street, by the lower end of Toronto, near drooping power lines and oak tree-like transformers. At Risto's parties, he offered up chicken and rice, stuffed peppers, and varieties of *zilnick*, a thin-doughed pastry crammed with leeks, cheese or spinach. All of the relatives talked in snatches of Slavic, and sang old songs such as the one about the woman by the water, whitening her clothes on the rocks. Anyway, Mom had a grip on the gray fringe of Babo's dress and she wasn't about to let her hands stutter away. The Petroves just had to get home.

Babo smiled at Jeannie but she was slightly annoyed. "*Malatah*. We'll go home soon. After Tata has thanked Risto and we've visited for awhile," she said in Macedonian. "Have some *mauslinkee*. And there's 7-Up, too." My use of the language isn't as good as Babo's nor my bilingual mother's, so I'm telling most of this story in English. Babo didn't speak much English, really. Mainly Macedonian, with a little Esperanto, French, and Russian sprinkled here and there.

Anyway, Babo was slightly frustrated with Jeannie because Mom should have been more content. She had just gotten a new doll, a Betsy-Wetsum from Dedo Risto. The doll was expensive—the Petroves couldn't afford such luxuries—but Jeannie had wanted it and Risto was always one to spoil his nieces and nephews, especially Jeannie who made him laugh whenever she did her Abbott and Costello "Who's on First" routine. All of Jeannie and Al's friends visited Thursdays to hear the A & C show and Wednesday and Saturday nights to listen to the hockey broadcasts over the store's radio. The neighborhood kids figured that Babo's kids (three girls and two boys) had it the best of anyone because their parents ran a Mom and Pop Variety. Not so. They may have had a radio, but when the Mom and Pop store first opened, the Petrove kids often asked Dedo Chris for candies, popcorn, or some of the comic books, and he always had to say no—it cut into family profits.

"Don't you like your doll, *Malatah*?" Babo thought the tank top was a little too glaring, the panties with pink ribbing a little too crass, and the doll's hard vinyl head surely might give somebody, one of Jeannie's annoying brothers, a black eye someday.

"Yes," Mom said, the doll trailing from her hand like a stiff ironing board. "But something has happened, we have to go." I can just imagine Mom's black hair dripping like thin pieces of cloth around pleading brown eyes, and Babo softening slightly at Mom's sincerity.

And no doubt, Babo felt a crisp tingle in the high part of her cheekbones. *Malatah* had prescient powers. She was always the quiet one, reserved, "a little lady," but a few months before Risto's party Jeannie almost ran right through the screen door screaming that she had seen "bones driving a car." Babo was scrubbing away bits of hardened grit from the raw *bobies*, white beans, that she was preparing for dinner, and Jeannie was flushed, her eyes expansive. A skeleton was driving a black car on Weston Road! And then Mom gave the license plate number, and in the next day's *Toronto Star*, Babo saw a grainy picture of an accident, the back end of a car cramp-crushed like one of the trash can lids at the side of the store. The car matched Jeannie's descriptions.

"Okay, okay." She nodded and kissed her daughter on the forehead, and when there was a gap in the conversation between Dedo Chris and Dedo Risto, Babo approached her husband. "*Malatah, Sakae a ode, doom.*"

Dedo Chris looked askance, his dark eyes puzzled by his daughter's demands, and Risto smiled, snatching up the doll. I think he was proud of getting it for her. "*Malatah, yahdee.* Go home later," Risto said, noting that she hadn't eaten much. He also said something about the doll being heavy. And then he squeezed the doll's vinyl cheeks, mumbled "good girl, good girl" and gave it a quarter, which was really an extra gift for my Mom. Risto was always joking around that way.

"*Neschoo ema stannatah,*" Babo told Dedo. The little one says something has happened. I believe her, let's go home.

Dedo knew his wife and that it was time to leave.

He hugged Risto, and as the Petroves gathered their coats, the other families sang lush carols about Christ's arrival on earth. The vocal harmonies sounded like rushing water capping over croppings of rock.

Dedo wasn't sure what to do with the man asleep in their kitchen.

Outside, he had seen the hole in the lower part of the front window, and the splatters of blood along the porch's hard concrete. And with caution, he told his wife and family to wait by the front door as he would survey the house. After quietly entering, Dedo calmly rushed to the back, by the store entrance, and unlocked the side door, in case he too needed a secondary exit.

Later, in the kitchen, Dedo watched a man with thick gray-black hair gurgle and mumble, his head tossed over the chair like a faded flannel shirt. Broken window shards glittered across the oval table alongside faint spots of blood. A tool belt—screwdrivers, hammers, and drills—also fanned the table.

"What is it?" Babo asked, entering the kitchen, her hair flat in the low-level light.

"Are you all right?" Dedo asked the man, gently pushing his shoulders. And he repeated the phrase several times. His English was inflected with gravel-filled words. "Are you all right?"

"Now wait a minute," Maggie interjects, her legs curved under the dusky brown sweater that wraps her thighs. "If I saw a stranger in my kitchen, I'd be out of there. With the kids. Matt, too." She sips from her dark mug of apple cider.

"But this was before faces on milk cartons," I say.

My mother smiles, shrugs her shoulders, and punches up the pillow she has crunched in the corner of the couch. "We were taught not to talk to strangers, too, but Dedo ran a variety store. We saw strangers all the time. The unemployed. Transients. People in the neighborhood. Fellow immigrants. I think to be afraid you have to have a lot. We never had much, and I can honestly say none of us were afraid of that man."

"Wow. Maybe so," Maggie says, sweeping back strands of her auburn hair, and stirring cider with a cinnamon stick. "Maybe so," and then Mom continues her story.

Jeannie tipped forward, the doll clutched to her chest. The man flashed his head from side to side and flailed his arms as if he were drowning. He sat up, lurched, and collapsed face down. He was whispering something about his wife, or missing his wife, or losing respect or something. His breath, squeezing from a half-pressed face, left a pond-shaped stain on the table. Mom says that years later she still can't tell what background the man was. He was nondescript— neither English-looking nor Eastern European. Something in-between. His eyes were veiled with dust, his face covered in a smeared charcoal of stubble. And he had a gash on the top of his head.

Babo snapped a tea towel from the rack on the door of the oven and pressed it across the man's head, but the cut had pretty much coagulated into a syrupy stickiness.

"Did she wet the towel?" Maggie asks, a perforated line of cinnamon along her lower lip.

"Yes. I guess so. It wasn't one of her best towels, but she would have wet it first. I forgot that detail," Mom says. "It was a plain tea towel with some embroidered birds or something along the edges. And it was wet. You're right, Maggie."

As Babo stood over the man she watched his shoulder blades angle up and down, and she recalled troubles she and the family had encountered upon first moving into the all-English neighborhood. But she hadn't seen this man anywhere before, and she didn't think this was something like that. Yes, people had called the Petroves many names including "niggers" and avoided them at first. Her neighbor, the widow Mrs. Tomlinson, had a Union Jack card pasted in her front window, and she used to scowl whenever Babo's kids ran across her front lawn, pointing toy guns and shouting "down with the Krauts!" But people came to the store, and started to accept them, and every year Babo insisted that Jimmy (her eldest son) leave bags of fresh peppers, grapes, and tomatoes that the Petroves had raised in their garden on Mrs. Tomlinson's back porch. "You're crazy, Ma. Why worry about her?" Jimmy said. But Babo insisted, and she also instructed the older kids to shovel the old woman's sidewalk in the winter. Canada was their home, and the Petroves were going to be welcomed by the English. In time, Mrs. Tomlinson invited Babo over for tea and they eventually became friends.

"Are you all right?" Babo asked.

The man, once again, sat up. "Leave me alone. Leave me alone." He shambled from the chair, leaned into the kitchen sink, and his legs buckled behind the knees.

"Sit down," Dedo said. "Rest."

"No. I gotta go somewhere. I need to get back." He smiled at my Dedo and then my mother. He pushed off from the sink, swung about his arms to give himself ballast, forgot the tools on the table, and slapped his way through the front door. Dedo quickly picked up the phone and dialed the police, giving them his address, "4-2-7 Weston Road," and a quick description of what had happened, and what the man was wearing—blue overalls, work boots, a plaid shirt—and then he told his family to wait, as he headed outside and tried to coax the man back in.

"What about the tools on the table? I bet you and Alec played with them, while Dedo was on the phone," I say.

My mother laughs, her eyes creasing into slivers of moon. "Actually we did. And Tata scolded us, in mid-sentence, while giving a description of the stranger to the police."

On the porch Dedo saw that the street was empty, and the sky had darkened into a plum black. Dedo wished his other three children—Frances, Lucy and Jimmy—would come home from their friends' houses and parties. They were young teenagers and the ways of the old world weren't their ways. They were growing up, spending Christmas Eves at the homes of the English. But he wanted his family around him now. He wanted his family.

But where was the strange man? He couldn't have gotten very far and the streetcar wasn't due for another fifteen minutes. Dedo walked down the steps to the edge of the murky street. The homes across the way cast arcs of light that looked like haloes.

And then he heard a kind of mewling grumble like a cat scarred in a fight. The man was groaning and swearing and groaning some more from the side of the house, near the back of the store. Dedo ran along the bricked alleyway, passing the coal chute, and stopped at the store windows that fronted Weston Road. Blurred lines of cars seamlessly blended with the snow on the street.

"Help! Get me out," the man said, crunched in the window well, his back flat against concrete, his feet reluctantly tossed up over his head. The bottoms of his black boots were worn.

Somehow, this man, had fallen into the shallow well. And although, if he had been sober, Mom explains, it would have been easy for him to climb out, in his drunken state, he was clearly lost. Dedo hoped he hadn't cut himself again or broken an arm or something. "Take my hand," he said.

"Huh?" The man couldn't quite understand Dedo's words. "Where am I?"

"You're at 4-2-7 Weston Road." Dedo showed him his hand, flexing his fingers, but the man couldn't reach them, so Dedo gingerly dropped into the well, and rousted the man up from under the arm pits, and coaxed him back into the house, promising him a cup of tea.

"Tea!"

Dedo told him that he had some rye, too.

"I like you, little guy. Where you from? Do I know you?"

The police wanted Dedo to press charges.

But after watching the man drink and talking to him for twenty minutes, Dedo empathized with him. They talked about the Maple Leafs and what a strong second line they had with Teeder Kennedy. They also discussed why second marriages weren't so bad (Dedo's was arranged, and the man thought that was weird, but 'Hey, whatever works, little fella. You're in love and that's real beautiful, you know?'). Besides, it was Christmas, his wife had left him, they had lost respect, and he didn't have a family. Why make his day worse? Babo agreed and together they wished that they had never phoned the police in the first place. Mom says that both cops were Irish or Scottish or some combination and they were getting kind of impatient with my grandparents.

"Look, ma'am. Look at that tool belt," one of the plain-clothed detectives with red hair said. His hat was pushed back with a hurried nonchalance. The other detective, with dim blue eyes, talked to the burglar, who was sitting in a chair, a towel pressed against a second cut to his head. "You two have kind hearts, but this guy is a professional. B and E. Break and Enter. Look at those tools—the drill bit, the screwdriver. The level. Does that look like the property of an amateur? Well, does it?"

"A level? Why would a burglar carry around a level? That's absurd, he's no burglar," Maggie says.

"Yeah," I say. "But then why did he break into the house?"

"He said that he wanted to get warm, to find a place 'to be,'" my Mom says with doubtful hesitancy.

"I don't get it," I say.

It seems Uncle Jimmy didn't either. He was back from a party and he leaned between his parents, his hands deep in his pockets. His hair was combed back with Frank Sinatra crooner cool. "He's right, Pop.

You gotta press charges," Jimmy implored his father, and then he glanced down at the pin-sized holes in his tan and white wing tips. My mother and Uncle Alec stood by Babo's side, watching, waiting. Mom figures that Jimmy had sensed his parents' foreignness made the police edgy and he was trying to smooth everything over. Frances and Lucy were still out visiting friends. "Teeder Kennedy is the best player on the Leafs," Dedo said.

"I agree, the best," said the stranger. "He has heart. He always mixes it up in the corners."

"Mr. Pe-tro-vy, listen to your son. This character here wasn't messing around. And he's probably done this kind of thing before," the red-haired detective said, pointing a stubby-squared finger for emphasis, and then tapping the edge of his stiff hat.

"I don't want to," Dedo said. Perhaps Grampa was offended that the cop didn't know how to pronounce his name, or at least didn't have the decency to even ask how to pronounce it. Petrove is Pe-troff, not Pe-tro-vy, I explain to Maggie, but she nods already aware of these distinctions in enunciation based on last winter's discussion of the Toronto Raptors' current owner, and fellow Macedonian, Paul Bitove.

"It's Christmas," Babo said, her left hand tight in her husband's.

"You gotta do it, Ma. Dad," Jimmy said.

Dedo glared sternly at his oldest son for disagreeing with him before the police. Macedonian children aren't supposed to disrespect and embarrass their parents before others, especially non-family. Dedo said nothing more, but as he stood straight, his shoulders hunched and the tips of his ears reddened.

The detective waited and waited and then pressed his lower lip into his upper teeth. "Well, we're going to arrest him for being drunk and disorderly. And I'd advise that overnight you two think about this incident and press charges in the morning. It's your duty."

Dedo knew about duty. As a store owner, especially during the wartime rationing, he often had angular shadows knocking at the back door, offering black-market beef at cheap rates to sell over the counter. "All of it is checked, it's safe," they'd say. And Dedo, quietly and with respect, always asked, "Is it government inspected? I don't see the blue stamp with the crown on it." "No." "Thank you very much, but I'm not going to take it. I'm not going to have peoples' lives on my conscience." And now his conscience was being asked to decide what was right in a case that didn't make a lot of sense. And it doesn't make complete sense for Maggie and me either. As Mom heads into the final turn of her story, Maggie and I can sense that not all of the themes will be linked into one foolproof lesson or epiphanic moment of urgency. Maggie's eyes gleam with this knowledge of open-ended wonder, but the flecks of joyous confusion underneath those eyes highlight shifts in details, pieces of a parable to pass on to our generation of children, for them maybe to tell, and to write, and to understand, in their own voices.

The man with the cuts, according to Mom, still hadn't really sobered up and it wasn't clear how much he knew about what was happening to him or really cared for that matter. He was sitting in a gold-flecked Formica chair, and mumbled a song about a boy lost on a hillside looking for his flock, his home. Dedo, over shots of rye, had also discovered that the man had worked on the waterfront docks, in construction, and as a part-time carpenter building homes and furniture. Funny, Dedo's father, in the old country, was a carpenter, too. But Dedo never did find out this man's name.

"Officers, I will think about this and I will let you know in the morning."

The blue-eyed detective nodded, mumbled something about "okay, it's your choice, pal," and pulled the tool belt up from the table as if it were grappled fishing lines. Then he and his partner shoved the man away. On his way out the door, the stranger told Dedo that the "Petroffs" were a wonderful family and he begged my grandparents to never lose respect for each other.

Dedo wished him a Merry Christmas and told the police not to return the towel. "I don't want back what I don't need."

Work in the Garden

Stan Traicheff sat in his Christies bread truck, his feet slapped against the thin-railed handles of a stack of metal trays. It had been a cold, slow morning, and Slava Kouras, the manager of the Queen and Parliament A&P, had yet again given Stan a hard time. Slava didn't want loaves of Small Crusty or Large Crusty. Just Fancy White, Fancy Wheat, Golden and Brookside White. That's all. But Stan knew that the Crustys would be a big seller for Slava. Stan had put 10% more business on Route 174 since taking it over, and he knew the people of this area, many of them the children of Eastern-European immigrants like himself, and he knew what they liked: fatter, heavier breads, with thicker crusts, good for soaking up olive oil and the various tomato-based sauces in okra and bean dishes.

The Crustys also brought in a higher commission. They sold for 23 and 27 cents as opposed to 19, 19, 19 and 23 for the other four. And the Queen Street A&P stood just blocks away from Eastern Variety and Highland Farms who sold large quantities of Christie's higher-end products. So why not along this immigrant quarter? Slava also accused Stan of cheating him on deliveries. "I know, I know. You're doing it somehow. You're cheating me," he'd yell in snatches of conflicting Greek and Macedonian.

Stan lit a cigarette. One of these days he was going to pop off and tell Slava to shove it. Stan never stole from nobody. Sure, some of his buddies like Jack Cadaret and Gord Isles, stole from the company, tweaking their books, charging more for less to the retailers and pocketing the margin difference, but not Stan. The temptation was there but he didn't do it. Before Christies, Stan had worked construction at the CN Railroad, but at Christies he was his own boss, and he was proud to have his name inscribed within the company's red embroidery on his brown work shirt.

He took a long, slow drag. The taste of the cigarette was bitter and bright and he was glad to rest. It was surprisingly cold for mid March and the tips of his fingers were stiff and partially numb. He stood up, checked his next call, Dominion Meats—Lemon Dels and Happy Snack six packs: butter tarts, pecan tarts, lemon tarts, brownies, snowballs, chocolate delights and creams flips. All thirty-six cents.

During a second cigarette drag, there was a sturdy rap on the passenger side of the truck. Stan tugged up his brown trousers, tucked in his work shirt, readjusted to a higher notch on his frayed belt, and opened the sliding door.

Nine-year old Cathy Cerlon leaned like a curled wave, her backpack hanging limply over her left shoulder, her blue-rimmed glasses not quite resting squarely on her nose. Her right ankle was turned over. "Hey, Stan," she hollered in an attempt at a casual greeting. The kid had an outgoing personality, and she loved to tease and be teased.

"What are you up to? I guess school's not started yet, huh?"

"Yeah." Her brown eyes squinted in the glimmers of sun. Her hair was pulled back off her forehead and she had a black Beatles button attached to one of the pockets of her faded Jean jacket.

Stan butted his cigarette against the truck's dull metal ceiling and invited her in. It was too cold to be standing outside. Actually, it wasn't that warm in the truck either. All of the heat blew down by Stan's legs and that was it. It never circulated upwards. In the cold winters Stan's right leg was always warm, and the heat off the accelerator burned holes in the soles of his shoes. He pointed at Cathy's button. "Is that a political candidate you're voting for?"

"No. It's the Beatles." Cathy shrugged her shoulders with heavy emphasis. "They were on Sullivan a couple of weeks ago?"

"Oh. I bet you like Paul. He's the cute one."

"No. I like Ringo. He's goofy."

"Well, goofy has its charm, I guess."

"You got any day olds," she asked, sitting on the right wheel hub below the dashboard. Her knees were tucked up to her delicate chin, and her voice was full of playful mischief.

"Sure. I've got some lemon tarts. I got some bread, too," Stan said pointing to five loaves that were pot-holed in the center. "Help yourself."

"Boy, that's some guilty bread. Guilty! Did you need somewhere to sit down, pal?"

"I dropped a tray on it." Stan shook his head. "Clumsy old Stosh." Cathy laughed as she folded back the slick cellophane on a lemon tart Happy Snack. The lemon topping had smashed against the wrapping like a popped blister, and she licked it off with her tongue.

Stan had first met Cathy about six months ago, when during a call at Highland Farms he caught her hopping out of the swinging back doors of the truck, a stack of cakes like record platters, shifting in her arms. He yelled at her, hauled her to the truck's diamond-tread floorboards, and threatened to call the police. She cried and he found out that her parents were divorced, and that her mom kept long hours as a bartender, and that her refrigerator was often empty.

Cathy bit into the lemon tart. Paste hardened at the corners of her lips as she talked with a loping, hesitant speed, some of the words mannered, others quick and rushing by like Maple-Leaf winger Frank Mahovlich busting down ice on a breakaway. At school her fourth-grade class was learning about inventions and was encouraged by Mr. Yorke to create their own for an invention convention and Cathy had a project she wanted to make. A clamp jaw.

"What's a clamp jaw, kid?" Stan placed his hands on his hips.

Cathy reached into her duffel bag and scratched out a drawing done in dark, pencil lines on thin-ruled paper. There were several smears from corrections, or what Cathy would call "do-overs," and Stan looked carefully at the illustration. The invention borrowed its design properties from the hole-punch, except the top arm of the pivot device had the crowded flat teeth of a meat tenderizer, and the lower arm was equipped with a short, shallow pan.

"It's for work in the garden," she said, shrugging and impishly smiling, friendly forehead wrinkles rippling above her glasses.

"You got a garden?"

"No. But, that's what it's for. You know? Those clumps of dirt that need to be broken up? The clamp jaw breaks them."

"What if the dirt gets wet. Can it break up those bits of dirt? If they're wet?"

"I wouldn't work in the garden, if it's wet."

Stan laughed. "You don't even have a garden." He handed her back her illustration. Clamp Jaw was written above the blueprints in big block letters. Some of the letters were filled in with hard rain-streaked lines, curving snakes and blue-flowered blossoms.

"I guess, I'd have to test it in wet dirt," she said, taking the picture back, and rubbing it against her thigh to remove some of the sticky lemon residue that had glued to the paper's edges

"Well, how are you going to make this clamp jaw thing?"

"I don't know."

Stan had an idea. Nick Turco, who managed Dominion Meats down the road, owed Stan a favor since Stan gave Nick a pair of gray tickets to the Leaf game last Tuesday, a 4-4 tie with the Bruins, a game in which the Leafs came back from a 4-0 hole. Newly acquired winger Andy Bathgate netted a goal and an assist. Stan also had tickets for the Saturday game in ten days at the Gardens, but this time he was going to take his four-year old son to his very first hockey game. Maybe Stan could lean on Nick to have his son, who was a welder, jiff up some gizmo for the contest. As long as Cathy designed the clamp jaw, surely it would be okay to get an expert to make a model from her blueprints. "I get off work at two. I'll pick you up at your school and we'll see Nick. Call your mom and make sure it's okay."

"'K."

Stan's route finished up at 1:30. At two, Christies had a mandatory meeting in which the salesmen and supervisors discussed new cake designs. Stan thought an orange, clover-clustered prototype looked "Faggy." He shouted his opinion at the meeting, much to the arched-eyebrow dismay of his supervisors. "Hey, you asked my opinion. I'm telling ya. Under the store lights, that cake's sticky oozing guzz will look like lava, molten fagdom courtesy of Christies." His fellow employees laughed while several district managers shot Stan a series of sharp looks. If they don't want to hear what I have to say, then don't invite me to these damn meetings, thought Stan. Shit, it's this kind of honesty that probably accounts for why in five years I've never been promoted. After the meeting, Stan, Jack and Gordie vented their frustrations at the Legion over four or five beers, and then he picked up Cathy outside of Rose Ave. Public School near Parliament and Bloor. Within minutes they were at Nick's Dominion Meats. All three sat in an upstairs office, where below they could see many of the aisles, the shoppers, and red and yellow pennant banners inscribed with "Dominion: Mainly Because of the Meat!" Many of the women had their hair up in pink and pale blue bandannas and were pushing carts with young toddlers sitting upright, reaching out for cereal boxes and other bright packages. Cathy was drinking an orange soda.

"Hey kid, I better get you a shaving kit," Stan said, pointing at her upper lip.

Cathy made a bemused face. "Sooo. I like Orange Crush."

"I think my son can help," Nick curled back a shirt sleeve. His hands were scrubbed clean, but the cuffs of his shirt were dotted with nubs of black marker. His face was long, his cheek bones wide set and high. "So, you lika to make these kind of things, huh?" He studied her clamp-jaw illustrations.

Cathy nodded, her feet tapping out a rhythm under a lime-flecked Formica chair.

"She's pretty good," Stan said. "The invention's all her idea. She just needs someone to realize her blueprints, I guess."

"I'll talk to my boy. He loves doing things like this." He looked over at Stan. "And you promise me a free fruitcake at Christmas?"

"Yes, Nick. Two fruitcakes."

"Good. Good."

Below them a kid cried. She wanted something her mother wouldn't let her have, and she lunged against the cart's handle, reaching for a brightly colored box. Another kid had dropped a jar of Gerbers out of the cart, and a smear of peas splattered the floor. Glass shards glinted in the light. Nick picked up a sandy-colored phone with grime on the handle and told someone to go clean up aisle four. Stan looked over at the large white clock with Dominion D, soundlessly ticking. 4:30. By five, five-thirty, he'd be back at the bar, having a few more drinks, and maybe playing a game of darts or two.

It was ten after eleven by the time Stan reached the back veranda of his two-bedroom house on Sudan Ave. Everyone was asleep, and Stan was more than tipsy from the ten or twelve beers he had. How the hell was he able to drive home so easily? Maybe it was all the salt and vinegar chips he ate to offset the alcohol. A low-watt kitchen light briefly lit the back corner of the house, but the rest was dark. He gently slid the screen door shut and crept across faded linoleum to the fridge, but he wasn't sure if he was really creeping. His steps were clumsy slow, and he feared that he was actually thudding. The whole house felt like a constricting tunnel, and he wasn't sure if he was being subtle at all. He reached for the heavy handle of his refrigerator and then searched over milk, cold cuts and raw chicken thighs, for leftovers. He didn't find anything. "What the hell?" Did he say that out loud? Or did he just think it?

On the center of the sparkling kitchen table was a box of Pablum, a bowl, and a spoon. A recipe-card note was propped against the china bowl. The dried cereal was poured into the bowl like pencil shavings emptied from a sharpener. "Stan—if you're going to act like a baby, you'll be treated like one. Enjoy your dinner—Jean."

He sat at the gray formica table, the card twirling in the fingers of his right hand, his left hand pressed into his cheek. I guess I deserve that. Stan enjoyed drinking after work—he figured it was his right. He was bringing home the money. But eleven o'clock was awfully late. He just lost track of the time. Maybe he had fourteen beers.

He struggled from the table, chuckled at the dim box of Pablum, and quietly, (at least it seemed quiet, maybe it was exuberantly noisy) stumbled down the hallway and upstairs to the two bedrooms. The boys were sleeping. Matt had a hand over his head, a blue pajama sleeve curling over his left wrist, a little trickle of saliva pooling at the dip in his chin. Pete was asleep on his side in the crib. The mobile of little plastic stars was still twisting. Jean must have just got to bed. And Pete must have just got to sleep.

Stan slipped open the door to his bedroom and leaned into the frame. His forehead was thudding.

Jean was sitting up, two pillows billowing her back, as she read a Morley Callaghan novel. "Where the hell were you?" Sheets bundled her legs and gathered at her hips.

"I'm sorry, Honey. Me and the boys, we had a couple of drinks and— "

"You have a family here, you know? These boys. They never see you. And when you are home, you're asleep." She looked at him with a tired intensity, a kind of weariness that had been down this side path too many times.

"I work hard, okay. I provide don't I? Give me a break."

"Stan." She brushed black hair from the side of her face. "We're a family. You just don't do what you want to do. The money's not all yours to spend how you want."

"I know."

"I need money to buy the kids clothes. I need— " She gestured with her hands, unable to look at him. "You were going to help me today with the garden."

"I know, I know. But it's too cold to plant anything, anyway."

"We can plant bulbs."

"Okay, I'm sorry. I'll be home early tomorrow. And I'm going to take Matt to the game next Saturday."

"He watched the game tonight, wishing you were here."

"Yeah. I watched it at the Legion." Coach Imlach had played with the lines again, putting Mahovlich with Shack and Kelly, and Keon with newcomers Bathgate and McKenney. "Mahovlich didn't score. But McKenney got two. He's averaging a point and a half a game since the trade."

"Stan—"

He sat on the edge of the bed, trying not to tumble over. "What a day I had. That prick, Slava Kouras. Won't carry breads I want him to. I know they'll sell. I'm a good salesman."

"Yes, you are."

"Guy accused me of cheating him. I don't cheat nobody. Cheat. Sonuvabitch." Stan clambered to his feet and gently paced the room, each step measured. He told Jean that he wanted her to go shop with the boys at the A&P tomorrow or the day after. Fill the cart up with non-perishables. But fill it. And then ask the manager why they aren't carrying any of Christies' Crusty Breads. When Kouras fails to give a satisfying answer, Jean's to throw her arms up and abandon the packed cart right in the middle of an aisle as she dramatically exits the store with their two sons. "That'll leave an impression." He started laughing and couldn't stop.

"Yes. I'm sure it will." Jean smiled.

"Will you do it," Stan pleaded though half-chuckles.

Jean nodded, her arms against her chest, her blue nighty slightly open, revealing the narrow ridges of her collarbones.

"You're still mad at me, aren't you?"

"Yes," she said.

"I can't sleep when you're mad at me."

"Well then, don't make me mad."

He huffed, his hands pressing into his upper thighs. "Pete just got to sleep, didn't he?"

"Enjoy your dinner, Stan." Jean grabbed the pillows from behind her back and turned away from him in the bed. "Good night. Shut off the light, please."

He watched her shoulder blades shake slightly with each breath. He'll be home early tomorrow. "I'm sorry."

"I know."

"Good night."

He shut off the light and walked back into his boys' bedroom. He reached into his pants pockets and pulled out a couple of waxed packs of hockey cards. The corners of the packs were scuffed slightly, and he left the packages by Matt's bedside table. And then he moved over to Pete who now slept like a bent elbow. He watched his younger son's breathing as the stilled stars dangling over his crib glittered with street light.

Four days before taking his son to his first hockey game at Maple Leaf Gardens, Stan leaned back in his truck, a hot cup of coffee in his right hand and a cigarette in his left. He had been sitting outside of the Queen A&P for twenty minutes. Dramatic emphasis. Slava Kouras had pleaded for some Small and Large Crustys. Slava didn't say why the sudden change in his managing policies, but he wanted Crustys bad. Stan knew why, and he had ordered an extra twenty loaves of each for today's run, but he was acting like maybe he didn't have them. He took a final short drag off his cigarette and a long pause between slurps of coffee. He hitched his pants, grabbed two metal trays, balancing them against his upper thighs, and walked into the store. Kouras waited by the sliding doors. His hair was slicked back and parted to the right. His forehead was heavily wrinkled, his upper cheeks pock-marked. "You're in luck," Stan said. "Got some extras."

"They're not day olds?"

"Would I give you day olds? C'mon, Slava. Now don't be a prick. I'm always treating you with respect. Now you treat me with some." Stan flexed a finger at Slava.

"You shouldn't talk to me like that." Slava backed up, looking at Stan's name tag surrounded in Christies's red trim.

"And you shouldn't accuse me of things I don't do. I don't cheat. I've never cheated you. I could. But I'm honest. Now let me put the bread on the shelves, if you don't mind." Stan hefted the trays to the far right of the store, next to the donuts and pies and other baked goods. Red-and-white ribboned bunting dipped from the ceiling. Stan let out a slow huff, and then handed Slava the order sheet, showing him the sell-by codes, counting all of the loaves of bread on each tray, and then placing them on the shelves. He stacked them in uniform rows, all of the brown-packaged breads in one row, all of the white packaged ones in another. He liked the rainbow tiers.

"My boys can do that."

"No, no. I do it. I make it attractive to the eye. They sell better." Stan was a little cocky about his job. He knew he was good. "All right. And I gave you some credit for the returns. Here's the return slip." Stan placed his hands on his hips. "The Crustys look nice?"

"They look nice," Slava nodded, his nose scrunching in the middle.

"So what finally brought you around? Customers been asking?" Stan suppressed a chuckle as he thought of his wife who yesterday had left a full cart of groceries in aisle seven when she wasn't able to get any Crusty bread. Stan couldn't resist needling Slava just a little bit.

"No, no. My wife thought it would be a good idea."

"Listen to them women folk, huh?"

"Yeah."

"Well, thank you for your business, Sir. I'll see you tomorrow." Stan shook Slava's hand. His fingers were dry, nubby and thick. Stan smiled, and then briskly paced back to his truck where his styrofoam cup of coffee would still be warm.

Outside the March air was crisp and bitter, and felt snappy like sharp, slapping newsprint. Cathy was standing by the door of his truck, her jean jacket a size or two too big for her body, her green back pack hanging languidly over her left shoulder.

"What's up with you? You're going to be late for school, waiting on me."

Cathy looked at the ground, an orange and blue-tinged welt was raised under her left eye. "I wanted you to know that that friend of yours finished the clamp jaw and he called me at home, and I got it, and well, anyway, yesterday it was nominated by some judges at my school to move on to the next level."

"What level? The inventors of the future?"

"Southern Ontario Regionals. The Invention Convention."

"Wow. That's great." Stan patted her on the shoulder, feeling the girth of the back pack against his finger tips. He wondered about that eye. Did she get in a fight? Did her mother hit her? Just the other day in the paper he read something about parents crossing the line and the role of the Children's Aid Society in protecting beaten children. "Whattaya got in there? Test tubes and Bunsen burners? That back pack must way a ton."

"Just books and my lunch, and my rock collection." She wasn't joking. She reached into her bag and pulled out several rocks. They were all smooth, and seemed to slip between her fingers like wet soap. And each rock had a Christmas ornament-type sheen. "I have a rock polisher and me and my friends trade them at school."

"I used to trade marbles, hockey cards, army men. But rocks? That's a new one. What happened to your eye?"

"What?" Her eyes had a guilty glaze. "Oh, I fell at home."

"Fell?" Stan wasn't too convinced by her answer. "Over what? Your big feet?"

"No. I tripped and banged into a doorknob. And my feet aren't big. They're luminous."

"Luminous?"

"Yes. I want to dance with these feet." Cathy did a quick little lightning pirouette her feet flashing like shifting sand dunes. "They're star's feet."

"Oh, I see. The dancing inventor."

"Yes. I am." Cathy flung her hands over her head, her fingers stretched stiff like taut veins of spider webbing, and then spun again, losing her balance and stumbling into the side of his truck, her body listing.

"You okay?'

"Yeah."

"Whatever you do, kid. Don't quit your day job. Stay in school."

"I wish my mom could afford lessons."

"What door knob did you hit?"

"The bathroom. No, the back one."

"The back one's a sliding door. I've been to your townhouse."

"Oh, yeah. The one that leads to the basement." Cathy shrugged, and readjusted her backpack on her left shoulder. Her Beatles button didn't look as shiny as it did a few days ago.

"Did your mom hit you?"

"No." She looked away, her eyes on the frayed laces of her blue Keds.

"Well," Stan paused, awkwardly. "Congrats on the Clamp Jaw. That's really something. Do something with your life. Get an education. I never did. Look at me."

"Anyway, thanks for your help with the Clamp Jaw. I better run."

"Yeah. I got some butter tart returns. You want one?"

"No, thanks. I'll see you tomorrow."

"Sure."

Two days before taking his son to his first hockey game at Maple Leaf Gardens, Stan parked his truck at the El Mocambo at Spadina. He had just finished his route and he wanted to talk to Lana Cerlon, Cathy's mom.

Stan hitched his pants up, smoothed out the wrinkles in his shirt, and hopped out. Last night Mahovlich scored the only goal in a 1-0 win over Montreal. Stan watched the first period of the game at the Legion before catching the second half of the second with Matt.

Mahovlich's goal, a low rising wrister, caught Charley Hodge on the short, stick side. Stan rubbed his throbbing right knee. He had to lose some weight. At 225, hopping on and off his truck was killing his knees.

The inside of the bar was dim and dark, with patches of conical light glinting over plastic palm trees. A black stage loomed off in the far end, bamboo drapes flapped behind the wet bar, and a burly guy with folded-up sleeves sat with his arms squatting over the cash register. "Can, I get you something, pal?"

"Yeah. I'll have a Canada Dry," Stan said.

"I've only got Wink"

"Sure. That's fine." The black bar top sparkled with slivers of metallic crescents burrowed under glass. "Is Lana, here?"

"Yeah. What's up?"

"I want to talk to her about her daughter Cathy. I'll be over at that table. The one with the pictures of Elvis on the wall."

The bartender nodded and Stan briskly moved through a scattering of chairs to the west corner. He sat with his back to the photographs. He didn't like Presley. He was a Johnny Cash fan. Impatiently, Stan tapped his finger along the table's chrome siding. Palm leaves reflected off the table's black-lacquered finish.

In two minutes his drink arrived; in ten, Lana. She wore a black dress, with ruffles around the shoulders that complemented thick black hair that was cropped just above her jaw lines. Her face was smooth, obscuring her thirty or so years. She had heavy eyebrows and a warm light in her eyes. She smiled and thanked Stan for his help with Cathy's clamp jaw. Her daughter was so excited about going on to regionals, and Lana was glad that her daughter had people in the neighborhood like Stan helping.

"Thanks. I don't know how to ask this," Stan said hesitantly. His usual disposition was to be blunt and direct. "But, anyway. Is everything all right? Cathy had a welt under her eye, and, well she tried to tell me that she banged it on a doorknob, but I knew she was lying. What happened?"

"What do you think happened?" Lana's upper cheekbones hardened as her mouth parted slightly, and the youthful gleam on her face faded. "Do you think I hit her?"

"No. I-I don't know. That's why I wanted to talk to you."

"You're not her father."

"I know that. I just—"

"I didn't hit her." Lana leaned forward, her shoulders sharp, angular, erect. Her shifting motion broke up the lazy reflections of palm leaves in the table.

"I'm sorry. I like the kid. I just want to—"

"Well, then just mind your own goddamn business, okay?" She sat back and flipped hair from her dark eyes. There was a pale white line where her wedding band used to circle her ring finger.

"Okay." Stan shrugged and played with the lip of his glass, running his finger around the edge. "I'll finish my drink, and I'll be gone."

Lana pursed her lips together, and placed her hands flat on the table. "Cathy was supposed to meet her dad last weekend for a visit. And the bastard canceled at the last minute. Cathy went nuts. Tore up her room. Everything. Art projects, the hair on her dolls' heads, blankets piled in the center like a teepee. And then she started hitting herself, and I tried to stop her. She even hit me." Lana jerked down the left edge of her dress's neckline and there were a series of small plum marks around her collarbone. "I finally got her calmed down. And we had some tea and she cried for a long time."

"I apologize for what I was thinking. I really do."

Lana shrugged and said nothing.

"Can I buy you a drink?"

"No, I'll buy you one," she said.

On Saturday Stan took his son Matt to Maple Leaf Gardens to watch the Leafs face off against the New York Rangers. All week long, radio announcers, columnist Dick Beddoes, and the Hot Stove League on *Hockey Night in Canada*, had been playing up the trades for ex-Rangers Andy Bathgate and Don McKenney, and how the Leafs traded away the future—including bright Junior A prospect Rod Seiling—for a push at a third cup in a row. First Coach Imlach put Bathgate and McKenney with Mahovlich, moving the big winger to center. But that never clicked. With Davey Keon, they did. Stan and Matt huddled in the halls of the Gardens looking at the past 9 cup winners, and Stan imagined Bathgate and McKenney's photographs up there on the wall next year. Water stains ran across one of the blue concrete walls as fans pushed forward to their seats. One more cup in 1963-64 would make it ten.

"There's Frank," Matt said, staring at the Big M's individual photograph with the 1962-63 Cup team. Matt was skinny, small for his age, and his brown hair bristled in several directions like a flickering weather pane.

"Yup, and he's over there too," Stan said, guiding his son's sight along his fingers to the adjacent 1961-62 team. "And Bob Pulford, Bobby Baun, goalie Johnny Bower, and the captain, George Armstrong."

Stan had a better day with Jean yesterday and Saturday. He got home early both days, cut the grass Friday afternoon, helped Jean with the kids and planting some bulbs in the garden, and didn't drink as much. They even made love last night.

"Who's your favorite player after Frank, Daddy?" Matt turned his head sideways to the left to get a better look at all of his favorite Leafs.

"Armstrong. The "C" he wears on his sweater doesn't just mean captain, it also means 'Chief.'" Stan chuckled. He loved pulling his son's leg. "That's his nickname. The Chief because he's a strong leader and an Indian. No other captain in the league can also claim that his 'C' stands for 'Chief.'"

"I like Davey Keon."

"Keon? He's nothing compared to Frank. Mahovlich is the best. Keon!" Everyone in Toronto loved "little Davey Keon," the slick-skating center from Noranda, Quebec. He was fast, gritty, hardworking, and an over achiever. But Frank, a Croation and the closest thing to Macedonian in the NHL, never got the credit he deserved. He was big, strong and fast from the blueline in, but the fans felt Frank never did enough. When he scored two goals, they wanted three. "Keon! Keon's not even half as good as Frank. Or the Chief for that matter. Or Allan Stanley." Stan liked Stanley. He was a stay-at-home defenseman, and he had a great last name.

Matt nodded, and his father grabbed his hand. "C'mon. I'll show you some other photographs." They walked down another blue-and-white hallway, through a series of ushers decked in freshly pressed blue sport jackets, each crested with crisp maple leaves. "Program! Program!" they hollered. "I walked out here in 1962. The Leafs were in overtime against Chicago, and I couldn't stand the pressure. So, I left my seat, walked around and looked at all of these photographs, and Dick Duff scored in overtime. I knew we had won the game because of the loud noise," Stan said, as he and his son slipped between large clumps of shoulders crowding the concession stands. "There's Bill Barilko. He scored in overtime against Montreal to give the Leafs the 1951 Cup." Stan directed Matt to the photograph of

Number 5, and he felt his son's excitement, sparking through his fingers as they studied the defenseman seemingly suspended in mid-air, the puck wedged over goalie Gerry MacNiel's left shoulder. MacNiel's beaten face was a combination of blinking sadness and astonishment. "And here's Teeder Kennedy, great Leaf Captain, shaking hands with the Queen."

Matt paused reverently, and then his father guided him to the escalator. Once they reached the top level by the grays, Stan bought his son a 35-cent program and an Eskimo pie. "Hurry. Eat up. You don't want to get chocolate all over the seats."

"Okay." Matt tried to study the stats inserted in the middle of the program, but he couldn't hold the pages open because his hands were sticky. Stan took the program and showed Matt the cover. "Tim Horton. The only player I've ever seen take the puck from behind his own net and as he rushes up ice, each section of the Gardens slowly rises as he passes by. An awesome rushing defenseman, kid. One of the best."

Matt finished his Eskimo pie, his chin dotted with chocolate smears, and Stan nudged his son from behind as they entered the aisles and made their way to their seats at the top of the Gardens. On the way up, Stan promised his son that he'd help him score the game. He brought three pencils with him, but Matt was no longer moving. Below, players, warming up, skated at opposite ends, peppering Jacques Plante and Johnny Bower with shots. The Leafs Bower seemed clumsy in the upper body, but nonchalant on his skates. Plante, hunched in his perfect three-quarter stance, looked a little tense, even with a mask on. "Dad. It's in color!" Matt exclaimed.

Stan laughed out loud, grabbing his sides. "Yes. Not like on TV, huh?"

Matt's eyes skipped across several pucks, especially those in the Leaf end. His eyes quickly adjusted to number 27, Mahovlich, straddling inside the blueline, swinging up his left shoulder, and ripping a slap shot past Bower. "Frank just scored," he said.

"That's nothing. One time in warm-ups, I saw him fire a slapper so hard that he sent Bower's trapper mitt flying into the crowd."

"Really?"

"Really." Stan laughed. "C'mon, kid. Let's sit down." Again, he reached for his son's hand. The inside was coated with a drying layer of slick chocolate and it smeared Stan's left palm. Stan studied the stain that stretched like dirt across the lines in his skin, and he thought about the rows of plants in his backyard, and the city grid lines across houses, and he saw Cathy Cerlon's clamp jaw breaking up matted dirt in Lana's yard, and the bulbs in his wife's garden pushing their way through the earth to the sun, and he remembered how last year Jean's tomatoes and peppers started slow but grew well, and then he thought about all of the gardens in his neighborhood, and all those lives and stories that flourished in the light and those that struggled to breathe but still grew in wet, dim-lit patches of warm shadows.

About the Author

Grant Tracey was born in Toronto, Ontario in 1960. From early on he was brought up in a hockey culture. Every Wednesday and Saturday night his family watched Hockey Night in Canada and cheered on the Leafs. "You can come over this Saturday, but I want you to know one thing, the hockey game will be on," his father often told friends and family who wanted to visit. In 1972, Grant watched his boyhood heroes, Canada's greatest hockey players including Phil Esposito, Ken Dryden, and Yvan Cournoyer, tackle the awesome Soviet juggernaut in an eight game Summit series. This series was a turning point in the formation of Canadian identity. Grant fondly recalls watching three of the four games from Moscow at school. Classes were dismissed to the library and gym, as young Canadian boys and girls cheered Canada to victory. Grant writes about this experience in the collection's debut story, "Hockey Canada."

After receiving his BA in English and History from Trent University, Grant went to Kansas State to earn a Masters in English and to learn to be a writer. There, he worked with Ben Nyberg and discovered the joys of the short story form. While at Kansas State, Grant also met his future wife Karen (a native Kansan), and they played intramural softball together and fell in love. After their MA's, Grant and Karen attended the University of Illinois to pursue Ph.D's.

After finishing his Ph.D. Grant decided to wed his love of hockey with his desire to write literate, mostly upbeat, character-driven stories. Over a period of eight years he wrote many of the stories featured in *Parallel Lines and the Hockey Universe*. Currently, Grant is Fiction Editor of the *North American Review* and he and his wife are Associate Professors of English at the University of Northern Iowa. They have three daughters. And every Saturday at the Tracey household, like it was for the generation before, is still hockey night!

Pocol Press

6023 Pocol Drive, Clifton, VA 20124
703-830-5862
chrisandtom@erols.com
www.pocolpress.com

Striking New
Fiction for 2003

Parallel Lines and the Hockey Universe by Grant Tracey, 198 pp., $12.95. The 21 stories in *Parallel Lines* are set against a backdrop of parallel universes—sports and families—linked by the life of Matt Traicheff. His parents, second-generation immigrants, are splitting apart because of marital discord, but through sports—hockey, football, and public speaking—each member of the family seeks some type of transcendence. Matt's work as a sports reporter sets up stories focusing on the Waterloo Black Hawks, a losing Junior A hockey team struggling for wins in the highly competitive United States Hockey League, while the Traicheffs try to remain a family. Cover art by Gary Kelley. ISBN: 1-929763-13-1.

Lost People by Paul Perry, 180 pp., $14.95. As a follow-up to his acclaimed *Street People*, Paul Perry returns with another short story collection about life's downtrodden. Perry's portrayals of sympathetic characters is dead on, and he creates a remarkable cast of people caught up in everyday struggles for survival. The stories work by themselves, but are more powerful as a whole. Abraham Maslow identified Food, Clothing, and Shelter in his Hierarchy of Needs. Yet, these people, as we all do, need far more than that. Like all of us, they need love and affection, and safety, and a sense of self and self worth.

In this book, Mexicans try to cross the border, people live in buses, in parks, prisons, half-way houses, under bridges, even cardboard boxes. A profound sense permeates these stories that the author is grateful and so should we all be for the gift of life, for roofs over our heads, for the ability of good and ordinary people to care for others. In a secular way, these tales are a metaphor for good works. There's a lot of befriending to be found inside. The endings remain hopeful, contemplative, introspective, and courageous, like many of the wonderful characters. ISBN: 1-929763-15-8

Best Bet in Beantown by G.S. Rowe, 210 pp., $17.95. The year is 1897. The place: Boston, Mass. Star short stop Herman Long has just been beaten and left for dead, alone and in the locker room of the Boston Beaneaters National League base ball team. But, who-dunnit and why? It's up to ne'er-do-well Will Beaman, who stumbles across Long while trying to secure a front office position with the ball club, to solve the case. Filled with romance, red herrings, exciting game reportage, heart-pounding chases, and shady characters, *Best Bet in Beantown* dives deeply into the sordid world of 19th century base ball. Cover art by Todd Mueller. ISBN: 1-929763-14-X.

Send check or money order to above address. Add $2.00 shipping per book. Priority Mail $4.00 per book. Foreign orders extra. Also available on website for credit card purchase.

Lillian Wald

The University of North Carolina Press

CHAPEL HILL

Lillian

Marjorie N. Feld

Wald

Designed by Courtney Leigh Baker
Set in Scala by Keystone Typesetting, Inc.

The paper in this book meets the guidelines for permanence
and durability of the Committee on Production Guidelines
for Book Longevity of the Council on Library Resources.

The University of North Carolina Press has been a member
of the Green Press Initiative since 2003.

Library of Congress Cataloging-in-Publication Data
Feld, Marjorie N.
Lillian Wald : a biography / Marjorie N. Feld.
p. cm.
Includes bibliographical references and index.
ISBN 978-0-8078-3236-3 (cloth: alk. paper)
1. Wald, Lillian D., 1867–1940. 2. Feminists—New York
(State)—New York—Biography. 3. Social reformers—
New York (State)—New York—Biography. I. Title.
HQ1413.W34F45 2008
361.3092—dc22   2008019176

12 11 10 09 08   5 4 3 2 1

Contents

Illustrations

Acknowledgments

I have traveled with Lillian Wald for a long, long time and have been lucky to have had the assistance of many helpful people along the way. Kathryn Kish Sklar first introduced me to Wald when I was an undergraduate at the State University of New York at Binghamton. She and Allan Arkush guided me through a senior honors thesis on Wald there. At Brandeis University, I had the sound advising of Joyce Antler and Morton Keller.

The summer before I began my graduate work, I secured a job at Henry Street Settlement, which Wald founded in 1893. I headed the Greening Challenge, a summer recycling program. My students that summer taught me about urban life, and I am grateful to them; my boss, Christine Koenig, taught me about politics, reform, and professionalism. She and Catherine Cullen, both open about their admiration of Wald, gave this project momentum by alerting me to the role settlements can *still* play in urban transformation.

Every historian is indebted to talented librarians, archivists, and administrators. Jim Baillie at Brandeis and Barbara Kendrick, Kate Buckley, and Hope Tillman at Babson found me the sources I needed on so many occasions. Sari Weintraub at Henry Street, Michael Delaney and John Belleci at the Visiting Nurse

Service of New York, and Laurie Deredita at Connecticut College, along with Mary Driscoll, Pat MacAlpine, and Sheila Dinsmoor at Babson, offered crucial assistance to me at various stages of this manuscript's preparation.

I am truly grateful to colleagues who took time to share their thoughts and suggestions with me over the years: Jonathan Sarna, Riv-Ellen Prell, Jane Kamensky, Kandice Hauf, Daniel Soyer, Louis Kampf, Saul Slapikoff, Tom Dublin, Kathryn Kish Sklar, David Engerman, Michael Staub, Rachel Rubin, and Erica Rand. For allowing me forums for my work, I thank Debbi Simonton at the *Women's History Magazine* and Maureen Flanagan at the *Journal of the Gilded Age and Progressive Era*. Conversations with Leo Nevas helped me map out the landscape of Westport, Connecticut. Annie Polland and Miriam Leberstein combed the Yiddish archives for Wald and Henry Street and then helped me theorize why she simply wasn't there.

This work benefited immeasurably from a semester spent writing and researching, afforded by a grant from the Babson Faculty Research Fund. A Koret Foundation Jewish Studies Grant helped make the illustrations possible and assisted in this book's publication. I also thank Chuck Grench at the University of North Carolina Press for shepherding this manuscript through to its completion.

Friendships have helped to make these years enjoyable. For their friendship, I thank Tobin Belzer, Ellen Tanowitz, Ann Trinh, Jenna Tranh, Missi Diamond, Meenakshi Khanna, Michelle Cheeseman, Julia Resnitsky, Ankit Jain, and the board of *Radical Teacher*. At Babson, Jeff Melnick has been a great friend and mentor and a reminder that juggling parenting, politics, teaching, and research is possible. I'm also grateful to Kevin Bruyneel for his warm friendship and calm advice.

I thank my family for their support and encouragement: Arthur and Eena Feld; Debra, Greg, and Rubin Harris; Marvin and Soni Feld; Sunny and Maier Fein; Matt, Lisa, and Corey Fein; and Joseph and Sylvia Fein. The memory of my mother, Rosalind Sperling Feld, never fails to inform all that I do.

My husband, Michael Fein, brings light to every one of my days. Our sons, Izzy and Nathan, know little of Wald, but their beauty, sweetness, and grudging acceptance of "Mommy's work" bring me great happiness. I have traveled far from my own hometown, and they have shown me just how joyful life can be.

Lillian Wald

Claiming Lillian Wald

In 1965, in the middle of a decade of liberation movements that challenged and reinvigorated American democracy, the Committee for the Election of Lillian Wald to the Hall of Fame for Great Americans compiled a list of the many reasons she deserved to enter this pantheon. Wald's advocates praised her work in arousing "public opinion and legislative power to pass laws to assure pure milk, protection for immigrants, better housing, minimum wages, better sanitation and fire protection." They trumpeted her work in public health, her campaigns for world peace, and her leadership in the settlement house movement. But Adolf A. Berle, a member of President Franklin Roosevelt's cabinet and chair of Wald's committee, went further. He lamented that most knew her only as a "pioneer social worker," a "great nurse," or as someone who "spearheaded social reforms." "It is time," he proclaimed, for all to see her as a "great American."[1]

This compilation of Wald's accomplishments appeared in a biographical pamphlet that spanned Wald's lifetime, from 1867 to 1940, beginning with her Jewish background and her nurse's training. A section entitled "Lillian Wald's Genius" followed, in which committee members enumerated the achievements that had earned her a place among the Hall of Fame's great American patriots: in 1893, she founded a nursing-center-turned-settlement house—Henry Street Settlement—to serve the immigrant poor on New York's Lower East Side; she had moved from nursing and social work to advocating for the rights of women, workers, immigrants, and African Americans, for antimilitarism and global public health. Like Wald's two books, *The House on Henry Street* (1915) and *Windows on Henry Street* (1934), nearly every page of the pamphlet for her candidacy contained anecdotes, these authored by colleagues, politicians, and other public figures. The composition of the committee reflected Wald's long-standing ties to various communities in New York and around the nation: it included Robert F. Wagner, mayor of New York City; Frances Perkins of Cornell University, the first woman cabinet member as secretary of labor under President Franklin Roosevelt; descendants of the Warburg, Schiff, and Sulzberger clans, some of the most powerful Jewish families of New York, who had befriended Wald on the common ground of culture and class; and officials from medical and social work schools, law firms, and government agencies who had been Wald's professional colleagues and allies.[2] Neighbors from Wald's retirement town of Westport, Connecticut, also signed on to earn her the honor of election to the Hall of Fame.

All contributors to the pamphlet sang her praises using patriotic flourishes. All testified to her work toward universalism, her success in bridging the divides of class, ethnicity, race, and religion among people worldwide. The final tribute to Wald was reserved for American critic and author Van Wyck Brooks. Brooks called Wald "the fulfillment of the American promise," her house on Henry Street "the interpreter's house where Americans, new and old alike, learned the meaning of their country." Wald was a "glowing presence" who "vindicated America as the Land of Promise."[3]

Administrators of New York University founded the Hall of Fame, located on their campus (now Bronx Community College), in 1900, just as

Wald rose to public visibility, in order "to honor prominent Americans who have had a significant impact on this nation's history." Designed by the celebrated American architect Stanford White, the hall is, according to its Web site, "a unique and patriotic reminder that this country's phenomenal growth has been due to the vitality, ingenuity, and intellect" of its honorees.[4] Those first inducted included George Washington, Daniel Webster, and Nathaniel Hawthorne, with new inductees elected every five years. Berle echoed the sentiments of Brooks and others when he wrote that Wald deserved the honor because "her achievements in rich abundance form an everlasting heritage to this nation, and her friends feel that her fame and memory should now be forever enshrined."[5]

Over the years, electors of the hall—college presidents and academics, noted public officials, activists and intellectuals—had inducted only a few women, including Harriet Beecher Stowe and Susan B. Anthony (whose grave lies not far from Wald's in Wald's hometown of Rochester, New York). In 1965, though Wald was on the ballot, she lost out to her good friend Jane Addams, a Chicago social worker, settlement house founder, and Nobel Prize winner. Real estate mogul Aaron Rabinowitz, who spearheaded the campaign for Wald's election, believed that this was because "most of the electors [were] from the west . . . and thus knew Miss Addams's work better than Miss Wald's."[6]

Rabinowitz continued his campaign with renewed energy during the late 1960s. He had emigrated from Russia in 1884 and was a young client of Wald's Henry Street Settlement before he became the first commissioner of the state board of housing, a wealthy real estate developer, owner of Tudor City, and a pioneer in public housing, a cause close to Wald's heart. He had moved to Westport, Connecticut, near Wald's retirement home, to be close to one of his childhood heroes. To prepare for the 1970 election, Rabinowitz called again upon the members of the Committee for the Election of Lillian Wald. Together, under Rabinowitz's direction, they "bombarded the electors with special pamphlets and letters of recommendation." Rabinowitz would say only that the cost was "considerable." At age eighty-seven, he clearly felt strongly about honoring the woman who had done so much to help him achieve success.[7]

Wald was elected to the Hall of Fame in 1970. One of the first two Jews to enter the hall (alongside German-born physicist Albert Michelson), hers was the first ceremony to have a rabbi provide the invocation. Wald would no doubt have preferred a representative of the secular Ethical Culture Movement, such as her friend and settlement colleague John Lovejoy Elliott, who officiated at her private funeral. But she probably would have accepted the rabbi chosen: the senior rabbi of Congregation Emanu-El. This was the temple her benefactor and friend Jacob Schiff supported for many years. The musical selection for the event was more in keeping with Wald's universalist sentiments: Henry Street's community chorus sang a Hebrew melody and an African American spiritual.[8]

Wald's election to the Hall of Fame marks a fitting starting point to a biography that charts competing claims on Wald's work and analyzes Wald's life alongside how individuals have remembered it. The event remains significant not least because it reinforced the claims Berle and Brooks placed on her legacy. In this memorial, they claimed her work for social justice and social welfare as the truest expression of American ideals. Despite Wald's vast contributions, and despite her visibility in the Hall of Fame, she is today, as Berle lamented in 1965, less often positioned with other patriotic Americans than she is with more narrowly defined groups: as a footnote to other social work and settlement luminaries; as a friend of the more famous Jane Addams; or, most visibly in the last few decades, as a Jewish leader whose contributions were to Jewish America. The latter claim is made despite Wald's lifelong rejection of Jewish claims on her work and her insistence that her work served universal, rather than particularist, ideals.

In 1970, the popular press paid little attention to Wald's role as one of the first Jewish inductees. Indeed, the medal issued in her honor received more column space in the coin collectors' section of the *New York Times* than did Wald's election in its front news sections.[9] Over the next generation, however, the Jewish community broadly, and the field of American Jewish women's history in particular, began to "count" Wald's achievements, with increasing regularity, as Jewish ones. Locating her in these areas, one finds Wald "Jewhooed," to use a contemporary term, with startling frequency, her difference consistently accented. Borrowing the term "Jewhoo" from a Web site with the same name, Susan Glenn studies the history of Jewhooing, defining it as "the social mechanism for both private and public naming and claiming of Jews by other Jews." Though the term "Jewhooing" is a modern one, the practice it describes dates to the early twentieth century, as Jews integrated into mainstream America and used the acts of claiming and naming to reinforce "tribal membership" through "blood logic."[10]

The history of Jewhooing, of Jewish claiming, provides a telling and compelling portrait of American Jewish concerns across the past century. "It is one of the ironies of modern Jewish history," Glenn writes, "that concepts of tribalism based on blood and race have persisted not only in spite of but also because of the experience of assimilation." Motivating the many Jewish encyclopedias, who's whos, biographical dictionaries, and other scholarly and nonscholarly works compiled since 1900 is an agenda of "Jewish public relations": they serve as both "a method for promoting the acceptance of Jews and an ambivalent response to the absorption of Jews into mainstream American society." They codify Jewish contributions to that mainstream and inscribe the contributors as acting solely as Jews.[11]

The philosophy behind these works is that descent (biology, genetic background, blood) trumps consent (choice) in the matter of group belonging.[12] Examples of these claims on Wald—when she has been positioned among other Jews in biographies, dictionaries, encyclopedias, and databases, often with little mention of her ambivalence toward Jewish belonging—are many. She can be found in the Jewish Women's Archive, an online database; in *Jewish Women in America: An Historical Encyclopedia*; and in multiple surveys of American Jewish women's history.[13] In an interesting bookend to her induction into the Hall of Fame for Great Americans, Wald's most recent mention in any media was her spring 2007 induction into the Jewish-American Hall of Fame, a "Jewish museum in cyberspace." The hall began honoring individuals in 1969, highlighting the Jewishness of Americans from diverse areas of American life—from Louis Brandeis to Golda Meir to Arthur Miller. When the hall announced Wald's induction by labeling her a "Jewish Florence Nightingale," it pulled her into the prioritization of descent in ways that would have greatly disappointed her.[14]

Indeed, these claims ill suit Wald's legacy and are a source of great irony. Wald dedicated her life to the triumph of consent, to an ideal or vision wherein people would transcend all that divided them and bring about universal belonging. Her own description of this vision is inscribed on her statue in the Hall of Fame for Great Americans: "The Social Workers of Our Time Are Dreaming a Great Dream and Seeing a Great Vision of Democracy, a Real Brotherhood Among Men." Wald self-consciously borrowed these words, and this vision, from the Protestant Social Gospel, a movement among religious leaders that addressed the social problems accompanying rapid industrialization in England and the United States.

Jewish claims on Wald rarely mention her ambivalence toward Jewish affiliation, and so the majority of these sources fail to take her on her own, more complicated, terms. Indeed, Wald saw herself as so much a part of the Social Gospel movement, and so dedicated to this ideal of brotherhood, that she specifically rejected inclusion in a collection entitled *Jewish Women in America* on the ground that "the title suggests work done by women as Jews."[15] Even when invited to a Jewish gathering as a Jewish social worker who worked among Jewish clients, Wald took great pains to present herself as a universal representative of all of the urban poor. As these invitations were frequent, so too were Wald's insistent statements of her secularism— her lack of adherence to Jewish religious tradition, but also her solely informal connections to Jewish communal or religious organizations and institutions, her refusal to think of herself as doing "Jewish work."

Moreover, Wald even maintained deep apprehensions about her own image—possibly because her dark features made her look conspicuously "oriental," a fear linked with her ambivalence toward her Jewishness. Laudatory portraits of her, even in mainstream magazines, often took note of her dark complexion, such as when the *New Yorker* described her as the "dark-eyed girl in the nurse's uniform."[16] Wald went to great lengths to ensure that her photograph was reproduced as infrequently as possible.[17]

Works of U.S. women's history, like public and academic American Jewish histories, also neglect critical aspects of Wald's life. Whereas American Jewish historians tend to rely on some essential "Jewishness" as the primary means of interpreting Wald's life (ignoring her more complex ethno-religious identity), women's historians often sidestep the issue of Wald's ethnicity altogether. They approach her with agendas that limit their purview of her accomplishments and legacies, focusing only on isolated aspects of her life and career. First, they emphasize her education at the New York Hospital Training School for Nurses and its importance to the development of her gender consciousness and support for women's rights issues. Though there are no extant Wald writings from her two years of clinical training, these scholars note those years' importance as Wald's first immersion in a women's network.

Certainly, Wald was a firm believer in women's biological differences. She presented herself as a maternalist figure, interested in nursing as an extension of women's moral duty to heal, but also as a women's profession. Importantly, though, she viewed her work for all maternalist causes—for playgrounds, milk stations, and school nurses, to cite just three early examples—as growing naturally out of her commitment to international public health, a commitment that, for Wald, emanated from her lessons in gender and ethnicity. By examining aspects of Wald's worldview only as they line up with others' crucial contributions to women's political culture, and by failing to place Wald's worldview at the center of their analysis, women's historians have not yet presented a complete portrait of her motivations.[18] They pay little heed to the way gender and ethnicity intersected in important ways during Wald's formative years in Rochester, and they stop short of considering her subsequent exposure to, and work with, mixed-gender networks of Progressives and American Jews.

Another area where historians of women sometimes isolate issues of gender is in discussions of Wald's sexuality. In 1979, for example, Blanche Wiesen Cook first drew attention to Wald as a lesbian based on collections of intimate letters. These letters demonstrate the acceptance of loving women's relationships in early-twentieth-century women's activist networks and the importance of those relationships in enabling the Progressive political work of Wald and other women.[19] Claiming Wald as a lesbian sheds light on the sustaining, intimate, and very private relationships she had with other women and is part of a larger project of striving for a more complex and complete history by naming gay, lesbian, bisexual, and transgender individuals from the past. It also challenges us to think about the ways in which her assumed heterosexuality (and assumed sexual passivity) underscored her self-presentation as a maternalist figure, the "mother of Henry Street."[20]

Focusing on women's issues—maternalism, nursing, sexuality—highlights many of the important components of Wald's life. Isolating women's issues, however, also reveals the danger of seeing those components as far too self-contained. Thus, though women's history scholars raise important points about Wald that draw us closer to a fuller understanding of her biography, they too have distorted her life history by dismissing certain aspects of her life and legacy. While American Jewish community members and scholars misread Wald's Jewishness, women's historians ignore her

Jewishness in focusing exclusively on issues of gender, sexuality, and power. The story of Wald's election to the Hall of Fame for Great Americans alerts us to the importance of making sense of Lillian Wald on her own terms, and in the broadest context. Should her fame draw only from her achievements in and around New York? Her membership in a Progressive women's community? Her connection to Jane Addams? Should she be known as a Jewish Jane Addams or Florence Nightingale, or a protofeminist? This study takes the widest possible view in analyzing the moments in Wald's career, and the moments since her death, when Wald has been seen through those lenses. Precisely because she long faced (and continues to face) these competing claims, I describe Wald in these pages as an "ethnic Progressive." Though Wald herself may have bristled at the label, it alerts modern readers to the important ways in which Wald's ethnic background *and* the women's political culture she joined combined to shape her identity.

This study analyzes the tensions Wald encountered in her approach to ethnocultural and gender difference in her public career, as the landscape of modern identity politics was just emerging. Placing Wald at the center of historical analysis, it focuses on the history of Jewish claims on Wald as they intersect with her life and legacy, and on the history of social reform strategies grounded in gender difference. Beginning in Wald's hometown of Rochester, tracing the complicated ways she connected to American Jewry, this study ends with an analysis of why Wald is now most often found in books with titles such as *Rebels and Reformers: Biographies of Four Jewish Americans* (1976), *Daughters of the Covenant: Portraits of Six Jewish Women* (1983), *Her Works Praise Her: A History of Jewish Women in America from Colonial Times to the Present* (2002), and *In the Promised Land: Lives of Jewish Americans* (2005).[21] What emerges from this twenty-first-century study is a portrait of Wald at a fascinating crossroads, standing at the intersection of two historical conversations: one within American Jewish history, the other within American gender history.

Scholars see the Progressive Era as a defining historical moment, a time of tremendous experimentation with governmental power, social relationships, and economic arrangements. Wald's committed involvement in these areas of experimentation unquestionably qualifies her as a Progressive. She thought of herself as belonging to a global community of those working toward progress in public health, diplomacy, and peace. I label Wald an *ethnic* Progressive because she had to navigate claims of ethnic belonging in ways that other Progressives did not.

As chapter 1 makes clear, Wald's Progressivism was tied to the strivings of her family's immigrant beginnings. Though her later fellowship among women reformers and other Progressives, along with uptown Jewish patrons and friends, profoundly affected her worldview, Wald's lifelong approach to reform began with the universalism that was the zeitgeist of Rochester's nineteenth-century German Jewish community. That community's insistence on a future of universal belonging was a means for its members to make room for themselves in mainstream America on the terms set by mainstream America. They embraced the idea that Jewish difference could be undone to meet with acceptance, and that gender difference could be reinforced to match the perceived needs of the capitalist marketplace. This chapter begins with Wald's family history in Rochester and argues that Wald began her public career very comfortable with these ideas. Ethnic universalism and gender difference continued to be key components of her approach to reform, as the emphasis on collective acceptance prepared her for the Social Gospel's vision of a brotherhood of man. Wald gave voice to these ideas in frequent references to her philosophy of "mutuality," her notion of universal human interdependence.

Perceptions of Wald within her multiple communities reveal the ethnic aspect of her Progressivism, a topic introduced in chapter 2 and examined throughout the text. She had multiple audiences, portraying herself differently to—and being perceived differently by—American Jews within the organized American Jewish community, American Jews outside of the organized Jewish community, and non-Jews. With a focus on these audiences and on the tensions she encountered in her approaches to gender and cultural difference, chapter 2 moves from her Rochester beginnings to her first immersion in mixed-gender Jewish and non-Jewish networks in New York in 1891, as she founded what was first known as the Nurses' Settlement. This chapter locates Wald's approach to gender difference within her nursing and Progressive communities. It examines her stunning achievements in coalition building for maternalist causes and her rich exchanges over women's responsibilities and Jewish communal boundaries. As her institution grew to be Henry Street Settlement, Wald faced questions about what role religion—and the Jewish community—would play in her work.

To American Jews who, unlike Wald, claimed membership among the organized Jewish community in social, religious, political, or professional organizations, Wald was a maternal *Jewish* figure, a mediator between rich and poor Jews, one of their own. The Jewhooing, or Jewish claiming, of Wald by this community began formally in 1905, when she was first quietly mentioned in the *American Jewish Yearbook*. She relied on her belonging to Jewish networks in order to raise funds for—and awareness of—her work for immigrants (many of them Jewish) on the Lower East Side. Periodically, as this study shows, some American Jews demonstrated their investment in her settlement work by criticizing it as not Jewish enough.

Members of the Jewish community watched as Wald integrated herself completely into Social Gospel and Progressive reform networks—so completely that she joined international campaigns and associations without a mention of her Jewishness. The positive reception of Wald's universalist work afforded her access to these transatlantic communities. Chapter 3 charts the application of Wald's vision of a brotherhood of man to international reform efforts before World War I. The chapter ends in 1920, with Wald's personal conflict over how to memorialize one of the most prominent American Jews of that era, her close friend Jacob Schiff. Should his legacy be recorded as a specifically Jewish legacy? This conflict foreshadowed the many claims that individuals would make on Wald's own achievements, often remembered more as Jewish work than in the way she would have preferred: as internationalist work toward a universal vision. During the conservative years following World War I, Wald found herself in the center of anguishing debates over issues of special import to Jews and non-Jews alike as a result of these claims.

Wald's approaches to ethnocultural and gender difference led to her most difficult challenges: confrontations over the Equal Rights Amendment, Russian revolutionary politics, and Zionism, the subjects of chapter 4. Her time-tested methods and strategies proved less and less successful in the modern era, as her ideal vision of modernity did not come to pass. Instead of a continued reliance on gender difference, a new generation of feminists agitated for gender equality by emphasizing the sameness between the sexes; instead of cultural differences becoming obsolete, as she had hoped, they became more pronounced through cultural movements, identity politics, and ardent nationalism.

Nineteenth-century German Jewish communities like that of Wald's early years established the paradigm for American Jewish identity. It encompassed the "soft permissive Judaism associated with the Reform movement, its federated organizational structure, its energetic commercial activity and rapid professionalization, [and] its liberal political culture." The eastern European Jewish immigrants with whom Wald worked in the 1900s and 1910s "adopted the terms of that transaction, giving it their own far more secular twist." (Reform Judaism played the important role for German Jews in the nineteenth century, for example, that Zionism would play for Jews from eastern Europe in the twentieth.)[22] Many members of the American Jewish community in the early twentieth century maintained optimism that full acceptance in America was possible, even inevitable.

In the 1930s, however, the global rise of anti-Semitism made many American Jews skeptical that this more secular formula could ensure the survival of Judaism. The Nazi Holocaust in Europe made survival itself a top priority, and American Jews subsequently began to change the terms of mainstream Jewish identity. As the brutalities of the twentieth century slowly eclipsed Wald's universalist approach, so too were Jewish identities like hers—those based on secularism, informal belonging, and a commitment to universalism—gradually marginalized. For many American Jews, Jewish belonging grew to be synonymous with formal affiliation and, in time, an embrace of Zionism.

The final chapter of Wald's life, after her retirement in 1933, offered her a chance to reflect on her life and legacy in the new era. Though she never fully recovered from an operation in 1932, Wald was exhilarated by the possibilities for state social welfare put forward by President Franklin D. Roosevelt. Chapter 5 examines Wald's thoughts on the New Deal, along with her recollections of her neighborhood and international reform work. In words and symbols, she carefully laid out her own hopes for her legacy. This chapter measures her hopes up against the commemorations that began after her retirement and then followed her death and public memorial service in 1940.

Studying Wald's place within the ethnic landscape of the early twentieth century offers us a fascinating perspective on that era, and studying her place in the modern ethnic landscape offers us a valuable perspective on our own. The conclusion surveys scholarly and popular debates that have invoked and analyzed Wald's life in the last seventy years. It follows the rhythm of interest in Wald, asking why she's more often studied in some eras than others, and from some vantage points and not others. Wald was not defined solely by her gender or her Jewishness, and yet nearly every past study privileges one at the expense of the other. This biography corrects the imbalance by examining how she contended with both in compelling ways throughout her lifetime.

This work is, ultimately, a biography of Lillian D. Wald that traces her public life while measuring how her accomplishments have been remembered. Two biographies precede this one. *Lillian Wald: Neighbor and Crusader* was written by Wald's close friend and neighbor in Westport, journalist Robert L. Duffus, in 1938. Based on interviews with Wald, along with ample research, Duffus offers a wealth of information in his hagiography, but it is not an analytic study. In *Always a Sister: The Feminism of Lillian D. Wald*, Doris Groshen Daniels carefully examines the life of Wald through the lens of feminism, documenting Wald's contributions to the advancement of gender equality. Both of these texts dismiss Wald's Jewishness as unimportant to her worldview and her life work; indeed, neither analyzes Wald's place on the ethnic landscape, save to place her among those with more gentle approaches to bringing about the assimilation of the immigrants who entered her Henry Street Settlement.[23]

This biography traverses new territory in its examination of Wald. Its chapters document Wald's public life and legacy to analyze the fluid and contested nature of the ethnic order, from her time to our own. They capture as well the changing views of women's difference that marked crucial shifts in strategies for attaining gender equality. I analyze, for the first time, how Wald's approach to woman's distinct nature and her personal experience with assimilationist strivings proved essential ingredients to her universalist worldview.

This study also makes clear the profound impact of Wald's lifelong struggles with particularist communities, specifically her struggles with members of the Jewish community who claimed her with little regard to her own sense of Jewishness. Their claims were in some ways reinforced by her maternalist presentation, in other ways buffered by them: as a Jewish woman, modern arrangements made her responsible for the Jewishness of her "house," but she also accented her maternalism to deflect criticisms of her as not being Jewish enough. These crucial negotiations made her universalist work, her multiple allegiances and wide access to diverse networks, possible. Indeed, these negotiations were the foundation to her work as an interpreter among diverse groups.

Just as many American Jews made unfounded assumptions about Wald's Jewish identity, so too did secular Jews and non-Jews fail to see the significance of her informal connections to uptown Jews and Yiddish intellectuals. The narrative of Mamie Pinzer, a contemporary of Wald's, serves as one example. A secular, assimilated Polish Jew and former prostitute who dedicated herself to aiding other women prostitutes, Pinzer respected Wald's work for years before she sought out Wald's guidance in person. "I was surprised to learn that Miss Wald was a Jewess," she wrote, "though now that I think of it, I should have guessed it, as her name is quite 'Yiddish.' . . . I knew families by that name when I was a child and lived among the Jews."[24]

Just as Pinzer, a distant colleague, was surprised that Wald was Jewish, many of Wald's close colleagues were surprised by the *ways* in which she was Jewish. Writer, social worker, and non-Jewish reformer Bruno Lasker, Wald's colleague at Henry Street in the 1910s and 1920s, offered a fascinating portrait of her in an offhand remark in his oral history. "By the way," he began,

> I remember one night going home from this Central Park affair at two o'clock in the morning with Miss Wald. We always had to see that the children and young people were properly taken care of and went home, you know. Well, on the way back, Miss Wald said, "Let's stop at such-and-such a place on Second Avenue." That was the headquarters of the Jewish press after midnight, and everyone knew her and crowded around her. It was a very entertaining and an interesting side-light on a side of her activity that I did not know anything about. I did not know she was interesting herself in Jewish affairs as such, or that the Jewish educators were particularly interested in her, but it appeared that they were very enthusiastic about her and about what she had done for the East Side.[25]

Lasker probably referred to the Café Royale, one of the centers for Yiddish intellectuals.[26] Though Lasker knew that Wald was Jewish, he had not expected her close relations with the Yiddish intelligentsia. He expected that the distance she kept from formal Jewish affiliation would be reflected in her equal distance from leaders in the Yiddish community, many of whom extended their political critiques of charity to the work of settlements.

As these quotations suggest, and as this biography confirms, Wald was not clearly and publicly identified with the organized Jewish community in the eyes of mainstream America. But neither was her Jewish identity of no significance. She expressed her Jewishness through friendship, culture, and class, through professional interests and expertise. Her deep connection to Jacob Schiff and his family, her collegiality with Yiddish intellectuals, her access to Jewish organizations to advance her work for the Jewish poor: these were crucial, meaningful parts of her world, and they were the sum total of the Jewish identity she constructed amid her society. But, as she emphasized consistently throughout her career, she saw all of these connections as bound up in her universalist work toward a brotherhood of man. Unlike members of the organized Jewish community, unlike Schiff, she did not think of herself as acting *as* a Jew, nor *for* the welfare of Jews, in her work.

Wald was in many ways like philosopher Isaac Deutscher, a self-described "non-Jewish Jew" who had "gone beyond Jewry." Both considered themselves internationalists, eschewing divisive uses of nationalism; both maintained a dislike for organized religion. While acknowledging that there was no single Jewish identity, in his book *The Non-Jewish Jew* (1968) Deutscher embraced "the moral and political heritage that the genius of the Jews who have gone beyond Jewry has left us—the message of universal human emancipation."[27] Never denying her Jewishness, Wald clearly did not see universalism as an outgrowth of Jewish particularism. Her journey to universalism originated with the assimilationist energy of Rochester and the reform energy of New York City.[28] Still, her universalism contained this same message of human emancipation.

Modern realities interrupted Wald's pursuit of universalism: world events and new generations' quests for firmer ethnic boundaries. Beginning in the 1920s, mainstream Jewish communities' desires for identification with Jewish particularism, religious observance, nationalism, and formal affiliation competed against the ideals of universalism. In the 1930s and 1940s, the failure of Jewish liberalism and universalism in Europe often meant the marginalization of these ideals in the United States.

Werner Sollers writes that "somebody's claim to universalism may easily become somebody else's restriction to particularism, as long as an ideal is identified not with total human striving but with a place on the map or a secular interest."[29] The American Jewish community once accepted universalism as within the spectrum of approaches to Jewish expression. In these early years, many Jews in the organized Jewish community continued to claim Wald's universalism as Jewish (despite occasional criticisms that she should demonstrate a clearer commitment to Jewish religiosity). But by the end of Wald's life, they saw it as too weak an expression of Jewishness; indeed, they saw it as an obstruction to their own reinvigorated, more "Jewish" expressions. Stuart Svonkin and Michael Staub record this shift "from liberal universalism to ethno-religious self-assertion" as beginning in the 1950s and 1960s. Susan Glenn links it to the "status anxiety" that emerged from the horrors of World War II.[30] This biography locates early signs of the shift throughout Wald's career, with its strongest impetus during and after World War II, as reflected in the claims on Wald's life by the Jewish community. Predictably, these claims appear most often in times of group anxiety, when American Jews have faced outside hostility, intolerance, and racism.

The conclusion to this study asks why these claims have long outlived such intolerance. Today, those who claim Wald for the Jewish community, who position her solely among other Jews with no regard for her own self-presentation, tend to reduce Jewishness to blood logic, religious tradition, nationalism, or a specific vision of social justice grounded in religious Judaism.[31] They suggest that Jewishness is "timeless," collapsing both time and space to demonstrate that all expressions of Jewish identity, past and present, share a core, common essence. They ignore the varied and diverse expressions of Jewishness throughout history: through formal affiliation and religiosity as well as through informal connections and ambivalent feelings about belonging.

In claiming Wald and others with no regard to complicated notions of Jewishness—in simplistically "counting" her in databases, encyclopedias, dictionaries, and other sources—American Jewish history scholars and community members are more true to their ethnic projects than to the historical record. Their projects share an agenda in their claims on Wald, one now quite separate from the early and mid-twentieth century's need for Jewish "public relations" to non-Jewish America. Their claims serve instead as assertions of a distinct position in today's intra-Jewish contests over what constitutes authentic Jewish identity. They endorse an essentialist notion that reinvigorates the boundaries of American Jewishness, ignoring the (often painful) historical and contemporary contests over what constitutes Jewish identity. To claim Wald and others is to incorporate forerunners into a position of sweeping modern consensus on Jewishness—when Jews today remain far from consensus.

American Jewish women's historians, in particular, face the challenge of deconstructing this idea of a consensus on American Jewish identity. When the recent 350th anniversary of Jewish life in America gave cause to assess this subfield, scholars rightly celebrated the proliferation of Jewish historical work that now incorporates gender and sexuality as central to its analysis. In one survey, Pamela S. Nadell notes that the "diversity of America's Jewish women makes it difficult to construct a single, overarching narrative." She records the ways in which Jewish women do, and do not, fit into paradigms of American women's history. She dedicates attention to the linguistic turn in history by noting that even the term "woman" needs to be examined through the lens of gender's construction across time and space. American Jewish women's history will soon build, too, on the diversity of approaches to the category of "Jewish" in monographs, encyclopedias, databases, and dictionaries, for only then will the full complexity of American Jewish women's life narratives begin to be clear.[32]

This biography's approach to Wald's Jewishness is a product of its historical moment, when the multidisciplinary field of Jewish studies is wrestling with gender, race, class, sexuality, ethnicity, and religion in new and complex ways. The scholars working in this field are slowly destabilizing and complicating our understanding of what "Jewish" has meant to historical subjects on their own terms. At the turn of the twenty-first century, this scholarship uses the insights of cultural, Jewish, and American studies to open up crucial questions about identity and belonging. It challenges the notion of a consensus on what constitutes authentic Jewishness, offering models that compete with the ethnic projects of much of American Jewish history.[33]

This work, then, joins the recent, lively conversation among public intellectuals and scholars of all disciplines about what constitutes Jewish identity and Jewish work. It investigates one of the "non-Jewish Jews" of the last century, relying especially on pathbreaking studies of gender and Jewish assimilation that first began to analyze intra-Jewish contests over the meanings of Jewishness.[34] It presents the world in which Wald relied on Jewish networks while self-identifying primarily as a maternalist Social Gospel reformer, and it explains what factors made that identification possible.

This biography stands, too, on recent developments in American women's history, even as it offers a corrective to the field for its singular focus on certain aspects of Wald's life. The first to use gender as a salient category of analysis, scholars in women's history then began to investigate the intersections of gender with race, class, and sexuality.[35] Importantly, American Jewish women's historians contribute insights into how American women's lives are inflected by their ethnic and religious identities as well. This volume relies on those insights as it offers a biographical portrait of a political activist, and thus a window onto the gendered political landscape of the last century.[36] It insists, then, on an ethnic and gender analysis, working from two mutually constituted categories to present Wald's public life.

In building on developments in the fields of Jewish and women's history, and in presenting Wald's public life in a narrative, *Lillian Wald: A Biography* is, of course, a product of its time. In our biography-saturated twenty-first-century American culture, this historical biography demonstrates what an exceptional individual Wald was, even as it also makes clear why Wald's Jewish and gender identities—seen in their full complexity—remain critical to understanding her life and times.[37] It records Wald's successes and failures sympathetically, for this biographer finds Wald's goals of peace and progress laudable in our contemporary world. Finally, then, this volume situates itself in today's currents, offering conclusions as to what Wald's public life has still to offer us.

Lillian Wald: A Biography repairs the legacy of Wald, fractured across disciplines that focus exclusively on her contributions to women's rights and to Jewish America. It travels from Wald's espousal of professional nursing as linked to "that century-cherished prerogative of women [to heal]" to debates over the Equal Rights Amendment, and from Wald's refusal to be in a book about Jewish women's work to an obituary that memorialized her as a "Great Jewish Social Worker" who "gave up wealth to serve all groups."[38] It follows her legacy through the Hall of Fame for Great Americans and into the pantheon of "great Jewish women" (the title of a book that included a portrait of Wald, published in 1994). Wald held in balance commitments to communities of particularist and universalist worldviews. This biography of Wald holds in balance a commitment to present Wald's words alongside a contemporary analysis of why her words—and the contests over them—are so important.

Wald's Hometown Lessons

The late 1870s were a time of national upheaval, when interconnected struggles over the boundaries of class, race, and ethnicity were increasingly fought in public spaces. Massive strikes shook the railroad industry, and the struggle for control over workers' lives moved into the streets. Radical Reconstruction ended in the former Confederacy, and Jim Crow legislation reinforced the savage inequality of the color line. Ethnic "whites"— among them, American Jews—negotiated their racial belonging in this setting, striving for the privileges of belonging in white America.

Lillian D. Wald and other Progressive reformers, including Jane Addams and Florence Kelley, were born in the midst of these struggles. As adults, they emerged as active participants, inspired and motivated by visions of universalism and unity as their efforts pushed the boundaries of women's public roles. But unlike her colleagues Addams and Kelley, who arrived at universalist visions through Protestantism, educational reform, and political legacies, Wald's vision first emerged through her family's experience with overcoming ethnic difference. As German Jewish immigrants in Rochester, New York, in these years, the Wald family strove to integrate themselves into the town's white elite: her father and uncles by way of economic success in the marketplace and her mother and aunts through public charity work. Their assimilation had distinctly gendered economic components, and they offered important models of how to contend with cultural, class, and gender difference.

Their social and economic strivings and their modeling of an approach to difference comprised Wald's hometown lessons. These lessons grounded what she referred to as her universalist vision of "mutuality," the idea that "no one class of people can be independent of the other."[1] Though rooted in the particular atmosphere of Rochester's German Jewish community, these lessons prepared her to adopt the Protestant quest for universal brotherhood, the Social Gospel's motivating vision, which she did while working among her Progressive allies in Manhattan.[2] This quest became the foundation of her lifelong reform efforts.

Wald viewed the turn-of-the-twentieth-century wave of immigrants, the individuals she worked with at her Henry Street Settlement beginning in 1893, through the lens of her own family's immigration and assimilation experience. She consistently downplayed differences between people, highlighting the cultural adjustments that would aid the integration of all newcomers into a modern, pluralist landscape. These same experiences informed her self-presentation. Even as she immersed herself in Manhattan's German Jewish subculture, she downplayed her own ethnic difference and belonging among Jews.

Wald's universalism—and the expertise that grew out of her life work—was built upon the reification of another category of difference: gender. She routinely emphasized the natural difference women possessed, and so relied on a traditional concept of gender; yet she simultaneously used that concept to expand the scope of activities and professional roles within women's realms of expertise. Thus, all of Wald's professional work (as a public health nurse, a settlement house founder, a member of numerous state commissions, and an international crusader for peace and public health) emerged from a commitment to women's "domestic" authority. Her faith in static concepts of womanhood proved to be an essential corollary to her belief that ethnic differences could be diminished.

In contrast to the masculine cultural values of unforgiving competitiveness she saw at work first in Rochester's marketplace, Wald came through her nurse's training and Progressive alliances to endorse components of a more liberal worldview: a liberal assimilationism, a more restrained version of capitalism, indeed a pro-labor humanitarianism. Wald's universalism drew from the social currents of nineteenth-century German Jewish assimilation in America, its constructions of difference with regard to gender, class, and culture. These lessons served her well in the community of urban Progressive women and men reformers she met in New York City, who profoundly shaped her life work. Among them, she balanced belonging to a particularist group with her striving for a universalist vision.

It was these reformers—especially the women of the "female dominion of American reform"[3]—who helped her to reinterpret her hometown lessons. They presented her with a new understanding of poverty, one that emphasized the active role that she and other women could play in shaping modern social, political, and economic arrangements. She took her hometown lessons far from their particularist moorings, expanding her worldview and the inclusiveness of her universalist philosophy. Wald played an important part in the negotiations over modern boundaries of class, race, and ethnicity. Her hometown lessons challenge our conventional understanding of the roots of Progressive-era reform; they also demonstrate the interconnectedness of gender, race, and ethnicity in American nineteenth- and twentieth-century assimilation.

Rochester's German Jewish Community

Any story of Wald's Rochester lessons must begin with her parents and grandparents, who arrived from Europe with their own hometown lessons. Wald's ancestors were rabbis, scholars, merchants, and professionals, and some were well integrated into the networks of Europe's social elite. When her grandparents and parents, the Schwarzes and the Walds, emigrated from Germany and Poland around the time of the revolutions of 1848, they brought with them beliefs and assumptions shaped by the debates surrounding Jewish emancipation that had repeatedly erupted in Germany in the 1830s and 1840s.

The liberalism endorsed by German pro-emancipationists had two sides: while its rhetoric of liberty, equality, and rights could be empowering for the disadvantaged, its working vision of the universal rights-bearing individual was a white, male Christian. Those who stood outside of this category struggled to be accepted as equals.[4] Like other western European Jews, German Jews formed their own "variant of bourgeois existence," emphasizing universalism in their attempts at assimilation and acceptance.[5] They transformed their subculture—their religious worship, their lifestyles—to mimic the Protestant norm. Because social pressures continued to be channeled into anti-Semitism, theirs was, ultimately, a hopeless attempt to win acceptance and achieve civic integration. In this environment, their subculture, with its conspicuous emphasis on the universal, came to sustain their own group particularism.[6] Unlike most German Jews, however, some members of Wald's family did indeed leave behind their membership in this particularist group and join the Christian majority. Her mother's brother, for one, converted to Christianity to marry.[7]

When Wald's family arrived in the United States, American Jews comprised a minority reviled by the majority, facing exclusion and prejudice. Though legally free, they encountered malicious stereotypes and persecution;[8] social services to Jews were often accompanied by Christian missionary efforts. Even within this turmoil, though, as the social arrangements of the modern United States emerged, American Jews hoped to find prosperity and success on their own terms. In 1878, Lillian Wald and her family moved from her birthplace of Ohio to Rochester, New York, in search of this success.

Rochester was a bustling industrial city with a growing and powerful middle class. Amid the renegotiation of color and class lines, it held for elite Jews like the Walds the promise of integration into the white elite. There was, too, a liberal spirit to the city, the origins of which lay in the Christian religious revivalism that swept through it in the eighteenth and nineteenth centuries. These revivals left in their wake liberal reform campaigns for charity, abolitionism, women's rights, temperance, and other causes, with women as central figures in each campaign.[9]

Rochester was the ideal setting for a group striving to make culture (and not biology) emblematic of their racial belonging. Behavior in religious and household settings—both the provinces of women—set the parameters for middle-class white Americanism. In this period of what Matthew Frye Jacobson calls their "probationary whiteness," German Jews encountered an American society increasingly defined in the scientific terminology of race.[10] Their strivings toward the social perception of whiteness, toward assimilation and acceptance, proved urgent and timely. While they formed their own subculture as a response to anti-Semitic exclusion and as an assertion of identification, they simultaneously followed the patterns they had set in nineteenth-century Germany, especially in the movement of Reform Judaism: they mimicked the culture of the Protestant elite. In the United States, though, these assertions held additional import: as the color lines hardened, American Jews' integration meant that they fell within the parameters of accepted whiteness.

The Wald family "were mellowed," writes Robert Duffus, Wald's friend and first biographer, who interviewed her about her life; they were "cosmopolitan without being sophisticated, seasoned in more than one national culture over and above their Hebraic substratum."[11] This family legacy, this transcendence "above their Hebraic substratum," fit well within the liberal zeitgeist of Rochester, New York. Its liberalism, its version of the Americanism that would result in the integration of nonnative whites, was also based on the ideal of white Christianity. Even as their German Jewish subculture reinforced some level of American German Jewish group identity, the men and women of Wald's family advocated for the eradication of boundaries around the Jewish community, its assimilation into the Protestant mainstream. In Werner Sollers's terms, they endorsed consent over descent, culture over biological concepts of racial Jewishness, as they embraced a liberal Americanism based on a white Christian norm.[12]

While balancing the particularism of this subculture against the universalist appeal of white Protestant Americanism was a personal, individualized effort, two institutions highlight the encounters of German Jews with Rochester's universalist spirit. The institution that most clearly mirrored this tension was Temple B'rith Kodesh, to which some members of the Wald family belonged.[13] It was, first, a place for worship. It also served both as a gathering and networking center within the boundaries of the German Jewish community and as an active contributor to the tearing down of those boundaries. Indeed, Temple B'rith Kodesh, founded in 1848, was a focal point in the rapidly liberalizing movement of Reform Judaism, which sought to acclimate Judaism to the Enlightenment and, especially in the United States, to mainstream Protestantism.

B'rith Kodesh's universalism was a means to those ends. Its members began the decade of the 1870s with an unprecedented invitation to a Unitarian minister to speak from their pulpit. Soon after, the temple became the first synagogue in the nation to permanently adopt English instead of Hebrew as its language of ritual.[14] In 1876, at the dedication of the temple's new building on St. Paul Street, the mayor, temple members, and others gathered to hear the esteemed Reform rabbi Dr. Max Landsberg offer his dedication. Trained in Germany, Landsberg was a radical assimilationist, a leader in the Reform movement, and one of a few rabbis in that era to officiate at marriages between Jews and non-Jews.[15]

Landsberg's dedication speech was "very liberal in tone," as reported by the *Rochester Daily Union Advertiser*. The report noted that the rabbi's sermon made clear that he was "not . . . in sympathy with those who would claim for themselves the exclusive care of the Almighty." He spoke of the temple's "new mission": "It is to dispel prejudice; non-Jewish brethren can come there and hear us pray and be surprised how little difference there is between them."[16] Landsberg's goal, like many in the German-founded Reform movement, was to adjust Jews to their American setting by removing Judaism's "orientalisms."[17] Only when American Jews abandoned traditional Jewish rituals could they fulfill their mission and achieve full acceptance and integration. In keeping with this ideal of the universal, of acculturating and assimilating, of consent over descent, the weekly newspaper the *Jewish Tidings* (called "the glorified house organ" for B'rith Kodesh) had as its masthead slogan "There is no Jewish race."[18]

The temple's prestigious German Jewish men's Eureka Club was the second institution that highlighted particularist and universalist tensions. Wald's uncles, her mother's brothers, were club members. They benefited from the spirit of the city and its German Jewish institutions. Leaders within the German Jewish community, they earned city leaders' respect in their successful business dealings.[19] The club was called "one of the most wealthy and powerful social organizations in the United States" by the local (non-Jewish) press. When members refurbished the club space, the site of meetings, weddings, and social gatherings, the mainstream non-Jewish press took note. The exhaustive descriptions of the new rooms highlighted both the reproduction of upper-class mores and the downplaying of Jewish difference. The membership's conspicuous consumption was evident, as consumerism provided an entrée into the American middle class: "expense was not considered" in the selections of "gorgeous furniture, satin curtains, steel engravings . . . resplendent crystal chandeliers and large and dazzling mirrors." The rooms provided ample space so that "members may bring their wives and pass their leisure hours in harmless amusement." The newspaper made no mention of the club's Jewish membership save for its celebration of "the annual Purim masquerade," the celebration of a Jewish holiday that was to be "one of the social events of the season."[20] What the members hoped to see in their "dazzling mirrors" were elite Americans, and that was precisely what they hoped outsiders would see as well.

The assimilationist energy of the club and the temple, the complicated balancing act of crafting a Jewish subculture while attempting to integrate Jews into the mainstream Protestant white elite: this energy permeated the city's wealthy Jewish community. In religious worship and social recreation, the community worked toward gradual inclusion and acceptance. Its members' strivings made them major contributors to the emergence of modern ethnic and racial arrangements. In these strivings, in their encounters with American culture, nineteenth-century German Jewish immigrants created the synthesis that set the foundation of twentieth-century American Jewish life.[21]

For most of these immigrants, their encounters with the United States stopped short of full integration, drawing the line at so-called intermarriage, or Christian worship. For them, "intermarriage" signified a rejection of all aspects of Jewish communal or individual identity, the complete triumph of consent over descent, which was unwelcome and unwanted. Accepting and even welcoming intermarriage, B'rith Kodesh and the Wald family, then, stood at the far end of the spectrum of belonging. As in Germany, Wald's family left their racial category of Jewishness behind, trafficking with relative ease in elite America. The terms of their synthesis, the optimism and striving that drove it, were crucial to the person Lillian Wald became. When the terms shifted midway through the twentieth century, she was at a loss to make sense of the new definitions of belonging.

Assimilation: Jewish Manhood and Womanhood

Importantly, the success of universalism and assimilation for German Jews in the United States at the turn of the last century was contingent on the fact that racial categories *and* class lines were both in flux. So while some in Wald's parents' cohort found their way into the white, Protestant mainstream society, that membership rested solidly on their distinctly gendered economic roles, on a specific brand of Americanism. Masculine American men and feminine American women had to fulfill specific roles in the emerging modern economy. Wald's aunts and uncles were members of the highly visible minority of these German Jewish immigrants who achieved economic success in the United States and sought to join the ranks of the native-born American upper classes. Their lifestyles, gender roles, habits of work, domestic arrangements, and even recreational patterns soon mimicked those of the native-born American elite.[22]

In Rochester, the success in clothing manufacturing that allowed German Jews the conspicuous consumption of the native-born elite also gave them key roles in the emerging modern marketplace. The men in Wald's family took strong antilabor stands in the industry strikes of the 1890s, locking out workers who attempted to unionize. Many of these workers were eastern European Jews, recent immigrants whose class and religious practices were at odds with the Wald family's cohort.

These actions secured the Wald men's claims to Americanism *and* American masculinity, founded on notions of individualism and competition that were crucial to Protestantism and industrial capitalism. As Jews' racial difference was historically pathologized and seen as ill suited to the demands of modern society, Jewish masculinity was the site of often violent contests over Jewish acceptance and integration.[23] European anti-Semitic portraits cast Jewish men as weak, indecisive, crass, and overly conspicuous. In the United States, one brand of Jewish masculinity became linked to class antagonism, preventing cross-class identification with newer, working-class Jewish immigrants. The outcomes of these struggles profoundly shaped assimilationist trends among nineteenth-century German American Jews.

The women in Wald's family also relied on models derived from modern economic and social currents. According to bourgeois culture, Jewish observance, now largely privatized and in women's household domain, became their responsibility. They were to make the home, and themselves, gentle buffers from market forces. Their natural difference meant that they were to be moral and generous, a delicate counterpoint to masculine hardness. In extending those sensibilities beyond the home, they carved out new roles for themselves as voluntarist reformers in the emerging social order.[24] Wald's aunts' Jewish charity work was their entrée into public society. Their feminine roles spoke to a more collectivist ideal than that of the men in the marketplace.

Male and female roles were, of course, interdependent. Wald's notion of what was possible for a Jewish woman grew out of her understanding of what was possible for Jewish men. Her extended family, important participants in Rochester's class conflicts and public charities, were her earliest models. In her first years in the city, battle lines were being drawn in the struggle for control over industries, and these struggles loomed large within the city's landscape.

The German Jewish community paid great attention. The *Tidings*, for one, reported increasing tensions in the city's garment industry because these struggles were an intra-Jewish affair between eastern European Jewish immigrant garment workers and German Jewish management. Wald's uncles were among those who managed garment firms.

As Lillian Wald arrived in Rochester, her uncles and other German Jews were investing huge amounts of capital into the mechanization of their successful clothing firms. They strove to meet the nation's growing appetite for inexpensive, ready-made clothing. The men and women who filled the factories, including immigrant Jews from eastern Europe, began to organize in order to protest their poor wages, unsafe working conditions, and lack of control over their work. This was the intracommunal tension between "uptown" German Jews and "downtown" eastern European Jews, named for their places of residence in Manhattan in a pattern reproduced in other cities like Rochester. This tension related to class and to industrial arrangements, as well as to the color line.[25] The new immigrants were largely poor, often more ritually observant, and decidedly "other" to the German assimilationist cohort.

Certainly, these immigrants threatened the status of the German Jews, their gradual integration into the white elite, their thriving and seemingly well-respected subculture. The positions taken by Wald's uncles Nathan

Levi, Morris Schwarz, and Henry Schwarz, and by the larger German Jewish community (including the *Tidings* readership and Rabbi Landsberg), were clear indications of their embrace of a decidedly middle-class, white Protestant Americanism. The certainty of their own insider elite white status rested on the outsider status of their working-class laborers.

The new immigrants became laborers, then, as American industrial relations were adjusting to mechanization and Taylorism, to working-class immigrant values and traditions, and to labor organization. Asserting the mutualism of their working-class community, and in response to degrading conditions, laborers in Rochester's garment industry began to listen to the Knights of Labor organizers who visited their shops.[26] The Knights envisioned a "workingmen's democracy" in which an inclusive labor movement would "champion and defend the public good within a regulated marketplace economy."[27] In 1881, three years after the Wald family had settled in town, several garment workers formed a unit of the Knights and called an unsuccessful strike.

One year later, German Jewish manufacturers, including Wald's uncles Morris and Henry Schwarz, founded a manufacturing organization called the Clothiers' Association. Members claimed the founding was in order to standardize their procedures.[28] But they followed the example of industry leaders across the United States who employed significant resources to engage in bitter battles against labor without much fear of state intervention. Although continued organizing attempts among laborers failed, the Knights took credit for the association's approval of the nine-hour day and pay increases for skilled factory workers.[29]

Soon after, the Knights succeeded in building the foundation of the first nationwide labor movement. Membership, strikes, and publicity reached a peak in the mid-1880s, as editorials expressed fears that the great "social question" of arrangements in capital and labor would lead to revolution.[30] In Rochester, after the Knights successfully organized garment workers, manufacturers responded by replacing the Clothiers' Association with the more hard-line Clothiers' Exchange. When Wald's uncle Henry Schwarz was asked if the Exchange "was intended to precipitate any conflict between the manufacturers and their employees," he replied: "The Exchange was not formed for anything but to promote harmony between employers and employees. We have nothing against the Union, and recognize its benefit. We simply intend to promote our own interests, and consequently the interests of our employees."[31]

Tensions boiled over, however, when union officials refused to permit the overtime hours that the manufacturers felt they needed—and were willing to pay for. Still insisting that they were not entirely "opposed to organized labor," Exchange members locked out union laborers.[32] While all of the local trade organizations initially supported the organized garment workers, alleged wrongdoing on the part of Knights leaders and Clothiers' Exchange members resulted in indictments on both sides.[33]

The Haymarket bombing in May 1886 had already contributed to a fierce antiunion sentiment that gradually undermined the Knights' growth nationwide. The Rochester indictments four years later further diminished local union support. Ultimately, however, it was extreme pressure from the manufacturers—including another lockout in 1893—that severed the ties between workers and the Knights of Labor.[34]

As the mainstream presses across the country labeled the unionists "un-American," editorials in Rochester's *Jewish Tidings* extended that argument to their own audience demographic. They heralded the Americanism of the Jewish managers for crushing the organizing attempts of the Jewish workers. Just as the existence of a Jewish race was denied in their masthead, cross-class "racial" sympathy for the workers was enthusiastically discouraged. The workers' radicalism was, in fact, defined as antithetical to the masculinity of the owners. Gender and economic roles were seen as mutually reinforcing: the middle-class masculine individualism of the owners was defined in contrast to the feminine mutualism of the workers' organizing efforts. Only the charity of women's organizational work bridged the two populations.

In 1891, the *Jewish Tidings* noted that the clothing manufacturers had in the past been "led around by the nose by their employees." But now, they boasted, "Now they act like men!" Using the language of the conventionally female role, the editors claimed that the manufacturers had been emasculated as "the subject of ridicule throughout the country on account of their humble submissions to the demands of irresponsible blackmailers." Management's success in crushing labor's organization marked its members' success in achieving white middle-class masculinity, and the *Tidings* congratulated the men on "their firmness and courage."[35] Management's newfound power over workers was the key to this masculinity. The editors disparaged the assimilationist potential of the workers, however, asking only, "Is there any manhood in the[se] Jews?"[36]

While Wald's uncles served as models of masculine individualism, competitive capitalism, and assimilation, her father remains largely absent from her life story. Marcus (Max) Wald sold optical goods, an industry pioneered in the 1870s by Rochester's own John Jacob Bausch and Henry Lomb. That he was a traveling salesman, moving the family from Ohio to Rochester and then traveling for business, suggests his absence. It also suggests that he lacked the very visible sort of success possessed by his brothers-in-law. His death in 1891 left only those men as Wald's family patriarchs.

The wives of these businessmen, Wald's aunts, followed the examples of their Christian counterparts. They took leadership positions in philanthropies—the Ladies' Aid Society and the Jewish Orphan Asylum—as their first foray into the public realm, embodying a gentler alternative to the increasingly impersonal and mechanized world of industrial and competitive capitalism.[37] While such work offered newfound public power for Jewish and non-Jewish women, it did not challenge this new world. Instead, the women's adoption of social roles as charity workers with Rochester's poor softened the roughest edges of the new economic arrangements. It also tapped into the predominant current in the uptown/downtown relationship, as their charity work aimed to Americanize the downtowners: they hoped to assimilate the immigrants rapidly, using themselves as models. Wald's aunts' public charity work—in association with other German Jews, and on behalf of eastern European Jews—was likely with the families of those locked out of her uncles' factories.[38]

Within the assimilationist German Jewish subculture, the bounds of middle-class respectability were more expansive when it came to women's new roles. In the 1890s, for example, even as B'rith Kodesh remained staunchly antilabor, members cited arguments grounded in essential notions of women's difference to support another of the era's social movements: woman suffrage. Rochester resident Susan B. Anthony relied on those arguments to win support for suffrage from the rabbi and the congregation.[39] Even as class divides were reified, then, middle-class notions of women's positive influence—on the poor, on the body politic—were changing the boundaries of what was acceptably feminine. That would have a profound effect on Wald's possibilities.

Of course, Lillian's mother, Minnie Schwarz Wald, was until her death in 1923 Wald's most immediate model of femininity. She worked at home to raise Wald and her siblings. Duffus's portrait places her firmly within the middle-class culture of women's charity. Her "other-worldly kindheartedness" stood in contrast to her brothers' antilabor stands. One often-told story demonstrated her kindness to the poor. She offered food to unemployed men who stopped by the house; so many began to show up on her doorstep that the police eventually had to ask her to stop. While Lillian listened to the recitation of literature at the breakfast table, one story goes, her mother was "anxious to be at her household duties." Her mother was known for refined taste in home decorating and for embroidery that "rose to high art." Duffus notes Wald's mother's most important characteristic: Lillian Wald's impulse to give things to people who needed help, he said, "was the same as her mother's."[40]

The members of Wald's immediate family, though enmeshed in the culture of the German Jewish community, were not active in its formal organizations. Their membership in B'rith Kodesh lapsed in the 1890s;[41] her father and brother did not join the Eureka Club. Wald received no formal Jewish education whatsoever. Her education outside of her household was at "Miss Cruttenden's English and French boarding school for young ladies." The classical school accepted students recommended by clergy of elite churches and of B'rith Kodesh. It was known for its "liberal and humane spirit," and there Wald learned the conventional lessons befitting her age and class status.[42] She recalled her childhood as full of "books and music," Shakespeare and Marcus Aurelius, Bach and Mozart. These lessons in gender and culture, taught in a secular, universal setting, hold a key to Wald's life trajectory: they allowed Wald to fit comfortably among the wealthy, usually Protestant networks of women and men to which she eventually belonged.

The lives of Wald's siblings were also crucial to her life trajectory. Wald's older brother, Alfred, drowned in 1885, at the young age of twenty-five, while living in California, where he was helping another uncle with a clothing business. His death left Wald with the desire to make her mark on the world as he might have done, perhaps imparting to her the ambition typically linked with conventional masculinity, attributed only to middle-class, white, Christian men.[43]

According to Wald's telling, it was during the childbirth experience of Julia, her older sister, that she met a nurse and decided that nursing would be her life career. But this meeting of Lillian and Julia Wald was not the only critical event shaping Wald's life. Julia's life choices in fact offered Lillian a model of Jewish integration into Rochester's Christian upper class. Two years Lillian's senior, Julia followed a more traditional path, marrying a prominent Catholic man in 1888 at age twenty-three.

Of her marriage, the *Jewish Tidings* said only: "Miss Julia Wald and Charles P. Barry were married at the Cathedral Saturday. . . . Miss Wald's parents are Jewish, but they have offered no objection to her marriage."[44] The *Tidings*, following Rabbi Landsberg's lead, embraced marriage between Jews and non-Jews as a means to Jews' complete assimilation. Certainly, Julia Wald's marriage meant that she had permanently "transcended" her "Hebraic substratum." Charles Barry hailed from one of the most prominent Christian families in Rochester. Julia's father-in-law was Patrick Barry, an Irish immigrant whose horticulture and nursery work promoted Rochester's growth and helped earn the city its nickname of the flower city.[45] Julia, Charles, and their three children—who were raised within the Catholic faith—lived not far from the Walds on East Avenue in a beautiful Georgian mansion.[46]

The urban, comfortable living arrangements of Wald's parents, sister, aunts, and uncles presented her with other possible models. Reproducing her own childhood, she could marry, have children, and tend to a middle-class home. She could join the German Jewish subculture, holding her wedding at the extravagant Eureka Club and subsequently visiting there with her husband for social occasions. She might meet other Jewish ladies in a voluntary society. Or, if she married a non-Jew, she might choose to immerse herself in mainstream Christian organizations.

Wald chose none of these paths. In Duffus's telling, her sister Julia's birth experience was the "act of fate" that propelled Wald to nursing. He writes: "If it is chance that guides human lives, this was the stroke of fortune that led Lillian Wald into the road she was to follow."[47] This telling of the narrative betrays Wald's desire to hide her own ambition—ambition she made clear in her letter of application to nursing school. After being rejected from Vassar College at age sixteen because of her youth, she spent the next six years in her private French school, attending parties and working. She remained close to home and with her mother, who required a great deal of care after the death of her brother. In May of 1889, just as tensions between Rochester's garment manufacturers and laborers were heating up, she wrote to the superintendent of New York Hospital in Manhattan. This first record of her strong voice reveals a great deal about Wald's young hopes: "My life hitherto has been—I presume—a type of modern American young womanhood, days devoted to society, study and house keeping duties such as practical mothers consider essential to a daughter's education. This does not satisfy me now, I feel the need of serious, definite work. A need perhaps more apparent since the desire to become a professional nurse has had birth."[48] In Wald's telling, the catalyst to leave all that was familiar was not the birth of her sister's child, but the genesis of her ambition. "The need of serious, definite work" awoke in her a desire to travel beyond the traditional parameters of white, middle-class womanhood. Whether Vassar or nursing school, hers was the choice of a women's world: there, she would be nurtured by her relationships with other women and defined not by her marriage but by her education and accomplishments.

This ambition took her, the next fall, to the New York Hospital Training School for Nurses, on West 50th and Fifth Avenue. There she entered a woman's professional world—and a big city—for the first time. The field of nursing was comprised entirely of women, almost all of whom were Christian. Indeed, nursing schools at Bellevue Hospital and the New York Hospital together graduated only four Jewish students from 1875–1920. Jewish presses noted the negative feelings Jewish women had for the nursing profession—some associated the profession with a Christian calling, others felt the work unfit for the daughters of a striving ethnic group—even as they urged them to embrace the profession's potential for women's autonomy and fulfillment.[49] The spirit of Wald's upbringing served her well as one of the first Jewish women in nursing.

Following her graduation from nursing school in 1891, Wald told Duffus, "her natural love for children" led her to the Juvenile Asylum on 176th

Lillian Wald's 1891 yearbook photograph from the New York Hospital Training School for Nurses. (Courtesy Medical Center Archives of New York–Presbyterian/Weill Cornell)

Street. This telling again masked her ambition and provided a conventionally feminine interpretation to her wage-earning, professional work. She situated herself within the boundaries of middle-class, white Americanism even as she pushed at the boundaries of what was possible for women's professional lives. After one year there, she became increasingly critical of institutional care. She decided to continue her education—and perhaps become a physician herself—by entering the Woman's Medical College in lower Manhattan.[50]

The impact of these years on Wald's life was significant. Surrounded by women who had made choices different than those of her mother, aunts, and sister, Wald no doubt felt nurtured in her professional and personal development. Mary Brewster, Lavinia Dock, and other nursing colleagues, along with women she would later meet, including Jane Addams, Florence Kelley, and other settlement house experts: Wald described herself as completely fulfilled by these friendships.[51] Throughout her life, she was sustained too by her intimate, physical relationships with women, including socialites Mabel Hyde Kittredge and Helen Arthur.[52]

Wald's choice of this community of women meant her outright rejection of a heterosexual—and even, within her residence, heterosocial—world. In this alternative community, she had access to alternative worldviews of modern society. Her thoughts on the need for cross-class and cross-race cooperation, for restraints and regulations on capitalism, and for active women's roles crystallized in this setting. This community helped to further expand her knowledge of the possibilities for women. Importantly, though, she continued to present women's public and professional possibilities as stemming from their "natural" roles as caretakers and generous givers.[53]

While Wald was ensconced in a women's world, with new role models and new possibilities before her, an older set of connections changed the course of her life. Her German Jewish background played an integral role in her first exposure to the lives of downtown Jewish immigrants. This encounter set the stage for her universalist, lifelong reform work and public negotiations between universalism and particularism, between her worldview and the worldview of her clients and the Jewish community. An analysis of Wald's balancing act begins with Rochester and then moves forward to this moment, when she first walked onto the public stage to meet the gazes of her diverse publics, Jewish and non-Jewish, social workers and Progressives, women and men. Jacob Schiff, American Jewish leader extraordinaire, stood on the stage with her from the moment the curtain rose. Their alliance had a profound effect on who she was and how she was perceived.

A Baptism into the Universal and the Particular: Schiff, Wald, and Religion in the Settlements

In Rochester, Wald had remained sheltered from the industrial poor whom fellow Rochester citizen Emma Goldman later described in her autobiography.[54] They affected her life indirectly through their complicated economic relationships to her uncles' businesses and her aunts' charity work. In Manhattan, when Minnie D. Louis, representing a Jewish philanthropy later named the Minnie Louis Sabbath School, sought the services of a nurse to give home nursing classes to Jewish immigrants, she hoped for a Jewish nurse such as Wald who would be sensitive to the observances of Jewish women. After teaching one class, Wald was taken by a child to a sick woman in a tenement. There, she first saw the lives of the industrial poor. These were the cohort who in that same year struck against—and were once again locked out by—her uncles in Rochester's garment strikes.[55] Wald's public narrative of this first encounter comprises an oft-quoted section of her first book, *The House on Henry Street*. She wrote: "To my inexperience it seemed certain that conditions such as these were allowed because people did not know, and for me there was a challenge to know and to tell. . . . My naïve conviction remained that, if people knew things—and 'things' meant everything implied in the condition of the family—such horrors would cease to exist, and I rejoiced that I had had a training in the care of the sick that in itself would give me an organic relationship to the neighborhood in which this awakening had come."[56] While drawing from her hometown lessons in reifying gender difference, Wald used maternalist notions to expand women's public roles. The "organic relationship" of her women's community to the neighborhood stood in contrast to the increasingly mechanized, masculine, modern capitalistic society. In constructing a new interpretation of class difference, one that emphasized the mutual responsibility between classes, she illustrated her departure from those same lessons. "All the maladjustments of our social and economic relations seemed epitomized in this brief journey and what was found at the end of it," she wrote. She criticized class inequality instead of naturalizing it as her aunts' philanthropy had done.[57]

Crucial to Wald's narrative is how she named this transformative moment: throughout her career, she referred to it as her "baptism of fire." With these words, Wald identified herself as part of the Social Gospel movement.[58] This movement grew out of Protestant churches, as church leaders in England and the United States strove to address the growing social problems of rapid industrialization and urbanization. Christian teachings, they believed, could bring about the kingdom of God, the brotherhood of man, on earth. The Social Gospel injected relevance into a church that was losing power in the new social order. It also served as a critique of the individualism of laissez-faire capitalism. Wald and other women felt a natural affinity for this critique and carved out a space for their work within it.

Not the Hebrew Orphan Association or the Sabbath School, Wald's was to be a nonsectarian institution devoted to ameliorating the lives of the poor. The currents of the day, however—accepted notions of religion and charity and peoplehood—allowed her only so much room in defining the terms of "nonsectarian." For just after she had her spiritual awakening and began to locate herself in another spiritual community, Wald formed crucial ties to New York's Jews. When Louis found that Wald was interested in offering full-time health care to the immigrants, she introduced Wald to Betty Loeb, who turned to her wealthy son-in-law, Jacob Schiff, a prominent leader in the uptown Jewish community, for funding.[59] Schiff became Wald's mentor, benefactor, and close ally. This sequence of referrals guided Wald into an interconnected network based on ethnic, religious, and cultural ties, and it familiarized her with the contours of New York's Jewish community. On this occasion, as on many others, Wald was seen as one of the German Jewish in-group, one of the uptown Jews.[60] This status gave her access to the people and resources that would keep her work afloat for decades. Her ideas about class and gender struck them as modern and even radical; still, for the moment, this particularist community thought of Wald as someone whose worldview and synthesis of Americanism and Jewishness mirrored their own.

This was decidedly true of Schiff. Wald recalled her first meeting with Schiff in 1893, arranged by Loeb, as an exchange between "an inexperienced girl" and a "busy banker."[61] He must have reminded her of her uncles, patriarchs with power over their families and their workers, prosperous businessmen who spent most of their time among other businessmen. Like them, Schiff trafficked in upper-class society. Indeed, Schiff cut an even more conventionally masculine figure, because he had attained far greater stature in the American financial world as a banker at the helm of the firm of Kuhn, Loeb and Company beginning in 1885. He socialized with Rockefellers and Rothschilds as well as American presidents; on visits to Europe, his family had audiences with the German emperor and the pope.[62] His wealth and power allowed for his "undisputed elitist leadership" of the American Jewish community.[63]

Schiff served as a father figure to Wald, whose father had died only two years before she and Schiff met. He was twenty years older than Wald, married to his business partner's daughter, Therese Loeb, and the father of two children. Wald and Schiff met on the common ground of culture, though they had divergent views on Jewish difference. Wald had experienced and benefited from a universalism in which Jews hoped to assimilate completely into a white, Christian, mainstream Americanism. Schiff ascribed great importance to perpetuating Jewish religious difference. He strongly disapproved of Jewish conversions, for example, and of marriage between Jews and non-Jews.[64]

Schiff saw Jews as a group united by faith, not race, and he prioritized the continuance of that faith in generations to come through his philanthropy. Indeed, he felt philanthropy to be his religious obligation, in line with the biblical tradition of setting aside funds for the less fortunate and the Jewish spiritual tradition of *tikkun olam*, repair of the world. Schiff's religious knowledge and observances had long served as his bridge to the new immigrant population: he began donating funds for free Jewish schools with libraries beginning in the 1860s.[65]

In 1893, after their meeting, Schiff funded Wald's entrepreneurial venture, a visiting nurses' service called the Nurses' Settlement, with nurses who lived together and "visited" the Lower East Side tenements, dispensing health care. Their institution grew, as the years passed, to offer classes in English, citizenship, and domestic science, to name just a few examples. It became known as Henry Street Settlement, part of the Social Gospel–inspired settlement house movement in which middle-class, educated women and some men moved to urban, low-income neighborhoods to address the prob-

Jacob H. Schiff and his wife, Therese Loeb Schiff. (Library of Congress, Prints and Photographs Division, LC-DIG-ggbain-30017)

lems of poverty. Mostly nonsectarian settlement houses offered their clients education and socialization opportunities, cultural outlets, and medical care. The resident workers of these houses gained professional experience, recording data and testing theories and methods for the rising field of social work. In the early part of the movement, they encouraged immigrants— who comprised the majority of their clientele—to adjust to American life, prioritizing Anglo-American culture.

The massive immigration of the late nineteenth and early twentieth centuries first drew attention to the huge gap in social services among the urban poor. Before settlements like Henry Street appeared on the urban landscape, religious groups had built institutions for downtown outreach and charity, and these were often sites of Christian missionary activity. The settlements, then, raised important questions about the separate roles of religious and secular institutions. In their survey of North American settlements, movement leaders Robert A. Woods and Albert J. Kennedy found that most houses affiliated with the settlement movement kept these roles distinctly separate and provided "neutral territory traversing all lines of racial and religious cleavage"; Woods and Kennedy also noted, however, that a "considerable number" did include "some of the functions distinctive of a particular . . . division of the church."[66]

In a forum on religion and social settlements in the *Journal of the Religious Education Association*, settlement workers, liberal religious leaders, and scholars weighed in on the issue. One settlement headworker described how settlements, boards of education, municipalities, and other agencies at first had "too many duplications . . . too many charitable institutions working on the same family to the great detriment of the family." To diminish these overlaps, settlements withdrew from religious services when it became clear that churches were "better fitted and better equipped" to do such work.[67] Graham Taylor, a Congregational minister and settlement house founder, wrote that the church and synagogue sought to realize "those divine ideals of relationship to Father God and fellowmen." They must necessarily divide the community according to religious tenets, while "the settlement comprehends and unites all these groups and others besides, on the common ground, and with the all-embracing frame-work of neighborhood and fellow-citizenship."[68] The forum contributors largely agreed that social workers shared the same goal with religious leaders and with the "born again": to set up "a new social order on earth and call it the City of God."[69] What was most important in all efforts for social progress was the "common Christianity" of those involved.[70]

Wald's clients shared with her donors—the downtown and uptown Jewish Americans, respectively—a natural skepticism of Social Gospel followers such as these, who purportedly used "Christian" synonymously with "ethical."[71] Given the widespread acceptance of social anti-Semitism and the history of Christian missionary efforts among Jews, they questioned the terms on which unity might be established among downtown groups. Because so many settlement figures emerged out of the Social Gospel movement, religiously observant Jews often responded to secular settlement work with apprehension—even distrust and hostility.

Some found the class and cultural divides between workers and clients to be unbridgeable. The editors of the *Hebrew Standard*, a conservative New York City Jewish paper, for example, praised the closing of a settlement house: "As for the ornamental side-shows, such as dancing, music, 'uplifting' talks, etc., they are hardly worth the great amount of money spent in maintaining a horde of professional 'uplifters,' whose highest ambition, as a rule, is to prate and write glibly about the 'ghetto people.' . . . The sooner we get rid of them the better."[72]

American Jewish immigrants and established elites—including Schiff—also strongly rejected Christian proselytizing among the Jewish poor. Their institutional strategies were clear: esteemed lawyer, philanthropist, and Jewish communal leader Louis Marshall, for one, challenged his community to think about how best to "re-Judaize" institutions, either nonsectarian or Christian-based, that catered to Jewish clientele. That alone would effectively counter missionary work.[73] But should staff be restricted to Jewish workers? What sort of traditions, if any, should be observed in these institutions? Moreover, just who possessed the power to decide when an institution was "wholly un-Jewish"?[74] Boisterous conference debates on these topics spilled onto the pages of local newspapers.

By her own admission, Wald knew nothing of these debates when she founded Henry Street Settlement. Funded by Schiff—by Jewish capital—and catering to a Jewish clientele, Henry Street also showcased the talents of a Jewish leader. As the settlement grew in size and reputation, Wald appeared frequently in the public eye and eventually was asked to identify her position on the role of religion in her work. Even as she held fast to her universalist vision, even as she retold the story of her "baptism," she later became embroiled in these conflicts over assimilation and Jewish peoplehood.

In her public talks, Wald pointedly prioritized her community of women, her sisterhood, above any religious affiliations. To a Jewish organizational gathering, she once referred to herself and her first colleague, Mary Brewster, as "sisters without religion." She even granted credit to the nonsectarian nature of the work for its early and lasting efficacy. These founding "sisters," Wald continued, directly contributed to the "developing of tolerance, that sense of brotherhood which has been one of the most significant features" of Henry Street Settlement.[75]

In keeping with her description of her baptism of fire, Wald consistently included herself not as part of organized Judaism but as within the Social Gospel movement. She spoke often of the spirituality evident in the era's "reawakening on matters of social concern," in which religious institutions began to contend with the social problems that accompanied industrialization and urbanization. Other figures entered the movement by way of their Protestant and political backgrounds—biographers point to the Quaker teachings in Jane Addams's past and her father's political work, for instance[76]—but Wald entered the Social Gospel movement by a different route. She described the "power of extending human relationships" as a progressive and humanizing force. Since "the American has been favored beyond all men since [the] history of mankind in his opportunity to have the wide view of humanity," she argued, "his privilege brings its obligation."[77] Her own sense of obligation originated in her family's successful experience with a liberal Americanism in Rochester, and she gained a wider view from her Social Gospel reform colleagues.

Wald employed the images of the Protestant millennium in describing settlement work as fulfilling the "prophesy" of the new civilization, "uniting people across the lines of religion, class, and race."[78] The settlement was a "new impulse to an old gospel," a modern application of the New Testament's teachings of brotherhood. It transcended "in a kind of spiritual value, which is also of social importance, other efforts for human betterment." Within those efforts, Wald indicated a new role for women, relying on traditional notions of women's morality to carve out a space for the professional settlement work of herself and her colleagues. She claimed that settlement house residents were on a "moral adventure" and that they "affected the morals of their generation out of all proportion to their numerical strength."[79]

The origins of her own work were a "baptism of fire." When asked what role religion played in her work, she replied: "The good will, the humanitarianism, the very strong desire to achieve justice and equality of opportunities, to eliminate from the lives of men, women and children the sordid conditions that drag them down spiritually, to lessen the greed of people, to place the highest value upon tolerance, kindness and love would be the motive of the thoughtful people who live in Settlements and who by their daily lives exemplify this creed in so far as it lies within their power."[80] Without formally endorsing any dogma or creed, Wald chose both an ethical and moral imperative for justice and a millennial Protestant spirituality as key ingredients to her new, ambitious endeavors.

Like Wald, Schiff imbued his public and private writings with religious and spiritual language. While Wald's words were those of the Social Gospel, Schiff assigned the settlement religious significance with effusive quotations from the Hebrew Bible. "Verily you have had the blessing of the Almighty," he wrote to Wald in one admiring New Year's recollection, "for to be given such satisfaction in one's work, as you and your co-workers enjoy, is the greatest blessing one can receive."[81] He even claimed Wald's universalist work for Jewish history, comparing her mission on earth to Moses's obligation to God: "When God promulgated his law to Israel, Moses in His name prohibited the erection of an altar of gold and silver: Of earth, thou shalt build your altar to me; that *you* have done, and because of it, your work has been blessed!"[82] Wald thought of Schiff as the spiritual center of the house. She celebrated that contribution from the financial giant: "It is a great spiritual community and I am always very grateful that from the very beginning, we had your comprehension and ardor to keep us from falling into materialistic pitfalls."[83]

Wald consistently relied on Schiff and other Jewish connections to help her bridge the gap of religious knowledge and observance between herself and her clients. Her first contact with strict Orthodox observance indicates that she did not recognize the culture she saw as even remotely related to her own upbringing.[84] It was Schiff who informed Wald of the approaching holidays of Rosh Hashanah and Yom Kippur.[85] On one occasion, in preparation for a speech on woman suffrage, she asked him for quotes from the Talmud or Hebrew Bible, quotes "out of your lore," separating herself from that group's membership because of her lack of Jewish education.[86] To Schiff, she vented her early frustration over her immigrant clients' religious observances: "The holidays have been and are yet rigidly observed," she wrote to Schiff in the fall of 1893, their first year working together, "and this has been unfavorable in many ways, the women not being able to do what scrubbing and washing they could—refusing to go to hospitals—the United Hebrew Charities closed many days."[87]

While Schiff gave generously to Jewish charities to support the perpetuation of Jewish religious difference, he hoped that his work with Wald would contribute to the undoing of religious prejudice among the world's peoples. Henry Street, in his view, built bridges among those of all backgrounds. He once lamented the many lives lost in religious crusades by those who believed their ideals "to be the only true gospel." Schiff was thankful that God's message was "beginning to be better understood" and that individuals like Wald, with her universalist message, now worked for the "permanent happiness of mankind." He foretold, "In centuries to come the walls of 265 Henry Street . . . will be shown by guides to a gazing and admiring multitude . . . and have its monuments in posterity and in better and happier men and women."[88] Schiff saw Henry Street as a place where people could surmount differences and unify across boundaries of class and race.

Unlike other religiously observant Jews who later bristled at Wald's lack of connection to their community and to religious Judaism, Schiff respected Wald's Protestant-inflected universalism. This insight runs counter to the traditional portrait of Schiff as the "defender of the faith" at Henry Street.[89] In an often-cited December 1914 letter to Wald, Schiff objected to the placement of a Christmas tree at Henry Street. As chief donor and the patriarch of the house, he worried that Wald was "tempting Jewish children away from their faith at an impressionable age."[90] But, importantly, two days earlier he had written to Wald, "I have the greatest respect for *every* religion, for traditions, customs, and even prejudices in whatever religion these may be found." He objected only to the fact that the kindergarten in which the tree stood was "*altogether* frequented by Jewish children"; he never intended to "deprive" Wald's "gentile coworkers from the pleasures of a festival."[91]

Wald's ambivalence about a symbol she saw as secular (and therefore universal) almost crossed the threshold of Schiff's tolerance for that secularism. He felt rebuffed by Wald's attributing to him interests that were *purely* particularist and not pluralist.

Indeed, Schiff had to defend his nonsectarianism at times. He did not share the view of some of the more conservative Orthodox Jews who, out of concern for Judaism's future, disparaged secular institutional work with Jewish immigrants (similar to those who lamented the futile work of the "uplifters"). When reformer journalist Jacob Riis appealed to Schiff for a donation to lessen the debt on his settlement, for example, Schiff was insulted that Riis felt compelled to mention that the project would "increasingly benefit Jewish children." Schiff replied that it was "unworthy" of people like Riis, who had "the good of their fellows at heart," to appeal to a donor on sectarian grounds. Schiff counted himself among those "big enough to ignore race or sectarian divisions." He was interested in philanthropy broadly, not only through "racial or religious ties."[92] A rift developed between Schiff and Riis in this exchange, and Schiff forwarded the entire correspondence to the only person who he felt could help mediate: Wald. Schiff relied on Wald to testify to his nonsectarian sensibilities.

Their work at Henry Street Settlement House was, after all, proof that Schiff had just such broad ideals.[93] Because of Wald's striving to make the house a place where people overcame their differences, Schiff benefited from counting Henry Street among his secular causes. They generally agreed on how to present Henry Street to the wider public. Both were vehement about the settlement's secular nature. In fact, they consistently strove to make the institution appear *less* Jewish. Regarding the leadership of Henry Street's board of directors, Schiff wrote to Wald: "What we should put our heads together about is the selection of a President (preferably a Gentile, so as to emphasize the non-sectarian character of the work) who stands for something, and is well known throughout the city, and we should endeavor to establish the Settlement in the eyes of the public, just like any of the other great communal philanthropic societies, in order to evoke a more general interest, both amongst the wealthy and the middle-class, [the] latter [of which] is, in reality, the backbone of all successful societies." Because so many Jewish names were associated with Wald's nursing and settlement work, Schiff believed they needed to strike a careful balance, tapping the funds of other populations, in order to achieve "general interest" and avoid the label of "Jewish work."[94]

In striving for this balance, Schiff echoed the concerns of many of his compatriots. According to Naomi Cohen, the prototypical German Jewish man in this period "walk[ed] an emotional tightrope, attempting to strike a balance between his dream of full integration, his religious-ethnic heritage, and the demands, rational or otherwise, of his gentile compatriots." Schiff followed the commonly understood set of guidelines formed out of fear of anti-Semitic hostility and possible reprisals.[95] He lived always with his mind attuned to how the non-Jewish world saw him as representative of American Jewry.

Though also considered in this same cohort of German Jews, Wald struck a very different balance. She did indeed traffic in the Jewish world. She expressly identified herself as a Jew on several occasions, usually to investigate anti-Semitic discrimination for a friend or colleague;[96] even more importantly, she frequently joined other Jewish speakers on the circuit of Jewish agencies and organizations. And though her intimate relationships (those of which there is extant evidence) were not with Jewish women, her deep friendship with Schiff and his family was grounded, too, in Jewish values and culture. Wald's Jewishness was expressed informally, through friendship and professional networks, not through public investment in formal Jewish affiliation.

So uncomfortable was Wald with more formal identification and affiliation, she once flatly rejected the chance to have her name as an entry in a book on notable American Jewish women.[97] To Wald and her family, universalism was the logical extension of the same energy that had allowed for their own acceptance. Once in New York City, she found the spiritual calling that best matched her own worldview and resonated with her sense of what needed to be done. The spirituality that guided her work, then, derived from the movement she encountered once she had left her hometown: the universalism of the Protestant Social Gospel of her New York connections.

Though the work of Wald and Jacob Schiff began with their very different spiritual groundings, their institution's nonsectarianism created little friction between them. "It is your House as well as my House and our House," she once wrote to Schiff, emphasizing just how crucial were his contributions at the settlement's beginnings and throughout its existence.[98] Her authority grew, and her relationship with Schiff, her first friend, became more reciprocal. As he continued to mentor her with funds and advice, and as new situations drew her into controversies over her "Jewish work," she taught him the new lessons she was learning from her women's community. As the years passed, Wald's universalism kept her door open to campaigns affecting all facets of her neighborhood—even as her concept of the neighborhood grew to encompass a global community.

The open door was, to Wald's mind, important in welcoming uptowners like Schiff to her settlement so as to introduce them to the lives of the downtown poor. At Wald's dinner table, according to Schiff's first biographer, he "came into contact with the laboring man and the immigrant, and obtained their point of view."[99] Schiff himself spoke with great emotion about how much Wald had schooled his family in universalism. "We gained by your friendship for us," he wrote, "and have become more imbued with the spirit of responsibility wealth should impose upon those to whom it is given by Providence, through the opportunities you have often made for us to better understand the life of those who have to struggle."[100] This was the goal of many of Wald's uptown appeals. They were all built on the foundation of her strong kinship with Schiff and the nonsectarian character of their work at Henry Street.[101]

If in the business world Schiff was compelled to wield his financial power with ruthlessness and a certain hardness, he credited Wald with creating a house—with all of the attributes of a home—where he could shed some of that disposition. Not only did Wald act as the woman of the house, a buffer from the outside forces of competitive capitalism, she also brought into the house individuals who had suffered from capitalism's abuses. For at Henry Street, Wald supported laborers' strike actions. As her relationship with Schiff developed, she brought him into sympathetic understanding as well. (Of course, as a banker, his investment in labor struggles was considerably less than that of her uncles, who were manufacturers.) Using his religiosity as a bridge to the new wave of immigrants, Schiff once "exchanged quotations from the Hebrew" with a striker who "knew his Scripture." In the name of protected womanhood and of unionism, Wald defended the right of local women workers to strike without police harassment. Schiff's support meant that he was applying the lessons he had learned from her at Henry Street.[102]

Indeed, one Russian immigrant and union activist who had been Wald's client wrote of Henry Street in these early years as a place "where rich and poor [were] made to forget their material difference." He called the settlement "[Wald's] house . . . a veritable *salon* where distinguished artists, intellectuals, statesmen, captains of industry and proletarians meet and converse without formality or affectation." Surely to Wald's satisfaction, he claimed her work on behalf of the "underdog in life's battles" as in keeping with "the old-fashioned American ideas of free speech, free press and free public assembly."[103]

Wald's work earned the admiration of union activists, academic sociologists, and politicians in the pages of publications from the liberal *Nation* magazine to *Newsweek*. Her work at Henry Street was hailed as "one of the most hopeful developments in American municipal life."[104] The *New York Times* considered Wald a "sensitive and refined organism" for whom "modesty" was "not a pose." Highlighting her Victorian womanhood, the *Times* article offered testament to "the quickness of her sympathy, the gentleness of her nature, and the remarkable qualities of mind and heart which have enabled her to establish the great work to which her life has been devoted."[105]

Her place in the early conversations of prominent reformers testifies to her success in laying claim to the vision of the Protestant Social Gospel. Robert Woods, founder of South End Settlement House in Boston, noted that the settlement movement made a "definite contribution toward practical Christian unity, by bringing together Christians of every name into enthusiastic joint action toward the bringing in of a more Christian city." Wald herself had "a peculiar quality of genuineness and inspiration" in her efforts toward that goal.[106] Woods's inclusion of Wald in an article on the progress of the settlement movement testified to her unqualified membership in the Social Gospel community of settlement workers, whose visions encompassed assimilation as well as broader reforms.

To the ears of a population striving to achieve a place in the annals of American history—including, and perhaps especially, Jacob Schiff—all such praise must have been pleasing indeed. To Wald's ears, though, such praise surely just confirmed what she had already believed: that her work was American work toward the realization of her vision of universal brotherhood. Wald also took pleasure from the assertion that material differences among visitors and residents evaporated in the Henry Street house, with its middle-class furnishings imported into a working-class neighborhood.

To contemporary listeners, of course, that notion sounds as though it served the privileged far more than it served the poor. Why would the rich, after all, need ever to forget their material differences? Yet Wald and her crusades reaped great benefit from the idea that her maternalist leadership was solely responsible for the collapsed distance between uptown and downtown, that she alone could interpret the poor to the rich.

Like their friendship and their dedication to the industrial poor, the nature of Wald and Schiff's exchange was clear. The "busy banker" and proud Jewish American provided the "inexperienced girl" with funds, Jewish knowledge, financial advice, a new building, land for convalescent and summer children's camps, horses, and, several years later, a "Ford machine" for settlement transportation.[107] In return, and true to the spirit of Rochester's German Jewish community, Wald did the work of proving Schiff's broad-mindedness through her work at the settlement. Within its walls, she also provided him with an education in universalism. Theirs was in some ways a typical gendered household arrangement, with key modifications that equalized their relationship and allowed for the freedom of the woman-run and women-centered household.

Wald's Interpretive Work:
The Distance between Uptown and Downtown

Wald was invited to uptown Jewish meetings specifically because she was seen as both a Jewish uptowner and a true representative of the new downtown Jewish immigrants. Uptowners at times disputed the nonsectarian character she and Schiff had crafted for their settlement work. They cited two facts. First, she allied, dined, traveled with, and took advice and funds from the German Jewish community. Second, her work was largely with eastern European Jews. The Jewish community relied on these facts as the basis of their Jewish claims on her work. Coupled with faith in her authority to interpret the lives of the poor, those claims earned her a platform to inform and raise funds. No matter the discomfort she felt with Jewish claims, she took full advantage of this platform.

In 1896, for example, only three years after her baptism into urban life, Wald received an invitation to speak at the first nationwide meeting of the National Council of Jewish Women (NCJW) as an authority on industrial poverty and the lives of those forced to live within it. The NCJW was founded in 1893 as an "offspring of the economic and social success achieved by German Jewish immigrants in the United States."[108] Modeling themselves on Protestant women's charity organizations, NCJW members were for the most part wives of successful businessmen. Their engagement with philanthropic work befitted their social and economic status, just as it did the status of Wald's aunts in Rochester. The women of the NCJW also came together as Jewish women, and their benevolent work was largely with eastern European Jewish immigrants: in these ways, they reinforced the boundaries of their Jewish community. The setting, then, was familiar to Wald.

In her talk, titled "Crowded Districts of Large Cities," Wald appealed to the conscience and ideals of the privileged women in the audience—with whom she shared upbringing and culture—by asking them (as she had asked herself and Schiff) to look at their lives and consider, "What is my responsibility?"[109] Wald challenged those who felt that conditions on the Lower East Side constituted a "Jewish problem," a common anti-Semitic accusation built on notions of Jews' negative racial characteristics. She disputed racialized categories. She emphasized that the problem was one of poverty, of environment, not specific to any one population: "An equal degree of ignorance and an equal depth of poverty will create the same conditions" among "Russians, Italians, or Irish," she asserted.

Wald's words suggested that she set herself apart from the ideas and politics espoused by the majority of NCJW members.[110] They also demonstrated that she had departed from the worldviews of her uncles upstate and that she had taken the public charity work and communalistic models of her mother and aunts one step further. She issued a powerful appeal to her wealthy listeners to understand the issues surrounding unionism and labor agitation, to overcome the prejudices of their class: "You can help the labor difficulty by comprehending what a fair condition of labor is. . . . If there is a strike, try to discover both sides of the question, not only the one vulgarly holding your butter, but the other's grievance also; not rejoicing in the workingman's failure without understanding (if that is possible) what was behind the discontent. Be fair enough to help that workingman in his way, if you can see that his way is right."

She focused on the need for her audience to learn about the humanity behind the statistics of overcrowding, crime, and labor strife in her neighborhood. Wald relied on her faith in culture, and not biology, as emblematic of a group's integrity. She challenged her audience to observe immigrants' "nobility of character," the degradation they faced in living and working in unregulated tenements, the "inhumanity" of "grinding work and small pay."

Wald's last question asked the women to consider a still closer working relationship: she argued that they should treat their domestic workers justly by giving them reasonable hours and "some privacy." "There is often as great a distance between drawing room and kitchen," she said, "as between up-town and down-town." Wald felt she had now traversed that distance. Her house's drawing room and kitchen, though occupied by middle-class ladies and full of mahogany furnishings, were frequented by the poor. And as lady of the house, Wald had made these visits the basis of a new professional role for herself and other women.

In the final moments of her speech, Wald chose to "retire as witness" for the industrial poor and instead conclude with "inspiration and right understanding." She quoted a lengthy passage by Phillips Brooks, an American Episcopal bishop who had died three years before. Given the tensions surrounding Christian missionary work among Jews, her choice was a pointedly risky one. The topic: "Mutualism." She quoted at length universalist ideas that paralleled her own: "The universal blunder of this world is in thinking that there are certain persons put into the world to govern, and certain others to obey. Everybody is in the world to govern, everybody to obey. Men are coming to see that beyond and above this individualism there is something higher—Mutualism. Don't you see that in this Mutualism the world becomes an entirely different thing? Men's dreams are after the perfect world of Mutualism. . . . This is new life, where service is universal law."

The speech could easily have been given in the sanctuary of B'rith Kodesh by a visiting Protestant clergyman who similarly privileged consent over descent. It spoke well to the currents and events of Wald's lifetime to that day. She had begun her own voyage out of Rochester by challenging the notion that gender determined one's role and one's place in the world. Drawing from the Americanism that was endorsed by the women of Rochester's German Jewish community, taking it past its particularist moorings, she created a household where it was applied to a wider range of issues. Her dream of this "perfect world" of universal brotherhood began with her first steps into the neighborhoods of Manhattan's industrial poor. With Schiff and her colleagues, she earned the authority to interpret her neighbors' experiences to the larger world. And this was her new life—her service for the realization of this vision, an active role in the tumultuous negotiations over the emerging racial, class, and ethnic arrangements in modern America.

2

The Woman at the
Head of the Table

NEGOTIATING UNIVERSALISM *and*
DIFFERENCE *at* HENRY STREET

Wald's hometown lessons served her well as she began to build coalitions in the wider world of Progressive reform, joining others who addressed the problems of industrial poverty. Representative of her skill in coalition building was the story of her settlement's large dining room tables. As soon as Wald moved into the house on Henry Street in 1893, the mahogany doors that graced the front entrance fell victim to her practicality, and she had them made into huge tables around which residents and visitors could gather to educate each other as to what was needed to effect change.[1] In their biographies and autobiographies, various Progressives (and Jacob Schiff) credit Wald's dining room meetings for opening up new worlds of ideas.[2]

Presiding over dinner and often serving her guests, Wald was very much the woman of her house. Her serving of the food is symbolic of her unthreatening, conventionally feminine self-presentation, even as her sitting at the table's head—where the man of the house would traditionally sit—demonstrates her challenges to these conventions of gender and power. Indeed, Wald's philosophy, her universalist vision, was grounded in a gendered notion of power, one based on women's difference. That vision became the engine of the institution, and it provided the foundation upon which she, her colleague Mary Brewster, and her nurses built Henry Street Settlement.[3]

Wald's approach to gender difference in her role as the woman of the house also proved indispensable to her coalition building. She used traditional notions of women's roles as helpmeets to explain the newfound public power of herself and others in her women's reform network. Even as she often justified her activism by citing traditional notions of women's caring, moral natures, she pushed hard at the boundaries of what professional women could do. She encouraged all women, especially those with nurses' training, to engage in broader reform work that sought to undo larger social problems associated with poverty. She and her Progressive colleagues blazed trails that forever altered the landscape for women professionals.[4]

The term "Progressive" encompasses a decidedly varied collection of turn-of-the-century reform efforts. For Wald, it described the group of middle-class Americans—including herself and her cohorts—who at the turn of the last century drew on older conceptions of government, charity, and gender roles in creating new institutions to contend with the circumstances of their "new society." In crafting her universalist vision, Wald moved beyond the Jewish, Social Gospel, and settlement communities and tapped into the social currents of the broader Progressive movement: thousands of middle-class, native-born citizens called for a more expansive and interventionist government to mitigate the harsh forces of industrialization and the violent class conflicts engendered by those forces.[5] As a nurse, at Henry Street Wald first joined forces with Progressives to work for society's health in the broadest sense.[6] Her vision encompassed a civic universalism wherein professional women represented the interests of all citizens in lobbying for public resources and civil rights. Relying on firm notions of women's distinctive natures, Wald and her colleagues argued for the insertion of the ethic of care into the political structures of their era.[7]

Because her Progressivism was tied to the American strivings of a previous generation of immigrants, because her interpretive work was tied to her balancing commitments to particularist and universalist communities, Wald was indeed an ethnic Progressive.[8] She modeled her approach to immigration on her own family's successful integration in Rochester, believing that all individuals could join—and contribute to—America's diverse ethnic landscape. Her faith that culture, and not race, was emblematic of a people's potential drew, too, from these lessons. Her networks in New York nurtured and sustained her vision. She took her place alongside other settlement workers, on the liberal end of the spectrum—opposite zealous Americanizers who organized racist and xenophobic "100 percent American" campaigns—in her approach to Americanizing new immigrants.

Just as Wald's early career straddled traditional and modern ideas about women's gender roles, so too were older and newer conceptions of ethnocultural American identities competing in those years. What would it mean to be an Italian American, a Greek American, or, in Wald's case, a Jewish American? The same assimilation project that led to the economic success of Wald's and so many other Jewish families—and to Wald's and other Jewish women's unprecedented access to public power—created widespread anxiety within the Jewish community. The massive Jewish immigration from eastern Europe heightened anxieties about what would constitute Jewish values and who would transmit them.

If Jewish difference were to be nearly invisible in the public realm, as the assimilation project entailed, it had to be confined to the household. No longer would men's learning and worship be indicative of Jewish belonging. How would the Jewish woman adjust to her new role as the transmitter of Jewish cultural and religious values? Jewish men, ambivalent over the loss of Jewish learning, focused on their own economic success; they structured their personal authority in part by criticizing Jewish women over the new gendered division of responsibilities.[9] When conservative (male) leaders pressed for the need to "re-Judaize" institutions that catered to the urban Jewish poor, for example, they made clear who was to blame for the waning of Jewish tradition: as one editorial in the local press argued, "the attack . . . must be delivered on the Jewish home, and if we are so ungallant to say it, upon the Jewish woman."[10]

Settlements, which were both institutions and homes, were often flash

In 1908, Wald attended a planning meeting in White Plains, New York, with many
of her close friends and colleagues from the settlement movement. The meeting resulted
in the National Federation of Settlements. Front row, left to right: Graham Taylor,
Mary McDowell, Robert A. Woods. Middle row: Cornelia Bradford, Jane Addams (in
striped blouse), Lillian Wald (seated), Elizabeth Williams, Dr. James Hamilton. Back
row: Helen Greene, Helena Dudley, John Lovejoy Elliott, Meyer Bloomfield, Mary K.
Simkhovitch, Ellen W. Coolidge. (Union Settlement Association Records, Columbia
University Rare Book and Manuscript Library)

points in the struggles over these issues, because many downtown settlements had women residents and catered to a Jewish clientele. When the
head resident was a Jewish woman, as was the case with Henry Street, she
and her institution were judged according to the standards of the newly
privatized, domesticated religion. The Jewish community, with an eye on its
"own," held Wald to measures that other (Christian) Progressive leaders did
not have to meet; they also approached her in ways that were distinctly
gendered. While all institutions were to respect Jewish difference, her critics
pressed her in ways that marked their particularist investments and their
expectations of her as a like-minded community member. They assumed
that Wald defined and expressed her Jewishness in the same ways they did.
Surely hers was, they pressed, a *Jewish* house?

In the Progressive moment, at the intersection of currents moving toward modern feminism and modern Jewish identity, Wald's early career
found her in the center of debates over what was possible—for women, for
American Jews, for Americans, and, eventually, for world citizens. She combined a zeal for professionalizing nursing with faith in women's natural
difference, inclusion in Jewish networks with a preference to avoid the
formal category of Jewish, respect for some level of ethnocultural difference
with a fervent faith in assimilation. Wald carefully balanced her commitments to universalist and particularist communities, growing Henry Street
and all of her work to be the fullest expression of her faith in a brotherhood
of man.

The "Raison d'Être of Our Existence": Wald and Nursing Work

Following her baptism of fire, with the financial support of Jacob Schiff,
Wald and Mary Brewster, a descendent of the Pilgrim leader Rev. William
Brewster and a fellow graduate of the New York Hospital Training School for
Nurses, took up residence at the College Settlement on Rivington Street on
Manhattan's Lower East Side in 1893. This settlement, founded in 1889, was
the first product of the College Settlement Association, a group with chapters of reform-minded students at Smith, Wellesley, Vassar, Bryn Mawr, and
other women's colleges. These students were educated in the new ideal of
womanhood, which Wald took as her own. Instead of sheltering women
from the harsh realities of life, this new ideal emphasized that women had a

special interest in—and special skills to apply to—those realities. Indeed, they could play important roles in the progress of civilization by acting on their natural sensibilities and their new educations to remedy social ills.

Here, Wald and Brewster met women from similar class and educational backgrounds who took seriously this call. They had already been immersed in the women's professional world of nursing. Now, College Settlement residents introduced them to the Lower East Side, to the suffering that accompanied industrial poverty, and to the goals and philosophies of the settlement movement. Their primary activities were leading learning clubs, in which a resident would instruct a group of clients in a gender-appropriate area, such as domestic science.[11] Life alongside the women of College Settlement offered Wald broader contact with the "female dominion of American reform": women whose activities were still seen as acceptably feminine, yet who lived independent of male companionship, leadership, or supervision.[12]

Nursing, Wald later wrote, served as "the 'raison d'être' of our existence from which all our other activities had had their natural and unforced growth."[13] Grounded in her ideas about women's distinctive nature, Wald's nursing provided her first encounters with women's professionalism and expert political power. She credited her colleagues from the New York Hospital Training School for Nurses for their continuing support—their professional cooperation, as well as their small financial contributions—as she made her forays into the wider world of reform.[14] In this world, she advocated for the agenda of an ethic of care and balanced her clients' ethnic strivings with her own universal commitments.

Though her settlement work, like her nursing career, was women-centered, Wald's funds originated with Schiff, and he asked (in the early years) for an accounting of how she spent his donations. After two months on Rivington Street, Wald wrote to him to inquire about establishing a settlement of her own. The nursing work that she and Brewster did was "not identical with the work of the College Settlement," she explained, continuing, "and now that their regular work begins, the rooms that we occupy should be used for workers who can give their time to the specific work of the house."[15] In September, she and Brewster found a house on Jefferson Street that suited their needs and taste. "Some assurance as to our material comfort was given to anxious, though at heart sympathetic, families," Wald wrote, including "windows curtained with spotless but inexpensive scrim" and "a tiny bedroom which we two shared." They imported some of their class markers with them to the house. They were pleased, for example, that they had "a small dining-room in which the family mahogany did not look out of place, and a kitchen."[16] At Schiff's insistence, Wald and Brewster chose this first home in the tenements in part because of these genteel accoutrements, including an indoor bathroom suitable for two ladies.

Viewing her home from the perspective of her neighbors and clients, Wald was sensitive to her importation of a middle-class lifestyle into the neighborhood of the industrial poor. After their first day there, Wald recorded, a small child who lived in the basement of their tenement reported to his mother, "Them ladies live like the Queen of England and eat off of solid gold plates."[17] In 1893, Schiff provided sufficient funds for Wald and Brewster to move to Henry Street, into another "fine old house, once the abode of the wealthy, but long abandoned to the poor of the city."[18] Made of brick and three stories high, 265 Henry Street also had all the marks of a genteel home—even without the huge mahogany doors.

Though their class origins set them apart from the neighborhood's residents, the nurses had a crucial—and "natural"—role to play in a city adjusting to the "unnatural" growth of industrial capitalism. "Our basic idea," wrote Wald, "was that the nurse's peculiar introduction to the patient and her organic relationship with the neighborhood should constitute the starting point for universal service to the region." The inequality that accompanied American industrial growth, Wald implied, was dehumanizing and uncivilized, and her nurses worked against those forces. She and her nursing colleagues, as trained professional women, were uniquely prepared to do such work. Her training in nursing, she believed, collapsed the class difference between herself and her clients and gave her "an immediate avenue of approach."[19]

The visiting nurses, whose activities were privately funded, dispensed health care in a personalized way. Immediately after her graduation from New York Hospital Training School for Nurses, Wald had spent a year at the Juvenile Asylum on 176th Street and had been horrified by the cold, indifferent health care she felt was provided by that institution; she thought of her nurses' methods as directly opposed to those at the asylum.[20] She also noted that "ninety per cent of the sick people in cities were sick at home"

Henry Street visiting nurses leaving an old settlement building early in the twentieth century. (Copyright Bettman/Corbis)

and that "there were large numbers of people who could not, or who sometimes would not, avail themselves of the hospitals." Above all, she asserted
that "a humanitarian civilization demanded that something of the nursing care given to those in hospitals"—those who made use of the "valuable and expensive hospital space"—should be "accorded to sick people
in their homes."[21] All citizens, she believed, were entitled to professional
health care.

In keeping with the civic element of Wald's universalist vision, the
Nurses' Settlement—soon to be known as Henry Street Settlement—was
the first visiting nursing service without formal ties to religious or charitable
institutions. "We considered it proper," she later recalled to Schiff, "that
patients should secure nursing on the most dignified basis . . . and that
their care should not be dependent upon racial or religious distinctions."[22]
In order to serve the working poor, nurses responded to calls from physicians, charitable agencies, and individuals in need; cooperated with hospitals when necessary; and offered services on a sliding fee scale. While the
nurses of charity organizations put "a premium upon the use of the service
by the very poor," Wald's nurses catered to "a growing class of people," she
wrote, "who pride themselves upon independence, who belong to lodges
and benefit societies and who engage their own physicians and pay for
them."[23] With their mission, these "sisters without religion" carved out a
new niche for their work.[24]

Implicit in this mission was the prioritization—even romanticization—of
the home and family as the place where recovery could best be encouraged.
Using the language of morality, Wald placed "the social, moral, and economic value of the home life first and foremost," warning that separation—
especially of children from parents—would lead to "demoralization of the
family group."[25] Women, of course, played a crucial role in times of sickness: the mother of the family tendered the treatment of the patient in need
of health care. In arguing for the need of an expert nurse, Wald extended the
maternal role into the professional realm.

Importantly, the nurse's mission grew out of a female culture. The language and ideas of this mission excited Wald. Endorsing the traditional
view of evangelical Protestantism of women as moral guardians, Wald envisioned her nurses fulfilling their feminine mission by crusading for the
health of the poor. They demonstrated "the modern aspect of an old profes-

sion that has evolved . . . without doubt because of the development of social self-consciousness on the part of women."[26] She wrote that "the visiting nurses throughout the country have been inspired to dignify and lay true value on their service, coveting for themselves the privilege of relieving pain, and linking to that century-cherished prerogative of women the new note of education and civic beauty."[27]

Wald's maternalist rhetoric located her within—and eventually led her to—a community of women reformers.[28] Historians often label Jane Addams's Hull House as the laboratory in which the founding members of this community joined forces to articulate a political agenda. Wald's residence at the College Settlement brought her the connections that led to meeting Addams, one of the most dynamic forces in women's reform. Upon departing from Hull House with her colleagues in 1899, Wald wrote to Addams of her gratitude. "It may be of some little service to you that one small group has a deeper desire than ever to press its service into and for a fairer society for having touched you. . . . we want to do *good*, and, like children, look to you for guidance."[29]

Wald's connection to Addams and Hull House grew even stronger when reformer and activist Florence Kelley moved into Henry Street in the summer of 1899.[30] Wald's platform of maternalist concerns fit well with those of Addams and Kelley: in New York City, she was already working for the institution of school nurses, classes for disabled students, free school lunches, clean milk stations, and more playgrounds. Together, these women comprised a powerful force in early-twentieth-century politics, recorded and interpreted by historians as an early apex of women's political power, the foundation of New Deal social welfare policies, and a part of the increasing reliance on social science and advocacy in governmental institutions.[31]

Within this new rhetoric of social science, Wald's voice stands out as the voice of a trained nurse, one whose career spanned the transition from the more traditional conception of nursing to its new professional status. In tracing the history of the field, historians often locate figures in "traditional" and "professionalizing" camps: traditionalists viewed women as naturally empathic and altruistic, and nursing as the logical service for women based on these qualities; professionalists focused more on rigorous training, just wages, and respect for nurses as experts.[32] The New York Hospital Training School for Nurses, which Wald entered in 1889, was one of the first schools in the United States to pull women (nearly all Protestant) from the middle and upper classes, as opposed to the working-class, "untrained" nurse of the past.[33] Wald's rhetoric and practice reflected this transition: while endorsing the more traditional view of woman's mission as a helpmate, she also worked with her colleagues to professionalize nursing.[34] She employed a lofty and spiritual language even while shoring up the professional boundaries of the field. She expanded women's professional roles while reinforcing patriarchal notions of women's natures.[35]

Wald framed her efforts to standardize nurses' training, one aspect of the process of professionalization, in terms of her fear of the exploitation of the poor. In contrast to the poor, she explained, the "well-to-do . . . have other resources and careful physicians, who know the nurses whom they recommend." Wald once wrote a letter to Schiff in support of a law that would bring state supervision to nurses' training. In it, she called his attention to an advertisement for a correspondence training school for nurses that declared its graduates earned twenty-five dollars a week. "So why should women spend years in training, when they can do as well by correspondence?" she asked in dismay.[36] To bring better-trained women into the field, Wald helped to initiate a public health nursing lecture series at Columbia's Teachers College in 1899, which led to the formation of the university's Department of Nursing and Health in 1910.

Wald's lobbying for a professional public health organization was in the spirit of her building coalitions and expanding women's professional roles. She coined the term "public health nurse" to replace "visiting nurse" in order to emphasize the extent to which nurses joined forces with private *and* public agencies in efforts "for social betterment."[37] The public health nurse would devote her professional status to the civic culture, to the more even distribution of resources such as health care to all citizens. The National Organization of Public Health Nursing, which Wald cofounded in 1912, hoped that "the leaders in the various movements of the profession may get to know each other, may sit at [a] table together, may have . . . informal contact."[38] She sought to unite nurses across institutional lines, from settlements to industrial locations, and ally with other public health reformers to preach what one historian called the "gospel of health."[39]

Importantly, Wald's attempt to unify professional nurses included the crossing of the color line. The National Organization of Public Health Nursing strove for racial inclusiveness, counting African American and white nurses as members. The organization also lent its support to the National Association of Colored Graduate Nurses, founded in 1908.[40] Wald was seen as a "staunch friend of black nurses" and was one of the first white leaders in nursing to recognize the NACGN. Some aspects of the color line still held sway at Henry Street: Wald's twenty-five black nurses were not allowed to visit white homes nor be promoted to supervisory ranks. But she "paid them equal salaries, and accorded them identical professional courtesies and recognition."[41]

Wald consistently emphasized the expansiveness of public health nursing's areas of concern. They included prevention—teaching hygiene classes, establishing milk stations, working for the health and safety of people at work and at school—alongside the treatment of disease. During monthly staff meetings at Henry Street's dining room table, Wald scheduled lectures by "people prominent in some Allied Field of Activity" in order to link efforts with other reform organizations.[42] Her nurses "came to seek to relate the interests and the problems of the neighborhood to the life of the city as a whole . . . gaining knowledge of conditions that will eventually lead to measures to fit the case."[43] In these efforts, the impact of her broader Progressive connections was clear.

Education was central to her work. Indeed, Henry Street Settlement and its satellites provided field training to (mainly) women from around the world who were enrolled in public health nursing programs. Individuals from all backgrounds visited to learn about the industrial poor and to observe the treatment of disease among the poor in its "social, economic, and moral aspects."[44] Several young, wealthy Reform Jewish women in New York, including Schiff's granddaughter and the daughter of *New York Times* founder Adolph Ochs, spent time at Henry Street as rites of passage in their civic educations.[45]

Combining the zeal of moral reform with the Progressive faith in solutions devised by experts, Wald built Henry Street on the solid foundation of her universalist philosophy and her medical training. Her activism expanded incrementally in and around Henry Street, and with it her own political power and commitment to universalism. To the moral language of the Social Gospel, to the rhetoric of Progressivism, she added her trained nurse's view of what measures were needed to ensure the health of her ever-expanding constituency. She linked her nursing with work for other maternalist causes, always emphasizing the special role of women in public affairs.[46]

Efficiency, Morality, and Democracy: Women's Campaigns

Out of the feminine mission in nursing, Wald envisioned and realized broader social roles for herself and her women's reform community. They were to soften the rough edges of industrial capitalism, to protect children, women workers, and immigrants. She used her contacts in the settlement, nursing, and Jewish communities of New York to create opportunities for her women colleagues.

From the beginning, Wald demonstrated her Progressive faith in governmental solutions by linking her efforts to the municipality. The city's Department of Health was receptive and provided Wald and Brewster with badges that declared them to be visiting nurses under the department's auspices in order to ease their admission into the tenements.[47] She also skillfully used her influence with civic officials to advance her causes. One example was when "the Commissioner of Health, a semi-invalid, felt gratitude to a trained nurse who had cared for him." Wald took the "opportunity to approach him" regarding the desperate need for neighborhood playgrounds. She and the University Settlement's Charles Stover had cofounded the Outdoor Recreation League in order to secure safe public spaces for this purpose. Wald recounted that the commissioner "promised (and he kept his promise) to use his influence to get an appropriation on the score of the menace to the health of the city."[48] In 1902, Seward Park was established a few blocks from Henry Street.

Asserting her gendered professional expertise, Wald also began the work of caring for children in the public schools. Following the 1896 report by the city's Department of Health on contagious sickness and absenteeism in the schools, the city hired outside medical inspectors to examine every schoolchild. In the first five and a half months of inspections, 57,986 children were excluded from school due to measles, diphtheria, mumps, trachoma, chicken pox, and other contagious diseases. As a result of the great number of "exclusions," the department was charged with "demoralizing the department of education by emptying the school rooms." Wald lamented that "well-meaning but overworked mothers were not able to properly care for their children."[49]

According to Wald, the Nurses' Settlement stepped in to heal this breach between the men of the medical establishment and those in City Hall in 1902. To the Department of Health, Wald offered the services of Lina Rogers, one of her residents.[50] New York was the first city to have municipal school nurses with gold badges from the Board of Health.[51] The *New York Times* noted that the "city fathers" did not favor public inspection of school-children until Miss Wald "loaned a nurse."[52]

Wald lent a moral cast to the mission of medical inspection and spoke to the broad success of educators in Americanizing new immigrants: "The State recognizes its responsibility for the development of its citizens," she wrote. "To meet this responsibility, the school is its most efficient agency," and it was to be credited for making "a single advance in the growth of civic conscience."[53]

Drawing from the civic and ethnic dimensions of this vision, Wald spoke out on public schooling for two reasons: she hoped these schools would diminish class divides and provide education and health care to all children, and she also endorsed their assimilationist potential while encouraging respect for some cultural differences. When the economic depression of 1905–7 left many school students undernourished, Wald worried that "relief measures" from private charities burdened students with the label of coming from a "poor school." Moreover, some efforts in New York failed because of the religious and national customs of the children: Jewish children suspected that food provided was not kosher, Catholics could not eat meat broth on Fridays, and "the Italian children [found] the American method of seasoning flat and tasteless." She noted successful school meal programs in France, Norway, and Italy, a clear sign that Wald was beginning to connect to international campaigns. The responsibility of the American state as "the stronghold of democracy" was to maintain "the absence of class distinctions" and the students' "sacred right of privacy."[54]

Borrowed from Social Gospel visions of a brotherhood of man, Wald's language in this and other campaigns reflected her sense of the moral issues at stake in state protection of men and women workers, mothers, and children. When the city granted funds for milk stations to prevent infant mortality, she wrote that there was "a grave ethical question involved" and that the city had taken "its proper and dignified position."[55] Maternity legislation and workmen's compensation, she argued, should be based "upon modern medical and social convictions."[56] Her observations about women workers led her to conclude that it was "the moral obligation of those indirectly involved" to advocate for "guarding and advancing the interests of the workers themselves."[57] She became involved in politics when Seth Low ran for mayor on the independent reform ticket as an anti-Tammany candidate, arguing for a "clean mayoralty" free from corruption.[58]

Wald lobbied for these causes in appeals that drew on a gendered notion of moral authority. Of Tammany's disregard for building codes, for example, she wrote that the machine's corruption was a "hideous disease" of the municipality and that "women realize, perhaps even more than men, the community value of protection for health." She continued: "It is of vital importance to women, the home makers of the city, to know that the building laws . . . should be administered by those who understand that they have been elected by citizens." Wald used rhetoric that drew on traditional notions of womanhood and simultaneously justified women's new public roles: she appealed to the "home makers of the city" to better their communities.[59]

Women's magazines, building on and reinforcing the idea of middle-class white women's homemaking roles, praised the leadership of Addams, Wald, and others in maternalist concerns. *Harper's Bazaar* called their efforts to ban child labor "a big, necessary, national movement, concerning the very life and safety of American children." The editors urged their readers to "become an associate member" of Wald's organization, the National Child Labor Committee. "Every woman should use what powers she has to protect and help children," they argued.[60]

Even as Wald linked her nursing work to other areas of reform by speaking in the broadest terms about a brotherhood of man, all of her work reflected distinctly gendered ideas of civic improvement and character. She and her colleagues participated in movements for child labor restrictions, parks, trade unions, public inspections of schools, professional nursing, kindergartens, child-study classes, and supervision of public school nurses. At Henry Street, they offered female clients instruction and club work in the areas of manual training (housekeeping, sewing, basketry), dancing, and literature.[61]

Building on the lessons of her mother and aunts in Rochester, as well as those of her nursing and settlement colleagues, Wald fit comfortably into the female dominion. She pushed at the boundaries of middle-class domesticity—though never challenging their existence—and was a powerful advocate in numerous women-centered campaigns. Her approach to gender difference met with widespread public approval, as was evidenced by her growing visibility and support. The ethnic and civic components of her universalism, its distinction as an ethnic Progressive vision, worked effectively in her maternalist campaigns. Back at the house, however, particularism posed a challenge to the foundation of Wald's work.

"Jewish Goodness": Settlements and Religion, Wald and Jewish New York

Wald's settlement colleagues, like men and women at all social work institutions that counted religious families among their clientele, were held to the task of respecting religious particularism. By the 1910s, with American settlements growing into their second or third decade of work, many staff members had learned from their conflicts with immigrant clients of the need to heed the particular concerns of all religious and cultural groups. Staff members tried to listen to and respect group traditions. Pulling away from their model of Christian Anglo-Americanism, they began to draw on the concept of pluralism in their approach to assimilation and Americanization. In this spirit, minister and settlement house leader Graham Taylor proposed four distinct (and finite) roles for religion to play in nonsectarian settlements: in a silent or oral "grace" at meals and in household prayer; in giving "the same respect and encouragement for every neighbor's faith"; in "active cooperation with the churches and ministers, priests and rabbis of the community"; and in "respecting and encouraging" the religious convictions of all resident workers.[62]

Jane Addams and her colleagues at Hull House settlement in Chicago followed Taylor's guide, even as they saw their settlement work as sharing the goals of the liberal churches: those of broadening the definition of religion and working from Christian ideals to form a more just society.[63] Beginning in the 1910s, the settlement faced a challenge to its liberal, Protestant-based vision of unity from the religiosity of the neighborhood's Catholic immigrants from Mexico. Though there were conflicts, Hull House staff generally respected the religion and culture of their clients and even did the work of "cultural rebuilding" when the United States adopted harsh repatriation measures in the decades that followed.[64]

Even with these efforts in cooperation, settlement residents were easy targets for blame when the second, American-born generation drew away from the religion and culture of their immigrant-born parents. Because an established Jewish community had long set the terms for Jewish identity in the United States, that community felt invested in the identities of this new American-born generation—even as that established community encountered the agency and competing ideas of the Jewish immigrant families themselves. Downtown Jewish clients in settlements that were funded by uptown Jews, then, were a special case in settlement work, with special tensions in their approaches to religion.

In considering this case, Hull House provides an instructive point of comparison with Henry Street, with immigrant narratives offering useful glimpses of residents' concerns with these tensions. In *I Came a Stranger: The Story of a Hull-House Girl*, Hilda Satt Polacheck chronicles her family's immigration from Poland to Chicago and the opportunities she found at Addams's Hull House. On the day she told Jane Addams of her impending marriage, Polacheck writes, she was surprised that Addams's immediate response was to ask if her future husband was Jewish. Relieved to find out he was, Addams recounted the reason for her question: a "distressing" incident in which a "young Jewish girl who had been attending classes in a settlement . . . had married a non-Jew and the people of the neighborhood had blamed the settlement for the girl's 'downfall.' "[65]

Jewish settlements—those with uptown Jewish donors, downtown clientele, and explicitly Jewish-informed missions—were founded, in part, as an institutional remedy to perceptions of problems with religious sensitivity.[66] Their numbers increased nationally from four in 1895 to twenty-four in 1910.[67] Importantly, though, they also tapped into the deep tensions between uptown and downtown.[68] For just as nonsectarian settlement houses at first accepted immigrants' cultural contributions only if they fit within an Anglo-American model, Jewish institutions first accepted Jewish practice only if it fit the uptown model of assimilated, religiously observant American Jewry. The approach of uptown Jewish donors assumed middle-class mores and embraced a more liberal Reform Judaism.

New York City's Educational Alliance, though not officially a settlement house (it lacked residents), serves as one example. It was founded in 1889 out of several downtown charities, including the Hebrew Free School Association that Jacob Schiff had long funded, and it was (and is) located only a few blocks from Henry Street. The Alliance's first annual report of 1893, Wald's first year on the Lower East Side, stated its goals as the "Americanization of [the] down-town population, the spread of distinctively American ideas on government, polity, and civil life." The Alliance was to be "a centre of sweetness and light, an oasis in the desert of degradation and despair . . . which may serve to elevate the distinctive and moral nature."[69]

Invested in the rapid Americanization of the immigrants, the board's condescending attempts at "elevation" encouraged the center's clientele to shed traditions and allegiances. Though it offered Jewish education and Hebrew instruction, Yiddish was banned in Alliance buildings. No socialist or anarchic groups were permitted to use the facilities. One *Hebrew Standard* editorial recorded the concerns of community members: "The Alliance does not link up its work with the olden Jewish customs and traditions . . . [and] a wide, impassable gulf is made to stretch between the young people coming within the scope of its influence and their immediate progenitors."[70]

At an early meeting of the National Conference on Jewish Charities, Jewish communal leader Abraham H. Fromenson blasted the Alliance for its "invertebrate, anemic, condescending, patronizing sentimentalism," as well as its lack of respect for "Jewish ethics and Jewish ideals." "It is unnecessary to present proof that the East Side is Jewish," he said, "but that is not a Jewish institution which suddenly grows ashamed of the name 'Hebrew Institute' graven over its portals and covers it over with a sign-board bearing the noncommittal phrase: 'Educational Alliance.' "[71] Beyond the *Standard*'s wish for bridging the generation gap, Fromenson urged ethnic pride.

The Alliance, like other social work institutions, altered its character and programs to address these criticisms. The board hired David Blaustein, a Russian-born rabbi, as superintendent. Blaustein lifted the ban on Yiddish and tied the Alliance more tightly to community activities. His gentler version of Americanization made him an important link in Jewish New York between the Alliance's uptown donors and its downtown clientele.[72]

Prominent Jewish leaders held Jewish social workers in nonsectarian settlements to similarly strict standards in approaching the widening gap between first- and second-generation Jewish immigrants. As with Minnie Louis's initial feelings toward Wald, Jewish leaders expected Jewish social workers to be more sensitive to the impact of Americanization on parents and children, clients of the settlement house. They assumed, first, that all Jewish individuals had training in Jewish religious ritual and knowledge; they also assumed that all Jewish individuals shared their powerful sense of investment in perpetuating some level of religious particularism. Even "without residing in the community," wrote Boris Bogen, a leader in Jewish social work, "the Jewish social worker . . . may know [the community] more intimately, and exert his influence more effectively than the stranger who happens to choose to live among these people."[73]

Charles S. Bernheimer, a Jew and therefore (according to Bogen) no "stranger" to Jewish tradition, encountered these expectations as assistant headworker at the nonsectarian University Settlement in New York City. He described himself to the assimilated readers of the *American Hebrew* as "living in a settlement, nonsectarian, dealing entirely with Jews," and he diplomatically suggested that all settlements needed to set policy about religion, "either negative, positive, or compromised." At his own institution, he had decided to employ "cultivated Jewish rabbis and laymen" to present "Jewish ideas" in English.[74] Bernheimer crafted for himself a careful endorsement of Jewish particularism, though within a framework that suggested the appropriate level of assimilation and "cultivation."

In a column for the conservative *Hebrew Standard*, a New York City–based weekly that catered to its conservative-leaning Orthodox audience, Bernheimer presented his work in a different light. He first enumerated the many "Jewish activities" at his settlement. Assuaging fears about Christian missionary efforts, he emphasized the fact that a majority of settlement workers were Jews, even as he made clear that those who were not Jewish "respect[ed] the convictions of the members and [made] no attempt to impose their religious views on the young people with whom they [came] into contact." He identified David Blaustein of the Jewish Educational Alliance as the rabbi who taught the teachers and residents of his nonsectarian University Settlement about the "life and characteristics of the Jewish people."[75]

Most pointed in Bernheimer's *Standard* column, though, were his final statements, in which he explained why he was writing "somewhat on the defensive." It was the generation gap, and it was his Jewishness. He was defensive, he wrote, "because criticisms of this and other settlements have been made respecting their attitude toward the Jewish young people who come to them." He elaborated, "I have felt called upon to make some explanation in regard to the University Settlement because I am a Jew and an official of the Settlement."[76]

Unlike Wald, Bernheimer hailed from a ritually observant, synagogue-affiliated Jewish family. Unlike Wald, he was a leader in Jewish social work meetings and organizations (such as the National Conference on Jewish Social Welfare and the National Association of Jewish Social Workers). Because he worked at a nonsectarian institution, he often spoke to these organizations' members, answering their pressing questions about the role of religious Judaism in settlement work, about Americanization and the generation gap. His speeches to these groups told of his strategies as he navigated the somewhat treacherous waters of these conflicts.

As someone who had no Jewish education, Wald often had to rely on others for assistance in navigating such issues. Her background simply did not allow her the sensitivity that Bogen assumed and Bernheimer evidenced. While her approach to immigration reflected a liberal, largely respectful pluralism that allowed room for religious difference, she clearly struggled to accommodate the particularist needs of her neighbors. In 1909, for example, Wald wrote to a friend to ask if he and his wife might take one of the settlement children in for a short time. The Jewish High Holidays were approaching, and Wald explained that to place the child with his mother would only provide him with a "loose street holiday." Wald asserted her strong conviction that she and her workers felt "an obligation to have them [the children] get such religious instruction from their own religion as they are entitled to."[77] Wald's language attests simultaneously to her respect for that religion and to the distance she maintained from it.

Even with that distance and her lack of affiliation, Wald's expertise and rising visibility continued to earn her invitations from uptown Jewish donors, rabbis, and communal leaders. They invited her to join their strategizing about the religious training and observance of second-generation immigrants. In February 1904, the Jewish Endeavor Society was attempting to raise funds to establish a young people's synagogue on the Lower East Side. In keeping with the society's goal of retaining Hebrew learning and Jewish observances among the second generation, its president proposed that the services of this synagogue be Orthodox, the denomination with the highest level of observance.

While Wald's presence suggested that religious Jews saw her as a Jewish social worker, one who shared their concern about the perpetuation of some degree of religious observance, her self-presentation struck a balance that her audience did not expect. To begin, the *American Hebrew* noted, nearly "all the speakers emphasized the need of an orthodox service—even . . . Miss Wald." But Wald took the discussion in an interesting direction and supported the synagogue for a reason separate from the rest of the attendees: "Christian ministers had told her of the need of a religious center, to which they might direct persons of our [Jewish] faith who come under their observation and require some religious attention."[78] The Orthodox Jews in attendance, ever vigilant of missionary efforts among Christian groups that served Jewish clients, searched for the motives behind her risky statement. Following Taylor's guidelines on active cooperation among religious leaders, Wald took a stand on interfaith relations by demonstrating *her* faith in the sincerity of the local ministers. She also highlighted her distance from the Orthodox Jews' concerns about Judaism and the second generation.

Occasionally, Wald's stands earned her an opportunity to respond with the same defensiveness Bernheimer showed to the readers of the *Hebrew Standard*. In fact, her gender made her a target for Jewish men's criticisms— criticisms based on expectations that ran deeper than those of Bernsheimer's critics. But Wald's maternalist self-presentation also provided her with a means to soften these criticisms. When she made it clear that, unlike Bernsheimer, she had no investment in Jewish difference to defend, her Jewish audience simply did not listen; for them, her identity as a Jewish *woman* and a Jewish social worker did not allow for the universalism she espoused.

A telling example of this appeared in a 1903 column entitled "Voices of the Ghetto," in which the English-only page of the *Yidishes Tageblatt (Jewish Daily News)* adopted the rallying cry, "Judaize the Settlements!" The Orthodox paper vilified figures who, like Wald, espoused "the platitudinous preachings of 'the brotherhood of man,' the empty phraseology of 'the broad platform of humanity.'" Jews in the settlement movement who espoused these ideas and worked with Jewish children were, according to the piece, "more dangerous than . . . missionaries!" Editor Abraham H. Fromenson, the Jewish communal leader and critic of the Educational Alliance, concluded, "WORK AMONG JEWS MUST BE DONE BY JEWS—good Jews."[79]

In the following week's column, Fromenson softened his tone a bit and explained that his slogan meant simply "that the leaders in Settlement work" ought to "invite and secure the cooperation of such associates who combine in their souls a thorough knowledge and sympathy with Settlement work and a thorough knowledge and sympathy with Jewish needs."[80] Like Boris Bogen, Fromenson assumed the presence of that knowledge and sympathy in all Jewish social workers. Also like Bogen, he feared the loss of religion among the younger generation.

While Bogen targeted male social workers (as his use of the male pronoun made clear), Fromenson aimed his disapproval at women workers in settlement houses. In this, he was a part of a larger movement among men in Western nations' assimilated Jewish populations. They adopted the bourgeois ideology that made Judaism exclusively the province of the domestic sphere, with wives and mothers bearing sole responsibility for its continuity in private.[81] Jewish men, in contrast, sought to prove their success in the public marketplace. Because Fromenson felt invested in perpetuating Jewish religious difference, his pronouncements reveal his ambivalence about losing the status of masculine Jewish learning. He saw Wald as the gatekeeper to Judaism for the downtown population's second generation, and so he approached her with criticism and paternalism.

In addition to shedding light on the gendered nature of the assimilation project for American Jews, Fromenson's comments and the exchange that followed locate Wald within that project. Because some controversy grew out of these columns, the *Yidishes Tageblatt* chose to send Rose Harriet Pastor to interview Wald, the Jewish settlement worker who was to speak for her colleagues and coreligionists. Pastor was a Jewish immigrant from Russia who labored for years in cigar factories, became an avowed socialist, and later married the (gentile) millionaire James Phelps Stokes, a fellow socialist; eventually, the Stokeses rejected settlement work altogether due to their political convictions.[82]

Wald relied on two familiar strategies in her interview with Pastor: downplaying Jewish difference and asserting traditional notions of gender difference. First, when asked to define a settlement, she simply replied that it "is a renaissance of democracy." She then went on to assure the *Tageblatt*'s readers that all religions were respected at the settlement. "What do you think of Judaizing the settlements?" Pastor asked. Wald "looked quizzically . . . and smiled," Pastor wrote, "answering my question with a question: 'What would you say to Catholicizing the settlements?' " Wald's ironic reply stopped short of suggesting that any religious content in settlement work contradicted what she saw as its universalist philosophy. She identified herself as a "Jewess" but said she felt more a part of the "unit" of the house, made up of residents of all faiths; each found the Jews "a particularly satisfactory people to work among," as they were "eager to learn and . . . quick and apt."

Wald's maternal self-presentation proved successful. Allaying her readers' fears, Pastor fell back on Wald's maternal appearance and style, which she perceived as traditionally feminine and therefore not threatening: Wald, Pastor wrote, "was loved by all those who come in contact with her."[83] Fromenson asserted, however, that Wald's views were inconsistent with her practices. Specifically, he protested her rejection of the "Judaizing of settlements," for, as anyone could see, "*she* makes it a 'Judaized' settlement": "The influence that she exerts is a Jewish influence, the goodness that emanates from her being is Jewish goodness, and those who come under her influence, and those who benefit by her goodness, must and do feel grateful to the race or nation that has given such a daughter to the world for the service of humanity." Fromenson wrote that his community preferred settlement headworkers to be "like Miss Wald—Jewish."[84] His statements were suffused with assumptions about Wald's nature and the essential Jewishness of all that she accomplished. His only criticism, then, was that in her universalist outlook, in the distance she kept from Jewish religious difference, she was not loyal to what he defined as her true nature.

Criticisms of Henry Street's work, though few, suggest that Wald's universalist approach made her seem foreign, even dangerous, to some neighbors and prospective clients. Irving Howe mentions that "some of the immigrants kept themselves apart from Miss Wald's nurses—there were rumors they were secret agents proselytizing for Christianity."[85] In *Bronx Primitive*, a narrative of early-twentieth-century tenement life, Kate Simon writes that her neighbors worried about the power of Henry Street staff:

they had "fearsome stories of brushes with truant officers, visiting nurses, people from naturalization offices, *Them* of the bewildering powers, and uncomfortably close."[86]

Yet Wald's approach also met with enthusiasm. Many observers counted the settlement's phenomenal growth as the result of clients' voting with their feet. Other immigrant memoirs, too, testified to earnest appreciation for Henry Street's work. Rose Cohen's immigrant narrative, *Out of the Shadow*, records Wald's glowing reception among Cohen and her family: "Miss Wald comes to visit, and a new world opens to us," she writes.[87]

Leaders of institutions in the Yiddish community left little record of their sentiments toward Wald's work, and Henry Street's community celebrations were largely not covered in the Yiddish press. This speaks to Wald's success in locating herself among New York's mainstream—and not Jewish—social work institutions. Still, she allied with Yiddish leaders and clearly won their professional respect. The liberal Yiddish journal *Der Tog* offered occasional comment on Wald's "very useful and varied range of activities," praising Henry Street as "one of the most important institutions of the East Side."[88]

Wald's friendship with members of the Yiddish intelligentsia, including Herman Bernstein, founder of *Der Tog*, demonstrates that respect, even among those whose radical politics extended into a class critique of settlement work. These individuals often echoed the sentiments of anarchist and feminist Emma Goldman, who wrote famously of settlements: "Teaching the poor to eat with a fork is all very well . . . but what good does it do if they have not the food? Let them first become the masters of life; they will then know how to eat and how to live." Indeed, Goldman wrote these words after a visit to the settlement house of Lillian Wald, whom she considered "genuinely concerned with the people of the east side," though Goldman felt that settlement work was generally "palliative" and did "more harm than good."[89] Goldman worked with Wald on several initiatives, and they shared enthusiasm over Russia's revolution as well.

Wald's Jewish connections, all told, were diverse and complex, products of personal friendships and professional interests and allegiances. The most difficult struggle she encountered among those connections was that between her own self-perception and the Jewish community's sense of her person and work. She appeared to shrug off—quite pointedly—any association with Judaism, even in response to Fromenson's pronouncements, and yet her inclusion in the *Tageblatt* originated with her acquiescence to being seen as part of "Jewish New York." Clearly, Wald did not subscribe to the Jewish community's fear that immigrants would lose their Jewishness through assimilation.[90] Because she relied on her gendered self-presentation in her reply—she was a teacher, a supporter, a "Jewess," and an expert at once—attempts to target her institution for not subscribing to the new goal of preserving immigrants' Jewish particularism fell far short of their mark. Still, the pressing need for Jewish content, as perceived by audiences of Henry Street, the Educational Alliance, Hull House, and other institutions, testified to a shift in American Jewish identity, as some American Jews began to measure Jewishness (in individuals and institutions) exclusively in terms of religious content and observance.[91]

On her own territory at Henry Street, and specifically in her building of the nearby gathering place of Clinton Hall, Wald's feelings about religious particularism were gradually becoming clear. The idea for the hall arose early in Wald's career with her first observations of the lack of public space for weddings and other social gatherings. "Every time we attended a wedding," she wrote, "it shocked us anew that these sober and right-behaving people were obliged to use for their social functions the offensive halls over or behind saloons." Wald asserted, in the language of morality and with condescension, that "an entirely innocent and natural desire for recreation afforded continual opportunity for the overstimulation of the senses and for dangerous exploitation" in dance halls and bars.[92] A visit to "a simple Scandinavian village"—another sign of her internationalist thinking—offered the idea of an alternative meeting place.[93] In 1901, to raise money, Wald organized the Social Halls Association, an incorporated stock company with a thousand shares of one hundred dollars each. Shares were bought by local merchants and other members of the community, as well as by wealthy donors (including Jacob Schiff, John D. Rockefeller, Benjamin Guggenheim, and George Foster Peabody).[94] "The history of this building has justified our faith," she wrote, "that the people are ready to pay for decency."[95] Ultimately, when it opened in 1904, Clinton Hall contained two restaurants, bowling lanes, billiard rooms, and a large auditorium that could seat 750 people. Settlement clubs and trade unions were to utilize its meeting space.[96]

Wald emphasized in public writings that the building would be "strictly non-sectarian . . . and any and all creeds will be admitted."[97] Behind the scenes, though, she lobbied for what she perceived as a need of the younger generation of Jewish immigrants on the East Side: they required a more liberal Judaism than traditional Orthodox observance. She relied on an uptown connection, Rabbi Stephen Wise, a friend and fellow reformer. Wise represented the enlightened Reform Judaism Wald admired. A scholar of Latin and Greek, Wise in 1907 founded the Free Synagogue, a liberal institution where prayers were said on Sunday (and not the traditional Jewish Sabbath of Saturday), English replaced Hebrew as the language of ritual, and a social services division was formed to meet the challenges of the new wave of immigration. By 1908, Wise had received numerous requests to found a second Free Synagogue on the Lower East Side. "These requests were fortified," Wise wrote in his autobiography, "by a meeting held at the Henry Street Settlement, suggested, if not called, by Lillian Wald."

When Jacob Schiff offered funds to build a Free Synagogue branch downtown, Wise refused Schiff's offer. He felt he could not work with a population that had not asked for his services; the downtown neighborhood would in such a case be "served" and not "consulted with," and he would not preach to them in services "subventioned by the well to do."[98] That Wise felt more at ease using Wald's institutional base suggests that he saw her as a true representative of the needs and desires of downtowners. He agreed to use Clinton Hall to communicate the "teaching and influence of the Free Synagogue" to those "who had not forsaken their Orthodox Jewish moorings and yet were eager in the midst of their humbler milieu to hear the words and the message of an intensely loyal Jewish liberal."[99]

Wald and Wise mapped their own assumptions about their clients' needs onto the offerings of Clinton Hall. Yet again, Wald couched her work in traditional terms of morality and mothering, and this diminished any criticism. The *Hebrew Standard* often attacked Wise for "reforming and deforming the synagogue and the religion of Israel beyond all recognition" while praising Wald's feminine skills that fitted her to head a "national department of public welfare."[100]

Similarly, sympathetic chroniclers of the immigrants' histories such as Irving Howe were quick to use the story of the hall as a clear illustration of downtown immigrants' subversion of uptowners' plans. Howe was a

Yiddish-speaking socialist whose record of the Yiddish community is both proud and nostalgic. He lauds the young immigrants for rejecting Wise's "spellbinder antics," his "mission of conversion," and for instead forming their own Orthodox institutions.[101] In contrast, he praises Wald and her "implacability of gentleness." Though Wise's work at Clinton Hall was in fact Wald's idea, she earned Howe's respect as a selfless, maternal representative of downtowners' earnest interests. In a humorous reference to Wald's radical (pro-labor, pro-peace) stands, Howe calls the settlement an "anarchic matriarchy" and describes her as "tender, sensitive, and sympathetic."[102] Howe misdirected his criticism of Wald's assimilationist expectations—aiming them instead at Wise.

In the early days of her career, Wald most often earned praise and recognition for her precise balancing of the particular and the universal. Congregationalist Rev. Raymond Calkins, for example, highlighted Wald's work for Clinton Hall in his newsletter column. Calkins urged others to follow Wald's example in providing urgently needed sober social activities for the urban poor. "The solution of this problem," he wrote, "presents one of the most practical and pressing forms of civic and Christian service."[103] Wald surely counted this among her successes.

"The Real Americanization Work"

Wald's political authority grew as her work earned successful receptions from all corners of New York. One clear indicator of Wald's growing authority as an expert on all immigrants' assimilation was her position on a state commission, from which her vision of universalism, of the role of cultural difference, gained a still wider audience. Predictably, the position originated with her invitation—this time, to Governor Charles Evans Hughes—to dine at her mahogany tables so that Wald might express her concern about an issue that fused her interests in health care, maternalist campaigns, labor, and immigrant rights and assimilation: the exploitation of immigrant laborers upon their arrival at the port of New York. At her table, Hughes could "meet the colleagues who could speak with authority on these matters."[104] The presentations that evening swayed the governor to create the Commission of Immigration of the State of New York and to place Wald on it as someone with intimate knowledge of immigrant life. Lawyer,

Progressive, and Jewish communal leader Louis Marshall chaired the commission; Frances Kellor, Wald's colleague and director of the Intermunicipal Research Committee, also served on the committee, and the two investigated the "condition, welfare, and industrial opportunities of aliens in the State of New York."[105] The women set out to rectify "the failure of existing agencies, public and private, properly to protect the alien immigrant from exploitation."[106]

Wald, Kellor, Mary Dreier of the Women's Trade Union League, and Lewis Hine, staff photographer of the *Survey*, set out on their "automobile tour of investigation." Over fourteen days in November, often in the rain and mud, they drove 1,286 miles along the path of the Erie Canal (which was being enlarged) and the new Barge Canal, and along the path of construction of reservoirs and aqueducts designed to provide a new water supply to the growing population of New York City. Immigrants from Italy, Poland, Hungary, Russia, and Sweden worked alongside native-born African American laborers on these projects.[107] Committee members examined the hiring, housing, and labor systems of the engineering labor camps to ensure that workers and (in a few cases) their families received fair treatment and lived in adequate housing. Wald was near her hometown of Rochester, but the camps offered little to remind her of her own comfortable childhood.

Wald and Kellor wrote a detailed description of their tour for the *Survey*, in which they expressed their concern for women and children in the labor camps, as well as their hope for "special protection" for new immigrants "to encourage confidence in our institutions, and to promote assimilation."[108] Juxtaposed with Lewis Hine's striking photographs of workers and their children, their words emphasized the state's responsibility to reduce the moral and physical risk to workers through employer liability laws, labor reform, housing and sanitation standards, medical facilities, education for children, bans on liquor and gambling, and provisions for recreation.[109]

After 42 meetings, 9 conferences, 37 hearings, and 193 interviews, the committee submitted its comprehensive 247-page report—of which the "automobile tour" was only one part—to the state legislature in April of 1909.[110] Though Wald was only one of nine authors of the report, her voice comes through clearly in certain sections. Under the heading "Forces of Assimilation," for example, the section on settlements reads: "In the opinion of these friends of the alien [settlement workers], respect for his fine

traditional qualities tend more rapidly to make of him a good American."
With a welcoming reception, the immigrant is more likely to "understand
the genius of our institutions than he would by attempts to instill American
traditions and nothing else." The main task of settlements, the report notes,
has been "interpreting the alien to the community at large."[111]

Drawing on the Progressive faith in data gathering and state solutions,
and on expanding women's public power, the commission was a success in
multiple ways. New York established the Bureau of Industries and Immigration, with Kellor in charge as the first woman to direct a state agency.[112] The
Public Health Council of the New York State Department of Health adopted
a sanitary code for all labor camps. The state also "legislated out of existence" fraudulent banks, express companies, and steamship agencies that
preyed on new immigrants.[113]

For Wald, the commission's report meant that a wide audience of citizens
and policymakers had an opportunity to read her gentler views on Americanization. No longer was she centered only in New York City debates over
Jewishness and the immigrants' generation gap. Bolstered by her position
at the state commission, by her experiences in Rochester and Manhattan, by
her nurse's training and her universalist philosophy, she entered into the
national conversation about the role of all immigrants in American society.
As she wrote to Schiff, "Settlement people are aware that they are doing the
real Americanization work."[114]

Wald began this work at a time when many native-born Americans reacted to the challenges of the new society—increasingly powerful industry,
foreign threats, and a new wave of immigration from southern and eastern
Europe—by turning to nativism and jingoism.[115] As more militant advocates pressed for complete assimilation, she distanced herself from their
movement and fought against immigration restriction. She worked for immigrant rights and later lobbied against the xenophobic 100 percent American campaigns of World War I, against literacy and other qualifications for
citizenship, and against restriction in general.[116] Her letters of protest over
such exclusions reached presidents, senators, and congressmen.[117]

As their early experiences indicated the practical need for a more plural-
ist approach, and in an environment of rising Anglo-Saxonism and anti-
Semitism, "settlement workers were among the first to appreciate the Old
World cultural survival in the immigrant colonies."[118] The settlements'

working philosophy—dubbed "immigrant gifts" for the respect it granted to the gifts immigrant cultures offered to America—carved out a space for European cultures. But simultaneously, settlement workers romanticized these cultures as nobler and simpler than the complex modern American lifestyle, the adoption of which they saw as the goal of the immigrants' adjustment to the United States.[119]

Wald's approach to the cultures of the new immigrants paralleled her philosophy of nursing, which began with the idea of reciprocity: "The patient should know the home of the nurse, and . . . the nurse should be intelligent about the housing conditions, the educational provisions, and the social life of the neighborhood in which she works and lives."[120] Her 1896 speech to the National Council of Jewish Women had also sounded this theme. In it, she urged the elite female audience to learn about the working conditions of those who made the products they consumed. As the settlement's services expanded, she adapted her faith in reciprocal relationships into a liberal view of Americanization as a cultural exchange.

Wald used her connections to the uptown Jewish community to speak to its members about immigration. Separating herself from that community, and feeling less of an investment in the Americanization of downtown Jews (the investment felt by many in the uptown Jewish community), Wald spoke about the mutual responsibilities of the native born and the immigrant. In an early speech to the uptown Jews of Rabbi Wise's Free Synagogue, Wald proposed that settlement residents needed to learn the cultures of their immigrant clients: "Education is called for on our part in their traditions, their motives for coming, their motives in leaving their own country, their political, industrial and aesthetic heritages. . . . to be most helpful, and likewise to establish a relationship of mutual respect and advantage, [a resident] must obtain the historic perspective of these new acquaintances." True to her vision, Wald directed settlement residents to assist in the development of "the powers of the neighborhood . . . through cooperation, not philanthropy."[121] She saw immigration as "new life and new blood for the nation."[122] She cited above all a sincere need for "recognition of mutuality" among the foreign and native-born.[123] While all individuals brought "a dower of great value to America," Wald observed, all were tied together as a "national family" through "passionate devotion for the theory of government expressed by the creators of our Republic."[124]

Wald saw dramatic performances and festivals as opportunities to "interpret anew to the community the rich inheritance of our neighbors."[125] Wald's settlement, like others, offered its clients classes in English and citizenship. But she believed that "popular dramatic and cultural exhibitions" demonstrated Henry Street's "interpretive function" most clearly.[126] Rita Teresa Wallach, a settlement worker, wrote that "in an age of hurry and materialism," when "we moderns . . . interpret all things according to scientific law," it was necessary to acknowledge the importance of integrating the artistic yearnings of the newcomers, which originated in times "unspoiled by the commercial spirit." Romanticizing the supposed simplicity of immigrant cultures, she urged her reader—the "unimaginative American-born citizen"—not to forget that in "some of the less sophisticated spots of the old world these festivities still play their part."[127]

The Neighborhood Playhouse, built with funds from Alice and Irene Lewisohn, two of Wald's good friends from her uptown Jewish network, produced performances that relied on the native heritages of the neighborhood, including Russian, Jewish (from the Hebrew Bible), Japanese, Native American, Celtic, and Native American plays and dances.[128] Wald and the Lewisohns attributed the Playhouse's success to the fact that its work "touched some common ancestral chord."[129] They believed that the reciprocal relationship between the settlement house reformers and the neighborhood could be realized through shows like *Jephthah's Daughter*, a play based on the Hebrew Bible that dramatized what settlement workers saw as the Old World customs of the neighborhood residents.[130]

Just as Wald's work for Clinton Hall drew attention to the balance of this reciprocal relationship and to her thoughts on immigrant gifts, so too did the Playhouse's offerings occasionally engender interesting controversy. Wald and the Lewisohns envisioned *Jephthah's Daughter* as a gift from the neighborhood that they could spotlight. According to Alice Lewisohn Crowley, however, "*Jephthah's Daughter* bore much criticism." Crowley explained: "Our orthodox Jewish neighbors were scandalized at the free interpretation of the Bible text. Caricatures of us appeared in the Yiddish Press showing 'Miss Neighborhood Playhouse' slamming the door in the face of the Yiddish playwright. The radically inclined were disappointed that the Old Testament was used as a source, rather than Andreyev or Gorky, and the conventionally minded were shocked at the bare feet of the dancers. Still another chorus raised its voice in behalf of American culture, protesting that only poor material and no good could come from this East-Side venture."[131] After the Yiddish press accused the Lewisohns of drawing audiences away from the Yiddish theater, the Playhouse produced a few Yiddish plays and even allowed the Folksbuhne—the Socialist Workmen's Circle troupe—to perform, to the dismay of the more conservative uptown contributors.[132]

Indeed, Wald's relationship with Jacob Gordin, "the dominant figure in Yiddish theatre in America," speaks again to her successes in reaching out to the Yiddish radical intelligentsia and the broader Yiddish-speaking community.[133] She and Gordin exchanged correspondence about their mutual interest in the theater and about what plays would most interest "our East Side neighborhood."[134] Wald described Gordin as one of the settlement's "early friends." He contributed to their stage despite what Wald described as the "fear, on the part of the older Jewish communities, that the Yiddish theater might retard the Americanization of the immigrant."[135]

Wald's willingness to address criticism, and to display earnest respect for the native languages and alliances of her clients, set her apart from zealous, conservative Americanizers. It also divided her from uptown Jews who held fast to their refusal to craft American Jewishness using any of the newcomers' cultural gifts. In acknowledging and gently dismissing uptowners' fears, Wald placed herself outside of their cohort.

Wald's vision of the relation of individual citizens to the collective whole of America, as reflected in her theater work and her settlement methods overall, locates her somewhere between cultural pluralism and the melting pot.[136] First proposed by Horace Kallen, cultural pluralism presented a vision in which the political and economic systems of the United States would provide the unifying foundation for different cultural groups to create a "multiplicity in a unity, an orchestration of mankind." Like Kallen, Wald opposed militant Americanizers and consistently said that she respected the ethnic inheritance of each individual.[137] "If by 'assimilation' is meant a complete physical and cultural reduction of the different ethnic groups in America to an American common denominator—then I am against it," she wrote. "But if it is meant as a process of exchange, of mutual advantage . . . then I am for it with all my heart." She called her vision of Kallen's pluralism "mutuality in race relations."[138]

But Kallen was an antiassimilationist, and Wald saw some degree of change as welcome and even necessary: "Assimilation is a *merging* (not an absorption)," she said.[139] This brought her closer to the concept of the melting pot, put forward by Israel Zangwill in his play of that name in 1909. Zangwill proposed a tolerant appreciation for difference, with the fervent hope (and assumption) that American nationality would eventually absorb new ethnic elements to form a culturally unified society: "The process of American amalgamation is not assimilation or simple surrender to the dominant type," he wrote, "but an all-round give-and-take by which the final type may be enriched or impoverished."

America, for Zangwill, was "the crucible of love" in which "past may be fused into a higher unity."[140] Interestingly, in Zangwill's play *The Melting Pot*, Vera Revendal, a former Russian revolutionary-turned-settlement-worker and a young Christian woman, falls in love with David Quixano, a Russian Jewish violinist in New York City. Her parents were formerly royalty under the czar; his parents were killed in a czarist-sponsored pogrom. In the final scenes, on the rooftop garden of the settlement, the two pledge their love as they reaffirm their faith in the "purging flame" of America, where "all races and nations come to labour and look forward."[141]

Zangwill's play endorses intermarriage between Jews and non-Jews. When faced with the fact that her father was directly involved with David's parents' deaths, Vera cries: "I say in the words of Ruth, thy people shall be my people, and thy God my God!"[142] The two meet, then, in a "universal" religion "that will transcend the Jewish-Christian antitheses of the past." Zangwill's ambivalence about difference is overshadowed by his positive feelings about the rational, universalist elements he finds in Judaism and Jewish culture.[143] That Vera works at a settlement demonstrates Zangwill's faith that settlement work will bring out these elements in each culture as the United States strives toward the melting pot.

Wald clearly endorsed a gradual process of absorption that stopped far short of prioritizing Jewish culture and identity. Yet some Western Jews continued to claim her and her work for the Jewish community. On one occasion, far into her career, she encountered the claims of Zangwill himself. She disputed his labeling of Henry Street as a "Jewish institution." His comments tapped into her deep discomfort with Jewish particularism, and so she responded with her own brand of universalism. "It has been our pleasure to prove on the neutral ground of the settlement how many are the things that bind people together and how few are the things that divide," she said, in the very spirit of Rabbi Max Landsberg at Rochester's Temple B'rith Kodesh.[144] She insisted he retract his label, and he apologized: "What I probably said was that both these institutions [the settlement house and the Playhouse] were run by Jewish workers and to a large extent by Jewish capital. And when so much insistence is placed upon our Shylockian character and every shady financier is credited to us, I felt it necessary to boast that members of my race were doing such truly Jewish work as promoting the Settlement and the Playhouse."[145] Transcending such labels altogether, Wald believed, was the only way to end attacks on any one group. This exchange highlights how public was Wald's Jewishness, how commonplace was the attribution of negative racial characteristics to Jews, and how deeply ambivalent Wald was toward entering into any conversation that invoked exclusive claims by a particularist group.

While active in the "real Americanization work" of that era, helping newcomers negotiate their past and present, Wald was herself an ethnic working among ethnics—her family had negotiated its own sense of belonging. Western Jews like Zangwill, Kallen, and Wald were defining many of the terms in debates over immigration and national character. They surveyed the landscape of immigration and assimilation and earned expertise from both personal experience and research. They were, at one level, making space for themselves in that landscape. Yet Kallen and Zangwill spoke from within and to their Jewish communities, and were therefore invested in Jewish assimilation. Wald did not feel a sense of belonging to the Jewish community that may have elicited in her this feeling of investment. In its place stood a faith in the Protestant millennial vision of the brotherhood of man. Most important to Wald in striving toward that universal vision was that men and women of all backgrounds stood shoulder-to-shoulder.

1909: The Distance between Hometown and Henry Street

After sixteen years of leadership at the head of Henry Street's table, Wald brought Schiff with her into two historic events that mirrored her growing reform agenda, her successes in balancing her community commitments. Her roles in both the 1909 garment workers' strike and the founding of the National Association for the Advancement of Colored People (NAACP) offer evidence of just how far she had traveled from her hometown lessons, how strong an influence were her Progressive connections. Her 1909 roles also demonstrate her profound skills in negotiating particularist commitments and universalist intentions, maternalist and modern ideas.

The 1909 New York City garment workers' strike placed Wald and her institution in the center of a struggle that surely reminded her of her final years in Rochester.[146] Again, the laborers were underpaid immigrant Jewish and Italian garment workers, and several of the bosses were German Jews. This time, she did not remain on the periphery. Indeed, she fully involved herself and Schiff, reporting that "he presided at my request at labor disputes." Using his religiosity as a bridge to the new wave of immigrants, Schiff "exchanged quotations from the Hebrew" with "the little tailor who knew his Scripture." In the name of protected womanhood and of unionism, Wald defended the right of the women workers to strike without police harassment. In this strike (and then again when a strike was threatened in 1915), Schiff joined Wald to serve as "literally walking delegates" to both sides of the conflict.[147] The backyard of Henry Street Settlement was used as a meeting place for the striking workers. As testament to her efforts on the workers' behalf, she was appointed as a public representative to the Joint Board of Sanitary Control established by the Protocol of Peace that marked the settlement of the strike; she and other board members monitored workplace conditions for the women laborers. Relying on her sense of women's right to special labor protections, along with her close connections to the downtown residents, Wald took part in one of the first industry-wide collective bargaining successes in the United States.[148]

Wald also brought Schiff along with her as she extended the boundaries of her universal vision across the color line in her organizational work. It was in her earliest years that separate but equal became the reigning racial paradigm in the United States. Yet Wald worked to integrate her table at Henry Street. In 1901, Wald gave Schiff and his wife a copy of *Up From Slavery*, the autobiography of Booker T. Washington, the leading African American intellectual. Two years later, Wald broached the idea of dinner with Washington first with Schiff's wife, testing the waters with someone she thought perhaps more sympathetic to the cause of racial equality. Schiff mildly reproached her: "Of course I would be very glad to meet Booker T. Washington at your dinner table, nor would I hesitate to ask him to my own.

You ought to know me well enough, not to have made the inquiry from Mrs. Schiff necessary."[149]

Both Schiff's and W. E. B. Du Bois's biographers credit Wald with interesting Schiff in civil rights. Schiff's first biographer, Cyrus Adler, notes that Schiff "frequently came to meetings [of African Americans] at Henry Street Settlement and made a stirring address at one meeting held in honor of the birthday of Dr. W. E. B. Du Bois." Du Bois's biographer David Levering Lewis records that in 1910, "Lillian Wald secured a small donation from Jacob Schiff" for the NAACP. Lewis labels this a "major defection from Bookerite financiers," those who had earlier supported the efforts of Booker T. Washington. Indeed, Wald succeeded only after Du Bois himself had failed to interest Schiff in his campaign. In these years—before World War I, and before Washington's death in 1915—Du Bois struggled to gain support from African Americans, and he relied on funds raised by Mary White Ovington, Wald, and other white women in the settlement movement to raise him to prominence and gradually shift allegiances toward his leadership and the National Association for the Advancement of Colored People.[150]

On the one hundredth anniversary of President Lincoln's birth, when Du Bois and Ovington headed an effort to issue a protest statement entitled "The Call" in the *New York Evening Post*, Wald joined fifty-nine other signers, many of whom she had worked alongside in her sixteen years in Manhattan: Jane Addams, Florence Kelley, Rabbi Stephen Wise, and John Dewey were among the white Progressives who signed. "The Call" cited the racial segregation and racist oppression of contemporary America as evidence that the nation had failed to live up to "the obligations imposed upon it by the Emancipation Proclamation . . . [especially] for equality of opportunity and equality before the law which underlie our American institutions and are guaranteed by the Constitution."[151] Wald's devotion to these civic ideals traced back to her family's opportunities, to her hometown community's insistence that culture, and not biology, shaped an individual's potential; her Progressive education among her peers in New York had only enhanced her devotion to this idea.

Those who signed "The Call," a group that eventually developed into the National Association for the Advancement of Colored People, held its first meeting at Henry Street Settlement in late May 1909. Wald's desire to integrate her mahogany table proved tricky, as supporters worried about what the public would say were African Americans and whites to dine together. Ever imaginative, she devised a solution: to serve food to standing activists instead.[152] That the event was held at her institution, with her as hostess at the head of the table of standing guests; that she was among black and white Progressives who attended, several of whom were Jewish; that she counted herself, above all, within the women's community of activists who decried the "present evils" of race relations: the moment reflected on Wald's successful negotiations with gender and cultural difference.[153]

In those moments, during the strike and at the founding of the NAACP, how can we best understand Wald's motivation or categorize her actions? Studying her approach to Jewish difference, for example, makes clear that she was not acting as a Jewish communal leader in the narrow sense that "Jewish" was defined by some members of the Jewish community in the early twentieth century. She was not religiously observant, nor was she invested in the continuity of Judaism as a religion. She is similarly ill-suited for the category invented in the twenty-first century, that of an American Jew for whom "involvement with African American causes could serve as a potent means of mitigating the emotional trauma of the assimilation process."[154] Wald's lifelong faith in and work for assimilation belies this statement. Indeed, this theory reinforces still another narrow definition of Jewishness, because it measures only an individual's distance from a religious, particularist norm. Wald's life requires a more complicated examination of the ways historical actors crafted and expressed their Jewishness.

Was she, then, foregrounding her identity as a woman? This chapter traces the outlines of Wald's own self-presentation: her citing of the lessons of her Rochester beginnings, her emphasizing her universal vision and its links to her feminine ideals. It analyzes Wald's faith in women's biological difference and how her nursing and maternalist activism grew out of that faith.

Looking at her approach to gender and cultural difference in this moment alerts us to a society transitioning to modern gender and economic arrangements. She opened doors for women professionals even as she relied on traditional notions of woman's distinctive nature. She modeled for others how to balance commitments and loyalties, how to integrate into the mainstream while remaining true to a Jewish community of friends and professional colleagues. She did this even as the ways in which she expressed her Jewishness increasingly came under scrutiny and met with criticism from religious particularists—those who made faulty assumptions about her priorities because they saw her first and foremost as a Jewish woman. In a nation of diverse people with deep social commitments, Wald's ethnic Progressivism became a site of controversy precisely because of its universal ideals.

Wald's ethnic Progressivism, then, encompassed complicated tensions over gender and cultural difference. It was the foundation for her expanded political powers. As a leader in the nation's "real Americanization work," she began to present herself as a representative of the disempowered on a broader stage. She soon began to separate that work out from debates over gender and culture in the United States. Global work seemed to her its most logical extension. Born into a family of assimilationist striving, she saw herself as opening the door for other individuals to walk through.

Universal Peace
and Brotherhood

3

Wald saw her authority as a Progressive reach its zenith in the 1910s. While Henry Street remained her home base, the place where her vision succeeded locally, in these years she took her expertise to the international level. Debates about the Jewishness of her work did not travel across the Atlantic; only in New York did she tap into Jewish networks, where they were the foundation of her efforts. These new campaigns, then, granted her more freedom to interpret immigrant experiences to the world at large. She built on her own maternalist authority and contributed to the growing political power of women. In the middle of this decade, she published her thoughts on immigrant and women's rights, on assimilation and suffrage, in a book heralded as the product of firsthand expertise.

With this authority, Wald gradually became a

"broker" in the early-twentieth-century transatlantic exchange of ideas, a contributor to the quest for "models and allies" for American social policy in Progressive Europe and Asia.[1] Many international figures had "crossed the threshold" of Henry Street and dined at Wald's long mahogany tables, teaching her and others about world politics and human rights.[2] Vida Scudder, socialist, English scholar, and settlement house founder, writes in her autobiography: "Lillian Wald of Henry Street showed me her guest book lately; to turn its pages was to review international history."[3] When Wald returned from a 1910 trip to Europe and Asia, her first formal international work, the press recorded her thoughts about the people and social welfare systems of the nations she had visited.

As she continued to interpret American immigrant experiences to the native-born, always emphasizing the potential for assimilation, so she tried to interpret other nations to American audiences. She hoped to encourage understanding between nations as a way to avoid conflict and promote peace. Her steadfast faith in her universal vision of a brotherhood of man led her to observe and crusade on behalf of international causes, none of which attracted as much attention as her antimilitarist stand during World War I.

Wald's allies in various networks continued to inform her perspective on all of these campaigns. As her main connection to the cosmopolitan world of New York's wealthy German uptown Jews, Jacob Schiff was instrumental in helping to arrange her 1910 voyage to Asia and Europe. His own international concerns centered mainly on the condition of Jewish citizens of all nations. She continued to rely on him, though with less urgency, as the years passed and her international networks expanded. Jane Addams's views on war and peace were also crucial to Wald's education. Addams mentored Wald in European Progressive politics, introducing Wald to the figures who had inspired her own conversion to settlement work in 1888. While Wald most often identified herself as a nurse, working for the health of society, she began to portray herself as part of a broader movement of social workers who used their firsthand experience to lobby for global social welfare and peace.

When grieving for Schiff, her dear mentor and friend, who died in 1920, she hoped to memorialize him as part of this same movement—not, as some wanted, strictly as a hero to the Jewish community. Old tensions between Jewish particularism and her own brand of universalism, tensions that had ebbed during the world crisis of war and the local crisis of an influenza epidemic, arose once again. Though she now struck a more confident figure, Wald also faced new challenges over her worldview. Among her colleagues, faith in government experimentation for positive good waned; among her diverse neighbors and donors, the tribalism she had so carefully avoided increased. Respectful of the heritage of their ancestors, fearful of a loss of religious and cultural particularism in the American melting pot, American Jews and other religious and cultural groups began the process of ethnicization, of reinvigorating and sometimes reinventing the ethnic, cultural, and religious boundaries around themselves. Important to Wald's story is that contrary to her vision, in which modernism would be tied to universal belonging with few particularist boundaries, modernism was tied inextricably to ethnicization for peoples all across the world.[4]

The 1910s began with a great feeling of possibility for Wald. She hoped that her universalist experiment could be expanded successfully from her local to a global neighborhood. Henry Street was, after all, where she had broadened the inclusiveness of her universalism across class and racial lines. She had hoped that modern realities would match those inside of Henry Street Settlement. The 1910s ended, though, with signs that her broader experiment would fail, would fracture along those same lines of race, class, and ethnicity that would mark the modern era's crises of politics and identity, nationalism and xenophobia.

Placing Wald center stage in an examination of these years offers a revealing look at Progressivism's challenges in the 1910s. Indeed, because Wald's was an ethnic Progressive vision, grounded in a universalism tied to personal strivings, she felt those challenges even more deeply. They proved just how tenuous was the coexistence of her commitments to universalism and internationalism on the one hand and to local ties and particularism on the other.

Universal Peace and Internationalism

A speech Wald gave early in the 1910s demonstrates the nascent internationalism in her thought. She continued to use her connections to the Jewish community to educate and to insert herself into a crucial national conversation about immigration's effects on American society. Addressing the Baltimore chapter of the National Council of Jewish Women, she began, as she so often did, by taking up "the question of the immigrants or foreigners" and describing the "dream of the brotherhood of man" that had "spiritualized the world" and encompassed her universalist philosophy. The settlement house, she told these upper-class Jewish women, is where "democracy can be tested in a measure not only politically but socially." Her own authority to speak about immigration rested on "the experiences obtained through direct human relationships."[5]

Wald challenged the Dillingham Commission report that had just been delivered to Congress. The commission found the newer waves of immigrants (consisting of people who had arrived from 1885 through 1910) from southern and eastern Europe less desirable than earlier waves of immigrants (1819–85) from northwestern Europe: newer immigrants adjusted and assimilated to American society less easily, were less intelligent, and had fewer skills as laborers. The report argued that newer immigrants would shortly push out the old labor force, as they would work for lower wages. Therefore, the Dillingham Commission endorsed a literacy test and a higher head tax to further restrict immigration.[6]

Wald was one of the few women Progressives who worked with the "new" immigrants and whose family were "old" immigrants. She told the NCJW members that the report lacked credibility: the commission "might have gone about to get the facts to prove their conclusions." The New York State immigration commission's report, to which she had contributed, recommended protective measures for newly arrived immigrants who were laboring in public works projects. Reflecting both her faith in immigrant assimilation and her belief that the government had a responsibility to provide opportunities for such a process, Wald saw the committee's recommendations as a means to promote immigrants' adjustment to America.

Concerned that prorestriction advocates would make "illogical deductions" from the Dillingham Commission's data, Wald disputed the "intimation" that immigrant labor "underbid" native-born labor. "It is fairer to say," she corrected, "that advantage is taken of his ignorance to pay him a small wage, and that as soon as he becomes familiar with the country and its customs" he asks "for the rate that the American laborer considers necessary for the maintenance of his family." She drew attention to the other side of the issue: "Not until the creation of the Bureau of Immigration in New York State (under Judge Hughes' renowned governorship) has there been any legislation that took cognizance of the obligation of the U.S. to protect the stranger from exploitation." She praised Hughes for establishing the bureau without mentioning that he was acting on her idea, proposed to him on a visit to Henry Street in 1908.[7]

Wald spoke of immigrants' contributions to American society and culture. She endorsed the liberal Americanization philosophy of the settlement movement, that of immigrant gifts. It was a proassimilation variant of cultural pluralism that emphasized the reciprocal obligations between immigrants and the native-born. "American complacency needs divine discontent and enthusiasm," she said, "and those of us who are in the Settlement believe that the nation's interests are getting a very definite contribution from these young immigrants." She noted that, contrary to nativist rhetoric, the Dillingham Commission found a lack of crime and immorality among immigrants. Immigrants' children attended school, and immigrant workers faithfully "built the railways, contracted the roads, dug the tunnels" that all Americans used.

Wald positioned herself as within the vital series of connections that illuminated social wrongs. She dwelt on the "degree of unselfishness, and large social conscience" of the men and women she had met in the recent New York City garment workers' strike. They "had the power to comprehend the social effect of their bad conditions, and . . . could interpret it for the city[,] and from them the understanding of labor has come that no course in social science could possibly have given."[8]

In addition to attempting to draw her audience of NCJW members into sympathy with the immigrant workers' struggle—her long-standing task— Wald spoke "of the country's moral and economic responsibilities to itself and the new-comers and theirs to us" in a way that indicated a broadening of her perspective since the early 1890s: "To interpret and to relate each of the nations to the other that we may together reach a higher understanding of life; an actual working out of internationalism which will fit into and be a preparation for the universal Peace that this generation is going to assure to the next—we all devoutly hope. This indeed becomes the obligation of those who are accustomed to act upon thought and to follow the direction of sentiment and affection."[9]

These comments reflect the evolution and development of Lillian Wald's thinking during her years of work on the Lower East Side. They convey the gendered ideal of authority emerging from sympathy, the trademark optimism of her Progressivism, and a pro-peace stand soon to be tested by American involvement in World War I. Her speech also pointed the way toward a broader, more sophisticated universalism, as she applied what she had learned to situations beyond New York City and New York State. Now that she had built successful coalitions with local public and private agencies, she sought to expand her neighborhood and her interpretive work.

Wald's Neighborhood Philosophy Abroad

In 1910, Wald prepared for a transatlantic voyage, both to vacation and to experience more of the world. Predictably, she relied on the connections and advice of Jacob Schiff, a world traveler. As financial advisor to Henry Street and as a protective friend of Wald's, he encouraged this "time off" and tried to assuage her fears of neglecting Henry Street business for six months. "I am sure the world in which you . . . move will get on even when you are away," he wrote, "and it will teach your worthy associates the self-reliance which is the first condition of all good work that is permanent."[10] He provided her with letters of introduction to prominent figures in Japan and elsewhere. He wrote a fairly detailed itinerary, designed, he said, "to somewhat advise you and [traveling partner] Miss Waters in your movements in Japan." His instructions combined protective warnings ("Tokio in February and March is raw and cold, and I would advise you to stay there only a few days") and self-referential tips ("Stop, if possible, for a day at the sacred Isle of Miyashima, which is quite interesting with its Temples and sacred forests, where you may be shown a tree planted by Mrs. Schiff, and of which you might take a snap-shot and bring it home to her").[11]

Wald's response to her travels demonstrated the impact of her seventeen years of experience on the Lower East Side. Public health, workers' safety, women's social and professional status, civil freedoms and rights: for her, each was a crucial component of a society's well-being. Like Jane Addams, Paul Kellogg, and so many others, Wald idealized the social organization in prewar Europe, and in her travels she joined other "American progressives, strung out all over Europe, foraging for what many of them hoped would be their future."[12] Wald's travels to Asia and Europe connected her to a cross-continental network of like-minded people who worked toward a similar vision.

Wald set off on her voyage with three women who shared her worldview: Irene Lewisohn, a founder of the Neighborhood Playhouse, Henry Street's theater, and nursing colleagues Ysabella Waters and Harriet Knight. During their brief stop in Hawaii, Wald took note of the "labor problems" of Japanese, Russian, and Filipino workers and "the very obvious prejudice" of the planters.[13] Japan was the next stop on their itinerary. Schiff's interest in Japan dated from his support of that country's 1904 war with Russia (whose czarist policies against Jews angered Schiff and others); he was instrumental in providing loans to Japan through its special finance commissioner, Baron Korekiyo Takahashi.[14] Schiff notified Takahashi of Wald's visit, and Takahashi sent "the most polite and faithful of guides"—a "walking encyclopedia"—to accompany Wald and her companions during their stay in Japan. Ysabella Waters wrote faithfully to "the family" at Henry Street, reporting how Wald stumped their guide by asking what percentage of Japanese men had the vote. When (after consulting sources) he informed her that the answer was 5 percent, she and her colleagues expressed their dismay.[15]

Schiff's introductions afforded the women entry into the "houses of millionaires and princes," but the travelers also viewed the "social conditions" in Japan.[16] Wald felt "grief" over the introduction of the factory system and worried over the lack of "inspection and scientific care of their little ones." Overall, though, she thought that the nation's social organization was "near perfection in so many ways."[17]

The party then went on to China. Though Wald was discouraged by the poverty she encountered, she was pleased, she wrote, that the "same good fortune followed us . . . where we met people interested in all progressive movements in the diplomatic circles and the educational centres." She remarked on the country's public education, public health, and the need for "women teachers, trained nurses, women physicians, [and] domestic science teachers."[18]

Next, they set out across Russia on the Trans-Siberian Railway, and in the course of this journey Wald observed the threat of deforestation.[19] Wald thought that "progress was beginning" in Russia, though she was well aware of the repressive government policies that led to overcrowded prisons and limited freedom of speech. She had hoped to see Catherine Breshkovskaia, the "grandmother of the Russian Revolution" of 1905.[20] Breshkovskaia had visited Henry Street and was introduced to Schiff in 1905, but she was an exile in Siberia the year Wald and her friends arrived in Russia.[21]

Many of Wald's Russian immigrant clients and neighbors shared her political sympathies with Russian radicals,[22] as did American Jews who, like Schiff, were concerned about the treatment of Jews under the czarist government.[23] Anti-imperialist Progressive colleagues also shared her views, as they looked to Russia to realize (and justify) their vision of a true working democracy.[24] Members of Wald's numerous networks must have been pleased by her testimony that the revolution was not dead, that "there is still heart in the Russian people, and they will fight again for their cause."[25] Even at their final tour stop in England, she and her colleagues visited several exiled Russian revolutionaries, including Prince Peter Kropotkin.[26]

The *New York Times* found Wald's report on her six-month trip the work of a "trained observer." Expressing a broader, international conception of her universalist idea, she told a *Times* reporter: "We brought back new friendships and pleasant memories. These are very personal and precious. The really vital thing is to come back with a conviction of the many big causes that we, as Americans, have in common with the peoples of all lands."[27] This conviction, which came from experience and "not through the written word or through abstract theses," led her to call her Henry Street colleagues "internationalists."[28] In keeping with that idea, Wald brought back a symbol for the settlement. She later explained its story: "Some years ago in Japan, desiring to acquire a suitable symbol for the Settlement decoration, I found it difficult to convey our idea to the Chinese designer. I called upon a young Japanese woman, who had lived at our Settlement, to describe it to him, and in the evening he brought the design which is on the Settlement banner. It was his understanding of our Japanese visitor's story. The symbol reads Universal Brotherhood."[29] The product of a visit to the East, this symbol represented the creed of the Western Protestant social gospel. For Wald, it translated into working toward universalism's victory over narrow particularism. She saw internationalism as her universalism's logical extension and truest expression.

With the adoption of this symbol, the settlement asserted its own important role in the bringing about of Wald's vision of universal brotherhood;

On her 1910 trip to Asia,
Wald asked an artist to
create this stylized Chinese
calligraphy design of the
Chinese character Bao
(brotherhood), the meaning
of which she expanded to
"universal brotherhood."
(Courtesy Henry Street
Settlement and Visiting
Nurse Service of New York)

Wald incorporated that role into the mission of her institution, with nursing at its center. She continued to bring world figures to Henry Street's table for discussions of crucial issues. Wald's institution stood as an international model for similar programs, and nurses from all over the world visited the house to gain practical training in one of the world's pioneer nursing organizations. By 1926, nurses trained at Henry Street worked in forty-eight countries in Europe, Asia, and Africa.[30]

Wald not only led the house and nursing service in these efforts, she also served as a personal resource to others with concerns similar to hers. She retained her connections with allies abroad and lent her network-building talents to various international causes. She corresponded with Baron Takahashi, keeping him up to date on the projects of the house.[31] Emma Goldman asked her to protest a Japanese woman's death sentence.[32] Wald attempted to set up a meeting between a Japanese college president and Nelson Rockefeller, presumably to discuss a monetary gift.[33] British suffragist Christabel Pankhurst lobbied Wald to support women's suffrage, along with Irish home rule. "Will you send us a message to 'Votes for Women' and also one to the general English Press," Pankhurst asked, "and would you also be so kind as to use your influence with other people and induce them to do so? Of course the opinions of men are always important."[34]

Wald at the height of her career, ca. 1915. (Copyright Bettman/Corbis)

Wald brought her neighborhood philosophy to an international setting, connecting people to causes and interpreting experiences across boundaries of nationality. She balanced these broad issues with the exhausting day-to-day routine of an institution whose causes grew in number each day. While she continued to speak about universalism, her outlook was altered: she seemed more worldly, appeared more often in the public eye, and was more apt to draw comparisons with other nations' social welfare policies. In each cause she took on, for each issue she tried to interpret on behalf of laborers, immigrants, women, and children, she appeared an expert, globally minded representative.

The House on Henry Street *(1915)*

Wald's first book, *The House on Henry Street*, presented international audiences with her very local example in troubled times—in the context of the war in Europe and the accompanying xenophobia and Americanization campaigns at home. To Schiff, she stated her goals with more modesty: the twentieth anniversary of Henry Street Settlement approached, she said, and she had decided to give in to "the publishers who, from time to time, have asked me for a history of our Settlement." Wald hoped that the book would be "of general social value."[35]

The book also testified to Wald's emerging independence from Schiff and from Jewish New York, recently strengthened by her struggles over the 1912 presidential election. Her two closest friends and mentors had chosen different candidates: Jacob Schiff supported Democrat Woodrow Wilson, and Jane Addams supported Progressive Theodore Roosevelt, who had bolted from the Republican Party to run against the Republican incumbent, William Taft. Unlike Addams and scores of social workers who saw Roosevelt's campaign as high point of reform energy, Schiff called Roosevelt a "Caesar" and told Wald that he was "disappointed—in an impersonal way" with what he assumed was her pro-Roosevelt position.[36] Her social work colleagues urged her to the Roosevelt camp; Henry Morgenthau, another prominent Jewish financial supporter and adviser to the house, even lobbied Wald to publicly support the Democrats in order to "counteract" Jane Addams's endorsement of Roosevelt, which had "received so much publicity."[37] Though very ill with a lung infection and not active in the campaigns, Wald ultimately confessed to Schiff that she sided with Roosevelt for his reform energy, but also because Wilson had rejected women's suffrage.[38]

The decision marked a pivotal moment for Wald, an important presage to her first book's publication. Though Schiff connected her to friends throughout the world, in many ways he represented her very local New York Jewish connections, those who had brought her to the Lower East Side and first funded her work. Addams represented her connection to American women's reform networks, as well as to Progressive international causes and ideas. Wald's endorsement of Roosevelt signaled her growing independence, as she located herself among an international community of reformers. It was from that vantage point, soon after the election, that Wald recorded her recollections of Henry Street's first twenty years.

The House on Henry Street began as a series of essays for the *Atlantic Monthly*, with Wald exercising her independence and reaching out to a wide audience of reformers and citizens. The story of *The House on Henry Street* is the story of Wald's taking seriously her role as an authority on her neighborhood, as the interpreter of her neighbors' experiences. "I am very happy about this series," the *Atlantic*'s editor, Ellery Sedgwick, told her, "for it is an important public service that the *Atlantic* is enabled to do."[39] Echoing the sentiment Wald wrote about as her baptism of fire, Sedgwick was convinced that Wald's firsthand accounts of life on the Lower East Side would "prick the interest of the professors" and encourage others to study ways to improve the lives of Wald's neighbors.[40] The "kindly insistence" of Sedgwick and his staff eventually convinced Wald to give her essays "more permanent form."[41]

Writing the book absorbed much of her energy. She put her business savvy—networking and the other skills she had learned at the helm of her institution—to work in her dealings with her publisher, Alfred Harcourt of Henry Holt and Company, successfully using another offer as leverage for greater royalties. Two months later, the publisher and his wife joined the Henry Street family at their long mahogany dinner tables. Harcourt described *The House on Henry Street* as so "splendid" that he had "no suggestions" for improvement.[42] While Wald's decision not to attend the International Congress of Women at the Hague in 1915 was largely due to her many responsibilities at home,[43] she might also have been reacting to Harcourt's comment that her departure would be a "personal disappointment" to him and "a business disappointment to Henry Holt and Company."[44]

What was it that Harcourt found so "splendid" in Wald's first published work? The time in which she wrote was a crucial factor. The First World War had begun, and, as Wald's friend and first biographer wrote, "the tragic test of the Settlement's faith in human brotherhood was at hand."[45] In recording the history of her institution, built on "a new sense of responsibility" by people who "worked not only for each other but for the cause of human progress," Wald mourned the news from Europe.[46] The book also served as a "plea for a better understanding of the immigrant and a protest against parochialism" at home.[47] One key audience for this plea was a group of her colleagues who became involved with zealous Americanization campaigns. Inspired by the wartime fear of "divided loyalties," these programs subscribed to philosophies far distant from pluralism and the concept of immigrant gifts.[48]

The book's publication also coincided with a New York referendum on women's suffrage, so that Wald intended to highlight the patriotism of her upstanding neighbors. Wald was responding to fellow suffragists who vented their "disgust" at having to court the votes of foreign-born men downtown.[49] Long before the book's publication, Wald reached out to friends in high positions of American Jewish communal life to obtain information on the "foreign vote." Her friend Max Kohler, lawyer, historian, and defender of immigrant and Jewish rights, had, for example, sent her "valuable" information.[50] Now, in *House on Henry Street*, Wald asserted that "the conviction that the extension of democracy should include women has found free expression in our part of the city."[51]

While these elements are important to any consideration of *The House on Henry Street*, the book also stands as a Progressive and pragmatic document, the history of successful experiments of the settlement written to encourage like-minded citizens to take on the challenges of the age. Wald cited mortality and other statistics to demonstrate the settlement's efficiency and utilitarianism—high priorities in the Progressive lexicon. In her discussions of the nurses' role in the community, she reflected the new faith in social science: "The approach to the families through the nurse and her ability to apply scientific truth to the problems of human living have been found to be invaluable."[52] She included discussions of playgrounds, work in the public schools, and Clinton Hall; she took on the issues of child labor, vocational education, trade unions, and Americanization.

Throughout, Wald cited the importance of firsthand observation and experience. Such experience was crucial to the process of earning "sympathetic legislation," the passage of "ameliorative measures" by a government with a moral responsibility to provide opportunities for all of its citizens. While many of these "constructive programmes" began among "the people themselves," she wrote, "[s]ettlements have increasing authority because of the persistency of their interest in social welfare measures." Wald continued: "They accumulate in their daily routines significant facts obtainable in no other way. Governors and legislators listen, and sooner or later act on the representations of responsible advocates whose facts are current and trustworthy. The experience of the social worker is often utilized by the state."[53] Wald contrasted the theories of social workers with those of educators. While social workers "see conditions as they are" and "almost unconsciously develop methods to meet needs. . . . the school teacher . . . approaches the child with preconceived theories and a determination to work them out."[54] Her observations contributed to conversations about women's professional roles as social workers. In consistently asserting the primacy of her firsthand experience at Henry Street, Wald took part in women's efforts to expand their place within social science, "diversifying its research questions, investigative practices, and political commitments."[55]

Wald's thoughts on immigrant difference also comprise an important conversation that runs throughout the text. Her anecdotes argue for the humanity of the newcomers, and so for immigrant rights; they also document her approach to assimilation. Jewish difference is predictably the focus of much of her writing on immigrant gifts and the inevitability of cultural assimilation. When discussing the "difficulties of readjustment for the pious Jew," she observed the generation gap in Jewish religious observance: "Freedom and opportunity for the young make costly demands upon the bewildered elders, who cling tenaciously to their ancient religious observances. . . . although the *Barmitzvah*, or confirmation of the son at thirteen, is still an impressive ceremony and the occasion of family rejoicing, there is lament on the part of the pious that the house of worship and the ritualistic ceremonial of the Jewish faith have lost their hold upon the spiritual life of the younger generation." She continued with an optimistic prediction for that younger generation, less wedded to religious observance: "For them new appeals take the place of the old religious commands. . . . Zionism with its appeal for a spiritual nationalism, socialism with its call to economic salvation, the extension of democracy through the enfranchisement of women, the plea for service to humanity through social work, stir the younger generation and give expression to the religious spirit."[56]

In this passage, Wald recalled her own conversion experience to the Social Gospel movement, to social reform work. She felt no anxiety toward assimilation; instead, she saw it as pregnant with the possibility of a sort of modern spiritual rebirth. Immigrants would have their own consent, their own choices, take the place of deterministic descent in the passing on of religious traditional observance. Culture and environment would replace biology as the markers of individual potential, just as they had for her. Henry Street would aid members of the younger generation in finding a place for their spiritual allegiances.

Above all, the book was Wald's clearest articulation of her own spiritual journey and of a universalist approach to local and world affairs. Henry Street's internationalist symbol graced the cover of the book and also appeared on the book's final page. Wald's final lines expressed her hope that the working vision of her house on Henry Street could be applied to the global context: "The visitors who come from all parts of the world and exchange views and experiences prove how absurd are frontiers between honest-thinking men and women of different nationalities or different classes. Human interest and passion for human progress break down barriers centuries old. They form a tie that binds closer than any conventional relationship."[57]

The reception of Wald's book by members of her various communities reinforced her faith in human progress and her sense of her own role as a successful interpreter of social issues. Socialist Morris Hillquit chose *House on Henry Street* as his "book of the year" for the *Evening Post*, describing it to Wald as a "human document . . . a book with a soul."[58] Letters praising the book came from people as diverse as Arthur Murray, the dancer; William Dean Howells, novelist, journalist, and past editor of the *Atlantic Monthly*; and Alexandra Tolstoy, daughter of Leo Tolstoy, whose writings Wald greatly admired. The praise of her close friend Jane Addams must have been especially important to her: "I was . . . proud of my author's copy and have done little else but read it ever since it came," Addams wrote. "It is awfully good reading and I want to congratulate you with all my heart."[59]

Academic, political, and popular reviewers responded with similar praise, recognizing Wald's authority and welcoming her anecdotal, optimistic portrayal of the possibilities for those who lived in poverty on the Lower East Side. The *New Republic*, the voice of its editors' pragmatism and new liberalism,[60] spoke of the success of Wald's "laboratory of human research." Settlements, the reviewer wrote, often "are deemed to chase the poisonous mosquitoes of poverty without ever seeking to drain the swamps." But "direct experience" had educated Wald in the "structural problems of poverty," and as an interpreter, she "educated those higher up."[61] The *New York Times* said of Henry Street that "there is no single spot in New York City that so epitomizes the social life of the day, the city's progress in citizenship, the hope, nation-wide, of the nation's future."[62]

Academic journals echoed these praises, though gently qualifying them with implications of the book's lack of theoretical underpinnings. The *Journal of Political Economy* noted that Wald's "sympathetic interpretation" of her experiences made for "pleasant reading." The reviewer appreciated her "many examples of some concrete problem whose solution involved the solving of greater problems."[63] Scott Bedford, writing for the *American Journal of Sociology*, noted that the story of Henry Street is "humanly and interestingly related" in the telling of the "daily experiences of a practical social service worker."[64]

The greatest praise for *House on Henry Street*, however, came from J. Salwyn Schapiro, a historian, uptown Jew, fellow nonsectarian settlement house founder, and one of Wald's partisans at the *Survey*, who devoted nearly five columns to a dissertation on Wald's place in the world of Progressive reform. He claimed Wald's work not for American Jews but as in line with the "cooperative individualism" that is the "distinctive mark of the Anglo-Saxon world." No doubt to her pleasure, he claimed her for the world history of mainstream Protestants. Wald's philosophy—not obvious on a "cursory reading"—entailed confronting social problems "one after another" so that "the whole social organism will undergo a noiseless transformation into a new and better system of living."

Schapiro credited her settlement house with coalition building: she and friends like Jane Addams had "never for a moment lost sight of the fact that the settlement must hitch up with other social movements and with the government in order to accomplish anything really worth while." He called Henry Street a "moral powerhouse," bringing people from all around the world together for social change. And he praised the book's "lucidity and directness," observing, "The reader feels that the book was written especially for him."[65] Indeed, liberals and radicals alike seemed to agree. Written with the intention of interpreting the experiences of the poor to the middle and upper classes, of presenting Wald's theories on immigration and reform, *The House on Henry Street*, Schapiro concluded, had succeeded in its goals. It demonstrated her internationalist vision of peaceful coexistence as it sketched a portrait of her local neighborhood.

Antimilitarism and Preparedness for Social Progress

After Wald completed the writing of *The House on Henry Street*, she drew strength from that vision of peace in her new organizational work. All of the settlement house workers and other social reformers who gathered with her at the house on Henry Street in September 1914, soon after the outbreak of World War I in Europe, were confident that they could use their expertise to successfully reform international relations.[66] Citing their experiences in "lesser conflicts in industrial life," which "embraced groups as large as armies," they initially placed their faith in "treaty-making" as a viable alternative to the horrors of war.[67] In joining the antimilitarist, antipreparedness movement, Wald felt she was taking her role as an interpreter one step further: she was using her authority to preserve the lives of people of all classes and backgrounds when greater forces threatened.

Addams and Wald, who issued the invitation to the meeting together with Paul Kellogg of the *Survey*, were fresh from other pro-peace organizational gatherings. Wald had recently walked at the head of the Women's Peace Parade down Fifth Avenue, and Addams had just returned from the International Congress of Women at the Hague.[68] The group that assembled at Henry Street—including economist, activist, and social reformer Emily Greene Balch, as well as Florence Kelley, Paul Kellogg, and Rabbi Stephen Wise—called itself the "Anti-militarism Committee," a name they changed two years later to the American Union Against Militarism (AUAM). They concerned themselves with the effects of war "not only in the belligerent countries, but in the neutral countries as well." They feared that the purpose of the American preparedness campaign was "to divert the public mind from those *preparations for world peace* based on international agreement which it might be our country's privilege to initiate at the close of this War." They also protested the diversion of public funds into "the manufacture of engines of death" when those funds were "sorely needed in constructive programs for national health and well-being." At their second meeting six months later, they found "abundant confirmation of [these] forecasts."

The rhetoric of the organization conveyed the seriousness of its goals. In a pamphlet decorated with the symbols of Hull House (interlocking H's) and Henry Street (the symbol meaning "brotherhood of man" that Wald had brought back from her 1910 trip to Asia), the committee condemned the war for having "mutilated the human spirit" and "crushed under its iron heels the uprisings of civilization itself."[69] Both Addams and Wald were active members of the AUAM. The board chose Wald as chair in good part because of her residence in New York, where the group held weekly meetings.

The AUAM—like Wald herself now—was distinctly international in its outlook. It favored strengthening the Monroe Doctrine's insistence on the nonintervention of European nations in the Western Hemisphere and called for the formation of a pan-American union. More philosophically, the AUAM took the idea of universalism to a global level, focusing on the cultural and political interdependence between America and other nations, and even citing those nations' successful social welfare programs: "By our heritage from each embattled nation; by our debt to them for languages and faiths and social institutions; for science, scholarship and invention; by the broken and desolated hearts that will come to us when the war ends; by our kinships and our unfeigned friendships—*we can speak as brothers.* [The war] has set back our promptings toward the *conservation of life*; and in a decade when England and France and Russia, Germany and Austria and Belgium, have been working out social insurance against the hazards of peace, it throws back upon the world an unnumbered company of the widowed and the fatherless, and of aged parents left bereft and destitute."[70]

Lobbying for nonpreparedness and nonintervention in the war in Europe, Wald and her colleagues drew strength from their successful campaign to avert war with Mexico in 1916. President Wilson then hoped to topple the regime of Victoriano Huerta for the leadership of Venustiano Carranza, a popular opposition figure. The AUAM's publicity countered the "sensationalist" versions of the incidents and later organized a conference of Mexican and American representatives, including several AUAM members.[71] Finding the representatives of the informal commission "very sympathetic," Wald threw a party for them at Henry Street. When war between the United States and Mexico was averted, the AUAM cheered the victory of this conference. Wald claimed the success as proof that "a little group of private citizens . . . could sit down together and discuss the issues" and in so doing demonstrate "the influence of small minorities in affairs of far-reaching public interest."[72]

That same year, as president of the AUAM, Wald explained to government officials the organization's position in Senate hearings on the state of "Preparedness for National Defense."[73] Bills were before Congress calling for the reorganization of the army and the creation of a reserve army. Military officers, state and federal elected officials, labor leaders, and a few citizens presented their opinions to the Committee on Military Affairs. Wald first presented her qualifications to the committee. (Her testimony regarding her work in an "immigrant neighborhood" and her "communication with the working people and the immigrants in very many sections of the city and of the country" were placed in parentheses by the transcriber.)

Wald's introductory remarks in this most public of policymaking forums suggest precisely how she saw herself and her work—as in line with patriotic American efforts to secure social welfare for all citizens. "I have for a quarter of a century devoted all the energies, all the resources I could command, all that I have and all that I am, to measures that will build up the social welfare of this country," she said. Her task, of the utmost importance, was to "interpret to [the] newcomers the national ideals of this country." Fearing corruption and pork-barrel spending, Wald considered a "militaristic policy" to be "at variance" with these ideals. The money should be earmarked "for that great, real preparedness . . . for the things that we call social progress."[74]

She emphasized that her group was not extreme in its antimilitarism, categorizing its members' viewpoint as that of "reasonable . . . thinking Americans." They were not "representing any disarmament group." She demanded to know the facts of the dangers of the war for American citizens:

how much was to be spent, and on what. She rejected the use of "secret diplomacy," observing, "We hear from our friends in England that secret diplomacy at home is more to be feared than a foreign foe." When Senator Gilbert M. Hitchcock of Nebraska insisted that preparedness was necessary because war could arrive on American shores "like a bolt of lightning out of a clear sky," Wald expressed doubt. Military experts and other figures always knew what might happen, she said, but they chose to make "the matter very obscure to common people . . . ordinary working people."[75]

Wald spoke for—and introduced some of—these people to the committee. She acquainted the members with representatives from labor, from agriculture, and "from women." Though in the past she had employed her approach to women's difference, her faith in their moral natures and natural investment in questions of health and justice, at this hearing she was quick to point out, "We are not making this plea because of woman's point of view."[76] This thought parallels a line in a letter Wald wrote to Addams in 1914, at the beginning of the AUAM's antiarmament campaign: "What I have laid stress upon is that the opposition to the agitation for increased armament appropriations is a man's affair. I have no objection to women's making it their affair too, but I would not like to fix in the public mind that it is not a man's affair."[77]

Instead of identifying herself as a nurse, she located herself as "part of a growing group of people who call themselves social workers." Wald explained: "We are not theorists and do not present our views as academic people do. We present them based upon actual knowledge, years upon years of knowledge of what really affects the great mass of people, the working people and the people who are not always as articulate as they should be. . . . We say, go slow on preparedness. . . . We want investigations . . . on the present budget, and . . . we want a hundred cents for every dollar that has been invested. We stand for taking the private profit out of so-called 'preparedness.' "[78] After reading an antipreparedness statement from the president of the United Mine Workers of America, Wald introduced James H. Maurer, president of the Pennsylvania Federation of Labor; Florence Kelley; Mr. Frank Donnblazer, executive board member of the National Farmers' Union; and Sara Bard Field, a California citizen and suffragist.

The testimony of Florence Kelley, Wald's close friend and colleague and a resident of Henry Street, sheds light on the various strategies employed by women reformers in their work. Wald introduced Kelley as "the daughter of an American statesman, [William Darrah Kelley,] who for 30 years sat in the House of Representatives." In making a plea for a "patient hearing" of what she had to say, Kelley added that her grandfather had fought in the Revolutionary War, her uncles in the Mexican and Civil wars, and her brother in the Spanish-American War. In contrast, Wald, lacking a similar legacy of family sacrifice for the nation during wartime, had cited her life's work as the source of her authority. The Wald family's strivings, along with her reform work, also contributed to that authority.

While Wald asserted that her group did not base its plea for unpreparedness on a "woman's point of view," Kelley chose to use that point of view as her main strategy. She argued that "overpreparedness . . . is primarily the concern of women." Referring to herself as "a mother" and "an old woman," Kelley echoed Wald's demand for information as to how the money was to be spent. "I speak as a mother," she stated, "and I know what it means to women, to threaten us with becoming one of the military nations." She boldly urged the committee to stop wasteful spending and "redistribute the expenditures . . . to take care of the boys who will be soldiers and the women who may be soldiers' wives and who will certainly be valuable citizens if they are allowed to be alive and be educated."[79]

The differing approaches of Wald and Kelley reflect the diverse strategies women reformers used in their universalist campaigns for peace and justice. Kelley was a member of the AUAM as well as a socialist, and her greatest achievements were protective social and labor legislation on behalf of women and children. She spoke to their interests in her testimony.[80] Though Wald had participated in the Women's Peace Parade, she chose at this moment to speak to the concerns of those who believed that a commitment to preparation for war meant huge setbacks for all reform movements. Both Kelley and Wald sought to represent the common men and women who benefited from public commitments to social welfare and who could easily be deceived into supporting preparedness by specious information.

When the United States entered the war in April 1917, the AUAM held fast to its goal of "the ultimate abolition of war." Because armament meant channeling resources away from social programs, its members knew that war threatened to undo both domestic and international progress toward social welfare. In May, it listed the main points of its immediate program, many echoing the points in Wald and Kelley's testimonies:

1) to oppose all legislation tending to fasten upon the United States in war-time a permanent military policy based on compulsory military training and service
2) to test the conscription act in the courts
3) to organize legal advice and aid for conscientious objectors
4) to fight for the complete maintenance in war-time of the constitutional rights of free speech, free press, and free assembly
5) to demand immediate publication by the government of all agreements or understandings with other nations, and a clear and definite statement of the terms on which the United States will make peace
6) To keep the ideal of internationalism alive and growing in the minds of the American people to the end that this nation may stand firm for world federation at the end of this war

   OR

7) To keep the ideal of internationalism alive and growing in the minds and hearts of the American people, and to cooperate with similar organizations in other countries in developing a spirit of international fellowship strong enough to bring about world organization for lasting peace at the close of this war.[81]

The organization sent a letter to President Wilson, whom Wald and others had met several times prior to American entrance into the war, enumerating these points and emphasizing the "ideal of internationalism." Wilson replied that he would try to act "in the spirit of [their] suggestion."[82] This was now the spirit of much of Wald's global activity, drawn from her hometown lessons and her New York experiences among uptown and downtown Jews and Progressives.

Though Wald had long felt comfortable articulating her ideals through the AUAM, during the summer of 1917, she and several other members grew unhappy with the organization's radical turn.[83] The day after Congress passed the Selective Service Act, Roger Baldwin, like Wald a founding member of the AUAM, proposed the formation of a new bureau for conscientious objectors. Wald and Kellogg both feared that the bureau marked a "radical

change in the policy of the union." Wald protested, "We cannot plan continuance of our program which entails friendly governmental relations . . .
and at the same time drift into being a party of opposition to the government."[84] All members accepted the compromise proposed by Crystal Eastman, that an independent group called the Civil Liberties Bureau split off
from the AUAM. A few months later, the board—against the objections
of Wald and others—voted to send representatives to a conference of the
People's Council, an antiwar group.

Wald had spent much of her career cooperating with and serving government agencies in countless reform campaigns. Her Progressivism was
grounded in a faith in state solutions. What she saw as "anti-government"
moves by members of the AUAM convinced her to resign her chairmanship.
She wrote to Addams, "I am very, very sorry for I think that we have a
definite place in the position that some of us feel that we ought to hold:
namely, the holding on of the civil rights and opposition to militarism, but
not opposition to the government, not embarrassment to the government."
In part, she saw the problem as generational, telling Addams that the younger members only gradually detected problems that were "so obvious to the
older minds." Mainly, however, she saw the divide as a political one: she felt
that "a committee of liberals"—not radicals—was needed to achieve the
organization's original vision of peaceful internationalism.[85] Working with
governmental powers was a key component to the realization of this vision.

Wald's resignation marked the first sign of her difficulty in wrestling
with radically different ideas. Her universalist vision entailed a complete
faith in the goodness of mankind, in the rightness of institutions. Her sharp
criticisms of governmental preparedness notwithstanding, Wald was un-
willing to join the growing modern opposition to such policies.

Yet even her struggles with the AUAM did not slow down her pace. Wald
kept attuned to issues back home that emerged as a consequence of the
march toward war. She supported the Mothers' Anti–High Price League,
for example, a group of immigrant women who protested the city's high
wartime food prices. With the league, she approached the mayor and the
Board of Estimate. She joined her neighbors in lobbying for a policy change,
urging the city to allow these women to remain "self-supporting."[86]

Though she continued to work for the cause of peace at home and abroad,
soon after resigning from the AUAM, Wald had to once again shift her

energies to a local crisis, in this case a practical task of preparedness at which she clearly excelled: she was appointed chair of the Nurses' Emergency Council during the influenza epidemic, and she oversaw the coordination of services from hospitals, social work agencies, nursing schools, and religious institutions. The battle against influenza was waged by an "army in nurses' blue" under Wald's command.[87]

The influenza outbreak of 1918 threatened the lives of hundreds of thousands of people and strained the public health facilities of New York City to their breaking point. Hoping to raise support, Wald's Nurses' Emergency Council took out an advertisement announcing "A Stern Task for Stern Women," summoning nurses and even untrained volunteers to help the sick with the plea that "Humanity calls them" and "Lives depend upon their answer."[88] Wald initiated a distribution plan for the advertisements that brought the resources of the wealthy to bear on the crisis: "Dignified and discerning women stood on the steps at Altman's and Tiffany's Fifth Avenue shops and accosted passers-by." The ads were a success: "Before the day was half spent, hundreds of men and women came to the office to volunteer their services," she later recollected.[89] Wald used her authority as chair of the Nurses' Emergency Council to call for more organization and cooperation among doctors, hospitals, and nurses, and for more philanthropic support for her Visiting Nurse Service, on which the public was increasingly dependent for health care.

Only a few months after her letter to Addams on the radicalism of the AUAM, Wald attended daily afternoon meetings of the Executive Committee of the Nurses' Emergency Council; her secretary reported to many of her friends that she was working until ten or eleven each night and was unable to complete even the monthly Henry Street reports.[90] This was a familiar rhythm to her: pulled from an international crisis to a national or even municipal matter, she saw all as within the scope of her concern. In 1919, two large-scale conferences, one international, one domestic, pulled her in these two directions once again.

1919: The Year of "Questions Which Know No Boundaries"

The decade that began with Wald's idealistic voyage to Europe ended with a dispiriting look at what war had wrought there. The lessons she had learned during the war—how to shift the focus of an antiwar organization once the nation became involved in the war, how to mobilize for a massive public health emergency—she brought to bear on her participation in conferences on world public health, nursing, and the future of American industrial relations. Her experiences foretold the eclipsing of her universalist vision.

Wald represented the Children's Bureau[91] and the Red Cross Nursing Service at the 1919 International Health Conference in Cannes, France.[92] Expert medical and scientific professionals from France, England, Italy, Japan, and the United States attended; those "from the former enemy countries and Russia" were excluded until "mutual confidence and cooperation [could] once more develop."[93]

The conference participants proposed to pool the scientific knowledge and resources of all nations' Red Cross organizations by establishing the League of Red Cross Societies, with an attached bureau on hygiene and public health "in the interest of humanity."[94] This organization corresponded to Wald's vision of international cooperation, a vision she strove to realize at Henry Street and in the AUAM. Hers was the Progressive ideal of the scientific gathering of firsthand knowledge and the subsequent formulation of appropriate policies, an idea she had worked for since 1893.

At this international conference on the prevention of disease, Wald contributed to two sessions. She and her nursing colleagues proposed a nursing department within the Red Cross that would act "as an intelligence center" to gather data and "seek out personnel for training both in sick nursing and in public health work." In the session devoted to child welfare, Wald and her colleagues stressed the urgency of maternal and prenatal health, as well as the need to address crises of malnutrition and infant and child mortality.[95]

Wald sent a cable from Cannes to the New York office of the *Survey*, observing the fact that "doctors found agreement easier than diplomats." Echoing the pleas for earnest internationalism that she expressed before the war, she spoke of the serious need for such cooperation—including both the Allies and the Central Powers—in the face of epidemics: "The time must come . . . when all peoples of the world will combine to solve these questions which know no boundaries. Typhus and influenza have no respect for frontiers, and world-wide epidemics must be met by united force."[96]

While Wald believed in the potential of the International Red Cross, she was deeply saddened by the suffering that surrounded her in Europe. She had "a sense of frustration of social effort" when she saw the war's toll on the physical and mental states of French, German, and Russian citizens. She noted food, housing, and health care shortages, and she spoke especially about the suffering of children in these countries. She was troubled by the lack of cooperation between American and domestic social workers in France.[97] "The only refreshing optimism Miss Wald found," the *Survey* reported, "was among the smaller units of American social workers, mostly in more outlying communities, who were carrying on their work of relief and reconstruction in the spirit and by the method of early social settlement experience."[98] Wald had long believed that when social workers applied the lessons of Henry Street to a larger "neighborhood"—when information was shared and understanding among different groups was fostered by contact —success could be achieved. Only on the smallest scale, in the countryside of France, did she find proof of that.

Wald returned home to see the spirit of cooperation threatened throughout her more immediate neighborhood, as labor strikes broke out on a historic scale across the United States. The strikes of police officers, miners, and mill and factory workers (including the great steel strike), along with workers in railroads and harbors, led to fears of economic instability. After including an article on labor in the Treaty of Versailles, President Wilson called an Industrial Conference in Washington, D.C. He invited a delegation from labor (specifically, from the American Federation of Labor and the railroad brotherhoods; more radical unions—as well as the unorganized— went unrepresented), management, and individuals whom he felt would represent "the public interest." They were to begin a conversation that would, he hoped, form the foundation for more harmonious relations between labor and capital.

Fifteen years had passed since Wald's uncles had taken antilabor stands in her hometown of Rochester; a decade had passed since she played a role as a public representative of workplace safety in the Lower East Side garment strikes of 1909. Wald's opinion on the massive strikes of 1919 had been sought out since they began. At the beginning of the year, she received a letter from clergyman and reformer Charles Stelzle asking for a brief message that would be read by "a million workingmen in scores of industrial plants all over this country." The request would put Wald in the league of "some of the leading men of this country." While her message could "perhaps contain pathos or humor," Stelzle requested that she say "something about team work, personal efficiency, loyalty to employers . . . or whatever else you may have in mind." Wald's reply made her position clear: "Through ORGANIZATION men and women can most effectively bring about their purposes. . . . it is organization . . . that has made it possible to secure better conditions of labor and wage" and "must now, in equal degree, secure the advantages of spirit and mind."[99]

A few months later, Wald received a last-minute invitation to attend Wilson's labor conference, again as a representative of the public, in place of suffragist Carrie Chapman Catt. During the course of the conference, she corresponded with Schiff, asking his thoughts on the relationship between labor and capital, which she assured him would be "of value to the whole country." "I doubt whether *any* elaborate scheme will prove practicable," Schiff responded, "and I cannot find any other practicable substitute for the strike than arbitration, compulsory if it must be. In the end this must be the kernel of any scheme to assure industrial peace, all else will be only camouflage."[100]

Wald lent her voice to issues with which she was quite familiar as a nurse, public health advocate, and Progressive reformer. With two other representatives, she contributed to a proposal for a "ready and periodical adjustment of standards of pay of all federal civil service employees"; alone, she proposed a resolution "that child labor should be eliminated as a factor in American industry." She introduced resolutions for employing nurses in industrial plants, and she voted for a resolution that secured for laborers the right to have their own representatives negotiate with employers.[101]

In her second book, *Windows on Henry Street*, Wald refers to the conference as a "painful incident."[102] Wilson's Versailles treaty had already been repudiated, a Republican president had been voted into office, and American representatives of capital and labor simply could not agree. The conference ended without its delegates' passing a single resolution.[103] Wald's frustration mirrored the sentiments of conference representatives who had traveled from Europe to attend. As a "balm" for their pains, she invited them to a "supper" at Henry Street, "when they were encouraged to 'explode' their disappointment and to realize that, though Washington had failed, many Americans were deeply concerned with their mission and disturbed by the fiasco of the conference reception."[104]

Back on her home territory, sitting around the Henry Street table, Wald reassured the international conference representatives that her projects—the settlement and the nursing service—were in the spirit of their mission, proof of Progressive, practical idealism at work in the United States. Here, at least, in this small gathering, they could discuss and consider their ideas and then circulate them among Wald's many networks of men and women, Jewish and non-Jewish reformers, politicians, and philanthropists in New York, Chicago, and throughout the world. Henry Street—and Wald at Henry Street—stood at the nexus of these networks. She and her institutions continued to thrive despite the failure of her social vision on the world stage.

As the decade of internationalism and war drew to a close, Wald sensed that America, indeed the larger world, was in the midst of great social change. "The industrial conflict," she wrote to a local journalist, "is only one of the manifestations of the changing social order."[105] The era's labor relations and public health crises represented only two of the modern, serious problems now transcending national boundaries.

Henry Street's potential suggested to her a range of possible solutions, and she continued to draw on it as an example even as this "changing social order" emerged. As she had written in *House on Henry Street*, the Henry Street Settlement was a place where boundaries between individuals fell away, revealing universal commonalities. She had there formulated her own vision of modern times, which encompassed voluntary assimilation and integration alongside cross-class coalition building. Henry Street's community was the truest expression of her vision. It gave her the authority to speak about immigration and America's "national ideals" to congressional and other national leaders.

The decade that began with her first international voyage, however, ended with a drastic change in the shape of that community, and with a debate that foreshadowed new contests over the terms of her own and others' assimilation and integration. The debate drew her back into the boundaries of Jewish New York—the community that had introduced her to the needs she now worked to address—in a moment of grief.

"Mr. Schiff's Interests Were as Wide as the World"

In 1920, Wald's top professional priority was the growth of her own institution—the foundation of all of her work—and the need for funds that growth
entailed. She and her board planned a one-million-dollar fund-raising campaign for a week in the spring. The money would provide additional nursing
centers in Manhattan, the Bronx, and Staten Island; train undergraduate and
graduate nurses in public health work; and establish a night-and-day maternity service. Highlighting the partnerships between public and private
agencies that had worked for the settlement from the beginning, Dr. Royal
Copeland, the city's health commissioner, formally announced the campaign at a Bankers' Club luncheon on 29 February. He expressed his amaze-
ment that the "City Charter made no provision for the care of sick persons in
their homes," and he cited especially the efficacy of the nurses' work during
the 1918 influenza epidemic. The Campaign Commission was a who's who
of Wald's many overlapping networks, including the Schiffs and Warburgs,
as well as Commissioner Copeland, Ethel Barrymore, Bernard Baruch, Mrs.
August Belmont, George Gordon Battle, T. Coleman Du Pont, and other city
social workers and elite philanthropists.[106] General John Pershing, com-
mander of the American Expeditionary Forces during World War I, spoke at
the kickoff luncheon, endorsing the nurses' work based on his own experience: "The visiting nurse service here in New York City may very well be likened to that on the battlefields of France, and this city can do itself no higher
credit than to take up this cause and enable the service to enlarge its field."[107]

Jacob Schiff did not counsel Wald through this campaign (his firm's legal
adviser, Paul Cravath, chaired the committee),[108] in part because his atten-
tions were drawn to the suffering of Jews in central and eastern Europe, in
part because that year marked the beginning of his gradual retirement from
philanthropic leadership.[109] But he and his wife offered the first donation of
fifty thousand dollars, which set the precedent for Mr. and Mrs. Felix Warburg, followed by Mr. and Mrs. John D. Rockefeller.[110]

Schiff's death on 20 September 1920 was devastating to Wald. Paul
Kellogg, editor of the *Survey*, asked her to write an obituary for the journal. In it, Wald shared one memory of Schiff's support for measures that
were "strange and remote from [his] experience, interest, and traditions."

Though he rejected the use of strikes to settle labor struggles, she wrote (no doubt about the garment strikes of 1909), "he readily agreed to bring the manufacturers to a conference—the Settlement [was] to bring the workers and the contractors." Wald continued: "He left the conference convinced of the oppressive position in which the employees in this branch of the trade had been placed, and all through a long-fought out struggle furnished money to relieve the needs of the families of the strikers, until they, triumphant, were able to contract better terms for labor. His sense of justice offended repeatedly brought forth a gallant fighter for the oppressed, and his reverence for the sanctity of others was as marked."[111]

In private, Henry Street nurses and friends gathered to honor Schiff in a simple memorial ceremony a few weeks after his death. While expressing "loving sorrow" for her friend and reflecting on the role Henry Street had played in his life, Wald also memorialized Schiff's deep commitment to Judaism and the Jewish community.[112] She described him as "devout and steadfast in his own faith," lauding him for viewing "projects for help and education" as part of his "obligation and responsibility." "His conception of the obligations of citizenship," she wrote, "was in essence a religion."[113] Throughout his lifetime, no discussion of Schiff could ignore his commitment to what were seen as Jewish and American ideals, and Wald's careful writing conflated the two. In their founding of Henry Street, they had done the same.

After decades of working alongside Jews and non-Jews dedicated to social progress, Wald found herself pulled into familiar situations with familiar tensions when faced with early requests for help in building a public memorial to Schiff. Similar to debating the settlement's Jewishness with Israel Zangwill, a key figure as author of *The Melting Pot*, Wald in this moment debated Jewish memorializing with Isidor Singer, a Jewish history scholar and editor of the *Jewish Encyclopedia*. The encyclopedia was published between 1901 and 1905 to provide a "faithful record" of Jews' "prominent part in the development of human thought and social progress throughout the centuries."[114] Singer's encyclopedia, first among many such records, promoted mainstream acceptance of Jewish contributions; it did so with a degree of ambivalence, however, as it also highlighted the Jewishness of contributors in order to draw boundaries around a group blending quickly into that mainstream.[115] Interestingly, the Schiff family—along with Isidore

Singer himself—appeared in the encyclopedia, though the Wald family did not. This is not surprising, though, as few Jewish women are specifically mentioned, and the Wald men were not noteworthy from a Jewish communal perspective.

Singer wrote to Wald "as one of the most fervent admirers of Jacob H. Schiff." He hoped to memorialize Schiff as a "great American Maecenas of Jewish literature." Singer mentioned that the tribute would be a collective effort, by Jews and non-Jews. Wald's hurried reply, though, demonstrated her knowledge of Singer's projects, which prompted her fear that Schiff's memorials would celebrate only his Jewish contributions. "I do not . . . believe that it should be a purely Jewish memorial," she replied to Singer, "for Mr. Schiff's interests were as wide as the world."[116]

Wald might easily have been writing about herself. Like Schiff, she had ventured far beyond the boundaries of Jewish New York. Indeed, in his letter, Singer wrote about Wald, calling her and Rebecca Kohut[117] "a kind of sociological Yankee-Deborahs" and urging her to help Therese Schiff "play the role of a new sort of a Pieta, the Uxor Dolorosa, offering in this noble role material and spiritual comfort to the widows and orphans." For Schiff's own role in establishing and legitimating the Jewish presence in America, Singer hoped to establish a Schiff Foundation "on the style of the 'Rockefeller Foundation,' which ought to take under its wings those subjects and institutions which were dear to the heart of our lamented friend."[118]

Because she felt no ambivalence about the movement of Jews like herself into the mainstream, because she felt no investment in drawing boundaries around Jews as a modern particularist group, Wald moved in a different direction. She hoped to affix Schiff's name to secular and public memorials that honored the issues they had worked for at Henry Street. Schiff Parkway, the Delancey Street approach to the Williamsburg Bridge, was the first broad highway available to those coming and going to work from Brooklyn and the East Side. Wald wrote that it was "probably traveled by more workers than any area of equal length in the world." Once the parkway bore his name, she lobbied for trees to be planted in the park that ran beside it. In Schiff's memory, the city had to continue to recognize, she wrote, "the appreciation and love of green growing things by plain folk."[119]

Schiff's widow, Therese, decided that the proper memorial for her husband was an administrative center for the Visiting Nurse Service, which

Schiff had worked toward for several years before his death.[120] She donated a building at 99 Park Avenue.[121] The 260 nurses worked out of twenty-two nursing centers and visited almost 350,000 sick people in their homes each year, from Manhattan to Staten Island, beyond Yonkers and into West-chester County. The top floor of Henry Street was no longer sufficient as a central location for the nurses, and Henry Street Settlement grew larger each year as its own independent institution.

In a tribute to Schiff and to the connections Wald made between phi-lanthropists and activists, Jane Addams wrote the words for the dedication of the new administrative center that were then carved over the fireplace in the building's main conference hall: "This building is given in memory of Jacob Henry Schiff by Therese, his wife, and is dedicated to the cause of public health nursing, which he long fostered for love of progressive educa-tion, civic righteousness and merciful administration."[122] These were the priorities of Wald and Schiff, the reason they had formed a partnership in the settlement. Though the editors at the *Times* feared that the nursing institution might change now that it was on Park Avenue, they expressed their relief that "Miss Wald is here to see that this new centre of a larger service, whatever its physical location, is still, in spirit, in 'Henry Street.' "[123]

By then, Wald's commitments stretched far beyond the confines of the island of Manhattan. Still, the *Times* editors took a rather romantic view of Wald's "spirit" guiding Henry Street to keep its personal, humane, and distinctively feminine approach to local social problems. Many other con-temporaries of Wald—and indeed, many scholars of Wald's life today—echo this romanticized view, portraying her work on all levels as a series of unqualified successes.

But to trace Wald's life and career past 1920 is to see a gradual change in the nature of her contributions to public debates. With her wide travels and exposure to new ideas, her universalist social vision matured. As Schiff and a few other older friends passed away, she assumed an independence of thought and authority. Her vision remained rooted in a local experience at Henry Street, however, where individuals were brought together in com-mon cause. Wald continued to hold fast to this vision of what the modern world might be, even as the devastation of World War I suggested another, more brutal model of modern times, and even as the emerging ethnic landscape suggested new terms of difference in modern identities.

4

The Society We Might Be Living In

MODERN CHALLENGES *to* AN
ETHNIC PROGRESSIVE VISION

Progressives like Wald wrote of their profound disillusionment in the early 1920s. To her friend judge Charles Evans Hughes, who, as New York governor in 1908, had appointed her to her first state commission, she remarked: "I have never had a more serious time in all my years of service than to keep alive in the hearts of good Americans their faith in our country—particularly those who have come to us from other lands and who have worshipped America. . . . The best of us are bewildered these days, and it is no strain upon the imagination to perceive what an Un-American persecution might mean to the ordinary boy and girl."[1] As late as 1916, Wald testified before Congress about how she had interpreted "national ideals" to new immigrants. Four years later, she saw American commitments to a pluralist society give way to a rising conservatism in the United

States. Progressives had hoped that World War I would outmode nationalism and that experiments in massive government economic intervention, or "war collectivism," would embolden an activist peacetime state.[2] Instead, nativist and racist sentiments continued to be sanctioned by a government that promised not radical experimentation in social welfare but a return to "normalcy."

These shifts in national priorities were symptoms of what Wald presciently referred to in 1919 as a "changing social order." For her, the changes marked the gradual eclipse of her universalist vision and a decline in her public power. Tracing her work though the 1920s and 1930s, especially her positions on Stalinism and Zionism, brings into relief the difficulties she faced in applying this vision to developments in the conservative interwar years.

After Schiff's death in 1920, Wald appeared increasingly independent of New York's Jewish communities (both uptown and downtown), especially with regard to her public admiration for revolutionary Russia. While these communities carefully monitored the new regime's treatment of Jews, Wald insisted that her involvement stemmed instead from a more universalist set of concerns: she was a Progressive who looked to Russia as a model of democracy and equality. As Jewish communities and others sounded alarms about Stalinist abuses, Wald's faith in Russian collectivism remained unshaken, and her vision increasingly myopic.

In debates over the Zionist movement, Wald again maintained a calculated distance from the position of the major pro-Zionist Jewish organizations. Her public pronouncements on Zionism made clear her role as a public representative of American Jews: she carved out a middle ground on the issue, providing a forum for conversations between Zionists and anti-Zionists. In private, however, she criticized the movement as antithetical to her universalist ideals. Her fervent faith in transcendence of the boundaries of nationalism and ethnoreligious identities emerged out of her approach to assimilation. That faith made the "tribal twenties" in general, and Zionism in particular, incomprehensible to her.[3]

Though individuals had criticized Wald's balancing of universalist and particularist commitments since 1903, when Abraham H. Fromenson declared the need to "Judaize the settlements," these tensions were most obvious *after* World War I, when she applied her ethnic Progressive vision, by now largely successful on the local and national levels, to the world stage. James Connolly has ably demonstrated the importance of ethnicity to Progressivism in these years. He records how ethnic leaders employed an ethnic brand of Progressivism, which he defines as a "political language and style" that pits "the people" against "the interests" for successful "ethnic activism and [as] a tool of political insurgency."[4] Their politics was inextricably linked to ethnic particularism; indeed, it reinforced ethnic belonging.

By contrast, Wald's experiences as an elite ethnic woman activist complicate this notion of ethnic Progressivism's triumph in the 1920s. Wald's ethnic Progressivism grew out of her hometown lessons in assimilation and her New York conversion to the Protestant Social Gospel; its vision was one of a brotherhood of man, of declining particularism through assimilation and declining nationalism through peacemaking. Debates over Stalinism and Zionism, specifically, in which opposing sides often expressed their arguments in particularist *and* political terms, highlight the tensions between Wald's ethnic Progressivism—based on older conceptions of American identity and reform—and the modern political realities and cultural conflicts she encountered. Growing conflicts between Wald's universal vision and newer conceptions of ethnic identity marked not the triumph but the eclipse of her ethnic Progressivism and the emergence of a new order of ethnic relations. Contrary to Wald's fervent hopes, ethnic divides did not yield to universal ideals. Instead, multiple and complicated factors led to a reinvigoration of ethnic boundaries: ethnicization was tied tightly to modernization.

A new generation of women's rights advocates gradually drew away from Wald's approach to gender difference, as that too became outmoded. Wald sided with reformers and labor feminists who opposed the Equal Rights Amendment (ERA); these women advocated for "social rights"—"the social supports necessary for a life apart from wage work," such as accommodation for parenting responsibilities—while emphasizing differences between women and men. ERA proponents, in contrast, emphasized women's similarities to men in supporting individual rights, a free market ideal that endorsed competition and freedom of contract as the best means to equality. To be sure, the tension between the strategies of emphasizing women's difference and women's sameness carried forward to the next century. Still, modern feminists often worked for full equality with regard to wage work, education, political involvement, family life, and leisure all in the language of individual rights—the language of the E R A's supporters.[5] Wald's position in this debate demonstrates fault lines between reform traditions in women's campaigns. As with her vision of ethnic difference, her vision of gender difference did not always meet modern realities.

Though she was ill for many years prior to her retirement in 1933, and though she lived mainly at her "country" home in Westport, Connecticut, Wald remained engaged in these domestic and international campaigns and had access to world news. Throughout, she held fast to a vision that had been developed and tested at the local level. It was crafted out of a belief in the fundamental similarities between different ethnic and racial groups and the fundamental differences between men and women. Her positions on the major issues of her day reveal the fault lines between Progressive Era gender and ethnoreligious identities and their more modern counterparts.

Wald and Russia: A "World Movement for Freedom and Progress That Is Our Struggle Too"

Wald's embrace of Russia during the 1920s and 1930s captures well the growing distance between the ideal political arrangements she sought and the modern political realities she encountered. Her position on Russian politics begins at Henry Street, with Wald standing at the nexus of uptown and downtown Jewish communities, surrounded by Progressives and a tightly knit group of women reformers.[6] The Russian Revolution of March 1917 won the attention and support of many members of her various networks. Later, as the Bolshevik revolution replaced the Kerensky regime, the allegiances of these members of her networks splintered.

From the beginning, Wald aligned herself with Jane Addams, John Dewey, and other Progressive activists who saw Russia as a nation embracing its people's potential.[7] Social workers like Wald saw in Russian freedom the opportunity to achieve "Hull House on a national scale."[8] Dissatisfied with a society they saw as saturated with excessive competitiveness and individualism, Wald and others pursued their ideal visions in Russia.[9]

In her enthusiasm for what she saw as Russian democracy (under Kerensky, Lenin, and then Stalin), Wald joined voices with Progressives worldwide. Once again, she found herself explaining one group's concerns to another. Just as she served as an interpreter between the uptown and downtown Jewish communities, so her connections to both Russian Jewish immigrants and American Progressives first drew her into the cause of Russian reform well before the 1917 revolution.

The Russian Revolutionary Committee in New York knew of Wald because of her Lower East Side work with and for Jews active in anticzarist efforts. They saw her as a friend of their cause and asked her to present a statement to President Theodore Roosevelt, whom she knew from his days in New York municipal government.[10] Soon after, Wald joined the Friends of Russian Freedom, which included many of her male and female Progressive colleagues.[11]

Wald, Addams, and others in the settlement movement embraced Russian freedom and opened their doors to countless visitors representing the cause. Their unchecked enthusiasm for the Russian revolutionaries was due in part to the difficulty of getting unbiased information. Those Russian revolutionaries who visited the United States downplayed the bitter divides within the broader revolutionary movement; they were also silent on the role of violence in the realization of their revolutionary visions. Pro-peace democrats like Wald and Addams were an ideal audience for their stories.[12]

Predictably, as she asserted that her interest in Russia stemmed from her Progressivism, Wald rejected the idea that it grew out of any ethnic allegiance to Jewish communities. "I would not have our profound interest in the Russian Revolution entirely explained by the fellowship we have had with those who have participated in it . . . or by our actual experience with innocent victims of outrages," she wrote, referring to the Jews who made up her clientele at Henry Street. She carefully noted that her concern arose from a broad concern for humanity, warning that "the continuance of a policy of suppression of freedom infiltrates the social order everywhere." She believed "the gigantic struggle in Russia" to be a "world movement for freedom and progress that is our struggle too."[13] This movement reached its high point in revolutionary Russia, and she was one of many Jews and Progressives alike to be swept up in the enthusiasm.[14]

Wald continued to work for the Russian cause within communities of both women reformers and Jews. She lobbied fervently with Addams and other women for the release of Nicholas Tchaykovsky, a social revolutionary imprisoned for his political beliefs. The correspondence among Wald,

Tchaykovsky, and his daughter and wife demonstrates the closeness Wald felt toward him and his cause. When visiting America, he appealed first to the nation's "democratic forces" by emphasizing his party's links to the "peasant majority" and second to "Jewish groups by declaring that he and his party opposed the pogroms."[15] At Henry Street, he had access to both groups. So when he arrived at the settlement, Wald lined up an audience of "bankers, editors, [and] publicists" to hear his "impassioned plea not to lend money to the Tsarist government"—a cause then close to the heart of prominent uptown Jews, who hoped to punish the government for its anti-Semitic persecution.[16]

Another of Wald's networks, her circle of women reformers, saw in the Russian Revolution of 1917 the potential for an international women's movement. She was one of eighteen women—including Harriot Stanton Blatch and Carrie Chapman Catt—who signed a letter "glorifying . . . the Russian revolution." They wrote of their "confidence in the Duma" that the "supreme sacrifices of Russian heroines" would be rewarded with women's full political equality in the country's "first great scheme of self-government and democracy." They concluded: "Heroes of Russia, trust your women."[17]

Catherine Breshkovskaia was an especially loved Russian visitor who appealed both to Progressive women reformers and to Wald's Jewish clients. She was a socialist revolutionary who had survived political imprisonment at hard labor. Wald first met "Babushka," as her friends affectionately called her, when the Russian celebrity visited the United States in 1905.[18] Emma Goldman credited Wald's receptions for Babushka with "interesting scores of people in the Russian cause."[19] Wald later recalled to Breshkovskaia that at that time, "almost the only friends [Breshkovskaia] had were the Russian Revolutionists, practically all Russian Jews."[20] Wald introduced her to Jane Addams. Wald, Addams, and other women reformers (especially suffragist Alice Stone Blackwell) in turn introduced Babushka to important American figures, including Jacob Schiff, always praising her "selfless devotion to a noble goal."[21] In return, Breshkovskaia referred to the "goodness of American women."[22] Though she oversimplified the idealism—and understated the violence—of Russian revolutionaries, Breshkovskaia successfully appealed to the "high moral purpose" of her audiences.[23]

Wald and others corresponded with her and lobbied on her behalf when she was exiled to Siberia upon her return to Russia in 1908. In 1917, when the provisional government invited Breshkovskaia (who was again abroad) back to Russia, Wald rejoiced with her at the "birth of the new democracy" and viewed Russia as "leading the way in democracy . . . that is consecrated by the sacrifices that are made for it."[24]

Wald also celebrated the March Revolution within her Jewish networks. According to one American Jewish historian, the revolution "lifted the entire Jewish public to a state near euphoria."[25] Schiff compared it to the deliverance of Israel from Egyptian bondage.[26] Wald wrote to Schiff: "I know your heart must be rejoicing over the deliverance of a people . . . It makes me very happy and I send you and the dear lady [Therese Schiff] love and congratulations that . . . the cloud has broken and because you have played so great a part in helping bring it all about." Schiff responded: "Like you I am full of joy and gratitude that a great and good people after centuries of oppression have at last effected their deliverance and are coming into their own."[27] Through Schiff and Babushka, Wald's commitment to the Russian cause grew stronger.

Wald's personal and philosophical connection to Russia was further bolstered by the enthusiasm of her clients. No less a revolutionary than American journalist (and friend of Lenin) John Reed called Henry Street Settlement, energized by Russian Jewish immigrants and the support of the German Jewish elite, "the heart of Russian America" and "the American home of the Russian Revolution."[28] According to Wald, members of the provisional government called Henry Street "a shrine that had burned for Russian freedom."[29] The house celebrated the revolution with a performance at the Neighborhood Playhouse, where, as Wald described it, "people sang together and left the Playhouse going down the street still singing 'The Marseilles,' 'America,' Yiddish songs and revolutionary songs."[30]

Wald's support for Russia also reinforced her connections to the Yiddish community. Herman Bernstein, former editor of the Yiddish daily *Der Tog*, traveled to Russia in 1917 on assignment for the *New York Herald*. Wald invited him to dine at the settlement's table before his departure, to hear of his plans and talk of Russia's possibilities.[31]

Wald stayed especially close to the intense emotion accompanying the revolution. In the summer of 1917, Boris Bakhmeteff, the provisional government's Russian ambassador, visited Henry Street. A small, informal reception grew into a meeting of thousands on the streets. Women and men thronged to touch the hands of the ambassador, and one woman climbed up onto a window ledge and called out, "I greet you in the name of my sisters who were tortured in Russia; I greet you in the name of my brothers who slaved in Siberia; I greet you in the name of my dead father, whose eyes were burned out in a pogrom."[32]

Inside the house, the group meeting with Bakhmeteff to discuss Russian economic reform reflected Wald's wide range of networks: it included Crystal Eastman, with whom she worked on the American Union Against Militarism; V. G. Simkhovitch, economist and husband of Greenwich House's headworker, Mary; and Abraham Cahan, editor of the *Jewish Daily Forward*. The first to speak was Jacob Schiff, who had been traveling with the ambassador. Schiff emphasized how Wald's universalist commitments strengthened her interest in the revolution. He spoke of her "service to humanity" and explained that at Henry Street, "people do not meet . . . as aristocrats, nor as proletarians, but as human beings."[33]

Indeed, Wald gradually came to be seen as a go-between among American Jews, Russian activists, and American politicians. When President Wilson asked Henry Morgenthau, ambassador to Turkey and a longtime friend of Henry Street, to recommend an expert to send on the American Commission to Russia in the spring of 1917, Morgenthau turned to Wald for names. Some confusion arose as to whether Jews could serve on the commission; the decision was contingent upon the new government's treatment of Jews. Secretary of State Robert Lansing warned President Wilson of the "measure of danger in overplaying the Jew element." Wald keenly hoped for a "really informed expert" and disputed the exclusion of Jews, citing the appointment of several Jews to positions in the provisional government. She ultimately recommended Arthur Bullard, who "though not a Jew understands the Russian Revolutionists." Wilson chose American Federation of Labor president Samuel Gompers—who was Jewish—as a "representative of Labour," explaining that to his mind, it was most important "not to send a Socialist."[34]

When the revolution provided fuel for nativist fires, Wald joined the fray once again. Elihu Root, former secretary of state and chair of the 1917 American Commission to Russia, asserted that Russian immigrants were now leaving the United States "in swarms," deserting the nation that had opened its doors to them. Wald responded. She spoke of the "great many

Russians" she knew, of their "religious fervor for the country that promised freedom," and of their "deep and loyal gratitude" to the United States. Assuming her customary role as interpreter, she emphasized the gifts that Russian immigrants offered the United States and linked their goals to those of American Progressives. Russian immigrants understood "that our democracy is not complete" and that the "social conscience in the last two decades" was a force toward a more democratic society, "expressed in progressive social measures for the protection of the people and for the attainment of our own ideals."[35]

After the March Revolution, Henry Street opened its doors "to any who might interpret the purpose behind the astounding new regime." Tchaykovsky (later a member of the Duma's peasant group), George Kennan, Alexander Kerensky (head of the provisional government), Prince Peter Kropotkin, and Pavel Milyukov (foreign minister of the provisional government) all visited the house.[36] Wald invited Moissaye Olgin to speak to an audience she chose about his recent visit to Russia in early 1921. A prominent American Jewish Communist, Olgin authored detailed articles in the *Forward* that were pivotal to the Yiddish intelligentsia's positions on Soviet Russia.[37] At Henry Street, Wald wrote, Olgin "gave the impression of having witnessed the phenomenon of a new people risen from beneath the earth and standing up as human beings in the light of the sun." So "enthralled" was the audience that he answered questions "long after a respectable time for closing the meeting."[38]

As Henry Street's founder and headworker, Wald made the settlement a common ground for all networks interested in Russia. At the same time, she held tightly to her faith in the Russian experiment as an expression of her own ideals. "Faith" well captures her sentiments, as her language suggested a religious dedication to Russian democracy. After the November Revolution, even as word spread of the "ruthlessness of the Bolsheviki," Wald spoke of "the vast promise of the Soviet government and the strength and wisdom and social passion of Lenin."[39] Kerensky, whom she once saw as the embodiment of Russian idealism, she now described as "a pathetic victim of circumstances beyond his understanding or control."[40]

Wald testified to the "public spiritedness" of the Bolsheviks even while many (though not all) members of her various networks withdrew their support. Breshkovskaia condemned the Bolsheviks' "treachery."[41] Members of Wald's networks of women reformers grew skeptical of the Soviets as creators of a true expression of democracy, a model of state planning. Prominent American Jews—even those who had first seen the Bolsheviks as the only alternative to continuing anti-Semitic oppression—now increasingly backed away from supporting the Soviet regime. Paul Warburg expressed the outrage of American Jews over the wave of anti-Semitic pogroms that followed the November Revolution and was upset by Wald's subtle defense of the Bolsheviks in her letter to Breshkovskaia. He found the new regime "just as bad as the old autocracy."[42] Wald emphasized that she shared his concern over the new government. "I fully agree with you that the Soviet does not express the will of the people unless every class shares in the Government," Wald wrote, avoiding any reference to anti-Semitic violence. "I am far from a prophet when I say that they will fall," she continued, disingenuously, "as every Government must fall, because of the Extremists."[43]

Downtown Jews shared Warburg's sentiments. Cahan's *Forward*, the main voice of the immigrant community and the leading socialist daily in the country, was initially supportive of the Bolsheviks, but by late 1922 the paper grew critical of the Soviet regime.[44] Cahan ceased printing travel accounts as pro-Soviet as Olgin's had been. At home, American Jews were wary of the postwar rise of nativism, antiradicalism, and anti-Semitism that linked the "international Jew" with Bolshevism;[45] individuals rejected Bolshevism out of ideological differences and as a matter of survival.[46]

As particularist communities withdrew their support, Wald remained committed, affiliated with nonsectarian Russian organizations exclusively as a nurse and public health expert. She worked with the American Friends Service Committee to alleviate famine in Russia.[47] She did not contribute to the Joint Distribution Committee, an organization founded by Morgenthau, Schiff, the Warburgs, and other uptown Jews in 1914 to aid Jews in Russia.[48] When she wrote to Herbert Hoover, the head of the American Relief Administration, which worked with the Joint Distribution Committee to distribute funds in Russia, she carefully explained that she wrote on behalf of "residents of Henry Street Settlement" who were concerned about the possible withdrawal of American relief to Russia.[49]

In 1924, journalist and fellow traveler Anna Louise Strong, along with the Bolsheviks' public health service representative in America, Dr. Michael Michailovsky, asked Wald to visit the country to offer advice on public health.[50] The invitation reflected the historic strength of her Jewish connections, her proximity to and knowledge of Russian politics, and her authority as a pioneer public health nurse. It may have stemmed from the USSR's Fifth Congress of Health Departments in the summer of 1924, where experts drew attention to the need for preventative health work, one of Wald's specialties.[51] Wald reported that "the invitation was given to make possible contacts necessary to an exchange of ideas and to secure the benefit of observations and to discuss public health exchanges." She joined "medical and technical experts from the provinces and from many foreign countries, invited . . . to inspect, to confer, and to report."[52] Wald then became one of many Americans who, "like modern Magi," went to Russia both to learn and to offer as a gift her broad knowledge of public health problems and policies.[53]

Russia's New Economic Policy in 1921 allowed small-scale private industry and trade to revive, and a strong industrial and economic recovery in 1924 engendered optimism among Bolshevik leaders and their supporters abroad. This optimism may have encouraged the leadership to invite foreign visitors, witnesses to the successes of Stalin's policy of "Socialism in One Country."[54] Narkomzdrav, the People's Commissary of Health, formed immediately after the Bolshevik revolution of November 1917, reflected the Bolsheviks' "demand for [centralized] political control and . . . respect for technical knowledge," which impressed Wald on her visit. Indeed, at the time of her visit, Narkomzdrav's growth in terms of employees outpaced that of every other major branch of the Soviet government.[55]

The aim of her trip, an exchange of medical knowledge, fell neatly within her reciprocal approach and marked a continuation of her internationalist work. On their way to Russia, she and two colleagues, Elizabeth Farrell of Henry Street and Lillian Hudson of Teachers College, first stopped in London to visit premier Ramsay MacDonald, a close friend of Wald's. They then flew to Germany (Wald's first experience in an airplane) and traveled by train to Moscow.

Accounts of Wald's visit dismiss its political significance. Her friend and first biographer wrote that she knew of the intense struggle between Stalin and Trotsky that followed Lenin's death in January of 1924 but that "mainly her thoughts were occupied with the practical things that needed to be done."[56] The press echoed this theme. Though Wald was in Red Square during Lenin's burial, the small article in the *Times* about her trip (four paragraphs, compared to a full-page article about her world tour in 1910) began only with her observation, that "Russia has made great strides in the last two or three years in getting back to pre-war standards of cleanliness and comfort."[57]

Addressing audiences back home, Wald dismissed reports of religious persecution and inefficiency. She spoke of Russia's progress in building and organizing effective schools and hospitals. In the *Survey*, she described the Public Health Administration's elaborate organizational structure, which she compared to that of federal, state, and local agencies in America. She noted the respect accorded her by Russian medical professionals and their ignorance of developments in American nursing, to which Wald had contributed so much energy. "The general impression, when we got to Russian land," she wrote to her colleagues back at Henry Street, "was that we were doctors, and on research work." Indeed, their Russian hosts, she noted, "insist in regarding me as a doctor specialist in public health." "As to nursing in our meaning of the term," she confessed her fear that "they simply do not [know] what we are talking about." She also recorded other items of interest to her community on working women, schools, and ballet performances. And she spoke of her "great surprise" at the "evident religious expression" in Russia.[58]

Wald's use of religious imagery in describing her visit demonstrates her continuing deep commitment to the new Russian society and to the language and goals of the Social Gospel movement. She wrote of her poignant dream following Lenin's funeral of a wagon "overflowing with crosses": "When the driver turned," she said, "I saw the face of Christ, radiant."[59] In Russia, then, she saw the realization of her own "religion," a universalist vision. Russian society was reborn into righteousness and justice, into Christ's teachings, the goal of the Protestant Social Gospel. Her baptism into that religion in 1893 had marked a spiritual rebirth for her, and now she hoped all of Russia too would be reborn. Soon, the rest of the world would follow.

While Wald shared in the "religious exultation of the social workers" who saw their political visions realized in the new Russia at a time of rising conservatism in America, she was not entirely uncritical in her public writings.[60] In her second book, *Windows on Henry Street*, she "summed up" her impressions of Bolshevism by quoting a letter dating from the 1924 visit: "The dictatorship is firm, strong, and harsh, and coming from America one feels the lack of what we call democracy." Yet she hesitated "to be critical of Russia in this respect without interpreting the attitude and method of the Party in the light of other revolutions."[61] She reported that her group had traveled extensively and visited sites not on the official itinerary. In Moscow, "the Bureau of Greatest Interest" to her and her colleagues was the Division for the Protection of Mother and Child.[62] And while they were impressed with what had been accomplished in a few years, they criticized some of the policies of the training school of maternity and infancy, specifically its refusal to admit the daughters of the bourgeoisie or nobility.[63]

Continuing her professional estimation of Russia, Wald stressed "the imperative need for the well-trained public health nurse" outside of the major cities.[64] In Russia, she had heard about how her own institution's international work affected lives in remote areas of Asia. By train and automobile, she and her colleagues traveled over the Caucasus Mountains to the Georgian city of Tbilisi, where they encountered stories of local nurses who had been trained in New York at Henry Street Settlement. This was proof of the efficacy of Wald's internationalist vision. Working for Near East Relief, these nurses had been expelled from Turkey and Asia Minor, and Wald hoped that they would "find permanent dwelling free from persecution in the new Russia."[65]

Overall, her political critique after her visit to the new regime amounted to very little. After returning to New York, Wald continued her efforts to support the Soviet experiment. In 1925, she sent masses of information to health and social workers she had met there: pamphlets on topics ranging from infant mortality to public hygiene, her book *The House on Henry Street*, and films like *Care of the Teeth* (made by Colgate).[66]

With continuing faith, she remained active in pro-Soviet organizations. From 1926 to 1930, she was a member of the American Society for Cultural Relations with Russia in New York, for which she and John Dewey both served as vice presidents. The organization listed its main goals in a 1928 pamphlet:

1—To bring together those who are interested in Russian life and culture
2—To promote cultural intercourse between the two nations and especially the interchange of students, doctors, scholars, scientists, artists and teachers
3—To collect and diffuse information in both countries on developments in Science, Education, Philosophy, Art, Literature, and Social and Economic Life.[67]

These fit well with Wald's approach to international exchanges and diplomacy.

At this point in Wald's career, it is clear that her public health experience was enough to smooth over some of the differences between *her* feelings toward Russia—guided by a universalist vision—and those of the groups from which she was distancing herself. The knowledge she had gained as a Progressive public health expert fueled her political optimism, her deep faith in Russia's rebirth. To look ahead to Wald's position on Russian politics after 1924 is to see her fall further out of step with these groups, as each began to wrestle with the documentation of destruction in Russia. Indeed, she supported Lenin, and then Stalin, long after many Americans she knew indicted their repressive regimes.

While she continued to invest in Soviet partnerships, Wald displayed her naïveté on matters of Soviet politics. In 1931, she recommended to a friend the best-selling, pro-Soviet propaganda piece *New Russia's Primer: The Story of the Five-Year Plan*. The book was widely read in the United States, and though its theories interested Wald, she also clearly felt out of her depth. She called the book "an amazing approach to the mind of twelve year olds, which on this matter is my I.Q."[68] Like other Progressives of her generation, she responded to the plan "in the name of practicality," comparing its "pragmatic, sensible, even scientific" approach to President Hoover's failed attempts to contend with the economic crisis.[69]

Wald's self-proclaimed naïveté did not prevent her from getting involved in the debate over American recognition of Soviet Russia. In her second book, *Windows on Henry Street* (1934), she argued for the need to recognize "a responsible government." She understood "the distaste for Marxism and for the fixed objective of the Soviet government to enthrone the proletariat" but asserted, "There is no other government in the world that has done as well." Reflecting her schooling from Schiff, she observed, "With the wheels of American industry stalled because of the slack in our trade, we have not been able to take advantage of this potentially great market." Wald concluded in the familiar language of her worldview: "Internationally as well as nationally, it is a basic fact that you cannot build up any social structure on hatred and suspicion."[70] She advised President Franklin D. Roosevelt not to have formal recognition "collide in time with the agricultural program" (the Agricultural Adjustment Act, passed in May of 1933): she feared "potential alarmist farmer propaganda" and hoped he would communicate to farmers that "the big market over there will help them through their own economic problems."[71]

Wald remained silent about the death and destruction documented in Russia under Lenin's leadership, and she continued to support Russia well after many other Progressives began to indict Stalin's repressive regime.[72] As late as 1937, when the Moscow trials shook the faith of many on the American Left, she endorsed the reporting of Walter Duranty, the *New York Times* Moscow correspondent known at his death as "the No. 1 Russian apologist in the West" and by his biographer as "Stalin's apologist."[73] "I am entirely with Durante [sic] and was before I knew what Durante thought and said," Wald wrote to a close friend.[74]

In March of that year, Wald took her support of Stalin one step further, confronting those who criticized Stalin's treatment of Leon Trotsky. Wald reported that the Trotsky committee had "stirred [her] greatly"—a reference to the American Committee for the Defense of Leon Trotsky, a coalition of Trotskyists, dissident Marxists, socialists, and liberals who supported a fair trial for Trotsky after he was driven from Russia.[75] The committee, led by John Dewey, Wald's friend and colleague from the American Society for Cultural Relations with Russia, was the Left's leading voice of American anti-Stalinism. Wald joined other Progressive colleagues, including Louis Fischer, correspondent for the *Nation*, Anna Louise Strong, and James Waterman Wise, son of Rabbi Stephen Wise, to protest the American Committee for the Defense of Leon Trotsky. They asserted that Russia "should be permitted to work out its problems without interference from the outside world." The group urged the committee's members, many of whom were "identified in the minds of the American public with truly liberal and progressive ideas," to consider that any advocacy of Trotsky's right to free speech meant "the confusion and the distortion of true liberalism." They argued that "the Soviet Union needs the support of liberals at this moment when the forces of fascism, led by Hitler, threaten to engulf Europe."[76]

Wald's lobbying work with and for Lower East Side Jews led to her initial commitment to Russia, but it was her Progressive ideals that cemented those bonds. As her universalist vision bridged her ethnic loyalties and Progressive ideals, it also helped to bridge the interests of well-boundaried social groups and brought them together for a historic moment in support of Russia's political experiments. During an era studied for its fragmentation and search for order, then, Wald's efforts represented an alternative to those whose zealous exclusions left no room for a middle ground.[77]

Working out her place in Russian politics, she continued to claim herself for this middle ground even as it ebbed away, undermined by forces that her Progressive vision underestimated or dismissed. By the mid-twentieth century, Wald's universalist vision seemed increasingly out of step with the times. Though it worked well in holding together diverse coalitions, it also diminished her ability to take seriously the bonds of particularity. She too easily dismissed the deep connections and concern that at times offered a clearer worldview than her universalist lens. Modern brutalities—including Stalinism and then Nazism—chipped away at the Progressives' universalist and idealistic beliefs that were the basis of their romance with Russia's politics. Contemporaneous debates over the means to women's equality found Wald similarly out of step, as her approach to women's difference was gradually supplanted by an emphasis on the sameness of both sexes.

Wald and the Sameness versus Difference Debate

Wald's attempts to apply neighborhood methods on an international scale became increasingly difficult in later years. In 1928, her neighborhood allegiances again became paramount. Her position in the national election of that year reflected her continued prominence both as a public figure in New York politics and as a member of a national network of women reformers. How Wald negotiated those dual allegiances reveals much about the divide slowly emerging within the women's movement. Wald's role in the election, and in that growing divide, offers more insights into the state of her universalist vision, grounded in lessons about gender, ethnic difference, and class.

During his second term as governor of New York, Alfred E. Smith apologized to Wald that state business in Washington prevented him from speaking to the Henry Street children on summer vacation in Nyack. "You are my neighbor, Miss Wald, of the Lower East Side," he wrote. "Will you give the message for me?" She replied that she would "tell them you were an East Side boy, and that you are never ashamed of having been poor, or of having worked hard."[78]

Wald admired Smith's humble downtown origins, as well as his politics, and she supported his "program of progressive social welfare"—especially his concern for "health protection" and his work against "slanderous attacks upon the immigrants."[79] She publicly endorsed his reelection campaign in 1924, and he returned the favor a month later by asking all New Yorkers to aid Henry Street's work. "My memory goes back twenty-five years and over, when you began your work in a tenement in Jefferson Street," Smith recalled in a public fund-raising pronouncement. He declared, "I know of no single force for public health more worthy than the Henry Street Nursing Service."[80]

In supporting Smith's 1928 presidential bid, Wald endangered her ties to several colleagues with whom she had worked for decades. Smith's candidacy brought to a head major conflicts in American politics: urban/rural, immigrant/native born, Catholic/non-Catholic, middle class/working class. The issue of Prohibition best reflected those divisions. Smith made no secret of his opposition to Prohibition, although he promised to enforce the Eighteenth Amendment while working toward its reconsideration. Wald supported Prohibition and had recently written the preface to a study of the success of the so-called noble experiment.[81] Nevertheless, she joined with Eleanor Roosevelt (whose husband had just decided, at Smith's urging, to run for governor of New York) and Edith Bolling Wilson in working for the Democratic ticket. The *Times* reported Wald's enthusiastic response to Smith's acceptance speech: "Your directness, your integrity, your sincerity and your boundless human understanding have been most impressively portrayed."[82]

Wald and her friend and colleague John Lovejoy Elliott, founder of New York City's Hudson Guild Settlement, sent a pro-Smith circular letter to social workers throughout the country. They drew attention to Smith's career as a "vital humanitarian" who worked for "the needs of common men and women." They labeled his platform "intelligent and progressive" and declared, "His policies reach all classes." Wald hoped too that Smith's candidacy might contribute to the undoing of American anti-Catholicism and so contribute to her vision of a more unified humanity. She presented him as "a logical president for really democratic people who can bury their prejudices to place [him] in the White House."[83]

But Wald underestimated the power of those prejudices. Her hopes were dashed in the ensuing "storm of objection" that the letter brought upon the heads of its two authors—"particularly upon mine," she said. To Jane Addams, she confided, "the anti-Catholic [responses] make me quite sick."[84]

In contrast to her struggle over candidates in the 1912 election, when she pleaded with Addams to help her make up her mind, Wald broke with Addams and other women reformers in endorsing Smith in 1928. Addams sent her a simple telegram—"Voting for Hoover but send good wishes for Smith Campaign."[85] When Smith lost, Wald boldly defied those who had attacked her support of his candidacy: she asked him to join the settlement's board of directors, and he accepted.[86]

While Wald's support of Smith showed her growing independence from the networks that had sustained her, some of the language she and Smith used on that occasion (and future occasions) revealed that she remained firmly entrenched within an older, Progressive reform tradition. Organizations such as the National Woman's Party had thrown their support behind the Equal Rights Amendment, which provided for equal treatment for men and women under the law using the language of individual rights. Debate over the amendment marked a crucial divide within the women's movement in the interwar years. Smith opposed the amendment: " 'Equal rights,' I admit, is a rather catchy phrase, but when it is applied to my opposition to it, it should read that I am opposed to sweating women, that I am opposed to overworking women, that I am opposed to underpaying them, and I am opposed to working them in that line of business that interferes with their health."[87]

Wald had sought—and Smith had supported—protective legislation specifically for wage-earning women, and she opposed the ERA for fear that it would undo "all the protective measures that women require in order to fulfill their duties as women and as mothers." Using Protestant messianic language, she later wrote, "We [as women] certainly do require, until the millennium comes, such protection . . . and so I am very much opposed to the Equal Rights Amendment."[88]

Wald was not alone in her opposition to the ERA. Colleagues Florence Kelley and Jane Addams joined her in justifying the protection of wage-earning women workers in terms that echoed those used by the wage-earning women themselves: women workers deserved protection on the basis of their difference from men. Though she was the same age as many ERA supporters, Eleanor Roosevelt, active in the Democratic Party, also rejected the amendment as "politically premature."[89] Scores of women's organizations, including philanthropies, religious and secular groups, cross-class labor unions, and suffrage organizations, fought the amendment for the same reasons. While the National Woman's Party saw gender-based protective legislation as an "anachronism," Wald and others believed that it shielded women from the abuses of unregulated capitalism.[90] Many saw gender-based legislation as "an entering wedge for the extension of state responsibility to wage-earning men." In lieu of a strong and visible working-class movement for such protection, historian Kathryn Kish Sklar notes, "gender did the work of class."[91]

Sklar points out that supporters of protective legislation were united in their "reluctance to venture into new and more radical solutions to women's inequality."[92] Wald and her cohort knew that campaigns based on women's roles as wives and mothers had proven effective and that working conditions for both men and women had improved.[93] Wald and Smith saw eye-to-eye on this issue, even as a new generation of women began to articulate their strategies for equality in the language of individual rights. The use of maternalist strategies continued, but Wald and her colleagues were no longer alone at the forefront of all efforts for women's advancement. Other activists offered women a competing vision, one that major women's organizations accepted by mid-century.

So while Wald's support of Smith marked an important step in her independence, her concordance with him on the Equal Rights Amendment also signaled that she joined the majority of her peers in supporting the labor feminist position: that the best means to women's equality was through the recognition of women's difference from men. Like her position on Russia after her visit in 1924, her stand in the 1928 election signaled that her vision was slowly being eclipsed. Though ERA critics carried the day, and though protective labor legislation advocates' goals of social rights continued to hold a more expansive view of women's reform, Wald never experimented with more modern notions of women's equality. Her methods and strategies, based as they were on local applications of her vision, were losing ground in the modern United States.

Wald and Ramsay MacDonald: A "Modern Messenger of Peace"

Wald's relationship with James Ramsay MacDonald, the first Labour Party prime minister of England, also demonstrated her mixed success with modern ideas. Their decades-long friendship grew from their shared idealism and political beliefs; their exchanges over the years were part of Wald's education in politics and coalition building. Their contact during the 1920s and 1930s is evidence of her continued involvement in international affairs, just as it reveals her unshaken faith in the application of her local vision on a global scale.

During the 1920s, Wald corresponded with MacDonald about a variety of public issues, from the Soviet Union to Smith's candidacy. "I am afraid the defeat of Al Smith was a great disappointment to you," MacDonald wrote to her in late 1928. "It would have been wonderful if he had got to the White House." Preparing for his own election as a candidate for prime minister, he sympathized with her anger over the prejudices that surrounded Smith's defeat: it must "break the hearts of people who are serious and who wish to put high values upon a democratic verdict," he wrote.[94] Wald drew strength from MacDonald in her work for peace and international cooperation.[95] Their friendship was an important and early piece of her internationalism.

Wald first met MacDonald in the fall of 1897, when he and his wife, Margaret, spent their honeymoon traveling around the United States meeting reformers. The MacDonalds stopped at Hull House in Chicago, where Wald joined Jane Addams in greeting them. Wald invited the MacDonalds to Henry Street, and they stopped there later in their tour. They arrived in time for a local election, in which Wald and her nurses (all new to city politics) tried unsuccessfully to introduce a feminine "moral influence" as "leavening" to the "Tammany lump of New York City politics." Unimpressed, Margaret MacDonald wrote home that "the thoughtful folks here will have to work harder at public affairs before they gain the influence which they have let slip."[96] Wald recalled the early incident with humor in her second book, *Windows on Henry Street*: "Alas, we know better now than we did then what an election requires!"[97]

The friendship between Wald and the MacDonalds endured, and Wald mourned the death of Margaret with Ramsay in 1911. During World War I, Wald and MacDonald were active members of organizations dedicated to antimilitarism (Wald the American Union Against Militarism, MacDonald the Union of Democratic Control). Though their organizations stopped short of radicalism—neither one protested conscription or joined the campaign to support conscientious objectors—they were labeled traitorous for their stands.[98] *Labour and the New Social Order*, which MacDonald coauthored in 1918, captivated Wald and other Progressives on both sides of the Atlantic with its postwar plans for controlling industry and partnering intellectuals and workers in a "new social order."[99] MacDonald and Wald grew more politically savvy in these years, and they formed a close bond based on a shared vision.

MacDonald too had been enthusiastic after the Russian Revolution of 1917 and remained hopeful after the Bolsheviks came to power.[100] England's relationship with the Bolshevik government was an important issue in the upcoming elections, and MacDonald no doubt valued Wald's insights. She shared with him her impressions of the economic and political situation and her excitement over the schools and hospitals. On her 1924 visit to Russia, Wald addressed her longest letters—aside from those to her "family" at the house—to MacDonald, then the first Labour prime minister.

Wald expressed her thoughts more openly to MacDonald than to her friends in her networks, her fellow New York Jews and Progressives. In letters to him, she was more critical of the Soviet Union. She told him of "many pitiful experiments where even basic requirements are not met and of course where insufficient funds, inadequate and untrained teachers, [and] scarcity of housing accommodation, make it impossible for them to approximate their hope for the 'liquidation of illiteracy.' " Though she found much continuity of religious observance (among Christians), she feared the indoctrination of children with "the religious faith in Communism and wickedness of private ownership" in cities like Moscow and Leningrad, and she decried the fact that there was "no personal liberty" and "ruthless disregard of the rights of students if they were not of the Proletariat." Weighing the positive and negative aspects of what she had seen, Wald concluded, "I hope that this dictation will be of some help to you and I certainly feel that the whole truth of Russia cannot be told unless a report of its difficulties is associated with a report of its idealism and great improvement."[101]

Wald and MacDonald continued to correspond about events in Russia, and on his next visit to the United States in 1927—his first in twenty years— they attended meetings at which Russia was "a subject of paramount inter- est" among liberals and Progressives.[102] When MacDonald first arrived for his "pleasure trip," he answered questions from reporters (while disem- barking his boat and later at a conference at Henry Street) about the Labour Party's positions on Russia, China, and Palestine; British interest in Al Smith; women's suffrage; and the incompetence of the current British gov- ernment, which, he said, "represents a class."[103]

In between stops at City Hall, MacDonald accompanied Wald to a variety of meetings. One appointment was for MacDonald to speak at the thirtieth anniversary celebration for the *Jewish Daily Forward*. That Wald had helped to arrange this gathering offers continuing testimony of her alliances with Yiddish intellectuals.

At first, Wald attempted to keep MacDonald's 1927 visit with her a secret. She corresponded with Baruch Charney Vladeck of the *Forward* about her plans for a dinner in MacDonald's honor, "to include the settlement people" as well as "some of the outstanding colored people and artists." But when MacDonald "told the enterprising newspaper men over the telephone that he was to sup with me," Wald said, she faced overwhelming demand and feared "she would never have another friend." Wald hoped that Jane Ad- dams and her partner, Mary Rozet Smith, could attend a "little" dinner so that they could meet with MacDonald in an intimate setting. Finally, a luncheon for MacDonald was planned. Oswald Garrison Villard of the *Na- tion* composed a list of possible "invitees," including, in addition to Wald, Abraham Cahan and Vladeck of the *Forward*, Adolph Ochs of the *Times*, Ogden Mills Reid of the *New York Tribune*, Walter Lippmann of the *New York World*, Ellery Sedgwick of the *Atlantic Monthly*, Paul Kellogg of the *Survey*, Herbert Croly of the *New Republic*, and James Weldon Johnson of the Na- tional Association for the Advancement of Colored People, as well as other journalists and civic leaders.[104]

In the perilously tribal twenties, Wald was playing a by-now-familiar role as a facilitator, bringing diverse people together. She continued to supply MacDonald with a variety of American connections that represented all parts of her own life. She invited socialist labor leader Sidney Hillman, Villard, and Kellogg to lunch with MacDonald at the home of the Lewisohns, the wealthy German Jewish benefactors of the Neighborhood Playhouse.[105] Wald introduced MacDonald to Jacob Schiff's widow and to the Warburg family.[106] Wald had long benefited from the international connections of her uptown Jewish friends; now, with her public power and global Progressive network, she added to her friends' connections. At the gatherings, they discussed labor unionism, Communism, and the uphill battle of socialists and pacifists against conservatism and militarism in England and America. Later during that trip, when MacDonald became desperately ill at a stop in Philadelphia, Wald was sent for—this time in her capacity as a nurse. She sat by his bedside for days, helping him to convalesce.

After that visit, and especially after MacDonald again became prime minister in 1929, Wald's advice to MacDonald took on increased importance. Tensions between the United States and Great Britain over naval disarmament intensified in 1929, when the U.S. Senate passed a bill authorizing the construction of fifteen cruisers and an aircraft carrier. Hoover's victory over Smith meant the passage and signing of the bill. That summer, Wald warned MacDonald that a visit to the United States without an advance promise from Hoover to negotiate might suggest a "possible parallel between this visit and Wilson's to Versailles"; she feared "there might be an opening for thrusts between the ribs."[107] "Very privately," he confided in response, "I can tell you that I shall not go to the United States until I have something certain in my possession."[108]

Prime Minister MacDonald visited America that fall, this time on an official peacemaking mission to President Hoover. MacDonald made "an appeal to mankind to enthrone peace over the world." MacDonald and Hoover agreed on a plan to reduce the burden of debt and spoke of "moral disarmament before physical disarmament." They saw the need to limit arms as a step toward "mutual confidence and mutual good will." Speaking to the Council on Foreign Relations, MacDonald emphasized the success of person-to-person diplomacy, of honesty and forthrightness in international affairs.[109]

During the same visit, Wald introduced MacDonald, whom she called a "modern messenger of peace," to the Foreign Policy Association, an outgrowth of the American Union Against Militarism, of which Wald was a member. Echoing her Senate testimony on military preparedness before World War I, she expressed her faith in "open covenants openly arrived at" as well as "conferences, conversations, round tables, teas (for the English), dinner, camp-fire intimacies when men (and we hope in due time the women also) may recognize the essential points of a new humanity in a new form for arriving at international relations." MacDonald emphasized how this diplomacy marked another step toward peace, for which he and his fellow Progressives had long worked. He addressed his audience as "friends" and spoke of how much they had learned from the war about the need for "settling in detail, in practical detail, the problems of peace [so] that the next generation will never be deluded and allured into the frame of mind which is awakened by conceptions of the romance of war." Lieutenant Governor Herbert Lehman, longtime friend of Henry Street, also spoke, followed by Paul Kellogg.[110]

On their final day in the United States before traveling to Canada, MacDonald and his daughter Ishbel took a "day in the country" at Wald's home in Connecticut. This was the first (and last) time that events at Wald's summer home were covered on the front page of the *New York Times*, which reported that the prime minister's canoe—while out on Wald's pond—ran aground. A detective, "without bothering to remove his shoes, walked in and freed the canoe."[111] The MacDonalds' visit to Wald's home allowed them (some) respite from the press. But it also reminded the public of the importance of the friendship of these like-minded public figures. When MacDonald spoke about the strength of the diversity of nationalities in both Great Britain and the United States, the audience no doubt heard the influence of Wald in his words; what she witnessed at Henry Street certainly influenced Ishbel MacDonald's strong interest in child welfare. To thank Wald for her hospitality at Westport, the MacDonalds gave her a dog, which she appropriately named Ramsay.[112]

Wald's intellectual and political friendship with the MacDonalds never strayed far from her mind. During the rising tide of conservatism of the 1920s, it was a reminder that her house continued to be a Progressive sanctuary, sustaining coalitions of Progressives from all around the world. Indeed, it was also a testament to the limited success of her internationalist visions that she had built progressive coalitions across the ocean. Mac-Donald's final dinner in the United States in 1929—the year before his rejection by his own party over governmental controversy—was at Wald's table at Henry Street, where Wald and the MacDonalds were joined by some settlement residents and other "public-spirited citizens who assist in the work and make the settlement their headquarters." Wald took "an active part in preparing the dinner itself," reported the *Times*, with no exaggeration. So excited was she to entertain her old friends that she "had to cut short a conversation with newspaper men to rush in and finish making the salad."[113]

After MacDonald returned to England, tensions over war debts and their effect on international trade continued to mount, and Wald followed the news with growing alarm. Again, she began to cook up a plan to alleviate the tensions between the two nations. She wrote to MacDonald that she was beginning to concur with Felix Warburg's view "that you, and you alone, can touch the orbit and make it spin in the direction toward financial peace."[114] Sick in bed at her home in Connecticut, she devised a way to create such a situation. When MacDonald responded, professing his desire for "the closest harmony and cooperation with the United States," Wald asked to show his letter to her friend, president-elect Franklin Roosevelt.[115]

After a series of letters and telegrams, Wald succeeded in setting up a meeting between the two leaders, a manifestation of her hope that understanding could be achieved by right-minded individuals.[116] Anticipating the World Monetary and Economic Conference in London that summer, Mac-Donald and Roosevelt made some headway. They issued a joint statement that read, in part: "We have in these talks found a reassurance of unity in purpose and method. They have given a fresh impetus to the solution of the problems that weigh so heavily upon the most stable, industrious and deserving men and women of the world."[117] MacDonald left the meeting attracted by Roosevelt's personality and policies.[118] Wald no doubt took pleasure from the fact that her person-to-person diplomacy had connected two leaders whose politics she respected. It was proof that the coalition-building methods she had learned on the Lower East Side could bring about international change on a grand scale, that her local methods could still prove effective.

But the limits of those methods again became clear. The London economic conference, planned to create a unified program to combat the depression, was seen by many (including Wald) as an opportunity for peacemaking. MacDonald joined the conference confident that he and Roosevelt agreed on what needed to be done. But Roosevelt issued a "belligerent" statement—known as "the Bombshell"—that effectively ended the proceedings.[119] Wald, Addams, and others were stunned and disappointed, as complex formulas of nationalism, militarism, and partisanship rendered their own universalist and antimilitarist ideals irrelevant.

As these forces gained strength, after the Balfour Declaration of 1917, in which Great Britain declared its commitment to creating a Jewish home in Palestine, Wald had yet another international topic to discuss with Mac-Donald: Zionism. Their discussions again display her role as an interpreter —between uptown and downtown New York Jews, between British and American leaders. They also demonstrate the increasing difficulty she encountered in fulfilling that role as tragic events unfolded on the world stage.

Wald and Anti-Zionism

Wald's clients at Henry Street were the foot soldiers of the American Zionist movement, part of the secular, nationalist expression of Jewish freedom and progress and a response to the rise of racial anti-Semitism throughout the world. Eastern European Jewish immigrants founded American Zionist organizations as early as 1897, and other organizations appeared in the early decades of the twentieth century. Many American Jews encountered anti-Semitism and witnessed a narrowing of definitions of Americanism as they moved into the professional middle class in the 1920s and 1930s; for them, Zionism linked American and Jewish identities and became a component of American Jewishness. Memberships in Zionist organizations grew dramatically in these years.[120]

In bringing together her Zionist clients and non-Zionist benefactors, Wald stood on a middle ground at Henry Street. But, as was the case with Russian politics, that middle ground, where opposing ideas could be voiced and heard, disappeared in the wake of urgent events. And while some scholars mark the 1920s and 1930s as an era of increasing inclusiveness for approaches to American Jewishness, Wald's experiences suggest the contrary: a "shift from liberal universalism to ethnoreligious self-assertion"

concluded the negotiation over ethnic identity that was an integral part of
the Progressive Era's shifting ethnic order. Her universalist approach failed
just as the boundaries of modern American Jewish identity closed in around
a particularist, Zionist consensus. As a result, the protests and reservations
of early critics of Zionism such as Wald did not penetrate the larger Zionist
community's agenda.[121]

Uptown Jews like Jacob Schiff and his son-in-law and business partner,
Felix Warburg, both leaders and models in ethnic strivings within the Jewish community, greeted early political Zionism—the movement to create a
Jewish state in Palestine—with alarm. Products of the emancipation of Jews
in western Europe, they hoped that American Jewish immigrants would
embrace their brand of Americanism. They envisioned immigrants' rapid
assimilation and integration into the mainstream while retaining some
elements of Jewish religious particularism.[122] They saw Jewish nationalism
as an obstacle to immigrants' assimilation, as making American Jews a
target for accusations of dual loyalties. Rabbi Max Landsberg, Rochester's
Reform rabbi of Temple B'rith Kodesh, concurred.

In the settlement's early years, Wald and Schiff agreed on this issue.
In 1907, Schiff wrote to Solomon Schechter, founder of the Conservative
movement in American Judaism, that "nowhere is there anything in Jewish
Holy Scriptures which justifies agitation to reestablish a Jewish nation and
state by human endeavor." He did not support the state as a "refuge" for
persecuted Jews, as he felt that anti-Semitism had to be confronted on its
own ground. Echoing the philosophy that he and Wald put to work at Henry
Street, Schiff warned that in the United States, "the [Zionist] agitation is apt
to retard the perfect Americanization of thousands who, in recent years,
have come among us."[123] American Jews—immigrants and all others—were
a religious group like Protestants and Catholics, Schiff insisted, and not a
nation; Zionism's nationalistic particularism threatened Jews' American
loyalties and true American identities.

In balancing their Jewishness and Americanism, many American Jews
followed Schiff's lead. They rejected political Zionism and its nonreligious
Jewish nationalism and endorsed the idea of cultural Zionism, which envisioned Palestine as a home to Jewish religious thought and learning, the
solution to the problem of a disintegrating Jewish culture and spirituality.[124]
After the Russian Revolution, Schiff wrote of the need for such a solution.

The Pale of Settlement, where Jews had been forced to live "by unjust and oppressive laws," had provided a "Jewish center from which Jewry the world over drew to a very considerable extent the spiritual nourishment it ever needs for continued existence." A Jewish homeland under British protection could fill the void left by the end of the pale.[125]

Writing in the *Nation* in April of 1919, Schiff expressed his pleasure that Zionism had "awakened in the Jew self-respect, self-consciousness, and perfectly justifiable race pride," that it had unified world Jewry and provided persecuted Jews with a place to settle. He believed that Palestine could be a place where Jews would be "free from the materialistic influences of the western world." There, they could create "a reservoir for Jewish learning and for the further development of Jewish literature."[126] Furthering his commitment to Jewish particularism, he saw Palestine as a home for Judaism. He also hoped it would be part of a broad solution to the problem of eastern European Jewish refugees who strained the resources of American Jews.[127]

After Schiff's death, Felix Warburg remained uncomfortable with the nationalistic elements of Zionism. He worked for Palestine as a committed non-Zionist, as Schiff had. His efforts on behalf of "a cultural homeland instead of a Jewish state" were motivated by moral and humanitarian considerations. He continued to harbor deep reservations about the politics in Palestine, however, so while contributing thousands of dollars to Palestine, he also pushed for negotiations between Jews and Arabs in the region.[128]

In her public writings, Wald occupied a middle ground on the issue of Zionism, opposing neither the nationalism of her immigrant clients nor the cultural Zionism of her German Jewish benefactors. She wrote approvingly of Zionism's "appeal for spiritual nationalism," which would "take the place of the old religious commands," and she seemed to endorse Schiff's view of Palestine as a home for Judaism.[129] Wald reported that at Henry Street's table, "the Zionists, the Arabs, and the British have discussed frankly their views of the situation in Palestine, and have sometimes been in surprising agreement on fundamental points at issue."[130]

Wald offered additional contributions out of sympathy with her neighbors. She aided the settlement of Palestine by training some of the earliest nurses to arrive there. She spoke of this fact along with her hope that those nurses were "carrying with them not only the technical training, but the spirit of the work."[131] She also supported the first professional Hebrew-language performance group, Habimah, when it visited the United States in 1927. Later, many of the actors who performed on that U.S. tour continued on to Palestine, where they became the National Theatre of Israel.[132]

Privately, however, Wald rejected political Zionism as divisive, and she took this rejection a step further. Schiff and others saw cultural Zionism as compatible with Jews' American identities and endorsed it as a means to perpetuate Jewish religious particularism. Wald had no investment in that perpetuation, and so, in the name of her internationalism, she dismissed cultural Zionism as well.[133] In 1917, for example, the director of the Women's Organization for the American Jewish Congress asked her to join the organization's advisory committee. But Wald objected to the congress' heavily Zionist membership. Drawing on her universal vision, and noting that the World War was the result of "super-nationalism," she declined. "I am not sure that I can consistently be a part of a nationalistic movement as long as I feel that there ought to be a union of all peoples irrespective of nationality or religion," she wrote. "My influence is in the direction of my convictions," she noted, "that is, internationally."[134]

As the Zionist project continued, Wald was shocked by the conflict that arose in Palestine. She sympathized with Adolph Ochs, the uptown publisher of the *New York Times*, who considered himself an "anti-Zionist." "I have always consistently disagreed with the ardent Zionists . . . however good and pure their motives might be," she wrote to Ochs. Echoing Schiff and Warburg, Wald warned of the need for the Jewish settlers in Palestine to negotiate with the local Arab population and expressed her fear that "the [Zionist] movement could and would be a boomerang"—that it would hurt the very people it was supposed to help.[135] To her close friend Lavinia Dock, Wald wrote that she believed Jewish settlers in Palestine arrived "largely for sentimental reasons"; her own sympathy lay only in the movement's "cultural and spiritual significance," but even that was outweighed by her certainty that it would bring violence to the area.[136]

Wald's close relationship with Ramsay MacDonald, a pivotal figure in British policy toward Palestine, ensured her a special place within the international struggle over Zionism. She felt the pressure that accompanied her position. "I feel as if the planet were spinning and that I were involved in the spin": this is how she began her letter to Dock on the conflicts in Palestine.[137]

Navigating between the interests of her clients and her own belief in universalism, Wald used her friendship with MacDonald to lobby for the Arab cause in Palestine. On one occasion, she agreed to set up a meeting between him and Ameen Rihani, a Lebanese author who was "to head a delegation to go to London for the purpose of laying before the British Government the cause of the Arabs of Palestine." Rihani had visited Henry Street and admired Wald's work. Wald described him as a "Pacifist who deplores the massacres [of Jews in Palestine] but is convinced that the Arab must have recognition."[138] After he read *The House on Henry Street*, he wrote, "O, for a Lillian Wald in Arabia, or Turkey, in fact in all the nations of the East or West."[139] When Wald agreed to set up the meeting, he thanked her for her "interest in the Arab cause."[140]

Wald's role as an interpreter of multiple causes placed her in a conspicuous position during a moment of great tension between Zionists and British leaders. In October 1930, Zionists throughout the world reacted furiously against the Passfield white paper, named for the British colonial secretary and written in response to the 1929 riots in Jerusalem.[141] The white paper stated that the terms of the Balfour Declaration and the British mandate were to work for Jewish *and* non-Jewish peoples in Palestine. It rejected the idea that the passages regarding the Jewish national home were the main feature of the mandate, and it also limited Jewish immigration to Palestine. In protest, Chaim Weizmann resigned from the Jewish Agency, the administrative body for world Jewry provided under the British mandate and comprised of Zionists and non-Zionists. MacDonald faced calls for a British reaffirmation of the idea of a Jewish homeland.[142]

The public and private correspondence between MacDonald and Wald during this crisis testifies to Wald's balancing act with regard to the American Jewish community. Recognizing her role as a representative of American Jewish concerns, he reassured her that Britain's "dual responsibility of establishing a Jewish National Home in Palestine on the one hand, and of safeguarding Arab interests in Palestine on the other, was clearly stated in [the] Mandate." He gave assurances that "the check [in immigration] will not destroy the National Home purpose . . . [and] it is far from true that the Jewish National Home is to be crystallized at its present stage of development." He wrote: "I would beg of you and your friends to exercise patience and forbearance at this juncture."[143]

In his private letter, he told Wald that she should "make any legitimate use" of his official statement. "I assure you," he wrote, "I am as anxious as are all your Jewish friends that things go along amicably, but I must have regard . . . to our obligations to the Arabs as well as the Jews." He noted "for her private information" that he was trying "to sweeten the situation," and added: "What I would ask you to do in return, would be to try and pacify the American Jews who are, I gather, organising Funds, Demonstrations, etc., on a large scale, and by rushing at things in such a fashion may do untold harm to the cause they have at heart. Tell them that the British government has altered none of its ultimate intentions. They must know that we will do our best in all the difficult circumstances that present themselves to us, and these we must first of all get over."[144]

Wald replied, "It is possible that the misunderstanding may have come about through a bit of tactlessness in the formulation of the White Paper by the people in the Colonial Office." She told MacDonald that his meetings with the Jewish Agency and his letters to American leaders were "very comforting"; she had faith that his "patience, sympathy, and wisdom ought to extricate [Britain] from . . . trouble."[145] To Lavinia Dock, Wald lamented that MacDonald should be placed in such a position. After she "had the privilege of reading the White Paper, containing all the correspondence between Churchill and the Arabs and the Zionists," she concluded that it was "most unfortunate that MacDonald should be asked to straighten out a situation that cannot be straightened."[146]

Following MacDonald's advice to "try and pacify American Jews," Wald showed his letters to her close friend Felix Warburg. Warburg had also resigned from his leadership position in the Jewish Agency to protest the white paper, but he was ready to accept MacDonald's explanations.[147] Though Warburg called the white paper a "cruel blow," he told Wald that he appreciated that MacDonald "went to the trouble to write to you as he did to reassure us that an effort will be made to carry out constructive measures in Palestine, to the satisfaction of both the Jews and the Arabs."[148] Ultimately, in a famous letter to Weizmann on 13 February 1931, MacDonald effectively negated the anti-Zionist implications of the white paper. Warburg praised MacDonald's letter and urged support of its policies.[149]

In private and personal letters to MacDonald, when Wald represented no one's interest but her own, she confessed, "The whole Zionist propaganda has been distasteful to me." Echoing her letter to Ochs, she wrote, "I am, indeed, an anti-Zionist, for among other objections, I perceive boomerang possibilities."[150] A month before his letter to Weizmann, MacDonald confided in Wald his feeling that "the great storm which followed the issue of the White Paper was not altogether without reason, but it was very largely a stunt."[151] Wald responded that those "with broader views about the Palestine situation are loyal to you." She lamented to her friend that the "extremists among the Zionists are like all other extremists—unreasonable and unaware of the existence or the interests or the obligations of other people."[152]

Wald's exchanges with MacDonald in these years place her firmly on the map of international affairs and locate her in the camp of those who advocated for negotiations with Arab residents of Palestine. Her warnings join those of others with prescient concerns.[153] Yet they also demonstrate that her ethnic Progressive vision distanced her from any understanding of or sympathy with the Zionist cause. In striving for a universalist internationalism, she had lost sight of the justification for any particularism.

Wald's only discussion of Zionism in a Jewish publication highlighted this distance. It appeared in 1936, in the liberal *Opinion: A Journal of Jewish Life and Letters*. The issue was dedicated to the election of Rabbi Stephen Wise, a friend and ally of Wald's and editor of the journal, as president of the newly formed World Jewish Congress. Wise and others in the Zionist congress stressed Palestine's role in the solution to the German Jewish crisis. After the passage of the German Nuremberg Laws, they called on Jews around the world to defend Jewish rights in Europe.

Wald's piece followed an article by Horace Kallen, the philosopher of cultural pluralism. He wrote in the pages of *Opinion* that American Zionists must work with other Jews to destroy the "falsehoods with which anti-Semitism libels each and every Jew." He saw the Zionist movement as the unifying force for Jews around the world to rally against anti-Semitism. Jews, he wrote, must unite "not only because of their common history, traditions, faith, and sufferings; not only because of the historic attitude of

the Christian world, but because anti-Semitism is universal and endemic."
He believed that Jews belonged to a secular but national community, with
Zionism an important part of its existence. And he stressed the importance
of Jewish negotiations with Arabs in the region, so that the two populations
might live in "amity and cooperation."[154]

Wald's article followed soon after, sharing space with the poems of the
Zionist Hayyim Nahman Bialik. Asked to write as both a Jew and a social
worker, she chose to emphasize her professional identity. She titled her
essay "A Social Worker's Viewpoint." In it, she expressed her fear that
Nazi barbarism was undoing progress toward her universalist vision. She
underscored her commitment to that vision with words she so often used in
her talks about Henry Street Settlement: "We have learned that human
beings are linked to each other, that they are interdependent," and that "they
must stand together when wrong is inflicted upon any member of the
human family."

In keeping with that view, Wald emphasized that the "appeal of the
American Jewish Congress, addressed to the Jews of America, is accepted by
social workers as an appeal to them, not to Jews exclusively." Hoping to raise
"a protest not only by Jews . . . but by people everywhere," Wald asserted that
the unique, firsthand experience of social workers demonstrated that "there
can be no frontiers between like-minded people," disputing even Kallen's
pluralist idea of Zionism's compatibility with national (American) identity.
She cited the president of the National Association of Settlements, whom
she identified only as "not a Jew," who stated, "When we join in protesting
what is happening in those countries, we are standing out for what concerns
liberals not only in Germany but anywhere."

Wald's words reflect two competing agendas: a call for cooperative work
against Fascism and an argument against Zionist ideology. Only in her last
sentence did she directly (if cautiously) mention Zionism. "In testifying
here to my faith in the brotherhood of man to which with so many dear
comrades I have devoted the long, long years," she observed, "I do not wish
to deny the ancestral call to come to the rescue of the victims of political and
social wrong." But neither would she affirm it. Admitting that working
together in "mutual co-operation" with "diverse ethnic groups" may not
"meet the immediate needs," she expressed her sincere hope that today's
children would be raised in "world-mindedness": "The likeness of people

and not their differences must be emphasized" instead of groups' "cultivating their sense of separateness."[155]

With an ethnic Progressive universalism as her point of reference, Wald was clearly not among those who welcomed Zionism as a way to revitalize contemporary Judaism. But there were other paths that might have led her to support the movement. Many activists of Wald's generation viewed Zionism as an extension of their Progressivism: disillusioned with social experimentation in the United States, they looked to utopian planning in Palestine.[156] Several friends of Wald's, including Louis Brandeis, who participated in the 1930 negotiations with MacDonald, explicitly articulated this idea. Other American Jews came to support Zionism after European and American anti-Semitism caused them to rethink their assumptions about Jewish emancipation and integration.[157] For them, Zionism was "a modern substitute for their scorned ethnic otherness" in the United States.[158]

Wald's refusal to follow any of these pathways to Zionism was in keeping with the careful and calculated distance she kept from any direct, formal identification with Jewish particularism throughout her career. She had never felt such "otherness." Perceived as an ethnic Progressive, claimed, praised, and criticized by American Jews, she drew strength and resources from them even while she avoided what she considered their more "tribal" interests. She always justified her actions by her universalist philosophy, with its strong internationalist component. One final document strikingly reveals the foundation and limits of that universalism.

In 1934, Wald wrote a letter to Mrs. John D. Rockefeller Jr. of the Young Women's Christian Association. Wald recalled the propaganda she had fought so hard against during World War I and lamented that the "open and subterranean Nazi propaganda jeers at all the good and the spiritual that have been developed since the dawn of conscience." She likened the current situation to other incidents of oppression she had witnessed in her lifetime: "Though I think the Hitler anti-Semitism is more brutal than anything else they do, it is fundamentally not more dangerous than their other outrages; it is not more dangerous than their suppression of Catholic freedom and liberal thought and their suppression of the rights of women. But anti-Semitism is the easiest red herring to deflect people. It has been used effectively so many times that recurrence of the cry lends itself easily to the provocateur. Would it not clarify thought for men and women to declare this propaganda to be not anti-Semitism but anti-Christianity? . . . the emphasis upon this aspect should come in from professing Christians, from those who are banded together for its teaching."[159]

Shocking as this letter might seem from a post–Nazi Holocaust perspective, it fits with a view of Wald as someone whose experience had encouraged her to reject Jewish difference. Wald—along with thousands of other American Jews—saw herself as part of the white, Protestant mainstream. Her membership in a women's reform network with Rockefeller was proof of this membership.

In the face of overwhelming horrors across the ocean and deepening anti-Semitism in America and abroad, Wald walked alongside those who believed that making Nazism a Jewish issue somehow violated "good American behavior."[160] Indeed, prominent Jewish organizations like the German Jewish American Jewish Committee and Rabbi Stephen Wise's American Jewish Congress often sought to "de-Judaize" their campaigns against Nazism.[161] To avoid claims of dual loyalties or Communist sympathies, and to garner the widest possible public support, they spoke of it as a threat against the "fundamental values of Americanism."[162] Importantly, Wald's only anti-Nazi activism was with the Emergency Committee in Aid of Political Refugees from Nazism, a group that aimed to raise money for German political refugees "primarily among non-Jews" by emphasizing that the "consequences of Nazi 'barbarism' were not restricted to Jews."[163] Such language was felt to be absolutely necessary to the fragile balance of American Jews' comfortable integration in the broader society. While members of the American Jewish establishment avoided particularist language to further their protest against Nazism, Wald avoided such language out of her long-standing commitment to universalist goals.

This was the balance that Wald lived and modeled, one that allowed her to connect to distinct particularist communities even as she rejected membership in them. It helped her to navigate Progressive reform networks and led her to involvement in Russian politics and debates over Zionism. Yet her vision of individuals' working together for their mutual benefit did not leave room for those who hoped to agitate on behalf of collective rights.[164] In the end, her faith in Russia's potential to realize her universal vision was greater than—and ran counter to—the particularist commitments of those communities. So too did her approach to difference preclude her acceptance of Zionism as a potential solution to the urgent situations in Palestine and Europe.

In a 1940 review of Robert L. Duffus's biography of Wald in *Jewish Social Studies*, sociologist Sophia M. Robison praised Wald's universalist approach while noting Wald's insistence on separating her concerns out from those of the Jewish community. "Many people no doubt never think of Miss Wald as a Jewess," Robison began. She continued: "In her protest against the Russian pogroms and the more recent German pogroms she acknowledged a direct personal interest although she had never been identified with any Jewish cause. Her protest was on the violation of human rights and human dignity."[165] Robison overstated Wald's commitment to protests in Russia and Germany and equated her political convictions to a non-Jewish "personal interest." Still, Robison's record of Wald's activism is a reminder of just how carefully Wald presented her concerns.

Indeed, Wald carefully maintained her approaches to both ethnic and gender difference, key components of her ethnic Progressive vision. Their effectiveness depended on a singular strategy toward women's rights, one that emphasized women's natural differences. Modern feminism altered the ultimate effectiveness of that strategy. Her approaches depended, too, on a fluid ethnic order, one in which Jewish difference specifically could be expressed in myriad, complicated ways. Zionism and Nazism drastically altered the ethnic landscape. The modern identity politics that emerged out of these challenges tested the very foundation of her two approaches, and so gradually undermined her vision.

The stories above make clear Wald's contributions—sometimes behind the scenes—to modern politics. Examining how contemporary scholars discuss these contributions provides a window onto the current state of identity politics. Women's historians, for example, readily place Wald in the cohort of difference feminists: settlement house, social science– pioneering suffragists who endorsed women's difference and advanced the rights of women—though largely white, middle-class women. Wald's only recent biography, too, dedicates ample space to a studious discussion of her approach to women's rights.

In contrast, no scholar mentions Wald's Stalinism in the sweeping, critical studies of the era, nor do the many analyses of American Zionism mention her anti-Zionism. Her role in facilitating meetings between international leaders is likewise ignored. These absences occur despite the over-whelming amount of Jewish scholarship that claims Wald's life for American Jewish history.

Scholars fail to study these aspects of Wald's career in part because of a well-accepted, generally romantic view of her life and work, an exclusive focus on her many successes. But more poignantly, these failures are the result of deep struggles over the current boundaries around American Jewish identity. In an age in which questioning Zionism is seen as threatening Israel's right to exist, in which dissent on American Zionism is often seen as consent to anti-Semitism, Wald's anti-Zionism (and, to a lesser degree, her Stalinism) proves unpalatable to the mainstream Jewish community.[166] In presenting Wald's Stalinism and anti-Zionism here, I argue that they must be seen in all of their complexity, in line with her idealism and her approaches to all varieties of difference.

To examine scholarship on Wald is to jump ahead, however. The celebratory commemorations of her life began in earnest only after she retired, and only then did her many honors begin to suggest the contested nature of her legacy. The memorials, which began nearly a decade later, only furthered those contests.

Windows Opened Upon a Moving World

During the 1930s, even as Lillian Wald remained enmeshed in national and international debates over politics and welfare, her health forced her to inch closer to retirement. After a 1925 trip to Mexico with Jane Addams, infections and anemia periodically troubled her. Later, she had several operations. Wald convalesced in vacation spots like Lake George in upstate New York and in the home she rented (and then bought) in Westport, Connecticut. From these locations, she continued to offer counsel based on a career's worth of experience.

In the conservative 1920s, the energies of Wald and other Progressives had been dispersed onto scores of projects, including the formulation of a new internationalism. The worldwide economic crisis that began in 1929, in her view, meant that the need for her expertise at home was more urgent than ever. Her nurses helped their neighbors to deal with the deprivation of the Depression. And she and her friends then celebrated Franklin Roosevelt's leadership in these troubled times, as they witnessed many of their Progressive ideas codified in the New Deal.

Yet Wald's general outlook proved anything but new. She consistently drew from the vision that grew out of her family's experiences in Germany and Rochester and her own in New York City. Wald's universalist vision inspired approaches to gender and ethnic difference that now revealed their important limits. Her approach to gender was slowly being eclipsed by activists who emphasized women's sameness with men rather than their natural difference.

Wald's belief in gender difference was an essential corollary to her belief that ethnic difference could be overcome. Yet this view left no room for those with investments in a particular ethnoreligious community or in group rights. And here too, as with modern feminism, Wald grew increasingly out of step with the emerging concerns of the American Jewish community, which she had represented and interpreted for so many years. Following the Immigration Act of 1924, which limited immigration from southern and eastern Europe (and ended Asian immigration), American Jewish communities became predominantly native-born and middle-class. Zionism became (for many) the foundation of American Jewish identity. By the late 1930s, all denominations of organized Judaism accepted Palestine as the center of Jewish culture.[1] But Wald rejected the tenets of Zionism and became further removed from the ideals of her Jewish supporters and clientele.

In her retirement home in Connecticut, she lived among like-minded friends and colleagues who found common ground in their worldview. Her neighbors were Progressives, women reformers, uptown Jews, and even a few downtown Jews who had amassed enough wealth to join "our crowd." In contrast to her table at Henry Street, where individuals connected across classes and cultures, this community reflected her ease in a relatively homogenous socioeconomic group, made up of people whose backgrounds and politics for the most part mirrored her own. Here, racial and nationalist notions of Jewish identity were left behind, and an upper-class cosmopolitanism stood most prominent.

Reinforcing the fact that her ease in this community began with her hometown lessons in Rochester was an invitation from the Society of the Genesee in 1931. The society was an elite Rochester organization begun by a like-minded German Jew, Louis Wiley, business manager for the *New York Times*. At the society's annual dinner in January of 1932, its members honored Wald. Rochester, the invitation read, was responsible for Wald's "education of the courteous," an education that "might now be considered old-fashioned." Wald's work combined "an idealistic vision" and "practical and efficient business sense," and the society was pleased that its tribute would "take on an international aspect with world leaders acclaiming one whose achievements in social welfare work have raised her to eminence." The grandiose conclusion read, "The Society of the Genesee feels that Miss Wald perhaps has made the greatest contribution of any former resident of the Genesee Valley to society, not only in New York and throughout the country, but also in various other countries of the world."[2] From a town that boasted Frederick Douglass and Susan B. Anthony as past residents, such praise was striking indeed.

Amid this and other tributes, Wald recorded her thoughts on her career alongside her enthusiasm for the New Deal in her second and final book, *Windows on Henry Street*. As she entered into retirement, American Jewish identity took on a Zionist foundation, modern feminism reinterpreted Wald's approach as outmoded, and other transitions began, including the professionalization of social work and nursing, as well as newer, more modern approaches to social reform work. The choices of Wald's successors at Henry Street and the Visiting Nurse Service, the two institutions she had founded in 1893, spoke to these developments. The social order on which Wald built her universalist vision slowly lost ground to new arrangements in each of these shifts.

At the time of her death in 1940, Wald's peers, along with a few young people from the settlement, offered their thoughts on her legacy. They reflected on her work in the field of nursing, in American politics, for feminism and the American Jewish community, with Manhattan youth, for international peace. Each person's tribute saluted the faith in universalism that had allowed for her entrance into so many reform networks in the first place. These memorials—and even her gravestone in her hometown of Rochester, New York—spoke to that faith and what it allowed her to accomplish. They spoke to the success of her early lessons and her entire career.

Only in hindsight do all of Wald's memorials suggest the ways in which her legacy would be fractured as the modern century wore on.

Westport: The New Deal from the House on the Pond

Toward the end of World War I, when her mother, Minnie Wald, moved into Henry Street Settlement, Wald searched out a place in the country as a refuge for her from the hot city summers.[3] Excellent with children, well-loved by Henry Street clients and residents, Mrs. Wald was said to bear a striking resemblance to Jane Addams in profile—a remark that spoke to the fluid boundaries between her daughter's many networks and families.[4] Wald rented a country home in Connecticut for her mother on a small pond near the Saugatuck River. After her mother's death in 1923, and especially after her own health began to fail in the summer of 1925, Wald continued to summer and rest at the home that she then purchased: her "house on the pond" on Compo Road.

Westport, Connecticut, attracted a number of Jewish and non-Jewish reformers, artists, and writers. Karl Anderson, the artist brother of writer Sherwood Anderson, lived nearby, as did critic and author Van Wyck Brooks.[5] The town boasted a small artists' colony by the time of Wald's retirement.[6] Also represented were members of the networks with whom Wald had worked for decades. Howard Brubaker of the *New Yorker* and Adelaide Baker, a peace advocate, moved to Westport. Wald's first biographer, Robert Duffus of the *New York Times*, lived there as well.[7]

Westport counted many assimilated New York Jews among its residents, though due to anti-Semitic "gentleman's agreements" in Connecticut any "Jewish Jews" had to buy land directly from a seller, as the real estate boards would not sell to them.[8] Aaron Rabinowitz moved to Connecticut to be near Wald, who was one of his childhood heroes. Originally a downtowner, he had emigrated from Russia in 1884 and was a young client of Henry Street before he became a pioneer in public housing. Ben and Sidonie Gruenberg, a teacher and a book illustrator, respectively, and Louis Dublin, who worked with Wald on the partnership between Metropolitan Life Insurance Company and Henry Street's nurses, all bought homes there over the course of the next fifteen years.[9]

After decades of city living, Wald embraced country life and took great

For her 1938 holiday card, Wald used this portrait of her beloved "House on the Pond" in Westport, taken by photographer Arnold Genthe. She sent this one to activist and women's rights leader Mary Dreier. Genthe also took two portrait photographs of Wald that are often reproduced (not shown here). (Courtesy Schlesinger Library, Radcliffe Institute, Harvard University)

pleasure in sharing it with visitors. Jane Addams (who often stayed with Alice Hamilton at her house in Hadlyme, Connecticut, not far from Westport), the Warburg family, Eleanor Roosevelt, and many others came to spend time with her at her bedside or, when she was feeling well, in the garden. There, she grew fruits and vegetables that she used to bake pies and other treats for friends. She often took canoes out on her pond—the same pond in which prime minister Ramsay MacDonald's canoe ran aground in 1929.

Above all, she adored watching local animals, including her dog, Ramsay, as well as turtles, ducks, swans, and geese, and she wrote of their movements and migrations in her letters. When some of the species appeared to be engaging in Darwinian behavior—behavior she found abhorrent in human and beast alike, it seems—she employed time-tested activist methods to address the problem. On behalf of herself and her neighbors, she wrote to

James Silver at the federal Department of Agriculture to inquire how they could limit the damage done by muskrats and how they should keep their turtles from eating their ducks.[10]

Though she took joy in her new surroundings, she assured her friends at home and abroad that she had not lost touch with national and international news. "The times are not static and though I still linger in Connecticut, I am not separated from the efforts of the nation or of the state or of the town," she wrote to Ramsay MacDonald. "An overwhelming [number of] mail, telegrams and telephones seem to keep me more integrated than I could have anticipated."[11] *Survey* editor Paul Kellogg described Wald's situation to MacDonald in a slightly different way: "She lives radiantly in her correspondence with friends like you."[12]

Writing to friends the world over, Wald could hardly contain her enthusiasm for the New Deal after a decade of antigovernment conservatism.[13] "The alphabetized government" of Franklin Roosevelt renewed her faith in people and politics.[14] "Despite occasional lapses on the part of mankind, I haven't lost my optimism and I am as happy as happy can be at the good will and progress that are discernable in greater measure than before," she wrote. "I am very much for President Roosevelt and see many things developing that I feared we would live a long time to see throughout the country."[15] She called President Roosevelt "nothing less than a miracle," and was equally enthusiastic about the first lady.[16] For Eleanor Roosevelt, Wald reserved her highest compliment. She wrote to Jane Addams: "Mrs. R acts truly as if she had been brought up in the Settlement. All the things that we were wont to talk about in our conspiracies are important to her happiness."[17]

Wald was proud of the fact that a number of "Henry Streeters" were active in New Deal politics. She had originally met New York's Jewish governor Herbert Lehman through a member of Jacob Schiff's family in the 1890s. She invited him to lead a boys' club at Henry Street, and his four-year tenure there grew into their lifelong friendship.[18] State senator Robert Wagner, ambassador and diplomat Henry Morgenthau Sr., and treasury secretary Henry Morgenthau Jr. also had looked through the windows on Henry Street and sought to integrate that experience into their public service. She watched their work from a distance, she said, "as nearly as is permitted one who is obliged to maintain a horizontal position."[19] During the Depression, as before, Wald's influence extended far beyond the neighborhood view from the windows of Henry Street Settlement.

Windows on Henry Street *(1934)*

Against this backdrop, Wald collected previously published essays for her second book, *Windows on Henry Street*. In it, she depicted the settlement and the nursing service as a seedbed of current political arrangements, writing, "Our forty years have witnessed the inception of measures that helped prepare for the New Deal."[20] She rejoiced that one of the Progressives' goals—idealized and romanticized in revolutionary Russia—had been realized in the United States: "The newer concept of the obligation of the State to the economic security of the industrial worker bids fair to uproot the old American persuasion that success is a matter of individual effort."[21]

Many of Wald's like-minded Connecticut neighbors helped her to write *Windows*, which served as a vehicle for her recollections of forty years on the Lower East Side. Her foreword was again a who's who of her sprawling networks: she thanked her neighbors, including critic Van Wyck Brooks and Louis Dublin; the uptown Jewish family with whom she remained so close, the Warburgs; fellow Progressive Paul Kellogg (to whom she confessed that she hoped the book would sell well "because we need to have the barn shingled");[22] and many of her nursing colleagues, including Marguerite Wales, who later headed the nursing service. She wrote about changes in the neighborhood and in nursing, about Henry Street's connections to Russia and her feelings on Prohibition and peace work. On each page, predictably, was a local story that offered a lesson in the application of her universalist vision to the neighborhood and the world at large.

In the first chapter, "Why This Book Is Written," Wald recorded her outward progression: "Our experience in one small East Side section, a block perhaps, had led to a next contact, and a next, in widening circles, until our community relationships have come to include the city, the state, the national government, and the world at large." Her "real hope" in recording these years was "to encourage people—particularly young people—to participate more widely than they do in the affairs of the going world." "The harvest of such living," Wald concluded, "would be a faith in democracy, and an understanding of people that would count against the disastrous currents of indifference and ignorance and prejudice."[23]

Taking stock of the world from her vantage point in Connecticut, she did not embrace an unqualified optimism. Although she offered praise for the advances made by workers, women, and African Americans, she also expressed alarm that "the cloud of war darkens the horizon and the German influence cannot be ignored."[24] Just as *The House on Henry Street* addressed the urgent need for mutual understanding in the face of World War I, *Windows* called for mutual understanding and peace as Nazism, Fascism, and economic depression threatened international security and goodwill.

With such lofty hopes for the book's impact, Wald did not intend for it to be an autobiography. Even so, she offered countless personal tributes—to the advocacy of Alfred Smith, to the memories of Jacob Schiff's generosity and Florence Kelley's activism (Kelley died in 1932). Many other members of her networks for reform appeared in her pages. The entire book is remarkably personal, its voice and opinions clearly her own. Indeed, in a review of the book, Wald's colleague in immigration reform and child welfare Grace Abbott noted that the personal aspect to *Windows* made it "more interesting than the first one."[25]

Wald's voice comes through with special clarity as a record of her sentiments on difference among Jews and other immigrants. In her second chapter, "Change Comes to the East Side," Wald documented and applauded the fact that economic mobility had resulted in a decline in difference among immigrants. She recalled changes in the mothers' club, a group of nine women whom her nurses originally met and organized into a club while visiting homes in the neighborhood. At the mothers' first meeting, she related, "there was no indication of any experience with social usages, for they came in untidy clothes, safety pins holding together their overflowing blouses; and the talk, interspersed with stories to make instruction palatable, was what might have been given to little children." At the thirty-fifth reunion of the club, in contrast, the one hundred alumnae who attended won Wald's approval as "a meeting of sophisticates."[26] Poverty had given way to middle-class status, and with it middle-class mores. The most widely read review of the book in the *New York Times* quoted this passage in full, supporting Wald's idea that the club members had made use of the settlement in precisely the right way. These changes were necessary steps toward mutual understanding.

Wald expressed similar feelings regarding the decline in the observance of Jewish religious rituals. Fewer married Jewish women chose to "disfigure themselves with the *sheitel*" (a wig worn by Orthodox Jewish married women to cover their heads), a move that Wald thought marked the "emancipation of our neighbors from binding tradition."[27] But she respected the retention of some level of religious difference. She related the story of an "old man from a neighborhood tenement who chants the religious songs inspired for the occasion [of the Jewish holiday of Sukkot] hundreds—perhaps thousands —of years ago." She was clearly pleased with residents' "demonstration of respect for old customs," especially when conducted in accordance with middle-class standards. As she recorded: *"Changes in this observance symbolize the changes in the economic condition of the neighborhood.* When I first came to the East Side, I would see the pitiful, newly arrived immigrants bargaining with the pushcart dealers for . . . the greens and fruit traditionally associated with the festival. Having no place to build the ceremonial booth, as their forbears did, they would lay branches over the roof of an outdoor toilet, which bore a remote suggestion of the traditional *sukkah.* None of today's children know this sorry makeshift, and their reintroduction to the old customs of the festival comes from people who see the spiritual message and who love to have the beautiful preserved as an inheritance." Wald celebrated the economic mobility and the sharing of "immigrant gifts" that allowed religious practice to gain respectability. The festival of Sukkot, she wrote, gave "no sense of intrusion, but rather of hospitality, when guests who happen to be at the Settlement, though they know little of Jewish customs, join in the celebration and are moved by the beauty of this ceremony transferred from the Orient to New York's East Side." The festival gained respectability because it became seamlessly integrated into mainstream America; for Wald, it was easily described as something beautiful, even spiritual.[28]

The most compelling comment on Jewish difference in *Windows* is a story that Wald offered in her chapter titled "People Who Have Crossed Our Threshold." She wrote of a Passover service given by a local Lower East Side Jewish charity. Wald attended the seder with Mary Antin, author of *The Promised Land.* Other guests included immigrants detained at Ellis Island, for, as Wald explained, "it was the custom of this centre to gather [the needy] for the sacred festival." Surrounded mostly by "strangers from distant lands . . . all familiar with the ceremony," Wald clearly felt she had nothing in common with those practicing the religious rituals of Judaism. Though the charity staff invited her to the Jewish gathering as an insider, she described the seder from an outsider's perspective. Surely Antin's presence put her at ease, as many thought of Antin as a champion of assimilation and Americanization.[29]

More telling in the story, however, is Wald's description of the "Man from Dahomey" (a nation in West Africa), a "picturesque stranger" in attendance at the seder. After commenting to a friend about the presence of a black man at the seder, she was told that the man (whom she never names) was a Jew. She described him as a "tall, erect figure with dark skin, straight hair, and a nose slightly aquiline": he lacked all the racial features of Jewishness, features she may have disliked in herself. The man told her that his Dahomey tribe believed in one god, one wife, and rejected cannibalism (unlike many neighboring tribes). He had arrived in Scotland as a stowaway, "where a philanthropic gentleman took him under his wing and had him educated." This explained his speaking "English with a Scotch burr," which nearly caused Wald to lose her "equilibrium" when he spoke to her.[30]

Searching out affirmation of the unlikely story, Wald turned to the pioneering anthropologist Franz Boas. Boas's work, in the spirit of Israel Zangwill's melting pot, emphasized the instability of the concept of race, the profound influence of environmental factors on human cultural life. Himself Jewish, Boas represented the growing Jewish presence in American intellectual, literary, and reform networks, notable in schools of thought that would integrate Jews into the category of mainstream whites.[31] He was studying the man Wald had met, and so he "corroborated the fact," Wald said, that "the Jew from Dahomey with his Scotch burr was not spoofing me."[32]

Wald's encounter with the man from Dahomey was a reinscription of her own ideas. Of course, this man's experience was vastly complicated by the color line, then collapsing around ethnic whites as (Euro-American) Jews and other groups gained the privileges of whiteness. His experience, though, also confirmed that consent could trump descent.

Even before the rise of Nazism (contemporaneous with the publication of *Windows*), the idea of Jewish racial difference was losing ground. But this anecdote offers more than additional proof of the passing of a racial defini- tion of Jewish identity. Wald's experience at the seder confirmed her belief that economic mobility and education could lead to integration into middle- class, educated networks, and that with such integration came transcen- dence over difference. Wald attended as a Jew among Jews. But she was immersed in networks of Jews and Christians, women reformers and Pro- gressives, united by a shared universalist vision that placed consent over descent, environment over race.

Wald's colleagues expressed their devotion to that vision in reviews of the book. Journalist and feminist Florence Finch Kelly praised Wald's applica- tion of it in the "far-flung neighborhood of the country and the world."[33] John Lovejoy Elliott called the book, and Wald, "courageous and inspiring," her many illustrative anecdotes "like flashes of sunshine on every path."[34] "The important comment for a reviewer to make about any book that Lillian Wald may write," began social worker E. R. Wembridge in the *Nation*, "is that everyone interested in the development of social reform in the United States should read it." Wembridge confirmed this even as she admitted to finding herself "stimulated and depressed" by Wald's book, given its cele- bration of the work done alongside its indication of the work yet to be done. Still, she went on to list the many goals of Wald's work, last listing her "fight against sweated labor, race prejudice, and bigoted nationalism."[35]

In *Windows*, Wald wrote that the Dahomey Jew she had met at the seder "had always planned to return to Africa and give his people the benefit of his education." Some members of the Jewish community saw Wald's work in that same light. They were mistaken. She came to the Lower East Side—and forever wanted to be thought of—as a professional, a nurse, and a social worker. Yet those categories, too, were changing as she wrote her final book.

"A Nurse, Social Worker, and Social Reformer All in One"

In *Windows*, Wald offered her thoughts on changes in the profession of nursing, the service that she had brought to the aid of Lower East Side immigrants. As Wald and her peers envisioned it, nursing drew from both "the older values of women's culture and the newer aspirations of profes- sional ideology."[36] Indeed, she held that "the old and new" were "linked together" in her profession. She elaborated on this idea with words that were a fusion of the classic Progressive language of efficiency and Victorian notions of feminine duty: the "American development" of nursing meant "the spirit of consecration, the power of organization, the realization that the nurse is an effective and indispensable educator, and that her profession is of community importance." "Each advance," Wald wrote, "has been but a new graft on an age-old acceptance of her duties and devotion."[37]

Social justice goals formed the foundation of Wald's approach to nursing and her Progressivism. When she celebrated nurses' "broadening interests" into areas such as "social insurance, old-age pensions, [and] state aid," she took note of the many maternalist public issues that had injected women into political debates in the second half of the nineteenth century. Maternalist campaigns for playgrounds, milk stations, and school nurses were Wald's first points of entry into municipal politics; they were the causes through which she first linked nursing and social reform work. Wald connected her professional training in nursing to social activism under the broad rubric of public health nursing, a term she coined herself.[38]

As separate training schools came to mark the increasingly divided territories of nursing and social work, in the 1920s and 1930s the division of labor between nurses and social workers became more stark.[39] Public health nursing was increasingly professionalized; maternalist medicine faded from view. The decline of maternalist concerns was also linked to twentieth-century women activists' emphasis on the similarity of the sexes, the same changing dynamic that divided Wald's strategies for women's rights from more modern campaigns.[40] Boards of education and health departments took over nursing's preventive and educational work, while bedside nursing became part of hospital and clinic care. The change from "private duty" to hospital staffing constituted nursing's "great transformation."[41] And with it came the medical profession's "retreat from social activism."[42]

The field of social work, which began as a broad term consistently applied to Wald's settlement efforts, was also narrowing and drawing away from social reform. Instead of comprehensive social policy initiatives, it came to emphasize psychiatry, scientific management, casework, and the treatment of individuals. The settlement house that Wald founded with Jacob Schiff in 1893 began to divide its services, especially after Schiff's widow dedicated a separate building for the nurses on Park Avenue in

1921.[43] At the same time, Henry Street Settlement, like others across the country, increasingly hired professional social workers.[44]

But as hospitals and other institutions sought to serve broader populations, settlements remained focused on the needs of their immediate neighborhoods.[45] Running both Henry Street Settlement and the Visiting Nurse Service during these transitions, Wald was a special case. Unlike Jane Addams, John Elliott (founder of Hudson Guild Settlement), and others of Wald's colleagues who studied sociology and philosophy prior to their social work in settlements, Wald was trained in nursing and turned to social reform and social work to meet the needs she perceived in her community. She bridged the fields of nursing and social work as others could not; she moved in both professional communities with relative ease. That movement was possible only for the historical moment of Wald's forty years at Henry Street.

The struggle to replace Wald upon her retirement in 1933 demonstrated just how transient a time that was. In 1931, when bad health kept her mainly at home in Westport, the board divided her job as headworker into two positions: Karl Hesley took charge of Henry Street Settlement's affairs, Marguerite Wales those of the nursing service. Given the complex array of networks Wald had constructed and the significant institutional growth over the past four decades, no single person could easily assume her role.

When Wald finally decided to step down formally, the search for her successor proceeded delicately. The board hoped for someone who would serve as headworker to the settlement and oversee the nurses as well. In May 1933, Wald wrote excitedly to Jane Addams and Mary Rozet Smith: "The main news . . . is to tell you that Helen Hall of Philadelphia is coming to the Settlement. I know you'll be glad because she is a fine person and an enthusiast about the contribution of settlements."[46] Hall had worked at the University Settlement in Philadelphia and had attended the New York School of Philanthropy, later known as the Columbia University School of Social Work. She was also chairman of the unemployment division of the National Federation of Settlements, a professional organization formally organized in 1911 by Wald, Addams, and Elliott, among others. Hall represented a new generation of trained social workers, and she would head the settlement and supervise the Visiting Nurse Service.

Though Hall knew that "specialization was essential in the profession of social work," she also emphasized the need for "general practitioners" to help specific neighborhood problems. Inspired by Wald's generation of reformers, she linked her leadership with activism. Echoing the language of Wald and her cohorts, Hall prioritized "the settlement's job of interpretation," its duty to share information on the lives of the poor with the public at large.[47] The similarities between Wald and Hall's approaches surely drew the board to her candidacy.

Even with this similarity of worldview, Hall had big shoes to fill. She knew well that Wald had been "a nurse, social worker, and social reformer in one."[48] She recalled that residents and friends of the settlement were so devoted to Wald that one club had "planned to dislike" her, while another woman "cried herself to sleep every night at the thought of having [Hall's] furniture moved into what had been Miss Wald's apartment."[49] And Hall simply did not have access to the many networks Wald had worked with for decades. Within a few months of her taking over, in August 1933, Hall asked Wald if she needed to speak at a meeting of the Jewish Philanthropic Society. "I would rather not do it but I thought you might feel that it was wise to for some reason—will you tell me?" she asked. "I don't know Miss Lewisohn"—referring to Wald's old friend, the cofounder of the Neighborhood Playhouse—"and I knew you would."[50] Wald's personal relationships created Henry Street's connections to uptown Jews—they shared similar cultural and class backgrounds—and now those connections became more tenuous.

Hall soon discovered the degree to which Henry Street was rooted in Wald's persona. During her second year as head of the settlement and overseer of the Visiting Nurse Service, Hall delicately suggested to Wald that one reunion party, commemorating both Thanksgiving and New Year's Day, be held instead of the tradition of celebrating both at separate Henry Street parties. Most people on the guest lists now seemed to prefer to celebrate "in their own homes" if they could not come back "to have a reunion with" Wald.[51] A few years later, she still felt that "most of the people" who had been invited to a settlement gathering had come in the past to see Wald, and, she said, "I do not feel that it means quite the same to them now."[52]

From Connecticut, and mostly through the mail, Wald struggled to arbitrate between Hall and Marguerite Wales, who remained actively in charge of the nurses but under Hall's supervision. Wales chafed under the leadership of someone not trained in nursing. Months after Hall took her position, Wald reassured Wales in long letters that though the settlement and the nursing service were "mutually interdependent," Hall's role "in no way infringes on the autonomy and integrity of the nursing service." Wald compared Hall's job to that of a university president, with the headworker "as a member of each department." Hall "does not want to speak as a nurse or for the nurses," Wald assured Wales. Holding fast to faith in the links between public health and broader reforms, Wald rejected Wales's suggestion that the two services be divided, holding that their "inter-relationship" was "immensely important."[53] Wald in turn emphasized to Hall that "the nurses are never to be interfered with, are to speak for themselves and to cooperate with all who have the same idea." Maintaining her faith in the spiritual, feminine calling of nursing, she praised Wales for maintaining "the spirit and purpose of the nurses."[54]

Wald feared the loss of "the essential principles of public health work and social service in combination" just as the tension in that combination reverberated through the increasingly divided worlds of public health and social work.[55] In 1937, Wales resigned, and the administrations of Henry Street Settlement and the Visiting Nurse Service were separated. In 1944, four years after Wald's death, the two formed separate corporations under the names Henry Street Settlement and the Visiting Nurse Service of New York.[56] Straddling the worlds of nursing and social work for decades, Wald could not be replaced by a single representative from either of these increasingly specialized fields.

In 1933, while Wald and her board still struggled over the leadership of the two institutions, her colleagues, friends, and clients began to discuss her legacy. She had proposed her own thoughts on that legacy in *Windows on Henry Street*. Now, tributes in honor of her sixty-sixth birthday allowed others to assess her impact. Certainly, they reflected the many goals of the work she had done in seeking to realize her vision. But they also reflected the beginning of the fracturing of her legacy, as individuals from increasingly specialized networks based on ethnoreligious, political, professional, or even philosophical ties claimed her legacy for themselves.

A Woman of Valor

The *New York Times* ran a story on Wald's birthday celebration every year, but in 1933 the paper linked that event to her retirement and to the fortieth anniversary of Henry Street. President and Eleanor Roosevelt and Governor Lehman sent messages; secretary of labor Frances Perkins, Ishbel Mac-Donald, and Jane Addams sent telegrams to be read at the large celebration held at the settlement. All testified to Wald's efficacy as a public advocate for women, workers, and the poor.[57]

The more private booklet of birthday wishes compiled by Karl Hesley offered other testimony. On the cover of the booklet, Hesley printed the symbol for universal brotherhood adopted by Wald as Henry Street's symbol after her trip to Asia in 1910. Inside the booklet's pages, many children active in Henry Street's clubs signed their names. At least thirty-five clubs were represented, including the Variety Girls, the Henry Midgets, and the Astor, Pirate, and Helen Keller Clubs, as well as the Wald Club, named in her honor. Local organizations offered appreciation for Wald's neighborhood efforts, including workers from the Lower East Side Community Council, the Bowery Young Men's Christian Association, the Jewish Social Service, the Girl Scouts, the Charity Organization Society, and the Catholic Charities. Wald had joined forces with these organizations first in the name of maternalist issues such as playgrounds and milk stations. Later, they worked together for social welfare and municipal causes that encompassed all of their neighbors—women, men, children, workers, and poor people of all religions and backgrounds.

One of the most prominent signers of the booklet reflected Wald's ties to uptown Jews and Progressives. Rabbi Stephen Wise, fellow New York reformer, blessed Wald's "life-bearing, life-bringing spirit" and quoted the Hebrew Bible in calling her an "*ayshet chayeel* [written in Hebrew characters], a woman of valor whose price is far above rubies." He attributed Wald's strength to her spirituality and her ability to uplift others with her strong spirit. In doing so, he claimed her and her legacy for Jewish peoplehood.

Members of Wald's nursing network spoke of her integrating feminine spirituality and the spirit of self-sacrifice into her work. Friend, nursing colleague, and women's rights activist Lavinia Dock contributed a loving poem in which she compared Wald to the sun, claiming that "happiness, welfare, and mirth come from both." A group of nurses from Massachusetts expressed their appreciation of her use of the "old and new" in their shared profession:

You . . . reach out to the nurses
You teach us of love and its law
That our duty is to all mankind
Now and forever more
You teach us that self denial
Is of service the highest form
That our own small needs and wishes
Are not for what we were born
You teach us by your example
What Brotherhood can mean
You teach us that we a prop must be
That weaker ones may lean
In fact you teach us, every one that
Our duty is to give
That each and every soul on earth
May learn to know and live

In psalmlike form, the nurses' praise testified to the fact that Wald's professionalism encompassed her universalist philosophy of a brotherhood of man. The poem spoke as well to Wald's deep dependence on traditionally feminine notions of women's duty to serve others—and deny their own needs.

John Lovejoy Elliott, a settlement colleague who was also a leader in the secular Ethical Culture Movement (emphasizing social action, or "deed, not creed"), also honored Wald's humanity. A descendent of abolitionist Owen Lovejoy, he had worked with Wald on antimilitarism and for civil liberties, women's suffrage, and countless causes of urban reform. He spoke about her ability to connect to people and improve lives: "From this city of New York, which, big as it is you have made seem like home for so many people, and from the nation, and from places all around the world that are healthier and happier and better and infinitely more human for what you have done, there is going to you love and gratitude."[58]

A photograph pasted into the birthday book illustrated that happiness. Wald is seated in her garden, surrounded by friends, smiling broadly. The table is set for a celebration, no doubt in her honor. Guests brought to the table their thoughts on Wald's major contributions to the world: her efficiency at managing institutions and building coalitions, her professional skills in nursing and social work, her spirituality and humanity.

Tributes continued in ensuing years. In 1935, reformer Josephine Goldmark made a bold public claim on Wald's legacy in a radio broadcast. Goldmark was an expert on labor law, a published author on conditions for women workers, and a contributor to the field of nursing's professionalization. Like Wald, she was the child of Jewish immigrants who left Europe after the 1848 revolutions. Goldmark predicted that Wald's legacy would link her ideals and achievements, noting that nursing was her point of entry to her lifelong work for reform:

> When she transplanted nursing into the homes of a great urban population, when she made of it an agency of education in the ways of health as well as of healing, when she combined with it the life of a great social settlement, she came into contact with all sorts and conditions of men. It was the force and charm of her personality which drew to her and has made her the confidant . . . of governors and mayors and fire-captains, and ward-leaders, of rabbis and priests and ministers, of the policeman and of the banker, of British cabinet ministers and presidents of the United States. Out of these varied and intimate relations has grown the role by which I think Miss Wald will be remembered in the future as much as by her concrete achievements which make up so long a list, in behalf of causes local, state, national and international.

From her view as a fellow Jewish woman reformer, Goldmark focused on how far Wald's philosophy had allowed her to travel—into networks with members of all persuasions and to nations all over the world. She saw that philosophy as the source of all of Wald's practical accomplishments.

Goldmark stressed that above all those accomplishments was Wald's role at the nexus of so many varied groups of people, separated along lines of class and nationality, of religion and generation: "She has been the great interpreter of one social class to another, of the newcomer and the alien to the native-born, of people of different racial backgrounds to one another, of

This photo was pasted into a booklet given to Wald on her birthday in March 1933. (Courtesy Department of Special Collections and Archives, Charles E. Shain Library, Connecticut College)

the underprivileged to the overprivileged, of age to youth and youth to age."[59] Wald's universal vision had afforded her that role for over forty years.

Goldmark's proposed legacy fit well with what Wald herself considered the single most important lesson she had learned in her work. Wald concluded *Windows on Henry Street* with its story:

> We on Henry Street have become internationalists . . . because we have found that the problems of one set of people are the problems of all . . . and that the vision which long since proclaimed the interdependence and the kinship of mankind was farsighted and is true. All the varied experience of our intercourse with the many races, those who are expressive and those who are not, and who wait upon others for a formulation of what lies deep within their racial traditions or religious promises— such experience points to the inevitable: that people rise and fall together, that no one group or nation dare be an economic or social law unto itself. That has been the lesson we have learned in the years at Henry Street.[60]

The significance of connectedness among people and not their divisions: this was her most important lesson. Wald hoped to be remembered as an internationalist, and as someone who aided cultural groups in finding their true expressions. Tributes to her recorded her deep connections to the diverse communities for which she had worked throughout her career.

"An Enduring Faith"

Wald had long shared a fervent faith in humanity with her colleague John Elliott. Their correspondence in the 1930s reveals their close friendship and similar worldviews. About the same age, they shared a sense of confusion over current trends. "The thing that perhaps discourages me most," Elliott wrote to Wald in late 1933, "is that so many of the people, both young and old, have sunk into a kind of lethargy, not to say despair, about a really and truly better world. There are no end of schemes to patch up this, that and the other thing. There doesn't seem to be any real chart to steer by. Of course, a person doesn't expect a blueprint but the faith we have, and there is faith, is muddy. [Social worker] Edward Lindeman talked the other day about having faith in faith. If that phrase doesn't make me feel mushy, nothing ever did."[61] Wald and Elliott's shared faith drew from the currents of Social Gospel; their universal visions guided them in their work for change. As they neared the end of their public careers, and as Nazism and Fascism gripped Europe, they worried that the next generation of reformers would not see the spiritual potential in such work.

So close were Wald and Elliott that as Wald's health declined, she thought he would best be able to articulate that potential for her friends and family after her death: "I suppose we must arrange for formalities and my dear friends would be disappointed if we did not have a few sentences of good will. I would like my old friend John Elliott to be spokesman for me. He will be willing—if he can—and I will have the assurance of knowing that he will mention only that my message is of the worthwhileness of love and fellowship and mutual respect for each other—the world over. It is an enduring faith."[62] In that request, Wald expressed hope that her faith in universalism would transcend all of her individual achievements and be her most lasting legacy. When she died in September 1940, Elliott spoke at the private ceremony in Westport. In a published obituary, he praised her for "making that which was good the actual and the real," and for striving for "peace on earth."[63]

The public ceremony memorialized Wald's philosophy in a different way. On 1 December 1940, hundreds gathered in Carnegie Hall to hear nine speakers offer their thoughts on Wald's work and legacy. They worked for reform in separate ways and had distinctive connections to Wald's work. George W. Alger, lawyer, humanitarian, and president of the Henry Street board, began with a portrayal of Wald as "One Who Had Faith in People." That faith was "Wald's abiding message to us," he said, and was "the hope of the world today." Others remarked on her achievements in specific fields and within specific networks. Mary Beard spoke "as the representative of all nurses" to praise Wald as a pioneer in public health nursing. Rev. John H. Johnson called Wald a "Friend of the Colored People" for the settlement and nursing work she offered the West Side, and for her encouragement of African American nurses.

Henry Street club alumnus Abraham Davis called her "An Inspiration to Youth" in teaching children "faith in democracy." Alfred Smith's "Neighbor on Henry Street" was a "great power behind all social legislation." Paul Kellogg said that Wald's internationalism earned her the title of "Creator of Wide Horizons." Mayor Fiorello La Guardia testified to her work on behalf of those who suffered "misery and hunger" in New York.

Dr. C. E. A. Winslow of Yale University offered his insights on Wald and public health. But he paused to acknowledge what seemed evident at the end of the presentations: that no one thought of her "primarily as a nurse, or as a social worker, or a pioneer in public health, or a citizen or a states-woman. . . . She was all these things, but she was more than all of these things." Winslow hoped to rectify the fracturing of Wald's legacy into so many specialized fields.

From a similar perspective, Van Wyck Brooks, Wald's neighbor in Con-necticut, offered a brief message for the ceremony's program about her as "one of the great Americans of her time." He credited her "cosmopolitan sympathies" with helping her to become "the fulfillment of the American promise . . . a radiant incarnation of the beliefs and instincts expressed in the great documents of our Revolution, in the acts and speeches of Lincoln, in the poems of Whitman, at a time, in a place where these instincts seemed smothered and lost." Descended from rabbis and merchants in Germany and Poland, Wald represented to him the best of American idealism and humanism.

Wald's commitment to the promise realized in her family's assimilation experience, along with her deep faith in the vision of the Protestant Social Gospel: these allowed her membership in exclusive networks. Brooks praised her for putting that membership to work for people suffering throughout the world: "Whether in America, Russia, Mexico, or Japan, there was nothing human that was alien to her." Echoing Goldmark's words, he described Henry Street as "the interpreter's house where Americans, new and old alike, learned the meaning of their country."[64]

Written by Brooks, the quintessential American critic, who had just won the Pulitzer Prize in history for his passionate study of New England literature, such comments were powerful and meaningful. They reflected all of Wald's hopes for Henry Street—and, not incidentally, for herself—as a national symbol. She tells the following related story in *Windows*. A visiting South American commission "was under the impression," she wrote, "that there is nothing to be seen in the United States but the successful attainment of material ends." The delegation's leader thought it "important that they should see something of value other than those that are purchasable." That a visit to Henry Street remedied the situation came as no surprise to Wald, for she had long thought that her institution represented the best of America. Now, at her memorial ceremony, Brooks reinforced that idea.[65]

The final word of the ceremony, however, belonged to John M. Schiff, grandson of Jacob Schiff and president of Henry Street since Wald's retirement. His remarks were primarily focused on Henry Street's history, with only a brief mention of Wald. (He was, after all, just growing into the job.) He thought that a "really characteristic quality of [Wald's] was that her face was always turned toward the future, while the past served as her guide." This was perhaps the most appropriate ending for Wald's public memorial. The other contributors enumerated her good works, praised her spirit and kindness. Schiff's words highlighted another important aspect of Wald's career: that her far-reaching, twentieth-century achievements rested on the foundation of a decidedly nineteenth-century set of hometown lessons and Social Gospel spirituality.

Rochester

Wald was buried in the birthplace of her vision, her hometown of Rochester, New York, in the city's Mount Hope Cemetery. Founded in 1838, a decade before Wald's family arrived in the United States, it was the first rural cemetery sponsored by a municipality. Urban Americans like those in Rochester began the rural cemetery movement as a means to make sense of their new communities and changing nation, to demonstrate their continuing strong ties to their families and to the "virtue of rural life." It was a quintessentially American burial site.[66] The famous figures buried there pay tribute to the reform energies of the region, which continued to be a hotbed long after the "burning over" by the early-nineteenth-century's Second Great Awakening and the corresponding explosion of evangelical reform. Wald and her family had joined other immigrants in Rochester and experienced a new wave of that reform energy in the age of the Social Gospel, when the city experienced massive industrial growth. Her uncles' garment factories, and their antilabor stands in the strikes of the 1890s, were part of the city's growing pains, its transition to modern arrangements of capital and labor.

Mount Hope reflects the polyglot racial, ethnic, and professional collective identities, as well as the many organizational affiliations, of the citizens of a rapidly modernizing city at the turn of the last century. Plots at Mount Hope were purchased by the German Benevolent Society, the New Scottish Burial Plot, the State Industrial School, the Daughters of the American Revolution, the Society of Friends, the United Sons of Rochester (recorded as a "Colored Association"), and veterans of the Spanish-American War and World War I.[67] Temple B'rith Kodesh, where Wald's family were members, also owned a plot.

The records of the temple are predictably—even ironically—fuzzy on whether or not the Wald family bought its plot directly from Mount Hope or through the temple. Once again, the opposing poles of Wald's integration and affiliation, her particularism and universalism, were at work. The family chose a plot in the cemetery's Jewish section, though not within the official area belonging to Temple B'rith Kodesh. The temple records show that when Wald's brother, Alfred, died in 1885, a rabbi officiated at the burial. But at the funerals for Wald's father, Marcus, who died in 1891, and

Wald's gravestone at Mount Hope Cemetery in Rochester, New York, with the Henry Street symbol for "universal brotherhood." Directly behind the stone, also in the family plot, is the grave of Lillian's mother, Minnie Wald. (Courtesy Frank Gillespie)

for her mother, Minnie, who died in 1923, no representatives of the temple were present.

Wald's ashes—and it should be noted that cremation is strictly forbidden in traditional Jewish communities—are buried next to her mother and father, her mother's parents, her sister, and her brother. Her uncle Morris Schwarz, one of the leaders of the antiunion Clothiers' Exchange in the 1890s garment industry, is also nearby. Surrounding the Wald family plot are gravestones marked with Hebrew lettering. Across the small path are the tall mausoleums of the (non-Jewish) families of Bausch and Lomb, the pioneers of the optical goods industry that brought Wald's father to the city in the first place. Just over the hill are the graves of two of the most important leaders in nineteenth-century struggles for American equality: Susan B. Anthony and Frederick Douglass.

Wald's place after death is strikingly similar to her place in life: she is with her family, surrounded by other Jews, nearby to workers, industrialists, male and female reformers, and cosmopolitan urban citizens. On Wald's gravestone, where a Star of David might have been, is the symbol she adopted for Henry Street after her first trip to Asia in 1910. The characters represent the words "universal brotherhood." As she worked for universal understanding in her life, she hoped to symbolize it to future generations after her death.

She Is All Religions

As Wald had hoped, her message of universal brotherhood—best expressed in the symbol she chose for her gravestone—endured after her death in the two institutions she founded. The same icon remains on the entryway of 265 Henry Street, still the home of the headworker of the thriving Henry Street Settlement. Wald's universal philosophy of reform, though challenged in significant ways even during her lifetime, proved flexible enough to stand the test of time, and flexible enough to meet the challenges of postindustrial urban life. The settlement continues to work with neighborhood residents of all backgrounds, now providing day care, youth programs, and services for the elderly, homeless individuals, and AIDS patients. Social workers there provide mental health counseling and training for jobs and for the graduate record exam.[1] The Lewisohns' theater, now part of Henry Street's Abrons Arts Center, still presents community productions. The Visiting Nurse Service of New York, too, continues to live out Wald's legacy by providing health care to diverse populations. It is the largest not-for-profit home health care provider in the United States, helping thirty thousand patients each day.

The commitment of Wald and other Progressives to affordable housing also lives on in another of Wald's marked legacies. Helen Hall, Wald's successor at Henry Street, along with other Henry Street staff members, continued to advocate for new housing for settlement clients. It was Wald who suggested to Aaron Rabinowitz and Herbert Lehman—both of whom had been active at Henry Street and had great success in business and politics, respectively—that they invest capital in the first cooperative housing projects on the Lower East Side. In the summer of 1941, state financing laws made possible the continuation of Wald's crusade for affordable and safe housing.[2] New housing projects were built along the East River, named for Jacob Riis and Bernard Baruch; and in Chelsea, where John Lovejoy Elliott worked, the Elliott Houses were built. One development was also named for Wald.

At the laying of the cornerstone of the Lillian Wald Houses on East Sixth Street and Avenue D in 1947, Mary K. Simkhovitch, settlement house reformer and vice chairman of the New York City Housing Authority, spoke passionately about her friend's life and deep roots in the neighborhood:

> What a pleasure and satisfaction it would have been for Miss Wald to see this cornerstone laid today! She spent her young womanhood going in and out of the old tenements of the East Side. As a nurse she was close to countless families and all the great work she accomplished in her lifetime was founded on her day by day association with the families of the old East Side. Above all she was a practical person, and all her great talents were founded on facts—the facts of daily life as she saw them, understood them, and acted on them. When she saw something to do, she did it. . . . Miss Wald as a nurse knew that people's health was intimately related to the whole tone of neighborhood life, to its opportunities for education and outdoor recreation, but above all to the life of the home.[3]

Simkhovitch's words capture well Wald's commitments to professionalism and practice, to maternalist notions of home life and public health. Importantly, her words also begin the work of memorializing Wald's connections to the "old East Side." Those who understood firsthand Wald's "intimate" relationship to the families of the old neighborhood, like Simkhovitch and Wald's first biographer, Robert L. Duffus, were the first chroniclers of her accomplishments. Their words later evoked nostalgic recollections of when the East Side was the "Jewish East Side."

Beyond the built world, where we can see Wald's name, Wald's posthumous legacies—and the way each generation, beginning with that of Simkhovitch and Duffus, has come to see those legacies—are as numerous as they are rich in multiple layers of meaning. Students of Wald across the decades since her death have wrestled with the question of how best to capture and make sense of the life of someone whose work met the needs of such diverse groups, and whose loyalties were just as widely distributed among those groups. In addition to shedding light on the context of Wald's life, her relationships and her reform efforts, all studies, including this one, offer insights into their own era's priorities. The claims on Wald's life by feminists, public health experts, and scholars (in Jewish studies and other disciplines) have followed a certain cadence, in tune with historical events and trends that have left individuals searching for answers to vexing questions. In this conclusion, I review studies of Wald and analyze the rhythm of interest in her life. I end, finally, with a brief comparison of the legacies of Wald and her friend and colleague Jane Addams. This comparison serves as a means to access contemporary social and academic priorities, including those that motivate this biography.

Wald's Audiences: Wald, Gender, and Jewish Goodness (Reprise)

The first memorials to Wald's productive life were in public obituaries, and they followed the pattern of group claiming established during her lifetime. The main professional journals stood in stark contrast to those in Jewish media, as each of her audiences recalled her legacies. The *American Journal of Nursing* compared Wald to Florence Nightingale in her genius, statesmanship, and international influence; *Social Service Review* likewise called her a "statesman."[4] While the first mentioned the gendered nature of her work, neither referenced her ethnic background. In contrast, the *National Jewish Monthly* of B'nai B'rith not only memorialized her as a "Great Jewish

Social Worker" who "gave up wealth to serve all groups," it also altered her telling of her initial inspiration: it was her grandfather's "Talmudic stories . . . in which service to humanity was always extolled" that inspired her career, not the Social Gospel and her baptism of fire.[5]

What Susan Glenn would call the "Jewhooing" of Wald had begun: many American Jews laid claim to her, counted her as one among them, demonstrating both their ambivalence toward Jewish assimilation and their pride in Jewish contributions to mainstream America.[6] Technically, Wald had been claimed as early as 1903, when Abraham Fromenson advised her of her role in making settlements more Jewish. She was first mentioned in the *American Jewish Yearbook* in 1905, and she appeared in five yearbooks, all told, in her lifetime. Brief entries on her life appeared in Jewish encyclopedias, such as the 1935 *Biographical Encyclopedia of American Jews*.[7] In 1933, the Jewish Academy of Arts and Sciences, founded in 1927, elected her to honorary membership.[8] A 1937 article in the Orthodox journal the *Synagogue Light* labeled her "A Great Jewess" and noted that "the Jewish flair for healing and caring for those who are ill manifested itself in Miss Wald." Though author Stanley Garten stated succinctly that "Miss Wald's work was done, not for Israel alone, but for the world," he concluded with the following assertion: "Israel, however, is happy to have given this great woman to the world as one more example of Jewish idealism, self-sacrifice, and love of humanity."[9] As this study reveals, the Jewish world routinely pulled her into this circle of belonging. Whether through criticism, coverage at public Jewish gatherings, or in the Jewish press, Jewish advocates sought to define Wald's work as emerging only from Jewish roots.

Still, these claims were relatively quiet and not well publicized outside of Wald's immediate professional and personal networks during the early twentieth century. In the final decades of her life, and even into the 1940s and 1950s, the most visible celebrations of Wald more often resembled that of Walter Tittle in 1926. He sketched a portrait of Wald and included it in a *Forum* magazine series entitled "Four American Women." Wald was joined by portraits of Dr. Alice Hamilton, author Willa Cather, and artist Cecilia Beaux.[10] As was the case with her acceptance into the Hall of Fame for Great Americans, Wald was honored as someone who contributed to national life as an American citizen, with no reference to any group belonging that set her apart from those who shared her honor, and with no suggestion that her work was primarily in the service of religious rather than civic ideals.[11]

By the 1970s, the ethnic revival movements of the post–civil rights movement United States began to shape the way a new generation of American writers interpreted Wald's legacy. Both a sign and a product of this ethnic revival, Irving Howe's *World of Our Fathers*, first published in 1976, had a wide appeal among American Jews in these same years.[12] The book was a lament for the end of the immigrant world, the "old East Side" and its *yiddishkeit*, its socialism and secularism.[13] Wald had a telling role to play in Howe's recollections. She ran Henry Street as an "anarchic matriarchy" and offered "the implacability of gentleness" to her clients.[14] Her traditionally gendered self-presentation was well received in a book whose title referenced only fathers. As noted in chapter 2 of this study, gender was key to Howe's dismissal of any of Wald's more controversial positions or achievements. The success of Howe's approach to Wald and the entire old East Side signaled a key component that would play an important role in emerging ideas of the meaning of American Jewishness: nostalgia for the mythologized Lower East Side and its Jewish stories.[15]

Other watershed moments—the Nazi Holocaust, Israel's statehood and 1967 war, the liberation movements of the 1960s and 1970s—as well as the tremendous class mobility of many American Jews contributed to profound changes in the ways they understood their Jewishness.[16] The responses to these changes varied widely: Many American Jews drifted toward secularism and away from formal religious observance and identification in these years.[17] Others took part in a complex revival of American Judaism and asserted their difference in new ways. Some—such as feminist, gay and lesbian, and progressive Jews—rejected mainstream denominational Judaism and formed their own communities, actively redefining the tenets of Jewish religiosity.[18] Still others worked within denominational Judaism, especially within Orthodoxy, to oppose the rapid assimilation of American Jews with a different strategy for revival. Distressed by increased secularism and uncomfortable with new forms of Jewish expression that destabilized the category of Jewish identity, this group turned its attention to shoring up Jewish difference by conflating religious observance and unwavering support for American Zionism with authentic Jewishness.[19] As the twentieth century moved forward, this group's language about Jewish belonging had a profound influence on communal and academic conversations about who is a Jew, what Jewishness means, and how Jewish and American identities could be reconciled. Its growing influence meant the beginning of more formal, more forceful Jewish claims on Wald's legacy.

Conservative nationalism, religious observance, and nostalgia were all subjects of a communal debate over what a new, reinvigorated, mainstream American Jewish identity would look like. Practitioners of the gradually professionalizing field of American Jewish history played a role in this debate, even as their work bore the heavy responsibility, as scholar Salo Baron explained in 1950, of serving "a religious group which has a deep emotional stake in its very survival."[20] Susan Glenn has called the period of contests over Jewishness in the 1950s and early 1960s the "Jewish Cold War": alongside the deep scars of Nazi brutalities and the deep fears of Soviet domination, the heavy emphasis on American conformity in these years led to bitter divisions within the Jewish community about who spoke *for* and *as* American Jews.[21]

The particular claims on Wald in public and academic Jewish histories in the three decades following World War II meant that she had a small but important role to play in those contests. Because biographical studies, dictionaries, and encyclopedias emphasized what all Jews had in common, they neglected to examine the diverse ways Jews had historically expressed their Jewishness. The rich, complex Jewish identity of someone such as Wald, who expressed her Jewishness through informal networks and friendship, through class and cultural connections: this was simply ignored in these new claims. Missing too was an acknowledgement of the ways in which Wald did *not* express her Jewishness, evidence that she herself did not believe in a unifying Jewish essence.

Examples of Wald's inclusion in such works are many. In 1960, Albert Vorspan, a leader in Reform Judaism, included Wald in his book *Giants of Justice*. Like Howe, Vorspan did not acknowledge the return to religion among many American Jews. In his introduction, he lamented the more widespread drift toward disaffiliation and secularism, the "melancholy fact" that many Jews were "hardly conscious, in their daily lives, of religion, or mission, or Covenant." He admitted that the "giants" whom he chose for his book often had tenuous relationships to organized Judaism: Louis Brandeis, for example, "conspicuously avoided the synagogue and Jewish religious life"; Wald "was not active in the Jewish community" and had "little interest" in religious Judaism. Yet Vorspan claimed them for Judaism because of their "desire to build a better world." This desire, he writes, "has sunk deep into the chromosomes, the bones, the blood, the memory, and the soul of the Jew." A more straightforward example of what Susan Glenn calls the "blood logic" of Jewhooing would be hard to find.[22] Invoking her gendered self-presentation, Vorspan described Wald as "the Angel of the East Side," "the tall, dark Jewess" whose work for the poor was inspired by "a prophetic tradition . . . deep in the tradition of Judaism."[23]

A few years later, Wald was again powerfully pulled into the new definitions of Jewishness. In the (for Wald, ironically titled) 1969 *Universal Jewish Encyclopedia*, Libby Benedict's entry on Wald concluded with a slightly confusing yet aggressive assertion of Wald's belonging: "Miss Wald's many associations were never restricted to specifically Jewish groups," she writes, "but her identification with Jewish life was avowed even beyond the multiple bonds with which her work among immigrants evoked."[24] Similarly, historian Irwin Yellowitz's 1971 entry on Wald in the *Encyclopedia Judaica* pulled her into group belonging, even as he acknowledged that Wald's "close contact with the Jewish community of the Lower East Side" never prompted her to identify "with her coreligionists as such."[25]

The 1970s marked a turning point in writings about Wald, as many participants in communal conversations about Jewishness came to conflate Jewishness with religiosity. Through the 1970s, 1980s, and 1990s, these (somewhat awkward) mentions of Wald's lack of connection to organized or religious Judaism receded further in works that "counted" her among American Jews. These works, written for both scholarly and nonacademic audiences, never mention her anti-Zionism, her resistance toward Jewish categorization, or her self-professed inspiration in the Social Gospel. They invoke Wald in order to assert her as a model of Jewish womanhood, someone who drew on Jewish religious notions of justice and even holiness. Journalist Alberta Eiseman counts Wald among her group of "rebels and reformers" in her 1976 book of the same title, which includes biographies of four American Jews; American Jewish historian June Sochen enumerates her achievements in *Consecrate Every Day: The Public Lives of Jewish American Women, 1880–1980* (1981); American cultural historian and writer

Edward Wagenknecht includes her as a model of Jewish womanhood in *Daughters of the Covenant: Portraits of Six Jewish Women* (1983); Elinor and Robert Slater praise her achievements in her entry in *Great Jewish Women* (1994); historians Emily Taitz and Sondra Henry place her among other "remarkable Jewish women" in their 1996 book of the same title; and American Jewish historians Hasia Diner and Beryl Lieff Benderly include her as a reformer in their history of Jewish American women, *Her Works Praise Her* (2002). Slater and Slater even go so far as to state that "Wald did not think of herself as Jewish per se," but they do not elaborate on that statement or account for how that might impact her inclusion in a compilation that chronicles great work done *by* Jews and *as* Jews.[26] Though a few authors and scholars dedicate space to identifying Wald's complicated Jewish identity, the general silence on that aspect of her legacy can be seen as part of a much larger development: the failure of the mainstream discourse on Jewish identity in these years to account for the multiplicity of ways individuals chose to express their Jewishness throughout American Jewish history.[27]

This failure was the result of multiple, interrelated factors: increasing ambivalence toward assimilation, the growing influence of conservative forces in Jewish communal conversations about Jewishness, and developments in the field of American Jewish history. In writing about Wald in this way, communal leaders, popular authors, and academics indeed mirrored the consensus of many American Jewish historians, who have long emphasized the positive outcome of the synthesis between American and Jewish life. They tend to record the integration of Jews into the American mainstream while detailing the accompanying creation of Jewish institutions that continue to accent Jewish difference and unite American Jews.[28] These scholars' continued investment in the perpetuation of Jewish difference—according to some critiques, their investment in differentiating Jews from the white majority—means that they often claim the Jewishness of a historical figure while understating the powerful American influences at work in her life.[29] This has been the case with most historical treatments of Wald, despite the fact that her encounter with assimilation and the ideas of the Christian Social Gospel movement, to her own mind, made her Jewishness largely irrelevant.

Other social and intellectual currents prompted renewed interest in Wald after 1970. During the feminist movement of that decade, non-Jewish historical interest in Wald developed from women's historians' search for sisterhood in U.S. history. These pioneering scholars devoted ample attention to the Progressive Era's settlement movement. One important product of this interest was Doris Groshen Daniels's 1989 biography, *Always a Sister: The Feminism of Lillian D. Wald*, which explores Wald's commitment to gender equality.[30] Daniels's and other studies offered important insights into Wald's role in maternalist campaigns and female networks, into the intersections of gender, sexuality, class, and race at the turn of the last century.

Already in the Hall of Fame for Great Americans, Wald became (quite literally) much more visible as a result of these works: in 1976, she was one of the first fifteen women inducted into the American Nurses Association's Hall of Fame in Washington, D.C.; in 1993, she was inducted into the National Women's Hall of Fame in Seneca Falls, New York.[31] Yet in these new studies, the emphasis on her feminist legacy meant that her ethnoreligious background became virtually invisible.[32] As this biography has shown, that background profoundly shaped her approaches to assimilation *and* women's causes in the Progressive Era, as her gender and ethnoreligious identity were so closely intertwined.

Public claims on Wald's legacy came from women's and nursing historians in the early 1990s, and their political and professional agendas often necessitated a narrow view of Wald's accomplishments.[33] In the midst of a "health care crisis," for example, public health experts turned to Wald's vision of "public health nursing," a phrase she coined for a profession she pioneered. Wald had been elected into the Health Care Hall of Fame in 1988.[34] Now during an era of "nationwide exploration into health care structures and practices," one author praised Wald's enduring community health nursing programs as a model for "our nation's health goals."[35] Susan Reverby, historian of nursing, wrote a 1993 editorial in which she placed Wald in the company of that moment's crusader for fair health care: she titled her piece "From Lillian Wald to Hillary Rodham Clinton: What Will Happen to Public Health Nursing?"[36]

These historians also debated Wald's approach to gender difference in campaigns for women's equality, an approach that chose "to push but not to destroy the boundaries around acceptable women's work."[37] Wald's strategy of emphasizing women's difference proved successful in her contributions to reform and suffrage, to women's protective labor legislation, and to nursing's professionalization. She and her peers placed women's social rights on the national agenda. But a new wave of women's rights activists pressed their demands in the language of individual rights, emphasizing women's sameness to men, and not their difference. The tensions between the two strategies live on, though, and Wald's approach to gender—divorced entirely from her approach to ethnoreligious difference—features prominently in some arenas of debate within the field of social work.[38]

Those who came to consider the more radical elements of Wald's legacies in the final decades of the twentieth century contributed to the explosion of monographs that considered the intersections of gender with class, race, and sexuality. Elizabeth Ewen writes of Wald's modest success in bridging the class divide between herself and her clients, as she earnestly embraced working-class struggles.[39] Elisabeth Lasch-Quinn and Darlene Clark Hine considered Wald's "reputation as an advocate for blacks," especially black nurses.[40] Blanche Wiesen Cook first drew attention to Wald's intimate relationships with women in 1979.[41] By 1993, Dell Richards counted Wald alongside such luminaries as Florence Nightingale, Anna Freud, and Jane Addams in her book titled *Superstars: Twelve Lesbians Who Changed the World*.[42] None of these works placed Wald at its center, and each had its own crucial contribution to make. Only with hindsight is it clear that these claims all contributed to the fracturing of Wald's legacy, ultimately separating her approaches to gender and ethnoreligiosity in scholarly discussions.

In the 1990s, two of Wald's separate audiences appeared to overlap. Historians of American women and American nursing emphasized Wald's activism and politics and then also began to explore her ethnoreligious background. In a 1993 article commemorating the centennial anniversary of public health nursing, Evelyn Benson, a nurse and nursing school dean, tapped into this new set of questions. "The focus on ethnic identity in late twentieth-century American society has created an incentive to explore one's ethnic roots in various spheres of human activity," she wrote. She considered it "timely and appropriate to examine the Jewish contribution to the field," and she went on to trace the "Jewish threads" of a profession "whose roots have traditionally been identified as Christian."[43] Wald was central to her story.

Benson's article paralleled similar studies from scholars of American Jews, and of American Jewish women in particular. The field of Jewish women's history experienced tremendous growth in these years due to a number of interrelated developments: To be sure, the ethnic revival of the 1970s and the vast resources available to many American Jews after their meteoric rise in social class played important roles. So too did the rising number of Jewish women scholars, thanks to the feminist movement and the gradual broadening of the canon to include Jews as a culture represented in multiculturalism.

By the end of the century, Jewish nurses, feminist scholars, and community activists had laid claim to Wald's work as an instructive model for addressing contemporary social dilemmas and needs. Beyond that, they had begun to unravel the intertwined strands of Wald's gender, sexual, ethnic, and professional identities. Yet those who claimed Wald's history most visibly have largely failed to draw from scholarship in *both* women's history and Jewish history. The complexities of her feminism and her Jewishness remained unexamined. To investigate these developments, and to draw conclusions about these years from them, it is worthwhile to take a step back for the purposes of a brief comparison, to view how another of Wald's generation has been treated by scholars in the past few decades. No one could serve this purpose better than her friend Jane Addams.

Wald and Addams

There is a marked contrast between scholarly treatments of Wald and Addams: while Wald's appeal is now largely relegated to the subdiscipline of American Jewish women's history, Addams's life draws attention across multiple fields. The comparison suggests that, like all historical subjects, their contemporary relevance is dictated by the circumstances of the times. Following Wald's own authorial inclinations, we begin with an illustrative anecdote.

In 1935, only months after the death of her close friend Jane Addams, Wald was asked to write an afterword to Addams's book about Hull House. Wald collected stories and praise of Addams for the piece, connecting others' words with her own ruminations about Addams's accomplishments over the many decades they had lived through together. She used "we" and "our" to indicate how her worldview and life work paralleled Addams's and to link their legacies together as one of peacemaking and reform work in "the community, the nation, and the world."[44] "Each year events challenge our beliefs," Wald wrote, quoting a favorite saying of Addams's. They relied on their separate life experiences to make sense of those challenges.

To do justice to Addams's unique experiences, Wald relied on only a few biographical facts. Though she described Addams's philosophy of peace-making as "deeply planted in her Quaker heritage," her words instead pulled Addams from her beginnings in Cedarville, Illinois. She wrote of Addams in Chicago, in Washington, at the Hague. She called her "a friend of every-one . . . a good neighbor, a good citizen, a good American," and wrote that her death was "an occasion of international sorrow."[45]

Wald's own health was declining, many of her friends passing away. Given these circumstances, her words inevitably served as a record of her own thoughts on posthumous remembrance and legacies. The final story Wald told about Addams spoke most to Wald's hopes for her own legacy, her own sense of belonging among like-minded members of her various net-works. Wald described an event that occurred at Addams's funeral viewing: "One old Greek, gazing upon her lovely face, turned to a resident standing near. 'She Catholic?' he asked. 'She Orthodox? She Jewish?' To each ques-tion the resident said: 'No.' Whereupon the old Greek said, smiling: 'Oh, I see! She all religions!' "[46] Wald hoped that she too would be thought of as belonging to all categories, as being "in the struggle, and yet above it."[47]

Many years earlier, reformer and journalist Jacob Riis wrote to Wald: "I am glad to find you taking your place alongside of Jane Addams in the popular consciousness. That's where you belong, different as you are."[48] Yet Wald has never achieved the scholarly or popular attention of Addams. This has largely to do with Addams's superior visibility in her own era: she gained national and international attention when she nominated Theodore Roosevelt at the 1912 presidential convention and received the Nobel Prize in 1931.[49] Though Wald certainly traveled and testified to Congress on occa-sion, she most often took her stands in and around New York City.

Perhaps for these reasons, Addams's life and writings remain of broad interest in the academy. More recent scholarship on Addams considers the relevance of her philosophies to early-twentieth-century American intellec-tual history. Scholars argue for Addams's rightful place alongside pragmatist philosophers William James and John Dewey. Citing her "feminist" or "cultural" pragmatism, her "ethic of care," and her gendered social vision, in which women were to work toward peace, these sociologists, historians, and social workers posit her social vision as a model for today.[50] Other scholars examine her religious education—from early readings of *Pilgrim's Progress* to her community meetings at Hull House—to demonstrate the contemporary need for a language of social morality.[51] And she remains alive in the public imagination as well: a Web search for Jane Addams turns up 641,000 hits, with top billing for the Nobel Prize Committee's Web site and Hull House histories.

Compared to Addams's ten books of philosophy, Wald's two books— filled mostly with anecdotes about life on the Lower East Side—offer far less grist for the scholarly mill. And while Addams came from a political family and traveled to England for her first encounter with settlements, scholars deem Wald's merchant relatives and brief baptism of fire as largely unworthy of extensive analysis.[52] As Wald's friend, Westport neighbor, and first biographer, Robert Duffus, phrased it, "Lillian Wald [was] quick to see and act on the immediate need, Jane Addams coming to the same point out of the depths of her sad and tender philosophy."[53]

Nor did Wald achieve Addams's success of belonging to "all religions." Aside from a few studies of nursing in the past decade, as noted above, Wald is visible mainly in books dedicated to the study of Jewish women.[54] A Web search for Wald turns up 43,000 hits: those that focus on Henry Street and the Visiting Nurse Service aside, Jewish-sponsored sites, such as the Jewish-American Hall of Fame, the Jewish Virtual Library, the online *Jewish Magazine*, and the Jewish Women's Archive, are at the top of the list.[55] The Jewish Women's Archive serves as a good example of the phenomenal (and growing) interest in researching and documenting the lives of Jewish women. Women appear in the archive only if defined as Jewish, with little information about the various approaches women have employed to express their Jewishness across time. The archive's (seemingly) limitless space offers a superb opportunity to explore such complexity.

The singular grouping in the Jewish-American Hall of Fame, the Jewish Virtual Library, the archive, and other places suggests that something essentially Jewish links these subjects together. Just as modern Addams scholars' quests for historical models of moral visions and pragmatic philosophy drew them to their subject, Wald scholars' search for some central Jewish essence —a defining experience or simple commonality—stems from their own contemporary needs. Wald fills a modern need for Jewish, often female, role models: women who managed to balance idealism and good works with professionalism and, importantly, Jewishness with Americanism.

That some American Jews read back into history a firmer meaning for Jewish identity is, in some ways, surprising. Jewish claiming is linked to the need for Jewish "public relations" in eras of hostility and intolerance. Yet Jews have never had a more comfortable moment. Pluralism and tolerance toward Jews has allowed for rapid assimilation, and many American Jews have unprecedented power, wealth, and skills.

What many consider these successes of American Jews are simultaneously, though, at the root of Jewish claims on Wald and others. The fear of disappearing into the American melting pot—the very ideal for which Wald strove—has led some American Jews to claim a core difference among Jewish Americans. These claims assert and perpetuate a certain brand of Jewishness, often (though not always) grounded in Zionism, religious observance, the reassertion of traditional gender roles, and—in both historical and contemporary discourses—the erasing of more prismatic and pluralist conceptions of Jewish identity.[56]

In other ways, too, this reading back into history a Jewish essence is not surprising. The intra-Jewish contests of the 1950s continue, and the resistance to the equation of Jewishness with conservative religiosity is increasingly pronounced. Can Jewish identity be religious *and* cultural, expressed through religious observance as well as through politics and art? Nonwhite Jews and feminist Jews join gay, lesbian, and transgender Jews, secular Jews, and Jews by choice in challenging a singular definition of what constitutes Jewish identity.[57] Jewish identity has never been more fluid and multifaceted than it is in the postmodern United States, and claiming is one uneasy response to that reality.

How then can scholars look back at historical figures such as Wald? Instead of looking to the past *for* Jewish role models in ways that reinforce mainstream Jewish belonging, we need to look *at* these historical actors for what they have to teach us about the richness of past and present expressions of Jewishness. Paula Hyman and Riv-Ellen Prell began the project of examining competing visions of what constitutes Jewishness.[58] New conversations in Jewish studies push these inquiries forward: writing at the intersections of cultural, American, and Jewish studies, scholars of the new Jewish studies analyze these contests and diverse expressions of Jewishness to offer new perspectives on intra-Jewish tensions and American Jewish identity across time.[59] They interrogate the unstable categories of woman, lesbian, radical, and Jew in ways that have proved crucial to this study of Lillian Wald.

This study of Wald grew out of these questions and insists on the importance of clarifying (rather than erasing) the complexities of Wald's approaches to gender, ethnoreligious, and cultural difference. Wald's approach to gender alerts us to the strengths and limits of strategies of difference. Wald's relationship to her own Jewish identity problematizes the search for any solid definition of Jewishness, any quest for a Jewish essence—historical or modern.

Because Wald's own distinct, ethnic brand of Progressivism was in part a result of her struggles with differences of gender, ethnicity, religion, and culture, we can use it to study questions of difference and belonging across time. This study has found the roots of Wald's philosophy in her family's nineteenth-century lessons in shedding conspicuous difference to achieve successful assimilation and integration, and in her claiming the heritage of the Social Gospel visions of a brotherhood of man. Sustained by her loving relationships with women and her friendships in and around New York, citing her universal vision as the bedrock of her work at Henry Street, Wald mediated across lines of difference based on class, race, gender, ethnicity, and religion in order to build coalitions for change in the neighborhood and the nation. With her nursing and Americanization work as the source of her authority, she sought to apply her vision to the world stage. To ignore how her ethnic background affected her domestic and international reform work, how crucial an ingredient it was to her dealings with clients, peers, and the press, or to oversimplify what Jewishness meant to her and those who knew her: to do this is to miss significant lessons in American group and individual identity.

As someone who spent a lifetime striving to become American and to make Americans out of others, as an ethnic working on behalf of other ethnics, Wald reveals the difficulties of mediating across social tensions in efforts for social betterment. Certainly, her universal vision made her more fearful of the pitfalls of "tribal" crusades. Yet Wald's rhetoric in that time and place also shows the failure of her universal vision to accommodate crucial particularist challenges: of nationalism and authoritarianism, of anti-Semitism, and of Zionism as its possible solution. That failure exposes the real-world perils of investing in a universalist vision. For Wald, that investment came at the expense of understanding the need for, as well as the dangers of, particularist crusades. While acknowledging the myopia that accompanies all human decisions, along with the hindsight of our own contemporary position, this biography shows the origins of Wald's vision in part to document why it did not meet the tests of twentieth-century events.[60] Simultaneously, it documents the value of Wald's civic work as a universalist-minded interpreter among diverse groups.

In the twenty-first century, Wald's legacy has in part come to symbolize the contests over contemporary identities. Reducing Wald's legacy to one that is only feminist or essentially Jewish downplays how her gender and ethnic identities combined to shape her work as a social justice crusader—something for which she was honored at the Hall of Fame for Great Americans in 1970, where this biography began. Largely because of her experience wrestling with complex questions of Jewish difference and Jewish belonging, Wald helped to steer the entire Americanization project toward one of mutual interpretation across difference, rather than toward one of forced conformity to some fixed, core Anglo-Protestant identity. Viewing Wald as a central figure in her era, rather than as a footnote to Jane Addams, helps to inform a broader understanding of the Progressive Era and, indeed, the centrality of questions about difference and conformity to determining what it means to be an American.

Whether sympathetic to or distressed by the individual whose life she is hunting down, no biographer can hope to capture the essence of her subject. She can simply offer a fresh perspective on her subject's one and many lives. Here, I offer my own perspective on Wald's experiences inside and outside of the women's and Jewish communities, claiming her only for the space between them, the site of her lifelong interpretive work toward universal understanding.

Notes

ABBREVIATIONS

AJA   American Jewish Archives, Cincinnati, Ohio

BL   Butler Library, Rare Book and Manuscript Library,
        Columbia University, New York, N.Y.

CSL   Charles E. Shain Library, Special Collections and Archives,
        Connecticut College, New London, Conn.

ECA   Ethical Culture Archives, New York, N.Y.

HA   Hadassah Archives, New York, N.Y.

MCA   Medical Center Archives of New York–Presbyterian/
        Weill Cornell, New York, N.Y.

NYPL   New York Public Library, Manuscripts and Archives
        Division, New York, N.Y.

OHC   Oral History Collection, Columbia University, New York, N.Y.

PRO   Public Record Office, London, U.K.

SCPC   Swarthmore College Peace Collection, Swarthmore, Pa.

SWHA   Social Welfare History Archives, Minneapolis, Minn.

TL   Tamiment Library, New York University, New York, N.Y.

URL   University of Rochester Library, Special Collections, Rochester, N.Y.

WPL   Westport Public Library, Westport, Conn.

YIVO   YIVO Archives, New York, N.Y.

INTRODUCTION

1   Berle, foreword to *Memorandum in Support*, 3.

2   "Lillian D. Wald's Election to the Hall of Fame for Great Americans," pamphlet, 12 Sept. 1971, New York University.

3   Copy of speech made by Van Wyck Brooks at Wald's public memorial service in Carnegie Hall, 1 Dec. 1940, Wald Papers, NYPL. Cited in *Memorandum in Support*, 27.

4   Hall of Fame for Great Americans, Bronx Community College, <http://www .bcc.cuny.edu/hallofFame/>.

5   Berle, foreword to *Memorandum in Support*, 3.

6   Quoted in Grace Lichtenstein, "Hall of Fame Lobbying Pays Off," *New York Times*, 8 Nov. 1970, 47.

7   Ibid.

8   "Lillian D. Wald's Election to the Hall of Fame," pamphlet, New York University.

9   Thomas Haney, "Tribute to Miss Wald," *New York Times*, 7 Nov. 1971, D31.

10 Glenn, "In the Blood."

11 Ibid., 140, 142.

12 Sollors, *Beyond Ethnicity*.

13 Jewish Women's Archive, "JWA—Lillian Wald—Introduction," <http://www .jwa.org/exhibits/wov/wald/index.html>; Hyman and Moore, *Jewish Women in America*. I consulted on the former project and wrote the latter encyclopedia entry. Scholarly mentions of Wald in the field of Jewish women's history include Diner and Benderly, *Her Works Praise Her*. Jewish claims on Wald are cited and discussed in greater detail below.

14 On Wald's induction into the Jewish-American Hall of Fame, see Jewish-American Hall of Fame, "Virtual Tour," <http://amuseum.org/jahf/virtour/ page39.html>. On the origins of the Jewish-American Hall of Fame, originally sponsored by the Magnes Museum of Berkeley, California, see Fromer, "Creation of the Magnes Museum," <http://amuseum.org/magnes/index.html>. For references to Wald as the "Jewish Florence Nightingale," see the press release of the Jewish-American Hall of Fame, "Hall of Fame Inducts Wald," at <http://www.hofmag.com/content/view/713/190/>; see this reference also in New York Nurse News, "2007 Honoree," <http://newyorknursenews.blog spot.com/2007/03/2007-honoree-of-jewish-american-hall-of.html>.

15 Wald to Madison C. Peters, 13 Feb. 1918, Wald Papers, NYPL. Peters, a Baptist minister, had already published two texts that praise the contributions of Jews

to civilization (see his *Justice to the Jew* and *Jews in America*). The need for this new text in 1918 was made obvious by the fact that his previous books mentioned only men.

16   Anthropologist Riv-Ellen Prell first suggested to me that Wald's discomfort with her likeness may have been because she felt she looked too "Oriental" (e-mail message to author, 21 Nov. 2000). Helena Huntingdon Smith's profile noted that Wald came from a "cultivated Jewish family" and described her (twice) as the "dark-eyed girl in the nurse's uniform," while she described Wald's founding partner, nurse Mary Brewster, as simply "blonde." See "Rampant but Respectable: Lillian D. Wald," *New Yorker*, 14 Dec. 1929, 32.

17   In 1914, for example, when the writings that were to become her first book, *The House on Henry Street*, were published in the *Atlantic Monthly*, Wald became upset over a portrait of herself used to promote the essays. She consulted a lawyer, who informed her that she had no control over the use of her photo. George Alger to Wald, 5 Dec. 1914, Wald Papers, NYPL. Three days later, after receiving several insistent letters, Ellery Sedgwick, the *Atlantic's* editor, wrote to Wald: "Your portrait has been safely removed from our advertising pages; so do not give the matter another thought." 8 Dec. 1914, Wald Papers, BL.

18   Pivotal texts on this period in U.S. women's history (and on the settlement movement generally) that incorporate Wald into their analysis with little mention of the impact of her ethnoreligious background include Allen Davis, *Spearheads for Reform*; Carson, *Settlement Folk*; Ellen Fitzpatrick, *Endless Crusade*; Muncy, *Creating a Female Dominion*; and Walkowitz, *Working with Class*.

19   See Cook, "Female Support Networks." Recently, Michael Reisch and Janice Andrews included Wald in their compelling history of radical social work, noting the "radical implications" of the "lesbian relationships or simply lifelong intimate friendships" of Wald, Addams, and others. Settlement work allowed these women independence from marriage and traditional families, "unique and socially useful employment, communal living, . . . leadership positions," and freedom "from the constraints of submissive Victorian womanhood" (33).

20   "Mother of Henry Street," a poem to Wald for her sixty-first birthday from "the Kids on Henry Street," "Henry News" 25, no. 3 (10 Mar. 1928), Wald Papers, BL.

21   Eiseman, *Rebels and Reformers*; Wagenknecht, *Daughters of the Covenant*; Diner and Benderly, *Her Works Praise Her*; Rappaport, *In the Promised Land*.

22   Feingold, "German Jews," 10, 13.

23   Duffus, *Lillian Wald*; Daniels, *Always a Sister*. For two biographies listed as

juvenile literature, see Williams, *Lillian Wald*, and Siegel, *Lillian Wald*. Siegel's is the most extended discussion of the impact of Wald's Jewishness on her life and work, taking up about five of the book's first ten pages.

24   Rosen, *Mamie Papers*, 307.

25   Reminiscences of Bruno Lasker, 1956, p. 172, OHC.

26   Howe, *World of Our Fathers*, 237. I thank Daniel Soyer for helping me to identify this café.

27   Deutscher, *Non-Jewish Jew*, 41.

28   Though I do not agree with all of their conclusions about "authentic" Jewish self-identification and Jewish communal obligations, the following sources have shaped my understanding of universalism and Jewish identity: Seidman, "Fag-Hags and Bu-Jews"; Lafer, "Universalism and Particularism"; and Gordon and Motzkin, "Between Universalism and Particularism."

29   Sollors, *Beyond Ethnicity*, 260.

30   Quote is from Svonkin, *Jews against Prejudice*, 180. See also Staub, *Torn at the Roots*, and Glenn, "Vogue of Jewish Self-Hatred."

31   Debra Kaufman discusses the implications of measuring American Jewish identity using a male model of "essential" or "traditional" Judaism in "Measuring Jewishness in America." Other analyses of contemporary Jewish identity include Hyman, "Modern Jewish Identities"; Whitfield, "Enigmas of Modern Jewish Identity"; and Lindenbaum, Stavans, and Chevlowe, *Jewish Identity Project*.

32   Nadell, "On Their Own Terms."

33   Recent examples include Staub, "Smart"; Melnick, "Soul"; Itzkovitz, "Race and Jews"; and Shneer and Aviv, *Queer Jews*. Tony Michels offers an important critique of American Jewish history in the introduction to his study of Yiddish socialism, *Fire in Their Hearts*. Recent nonacademic discussions of Jewish identity include Mamet, *Wicked Son*, and Mallet, *Tevye's Grandchildren*.

34   Prell, *Fighting to Become Americans*; Hyman, *Gender and Assimilation*.

35   For a fascinating conversation on the field of U.S. women's history, its accomplishments and its continuing challenges, see Cott, Lerner, Sklar, DuBois, and Hewitt, "State of U.S. Women's History."

36   In "State of U.S. Women's History," Gerda Lerner voiced concern with the number of new projects in women's history that were largely biographical studies of subjects who were "not political persons"; biographies of political activists, she asserted, give a "total picture," a portrait of a "whole society." Ibid., 160.

37   In "Historians Who Love Too Much," Jill Lepore offers her thoughts on the difference between biography and microhistory: while biography is "largely

founded on a belief in the singularity and significance of an individual's life and his contribution to history, microhistory is founded upon almost the opposite assumption: however singular a person's life may be, the value of examining it lies not in its uniqueness, but in its exemplariness, in how that individual's life serves as an allegory for broader issues affecting the culture as a whole" (133). For a useful analysis of the nineteenth-century origins of American biography, including thoughtful discussions of the roles of sectionalism, gender, and sentiment, see Casper, *Constructing American Lives*. In his *Biography: A Brief History*, Nigel Hamilton parallels interest in biography with the West's increasing fascination with individuality. Several scholars at the Schlesinger Library Summer Seminar on Gender History "Writing Past Lives: Biography as History," held 25–29 June 2007, suggested that this extreme attention to biography and thus to individuality may come at the cost of social history's prominence. Americans' interest in biography may signal their willingness to see individuals as having free agency, acting outside of the social forces that, social historians make clear, are so important. By placing Wald firmly within her era's currents, by emphasizing her role in mass movements for change, this biography instead provides a window onto social history.

38   Wald, "We Called Our Enterprise," xiv; Oscar Leonard, "Death of an Angel: Lillian Wald, Great Jewish Social Worker, Gave up Wealth to Serve All Groups in New York's Teeming East Side Slums," *National Jewish Monthly*, Oct. 1940, 48, 59.

CHAPTER ONE

1   Wald, "The Nurse as Settlement Worker," *Cleveland Women's Journal*, 4 May 1918, Wald Papers, NYPL.
2   On the impact of the Social Gospel movement, or "applied Christianity," on the settlement movement, see chap. 2. See also Carson, *Settlement Folk*, esp. chap. 1.
3   Muncy, *Creating a Female Dominion*.
4   Herzog, *Intimacy and Exclusion*, 58, 137–39.
5   Kaplan, *Jewish Middle Class*, 7. Though Kaplan's study focuses on the period after Schiff and Wald's family emigrated, her background discussion of Jewish entrance into the bourgeoisie is instructive.
6   Sorkin, *Transformation of German Jewry*.
7   Duffus, *Lillian Wald*, 10.
8   The pivotal text on this period for American German Jews is Naomi Cohen, *Encounter with Emancipation*.

9   Nancy Hewitt writes that women's public work in these campaigns allowed for a "cultural redefinition of gender roles." *Women's Activism*, 39. On women and citizenship in this region, see Ginzberg, *Untidy Origins*.

10   Jacobson, *Whiteness of a Different Color*, 176.

11   Duffus, *Lillian Wald*, 4.

12   Sollors, *Beyond Ethnicity*.

13   B'rith Kodesh membership lists from the 1870s were destroyed in a fire. Records of deaths of temple members (in a book somehow rescued), however, include Wald's brother (who died in 1885), father (1891), grandfather (1892), and mother (1925). These records suggest that someone in the family belonged to the temple. For more on Wald's burial, see chap. 5. Stuart Rosenberg details B'rith Kodesh's development in a chapter titled "The Synagogue and Its By-products" in *Jewish Community in Rochester*. For a more recent work, see Eisenstadt, *Affirming the Covenant*. On Rochester's history, see McKelvey, *Rochester on the Genesee*.

14   *Rochester Historical Society Publication Series* 3 (1924): 174.

15   Eisenstadt, *Affirming the Covenant*, 63.

16   "Dedication of a Synagogue," *Rochester Daily Union Advertiser*, 16 Sept. 1876. On this point, see also Rosenberg, *Jewish Community in Rochester*, 91.

17   A plaque in Temple B'rith Kodesh (when it was on Gibbs Street in Rochester) "honored Landsberg for leading the congregation out of 'orientalism,' his disdainful term for Jewish ritual." Eisenstadt, *Affirming the Covenant*, 91.

18   Ibid., 63. Eric Goldstein asserts that Jews in the early twentieth century used racialized language as a "comforting means of self-understanding," a "rhetorical strategy" that asserted distinctiveness without jeopardizing inclusion. Clearly, the zeitgeist of Rochester's *Tidings* readers cut against this hypothesis. So too did B'rith Kodesh's Rabbi Landsberg's willingness to perform marriages between Jews and non-Jews, for, as Goldstein points out, most Reform rabbis saw "intermarriage" as the outside boundary to encounters with the non-Jewish population. *Price of Whiteness*, 89, 16.

19   For much of Wald's genealogy, I am indebted to an undated document compiled by Eileen Polakoff housed in the Genealogies File under "Schwarz" at the AJA. In *Jewish Community in Rochester*, Stuart E. Rosenberg credits Jews' participation in the Civil War with boosting their economic and social positions: many Jews were in the clothing industry, which boomed during the war, and they were active supporters of the Union cause.

20   "The Eureka Club: A Wealthy and Influential Social Organization," *Rochester Union and Advertiser*, 14 Mar. 1887. On the membership of Morris Schwarz,

Wald's uncle, see Wile, *Jews of Rochester*, 111. On consumerism and middle-class mores, see Scobey, "Anatomy of the Promenade."

21 Henry Feingold, a scholar of German Jewry, writes that "What American Jewry became in the twentieth century, its 'soft' permissive Judaism associated with the Reform movement, its federated organizational structure, its energetic commercial activity and rapid professionalization, its liberal political culture, are all anchored in the nineteenth-century German-Jewish transaction with America." "German Jews," 10. I discuss this synthesis in the introduction. On American Jewish history's focus on this synthesis, see the conclusion to this volume and Diner and Michels, "Considering American Jewish History."

22 For stories about these elite in New York City, see Birmingham, *Our Crowd*. Hasia Diner points out in *Time for Gathering* that only a small percentage of immigrants from what is known as the "German" period in American Jewish history, 1820–1880, were in fact from Germany and that few of those achieved the economic success of "our crowd" in New York. Although Wald's family fit the old paradigm of the German Jewish success story, this fact does not undermine Diner's important assertions of the complicated nature of this period of immigration. Tobias Brinkmann writes in "Jews, Germans, or Americans" that the term "German Jews" became increasingly suggestive of social status, and that definition fits in this case.

23 Gilman, *Freud, Race, and Gender* and *The Jew's Body*.

24 In *Gender and Assimilation*, Paula Hyman observes the gendered nature of the assimilation project for Jews in Westernized nations in the late nineteenth century. Women were increasingly responsible for the cultural transmission of Jewish values and were judged according to the levels of the next generation's observances of private Jewishness. In losing the status accorded to traditional Jewish learning, Jewish men were judged according to their achievements in the broader society, primarily the family's social mobility. This framework certainly applies to Wald's extended family, as her uncles modeled the behavior of the white elite in striving for that mobility.

25 The classic histories of New York's Jewish immigrants of this era are Rischin, *Promised City*, and Howe, *World of Our Fathers*.

26 Michael McGerr points out that low incomes "virtually guaranteed that Victorian individualism was impossible for the working class." *Fierce Discontent*, 16.

27 Voss, *Making of American Exceptionalism*, 89; see also Fink, *Workingmen's Democracy*, 228.

28   Morris Schwarz was elected to the executive committee of the Clothiers' Association in June of 1883. "Items in Brief," *Rochester Daily Union Advertiser,* 29 June 1883, 2.

29   McKelvey, "Men's Clothing Industry"; see also Voss, *Making of American Exceptionalism,* 204.

30   Voss, *Making of American Exceptionalism,* 75–79.

31   "Clothing Trade Matters," *Rochester Union Advertiser,* 8 Dec. 1890, 5.

32   "Manufacturers Speak: Statement from the Clothiers Exchange Committee," *Rochester Union Advertiser,* 26 Mar. 1891, 5.

33   Hawley, "Labor Movement in Rochester," 207–12. Hawley concludes that the Knights' master workman, James Hughes, who was found guilty of extortion for his dealings with the clothing manufacturers, as well as other Knights officers "sought the enhancement of their own position . . . rather than the welfare of the union membership" (228). The workers remained effectively unorganized until the Amalgamated arrived in 1914.

34   Voss's final chapter examines quantitative data on the Knights' final years. She notes that "employers' associations [like the Exchange] had a devastating effect on skilled-workers' locals," especially after 1886. *Making of American Exceptionalism,* 194, 199.

35   Editorial, *Jewish Tidings,* 13 Mar. 1891.

36   Ibid., 27 Mar. 1891. Daniel Boyarin argues in *Unheroic Conduct* that eastern European Jewish tradition prioritized an oppositional masculinity, emphasizing gentleness and scholarship; this tradition contrasted with violent Western conceptions of masculinity.

37   Though Wald's immediate family members were not consistently affiliated with the organized Jewish community, Paula Hyman's observations of the assimilation project for Jewish men and women fit well with their experiences: "The increased identification of Jewishness and femaleness that induced anxiety among Jewish men enabled Jewish women to lay claim to new public roles." *Gender and Assimilation,* 161.

38   Mrs. Nathan Levi was president of the (Jewish) Ladies' Aid Society and on the board of the Jewish Orphan Asylum. The family's social gatherings were recorded by *Jewish Tidings.* See "Ladies Aid Society," 7 Feb. 1890, and "Jewish Orphan Asylum," 13 Apr. 1888. Social events of the family were mentioned throughout the paper's existence from 1887 through 1894.

39   Eisenstadt, *Affirming the Covenant,* 83.

40   Duffus, *Lillian Wald,* 6, 5, 8, 15.

41   The temple records show that when Wald's brother, Alfred, died in 1885, a rabbi officiated at the burial. But at the funerals for Wald's father, Marcus,

who died in 1891, and for her mother, Minnie, who died in 1923, no representative of the temple was present. Record book of Temple B'rith Kodesh, Rochester, N.Y.

42 *Rochester Historical Society Publication Series* 17 (1939): 157–58.

43 Doris Groshen Daniels makes this point in *Always a Sister*, 12.

44 *Jewish Tidings*, 25 May 1888, 6.

45 See McKelvey, *Rochester on the Genesee*, 48, 49, 104, and Creek, "Family Story."

46 Julia and Charles's three children were Harriet (whose middle name was Lillian), Thomas, and Alfred (named for Julia and Lillian's brother). A report card from Alfred Barry's school remarks that he was anxious to return to the Catholic Church; a case of diphtheria there had kept him away. Choate School, Wallingford, Conn., Report of Alfred Wald Barry for Month ending 30 Nov. 1911, Ellwanger and Barry Papers, box 55, URL. When Charles Barry died in 1907, Julia, in the independent tradition of her younger sister, Lillian, began her own business, the Authentic Antique Shop, and held on to her Rochester mansion for six more years. Ellwanger and Barry Papers, boxes 55–57, URL. After Max Wald died, Minnie Wald lived with Julia on East Avenue. Though the Wald family home no longer stands on East Avenue, the house where Julia and Charles Barry lived remains as number 1163. Julia later married Frank Cordley, a banker, and lived in Pennsylvania. Her obituary in the *New York Times* lists her unmarried name as "Julia D'Waldo." 5 Dec. 1946, 29.

47 Duffus, *Lillian Wald*, 18. Jill Conway suggests in *When Memory Speaks* that in their autobiographies, women tend to make their own ambition invisible by presenting themselves as impelled forward by some force outside of themselves. Through her telling to Duffus, Wald presents two occasions when "fate" lends a hand to guide her to a career on the Lower East Side; both seem to have been times when she was exposed to new ideas and understood that following through on those ideas could serve her own interests.

48 Wald to George P. Ludlum, 27 May 1889, copy in Wald Papers, NYPL.

49 Benson, *As We See Ourselves*, 45–46, 59–60. Benson quotes from an 1895 article in the *American Jewess*, an English-language Jewish magazine devoted to the interests of Jewish women. The article's author, Johanne Moritzen, calls nursing "the most womanly of all womanly occupations" and laments that "Jewish women have been slow in possessing themselves of a calling for which they are eminently fitted." Still, she is hopeful for the "signs of awakening among the young women of Israel" to the possibility of joining the profession of nursing. "Where Woman Reigns Supreme," *American Jewess*, Dec. 1895, 164, quoted in Benson, *As We See Ourselves*, 45.

50 Duffus, *Lillian Wald*, 23. On nursing, see Melosh, *Physician's Hand*. While

Melosh focuses mainly on the twentieth century, Susan Reverby expands that perspective back into the nineteenth century and discusses the politicized nature of nursing's professionalization in greater depth in *Ordered to Care*. On nursing as a contributor to social feminism, and on the struggle for professional autonomy among nurses, see Lewenson, *Taking Charge*. On Wald's early nursing career, see Duffus, *Lillian Wald*, chap. 2, and Daniels, *Always a Sister*, chap. 2. Joyce Antler discusses the history of the New York Infirmary and its teaching adjunct, the Woman's Medical College, in "Medical Women," 11–16. Founded by Elizabeth Blackwell, the first woman doctor in modern times and later a close friend of Wald's, the college sought to extend women's sphere to the field of medicine—an easy task given Blackwell's belief that "the true physician must possess the essential qualities of maternity" (quoted on 12). For a discussion on Wald's ideas on women and medicine, see chap. 2 of this volume.

51 On the friendship of Wald and Dock from the perspective of human care theory, see Ott, "Friendship of Dock and Wald."

52 Cook, "Female Support Networks"; Alpert, *Like Bread*, 118–22.

53 Mina Carson discusses "a new rhetorical ideal of womanhood" in this era, in which women's education advocates added to women's "special burden in the progress and refinement of civilization": instead of being shielded from life's "harsh realities," women were be to educated in them. *Settlement Folk*, 23. On Wald's role in the dissemination of this ideal, and on her position in nursing's professionalization and how it fits into women's "natural" roles, see chap. 2.

54 Emma Goldman, *Living My Life*, vol. 1, chap. 2.

55 Morris Schwarz is listed as one of thirteen contractors who locked out their workers in May of 1893, feigning sickness. The newspapers hinted at the contractors' collusion, writing that "many of the bosses were seen later in the day by the men and did not look sick." Instead, the "men think [the bosses] have combined in order to down the unions." "Many Tailors Locked Out," *Rochester Democrat and Chronicle*, 2 May 1893, 10.

56 Wald, *House on Henry Street*, 7, 8.

57 Ibid., 6.

58 On the Social Gospel movement, see Hopkins, *Rise of the Social Gospel Movement*; May, *Protestant Churches*; Handy, *Social Gospel in America*; White and Hopkins, *Social Gospel*; and Crunden, *Ministers of Reform*. Richard Fox examines the complicated and important relationship between liberal Protestantism, Progressivism, and secularism in "Liberal Protestant Progressivism." Few scholars have attempted to examine the place of liberal Judaism in the Social Gospel movement. See the following: Feldman, "Social Gospel and the

Jews"; Mervis, "Social Justice Movement"; and Sutherland, "Rabbi Joseph Krauskopf."

59 Schiff wrote to Wald on 31 Dec. 1903, "Well do we remember your first visit with Mrs. M. D. Louis, and from which resulted the first start, on the top floor of the Jefferson Street tenement." Wald Papers, BL. Louis was president of the Louis Downtown Sabbath School, but, according to Duffus, it was Loeb who had "made possible those first nursing lessons on Henry Street." *Lillian Wald*, 35. See also *Jewish Women in America*, s.v. "Minnie Dessau Louis."

60 On the "homogenous," "tightly knit" social networks of German Jewish financiers in America, see Supple, "Business Elite." Searching out a looser categorical term to identify this and other similar in-groups, Milton Gordon coined the word "ethclass" in *Assimilation in American Life* to describe a uniformity of cultural values, when people of the same ethnic group and social class tend to share a sense of "peoplehood." Eli Lederhendler recently critiqued American Jewish historians in "The New Filiopietism" for applying the term "ethnicity" to individuals and events in Jewish history without using the "critical thrust" necessary for historical analysis. American Jewish historians' investment in validating Jewish life, he asserts, finds them mystifying the historical record. Though I do not agree with all of Lederhendler's conclusions about the role of authentic Jewishness in history, this study of Wald proceeds from the premise that a critical assessment of the unstable meaning of Jewish ethnic identity is essential to her demystification.

61 Wald, "Jacob H. Schiff," *Survey* 45 (2 Oct. 1920): 20.

62 On Jacob Schiff reporting to Wald about his meeting with the German emperor and his wife's meeting with the pope, see Schiff to Wald, 28 June 1911, 22 Mar. 1904, Wald Papers, BL.

63 Naomi Cohen, *Jacob H. Schiff*, 222.

64 On this point, see ibid., 50.

65 Ibid., 48; Bellow, *Educational Alliance*, 16. Cyrus Adler, Schiff's biographer, writes that Schiff gave at least one-tenth—but often much more—of his earnings to charity, based on a Jewish tradition that dates back to ancient tithes. *Jacob H. Schiff*, 1:354.

66 Woods and Kennedy, *Handbook of Settlements*, v.

67 Riddle, "Religion in the Settlement," 349.

68 Graham Taylor, "Is Religion an Element," 346.

69 Riddle, "Religion in the Settlement," 350.

70 Falconer, "Science and Religion," 344.

71 Carson, *Settlement Folk*, 18.

72 *Hebrew Standard*, 21 Jan. 1910.

73   Marshall, "Need of a Jewish Tendency," 112–22.

74   "Re-Judaisation," *Boston Jewish Advocate*, 15 May 1908, 7.

75   "Miss Wald's Speech to the Judaeans," 13 Dec. 1931, Wald Papers, NYPL.

76   Christopher Lasch writes that for Addams, "the social settlement . . . was . . . a secular outlet . . . for energies essentially religious," and Allen Davis calls "her decision to establish a settlement in a poor section of Chicago . . . essentially a religious commitment." Lasch, *New Radicalism in America*, 11; Davis, *American Heroine*, 51. See also Brown, *Education of Jane Addams*.

77   Wald, "The Utilization of the Immigrant," speech delivered at the Free Synagogue, New York, Dec. 1907, Wald Papers, NYPL.

78   Wald, "President's Address at the Conference of National Federation of Settlements," Pittsburgh, 24–26 Sept. 1913, Wald Papers, NYPL; Wald, "We Called Our Enterprise," xiv.

79   Wald, "Settlements," speech delivered to the Jamaica Women's Club, 12 Feb. 1913, Wald Papers, NYPL; Wald, *House on Henry Street*, v; Wald, "Standards and Stipends in Settlement Work," speech delivered at the Inter-Settlement Conference, Boston, Mass., 29 Mar. 1913, Wald Papers, NYPL. For theories on the intellectual origins of settlement work, see Hofstadter, *Age of Reform*, 198–214, and Carson, *Settlement Folk*.

80   Wald to Mr. Scherer, Syrian Protestant College, Beirut, Lebanon, 10 July 1908, Wald Papers, NYPL.

81   Schiff to Wald, 31 Dec. 1903, Wald Papers, BL.

82   Schiff to Wald, 2 July 1903, Wald Papers, BL.

83   Wald to Schiff, 28 Nov. 1911, Wald Papers, BL.

84   Jill Conway, in her pioneering study *The First Generation of American Women Graduates*, posits of the relationship between Wald and her immigrant clients, "Lillian understood and shared their faith" (97). Much evidence suggests the contrary, including one letter from Wald to an acquaintance in which she asks for the definitions and pronunciations of several fairly common Hebrew words, including Sephardim, shul, minyan, and chevra. See Charles Alowen to Wald, 19 Mar. 1915, Wald Papers, BL.

85   Schiff to Wald, 19 Sept. 1916, Wald Papers, BL.

86   Wald to Schiff, 1 Oct. 1917, Wald Papers, BL.

87   Wald to Schiff, 2 Oct. 1893, Wald Papers, NYPL.

88   Schiff to Wald, 22 Mar. 1904, Wald Papers, BL.

89   See, for example, Resnick, "Lillian Wald," 255.

90   This letter is pivotal to a one-act play about Wald. See Coss, *Lillian D. Wald*, 37–39. The quote is from Schiff to Wald, 22 Dec. 1914, Wald Papers, BL.

Coss includes Schiff's letter in her compelling collection of Wald's letters and speeches, 48–49.

91   Schiff to Wald, 20 Dec. 1914, Wald Papers, BL. Unfortunately, only one side of this exchange is extant.

92   Riis to Schiff, 20 Nov. 1906, Wald Papers, BL; Schiff to Riis, 22 Nov. 1906, Wald Papers, BL.

93   Schiff's biographer, Naomi Cohen, writes that "as an advocate of nonsectarianism in institutions he dominated, like . . . Henry Street Settlement, he knew that Jews who opened their charities to all creeds scored high marks for civic virtue." *Jacob H. Schiff,* 60. According to Cohen, then, in his nonsectarian charities, Schiff also worked to improve the public profile of American Jews.

94   Schiff to Wald, 6 Jan. 1916, Wald Papers, BL.

95   Naomi Cohen, *Encounter with Emancipation,* xii.

96   In 1915, Wald investigated the rumor that a New York hotel did not accept Jewish customers: "I am of that race," she wrote, "and want to understand the situation clearly." Wald to Asa Gallup, vice president, Hotel Gramatan of Bronxville, New York, 8 Apr. 1915, Wald Papers, NYPL. In 1931, she pledged to "draw the sword out of the scabbard" and investigate similar restrictions in sororities at Swarthmore College. Wald to Rita Morgenthau, 8 Apr. 1931, Wald Papers, NYPL.

97   This incident is described in the introduction.

98   Wald to Schiff, 9 Nov. 1915, Schiff Papers, AJA.

99   Adler, *Jacob H. Schiff,* 1:389. Ron Chernow, historian of the Warburg family (Schiff was a business partner of the Warburg men, and his daughter married Felix Warburg), notes that Wald was "a direct human link with the lower end of the social ladder . . . in what must have been sometimes awkward but moving confrontations of poor and rich Jews." *Warburgs,* 99.

100 Schiff to Wald, New Year's Day, 1905, Wald Papers, BL. Schiff spoke also to Wald of learning from her the "responsibility we have to our Maker." New Year's Day, 1906, Wald Papers, BL.

101 Naomi Cohen, Schiff's most recent biographer, writes that though Wald did not "convert the conservative banker into a Progressive," she and her work "deepened his sympathy for the have and have-nots and for government intervention on their behalf." *Jacob Schiff,* 94–95.

102 "Miss Wald's Speech to the Judaeans," Wald Papers, NYPL. See also Naomi Cohen, *Jacob H. Schiff,* 115–17, and Daniels, *Always a Sister,* 95–96.

103 Weinstein, *Ardent Eighties,* 102, 103.

104 Review of *The House on Henry Street*, by Lillian D. Wald, *Nation*, 6 Jan. 1916, 20.

105 "A Pioneer among Settlement Workers Is Miss Wald," *New York Times*, 23 Apr. 1905, SM4.

106 Woods, "The Social Settlement Movement after Sixteen Years," *Congregationalist* 86 (2 Feb. 1901): 182.

107 Schiff to Wald, 21 Oct. 1915, Wald Papers, BL.

108 Rogow, *Gone to Another Meeting*, 2.

109 Jill Conway believes Wald prepared "Crowded Districts" for testimony with Riis before the tenement commission in 1894. See *First Generation*, 212–13. In the copy Wald submitted to the NCJW proceedings, she makes reference to the tenement commission. While some of the material may overlap, Wald obviously altered the piece for the convention in 1896. See National Council of Jewish Women, *Proceedings*, 258–68.

110 Rebecca Kohut stands outside of this accusation of the class bias of the NCJW. In her paper at the founding of the NCJW in 1893, she scorned her fellow members for their avoidance of any direct work with the East Side Jewish population (using colorful language: "the opulent members of society, fancying themselves enshrouded in a pleasing halo . . . haughtily lift their heads in the gentle zephyr of prosperity and, for fear of contracting an inconvenient cold, take scrupulous care not to be ushered into the stiffly blowing gale of neglect and total abandon"). Still, Kohut subscribed to the popular notion of linking the Americanization of the immigrants to upper-class mores ("Why emphasize so unfeelingly the [immigrants'] dearth of refinement, the lack of culture?"). Solomon and Del Banco, *Jewish Women's Congress*, 189, 190, 194. Like Wald, Kohut was influenced by Josephine Shaw Lowell of New York City's Charity Organization Society in her thinking about work with the poor; Kohut also received financial backing from Jacob Schiff and his wife for the Kohut School for Girls. See Antler, *Journey Home*, 45–50. Interestingly, the NCJW continued to invite Wald to deliver speeches. In 1922, the president of the junior auxiliary of the New York section of the NCJW thanked Wald and called her talk "a spur to many of us to do bigger and better work." She praised Wald as "one who for so many years has pointed the way." Irma Hahn to Wald, 21 Oct. 1922, Wald Papers, NYPL.

CHAPTER TWO

1 Reminiscences of Bruno Lasker, 1956, pp. 169–73, OHC. The tables remain at the Henry Street Settlement, and employees there gather around them for lunch, meetings, and conferences. Christine Stansell's work on Greenwich

Village as a "liminal zone" of cross-class meetings has influenced my own thinking here. *American Moderns*, 16.

2   Clarke A. Chambers writes of Paul Kellogg, a New York reformer and editor of the social work journal the *Survey*: "At dinner at the Henry Street Settlement, with Lillian Wald at the head of the table ladling out the evening's soup, the young journalist met social workers, politicians, artists, labor leaders from all parts of Europe." *Paul U. Kellogg*, 71.

3   Duffus records one story of why Henry Street became the official name: When boys from the settlement's athletic clubs were involved in competitions with boys from similar organizations, "in moments of stress their opponents taunted them with cries of 'Noices! Noices!' Wald and her colleagues sought a formal name that encompassed their broad range of activities. For that and other reasons the name Henry Street came into use after a few years and was made official." *Lillian Wald*, 59.

4   Wald took part in the cohort of women who emphasized women's difference and advocated "separatism as strategy" in advancing women's power and influence. They later encountered those who used not difference but "same-ness"—the sameness of women to men—to advance gender equality. For the pioneering essay on this topic, see Freedman, "Separatism as Strategy."

5   While Peter Filene composed an obituary for the Progressive movement, asserting the lack of unifying, coherent reform energy necessary to a move-ment, I maintain that Wald and her cohorts were indeed classical Progres-sives. See Filene, "Obituary for 'the Progressive Movement' "; Keller, *Regulat-ing a New Society*, 1–9, 182–187; Rodgers, "In Search of Progressivism"; and McGerr, *Fierce Discontent*. I also rely here on Linda Gordon's conclusions as to the "common denominators" of Progressivism: a call for an expanded, inter-ventionist government, one that relied on data gathered by social scientists for policymaking. See "If the Progressives Were Advising Us."

6   Women's historians have long recorded the gendered nature of Progressive women's reform. See Sklar, *Florence Kelley*; Skocpol, *Protecting Soldiers and Mothers*; Muncy, *Creating a Female Dominion*; Ellen Fitzpatrick, *Endless Cru-sade*; and Flanagan, *Seeing with Their Hearts*. In "Building on the Romance," Barbara Levy Simon writes about the women's community at Henry Street as a model for contemporary social work practices that fully utilize women's innate and culturally specific skills.

7   Tronto, *Moral Boundaries*.

8   On ethnic Progressivism, see also Connolly, *Triumph of Ethnic Progressivism*, 163, 199. Chapter 4 details where my interpretation differs from Connolly's.

9   Hyman, *Gender and Assimilation*.

10   "Re-Judaisation," editorial, *Boston Jewish Advocate*, 15 May 1908.

11   On the founding of the New York College Settlement, see Woods and Kennedy, *Settlement Horizon*, 44–46, and Allen Davis, *Spearheads for Reform*, 10–12.

12   Muncy, *Creating a Female Dominion*, 9.

13   Wald, "The Nurses' Settlement," in *The Transactions of the Third International Congress of Nurses*, Pan-American Exposition, Buffalo, New York, 18–21 Sept. 1901, Wald Papers, BL.

14   In 1901, the Alumnae Association of the Training School set aside fifteen dollars a month for seven months for "singing lessons among the East Side children" and "Mothers' Classes" at the Nurses' Settlement. See Minutes, Alumnae Association, New York Hospital Training School for Nurses, 9 Oct. 1901, MCA. In 1905, Wald submitted a brief report on her settlement that was included in the Training School's annual report. In it, she expressed her gratitude for the "support" she received through "cooperation with the New York Hospital through its trustees, superintendent, official staff and training school." Report of Superintendent of the Training School, in Annual Report, Society of the New York Hospital, 1905, 85–87, MCA.

15   Quoted in Duffus, *Lillian Wald*, 38.

16   Wald, *House on Henry Street*, 11.

17   Ibid., 12. Daniel Walkowitz notes that social workers' status, as middle-class and as professionals, was defined in opposition to the working-class "other"-ness of their clients. Nowhere was the contrast more evident than in settlement houses, where the two contingent categories met face to face. Walkowitz is correct to point out, however, that the situation of settlement house head-workers like Wald differed from those of other social workers, in that they were independent of a higher institution's authority. See *Working with Class*, 36–41.

18   Wald, "Settlements," speech delivered to the Jamaica Women's Club, 12 Feb. 1913, Wald Papers, NYPL.

19   Wald, "The Nurse as Settlement Worker," *Cleveland Women's Journal*, 4 May 1918, Wald Papers, NYPL.

20   Duffus, *Lillian Wald*, 23. Wald writes of the disadvantages of institutional care for children in *House on Henry Street*, 126–32.

21   Wald, "Report of Henry Street Settlement," 14.

22   Wald to Schiff, 9 Nov. 1915, Schiff Papers, AJA.

23   Wald to Mr. Eugene Lies, 1 Dec. 1910, Wald Papers, NYPL. Lavinia L. Dock, who joined the Nurses' Settlement in late 1896, reported that due to the

poverty of the patients, their care was "freely given, with the exception of one [nurse] who devotes her whole time to a service among those of more means, who would not ask for free nursing." Dock also provides a description of the "daily round" at Henry Street. "The Nurses' Settlement in New York," in *Short Papers on Nursing Subjects* (New York: M. Louise Longeway, 1900), reprinted in James, *Lavinia Dock Reader*, 30–31, quotation on 30.

24   "Miss Wald's Speech to the Judaeans," 13 Dec. 1931, R26, Wald Papers, NYPL.

25   "A Pioneer among Settlement Workers Is Miss Wald," *New York Times*, 23 Apr. 1905, SM4.

26   Wald, "Nurse as Settlement Worker," Wald Papers, NYPL.

27   Wald, "We Called Our Enterprise," xiv.

28   Robyn Muncy uses the term "female dominion [of American reform]" to identify "an interlocking set of organizations and agencies" in "the mostly male empire of policymaking." *Creating a Female Dominion*, xii. Molly Ladd-Taylor describes the category of "progressive maternalists" as those who combined maternalist ideas—that women had special capacities for nurturing and raising children—with political commitments to suffrage, social justice, and democracy. Progressive maternalists also "rejected a sentimental view of motherhood and embraced science and professionalism as values equally available to women and men." "Toward Defining Maternalism," 111. As a nurse and suffragist, Wald certainly fell into this category. See also Ladd-Taylor, *Mother-Work*, and Clapp, *Mothers of All Children*.

29   Wald to Addams, 15 Nov. 1898, Jane Addams Papers, SCPC.

30   See Sklar, *Florence Kelley*, 311.

31   Muncy, *Creating a Female Dominion*, 42–45.

32   For such a division, see Melosh, *Physician's Hand*, esp. chap. 1.

33   Reverby, *Ordered to Care*, 87. On the history of Wald's nursing school, see Jordan, *Cornell University–New York Hospital School of Nursing*.

34   Susan Reverby points out that the transition to paid and trained labor "did not change the assumption that the work was based on womanly duty requiring service to others and acquiescence to the authority of physicians." *Ordered to Care*, 4. Wald stood outside of this paradigm, however, in that her visiting / public health nurses generally worked independently of physicians.

35   Patricia D'Antonio highlights the fact that nurses were "collectively rather conservative and sought primarily—and this was no insignificant achievement—to create their own influential place within established structures and traditions." "Revisiting and Rethinking," 281. Wald's conservative approach to women's power later met resistance from organizations like the National

Woman's Party, which emphasized women's sameness to men and not their difference. See chap. 4.

36   Wald to Schiff, 17 Feb. 1914, Wald Papers, BL.

37   Wald, "We Called Our Enterprise," xi–xiv; Dock and Stewart, *Short History of Nursing*, 305–7.

38   Wald to Adelaide Nutting, 16 Jan. 1912, Wald Papers, NYPL.

39   Melosh, *Physician's Hand*, 115, 113. Wald also used this term in *House on Henry Street*, 62. Regina Kunzel examines the complicated impact of professionalization on the field of social work, especially its contributions to women's cross-class conflicts, in *Fallen Women, Problem Girls*.

40   On Wald and the National Organization of Public Health Nursing's relationship to the National Association of Colored Graduate Nurses, see Carnegie, *Path We Tread*, 112–14.

41   The quote and statistics are from Hine, *Black Women in White*, 101. On Wald and National Association of Colored Graduate Nurses, see also Althea Davis, *Early Leaders in Nursing*, 90–91. Wald's commitment to civil rights for African Americans was also demonstrated in her early work for the National Association for the Advancement of Colored People, discussed below.

42   Wald, "Report of Henry Street Settlement," 15, 18.

43   Wald, "Settlements," Wald Papers, NYPL. See also Lewenson, *Taking Charge*, 120–31. As Joyce Antler points out, the out-practice department, or Tenement Home Service, of the New York Infirmary for Women and Children provided Wald (and others) with a model for linking illness, poverty, and morality. The infirmary, founded by Alice Stone Blackwell, a friend of Wald's, also "built on and sanctified women's recognized responsibility for domestic and spiritual matters," endorsing their active role in science while it projected middle-class values onto immigrant practices. "Medical Women," 11–18.

44   Wald, "Treatment of Families," 427.

45   Tifft and Jones, *The Trust*, 100.

46   On nurses' activism, see Roberts and Group, *Feminism and Nursing*.

47   Wald, "Report of Henry Street Settlement." See also *House on Henry Street*, 44–46. The badges were shortly found to be unnecessary.

48   Wald, *House on Henry Street*, 86; Duffus, *Lillian Wald*, 86–87; New York City Department of Parks and Recreation, "Playgrounds and Public Recreation," <http://www.nycgovparks.org/sub_about/parks_history/historic_tour/history_playgrounds_recreation.html>; Goodman, *Choosing Sides*. Wald remained a member of the Outdoor Recreation League through World War I. Charles Stover was appointed New York's park commissioner in 1910.

49 Wald, "Medical Inspection," 293.

50 Ibid.

51 Quoted in Duffy, *History of Public Health*, 254.

52 "One Woman's Services," *New York Times*, 9 Nov. 1909, 8.

53 Wald, "Medical Inspection," 293, 297, 298.

54 Wald, "Feeding of the School Children," 371–74.

55 Wald, "Put Responsibility on the Right Shoulders," 316.

56 Wald, "Health and Maternity Legislation," 11.

57 Wald's work for women's protective legislation and trade unionism took the form of participation in the Women's Trade Union League, in which middle-class women allied with working-class women "to give support and assistance . . . in their efforts for organization." Wald encouraged others to get involved and spoke to the urgency of the issue: "This seems to be a clear call," she wrote, "to that part of the community that with any seriousness concerns itself with the welfare and the fate of the women in industry." "Organization amongst Working Women," 639, 641, 645. On the history of the league, see Dye, *Women's Trade Union League*.

58 Allen Davis, *Spearheads for Reform*, 182. Davis recounts the story of Wald and other New York reformers involved in Low's campaign in his chapter titled "The Settlement Movement and Municipal Reform." Naomi Cohen discusses the investment of uptown German Jews in that election: while endorsing the need for "good government"—as opposed to Tammany's "scandal-ridden hold on New York"—German Jews also had in mind the cleaning up of the East Side. Improving the living conditions of the eastern European Jewish immigrants would mitigate uptowners' unease with the visibility of immigrants' poverty. *Encounter with Emancipation*, 329–36.

59 "Women in the Campaign: Miss Wald Tells Why They Are against Tammany," *Evening Post*, 3 Nov. 1913, Wald Papers, NYPL.

60 "American Women and Child Labor," *Harper's Bazaar*, Feb. 1908, 192.

61 Caroline Williamson Montgomery, *Bibliography of College, Social, University and Church Settlements* (Chicago: Blakely Press, 1905), Wald Papers, BL.

62 Graham Taylor, "Is Religion an Element," 345.

63 Stebner, *Women of Hull House*.

64 Badillo, "Incorporating Reform and Religion," 49.

65 Polacheck, *I Came a Stranger*, 122. To demonstrate her respect, Addams went so far as to serve kosher chicken at the Hull House reception following Polacheck's wedding. (Polacheck regretfully notes that the ice cream that was served at the same dinner—mixing meat and milk, and therefore not strictly

kosher for an observant Jew—meant her mother could not partake of the meal. That she herself ate the meal spoke directly to the generation gap in religious observance.)

66 On Jewish settlements, see Rose, "Sponge Cake to *Hamentashen*," and Alissa Schwartz, "Americanization and Cultural Preservation," 25–45.

67 Allen Davis, *Spearheads for Reform*, 15.

68 On the assimilation attempts of uptown, assimilated Jews on downtown, Orthodox Jews, see, for example, the work of Gerald Sorin, who labeled this relationship one of "mutual contempt, mutual benefit" in his article of the same title.

69 Educational Alliance, First Annual Report, 1893, *Minutes of the Meetings of the Board of Directors of the Educational Alliance, 1879–1980* (New York: Clearwater, 1987), microfiche collection.

70 Editorial, *Hebrew Standard*, 3 Mar. 1916.

71 Fromenson, "East Side Preventative Work," 121.

72 On David Blaustein's tenure at the Educational Alliance, see Miriam Blaustein, *Memoirs of David Blaustein*.

73 Bogen, *Jewish Philanthropy*, 247.

74 Bernheimer, "A Social Settlement for an Immigrant Jewish Population," *American Hebrew*, 16 July 1909, 268–69.

75 Bernheimer, "Jewish Activities at the University Settlement," *Hebrew Standard*, 3 Jan. 1908.

76 Ibid. For Bernheimer's more lengthy discussion of this, see *Half a Century*, 19–39.

77 Wald to Dr. Harris, 1 Sept. 1909, Wald Papers, NYPL.

78 Jeffrey S. Gurock tells the important story of this meeting in *American Jewish Orthodoxy*, 286. See also "Religious Centers Down-Town," *American Hebrew*, 5 Feb. 1904, 391.

79 *Yidishes Tageblatt (Jewish Daily News)*, 6 July 1903 (capitalization in original).

80 *Yidishes Tageblatt (Jewish Daily News)*, 22 July 1903.

81 Hyman, *Gender and Assimilation*, 45.

82 On the Stokeses' rejection of settlement work, see Zipser and Zipser, *Fire and Grace*, 62–63. Rose Pastor Stokes joined the Socialist Party when she concluded that settlement reformers were "well meaning and kindly . . . but blinded to the real issues of the unjust social system . . . which legalizes the taking of great wealth by the idle." "Stokes and Wife to Show Way to Live: Applied Christianity Now Socialist Doctrine, Denounce Idle Rich; Former Settlement Workers Say Scheming Few Subsist on the Laboring Class," *New York Press*, 20 Jan. 1907.

83   *Yidishes Tageblatt (Jewish Daily News)*, 29 July 1903.

84   Ibid.

85   Howe, *World of Our Fathers*, 93. Though Howe's work "lacks the substance of truly historical writing," his stories are based on first-person recollections; these capture historical sentiments, even as they are grounded in his own nostalgia. Heinze, "But Is It History?" 501.

86   Kate Simon, *Bronx Primitive*, 9.

87   Rose Cohen, *Out of the Shadow*, 231.

88   "The Henry Street Settlement," *Der Tog* 2, no. 78 (21 Jan. 1915) 5, col. 1. A search of Yiddish newspapers during a series of important moments in Henry Street's history (e.g., the visit of Russian revolutionary Catherine Breshkovskaia to Henry Street in 1905, the Henry Street anniversary celebration in 1915, or the Russian provisional government's visit in 1917) yielded no articles on Wald or the settlement.

89   Emma Goldman, *Living My Life*, 1:160.

90   On the changing institutional priorities in this period, see David Kaufman, *Shul with a Pool*, 112–27. On advocates for "Americanization with Jewish content," see Naomi Cohen, *Encounter with Emancipation*, 308–17.

91   Fromenson (1874–1935) serves as an excellent point of contrast, because his life paralleled Wald's for a time. Like Wald, he was born in the Midwest, though in Chicago, not Cincinnati. His journalistic ambition took him to Rochester, where he was editor of the *Jewish Tidings*, the antilabor, pro–woman suffrage serial of Temple B'rith Kodesh. Following that, however, Fromenson's Jewish affiliations, including his membership in a synagogue, set him apart from Wald and indicated their diverging life paths. He endorsed Jewish religious difference, as was made clear in his criticism of Wald and other Jewish settlement leaders. He rejected Wald's universalism in favor of Judaism's particularism. Later, these views led him to Zionism. On Fromenson, see the entries in the *Universal Jewish Encyclopedia*, the *Biographical Encyclopedia of American Jews*, and the *American Jewish Yearbook 6*.

92   Wald, *House on Henry Street*, 220, 225.

93   Wald to Social Halls Association, 11 Sept. 1921, Wald Papers, BL.

94   "Social Halls Association, Names of Subscribers for Ten Shares or More," 1914, Wald Papers, BL.

95   Wald, *House on Henry Street*, 228.

96   Ibid., 226.

97   "The Social Halls Association," *Charities* 6 (22 May 1901): 442–43.

98   Wise, *Challenging Years*, 103–4.

99   Ibid., 102.

100 Editorials, *Hebrew Standard*, 24 Sept. 1915, 11 Mar. 1921.

101 Howe, *World of Our Fathers*, 197. Other historians note that Wise's oratorical abilities, not his teachings of Reform Judaism, attracted his following. See Shapiro, *Reform Rabbi*, 190–95.

102 Howe, *World of Our Fathers*, 90–94.

103 Calkins, "The New Social Halls Association," *Congregationalist and Christian World*, 9 May 1903, 662.

104 Wald, *House on Henry Street*, 293.

105 Quoted in Duffus, *Lillian Wald*, 107.

106 Wald, letter to the editor, *Survey* 28 (25 May 1912): 347.

107 Jacqueline Jones discusses the competition for jobs between African Americans and European immigrants, so important because African Americans "lacked employment 'niches' of the kind that provided for upward mobility among individual immigrant groups." *American Work*, 306. This tension is not evident in Wald and Kellor's report; it is indeed surprising that they note the fact that the African American workers they encountered were "usually skilled workmen."

108 Wald, *House on Henry Street*, 293, 294.

109 All quotes are from Wald and Kellor, "The Construction Camps of the People," *Survey* 23 (1 Jan. 1910): 434–65.

110 Marshall, *Report of the Commission*.

111 Ibid., 23.

112 On Kellor's work on the commission, see Ellen Fitzpatrick, *Endless Crusade*, 142–45.

113 Wald, *House on Henry Street*, 298.

114 Wald to Schiff, 30 Sept. 1918, Wald Papers, BL. For a review of the history of the concepts of assimilation and Americanization in history, see Kazal, "Revisiting Assimilation."

115 Higham, *Strangers in the Land*, 77.

116 On Frances Kellor's 100 percent American campaign, see Ellen Fitzpatrick, *Endless Crusade*. On the movement, see also McClymer, "Gender and the 'American Way.'"

117 For just one example, see Wald to President Taft, Senator Elihu Root, and Senator James O'Gorman, 7 Jan. 1913, Wald Papers, BL. In this form letter, Wald protests the proposed literacy test for immigrant citizenship. "We speak from a continuous and intimate acquaintance with the immigrant population, covering a period of twenty years," she wrote, "and with a knowledge of the historic values that the immigrant has contributed to the making of the United States."

118 Carson, *Settlement Folk*, 103. Higham articulated this same point, that the "settlements pioneered because they respected foreign customs and approached the foreigners' problems in an empirical way." *Strangers in the Land*, 121.

119 Higham, *Strangers in the Land*, 121.

120 Wald, "Nurses' Settlement," Wald Papers, BL.

121 Wald, "The Utilization of the Immigrant," speech to the Free Synagogue, Dec. 1907, Wald Papers, NYPL.

122 Wald, *House on Henry Street*, 306.

123 Wald, paper delivered at the Conference on Immigration Policy, 10 Apr. 1929, Wald Papers, BL.

124 Wald, "Americanism," speech for Settlement Conference, 1 Mar. 1919, Wald Papers, BL.

125 Wald, *House on Henry Street*, 184.

126 Wald, "The Assimilation of the Alien," speech, 9 Apr. 1929, Wald Papers, NYPL.

127 Rita Teresa Wallach, "The Settlement Movement: The Social Value of the Festival," *Charities and the Commons* 16 (2 June 1909): 315–19.

128 Alice Lewisohn Crowley describes her first meeting with Wald in her book *The Neighborhood Playhouse: Leaves from a Theatre Scrapbook*. After traveling with her father "through streets littered with garbage," they were soon "waiting for the gong to announce dinner" with the nurses at the settlement, where "Lillian Wald played not one part, but innumerably changing characters." At the table, Wald's "hands seemed to work automatically as she mixed the crisp green leaves in the salad bowl, while she clarified some problem about unions, interlarding her conversation with whimsical stories" (5–6).

129 Ibid., 20.

130 Modern scholars, too, cite this play as proof of Wald's dedication to the native cultures of the settlement's clients. Using poststructuralist theory, Patrick Tuite locates Wald on the liberal side of the spectrum in approaches to assimilation. Wald's "immigrant gifts" philosophy, the organic relationship between the theater and the neighborhood, present her "as a model for producing meaningful multicultural theatre for children today." "Assimilating Immigrants through Drama," 17. Mina Carson describes settlements' dramatic work—including that at Henry Street—as in line with Victorian values, in which art served "as a vehicle of moral education, promoting the growth of individual character through social interaction, and as an effort to make culture truly democratic not by conceding dominion over taste and form to the vulgar majority, but by extending to everyone access to the 'best which has been thought and known in the world.'" *Settlement Folk*, 117. While Wald cer-

tainly hoped for education within the process of producing drama, she most often referred to the cultural exchange between the audience and the players, not to individual character education. Linda J. Tomko studies the historical significance of Henry Street's unique community productions—their experimentation with "new modes of theatrical expressions," their Americanization work, their capacity for neighborhood expression, their "example of women's innovation" and social engagement in the choreography of several Russian immigrant Jews, including Helen Taminis, Sophie Maslow, and Anna Sokolow. See Tomko, *Dancing Class*, 110, 134, 132.

131   Crowley, *Neighborhood Playhouse*, 40–41.

132   This story is told in Birmingham, *Our Crowd*, 332–33.

133   Steven Cassedy discusses Gordin's role as the leading playwright in the "realist" faction, which opposed the works of those in the "romantic" faction. *To the Other Shore*, 134–36. In "Reforming the New York Yiddish Theater," Bettina Warnke analyzes the division between the radical press, which largely praised Gordin's realist works, and the Orthodox press, which blamed radicals and realists like Gordin for the "decline" of traditional Jewish family life.

134   Wald to Jacob Gordin, Sept. 28, 1904, Jacob Gordin Papers, YIVO.

135   Wald, *House on Henry Street*, 271.

136   Philip Gleason provides a historical and analytical discussion of the concept of cultural pluralism and the melting pot in "American Identity and Americanization." In a comprehensive study of pluralism titled *Pluralism and Progressives*, Rivka Lissak argues that the settlement house concept of Americanization—specifically that of Jane Addams's Hull House—remained tied to Anglo-Saxonism, emphasizing the need for cultures to be modeled on Anglo-Saxon culture (see esp. her conclusion, 182–84). Yet she also found that their work "unintentionally paved the way for a more pluralist view of society in the 1930s" (184).

137   Kallen, *Culture and Democracy*; Ratner, "Kallen and Cultural Pluralism." Werner Sollors writes that Kallen ultimately "naturalized ethnicity [Jewishness] as an immutable category." *Beyond Ethnicity*, 183.

138   Wald, "Assimilation of the Alien," Wald Papers, NYPL. In her study of social settlements in Gary and Indianapolis, Indiana, Ruth Hutchinson Crocker finds that "the settlement workers of this study were not cultural pluralists, but missionaries for the American Way." They saw no opportunity for a "new synthesis" of American culture based on immigrant contributions. *Social Work and Social Order*, 212. Wald's rhetoric indicates that she opposed the extremes of this missionary approach.

139   Wald, "Assimilation of the Alien," Wald Papers, NYPL.

140 Zangwill, afterword to *Melting Pot*, 203.

141 Ibid., 185.

142 Ibid., 154.

143 Udelson, *Dreamer of the Ghetto*, 198. See also Rochelson, introduction to *Children of the Ghetto*. David Biale contends that Zangwill's ending suggests not the Americanizing of Jews but the "Judaising" of Americans. "Melting Pot and Beyond," 24. Zangwill's relationship to Zionism demonstrates his complicated relationship to Jewish peoplehood. Though once a Zionist, he later split with the movement over the question of a peaceful means of nationalist existence. See Faris, "Israel Zangwill's Challenge."

144 Wald to Zangwill, 13 Nov. 1923, Wald Papers, NYPL.

145 Zangwill to Wald, 19 Nov. 1923, Wald Papers, NYPL.

146 In his study of New York City workers in the Progressive Era, Melvyn Dubofsky notes that while "between the workers, immigrant and American, and the reformer, a real gulf existed," settlement house workers were among those who made contributions to "urban betterment" through "pragmatic cooperation with organized labor in lobbying for . . . protective labor legislation" and that they "were probably the most effective of the metropolis' diverse reformers at the human level." *When Workers Organize*, 26, 23, 49–58. See also Howe, *World of Our Fathers*, 295–304. For firsthand accounts of the strike, see Schneiderman, *All For One*, and Schofield, "Uprising of the 20,000."

147 "Miss Wald's Speech to the Judaeans," Wald Papers, NYPL. See also Naomi Cohen, *Jacob H. Schiff*, 115–17.

148 On Henry Street's role in the strike, see Wald, *House on Henry Street*, 206. The job of the Joint Board of Sanitary Control was to fix standards in the workshops, including standards on "fire drills, diminution of fire causes, cleaning of floors and walls and windows, adjustment of lights, improvement in ventilation, the introduction of the emergency kits, [and] the renovation of toilets." "The 'White' Protocol," *Survey* 29 (1 Feb. 1913): 557–59. On the protocol as "among the first industry-wide collective bargaining agreements in American economic history," see Dubofsky, *When Workers Organize*, 65. The same board later supervised the shirtwaist industry as well.

149 Schiff to Wald, 10 May 1903, Wald Papers, BL. See Schiff's thanks for Wald's sending *Up From Slavery*, 4 Aug. 1901, Wald Papers, BL.

150 Adler, *Jacob H. Schiff*, 1:314; Lewis, *W. E. B. Du Bois*, 402. Du Bois recollected decades later that he called on Schiff "for help in starting a monthly magazine on the Negro problem . . . [a]t his invitation"; Schiff ultimately "declined to help," and though Du Bois admitted he did not know for sure why this was, he assumed it was "because of the influence of Booker T. Washington and his

friends." Du Bois to Professor [Merle] Curti, 4 June 1958, in Aptheker, *Correspondence of W. E. B. DuBois*, 430. This magazine was no doubt the *Crisis*, which began in 1910, the same year Wald successfully convinced Schiff to donate funds.

151   On "The Call," published in the *New York Evening Post* on 12 Feb. 1909, see Finch, *NAACP*, 8–12, and Hughes, *Fight for Freedom*, 22–23.

152   The story of the reception at Henry Street is in Wald's *Windows on Henry Street*, 49.

153   Cheryl Greenberg lists Wald, along with Wise, Schiff, and others involved with the early NAACP, as "among the leading Jewish activists of their day." Her analysis contrasts sharply with Eric Goldstein's, discussed below, and her conclusions mirror those in this biography: in endorsing the liberal integrationist stance of the NAACP, she writes, many Jews (such as Wald) reflected both their "high mindedness" and their "self-interest"—the earlier simply redefining the latter more broadly. "Given their historical experience with persecution and the dangerous intolerance of parochial and authoritarian societies, and recognizing the security and freedom civil emancipation had brought them in Europe," Greenberg writes, "Jews understood their self-interest as rooted in liberal values of tolerance and broad access to the opportunities of civil society." She incorporates her discussion of Jewish liberalism into a chapter entitled "Settling In," which focuses on the Reform movement, the waves of German and eastern European Jewish immigrations to the United States, and the views African Americans and Jews had of each other in the early twentieth century. *Troubling the Waters*, 24, 31.

154   Goldstein, *Price of Whiteness*, 70.

CHAPTER THREE

1   Rodgers, *Atlantic Crossings*, 4, 75. Other scholarship focuses on the international women's movement. While such work suggests frameworks for understanding global coalition building, its focus on women's issues excludes Wald's internationalist health work in Russia. See Anderson, *Joyous Greetings*; Berkovitch, *From Motherhood to Citizenship*; D'Itri, *Cross Currents*; and Rupp, *Worlds of Women*. On Jewish women's organizational, international work, see McCune, *Whole Wide World*.

2   Wald, *House on Henry Street*, 238. Wald chose this title—"People Who Have Crossed Our Threshold"—for a chapter in her second book, *Windows on Henry Street*.

3   Scudder, *On Journey*, 156. Daniel Rodgers states that "the settlement house movement was one of transatlantic social Protestantism's most striking productions." *Atlantic Crossings*, 64.

4   Werner Sollors discusses how "ethnicization and modernization often go hand in hand" in *Beyond Ethnicity*, 246–47.

5   Wald, Speech to the Council of Jewish Women, Baltimore, 26 Feb. 1911, Wald Papers, NYPL.

6   The forty-two-page report of the Dillingham Commission took a "moderately restrictionist" position, including an endorsement of a literacy test for citizenship. Higham, *Strangers in the Land*, 189. See also Cafferty, Chiswick, Greeley, and Sullivan, *Dilemma of American Immigration*; Raider, "Race and Nationality"; and Handlin, *Race and Nationality*, esp. chap. 5.

7   See Duffus, *Lillian Wald*, 106–8, and chap. 2 of this volume.

8   Wald, Speech to the Council of Jewish Women, Wald Papers, NYPL.

9   Ibid.

10   Schiff to Wald, 27 Dec. 1909, Wald Papers, BL.

11   Schiff to Wald, 13 Jan. 1910, Wald Papers, BL.

12   Rodgers, *Atlantic Crossings*, 269.

13   "Sociological Conditions in the Far East: Miss Lillian D. Wald, the Famous Settlement Worker of New York, Tells Her Impressions during an Extended Trip around the World," *New York Times*, 10 July 1910, SM11.

14   Takahashi wrote to Cyrus Adler, Schiff's biographer, of his first meeting with Schiff. He noted that Schiff "was justly indignant at the unfair treatment of the Jewish population by the Russian government, which had culminated in notorious persecutions." Adler, *Jacob H. Schiff*, 1:217. Baron Takahashi's daughter spent two years with the Schiffs and referred to them as "Auntie and Uncle Schiff." Like Wald, Takahashi wanted his government to curtail military spending; he "opposed the militarists in their constant demands for increased military expenditure." He was murdered in 1936 by assassins associated with the ruling militarists. See "Mr. Takahashi: A Statesman of Courage and Genius," *Manchester Guardian*, [1936], Wald Papers, NYPL.

15   Waters to "the Family," 17 Mar. 1910, Wald Papers, NYPL.

16   Duffus, *Lillian Wald*, 123; "Sociological Conditions," *New York Times*.

17   "Sociological Conditions," *New York Times*.

18   Wald to Miss Tsuda, 23 July 1910, Wald Papers, BL.

19   "Sociological Conditions," *New York Times*.

20   Allen Davis, *Spearheads for Reform*, 110. Emma Goldman writes about Breshkovskaia as an inspiration to her. See *Living My Life*, 1:361–65.

21   Schiff wrote to Wald that he would come to the house to visit "the Russian
      lady" there. 13 Mar. 1905, Wald Papers, BL. Wald writes of Breshkovskaia's
      1905 visit to Henry Street in *House on Henry Street*, 240.

22   Cassedy, "Chernyshevskii Goes West."

23   Schiff began to make public statements on Russia's treatment of Jews in 1890.
      See Adler, *Jacob H. Schiff*, 1:114–15. In an interesting turn of events that
      highlights Wald's many allegiances, Schiff volunteered to pay for all Ameri-
      can magazine subscriptions that were sent to Breshkovskaia in Russia. Wald
      set up the subscriptions through Alice Stone Blackwell, a leading figure in the
      National American Women's Suffrage Association. The organization earned
      commission fees when Wald and Schiff ordered *National Geographic, Mc-
      Clure's, Life and Labor*, and the *Survey* for their Russian radical ally in 1912 and
      1913. See Blackwell to Wald, 26 Apr. 1912, Wald Papers, BL. Breshkovskaia
      wrote to Wald that the magazines kept her "au courant about the whole
      world," that they traveled all over Siberia, where she was in exile, and that
      others were "studying [them] in exile and in prisons." 10 Apr. 1913, Wald
      Papers, BL. Here, we see Wald's uptown Jewish connections (Schiff), her
      sympathies with Russian radicalism, and her loyalty to her women's network
      and its cause of suffrage.

24   To understand American liberals' attitudes toward the Russian Revolution,
      Christopher Lasch divided them into two groups in *American Liberals*: "war
      liberals" and "anti-imperialists." Wald's reactions to both World War I and the
      Russian Revolution locate her in the anti-imperialist camp, and her rhetoric is
      suffused with the romanticization and hopefulness Lasch describes. Like oth-
      ers in her camp, Wald thought of the revolution as "a great tidal wave of
      democracy." Wald to Schiff, 16 Mar. 1917, Wald Papers, BL. For more on Wald's
      relationship to Russia—specifically to Russian revolutionaries—see chap. 4.

25   "Sociological Conditions," *New York Times*.

26   Ibid. In *Mutual Aid* (1902), Kropotkin used anthropology and observations of
      different animal species to prove that mutual cooperation was the law of
      nature, as opposed to a Darwinian or Malthusian theory of nature. He be-
      lieved that this need for mutual aid propelled societies toward progress. While
      his faith in human connections mirrored Wald's universalist philosophy, he
      was an anarchist who decried "the crushing powers of the centralised State,"
      which of course ran counter to Wald's ideas. Woodcock and Avakumovic, *Peter
      Kropotkin*, 329–38, quote on 337. On Kropotkin's influence on Emma Gold-
      man, see Antler, *Journey Home*, 82. Interestingly, Breshkovskaia and Kro-
      potkin are the only two portraits in Wald's first book, *The House on Henry
      Street* (1915), aside from one of herself with Mary Brewster.

Untitled

27 "Sociological Conditions," *New York Times*. In fact, Wald hoped that the entire article would be more broadly conceived, with less of a focus on her own voice. M. D. Maclean of the *New York Times* apologized to her for not being able to "further eliminate the personal pronoun from the interview." She continued: "But you see the point of it was it was *you*, and you had to appear. But nobody except your modest self would have thought there was too much 'I.' " Maclean to Wald, 11 July 1910, Wald Papers, NYPL.

28 Wald, *Windows on Henry Street*, 337.

29 Wald, "Report of Henry Street Settlement," 26. The symbol remains on some Henry Street stationery, and a casting of it greets all visitors to the house. The symbol is also on Wald's grave in Rochester, New York.

30 In 1926, in a fund-raising letter to John D. Rockefeller Jr., Wald wrote about a "map of the world" they had at the settlement: "Buttons on it indicate the various countries of Europe, Asia, and Africa, 48 in all, who have sent women to us or to whom we have sent women equipped to establish public health work in their own countries." 30 Nov. 1926, Wald Papers, CSL. Henrietta Szold, who founded Hadassah, a women's Zionist organization, in 1912, had Wald's program in mind when she established a nursing program in the poorer areas of Jerusalem. Joyce Antler discusses this idea in *Journey Home*, 105–6.

31 Wald to Takahashi, 19 May 1911, Wald Papers, NYPL.

32 Emma Goldman to Wald, n.d., ca. Dec. 1910, Wald Papers, NYPL. Based on this and a letter from journalist and author Hutchins Hapgood, Wald asked Mr. Ichinomiya of Yokohama Specie Bank on Wall Street to write to the consul general of Japan about the Kataku case. The consul responded, "Neither political pressure nor public clamor will have any affect on the finding and decision of our Court." Wald passed this information on to both Goldman and Hapgood with characteristic optimism that the life of Miss Kataku would be spared. See Wald to Goldman, 5 Dec. 1910; Consul General to Mr. Ichinomiya, 8 Dec. 1910; and Hapgood to Wald, n.d., ca. Dec. 1910, Wald Papers, NYPL.

33 Wald to Mr. Starr Murphy [to arrange a meeting between Mr. Tasuka Harada and Mr. Rockefeller], 17 Nov. 1910, Wald Papers, NYPL.

34 Pankhurst to Wald, 30 Apr. 1912, Wald Papers, NYPL. Wald wrote to George Foster Peabody, who subsequently refused to support the causes of Irish home rule and suffrage together, arguing that the question of woman suffrage was an international one and only complicated the question of British control of Ireland. Peabody to Wald, 25 May 1912, Wald Papers, NYPL.

35 Wald to Schiff, 25 Nov. 1912, Wald Papers, BL. This exchange took place in the early stages of her writing the book.

36   Schiff to Wald, n.d., ca. Aug. 1912, Wald Papers, BL.

37   Morgenthau to Wald, 8 Aug. 1912, Wald Papers, NYPL.

38   "As you know . . . I am not an aggressive suffragist," Wald wrote to Schiff, "but the issue is too real for one who has declared herself to have taken that position." 12 Aug. 1912, Wald Papers, BL. Jane Addams wrestled with the issue of Roosevelt's militarism, as he pledged to build two battleships a year. See Addams, *Second Twenty Years*, 34–38. She also struggled with the exclusion of African Americans from the Progressive convention. See Milkis and Tichenor, "Direct Democracy," 315–20, and Gustafson, "Jane Addams." To Wald, she wrote: "You may imagine it was pretty hard for me to swallow warships. The negro situation is really much better than the paper makes out, but Mr. Moskowitz will tell you that." 17 Aug. 1912, Jane Addams Papers, SCPC.

39   Sedgwick to Wald, 7 Oct. 1914, Wald Papers, BL.

40   Sedgwick to Wald, 9 Dec. 1914, Wald Papers, BL.

41   Wald, *House on Henry Street*, v.

42   Harcourt to Wald, 24 Dec. 1914, 21 Feb. 1915, Wald Papers, BL.

43   Jane Addams and others in their network repeatedly asked Wald to attend the congress in Holland. "My leaving America at this time, even for a few weeks, would seriously affect responsibilities which I have assumed, and which I cannot feel that I can properly abandon," Wald wrote to Addams. 25 Mar. 1915, Wald Papers, NYPL. Doris Groshen Daniels includes an extensive discussion of Wald's views on the Hague in *Always a Sister*, 127–30. On Addams, Wald, and other women reformers' international peace work, see also Sklar, "Some of Us," and Alonso, *Peace as a Women's Issue*.

44   Harcourt to Wald, 22 Mar. 1915, Wald Papers, BL.

45   Duffus, *Lillian Wald*, 175.

46   Wald, *House on Henry Street*, v, vi.

47   Duffus, *Lillian Wald*, 173.

48   Frances Kellor, with whom Wald had worked in the past, spearheaded a National Americanization Day Committee in 1915. Though "the tone was still liberal," one historian observes, with the onset of the war "the impulse behind the new interest in Americanization was fear of divided loyalties." Higham, *Strangers in the Land*, 243.

49   Harriot Stanton Blatch, daughter of Elizabeth Cady Stanton, expressed these thoughts in an interview with the *Times* after a failed attempt at the suffrage referendum. See "Mrs. Blatch Pours Out Wrath on Root," *New York Times*, 4 Nov. 1915, 3. Wald responded the next day with a letter in which she stated that Blatch "did not thoroughly analyze the vote that was cast on the east side," and that she herself was "in a position to speak with greater authority on the

subject." She called attention to the support of the referendum in the "very foreign" districts—often higher than those where the "Anglo-Saxon naturalized citizens live." Wald wrote that Blatch and her colleagues were shown "great courtesy" while downtown, and that their East Side supporters were now "inspired to put forth greater effort in the future." Wald, letter to the editor, *New York Times*, 6 Nov. 1915.

50 Wald to Kohler, 8 Dec. 1913, Max Kohler Papers, YIVO. Wald's extant correspondence with Kohler stretches from her congratulations on his marriage in 1906 (on which occasion Wald invited him to dine at the settlement so that her " 'faculty' may declare their betrothals entirely sealed") through the years that immediately preceded his death in 1934. Wald to Kohler, 5 July 1906, Max Kohler Papers, YIVO.

51 Wald, *House on Henry Street*, 266.

52 Ibid., 54.

53 Ibid., 25, 261.

54 Ibid., 106.

55 Silverberg, "Introduction," 12. On the way women social scientists established their authority outside of formal university settings, and on how this development contributed to the diversification of the field, see Silverberg's introduction and Sklar, "*Hull House Maps.*"

56 Wald, *House on Henry Street*, 254. The transliteration is her own. For a discussion of Wald's opinions on Zionism, see chap. 4.

57 Wald, *House on Henry Street*, 310.

58 Hillquit to Wald, 30 Nov. 1915, Wald Papers, NYPL.

59 Addams to Wald, 12 Nov. 1915, Jane Addams Papers, SCPC.

60 Forcey, *Crossroads of Liberalism*.

61 F. H. [probably founding editor Francis Hackett], "The Permanent War," review of *The House on Henry Street*, *New Republic*, 8 Jan. 1916, 255–56.

62 "Story of the House on Henry Street: Miss Wald's Illuminating Record of the Work that Has Been Done by the Settlement Housed in an Old New York Dwelling," *New York Times*, 21 Nov. 1915, BR451.

63 Review of *The House on Henry Street*, by Lillian D. Wald, *Journal of Political Economy* 24 (1916): 416.

64 Scott E. W. Bedford, review of *The House on Henry Street*, by Lillian D. Wald, *American Journal of Sociology* 21 (1915–16): 705.

65 J. Salwyn Schapiro, review of *The House on Henry Street*, by Lillian D. Wald, *Survey* 35 (8 Jan. 1916): 437–38.

66 Marchand, *American Peace Movement*. Marchand focuses on the "interconnections of [the peace] movement with other contemporary social movements

and concerns" and how each activist's goals in the peace movement served as an extension of her or his other reform commitments (x). Addams writes about this meeting in *Second Twenty Years*, 121.

67 AUAM, "Towards the Peace That Shall Last," pamphlet, n.d., ca. winter 1915, AUAM Papers, SCPC.

68 Marchand discusses the "maternal instinct" in women's organizational work for peace in *American Peace Movement*, chap. 6. See also Alonso, *Peace as a Women's Issue*, chap. 3.

69 AUAM, "Towards the Peace," AUAM Papers, SCPC; "Anti-Preparedness' Committee Pamphlet," n.d., ca. 1915, AUAM Papers, SCPC.

70 AUAM, "Towards the Peace," AUAM Papers, SCPC (emphasis in original).

71 An AUAM flier demanded, "Shall We Have War with Mexico?" In the text of the flier, the organization wrote that "the American people will surely not be deceived by any attempt to alter the facts," for war with Mexico, a nation "undergoing a period of reconstruction," would be "a blot upon American history." Flier, 26 June 1916, Wald Papers, BL.

72 Wald, *Windows on Henry Street*, 295, 285, 298. See also Marchand, *American Peace Movement*, 242–44.

73 The AUAM billed the hearings as the opportunity to hear testimony "Against Universal Military Training." AUAM bulletin, 1916, AUAM Papers, SCPC.

74 Statement of Wald before the Committee on Military Affairs, in U.S. Senate, *Preparedness for National Defense*, 1030.

75 Ibid., 1032.

76 Ibid., 1031.

77 Wald to Addams, 24 Dec. 1914, Jane Addams Papers, SCPC.

78 Statement of Wald, U.S. Senate, *Preparedness for National Defense*, 1031.

79 Statement of Kelley, U.S. Senate, *Preparedness for National Defense*, 1039, 1041.

80 Sklar, *Notes of Sixty Years*. On Kelley's career, see Sklar, *Florence Kelley*.

81 "War Program of the AUAM," Committee Minutes of the AUAM, May 1917, AUAM Papers, SCPC.

82 Members of the AUAM to Wilson, 16 Apr. 1917, Jane Addams Papers, SCPC. For Wilson's reply, see Wald, *Windows on Henry Street*, 310.

83 The story of the transition into a more radical chapter of the AUAM's history is told well in Marchand, *American Peace Movement*, 253–61, and in Johnson, *Challenge to American Freedoms*, 18–25. Marchand points out that Schiff's 1917 shift to a pro-war stance undoubtedly put pressure on Wald to avoid radical antiwar organizations.

84 Wald quoted by Crystal Eastman in her letter to Emily G. Balch, 14 June 1917, in Cook, *Crystal Eastman*, 255.

85 Wald to Addams, 14 Aug., 1 Oct., 13 Nov. 1917, Jane Addams Papers, SCPC.

86 Mary Dewhurst, "The Food Demonstrations in New York," *Outlook*, 7 Mar. 1917, 405.

87 Wald, "Influenza: When the City Is a Great Field Hospital," *Survey* 43 (14 Feb. 1920): 581. See also Kolata, *Flu*.

88 A reprint of the advertisement appears in *Windows on Henry Street*, 98. Arthur Kellogg, Paul Kellogg's brother, reported to Wald that the ad had a "splendid response from women of all sorts." Arthur Kellogg to Wald, 15 Oct. 1919, *Survey* Associates Papers, SWHA.

89 Wald, *Windows on Henry Street*, 97.

90 Secretary to Miss Wald to Mr. Herbert Lehman, 18 Oct. 1918, Wald Papers, BL. She writes: "Everyone is working in one way or another on the epidemic, those who are not nurses trying to relieve the nurses wherever possible."

91 Wald and Florence Kelley, a resident at Henry Street since 1899, worked together to establish the Children's Bureau in Washington from 1903—when Wald brainstormed the idea at the breakfast table at Henry Street—until the bureau's establishment in 1912. Robyn Muncy titles her chapter on the establishment of the bureau "A [Female] Dominion Materializes." *Creating a Female Dominion*, 38. See also Lindenmeyer, *Right to Childhood*. The bureau was concerned with infant mortality, child labor, and children's health and welfare issues.

92 Wald's invitation must have arrived shortly before the conference began, for her secretary wrote both Felix Warburg and Herbert Lehman—two trusted friends and financial supporters of the house—to inform them of her hasty departure. See Wald (through Dorothy Caffin, her secretary) to Warburg, 26 Mar. 1919, Felix Warburg Papers, AJA, and Wald (through Caffin) to Lehman, 26 Mar. 1919, Wald Papers, BL. The *New York Times* reported her appointment to the position after she had already sailed for France. See "Miss Wald to Attend Convention," 1 Apr. 1919, 5.

93 "Sectional Reports of the Inter-Allied Committee of Red Cross Societies," *Survey* 42 (28 June 1919): 491.

94 "Blessing of Health for All the World: Red Cross to Turn from War to the Amelioration of the Tragedies of Peace," *New York Times*, 4 May 1919, 25. See also Hutchinson, "Custodians of the Sacred Fire," 206–12.

95 "Sectional Reports," *Survey*.

96 Wald, "The Red Cross and the Covenant," *Survey* 42 (31 May 1919): 333.

97 Ruth Gaines tells of the difficulties of coordinating the efforts of the American Red Cross under French leadership during and immediately after the war in *Helping France*. Daniel Rogers cites the American Red Cross efforts in France

as an "expedition" in which the American social workers tried "to reshape France on lines closer to the Europe of their own imagination," socially organized and socially responsible. *Atlantic Crossings*, 368–69.

98   "The Condition of Europe," *Survey* 41 (5 July 1919): 529, 658. After the conference in Cannes, Wald traveled with Florence Kelley and Jane Addams to Zurich for the Women's Congress, at which the Women's International League for Peace and Freedom was founded. See Duffus, *Lillian Wald*, 209, and Daniels, *Always a Sister*, 133. Wald wrote little about this trip or about the congress itself.

99   Stelzle to Wald, Jan. 1919; Wald to Stelzle, n.d., Wald Papers, BL.

100 Wald to Schiff, 8 Oct. 1919; Schiff to Wald, 14 Oct. 1919, Wald Papers, BL.

101 Duffus, *Lillian Wald*, 213–21; resolution is recorded in the *Survey* 43 (25 Oct. 1919): 42, 45.

102 Wald, *Windows on Henry Street*, 63.

103 A historian of the conference points to the antagonism of the two sides as an indication that "they understood the full meaning of each other's positions too well." He posits that two competing ideologies there became evident: one of welfare capitalism and one of a strong union movement, later strengthened by the Wagner Act of the New Deal. Hurvitz, "Ideology and Industrial Conflict." Daniel Rodgers compares the American Industrial Conference with that of Britain and finds that similar forces were at work in labor's postwar losses in both nations. *Atlantic Crossings*, 294–305.

104 Wald, *Windows on Henry Street*, 64.

105 Wald to Eva Clyde Clarke of the *Pictorial Review*, 21 Jan. 1920, Wald Papers, NYPL.

106 "$1,000,000 Nursing Drive," *New York Times*, 29 Feb. 1920, E3.

107 "Pershing Indorses Drive for Nurses," *New York Times*, 14 Mar. 1920, 8. The irony of Pershing's presence at the event was doubtless noticed, given Wald's antimilitarism and her objection to American involvement in World War I.

108 Paul Cravath, the "chief architect of the modern large corporate law firm," was a supporter of Henry Street Settlement, probably through his association with Schiff. Fourteen years after he chaired the Henry Street fund-raising campaign, he rescued the Metropolitan Opera from financial insolvency. See Mendales, "Paul Drennan Cravath."

109 Schiff had recently retired from his long-standing position as president of Montefiore Home, a hospital for chronically ill patients. At his retirement dinner in January 1920, a colleague referred to the preceding forty years as the "Schiff era in American Jewry." Quoted in Adler, *Jacob H. Schiff*, 2:293.

110 Felix Warburg to Charles Schwab, Esq. [acting for Henry Street Settlement], 17 Mar. 1920, Felix Warburg Papers, AJA.

111 Wald, "Jacob H. Schiff," *Survey* 45 (2 Oct. 1920): 20.

112 Wald to Mortimer Schiff [son of Jacob Schiff], 7 Oct. 1920, Wald Papers, BL. On Schiff's death, see Naomi Cohen, *Jacob Schiff*, 245–50.

113 Wald, "Jacob H. Schiff"; Wald to *American Hebrew*, 5 Oct. 1920, Wald Papers, NYPL.

114 The *Jewish Encyclopedia* is now in the public domain, and its original preface can be found at <http://www.jewishencyclopedia.com/preface.jsp>.

115 Glenn, "In the Blood."

116 Wald to Singer, 28 Oct. 1920, Wald Papers, BL. Schiff was one of the largest contributors to Singer's encyclopedia in the late 1890s. See Shuly Schwartz, *Emergence of Jewish Scholarship*, 28, 102.

117 With Schiff's help, Kohut had opened a Jewish girls' school. Unlike Wald, Kohut began public work in Jewish institutions and felt very much a part of the Jewish community. Kohut's family, too, received an entry in Singer's encyclopedia.

118 Singer to Wald, 15 Oct. 1920; Wald to Singer, 28 Oct. 1920; Singer to Wald, 31 Oct. 1920, Wald Papers, BL. In fact, Singer's views on Judaism were closer to Wald's own: he embraced a universalism that shed aspects of traditional Judaism in favor of an "intellectual world religion that would inaugurate an era of international peace." Shuly Schwartz, *Emergence of Jewish Scholarship*, 23. Still, his work for the encyclopedia indicated his commitment to the boundaries around American Jewry.

119 Wald, letter to the editor, *New York Times*, 6 Mar. 1923, 20.

120 Schiff to Wald, 28 July 1919, Wald Papers, BL.

121 Mortimer Schiff, speaking on behalf of his mother, first proposed the idea at the board of directors meeting on 19 Oct. 1921. Minutes, Felix Warburg Papers, AJA.

122 "Schiff Memorial Home for Nurses," *New York Times*, 7 Jan. 1923, X6. Wald includes this dedication in her second book, *Windows on Henry Street*, but does not credit Addams with authorship (110).

123 "Henry Street," editorial, *New York Times*, 10 Jan. 1923, 22.

CHAPTER FOUR

1 The chapter title was taken from the following quotation: "How far I have been and how far I am from realizing the vision I have of the society we might be living in. . . . [The] roots [of Henry Street's work] grow out of the conviction

from the very soil that the race must be cultivated so that civilization may move on out of brutality into the comprehension of the relationship of people to each other." Wald, "On the Presentation of Medals," speech to members of the Rotary Club, 4 Dec. 1923, Wald Papers, NYPL; Wald to Judge Charles E. Hughes, 16 Jan. 1920, Wald Papers, NYPL.

2   Link, "What Happened to the Progressive Movement"; Dumenil, *Modern Temper*, esp. chap. 1. On Progressive hopes for lasting collectivist experiments, see Rodgers, *Atlantic Crossings*, 290–317. In the final chapter of *Always a Sister*, Doris Groshen Daniels considers the fate of the feminist movement after 1920. Otis Graham notes that "the years after 1917 were years of deep attrition against [Progressives'] energy, their assumptions, their leadership, and, of course, their prospects." *Encore for Reform*, 16. He traces the long Progressive Era through to Progressives' influence in the New Deal. I discuss Wald's involvement in the New Deal in chap. 5.

3   The phrase is from Higham's *Strangers in the Land*.

4   Connolly, *Triumph of Ethnic Progressivism*, 163, 199.

5   On social rights, see Cobble, *Other Women's Movement*, 4, 57. For Cobble's superb discussion of the contests between ideologies of social rights versus individual rights, see 60–68.

6   On Wald's 1910 trip to Russia, see chap. 3.

7   While Christopher Lasch labels the "Russophilia" of liberals in the West as "a form of rejection of the gospel of progress," since Russia symbolized a romantic version of "backwardness," Wald's writings suggest instead that she saw Soviet politics as the fulfillment of Progressivism. *American Liberals*, 4, 24–26.

8   Feuer, "American Travelers."

9   Richard Pells writes that in the early 1930s, many Americans found in socialism "a modern version of Christian brotherhood . . . a sense of communal solidarity." *Radical Visions*, 355. The same may be said for Wald and other nonsocialist Progressives in their hopeful attitudes toward Russia beginning in the early 1900s.

10 Wald, *House on Henry Street*, 236–37.

11 On the Friends of Russian Freedom, founded in 1891, see Thompson, "Reception."

12 On this point, see Good, "America."

13 Wald, *House on Henry Street*, 248.

14 Certainly, any study of American support for Russia *and* American support for the Communist Party has to account for the disproportionate number of Jews involved in both causes and across so many generations. Irving Howe

posits that on the early-twentieth-century Lower East Side, poverty and struggle served as the catalyst to translate Jewish religious messianic visions into
political visions of revolution. Though he argues for Jewish radicalism (specifically socialism) to be confronted "on its own terms," he acknowledges that
such radicalism formed a chapter in Jewish immigrants' adjustment to American life. *World of Our Fathers*, 321–24. Tony Michels writes in *Fire in Their
Hearts* of the Jewish socialists' "German-Americanization," as urban Jews
learned socialism from German immigrants and brought to the Jewish labor
movement a Yiddish culture that sought cultural expression and social justice.

15   The correspondence (1908–15) sent to and from Wald by Nicholas Tchaykovsky, his daughter, and his wife can be found in Wald Papers, BL. The quotation
is from Thompson, "Reception," 463.

16   Wald, *Windows on Henry Street*, 254. Even after the 1905 revolution, when
American interest in Russian anticzarism waned, Wald continued to lobby on
behalf of social revolutionaries. Alexis Aladin was a relatively moderate revolutionary and a friend of Tchaykovsky's. In 1907, Wald wrote Aladin a letter of
introduction to Ramsay MacDonald, a Labour government official in England;
hearing that MacDonald spoke at the "Russian Socialist convention," she
hoped Aladin would "find a friend" in him. Wald to MacDonald, 6 June 1907,
MacDonald Papers, PRO. When Aladin later appealed to Wald from England
for support, she decided she should turn to another of her networks and
consulted with Jacob Schiff. They agreed that Aladin needed to have an audience with Claude Montefiore, member of a prominent Anglo-Jewish family.
Because of Jewish sympathy with the cause, she and Schiff felt he was "logi-
cally the one to appeal to." Wald to Aladin, 14 Jan. 1911; Aladin to Wald, 22 Feb.
1911, Wald Papers, BL.

17   Women of America letter, [1917], Wald Papers, BL. On the role of women in
the Bolshevik vision, see Wendy Goldman, *Women, the State, and Revolution*,
esp. chap. 1.

18   Wald tells the story of Breshkovskaia's visit in *House on Henry Street*, 238–48.
Jane Good points out that Breshkovskaia herself downplayed divisions in the
broader revolutionary movement and the role of violence she endorsed in
working toward her own revolutionary vision. Good writes that Breshkovskaia,
an "advocate of socialism and terror," relied on "wildly exaggerated stories"
and chose to ignore "theoretical and tactical issues." In addition, she used the
ten thousand dollars she raised from American audiences in 1905 to purchase
arms for revolutionaries in Odessa. "America," 286, 287.

19   Emma Goldman, *Living My Life*, 1:362.

20   Wald to "Babushka" [Breshkovskaia], 27 Feb. 1919, Wald Papers, BL.

21 Wald, review of *The Little Grandmother of the Revolution: Reminiscences and Letters of Catherine Breshkovsky*, by Alice Stone Blackwell, *Survey* 39 (9 Mar. 1918): 638.

22 Breshkovskaia to Wald, 23 Aug. 1919, Wald Papers, BL.

23 Good and Jones, *Babushka*, 89.

24 Wald to Breshkovskaia, 8 Aug. 1917, Wald Papers, NYPL.

25 Goren, *New York Jews*, 228.

26 Quoted in Adler, *Jacob H. Schiff*, 2:257.

27 Wald to Schiff, 16 Mar. 1917; Schiff to Wald, 17 Mar. 1917, Wald Papers, BL. On Schiff and his sentiments toward the Russian revolutions, see Naomi Cohen, *Jacob H. Schiff*, 242–45.

28 John Reed, "East Side Exiles Stirred by Russian Envoy's 'Welcome Home': Orthodox and Jews Alike Jubilant over Bakhmeteff's Message to Crowds That Swarmed around Henry Street Settlement," *Evening Mail*, 11 July 1917, Wald Papers, BL.

29 Wald, *Windows on Henry Street*, 255.

30 Wald to Schiff, 29 Mar. 1917, Wald Papers, BL.

31 Wald to Bernstein, 15 May [1917], Herman Bernstein Papers, YIVO.

32 "Russian Envoy Thrills East Side," *New York Times*, 10 July 1917, 3; Schiff to Wald, 28 June 1917, Wald Papers, BL. Wald also tells this story in *Windows on Henry Street*, 255–56, as does Irving Howe in *World of Our Fathers*, 326.

33 "Russian Envoy Thrills," *New York Times*. Schiff later wrote privately to Wald that that evening he and his wife had observed "so happy and gratified an expression on your face . . . that it looked to me as if you felt the reception to the Ambassador of new Russia was a heavenly reward to you for years of unselfish efforts in imbuing with courage and confidence in better things to come, those who were so sacrificingly struggling in the Russian darkness in order to reach the light." 11 July 1917, Schiff Papers, AJA.

34 Secretary of State Robert Lansing to President Woodrow Wilson, 12 Apr. 1917, in Baker, *War Leader*, 18; Wald to Morgenthau, 23 May 1917, Wald Papers, BL; Wilson to Lansing, [Apr. 1917], in Baker, *War Leader*, 28–29. Bullard had visited Russia in 1905 and began "muckraking against Czarism" after his return. Thompson, "Reception," 462.

35 "Social Workers Comment on Elihu Root Charges," *New York Evening Post*, 27 Aug. 1917, Wald Papers, BL.

36 Wald, *Windows on Henry Street*, 261. Jane Good discusses how on earlier visits to the United States to raise funds and support, Milyukov, too, was guilty of offering an "interpretation [that] did not prove to be an accurate analysis of Russian reality." "America," 281–84.

37   Soyer, "Soviet Travel."

38   Wald, *Windows on Henry Street*, 261.

39   Ibid., 256.

40   Ibid., 278.

41   Wald to Breshkovskaia, 27 Feb. 1919, Wald Papers, BL. A measure of the importance Wald placed on this letter is the fact that she included it in her second book, *Windows on Henry Street* (259–60). Wald wrote to her friend Arthur Bullard that Breshkovskaia was "not happy" to read Wald's reaction to her letter: "the world seems more complex to her in America than it did in prison or in exile," Wald reported. 12 Mar. 1919, Wald Papers, BL. Wald sent Bullard a copy of her letter to Breshkovskaia, in which he is cited as returning from Russia with evidence of the Bolsheviks' public-spiritedness. Upon reading this, Bullard protested his inclusion, writing that for "Lenin, Trotsky and their satellites, I have no more respect than for the Kaiser and his crew." He attested to the "dishonesty and brutality of the Bolshiviki," calling Lenin's a "Minority Revolution." Whether or not he knew of Wald's opinion, his comments provided Wald a different perspective by a recent visitor. Bullard to Wald, 31 Mar. 1919, Wald Papers, BL.

42   Warburg to Wald, 5 Mar. 1919, Wald Papers, BL.

43   Wald to Warburg, 6 Mar. 1919, Wald Papers, BL. It is important to note that beginning in 1919 Jacob Schiff (who died in 1920) and other prominent Jews were exploring various ways to support anti-Bolshevik leaders in Russia, often through supporting American military intervention. Clearly, Wald's support of the Bolsheviks was not shared by members of elite American Jewish networks. See Szajkowski, *Kolchak*.

44   Soyer, "Abraham Cahan's Travels," 60–61.

45   On "the international Jew," see Higham, *Strangers in the Land*, 277–86. On Jewish support for the Bolsheviks, see Szajkowski, *Attitude of American Jews*. On the culture of Yiddish Communism well into the 1930s, see Howe, *World of Our Fathers*.

46   Wald did not escape suspicion during this red scare. Interestingly, though, the accusations against her attest to her success in distancing herself from Jewish affiliation: critics located her in the secular network of "women dictators" including Addams, Florence Kelley, and others whose prosuffrage and antiwar stands were attacked as antifamily and anti-American. In the Lusk-Stevenson investigation, Wald was cited alongside friends and colleagues as one of the "leaders of the radicals and liberals and apologists for radicals." Quoted in "The Lusk-Stevenson 'Investigation,'" *Soviet Russia*, July 5, 1919, 4.

47   Wald's correspondence during the twenties includes scores of letters regard-

ing Russian affairs. On Paul and Felix Warburg's contributions to the American Relief Administration, see Chernow, *Warburgs*, 290.

48   The Joint Distribution Committee donated over eight million dollars to Russian relief between 1921 and 1923, "more than one-third of it through the American Relief Administration for nonsectarian purposes." Gitelman, *Century of Ambivalence*, 123.

49   Wald to Hoover, 3 Mar. 1923, Wald Papers, BL.

50   Strong was a prominent figure in the history of U.S.-Soviet (and U.S.-Chinese) relations. She was a close friend of Leon Trotsky's. Though no evidence suggests that Wald met Trotsky, her support of Strong's work continued at least though 1925. Wald sent flowers to Strong on a boat departing (probably) for the nationalist revolution in southern China, which Strong covered as a journalist. See Wald to Strong, May 1925, Wald Papers, NYPL.

51   Christopher Davis, "Soviet Public Health," 148.

52   Wald, "Public Health in Soviet Russia," *Survey* 53 (1 Dec. 1924): 270–74.

53   Feuer, "American Travelers," 120.

54   Sheila Fitzpatrick, *Russian Revolution*, 97–109.

55   Weissman, "Soviet Health Administration," 104–5, 108.

56   Duffus, *Lillian Wald*, 242.

57   "Found Russia Improving: Miss Wald Tells of Conditions There after Making Survey," *New York Times*, 14 Jan. 1925, 14.

58   Wald to "Beloveds," 12 June 1924, Wald Papers, NYPL.

59   Wald, *Windows on Henry Street*, 271.

60   Feuer, "American Travelers," 128.

61   Wald, *Windows on Henry Street*, 263. In this, Wald was not unlike muckraking journalist Lincoln Steffens. Though he spoke of Lenin's leadership as a "dictatorship"—and indeed as the inevitable outcome of a revolutionary democracy—he remained hopeful that other nations would learn from the promise of Bolshevik leadership. *Autobiography*, 757–63.

62   According to Wendy Goldman, in 1924 the progressive, women- and child-centered policies of the original Bolshevik vision—the "withering away" of the traditional family in order to liberate women—remained intact. She charts the conservative turn away from such policies beginning in the late 1920s, completed by 1936. Goldman locates the causes for this turn in the state's poverty and Stalin's "increasing reliance on repression." See *Women, the State, and Revolution*, esp. the conclusion. Quote from 342.

63   Wald tells of this frustration in *Windows on Henry Street*, 263. It is especially interesting given Wald's own background and her entrance into the

nursing profession just as American training schools began to specifically target middle-class and upper-class women for training. See also Duffus, *Lillian Wald*, 241.

64 Wald, "Public Health."

65 Wald, *Windows on Henry Street*, 274.

66 The list appears under the heading "Material Sent to Russia, 1925" in Wald Papers, NYPL.

67 American Society for Cultural Relations with Russia (U.S.S.R.), pamphlet, 1928, Wald Papers, BL.

68 Wald to John Wilkie, 18 June 1931, Wald Papers, BL.

69 Kutulas, *Long War*, 48. Kutulas's "Comparison of Subgroups within the Left Intellectual Community of the 1930s" (24) aided my thinking about Wald's political allegiances in the context of her generational, ethnoreligious, cultural, class, and educational/career backgrounds. Wald fits squarely into the Progressive category, and her political choices reflect those of others similarly situated.

70 Wald, *Windows on Henry Street*, 282–84. Wald was joined in this campaign by radicals and Progressives, including Jane Addams, who, while skeptical of the Bolsheviks, advocated official recognition. Wald tells of Addams's role in the campaign in her afterword to *Forty Years at Hull House*; Addams writes about Russia in *Peace and Bread*, 91–106. See also Levine, *Jane Addams*, 237. Like Wald, Addams was not well in the mid-twenties; she suffered a heart attack in 1926 that left her a semi-invalid for her remaining years. She died in 1935.

71 Wald to Roosevelt, 20 Mar. 1933, Helen Hall Papers, SWHA.

72 Jill Conway also makes this point in *First Generation*, 514. I have found no record of Wald's attitude toward the Popular Front, the Spanish Civil War, or the Moscow trials in her personal correspondence from this period.

73 Kutulas, *Long War*, 111. See also *Time*, 14 Oct. 1957, 110, quoted in S. J. Taylor, *Stalin's Apologist*, 355.

74 Wald to "Very Dear Grace" [Abbott], 18 Feb. 1937, Wald Papers, NYPL.

75 Ibid. The Dewey Commission, which grew out of the American Committee for the Defense of Leon Trotsky, held hearings on the charges made against Trotsky in Mexico in April 1937. See Dewey, Stolberg, La Follette, and Glotzer, *Case of Leon Trotsky*.

76 "An Open Letter to American Liberals," *Soviet Russia Today* 6 (Mar. 1937): 14–15, reprinted in Filene, *American Views*, 117–21; Lyons, *Red Decade*, 253–55. Lyons's is a highly partisan source, and for additional assistance I relied on Kutulas, *Long War*, 5, 110–22, and Engerman, "Modernization." Alan Wald

writes in "Memories" of the "aloofness and perplexity" of those who remained committed to Stalinist Russia, their "fear of confronting a truth which was likely to be profoundly disturbing" (440).

77   Christine Stansell links liberal support for World War I with the decline of the "middle ground" and "ambiguity" that had nurtured bohemian culture and its political critiques in New York. That Wald remained opposed to American involvement in the war suggests that her vision lasted long into the twenties, when, as Stansell writes, the "afflictions and catastrophes of modernity" changed the world "inalterably, but not in the ways that the moderns anticipated." *American Moderns*, 315–16, 337. Like the moderns, Wald never anticipated the shape and horrors of the modern world.

78   Wald told the story of this exchange in her speech to children in Nyack, 9 Aug. 1923, Wald Papers, NYPL.

79   Wald to Mr. Joseph Proskauer, chairman, Citizens' Committee for Alfred E. Smith, 8 Oct. 1920, Wald Papers, NYPL; Wald to Smith, 9 Jan. 1920, Wald Papers, NYPL.

80   "Endorse Governor Smith," *New York Times*, 21 Oct. 1924, 7; "Governor Praises Visiting Nurses," *New York Times*, 27 Nov. 1924, 3. In 1923, Wald wrote a speech in support of Smith using a text penned by Belle Moskowitz, Smith's adviser and a "guardian angel of the Lower East Side." The letter highlighted Smith's hard work after the death of his father when he was only thirteen years old, his reverence for his mother, and his love of learning. In addition to her own political reform work, Belle Moskowitz was married to Henry Moskowitz, a client and later an adviser to Henry Street. Their connections highlight the overlapping networks of liberal Jews, politicos, and women reformers. Belle Moskowitz to Wald, 7 Aug. 1923, in Perry, *Belle Moskowitz*, 219–20.

81   See Wald, foreword to *Does Prohibition Work?* The Study was conducted by the National Federation of Settlements' Committee on Prohibition, including Wald, John Eliot, Bruno Lasker, Jane Addams, Paul Kellogg, and others, and directed by Martha Bensley Bruere.

82   "J. W. Davis Praises Smith Acceptance," *New York Times*, 25 Aug. 1928.

83   Wald and Elliott to Paul Kellogg, 29 Sept. 1928, *Survey* Associates Papers, SWHA. Identical letters circulated to many social workers.

84   Wald to Mary R. Smith, 14 Sept. 1928, Jane Addams Papers, SCPC; Wald to Paul Kellogg, 31 Oct. 1928, *Survey* Associates Papers, SWHA; Wald to Addams, 15 Oct. 1928, Jane Addams Papers, SCPC.

85   Addams to Wald, telegram, 20 Sept. 1928, Jane Addams Papers, SCPC. Wald and Addams remained very close, as evidenced by the fact that they vacationed together in Mexico in early 1925. See Duffus, *Lillian Wald*, 243–47.

86   Duffus, *Lillian Wald*, 275.

87   *New York Times*, 1 Nov. 1928, 12. See also "Women to Combat Smith," *New York Times*, 15 Oct. 1928.

88   Wald to Senator George W. Norris, 23 Feb. 1938, Wald Papers, NYPL.

89   Cook, *Eleanor Roosevelt*, 1:356. Cook offers a useful discussion of Eleanor Roosevelt's place in the debate (see esp. 354–60).

90   Cott, *Grounding of Modern Feminism*, 125. Cott discusses the debate over the ERA within the women's movement (see esp. 136–42). It is important to note that the radicalism of the National Woman's Party specifically had well-defined limits. While the party continued to reject sex-based labor legislation into the 1930s, the organization's opposition to the Fair Labor Standard Act in 1938 served as evidence of its increasingly antilabor position. See Storrs, *Civilizing Capitalism*, 195, 241; see also Cobble, 60–66. The party's hostility to African American women's rights also speaks to its conservatism.

91   Sklar, "Historical Foundations," 73. Sklar notes that the work of women in settlements and political organizations before 1930—including efforts to pass and maintain protective labor laws for women—contributed greatly to the creation of the American welfare state.

92   Sklar, "Politically Active Women Opposed."

93   On comparative international definitions of maternalism, see Weiner, Allen, Boris, Ladd-Taylor, Lindenmeyr, and Uno, "Maternalism as Paradigm." On competing definitions in the United States, see Ladd-Taylor, *Mother-Work*.

94   MacDonald to Wald, 26 Nov. 1928, MacDonald Papers, PRO.

95   According to David Marquand, MacDonald's biographer, MacDonald was a "champion of reformism . . . a lonely David pitting his sling against the Goliath of authority." *Ramsay MacDonald*, 227.

96   Margaret MacDonald to Florence Gladstone, 16 Oct. 1897: "At New York we are going to another settlement, whose head we met at Hull House"; Margaret MacDonald to Florence Gladstone, 3 Nov. 1897 (from 265 Henry Street), both in Cox, *Singular Marriage*, 193, 195. On Margaret MacDonald, see Martin, "Gender."

97   Wald, *Windows on Henry Street*, 60.

98   On Wald's antimilitarism, see chap. 3. On MacDonald's antimilitarism, see Marquand, *Ramsay MacDonald*, 179–85. For a comparison between the AUAM and the Union of Democratic Control, see Cook, "Democracy in Wartime." On the Liberal-Labour coalition of the Union, see Swartz, *Union of Democratic Control*.

99   Rodgers, *Atlantic Crossings*, 296–301.

100 See Marquand, *Ramsay MacDonald*, 207–20, 227.

101 Wald to MacDonald, labeled "Private and Confidential," 2 Sept. 1924, Wald Papers, NYPL.

102 Wald, *Windows on Henry Street*, 276.

103 "MacDonald Arrives: Sees Labor Victory," *New York Times*, 16 Apr. 1927.

104 Wald to Vladeck, 26 Feb., 28 Mar. 1927, Baruch Charney Vladeck Papers, TL; Wald to Addams and Smith, 17 Mar. 1927, Jane Addams Papers, SCPC; Villard to Vladeck, 7 Mar. 1927, Baruch Charney Vladeck Papers, TL.

105 Paul Kellogg, "J. Ramsay MacDonald, Spring 1927," *Survey* Associates Papers, SWHA.

106 MacDonald wrote to Wald of his meetings with "your nice Mrs. Schiff and the delightful Warburgs." He said, "The day I spent with the latter I treasure amongst my best memories." 6 Dec. 1927, MacDonald Papers, PRO.

107 Wald to MacDonald, 13 June 1929, MacDonald Papers, PRO.

108 MacDonald to Wald, 25 June 1929, MacDonald Papers, PRO.

109 "M'Donald Appeals to the Whole World to Back His and Hoover's Peace Aims; Disclaims 'Exclusive Understanding,'" *New York Times*, 12 Oct. 1929. This pact is often seen as the culmination of the "feminization of foreign policy" by progressive internationalists. Scores of governments signed the pact to pledge themselves to renounce war as an instrument of foreign policy. See Dawley, *Struggles for Justice*, 323–24.

110 Wald, speech to the Foreign Policy Association, in *Meeting of the Foreign Policy Association*, pamphlet, 11 Oct. 1929, *Survey* Associates Papers, SWHA.

111 "MacDonald Relaxes at Country Home; Leaves City Today," *New York Times*, 14 Oct. 1929, 1.

112 A photo of Wald and her dog Ramsay is in the Wald file at Connecticut College. She wrote to a friend: "The dog, Ramsay MacDonald, is friendly to everyone who looks prosperous, and he has a scent for the beggars who come to town." Wald to John Wilkie, 18 June 1931, Wald Papers, BL. Four years later, Wald wrote to the dog's namesake to share some bad news: "One sad event was that Ramsey [sic] MacDonald left the place one snowy night and despite the fact that his shiny black body was against the white snow he was knocked into the next dog heaven by an automobile. We grieved and grieved and no one of course could take his place." 27 Mar. 1935, MacDonald Papers, PRO.

113 "MacDonald Relaxes at Country Home," *New York Times*.

114 Wald to MacDonald, 30 Jan. 1933, Helen Hall Papers, SWHA.

115 MacDonald to Wald, 7 Feb. 1933; Wald to MacDonald, telegram (copy), 21 Feb. 1933; MacDonald to Wald, telegram (copy), 22 Feb. 1933; Franklin Roosevelt to Wald, 16 Mar. 1933; Wald to Franklin Roosevelt, 20 Mar. 1933, Helen Hall Papers, SWHA. According to Blanche Wiesen Cook, Eleanor Roosevelt sought

out Wald's guidance for her husband on this occasion in order to contribute to the defeat of "isolationism and economic nationalism." "Ardent for peace," Cook writes, Roosevelt "astonishingly gave presidential correspondence to MacDonald's old ally, Lillian Wald." *Eleanor Roosevelt*, 2:49. Such a chronology does not quite fit, however, since Wald initiated the correspondence with Franklin Roosevelt.

116 Raymond Moley, Roosevelt's assistant secretary of state and a delegate to the economic conference, writes that in January, Roosevelt "had agreed . . . to receive a representative to discuss the British war debts." The president was not clear on the identity of that representative until March, when he indicated to Moley that he hoped MacDonald would come to Washington. This corroborates the idea that Wald's February correspondence with Roosevelt and MacDonald influenced Roosevelt's decision. *After Seven Years*, 199.

117 "Roosevelt-MacDonald Statement," *New York Times*, 27 Apr. 1933, 1. The *Times* also reported that Ishbel MacDonald "motored" out to Westport to visit her friend Miss Wald.

118 Marquand, *Ramsay MacDonald*, 734–35.

119 Raymond Moley wrote that because of the president's message, "Europe exploded with resentment and wrath," and "the Conference, in an uproar, refused to continue work." *After Seven Years*, 261. Blanche Wiesen Cook writes that after the conference, "FDR made it clear that international issues were not ER's [Eleanor's] business." *Eleanor Roosevelt*, 2:49.

120 See Raider, *Emergence of American Zionism*, esp. chap. 2, and Maier Fox, "American Zionism." Fox's data indicate that in 1921, Zionist organizations (including the Zionist Organization of America, Hadassah, and B'nai Zion) claimed thirty thousand members; by 1929, that number was sixty thousand (147). On the integration and institutionalization of Zionism into the diasporic identities of Western Jews, see Berkowitz, *Western Jewry*.

121 Svonkin, *Jews against Prejudice*, 180. Mark Dollinger writes that in the 1930s, "second-generation Jews crafted a liberal definition of Americanism, founded upon their optimism for inclusion in public life, their desire to maintain a distinct ethnic culture." This liberal Americanism "valued difference and understood the strengths of a multicultural approach to American democracy." *Quest for Inclusion*, 22, 25. Wald's experiences testify to more narrow definitions of liberalism and liberal Americanism with regard to American Jewish identity. Those who, like her, embraced a Jewishness based on informal belonging, not on religious observance or formal affiliation, were gradually marginalized. Kushner and Solomon's collection, *Wrestling with Zion*, presents historical and contemporary critiques of Zionism.

122   Some qualification must be made, though, in grouping Schiff and his son-in-law. According to one scholar, Warburg, unlike Schiff, "was not intrinsically interested in things Jewish"; his family "considered him somewhat of a universalist." Still, Warburg felt pulled in to Jewish concerns by his father-in-law. After Schiff's death in 1920, Warburg inherited Schiff's "mantle of leadership" in the German Jewish community. Kutnick, "Non-Zionist Leadership," 82, 86, 91.

123   Schiff to Schechter, 8 Aug., 22 Sept. 1907, in Adler, *Jacob H. Schiff*, 2:165-69.

124   On the origins of cultural Zionism in the thought of Ahad Ha-Am, see Friesel, "Ahad Ha-Amism." Friesel notes the fact that many cultural Zionists rejected the secular vision of Ha-Am; Schiff certainly saw cultural Zionism as the key to Jewish religious survival. On opposition to Zionism, see Menahem Kaufman, *Ambiguous Partnership*.

125   Schiff to Judge Julian Mack, 3 Dec. 1917, in Adler, *Jacob H. Schiff*, 2:313.

126   Schiff, "The Need for a Jewish Homeland," *Nation*, 26 Apr. 1919. See also Friesel, "Jacob H. Schiff," and Naomi Cohen, *Jacob H. Schiff*, esp. 229-37. On German Jewish opposition to Zionism, see Kolsky, *Jews against Zionism*.

127   In her biography of Schiff, Naomi Cohen maintains that Schiff's ideological differences with others in the American Zionist movement—cultural and political Zionists—had "little substance." All sides contributed to the development of a Zionist state, and "hardly any Zionist would have denied the security of American Jewry or posited the primacy of Jewish over American loyalty." More important than Zionist ideologies, she believes, were "clashes of personalities" and "competing claims to leadership" within the American Jewish community. *Jacob H. Schiff*, 236-37. Such clashes clearly played an important role. Because my focus is on how Wald and Schiff portrayed their public Jewish identities, I examine how they justified their ideas to the broader public in the language of ideology.

128   Chernow, *Warburgs*, 299-304. Kutnick believes that Warburg's support of Palestine stemmed "from the perspective of the non-Jewish Western culture with which he identified," from the Christian conception of Jerusalem and the rest of Palestine as "different from all other terrestrial places." "Non-Zionist Leadership," 169, 151.

129   Wald, *House on Henry Street*, 254.

130   Wald, *Windows on Henry Street*, 49. The only record of Wald's contributions to Palestine is after Schiff's death, when she contributed one hundred dollars to the American Palestine Campaign in honor of Mrs. Felix Warburg in 1931. Morris Rothenberg, national chairman of the American Palestine Campaign, to Wald, 30 Mar. 1931, Wald Papers, BL.

131 "Miss Wald's Speech to the Judaeans," 13 Dec. 1931, Wald Papers, NYPL. Along with five male doctors, Wald served on the medical advisory board for the American Zionist Medical Unit for Palestine, a Hadassah organization that left for Palestine in 1918. Henrietta Szold, founder of Hadassah, chaired the unit and modeled her nursing school there, at least in part, on Wald's Henry Street. See "Medical Relief for Palestine: The American Zionist Medical Unit for Palestine," flier, ca. 1917–1918, HA; see also Sarah Kussy, "When Hadassah Was Born," *Hadassah News Letter*, 70th birthday of Henrietta Szold commemorative issue, Dec. 1930, HA.

132 Wald wrote to Baruch Charney Vladeck of the Yiddish daily the *Forward* to ask him how best to support Habimah. Wald to Vladeck, 2 Dec. 1927, Baruch Charney Vladeck Papers, TL.

133 Ezra Mendelsohn writes that by the 1920s, "in the face of growing estrangement of American Jews from all forms of Jewishness, hostility to secular Zionism as an illegitimate form of Jewishness was now tempered by an awareness that any form of Jewishness was preferable to no Jewishness at all." *On Modern Jewish Politics*, 85.

134 Dr. Dora Askowith to Wald, 18 Feb. 1917; Wald to Askowith, 20 Feb. 1917, Wald Papers, BL. Askowith had been working on a presentation for the third convention of the Zionist Jewish women's organization Hadassah (summer 1916) on the actions of the American Jewish Congress. See McCune, *Whole Wide World*, 67.

135 Wald to Ochs, 10 Sept. 1929, Wald Papers, BL.

136 Wald to Dock, 10 Sept. 1929, Wald Papers, NYPL.

137 Ibid.

138 Ibid.

139 Rihani to Wald, 20 June 1929, Wald Papers, NYPL.

140 Rihani to Wald, 15, 21 Sept. 1929, Wald Papers, NYPL. The letters indicate that Rihani did not travel to England that year due to his busy schedule of speaking engagements.

141 On reactions to the 1929 riots, see Medoff, *Zionism and the Arabs*, esp. chap. 5. See also Naomi Cohen, *Year after the Riots*.

142 On the Jewish Agency, see Urofsky, *American Zionism*, 297–303. The so-called new historians of Israel challenge the long-accepted idea that the British were hostile to Zionist aims. See, most recently, Segev, *One Palestine, Complete*. MacDonald's letters, quoted here, are evidence of British support, but it is important to note that they were written mainly to reassure Wald's Jewish friends and clients of British support.

143 MacDonald to Wald, 30 Oct. 1930, Wald Papers, NYPL.

144 MacDonald to Wald, 29 Oct. 1930, Wald Papers, NYPL.

145 Wald to MacDonald, 10 Dec. 1930, MacDonald Papers, PRO.

146 Wald to Dock, 10 Sept. 1929, Wald Papers, NYPL.

147 On Warburg's leadership of the Jewish Agency, see Kutnick, "Non-Zionist Leadership," 172–99. Indeed, Warburg had also had a stake in MacDonald's 1929 visit. Just as MacDonald met to negotiate a peace pact with the American administration, spoke to the Foreign Policy Association after Wald's introduction, and met with Wald at Henry Street and in Connecticut, he also spoke with Warburg about the British commitment to its mandate in Palestine. "Premier Promises Order in Palestine," *New York Times*, 12 Oct. 1929, 3.

148 Warburg to Wald, 13 Nov. 1930, Wald Papers, NYPL.

149 Kutnick, "Non-Zionist Leadership," 313–15. Kutnick does not mention Wald's role in this event as a go-between for Warburg, MacDonald, and Roosevelt.

150 Wald to MacDonald, 10 Dec. 1930, MacDonald Papers, PRO.

151 MacDonald to Wald, 5 Jan. 1931, MacDonald Papers, PRO.

152 Wald to MacDonald, 30 Jan. 1931, Wald Papers, NYPL.

153 Those who were fearful of the implications of Jewish nationalism and territory in Palestine include Judah Magnes, Hannah Arendt, Albert Einstein, I. F. Stone, and others. See Kushner and Solomon, *Wrestling with Zion*, sec. 1.

154 Kallen believed Jewish life to be "national and secular." See his "Jewish Life" and "Zionism and Liberalism." See also Toll, "Horace M. Kallen."

155 Wald, "A Social Worker's Viewpoint," *Opinion: A Journal of Jewish Life and Letters* 6 (Aug. 1936): 16–17.

156 Sarna, "Projection of America."

157 Sarna, "Converts to Zionism."

158 Arad, *America, Its Jews*, 18.

159 Wald to Mrs. Rockefeller, 11 July 1934, Wald Papers, NYPL. Doris Groshen Daniels, Wald's most recent biographer, examines this quote in order to elucidate the role of women in antimilitarist and pacifist movements. Indeed, Wald assured Mrs. Rockefeller that both Jane Addams and Mary Beard concurred with her suggestion. See Daniels, *Always a Sister*, 134–35.

160 Arad, *America, Its Jews*, 108.

161 Wise drew much public attention to the cause of Jews and other minorities in Europe, to be sure. Arad discusses the tensions Wise faced and the resultant compromises he made in his positions of leadership, especially with President Roosevelt, in the final chapter of *America, Its Jews*.

162 American Jewish Committee appeal, quoted in ibid., 127.

163 "$250,000 Is Sought for Nazi Refugees," *New York Times*, 24 Nov. 1935, 26. Zosa Szajkowski records the tremendous burden on those who lobbied for aid

to German refugees—the burden to convince American Jews and non-Jews that the rise of Nazism posed an urgent threat. Leaders had to overcome disinterest and inertia in addition to deep-seated fear of anti-immigrant and anti-Semitic reprisals. "Attitude of American Jews."

164 In 1942, Reinhold Niebuhr wrote about the failure of liberalism to come to terms with collective rights. In "Jews after the War," he faulted liberals for assuming "that the Jewish problem was solved when Jews were guaranteed their rights as individual citizens." Certainly Wald fell into this category. *Nation*, 21 Feb. 1942, quoted in Richard Fox, *Reinhold Niebuhr*, 210.

165 Sophia M. Robison, review of *Lillian Wald*, by R. L. Duffus, *Jewish Social Studies* 2 (1940): 109.

166 One recent article that records these ongoing debates is Patricia Cohen, "Essay Linking Liberal Jews and Anti-Semitism Sparks a Furor," *New York Times*, 31 Jan. 2007, E1.

CHAPTER FIVE

1 Wenger, *New York Jews*; Goren, "Anu banu artza."

2 Thomas J. Watson, president, Society of the Genesee, to Edward Miner, 13 Nov. 1931, Edward G. Miner Papers, URL. See also "Miss Wald Honored by Genesee Society," *New York Times*, 26 Jan. 1932, 25.

3 The *New York Times* obituary for Minnie Wald states that she had lived at the settlement "for the last few years" (1 Dec. 1923, 13). Duffus, whose work was largely based on interviews with Lillian Wald, writes that Minnie Wald came to Henry Street "toward the end of the war." *Lillian Wald*, 234.

4 Duffus, *Lillian Wald*, 234. Addams wrote to express sympathy over the death of Wald's mother on 1 December 1923. Jane Addams Papers, SCPC.

5 Duffus, *Lillian Wald*, 248.

6 See Tarrant and Tarrant, *Community of Artists*.

7 I thank Louis Dublin's son, Amos Dublin, and grandson, Thomas Dublin, for providing me with this information (e-mail message to author from Thomas Dublin, Binghamton University, 6 June 2000). I also thank Leo Nevas, who opened his law office in Westport in 1936 and who knew Wald. His knowledge of the town's history was indispensable to my work (conversations with the author, 6 Nov. 2001, 14 Jan. 2002). Other names were mentioned in "The Way Westport Was," *Westport News*, 10 Apr. 1985, 4, Lillian Wald Folder, WPL.

8 Leo Nevas recalls that such agreements ended only after World War II, but even then Jews formed their own country club in 1946 because of their exclusion (conversations with the author, 6 Nov. 2001, 14 Jan. 2002).

9　In 1908, Wald, working with Louis Dublin and her friend (and fellow uptown Jew) Lee Frankel, arranged for Henry Street nurses to deliver health care directly to Metropolitan Life policyholders. According to Wald's biographer, within sixteen months, twelve hundred cities had begun to work out similar arrangements between insurance companies and nursing agencies. See Dublin, *After Eighty Years*, 40–42, and Duffus, *Lillian Wald*, 117–18.

10　Wald to Silver, 9 Nov. 1931, Wald Papers, BL. Silver answered that they could trap muskrats, but nothing could prevent the turtles from eating their desired meals.

11　Wald to MacDonald, 1 Mar. 1934, MacDonald Papers, PRO.

12　Kellogg to MacDonald, 13 Oct. 1937, MacDonald Papers, PRO.

13　Robyn Muncy describes the New Deal as "a culmination of female reform activity since the Progressive Era." *Creating a Female Dominion*, xi. Otis Graham writes that "women progressives almost invariably followed their progressivism straight into the arms of the New Deal." *Encore for Reform*, 169. See also Sklar, "Historical Foundations," and Ware, *Beyond Suffrage*.

14　Wald to MacDonald, 1 Mar. 1934, MacDonald Papers, PRO.

15　Wald to Judge Ben Lindsay, 29 Nov. 1935, Wald Papers, NYPL.

16　Wald to Joseph Levine, 5 Feb. 1934, Wald Papers, CSL.

17　Wald to Addams, 19 Dec. 1934, Jane Addams Papers, SCPC.

18　Allan Nevins, Lehman's biographer, writes that "Lehman always credited Lillian Wald with a large part in introducing him to social problems and hence to public affairs." *Herbert H. Lehman*, 77.

19　Wald to MacDonald, 30 Jan. 1933, Helen Hall Papers, SWHA.

20　Wald, *Windows on Henry Street*, 319.

21　Ibid., 326.

22　Wald to Kellogg, 13 Mar. 1934, *Survey* Associates Papers, SWHA.

23　Wald, *Windows on Henry Street*, 10, 11.

24　Ibid., 324.

25　Grace Abbott, "Miss Wald," review of *Windows on Henry Street*, by Lillian Wald, *New Republic*, 27 June 1934, 190.

26　Wald, *Windows on Henry Street*, 16.

27　Ibid.

28　Ibid., 21 (emphasis mine).

29　Antin was also a Zionist, a stance she saw as completely compatible with her American identity.

30　Wald, *Windows on Henry Street*, 67.

31　See Hart, "Franz Boas."

32   Wald, *Windows on Henry Street*, 67.

33   Florence Finch Kelly, "Henry Street Reflects the World," review of *Windows on Henry Street*, by Lillian Wald, *New York Times Book Review*, 18 Mar. 1934, 4.

34   John L. Elliott, "Home for a Community," review of *Windows on Henry Street*, by Lillian Wald, *Survey Graphic* 23 (Apr. 1934): 195–96.

35   E. R. Wembridge, "Patience on Henry Street," review of *Windows on Henry Street*, by Lillian Wald, *Nation*, 18 Apr. 1934, 451.

36   Melosh, *Physician's Hand*, 139.

37   Wald, *Windows on Henry Street*, 74.

38   Ibid., 77–78. See also More, *Restoring the Balance*, esp. chap. 3. Though Wald was not a physician, More provides a good discussion of the links between maternalist concerns and social activism.

39   Melosh, *Physician's Hand*, 149–50. On the gendered nature of early social science—including the work of Wald, Jane Addams, and Florence Kelley—see Sklar, "*Hull House Maps*." See also Ellen Fitzpatrick, *Endless Crusade*.

40   Cott, *Grounding of Modern Feminism*; Sklar, "Historical Foundations."

41   See More, *Restoring the Balance*, chap. 6; Reverby, *Ordered to Care*, 180.

42   Morantz-Sanchez, *Sympathy and Science*, 309.

43   In May 1939, the nurses' headquarters moved again, to 262 Madison Avenue.

44   Judith Trolander writes that by 1947, "one in eight workers in professional [settlement house] positions had an M.S.W. [masters in social work]." This change was heralded, she asserts, by the new crop of headworkers hired after so many Progressives retired in the late 1930s and early 1940s. *Professionalism and Social Change*, 39.

45   Ibid., chap. 2.

46   Wald to Addams and Smith, 15 May 1933, Jane Addams Papers, SCPC.

47   Hall, *Unfinished Business*, xiii–xiv.

48   Ibid., 7.

49   Ibid., 7.

50   Hall to Wald, 2 Nov. 1933, Helen Hall Papers, SWHA.

51   Hall to Wald, 19 Nov. 1934, Helen Hall Papers, SWHA.

52   Hall to Wald, 27 Oct. 1936, Helen Hall Papers, SWHA.

53   Wald to Wales, 1 Feb. 1934, Wald Papers, NYPL.

54   Wald to Hall, 11 May 1936, Helen Hall Papers, SWHA.

55   Wald to Hall, 19 May 1936, Wald Papers, NYPL.

56   Wald to Ellen Buell, 7 July 1936, Wald Papers, NYPL; Hall, *Unfinished Business*, 7.

57   "Miss L. D. Wald Ill; Is 66 Tomorrow," *New York Times*, 9 Mar. 1933, 15;

"Friends Visit Miss Wald, 66; Roosevelts Send Message," *New York Times*, 11 Mar. 1933, 15; "Henry St. 'Alumni' Mark Anniversary," *New York Times*, 30 Apr. 1933, 30.

58 "To Miss Wald on Her Birthday, March 10th, 1933: A Book of Letters from Friends," Wald Papers, CSL.

59 Josephine Goldmark, "An Appreciation," remarks on Lillian D. Wald broadcast on WMCA, Friday, 10 Apr. [ca. 1935], Wald Papers, NYPL.

60 Wald, *Windows on Henry Street*, 337–38.

61 Elliott to Wald, 10 Nov. 1933, Elliott Hudson Guild Collection, ECA.

62 Wald to "Folks," 27 July 1939, Elliott Hudson Guild Collection, ECA. The letter was forwarded to Elliott by Wald's sister after Wald's death.

63 John L. Elliott, "Lillian D. Wald," *Standard* (newsletter of the Ethical Culture Society) 27 (Oct. 1940), ECA. Rabbi Stephen Wise led a brief public service at Henry Street's Neighborhood Playhouse, where thousands lined the streets to pay tribute to Wald's life work. See "Thousands Mourn for Lillian Wald," *New York Times*, 5 Sept. 1940, 23.

64 Collection of documents from Wald's memorial service, Wald Papers, NYPL.

65 Wald, *Windows on Henry Street*, 56.

66 Sloan, *Last Great Necessity*, 56.

67 Thomas and Rosenberg-Naparsteck, "Sleepers' City."

CONCLUSION

1 On the relevance of, and need for, settlement house social services in contemporary America, see Fabricant and Fisher, *Settlement Houses under Siege*. Fabricant and Fisher emphasize the urgent need for settlements' community building to actively challenge privatization and corporatization, and to allow the project of "social and economic justice to move forward" (290).

2 "Contracts Signed for New Housing," *New York Times*, 28 June 1941, 32. The new, public, low-rent projects accommodated 3,492 families. Obviously standing up for the state's investment, the state housing commissioner "warned against advice that public housing must be sacrificed to the defense program at this time." Helen Hall indicates, however, that the actual building took place after the war. *Unfinished Business*, 237.

3 Papers of Mary (Kingsbury) Simkhovitch, 1867–1951, box 4, folder 64, Schlesinger Library, Harvard University. The event took place on 14 October 1947. Today, the Wald Houses contain several youth services programs of the Henry Street Settlement, including the Boys and Girls Republic, which hosts activities for students aged six to eighteen, such as tutoring, computer training,

counseling, arts education, and recreation; in the summer, it sponsors a summer camp upstate.

4   "Obituary: Lillian D. Wald," *American Journal of Nursing* 40 (Oct. 1940): 1180–82; "In Memoriam: Lillian D. Wald," *Social Service Review* 14 (1940): 755.

5   Oscar Leonard, "Death of an Angel: Lillian Wald, Great Jewish Social Worker, Gave Up Wealth to Serve All Groups in New York's Teeming East Side Slums," *National Jewish Monthly*, Oct. 1940, 48, 59.

6   Glenn, "In the Blood."

7   Glassman and Jacobs, *Biographical Encyclopedia of American Jews*. Wald also appeared in *Who's Who in American Jewry* in 1926, 1928, and 1938.

8   "Join Jewish Academy: Miss Wald and Dr. Klieger Are Named Honorary Members," *New York Times*, 2 June 1933, 14.

9   Stanley Garten, "A Great Jewess—Lillian D. Wald," *Synagogue Light* 4, no. 8 (Apr. 1937): 2, 16, Wald Papers, BL.

10   Tittle, "Four American Women."

11   For the history of Wald's acceptance into the Hall of Fame for Great Americans, see the introduction.

12   Hasia Diner explores the crucial importance of Howe's text to American Jews in "Embracing *World of Our Fathers*." Its appeal (no doubt to multiple audiences) was evidenced by the fact that the book was on the *New York Times* best seller list for thirty-two weeks. Justice, *Bestseller Index*, 157.

13   Importantly, Howe emphasized these aspects while largely ignoring the increasingly important role that Zionism, religious observance, and the Nazi Holocaust were coming to play in American Jewish identity. For a thoughtful discussion of Howe's book and his complicated relationship to Judaism and Jewishness, see Sorin, "Irving Howe's 'Margin of Hope.'" Sorin also notes these absences in Howe's text.

14   Howe, *World of Our Fathers*, 90–94.

15   Andrew R. Heinze notes the lack of historical methodology and rigor in Howe's work in "But Is It History?" On the role of the Lower East Side in American Jewish memory, see Diner, *Lower East Side Memories*, and Diner, Shandler, and Wenger, *Remembering the Lower East Side*.

16   Jacobson, *Roots Too*.

17   Lederhendler, *New York Jews*. The foremost observer of postwar American Jewry is sociologist Marshall Sklare, who observed waning synagogue attendance, declining membership in the Conservative movement, and a revitalization of Orthodox Judaism. He studied American Jews' sentiments toward Israel, correlating those sentiments with a commitment to American Jewish life; the impact of suburbanization and intermarriage on American Jewish

life; and American Jewish education. According to Jonathan Sarna, Sklares's work at Brandeis University, beginning in 1969, "marked the first time that the sociological study of American Jewry achieved recognition as a legitimate university discipline, and the first time that a sociologist of the Jews had ever been appointed to a chair at an American university." See Sarna, "Marshall Sklare," 34. Sklare's books and articles are too numerous to list here. For a useful edited collection (with a chronological bibliography) published posthumously, see Sklare, *Observing America's Jews*. Charles Liebman also contributed crucial observations on assimilation within the American Jewish community and the transformation of American Judaism. His works include *Ambivalent American Jew, Deceptive Images*, and *Choosing Survival*.

18   For use of the term "revival," see, for example, Jack Wertheimer: he juxtaposes the "erosion in Jewish commitments on the part of a significant proportion of the populace" with the "popular religious revival" of these and other groups in *People Divided*, chap. 4. See also Prell, *Prayer and Community* and *Women Remaking American Judaism*. In his masterful work *American Judaism*, Jonathan Sarna writes of the role of "the Holocaust, Israel, feminism, and spirituality" in calls for American Judaism's "Renewal" but states that the meaning of the term "remains elusive" (355).

19   Though they approach this point from different vantages, the following scholars discuss this shift in the American Jewish community: Staub, *Torn at the Roots*; Svonkin, *Jews against Prejudice*; and Glenn, "Vogue of Jewish Self-Hatred."

20   Quotation from Salo Baron, a historian at Columbia (and the first professor of Jewish history at an American university), to a meeting of the American Jewish Historical Society in 1950, in Diner, "American Jewish History," 471–90. In her overview of American Jewish historical writing, Diner writes that the professionalization of the scholarly field of American Jewish history originated in "two interrelated contexts, the traumatic events of the Second World War, and the changed nature of American society—particularly—although not exclusively—educational reforms" that allowed American Jews the freedom to engage in "the open exchange of ideas and the untrammeled search for information about the past" (473).

21   Glenn, "Vogue of Jewish Self-Hatred."

22   Vorspan, *Giants of Justice*, vi, vii, 74; Glenn, "In the Blood."

23   Ibid., 63, 74.

24   Benedict, "Lillian Wald."

25   Yellowitz, "Lillian Wald."

26   The following is a sampling of works that include brief biographical entries on

or mentions of Wald: Sochen, *Consecrate Every Day*; Wagenknecht, *Daughters of the Covenant*; Slater and Slater, *Great Jewish Women*; Taitz and Henry, *Remarkable Jewish Women*; Finkelstein, *Heeding the Call*; Diner, *In the Almost Promised Land*; Eiseman, *Rebels and Reformers*; Diner and Benderly, *Her Works Praise Her*; and Rappaport, *In the Promised Land*.

27 Joyce Antler notes Wald's detachment from Judaism in *Journey Home*; Mary McCune contrasts Wald with more "Jewishly identified women" in *Whole Wide World*, 191.

28 American Jewish historians Hasia Diner and Tony Michels emphasize the few dissenting voices from this synthesis, and write too about the recent interest among American Jewish historians in "the changing meanings that American Jews, or some subset of them, invested into their own history, communities, and place in American society." "Considering American Jewish History," 18. Michels offers a cogent and useful discussion of this synthesis in the introduction to *Fire in Their Hearts*, discussed below.

29 Eli Lederendler finds a "new filiopietism" in American Jewish history, a "new essentialism" in which Jewish ethnicity is found and labeled in "normative (i.e., widely shared) behavior patterns that are deemed to beget, enhance, or preserve difference." "New Filiopietism," 13–14.

30 Daniels's 1989 study of Wald, *Always a Sister*, focuses on her role in women's campaigns.

31 American Nurses Association, "Hall of Fame Inductees," <http://nursingworld.org/FunctionalMenuCategories/AboutANA/WhereWeComeFrom_1/HallofFame/19761982/waldld5595.aspx>; National Women's Hall of Fame, "Women of the Hall," <http://www.greatwomen.org/women.php?action=viewone&id=162>.

32 See Coss, *Lillian D. Wald*, and Robyn Muncy's pivotal text on female networks, *Creating a Female Dominion*. Educational biographies written in this era also pay little heed to Wald's ethnoreligious identity: see Conway, *First Generation*, and Lagemann, *Generation of Women*.

33 More recent books on nursing include Schorr and Kennedy, *100 Years*; Lewenson, *Taking Charge*; and Roberts and Group, *Feminism and Nursing*. According to Deborah Phillips, Wald served as the inspiration for the protagonist of a series of young adult novels entitled *Sue Barton: Visiting Nurse* (published in 1938 and again in 1991). Phillips writes in "Healthy Heroines" that Barton's character demonstrates to young readers that women can be "at the center of debates about the practice of health care, and offer a construction of nursing as a radical alternative to a 'scientific' domination of male professionalism in medicine."

34 "Health Care Hall of Fame Past Inductees," *Modern Healthcare* 34, no. 9 (Mar. 1, 2004): H10.

35 Jossens, "Of Lillian Wald," 102. See also Buhler-Wilkerson, "Bringing Care," and Halamandaris, "Tribute to Lillian D. Wald."

36 Reverby, "From Lillian Wald," 1662–63.

37 D'Antonio, "Revisiting and Rethinking," 283.

38 Barbara Levy Simon writes about Wald's community and its maternalist/ social feminism; Simon endorses it as a model for contemporary social work practices that fully utilize women's innate and culturally specific skills. See "Building on the Romance."

39 Ewen, *Immigrant Women.*

40 Lasch-Quinn, *Black Neighbors,* 29; Hine, *Black Women in White.*

41 Cook, "Female Support Networks."

42 Richards, *Superstars*; Alpert, *Like Bread,* 118–22. Recent conversations in queer theory draw attention to the difficulties in reading the category of lesbian back into history as a static concept. Annamarie Jagose asserts that this project can be seen as "derivative," as "the historical subject is rendered in terms that are not her own, in terms of the modern lesbian." Jagose, *Inconsequence,* 13, 23. See also Moore, *Dangerous Intimacies,* especially her introduction. Both Jagose and Moore respond to one of the most important pioneer books in lesbian history, Lillian Faderman's *Odd Girls and Twilight Lovers.* Faderman's study mentions Jane Addams, whose "romantic friendships" were well known, but not Wald.

43 Benson, "Public Health Nursing," 55, 57. These thoughts were then incorporated into Benson's ambitious book, *As We See Ourselves.*

44 Wald, afterword to *Forty Years,* 431.

45 Ibid., 454, 456.

46 Ibid., 454.

47 Ibid., 459.

48 Riis to Wald, 12 Feb. 1904, Wald Papers, BL.

49 Wald in fact wrote a letter of support for Addams's nomination, praising her as "our great internationalist." Wald to Nobel Prize Committee, 16 Jan. 1923, Wald Papers, NYPL.

50 A sampling of recent historiography of Jane Addams includes Leffers, "Pragmatists Addams and Dewey"; Schott, "Addams and James"; Mahowald, "Classical American Philosophers"; Deegan, "Dear Love, Dear Love"; and Lundblad, "Addams and Social Reform." See also Bush, "Jane Addams," and Deegan and Hill, "Symbolic Interaction," and "Working Hypotheses."

51   See, for example, Elshtain, *Addams and the Dream*; Brown, *Education of Jane Addams*; and Stebner, *Women of Hull House*, esp. chap. 4.

52   Allen Davis, *American Heroine*.

53   Duffus, *Lillian Wald*, 283. Jill Conway recounts the importance of the relationship between Addams and Wald: "In making Jane Addams her model Lillian Wald became her colleague and assumed the role of sage herself." *First Generation*, 222.

54   See, for example, Buhler-Wilkerson, *No Place Like Home*.

55   Wald was one of three women honored in the first Women of Valor project in 1998, sponsored jointly by the Jewish Women's Archive of Boston and Ma'yan: The Jewish Women's Project in New York City. I contributed to the material on Wald in this online exhibit. See material on the Web site of the archive at <http://jwa.org/exhibits/wov/>. See also Wald's entry, which I wrote, in the most recent comprehensive work of scholarship on Jewish women, Hyman and Moore, *Jewish Women in America*.

56   Recently, scholars and communal leaders have begun to comment on this trend and its impact on organized American Jewish life. Samuel Heilman studies the conservative response to modern assimilation within the Orthodox community in *Sliding to the Right*. Ma'yan, a Jewish women's organization, published a report in 2005 that highlighted the continuing challenges faced by feminism in organized Jewish life. See Ma'yan, "Listen to Her Voice," <http://www.jccmanhattan.org/category.aspx?catid=1013>. Eli Lederhendler critiques the misuse of the term "ethnicity" by American Jewish historians, whose work he labels "ideologically 'engaged,'" as its practitioners "viewed their task as not just explaining but also validating the persistence and evolution" of Jewish difference. "New Filiopietism," 3. Tony Michels also critiques American Jewish historians for excluding those who "had an ambivalent, tenuous, or even hostile relationship to things Jewish" (as his subjects, Jewish radicals, did). *Fire in Their Hearts*, 16–19.

57   On the challenges posed by these groups, see Feld, "Sexism Is a Sin." On the transformative work of Jewish feminists on Judaism, see Prell, *Women Remaking American Judaism*.

58   Prell, *Fighting to Become Americans*; Hyman, *Gender and Assimilation*.

59   A sampling of books most relevant to this study include many cited above. Other compelling new works include, but are not limited to, Chevlowe, *New Jewish Identity Project*; Boyarin, Itzkovitz, and Pellegrini, *Queer Theory*; and Boyarin and Boyarin, *Jews and Other Differences*.

60   Chernow, "Waking the Dead," 6.

Bibliography

ARCHIVAL COLLECTIONS

Cambridge, Mass.
  Schlesinger Library, Harvard University
    Papers of Mary (Kingsbury) Simkhovitch
Cincinnati, Ohio
  American Jewish Archives
    Genealogies File—"Schwarz"
    Jacob Henry Schiff Papers
    Felix Warburg Papers
London, U.K.
  Public Record Office
    James Ramsay MacDonald Papers
Minneapolis, Minn.
  Social Welfare History Archives
    Helen Hall Papers
    Survey Associates Papers
New London, Conn.
  Connecticut College, Charles E. Shain Library, Special Collections and Archives
    Lillian Wald Papers
New York, N.Y.
  Columbia University, Butler Library, Rare Book and Manuscript Library
    Lillian Wald Papers
  Columbia University, Oral History Collection
    Reminiscences of Bruno Lasker

Ethical Culture Archives
   John Lovejoy Elliott Papers
   Elliott Hudson Guild Collection
Hadassah Archives
Medical Center Archives of New York–Presbyterian/Weill Cornell
New York Public Library, Manuscripts and Archives Division
   Lillian Wald Papers
New York University, Tamiment Library
   Baruch Charney Vladeck Papers
YIVO Archives
   Herman Bernstein Papers
   Jacob Gordin Papers
   Max Kohler Papers
Rochester, N.Y.
  University of Rochester Library, Special Collections
   Ellwanger and Barry Papers
   Edward G. Miner Papers
Swarthmore, Pa.
  Swarthmore College Peace Collection
   American Union Against Militarism (AUAM) Papers
   Jane Addams Papers
Westport, Conn.
  Westport Public Library
   Lillian Wald Folder, Correspondence and Articles

PERIODICALS

American Hebrew
American Jewess
Boston Jewish Advocate
Charities
Charities and the Commons
Congregationalist
Congregationalist and Christian World
Der Tog
Harper's Bazaar
Hebrew Standard
Jewish Tidings
Modern Healthcare
Nation
National Jewish Monthly
New Republic
New Yorker
New York Press
New York Times
New York Times Book Review
Opinion: A Journal of Jewish Life and Letters
Outlook
Rochester Daily Union and Advertiser
Rochester Democrat and Chronicle

Rochester Historical Society Publication
  Series
Rochester Union and Advertiser
Survey

Survey Graphic
Who's Who in American Jewry
Yidishes Tageblatt (Jewish Daily News)

ENCYCLOPEDIAS AND YEARBOOKS

American Jewish Yearbook 6 (1904–05). Edited by Cyrus Adler and Henrietta Szold.
Philadelphia: Jewish Publication Society of America, 1905.
Biographical Encyclopedia of American Jews. Edited by Leo M. Glassman. New York:
Maurice Jacobs and Leo M. Glassman, 1935.
Encyclopedia Judaica. Edited by Cecil Roth. 16 vols. New York: Macmillan, 1972.
Jewish Women in America: An Historical Encyclopedia. Edited by Paula Hyman and
Deborah Dash Moore. 2 vols. New York: Routledge, 1997.
The Universal Jewish Encyclopedia. Edited by Isaac Landman. 10 vols. New York:
Ktav, 1969.

BOOKS AND ARTICLES

Addams, Jane. Peace and Bread in Time of War. 1922. Boston: G. K. Hall, 1960.
——. The Second Twenty Years at Hull House. New York: Macmillan, 1930.
Adler, Cyrus, ed. Jacob H. Schiff: His Life and Letters. 2 vols. Garden City, N.Y.:
Doubleday, Doran, 1928.
Alonso, Harriet Hyman. Peace as a Women's Issue: A History of the U.S. Movement for
World Peace and Women's Rights. Syracuse: Syracuse University Press, 1993.
Alpert, Rebecca. Like Bread on the Seder Plate: Jewish Lesbians and the Transformation
of Tradition. New York: Columbia University Press, 1997.
Anderson, Bonnie S. Joyous Greetings: The First International Women's Movement,
1830–1860. New York: Oxford University Press, 2000.
Antler, Joyce. The Journey Home: Jewish Women and the American Century. New
York: Free Press, 1997.
——. "Medical Women and Social Reform—A History of the New York Infirmary
for Women and Children." Women and Health: Issues in Women's Health Care
(July/Aug. 1976): 11–18.
Aptheker, Herbert, ed. Selections, 1944–1963. Vol. 3 of The Correspondence of W. E. B.
DuBois. Amherst: University of Massachusetts Press, 1978.
Arad, Gulie N'eman. America, Its Jews, and the Rise of Nazism. Bloomington:
Indiana University Press, 2000.
Badillo, David A. "Incorporating Reform and Religion: Mexican Immigrants, Hull-

House, and the Church." In *Pots of Promise: Mexicans and Pottery at Hull House, 1920–1940*, edited by Cheryl R. Ganz and Margaret Strobel, 31–49. Urbana: University of Illinois Press, 2004.

Baker, Ray Stannard, ed. *War Leader, April 6, 1917–February 28, 1918*. Vol. 7 of *Woodrow Wilson: Life and Letters*. New York: Doubleday, Doran, 1939.

Bellow, Adam. *The Educational Alliance: A Centennial Celebration*. New York: Educational Alliance, 1990.

Benedict, Libby. "Lillian Wald." In *Universal Jewish Encyclopedia*, edited by Isaac Landman. New York: Ktav, 1969.

Benson, Evelyn R. *As We See Ourselves: Jewish Women in Nursing*. Indianapolis: Sigma Theta Tau International Honor Society of Nursing, 2001.

———. "Public Health Nursing and the Jewish Connection." *Public Health Nursing* 10 (Dec. 1993): 55–57.

Berkovitch, Nitza. *From Motherhood to Citizenship: Women's Rights and International Organizations*. Baltimore: Johns Hopkins University Press, 1999.

Berkowitz, Michael. *Western Jewry and the Zionist Project, 1914–1933*. Cambridge: Cambridge University Press, 1997.

Berle, Adolf A. Foreword to *Memorandum in Support of the Candidacy of Lillian Wald of Henry Street for Admission to the Hall of Fame for Great Americans*, 3. New York, 1965.

Bernheimer, Charles S. *Half a Century in Community Service*. New York: Association Press, 1948.

Biale, David. "The Melting Pot and Beyond: Jews and the Politics of American Identity." In *Insider/Outsider: American Jews and Multiculturalism*, edited by David Biale, Michael Galchinsky, and Susan Heschel, 17–33. Berkeley: University of California Press, 1998.

Birmingham, Stephen. *Our Crowd: The Great Jewish Families of New York*. New York: Berkley Books, 1967.

Blaustein, Miriam, ed. *Memoirs of David Blaustein: Educator and Communal Worker*. 1913. New York: Arno, 1975.

Bogen, Boris. *Jewish Philanthropy: An Exposition of Principles and Methods of Jewish Social Service in the United States*. New York: Macmillan, 1917.

Boyarin, Daniel. *Unheroic Conduct: The Rise of Heterosexuality and the Invention of the Jewish Man*. Berkeley: University of California Press, 1997.

Boyarin, Daniel, Daniel Itzkovitz, and Ann Pellegrini, eds. *Queer Theory and the Jewish Question*. New York: Columbia University Press, 2003.

Boyarin, Jonathan, and Daniel Boyarin. *Jews and Other Differences: The New Jewish Cultural Studies*. Minneapolis: University of Minnesota Press, 1997.

Brinkmann, Tobias. "Jews, Germans, or Americans? German Jewish Immigrants in the Nineteenth-Century United States." In *The Heimat Abroad: The Boundaries of Germanness*, edited by Krista O'Donnell, Renate Bridenthal, and Nancy Reagin, 111–40. Ann Arbor: University of Michigan Press, 2005.

Brown, Victoria Bissell. *The Education of Jane Addams*. Philadelphia: University of Pennsylvania Press, 2004.

Buhler-Wilkerson, Karen. "Bringing Care to the People: Lillian Wald's Legacy to Public Health Nursing." *American Journal of Public Health* 83 (Dec. 1993): 1778–86.

——. *No Place Like Home: A History of Nursing and Home Care in the United States.* Baltimore: Johns Hopkins University Press, 2005.

Bush, Malcolm. "Jane Addams: No Easy Heroine." *Free Inquiry* 13 (Fall 1993): 48–49.

Cafferty, Pastora San Juan, Barry R. Chiswick, Andrew M. Greeley, and Teresa A. Sullivan. *The Dilemma of American Immigration: Beyond the Golden Door.* New Brunswick, N.J.: Transaction Books, 1984.

Carnegie, M. Elizabeth. *The Path We Tread: Blacks in Nursing Worldwide, 1854–1994.* 3rd ed. Boston: Jones and Bartlett, 2000.

Carson, Mina. *Settlement Folk: Social Thought and the American Settlement Movement, 1885–1930.* Chicago: University of Chicago Press, 1990.

Casper, Scott E. *Constructing American Lives: Biography and Culture in Nineteenth-Century America.* Chapel Hill: University of North Carolina Press, 1999.

Cassedy, Steven. "Chernyshevskii Goes West: How Jewish Immigration Helped Bring Russian Radicalism to America." *Russian History* 21 (1994): 1–21.

——. *To the Other Shore: The Russian Jewish Intellectuals Who Came to America.* Princeton, N.J.: Princeton University Press, 1997.

Chambers, Clarke A. *Paul U. Kellogg and the "Survey": Voices for Social Welfare and Social Justice.* Minneapolis: University of Minnesota Press, 1971.

Chernow, Ron. "Waking the Dead: The Biography Boom in America." *Culturefront* 9 (Summer 2000): 6.

——. *The Warburgs: The Twentieth-Century Odyssey of a Remarkable Jewish Family.* New York: Vintage Books, 1994.

Chevlowe, Susan. *The New Jewish Identity Project: New American Photography.* New York: Jewish Museum; New Haven, Conn.: Yale University Press, 2005.

Clapp, Elizabeth J. *Mothers of All Children: Women Reformers and the Rise of Juvenile Courts in Progressive Era America.* University Park: Pennsylvania State University Press, 1998.

Cobble, Dorothy Sue. *The Other Women's Movement: Workplace Justice and Social Rights in Modern America.* Princeton, N.J.: Princeton University Press, 2004.

Cohen, Naomi W. *Encounter with Emancipation: The German Jews in the United States, 1830–1914.* Philadelphia: Jewish Publication Society of America, 1984.

——. *Jacob H. Schiff: A Study in American Jewish Leadership*. Hanover, N.H.:
    University Press of New England / Brandeis University Press, 1999.

——. *The Year after the Riots: American Responses to the Palestine Crisis of 1929–1930*.
    Detroit: Wayne State University Press, 1988.

Cohen, Rose. *Out of the Shadow: A Russian Jewish Girlhood on the Lower East Side*.
    Ithaca, N.Y.: Cornell University Press, 1995.

Connolly, James J. *The Triumph of Ethnic Progressivism: Urban Political Culture in
    Boston, 1900–1925*. Cambridge, Mass.: Harvard University Press, 1998.

Conway, Jill K. *The First Generation of American Women Graduates*. New York:
    Garland, 1987.

——. *When Memory Speaks: Reflections on Autobiography*. New York: Knopf, 1998.

Cook, Blanche Wiesen. "Democracy in Wartime: Antimilitarism in England and the
    United States, 1914–1918." In *Peace Movements in America*, edited by Charles
    Chatfield, 39–56. New York: Schocken Books, 1973.

——. *Eleanor Roosevelt*. 2 vols. New York: Penguin Books, 1993–99.

——. "Female Support Networks and Political Activism: Lillian Wald, Crystal
    Eastman, Emma Goldman." In *A Heritage of Her Own: Toward a New Social
    History of American Women*, edited by Nancy F. Cott and Elizabeth H. Pleck,
    412–41. New York: Simon and Schuster, 1979.

——, ed. *Crystal Eastman on Women and Revolution*. New York: Oxford University
    Press, 1978.

Coss, Clare. *Lillian D. Wald: Progressive Activist*. New York: Feminist Press, 1989.

Cott, Nancy. *The Grounding of Modern Feminism*. New Haven, Conn.: Yale
    University Press, 1987.

Cott, Nancy, Gerda Lerner, Kathryn Kish Sklar, Ellen DuBois, and Nancy Hewitt.
    "Considering the State of U.S. Women's History." *Journal of Women's History* 15
    (2003): 145–63.

Cox, Jane, ed. *A Singular Marriage: A Labour Love Story in Letters and Diaries;
    Ramsay and Margaret MacDonald*. London: HARRAP, 1988.

Creek, Alma Burner. "A Family Story: The Ellwangers and the Barrys." *University of
    Rochester Library Bulletin* 35 (1982): 26–39.

Crocker, Ruth Hutchinson. *Social Work and Social Order: The Settlement Movement
    in Two Industrial Cities, 1889–1930*. Urbana: University of Illinois Press, 1992.

Crowley, Alice Lewisohn. *The Neighborhood Playhouse: Leaves from a Theatre
    Scrapbook*. New York: Theatre Arts, 1959.

Crunden, Robert M. *Ministers of Reform: The Progressives' Achievement in American
    Civilization, 1889–1920*. New York: Basic Books, 1982.

Daniels, Doris Groshen. *Always a Sister: The Feminism of Lillian D. Wald*. New York:
    Feminist Press, 1989.

D'Antonio, Patricia. "Revisiting and Rethinking the Rewriting of Nursing History." *Bulletin of the History of Medicine* 73 (Summer 1999): 268–90.

Davis, Allen F. *American Heroine: The Life and Legend of Jane Addams.* New York: Oxford University Press, 1973.

——. *Spearheads for Reform: The Social Settlements and the Progressive Movement, 1890–1914.* New York: Oxford University Press, 1967.

Davis, Althea T. *Early Black American Leaders in Nursing: Architects for Integration and Equality.* Boston: Jones and Bartlett, 1999.

Davis, Christopher M. "Economics of Soviet Public Health, 1928–1932: Development Strategy, Resource Constraints, and Health Plans." In *Health and Society in Revolutionary Russia*, edited by Susan Gross Solomon and John F. Hutchinson, 146–74. Bloomington: Indiana University Press, 1990.

Dawley, Alan. *Struggles for Justice: Social Responsibility and the Liberal State.* Cambridge, Mass.: Harvard University Press, Belknap Press, 1991.

Deegan, Mary Jo. " 'Dear Love, Dear Love': Feminist Pragmatism and the Chicago Female World of Love and Ritual." *Gender and Society* 10 (Oct. 1996): 590–607.

——. "Symbolic Interaction and the Study of Women." In *Women and Symbolic Interaction*, edited by Mary Jo Deegan and Michael R. Hill, 3–15. Boston: Allen and Unwin, 1987.

——. "Working Hypotheses for Women and Social Change." In *Women and Symbolic Interaction*, edited by Mary Jo Deegan and Michael R. Hill, 443–49. Boston: Allen and Unwin, 1987.

Deutscher, Isaac. *The Non-Jewish Jew and Other Essays.* New York: Hill and Wang, 1968.

Dewey, John, Benjamin Stolberg, Suzanne La Follette, and Albert Manning Glotzer. *The Case of Leon Trotsky: Report of Hearings on the Charges Made against Him in the Moscow Trials by the Preliminary Commission of Inquiry.* 1937. New York: Merit, 1965.

Diner, Hasia. "American Jewish History." In *The Oxford Handbook of Jewish Studies*, edited by Martin Goodman, Jeremy Cohen, and David Sorkin, 471–90. Oxford: Oxford University Press, 2003.

——. "Embracing *World of Our Fathers*: The Context of Reception." *American Jewish History* 88 (Dec. 2000): 449–62.

——. *In the Almost Promised Land: American Jews and Blacks, 1915–1935.* Westport, Conn.: Greenwood, 1977.

——. *Lower East Side Memories: A Jewish Place in America.* Princeton, N.J.: Princeton University Press, 2002.

——. *A Time for Gathering: The Second Migration, 1820–1880.* Baltimore: Johns Hopkins University Press, 1992.

Diner, Hasia, and Beryl Lieff Benderly. *Her Works Praise Her: A History of Jewish Women in America from Colonial Times to the Present.* New York: Basic Books, 2002.

Diner, Hasia, and Tony Michels. "Considering American Jewish History." *Organization of American Historians Newsletter* 35 (Nov. 2007): 18.

Diner, Hasia, Jeffrey Shandler, and Beth S. Wenger, eds. *Remembering the Lower East Side: American Jewish Reflections.* Bloomington: Indiana University Press, 2000.

D'Itri, Patricia Ward. *Cross Currents in the International Women's Movement, 1848–1948.* Bowling Green, Ohio: Bowling Green University Popular Press, 1999.

Dock, Lavinia L., and Isabel Maitland Stewart. *A Short History of Nursing.* New York: G. P. Putnam's Sons, 1920.

Dollinger, Mark. *Quest for Inclusion: Jews and Liberalism in Modern America.* Princeton, N.J.: Princeton University Press, 2000.

Dublin, Louis. *After Eighty Years: The Impact of Life Insurance on the Public Health.* Gainesville: University of Florida Press, 1966.

Dubofsky, Melvyn. *When Workers Organize: New York City in the Progressive Era.* Amherst: University of Massachusetts Press, 1968.

Duffus, R. L. *Lillian Wald: Neighbor and Crusader.* New York: Macmillan, 1938.

Duffy, John. *A History of Public Health in New York City, 1866–1966.* New York: Russell Sage Foundation, 1974.

Dumenil, Lynn. *Modern Temper: American Culture and Society in the 1920s.* New York: Hill and Wang, 1995.

Dye, Nancy Shrom. *The Women's Trade Union League, 1903–1920.* Madison: University of Wisconsin Press, 1974.

Eiseman, Alberta. *Rebels and Reformers: Biographies of Four Jewish Americans.* Garden City, N.J.: Zenith Books, 1976.

Eisenstadt, Peter. *Affirming the Covenant: A History of Temple B'rith Kodesh, Rochester, New York, 1848–1998.* Syracuse: Syracuse University Press, 1999.

Elshtain, Jean Bethke. *Jane Addams and the Dream of American Democracy.* New York: Basic Books, 2002.

Engerman, David C. "Modernization from the Other Shore: American Observers and the Costs of Soviet Economic Development." *American Historical Review* 105 (Apr. 2000): 383–416.

Ewen, Elizabeth. *Immigrant Women in the Land of Dollars: Life and Culture on the Lower East Side, 1890–1925.* New York: Monthly Review Press, 1985.

Fabricant, Michael B., and Robert Fisher. *Settlement Houses under Siege: The Struggle to Sustain Community Organizations in New York City.* New York: Columbia University Press, 2002.

Faderman, Lillian. *Odd Girls and Twilight Lovers: A History of Lesbian Life in Twentieth-Century America*. New York: Columbia University Press, 1991.

Falconer, R. A. "Science and Religion as Factors in Progress." *Journal of the Religious Education Association* 8 (1913): 340–44.

Faris, Hani A. "Israel Zangwill's Challenge to Zionism." *Journal of Palestine Studies* 4 (Spring 1975): 74–90.

Feingold, Henry L. "German Jews and the American-Jewish Synthesis." In *German Jewish Identities in America*, edited by Christof Mauch and Joseph Salmons, 8–20. Madison, Wisc.: Max Kade Institute for German-American Studies, 2003.

Feld, Marjorie N. " 'Sexism Is a Sin': Feminism and American Jewish Life in the 21st Century." Paper delivered at the 2006 Biennial Scholars' Conference on American Jewish History. Charleston, S.C., June 5–7, 2006.

Feldman, Egal. "The Social Gospel and the Jews." *American Jewish Historical Quarterly* 58 (Mar. 1969): 308–22.

Feuer, Lewis S. "American Travelers to the Soviet Union, 1917–1932: The Formation of a Component of New Deal Ideology." *American Quarterly* 14 (Summer 1962): 119–49.

Filene, Peter G. "An Obituary for 'the Progressive Movement.' " *American Quarterly* 22 (1970): 20–34.

——, ed. *American Views of Soviet Russia, 1917–1965*. Homewood, Ill.: Dorsey, 1968.

Finch, Minnie. *The NAACP: Its Fight for Justice*. Metuchen, N.J.: Scarecrow, 1981.

Fink, Leon. *Workingmen's Democracy: The Knights of Labor and American Politics*. Urbana: University of Illinois Press, 1983.

Finkelstein, Norman. *Heeding the Call: Jewish Voices in America's Civil Rights Struggle*. Philadelphia: Jewish Publication Society, 1998.

Fitzpatrick, Ellen. *Endless Crusade: Women Social Scientists and Progressive Reform*. New York: Oxford University Press, 1990.

Fitzpatrick, Sheila. *The Russian Revolution, 1917–1932*. New York: Oxford University Press, 1982.

Flanagan, Maureen. *Seeing with Their Hearts: Chicago Women and the Vision of the Good City, 1871–1933*. Princeton, N.J.: Princeton University Press, 2002.

Forcey, Charles. *The Crossroads of Liberalism: Croly, Weyl, Lippman, and the Progressive Era, 1900–1925*. New York: Oxford University Press, 1961.

Fox, Maier Bryan. "American Zionism in the 1920s." Ph.D. diss., George Washington University, 1979.

Fox, Richard Wightman. "The Culture of Liberal Protestant Progressivism, 1875–1925." *Journal of Interdisciplinary History* 23 (Winter 1993): 639–60.

——. *Reinhold Niebuhr: A Biography*. 2nd ed. Ithaca, N.Y.: Cornell University Press, 1996.

Frankel, Lee K. *In the Early Days of Charity*. New York: National Council of Jewish Social Service, 1930.

Freedman, Estelle. "Separatism as Strategy: Female Institution Building and American Feminism, 1870–1930." *Feminist Studies* 5 (Autumn 1979): 512–29.

Friesel, Evyatar. "Ahad Ha-Amism in American Zionist Thought." In *At the Crossroads: Essays on Ahad Ha-Am*, edited by Jacques Kornberg, 133–41. Albany: State University of New York Press, 1983.

——. "Jacob H. Schiff Becomes a Zionist: A Chapter in American Jewish Self-Definition, 1907–1917." *Studies in Zionism* 5 (Apr. 1982): 55–92.

Fromenson, A. H. "East Side Preventative Work." 1904. In *Trends and Issues in Jewish Social Welfare in the United States, 1899–1952*, edited by Robert Morris and Michael Freund, 118–23. Philadelphia: Jewish Publication Society, 1966.

Gaines, Ruth. *Helping France: The Red Cross in the Devastated Area*. New York: E. P. Dutton, 1919.

Gilman, Sander L. *Freud, Race, and Gender*. Princeton, N.J.: Princeton University Press, 1993.

——. *The Jew's Body*. New York: Routledge, 1991.

Ginzberg, Lori D. *Untidy Origins: A Story of Woman's Rights in Antebellum New York*. Chapel Hill: University of North Carolina Press, 2005.

Gitelman, Zvi. *A Century of Ambivalence: The Jews of Russia and the Soviet Union, 1881 to the Present*. New York: YIVO Institute for Jewish Research, 1988.

Gleason, Philip. "American Identity and Americanization." In *Harvard Encyclopedia of American Ethnic Groups*, edited by Stephan Thernstrom, Ann Orlov, and Oscar Handlin, 38–47. Cambridge, Mass.: Harvard University Press, Belknap Press, 1980.

Glenn, Susan A. "In the Blood? Consent, Descent, and the Ironies of Jewish Identity." *Jewish Social Studies* 8 (Spring 2002): 139–52.

——. "The Vogue of Jewish Self-Hatred in Post–World War II America." *Jewish Social Studies* 12 (Spring/Summer 2006): 95–136.

Goldman, Emma. *Living My Life*. 2 vols. New York: Dover, 1931.

Goldman, Wendy Z. *Women, the State, and Revolution: Soviet Family Policy and Social Life, 1917–1936*. Cambridge: Cambridge University Press, 1993.

Goldstein, Eric. *The Price of Whiteness: Jews, Race, and American Identity*. Princeton, N.J.: Princeton University Press, 2006.

Good, Jane E. "America and the Russian Revolutionary Movement, 1888–1905." *Russian Review* 41 (1982): 273–87.

Good, Jane E., and David R. Jones. *Babushka: The Life of the Russian Revolutionary Ekaterina K. Breshko-Breshkovskaia, 1844–1934*. Newtonville, Mass.: Oriental Research Partners, 1991.

Goodman, Cary. *Choosing Sides: Playground and Street Life on the Lower East Side.* New York: Schocken Books, 1979.

Gordon, Linda. "If the Progressives Were Advising Us Today, Should We Listen?" *Journal of the Gilded Age and Progressive Era* 1 (Apr. 2002): 109–21.

Gordon, Milton. *Assimilation in American Life: The Role of Race, Religion and National Origins.* New York: Oxford University Press, 1964.

Gordon, Neve, and Gabriel Motzkin. "Between Universalism and Particularism: The Origins of the Philosophy Department at Hebrew University and the Zionist Project." *Jewish Social Studies* 9 (Winter 2003): 99–122.

Goren, Arthur Aryeh. " 'Anu banu artza' in America: The Americanization of the *Halutz* Ideal." In *Envisioning Israel: The Changing Ideals and Images of North American Jews,* edited by Allon Gal, 81–116. Detroit: Wayne State University Press, 1996.

———. *New York Jews and the Quest for Community: The Kehillah Experiment, 1908–1922.* New York: Columbia University Press, 1970.

Graham, Otis L., Jr. *An Encore for Reform: The Old Progressives and the New Deal.* New York: Oxford University Press, 1967.

Greenberg, Cheryl Lynn. *Troubling the Waters: Black-Jewish Relations in the American Century.* Princeton, N.J.: Princeton University Press, 2006.

Gurock, Jeffrey S. *American Jewish Orthodoxy in Historical Perspective.* Jersey City, N.J.: Ktav, 1996.

Gustafson, Melanie. "Jane Addams and the Construction of Race and Gender in the Progressive Party, 1912." Paper presented at the Berkshire Conference on the History of Women, Chapel Hill, N.C., 7 June 1996.

Halamandaris, Val J. "A Tribute to Lillian D. Wald." *Caring: National Association for Home Care Magazine* 11 (Sept. 1992): 100.

Hall, Helen. *Unfinished Business in Neighborhood and Nation: A Firsthand Account by the Former Director of the Henry Street Settlement.* New York: Macmillan, 1971.

Hamilton, Nigel. *Biography: A Brief History.* Cambridge, Mass.: Harvard University Press, 2007.

Handlin, Oscar. *Race and Nationality in American Life.* Boston: Little, Brown, 1948.

Handy, Robert T., ed. *The Social Gospel in America, 1870–1920: Gladden, Ely, Rauschenbusch.* New York: Oxford University Press, 1966.

Hart, Mitchell B. "Franz Boas as German, American, and Jew." In *German Jewish Identities in America,* edited by Christof Mauch and Joseph Salmons, 88–105. Madison, Wisc.: Max Kade Institute for German-American Studies, 2003.

Hawley, Natalie F. "The Labor Movement in Rochester, 1880–1898." Master's thesis, Department of History, University of Rochester, 1948.

Heilman, Samuel. *Sliding to the Right: The Contest for the Future of American Jewish Orthodoxy*. Berkeley: University of California Press, 2006.

Heinze, Andrew R. "But Is It History? *World of Our Fathers* as a Historicized Text." *American Jewish History* 88 (2000): 495–510.

Herzog, Dagmar. *Intimacy and Exclusion: Religious Politics in Pre-revolutionary Baden*. Princeton, N.J.: Princeton University Press, 1996.

Hewitt, Nancy A. *Women's Activism and Social Change: Rochester, New York, 1822–1872*. Ithaca, N.Y.: Cornell University Press, 1984.

Higham, John. *Strangers in the Land: Patterns of American Nativism, 1860–1925*. 2nd ed. New Brunswick, N.J.: Rutgers University Press, 1992.

Hine, Darlene Clark. *Black Women in White: Racial Conflict and Cooperation in the Nursing Profession, 1890–1950*. Bloomington: Indiana University Press, 1989.

Hofstadter, Richard. *The Age of Reform: From Bryan to F.D.R.* New York: Vintage Books, 1955.

Hopkins, Charles Howard. *The Rise of the Social Gospel Movement in American Protestantism, 1865–1915*. New Haven: Yale University Press, 1940.

Howe, Irving. *World of Our Fathers: The Journey of the East European Jews to America and the Life They Found and Made*. 2nd ed. New York: Schocken Books, 1989.

Hughes, Langston. *Fight for Freedom: The Story of the NAACP*. New York: W. W. Norton, 1962.

Hurvitz, Haggai. "Ideology and Industrial Conflict: President Wilson's First Industrial Conference of October 1919." *Labor History* 18 (Fall 1977): 509–24.

Hutchinson, John F. " 'Custodians of the Sacred Fire': The ICRC and the Postwar Reorganisation of the International Red Cross." In *International Health Organisations and Movements, 1918–1939*, edited by Paul Weindling, 17–35. Cambridge: Cambridge University Press, 1995.

Hyman, Paula E. *Gender and Assimilation in Modern Jewish History: The Roles and Representation of Women*. Seattle: University of Washington Press, 1995.

——. "Gender and the Shaping of Modern Jewish Identities." *Jewish Social Studies* 8 (Winter/Spring 2002): 153–61.

Itzkovitz, Daniel. "Race and Jews in America: An Introduction." *Shofar: An Interdisciplinary Journal of Jewish Studies* 23 (Summer 2005): 1–8.

Jacobson, Matthew Frye. *Roots Too: White Ethnic Revival in Post–Civil Rights America*. Cambridge, Mass.: Harvard University Press, 2006.

——. *Whiteness of a Different Color: European Immigrants and the Alchemy of Race*. Cambridge, Mass.: Harvard University Press, 1998.

Jagose, Annamarie. *Inconsequence: Lesbian Representation and the Logic of Sexual Sequence*. Ithaca, N.Y.: Cornell University Press, 2002.

James, Janet Wilson, ed. *A Lavinia Dock Reader*. New York: Garland, 1985.

Johnson, Donald. *The Challenge to American Freedoms: World War I and the Rise of the American Civil Liberties Union*. Lexington: University of Kentucky Press, 1963.

Jones, Jacqueline. *American Work: Four Centuries of Black and White Labor*. New York: W. W. Norton, 1998.

Jordan, Helene Jamieson. *Cornell University–New York Hospital School of Nursing, 1877–1952*. New York: Society of the New York Hospital, 1952.

Jossens, Marilyn O. R. "Of Lillian Wald, Community Health Nursing Education, and Health Care Reform." *Public Health Nursing* 13 (Apr. 1996): 102.

Justice, Keith L. *Bestseller Index: All Books, by Author, on the List of "Publishers Weekly" and the "New York Times" through 1990*. Jefferson, N.C.: McFarland, 1998.

Kallen, Horace. *Culture and Democracy in the United States*. New York: Boni and Liveright, 1924.

———. "Jewish Life Is National and Secular." In *The Zionist Idea: A Historical Analysis and Reader*, edited by Arthur Hertzberg, 526. New York: Athenaeum, 1959.

———. "Zionism and Liberalism." In *The Zionist Idea: A Historical Analysis and Reader*, edited by Arthur Hertzberg, 528. New York: Athenaeum, 1959.

Kaplan, Marion A. *The Making of the Jewish Middle Class: Women, Family, and Identity in Imperial Germany*. New York: Oxford University Press, 1991.

Kaufman, David. *Shul with a Pool: The "Synagogue Center" in American Jewish History*. Hanover, N.H.: University Press of New England, 1999.

Kaufman, Debra. "Measuring Jewishness in America: Some Feminist Concerns." *NASHIM: A Journal of Jewish Women's Studies and Gender Issues* 10 (Fall 2006): 84–98.

Kaufman, Menahem. *An Ambiguous Partnership: Non-Zionists and Zionists in America, 1939–1948*. Detroit: Wayne State University Press, 1991.

Kazal, Russell A. "Revisiting Assimilation: The Rise, Fall, and Reappraisal of a Concept in American Ethnic History." *American Historical Review* 100 (Apr. 1995): 437–71.

Keller, Morton. *Regulating a New Society: Public Policy and Social Change in America, 1900–1933*. Cambridge, Mass.: Harvard University Press, 1994.

Kolata, Gina Bari. *Flu: The Story of the Great Influenza Pandemic of 1918 and the Search for the Virus that Caused It*. New York: Farrar, Straus, and Giroux, 1999.

Kolsky, Thomas A. *Jews against Zionism: The American Council for Judaism, 1942–1948*. Philadelphia: Temple University Press, 1990.

Kunzel, Regina G. *Fallen Women, Problem Girls: Unmarried Mothers and the Professionalization of Social Work, 1890–1945*. New Haven, Conn.: Yale University Press, 1993.

Kushner, Tony, and Alisa Solomon, eds. *Wrestling with Zion: Progressive Jewish-American Responses to the Israeli-Palestinian Conflict*. New York: Grove, 2003.

Kutnick, Jerome M. "Non-Zionist Leadership: Felix M. Warburg, 1929–1937."
     Ph.D. diss., Brandeis University, 1983.

Kutulas, Judy. *The Long War: The Intellectual People's Front and Anti-Stalinism, 1930–
     1940.* Durham, N.C.: Duke University Press, 1995.

Ladd-Taylor, Molly. *Mother-Work: Women, Child Welfare and the State, 1890–1930.*
     Urbana: University of Illinois Press, 1993.

——. "Toward Defining Maternalism in U.S. History." *Journal of Women's History* 5
     (Fall 1993): 110–13.

Lafer, Gordon. "Universalism and Particularism in Jewish Law: Making Sense of
     Political Loyalties." In *Jewish Identity*, edited by David Theo Goldberg and
     Michael Krausz, 177–211. Philadelphia: Temple University Press, 1993.

Lagemann, Ellen Condliffe. *A Generation of Women: Education in the Lives of
     Progressive Reformers.* Cambridge, Mass.: Harvard University Press, 1979.

Lasch, Christopher. *The American Liberals and the Russian Revolution.* New York:
     Columbia University Press, 1962.

——. *The New Radicalism in America: The Intellectual as a Social Type, 1889–1963.*
     New York: Alfred A. Knopf, 1965.

Lasch-Quinn, Elizabeth. *Black Neighbors: Race and the Limits of Reform in the
     American Settlement House Movement, 1890–1945.* Chapel Hill: University of
     North Carolina Press, 1993.

Lederhendler, Eli. "The New Filiopietism, or Toward a New History of Jewish
     Immigration to America." *American Jewish History* 93 (Mar. 2007): 1–20.

——. *New York Jews and the Decline of Urban Ethnicity, 1950–1970.* Syracuse:
     Syracuse University Press, 2001.

Leffers, M. Regina. "Pragmatists Jane Addams and John Dewey Inform the Ethic of
     Care." *Hypatia* 8 (Spring 1993): 64–77.

Lepore, Jill. "Historians Who Love Too Much: Reflections on Microhistory and
     Biography." *Journal of American History* 88 (June 2001): 129–44.

Levine, Daniel. *Jane Addams and the Liberal Tradition.* Madison: State Historical
     Society of Wisconsin, 1971.

Lewenson, Sandra Beth. *Taking Charge: Nursing, Suffrage, and Feminism in America,
     1873–1920.* New York: Garland, 1993.

Lewis, David Levering. *W. E. B. Du Bois: Biography of a Race, 1868–1919.* New York:
     Henry Holt, 1993.

Liebman, Charles. *The Ambivalent American Jew: Politics, Religion, and Family in
     American Jewish Life.* Philadelphia: Jewish Publication Society of America, 1973.

——. *Deceptive Images: Toward a Redefinition of American Judaism.* New Brunswick,
     N.J.: Transaction Books, 1988.

Liebman, Charles, with Bernard Susser. *Choosing Survival: Strategies for a Jewish Future*. New York: Oxford University Press, 1999.

Lindenbaum, Joanna, Ilan Stavans, and Susan Chevlowe, eds. *The Jewish Identity Project: New American Photography*. New Haven, Conn.: Yale University Press, 2005.

Lindenmeyer, Kriste. *"A Right to Childhood": The U.S. Children's Bureau and Child Welfare, 1912–46*. Urbana: University of Illinois Press, 1997.

Link, Arthur S. "What Happened to the Progressive Movement in the 1920's?" *American Historical Review* 64 (July 1959): 833–51.

Lissak, Rivka Shpak. *Pluralism and Progressives: Hull House and the New Immigrants, 1890–1919*. Chicago: University of Chicago Press, 1989.

Lundblad, Karen Shafer. "Jane Addams and Social Reform: A Role Model for the 1990s." *Social Work* 40 (Sept. 1995): 661–69.

Lyons, Eugene. *The Red Decade: The Stalinist Penetration of America*. New York: Bobbs-Merrill, 1941.

Mahowald, Mary B. "What Classical American Philosophers Missed: Jane Addams, Critical Pragmatism, and Cultural Feminism." *Journal of Value Inquiry* 31 (1997): 39–54.

Mallet, Eleanor. *Tevye's Grandchildren: Rediscovering a Jewish Identity*. Cleveland: Pilgrim, 2004.

Mamet, David. *The Wicked Son: Anti-Semitism, Self-Hatred, and the Jews*. New York: Schocken Books, 2006.

Marchand, C. Roland. *The American Peace Movement and Social Reform, 1898–1918*. Princeton, N.J.: Princeton University Press, 1972.

Marquand, David. *Ramsay MacDonald*. London: Jonathan Cape, 1977.

Marshall, Louis. "The Need of a Distinctly Jewish Tendency in the Conduct of Jewish Educational Institutions." *Fifth Biennial Session, the National Conference of Jewish Charities in the United States, 1908*, 112–22.

——. *Report of the Commission of Immigration of the State of New York*. Albany: J. B. Lyon, 1909.

Martin, Jane. "Gender, the City and the Politics of Schooling: Towards a Collective Biography of Women 'Doing Good' as Public Moralists in London." *Gender and Education* 17 (May 2005): 143–63.

May, Henry F. *Protestant Churches and Industrial America*. New York: Harper, 1949.

McClymer, John F. "Gender and the 'American Way of Life': Women in the Americanization Movement." *Journal of American Ethnic History* 10 (Spring 1991): 3–20.

McCune, Mary. *"The Whole Wide World without Limits": International Relief, Gender*

Politics, and American Jewish Women, 1893–1930. Detroit: Wayne State University Press, 2005.

McGerr, Michael. *A Fierce Discontent: The Rise and Fall of the Progressive Movement in America.* New York: Free Press, 2003.

McKelvey, Blake. "The Men's Clothing Industry in Rochester's History." *Rochester History* 3 (July 1960): 1–20.

———. *Rochester on the Genesee: The Growth of a City.* 2nd ed. Syracuse: Syracuse University Press, 1993.

Medoff, Rafael. *Zionism and the Arabs: An American Jewish Dilemma, 1898–1948.* Westport, Conn.: Praeger, 1997.

Melnick, Jeff. " 'Soul.' " *Shofar: An Interdisciplinary Journal of Jewish Studies* 24 (Summer 2006): 13–21.

Melosh, Barbara. *"The Physician's Hand": Work Culture and Conflict in American Nursing.* Philadelphia: Temple University Press, 1982.

Memorandum in Support of the Candidacy of Lillian Wald of Henry Street for Admission to the Hall of Fame for Great Americans. New York, 1965.

Mendales, Richard E. "Paul Drennan Cravath." In *American National Biography,* edited by John Garraty and Mark Carnes, 689–90. New York: Oxford University Press, 1999.

Mendelsohn, Ezra. *On Modern Jewish Politics.* New York: Oxford University Press, 1993.

Mervis, Leonard J. "The Social Justice Movement and the American Reform Rabbi." *American Jewish Archives* 7 (June 1955): 171–230.

Michels, Tony. *A Fire in Their Hearts: Yiddish Socialists in New York.* Cambridge, Mass.: Harvard University Press, 2005.

Milkis, Sidney M., and Daniel J. Tichenor. " 'Direct Democracy' and Social Justice: The Progressive Party Campaign of 1912." *Studies in American Political Development* 8 (Fall 1994): 282–340.

Moley, Raymond. *After Seven Years.* New York: Harper and Brothers, 1939.

Moore, Lisa L. *Dangerous Intimacies: Toward a Sapphic History of the British Novel.* Durham, N.C.: Duke University Press, 1997.

Morantz-Sanchez, Regina Markell. *Sympathy and Science: Women Physicians in American Medicine.* New York: Oxford University Press, 1985.

More, Ellen S. *Restoring the Balance: Women Physicians and the Profession of Medicine, 1850–1995.* Cambridge, Mass.: Harvard University Press, 1999.

Muncy, Robyn. *Creating a Female Dominion in American Reform, 1890–1935.* New York: Oxford University Press, 1991.

Nadell, Pamela S. "On Their Own Terms: America's Jewish Women, 1954–2004." *American Jewish History* 91 (2003): 389–404.

National Council of Jewish Women. *Proceedings of the First Convention of the National Council of Jewish Women, November 15–19, 1896*. Philadelphia: Jewish Publication Service of America, 1897.

Nevins, Allan. *Herbert H. Lehman and His Era*. New York: Charles Scribner's Sons, 1963.

Ott, Maureen. "An Analysis of the Friendship of Lavinia Dock and Lillian Wald, 1898–1930." Master of Science thesis, Community Health Nursing, D'Youville College, Buffalo, N.Y., 1994.

Pells, Richard. *Radical Visions and American Dreams: Culture and Social Thought in the Depression Years*. New York: Harper and Row, 1973.

Perry, Elizabeth Israels. *Belle Moskowitz: Feminine Politics and the Exercise of Power in the Age of Alfred E. Smith*. New York: Routledge, 1992.

Peters, Madison C. *The Jews in America: A Short Story of Their Part in the Building of the Republic*. Philadelphia: John C. Winston, 1905.

———. *Justice to the Jew: The Story of What He Has Done for the World*. New York: McClure, 1908.

Phillips, Deborah. "Healthy Heroines: Sue Barton, Lillian Wald, Lavinia Lloyd Dock and the Henry Street Settlement." *Journal of American Studies* 33 (1999): 65–82.

Polacheck, Hilda Satt. *I Came a Stranger: The Story of a Hull House Girl*. Urbana: University of Illinois Press, 1989.

Prell, Riv-Ellen. *Fighting to Become Americans: Jews, Gender, and the Anxiety of Assimilation*. Boston: Beacon, 1999.

———. *Prayer and Community: The Havurah in American Judaism*. Detroit: Wayne State University Press, 1989.

———, ed. *Women Remaking American Judaism*. Detroit: Wayne State University Press, 2007.

Raider, Mark A. *The Emergence of American Zionism*. New York: New York University Press, 1998.

———. "Race and Nationality in American Life: The Jews in the Mind of the Dillingham Commission." In *The Proceedings of the 19th Annual Conference of the Middle Atlantic Historical Association of Catholic Colleges and Universities* vol. 8, edited by Margaret E. Craft, 90–98. 1993.

Rappaport, Doreen. *In the Promised Land: Lives of Jewish Americans*. New York: HarperCollins, 2005.

Ratner, Sidney. "Horace M. Kallen and Cultural Pluralism." In *The Legacy of Horace M. Kallen*, edited by Milton R. Konvitz, 48–63. Rutherford, N.J.: Fairleigh Dickinson University Press, 1987.

Reisch, Michael, and Janice Andrews Reisch. *The Road Not Taken: A History of Radical Social Work in the United States*. New York: Routledge, 2001.

Resnick, Allan Edward. "Lillian Wald: The Years at Henry Street." Ph.D. diss., University of Wisconsin, Madison, 1973.

Reverby, Susan M. "From Lillian Wald to Hillary Rodham Clinton: What Will Happen to Public Health Nursing?" *American Journal of Public Health* 83 (Dec. 1993): 1662–63.

———. *Ordered to Care: The Dilemma of American Nursing, 1850–1945.* Cambridge: Cambridge University Press, 1987.

Richards, Dell. *Superstars: Twelve Lesbians Who Changed the World.* New York: Caroll and Graf, 1993.

Riddle, J. B. "Religion in the Settlement." *Journal of the Religious Education Association* 8 (1913): 348–50.

Rischin, Moses. *The Promised City: New York's Jews, 1870–1914.* Cambridge, Mass.: Harvard University Press, 1962.

Roberts, Joan I., and Thetis M. Group. *Feminism and Nursing: An Historical Perspective on Power, Status, and Political Activism in the Nursing Profession.* Westport, Conn.: Praeger, 1995.

Rochelson, Meri-Jane. Introduction to *Children of the Ghetto: A Study of a Peculiar People,* by Israel Zangwill, 11–44. Detroit: Wayne State University Press, 1998.

Rodgers, Daniel T. *Atlantic Crossings: Social Politics in a Progressive Age.* Cambridge, Mass.: Harvard University Press, Belknap Press, 1998.

———. "In Search of Progressivism." *Reviews in American History* 10 (1982): 113–32.

Rogow, Faith. *Gone to Another Meeting: A History of the National Council of Jewish Women.* Tuscaloosa: University of Alabama Press, 1993.

Rose, Elizabeth. "From Sponge Cake to *Hamentashen*: Jewish Identity in a Jewish Settlement House, 1885–1952." *Journal of American Ethnic History* 13 (Spring 1994): 3–23.

Rosen, Ruth, ed. *The Mamie Papers.* New York: Feminist Press, 1977.

Rosenberg, Stuart E. *The Jewish Community in Rochester, 1843–1925.* New York: Columbia University Press, 1954.

Rupp, Leila J. *Worlds of Women: The Making of an International Women's Movement.* Princeton, N.J.: Princeton University Press, 1997.

Sarna, Jonathan. *American Judaism: A History.* New Haven, Conn.: Yale University Press, 2004.

———. "Converts to Zionism in the American Reform Movement." In *Zionism and Religion,* edited by Shmuel Almog, Jehuda Reinharz, and Anita Shapira, 188–203. Hanover, N.H.: Brandeis University Press, 1998.

———. "Marshall Sklare (1921–1922)." *Proceedings of the American Academy for Jewish Research* 58 (1992): 33–35.

———. "A Projection of America as It Ought to Be: Zion in the Mind's Eye of

American Jews." In *Envisioning Israel: The Changing Ideals and Images of North American Jews*, edited by Allon Gal, 41–59. Detroit: Wayne State University Press, 1996.

Schneiderman, Rose, with Lucy Goldthwaite. *All for One.* New York: Paul Eriksson, 1967.

Schofield, Ann. "The Uprising of the 20,000: The Making of a Labor Legend." In *A Needle, a Bobbin, a Strike: Women Needleworkers in America*, edited by Joan M. Jensen and Sue Davidson, 167–82. Philadelphia: Temple University Press, 1984.

Schorr, Thelma M., and Maureen Shawn Kennedy. *100 Years of American Nursing: Celebrating a Century of Caring.* Philadelphia: Lippincott Williams and Wilkins, 1999.

Schott, Linda. "Jane Addams and William James on Alternatives to War." *Journal of the History of Ideas* 54 (Apr. 1993): 241–54.

Schwartz, Alissa. "Americanization and Cultural Preservation in Seattle's Settlement House: A Jewish Adaptation of the Anglo-American Model of Settlement Work." *Journal of Sociology and Social Welfare* 26, no. 3 (Sept. 1999): 25–45.

Schwartz, Shuly Rubin. *The Emergence of Jewish Scholarship in America: The Publication of the "Jewish Encyclopedia."* Cincinnati: Hebrew Union College Press, 1991.

Scobey, David. "Anatomy of the Promenade: the Politics of Bourgeois Sociability in Nineteenth-Century New York." *Social History* 17 (May 1992): 203–27.

Scudder, Vida Dutton. *On Journey.* New York: E. P. Dutton, 1937.

Segev, Tom. *One Palestine, Complete: Jews and Arabs under the British Mandate.* New York: Henry Holt, 2000.

Seidman, Naomi. "Fag-Hags and Bu-Jews: Toward a (Jewish) Politics of Vicarious Identity." In *Insider/Outsider: American Jews and Multiculturalism*, edited by David Biale, Michael Galchinsky, and Susan Heschel, 254–68. Berkeley: University of California Press, 1998.

Shapiro, Robert D. *A Reform Rabbi in the Progressive Era.* New York: Garland, 1988.

Shneer, David, and Caryn Aviv, eds. *Queer Jews.* New York: Routledge, 2002.

Siegel, Beatrice. *Lillian Wald of Henry Street.* New York: Macmillan, 1983.

Silverberg, Helene. "Introduction: Toward a Gendered Social Science History." In *Gender and American Social Science: The Formative Years*, edited by Helene Silverberg, 3–32. Princeton, N.J.: Princeton University Press, 1998.

Simon, Barbara Levy. "Building on the Romance of Women's Innate Strengths: Social Feminism and Its Influence at the Henry Street Settlement, 1893–1993." In *Building on Women's Strengths: A Social Work Agenda for the Twenty-First*

Century, edited by K. Jean Peterson and Alice A. Lieberman, 23–44. 2nd ed. New York: Haworth Press, 2001.

Simon, Kate. *Bronx Primitive: Portraits in a Childhood*. New York: Penguin Books, 1982.

Sklar, Kathryn Kish. *Florence Kelley and the Nation's Work: The Rise of Women's Political Culture, 1830–1900*. New Haven, Conn.: Yale University Press, 1995.

———. "The Historical Foundations of Women's Power in the Creation of the American Welfare State, 1830–1930." In *Mothers of a New World: Maternalist Politics and the Origins of Welfare States*, edited by Seth Koven and Sonya Michel, 43–93. New York: Routledge, 1993.

———. "*Hull House Maps and Papers*: Social Science as Women's Work in the 1890s." In *Gender and American Social Science*, edited by Helene Silverberg, 127–55. Princeton, N.J.: Princeton University Press, 1998.

———. *Notes of Sixty Years: The Autobiography of Florence Kelley*. Chicago: Charles H. Kerr, 1986.

———. "'Some of Us Who Deal with the Social Fabric': Jane Addams Blends Peace and Social Justice, 1907–1919." *Journal of the Gilded Age and Progressive Era* 2, no. 1 (Jan. 2003): 80–96.

———. "Why Were Most Politically Active Women Opposed to the ERA in the 1920s?" In *Women and Power in American History*, edited by Kathryn Kish Sklar and Thomas Dublin, 2:175–82. Englewood Cliffs, N.J.: Prentice Hall, 1991.

Sklare, Marshall. *Observing America's Jews*. Hanover, N.H.: University Press of New England, 1993.

Skocpol, Theda. *Protecting Soldiers and Mothers: The Political Origins of Social Policy in the United States*. Cambridge, Mass.: Harvard University Press, Belknap Press, 1992.

Slater, Elinor, and Robert Slater. *Great Jewish Women*. New York: Jonathan David, 1994.

Sloan, David Charles. *The Last Great Necessity: Cemeteries in American History*. Baltimore: Johns Hopkins University Press, 1991.

Sochen, June. *Consecrate Every Day: The Public Lives of Jewish American Women*. Albany: State University of New York Press, 1981.

Sollors, Werner. *Beyond Ethnicity: Consent and Descent in American Culture*. New York: Oxford University Press, 1986.

Solomon, Hannah G., and Miriam Del Banco, eds. *Papers of the Jewish Women's Congress Held at Chicago, September 4, 5, 6 and 7, 1893*. Philadelphia: Jewish Publication Society of America, 1894.

Sorin, Gerald. "Irving Howe's 'Margin of Hope': *World of Our Fathers* as Autobiography." *American Jewish History* 88 (Dec. 2000): 475–94.

——. "Mutual Contempt, Mutual Benefit: The Strained Encounter between German and Eastern European Jews in America, 1880–1920." *American Jewish History* 81 (Autumn 1993): 34–59.

Sorkin, David. *The Transformation of German Jewry, 1780–1840.* New York: Oxford University Press, 1987.

Soyer, Daniel. "Abraham Cahan's Travels in Jewish Homelands: Palestine in 1925 and the Soviet Union in 1927." In *Yiddish and the Left,* edited by Gennady Estraikh and Mikhail Krutikov, 56–79. Oxford, U.K.: European Humanities Research Centre, 2001.

——. "Soviet Travel and the Making of an American Jewish Communist: Moissaye Olgin's Trip to Russia in 1920–1921." *American Communist History* 4 (June 2005): 1–20.

Stansell, Christine. *American Moderns: Bohemian New York and the Creation of a New Century.* New York: Metropolitan Books, 2001.

Staub, Michael E. " 'Smart.' " *Shofar: An Interdisciplinary Journal of Jewish Studies* 24 (Summer 2006): 2–12.

——. *Torn at the Roots: The Crisis of Jewish Liberalism in Postwar America.* New York: Columbia University Press, 2002.

Stebner, Eleanor. *The Women of Hull House: A Study in Spirituality, Vocation, and Friendship.* Albany: State University of New York Press, 1997.

Steffens, Lincoln. *The Autobiography of Lincoln Steffens.* New York: Harcourt, Brace, 1931.

Storrs, Landon R. Y. *Civilizing Capitalism: The National Consumers' League, Women's Activism, and Labor Standards in the New Deal Era.* Chapel Hill: University of North Carolina Press, 2000.

Supple, Barry E. "A Business Elite: German-Jewish Financiers in Nineteenth-Century New York." *Business History Review* 31 (Summer 1957): 143–78.

Sutherland, John F. "Rabbi Joseph Krauskopf of Philadelphia: The Urban Reformer Returns to the Land." *American Jewish History* 67 (June 1978): 342–62.

Svonkin, Stuart. *Jews against Prejudice: American Jews and the Fight for Civil Liberties.* New York: Columbia University Press, 1997.

Swartz, Marvin. *The Union of Democratic Control in British Politics during the First World War.* London: Oxford University Press, 1971.

Szajkowski, Zosa. "The Attitude of American Jews to Refugees from Germany in the 1930s." *American Jewish Historical Quarterly* 61 (Dec. 1971): 101–43.

——. *The Attitude of American Jews to World War I, the Russian Revolutions of 1917, and Communism, 1914–1949.* Vol. 1 of *Jews, Wars, and Communism.* New York: Ktav, 1973.

——. *Kolchak, Jews, and the American Intervention in Northern Russia and Siberia, 1918–1920.* New York: privately printed, 1977.

Taitz, Emily, and Sondra Henry. *Remarkable Jewish Women: Rebels, Rabbis, and Other Women from Biblical Times to the Present.* Philadelphia: Jewish Publication Society, 1996.

Tarrant, Dorothy, and John Tarrant. *A Community of Artists: Westport-Weston, 1900–1985.* Westport, Conn.: Westport Arts Council, 1985.

Taylor, Graham. "Is Religion an Element in the Social Settlement?" *Journal of the Religious Education Association* 8 (1913): 345–48.

Taylor, S. J. *Stalin's Apologist: Walter Durante, the New York Times's Man in Moscow.* New York: Oxford University Press, 1990.

Thomas, W. Stephen, and Ruth Rosenberg-Naparsteck. "Sleepers' City: The Sesquicentennial History of Mt. Hope Cemetery." *Rochester History* 50 (Oct. 1988): 1–17.

Thompson, Arthur W. "The Reception of Russian Revolutionary Leaders in America, 1904–1906." *American Quarterly* 18 (Autumn 1966): 452–76.

Tifft, Susan E., and Alex S. Jones. *The Trust: The Private and Powerful Family behind the "New York Times."* Boston: Little, Brown, 1999.

Tittle, Walter. "Four American Women: Portrait Drawings." *Forum* 76 (Oct. 1926): 557–61.

Toll, William. "Horace M. Kallen: Pluralism and American Jewish Identity." *American Jewish History* 85 (Mar. 1997): 57–74.

Tomko, Linda J. *Dancing Class: Gender, Ethnicity, and Social Divides in American Dance, 1890–1920.* Bloomington: Indiana University Press, 1999.

Trolander, Judith Ann. *Professionalism and Social Change: From the Settlement House Movement to Neighborhood Centers, 1886 to the Present.* New York: Columbia University Press, 1987.

Tronto, Joan B. *Moral Boundaries: A Political Argument for an Ethic of Care.* New York: Routledge, 1993.

Tuite, Patrick. "Assimilating Immigrants through Drama: The Social Politics of Alice Minnie Herts and Lillian Wald." *Youth Theatre Journal* 12 (1998): 10–18.

Udelson, Joseph H. *Dreamer of the Ghetto: The Life and Works of Israel Zangwill.* Tuscaloosa: University of Alabama Press, 1990.

Urofsky, Melvin I. *American Zionism from Herzl to the Holocaust.* Garden City, N.J.: Anchor Books, 1976.

U.S. Senate. Committee on Military Affairs. *Preparedness for National Defense:*

Hearings before the Committee on Military Affairs, United States Senate, Sixty-Fourth Congress, First Session, on Bills for the Reorganization of the Army and for the Creation of a Reserve Army, January 18, 1916. Washington, D.C.: U.S. Government Printing Office, 1916.

Vorspan, Albert. *Giants of Justice.* New York: Union of American Hebrew Congregations, 1960.

Voss, Kim. *The Making of American Exceptionalism: The Knights of Labor and Class Formation in the Nineteenth Century.* Ithaca, N.Y.: Cornell University Press, 1993.

Wagenknecht, Edward. *Daughters of the Covenant: Portraits of Six Jewish Women.* Amherst: University of Massachusetts Press, 1983.

Wald, Alan. "Memories of the John Dewey Commission: Forty Years Later." *Antioch Review* 35 (Fall 1977): 438–53.

Wald, Lillian D. Afterword to *Forty Years at Hull House,* by Jane Addams. New York: MacMillan, 1935.

———. "The Feeding of the School Children." *Charities and the Commons* 20 (13 June 1908): 371–74.

———. Foreword to *Does Prohibition Work?* by Martha Bensley Bruere. New York: Harper and Brothers, 1927.

———. "Health and Maternity Legislation 'A Poignant Need.' " *American Labor Legislation Review* 60 (1911): 11.

———. *The House on Henry Street.* New York: Henry Holt, 1915.

———. "Medical Inspection of Public Schools." *Annals of the American Academy of Political Science* 25 (1905): 290–98.

———. "Organization amongst Working Women." *Annals of the American Academy of Political Science* 27 (1906): 638–45.

———. "Put Responsibility on the Right Shoulders." *Survey* 25 (26 Nov. 1910): 316.

———. "Report of the Henry Street Settlement, 1893–1913." New York: Henry Street Settlement, 1913.

———. "The Treatment of Families in which There Is Sickness." *American Journal of Nursing* 4 (Dec. 1904): 427–31, 515–19.

———. "We Called Our Enterprise Public Health Nursing." Foreword to *The Public Health Nurse in Action,* by Marguerite Wales. New York: Macmillan, 1941.

———. *Windows on Henry Street.* Boston: Little, Brown, 1934.

Walkowitz, Daniel J. *Working with Class: Social Workers and the Politics of Middle-Class Identity.* Chapel Hill: University of North Carolina Press, 1999.

Ware, Susan. *Beyond Suffrage: Women in the New Deal.* Cambridge, Mass.: Harvard University Press, 1981.

Warnke, Bettina. "Reforming the New York Yiddish Theater: The Cultural Politics of Immigrant Intellectuals and the Yiddish Press, 1887–1910." Ph.D. diss., Columbia University, 2001.

Weiner, Lynn M., Ann Taylor Allen, Eileen Boris, Molly Ladd-Taylor, Adele Lindenmeyr, and Kathleen Uno. "Maternalism as Paradigm: Defining the Issues." *Journal of Women's History* 5 (Fall 1993): 96–130.

Weinstein, Gregory. *The Ardent Eighties: Reminiscences of an Interesting Decade.* New York: International Press, 1928.

Weissman, Neil B. "Origins of Soviet Health Administration: *Narkomzdrav*, 1918–1928." In *Health and Society in Revolutionary Russia*, edited by Susan Gross Solomon and John F. Hutchinson, 97–120. Bloomington: Indiana University Press, 1990.

Wenger, Beth S. *New York Jews and the Great Depression: Uncertain Promise.* New Haven, Conn.: Yale University Press, 1996.

Wertheimer, Jack. *A People Divided: Judaism in Contemporary America.* New York: Basic Books, 1993.

White, Ronald C., and C. Howard Hopkins, eds. *The Social Gospel: Religion and Reform in Changing America.* Philadelphia: Temple University Press, 1976.

Whitfield, Stephen J. "Enigmas of Modern Jewish Identity." *Jewish Social Studies* 8 (Winter/Spring 2002): 162–67.

Wile, Isaac A. *The Jews of Rochester.* Rochester, N.Y.: Historical Review Society, 1912.

Williams, Beryl. *Lillian Wald: Angel of Henry Street.* New York: Julian Messner, 1948.

Wise, Stephen. *Challenging Years: The Autobiography of Stephen Wise.* New York: G. P. Putnam's Sons, 1949.

Woodcock, George, and Ivan Avakumovic. *Peter Kropotkin: From Prince to Rebel.* New York: Black Rose Books, 1990.

Woods, Robert A., and Albert J. Kennedy. *The Settlement Horizon: A National Estimate.* New York: Russell Sage Foundation, 1922.

——, eds. *Handbook of Settlements.* New York: Arno, 1911.

Yellowitz, Irwin. "Lillian Wald." In *Encyclopedia Judaica.* Jerusalem: Macmillan, 1971.

Zangwill, Israel. Afterword to *The Melting Pot: Drama in Four Acts*, 199–216. New York: Macmillan, 1914.

Zipser, Arthur, and Pearl Zipser. *Fire and Grace: The Life of Rose Pastor Stokes.* Athens: University of Georgia Press, 1989.

INTERNET SOURCES

American Nurses Association. "Hall of Fame Inductees." <http://nursing world.org/FunctionalMenuCategories/AboutANA/WhereWeComeFrom _1/HallofFame/19761982/waldld5595.aspx>. 11 Feb. 2007.

Fromer, Rebecca Camhi. "The Creation of the Magnes Museum." Jewish-American Hall of Fame. <http://amuseum.org/magnes/index.html>. 10 June 2007.

Jewish-American Hall of Fame. "Jewish-American Hall of Fame Inducts Lillian Wald." HOF (Hall of Fame Magazine). <http://www.hofmag.com/content/view/713/190/>. 10 June 2007.

——. "Virtual Tour." <http://amuseum.org/jahf/virtour/page39.html>. 10 June 2007.

Jewish Encyclopedia. Preface to the first edition. <http://www.jewishencyclopedia.com/preface.jsp>. 11 Feb. 2007.

Jewish Women's Archive. "JWA—Lillian Wald—Introduction." <http://www.jwa.org/exhibits/wov/wald/index.html>. 1998. Dec. 26, 2007.

Ma'yan. " 'Listen to Her Voice': The Ma'yan Report; Assessing the Experiences of Women in the Jewish Community and their Relationships to Feminism." Jan. 2005. <http://www.jccmanhattan.org/category.aspx?catid=1013>. May 1, 2006.

National Women's Hall of Fame. "Women of the Hall." <http://www.greatwomen.org/women.php?action=viewone&id=162>. 11 Feb. 2007.

New York City Department of Parks and Recreation. "Playgrounds and Public Recreation, 1898–1929." <http://www.nycgovparks.org/sub_about/parks_history/historic_tour/history_playgrounds_recreation.html>. 11 Feb. 2007.

New York Nurse News. "2007 Honoree of Jewish-American Hall of Fame: Lillian Wald." <http://newyorknursenews.blogspot.com/2007/03/2007-honoree-of-jewish-american-hall-of.html>. 10 June 2007.

Index